北京第二外国语学院人才培养规划
研究生质量提升计划优质课程建设教材

XIFANG XIANDAI WENLUN JINGDIAN DAODU

西方现代文论
经典导读

胡继华　杨　旭　张泽恒　李静宜◎编著

北京师范大学出版集团
BEIJING NORMAL UNIVERSITY PUBLISHING GROUP
北京师范大学出版社

图书在版编目（CIP）数据

西方现代文论经典导读 / 胡继华，杨旭，张泽恒编著. —北京：
北京师范大学出版社，2022.10
ISBN 978-7-303-28155-8

Ⅰ.①西…　Ⅱ.①胡…②杨…③张…　Ⅲ.①文艺理论－西方国
家－现代　Ⅳ.①I109.5

中国版本图书馆 CIP 数据核字（2022）第 169625 号

图 书 意 见 反 馈　gaozhifk@bnupg.com　010-58805079
营 销 中 心 电 话　010-58807651
北师大出版社高等教育分社微信公众号　新外大街拾玖号

XIFANG XIANDAI WENLUN JINGDIAN DAODU
出版发行：北京师范大学出版社　www.bnup.com
　　　　　北京市西城区新街口外大街 12-3 号
　　　　　邮政编码：100088
印　　刷：北京虎彩文化传播有限公司
经　　销：全国新华书店
开　　本：787 mm×1092 mm　1/16
印　　张：35.75
字　　数：900 千字
版　　次：2022 年 10 月第 1 版
印　　次：2022 年 10 月第 1 次印刷
定　　价：78.00 元

策划编辑：周劲含　　　　　　责任编辑：陈　倩
美术编辑：李向昕　　　　　　装帧设计：李向昕
责任校对：康　悦　　　　　　责任印制：马　洁

当代西方文论新趋势：
从语言论到文化论（代序）

德国早期浪漫主义诗人诺瓦利斯（Novalis，Georg Philipp Friedrich Freiherr von Hardenberg，1772—1801）对语言具有一种天赋的敏感能力。他提出诗的语言必须是有机的富有活力的语言。以诗为媒介，以语言为重心，他建构了一种浪漫的诗学，致力于"以一种惬意的方式陌生化"①，让一切熟悉而又陌生，灵动而又坚实。他也许没有想到，作为主体的诗人淡出、从表现论向语言论的转向将成为一百多年后文学理论的命运。延续着浪漫主义文学精神血脉却更迷恋词语抽象性的法国象征主义诗人马拉美一语道破了文学理论转向语言的必然性："虚无走了，纯洁性的城堡继留于世。"②"纯洁性的城堡"是一个隐喻，其本体即"词语"。诗人坚持认为，用来写诗的不是思想，而是"词语"。

20世纪30年代之后，欧洲人的精神生活陷入一种危机。现象学的创始人胡塞尔（Husserl，1859—1938）将这种历史危机转向现代"生活世界"。于是，"生活世界"（Lebenswelt）的概念以及"生活世界"的理论应运而生。按照胡塞尔的看法，"生活世界"是一个全新的哲学概念。"生活世界是原始明见性的一个领域"，以此为基础可望建立一种"关于先在世界普遍性原理的科学"。③ 而"生活世界"的危机必须归咎于近代以来自然科学的过分严谨，以及技术现代性对自我认知的压制。将"生活世界"概念引入哲学是胡塞尔的建树之一。德国哲学家布鲁门伯格（Hans Blumenberg，1920—1996）进一步将"生活概念"携入美学和修辞学论域之中，酝酿出"生活世界的理论"。在他看来，"生活世界"具有前逻辑性和前预示性，是一个不容哲学思辨侵入且不让哲学存在的世界，

---

① 刘小枫：《夜颂中的革命和宗教——诺瓦利斯选集卷一》，林克等译，176页，北京，华夏出版社，2007。

② 马拉美：《伊纪杜尔》，见《马拉美诗全集》，葛雷、梁栋译，305页，杭州，浙江文艺出版社，1997。

③ 胡塞尔：《生活世界现象学》，倪梁康、张廷国译，265页，上海，上海译文出版社，2002。

也是一个乌托邦式的审美世界、一个终极的创造世界。因而，基于"生活世界"的审美建构是一种防御性的建构。"生活世界"是一系列前哲学的"先入之见"或"秩序"与"制度"。以此为基础建立的乌托邦式美学宇宙将混乱、恐怖的自然状态放置在适当的距离之外，好让我们的世界宜于居住，好让生活变得舒适，好让社会秩序井然。[①]

正如诺瓦利斯所预感、马拉美所预言的那样，语言论转向（linguistic turn）不仅构成了 20 世纪文学理论的主导趋势，而且导致了整个人文学科范式的革命。美国哲学家柏格曼（G. Bergmann）、罗蒂（R. Rorty）在 20 世纪 60 年代中期用语言论转向来概括 19 世纪末 20 世纪初西方人文学科领域发生的语言取代理性而占据中心的转变过程。随着语言取代理性，主体渐渐淡出，在文学理论中，对于文学的词语、形式、结构的考虑渐渐获得了优先地位，甚至取代了对文学的情感、思想、意义的考虑。我们赞同德国解释学家伽达默尔、英国文学理论家伊格尔顿的概括，把语言论转向理解为：语言，连同其问题、秘密和含义一起，成为哲学关注的中心，成为 20 世纪精神生活的范型，成为文学研究优先考虑的对象。

在语言论转向大潮中，文学理论涌动着对语言的激情，通过对语言的深情凝视而追寻语言的胜境，语言乌托邦的光照笼罩着盛期现代文论。"盛期现代性"（high modernity），是社会学家吉登斯、拉什（Scott Lash）等人用来刻画现代社会发展的极限阶段、现代问题积累的复杂程度和现代精神气质的饱和状态的概念，其含义是指现代社会同古典的断裂抵达了极限，现代问题积累趋向于冲突，以及现代精神气质基本达到饱和状态而要求重新定位。

反映在文学理论话语中，盛期现代西方文论的演变大体上呈现出文学主体的淡出与复归的循环，语言学乌托邦从建构到解构的行程，以及走出"语言的牢笼"通往全球文化语境的趋势。拉什将"盛期现代"看作一个纯粹的社会学概念，将其追溯到西方启蒙运动与工业革命，同时将"盛期现代"的自我超越同文化理论的自我反思联系在一起。

① Hans Blumenberg, *Theorie der Lebenswelt*, Frankfurt am Main, Suhrkamp, 2010, pp. 123-124. 关于这个主题的论述，参见尼科尔斯：《神话及其政治意蕴——布鲁门伯格遗作研究》，刘静译，载《跨文化研究》，2019(2)。

就文化理论言之，社会学按照一种相同的合理性建构了"盛期现代"，但就社会学言之，文化理论则全然根据差异的问题意识解构了现代，并废黜了合理性。[1]

同一与差异的交替凸显、建构与解构的辩证节奏，便构成了盛期现代西方文论自我定位与自我超越的隐秘逻辑。

首先，通过追踪这一隐秘逻辑，我们看到了文学主体在文学理论的语言论转向潮流中的兴衰浮沉。在俄国形式主义、新批评那里，文学主体下降、文学形式上升已经成为明显的趋势。尽管形式主义关心词语的生命远甚于关心诗人的生命，尽管新批评的先驱者 T. S. 艾略特主张逃避情感，但文学主体并没有完全消逝，却在作为独创标志的"文学性"(literariness)概念和作为文学肌理(texture)的"意义"概念中留下了美妙的剪影。在心理分析批评和结构主义批评话语中，主体被看作"无意识语言结构"和"语言编码活动"的产物，几乎完全被剥夺了主动性而成为一种宿命的存在物。象征主义诗人"不是我说话而是话说我"的魔咒成为盛期现代西方文论的基本信念。峰回路转，柳暗花明，文学主体遭受了淡漠和抑制之后，又在解构理论、解释学与接受理论中获得了新生。解构理论强调批评主体自由游戏的策略，而阐释学与接受理论既重视读者的语言素质，又赋予了接受主体以创造性阐释的权力。

其次，通过追踪这一隐秘逻辑，我们可以见证语言乌托邦在西方现代文论话语中的建构与解构。俄国形式主义通过"陌生化"手段将艺术建构为一个"独立自足"的世界，通过形式的演变将文学历史呈现为一种不依赖于社会生活的独立精神王国的历史。"飘扬在彼得堡城市上空的旗子"，这个形象已经成为语言乌托邦的隐喻，意在表明文学话语相对于社会历史的独立性。在巴赫金手上，艺术形式的独立地位、文学符号的超然性通过复调、狂欢和对话的形式获得了丰富的内涵与具象的形式。比如，他对拉伯雷、歌德、陀思妥耶夫斯基文学世界的重构，就为我们提供了形态各异、色彩斑斓的语言乌托邦范本。而崇尚经典、带有浓郁贵族情调并充分展示了经验分析方法优势的英美新批评，通过运用悖论、反讽、含混等富有逻辑穿透力的概念把文学文本打造为"精制的瓮"，并以此来存留诗人爱的行迹和诗的冥想。心理分析从分析个体的梦境开始，把文学文本的原动力追溯到了深层"无意

---

① Scott Lash, *Another Modernity: A Different Rationality*, Oxford, Blackwell, 1999, p. 1.

识"和本能欲望，最后发现"无意识结构有如语言"，而穿越"显意"直达"隐意"的释梦之旅，也未尝不可以被理解为对梦境语言乌托邦的建构。心理分析批评的发展形态——原型批评或者神话批评，则从集体心理、文化无意识入手，将文学话语建构为喜剧、传奇、悲剧和讽刺的神话位移，同春、夏、秋、冬四季相对应，四种文学话语形式的循环构成了流动的语言乌托邦。结构主义理论运用人类学、符号学、民俗学、种族志等方法论工具去解读文化符号，将包括古代神话、悲剧以及现代流行体系在内的一切符号形式看作精神秩序的物质存在，从而将发现秩序、制服紊乱视为一切包括文学批评在内的符号实践的使命。这就把语言乌托邦建构在人类精神的普遍秩序之上，从而将柏拉图的理想城邦安置在文学话语之中。物极必反，语言乌托邦在罗兰·巴特的符号学冒险中已经表现出了破碎的迹象，而当他运用多种符码去分解巴尔扎克的小说《萨拉辛》时，我们看到了文学文本发生了灾难性的"聚变"——玲珑剔透的语言乌托邦支离破碎，并呈星型开裂，无中心地弥散开来。德里达采用自由游戏的策略放任能指的漂移，在无休止地生成和散播差异的过程中让文本自我裂变，演示建立在脆弱的"语音中心"基础上的"逻各斯中心主义"大厦的自我倾覆。他在解构之眼的逼视下，"目无全牛"。而在美国解构批评家看来，一切深文周纳的逻辑织体都在自我解构，因为文学"修辞性"时刻都如水银泻地一般地瓦解语言乌托邦的铜墙铁壁。语言论转向与哲学人类学在 20 世纪 70 年代的合流，迎来了"修辞学的复兴"。修辞论美学取代传统思辨美学、现代经验论美学，空前关注人类符号实践及其美的建构。语言论转向将语言运用置于美学建构的首要地位，哲学人类学则将修辞视为人类补偿天然人性匮乏的重要手段。德国哲学人类学家马克斯·舍勒（Max Scheler）、赫尔穆特·普莱斯纳（Helmuth Plessner）和阿诺德·盖伦（Arnold Gehlen）一致强调，人类的生物学本能与人类的社会性一样重要。但人类在生物学上天生匮乏，难以适应环境的复杂变化，故而必须以文化、语言、技术、修辞、象征等手段来补偿天生匮乏。布鲁门伯格将"修辞补偿论"追溯到柏拉图的《普罗泰戈拉篇》，把普罗米修斯从天神盗火、泽及人类的故事解释为一个修辞美学的隐喻：人类脱离了语言、技术等补偿手段，就无法生存。修辞的功用，相当于普罗米修斯之火的功用。布鲁门伯格将修辞论美学凝练为两个命题："人类作为匮乏的造物，需要修辞作为表面的艺术来应对自己匮乏真实的处境"①;"不仅人类的处境是潜在的隐喻处境,人类存在本身亦复如此"②。可见,修辞成为一种文学建构的基本媒介,在人类的符号实践中占有不可或缺的位置。

最后,通过追踪这一隐秘逻辑,我们还可以预测文学理论走出"语言的牢笼"通往全球文化语境的趋势。盛期现代西方文论顺应语言论转向,以语言为优先关注的中心,形成了有关文学的一系列基本共识。比如,认为文学之本是语言符号,文学的力量在于语言的力量,结构决定文学作品的意义,文学接受取决于读者的语言素质,等等。语言论批评关注语言结构与文学形式,其极端的形式是"试图将主体重新融入纯关系、融入语言或象征的体系"③,从而陷入了"语言的牢笼"。所以,尽管认为结构主义、符号学、形式主义"是一种观照探险",但德里达还是确信,这种探险引发了一种焦虑,而这种焦虑只能是对语言的焦虑。"结构主义意识是一种灾难意识,同时既摧毁而又建构,一点也不自相矛盾……"④德里达的这个看法启发我们去思考语言论文论的自我反思与自我解构的可能性。也就是说,文学理论应该从"语言的牢笼"中突围,汇入全球文化语境。全球文化本质上不应该以"同一的合理性"灭杀"差异的问题意识",它不是摧毁而是创生。因此,从盛期现代文论的语言论转向到全球语境下语言论文论的自我解构,可能是西方文论执行自我反思、展开自我超越的一种取向。事实上,俄国形式主义向巴赫金文化诗学的过渡,英美新批评所隐含的精英文化立场,心理分析理论越来越多的文化情怀,结构主义的整体文化意识,解构理论对伦理、政治、宗教文化的叩问,以及解释学与接受理论对文化视野的强调,都不仅预示着语言论解构的可能性,而且为这度转向开辟了道路。语言论自我解构以转向文化为具体标志:优先关注文化,以文化为文学的内省维度,寻求异趣沟通,通达"和而不同"的境界。这是西方现代文论自 20 世纪中期以来所表现的基本趋向。

---

① Hans Blumenberg, *Beschreibung des Menschen*, Frankfurt am Main, Suhrkamp, 2006, pp. 431-432.

② Hans Blumenberg, "Anthropologische Annäherung an die Akualität der Rhetorik," in *Ästhetische und metaphorologische Schriften*, Frankfurt am Main, Suhrkamp, 2001, p. 431.

③ 詹姆逊:《语言的牢笼——结构主义及俄国形式主义述评》,钱佼汝译,164 页,南昌,百花洲文艺出版社,1995。

④ Jacques Derrida, *Writing and Difference*, translated, with an introduction and additional notes, by Alan Bass, London, Melbourne and Henley, Routledge and Kegan Paul, 1978, pp. 5-6.

目　录
Contents

1. The Resurrection of the Word（1914）
   By Viktor Shklovsky ··· 1
1. 什克洛夫斯基：《语词的复活》
   (Viktor Shklovsky, "The Resurrection of the Word," 1914) ············ 10

2. The Language of Paradox（1947）
   By Cleanth Brooks ·· 18
2. 布鲁克斯：《悖论的语言》
   (Cleanth Brooks, "The Language of Paradox," 1947) ·············· 35

3. Word Magic（1925）
   By Ernst Cassirer ·· 42
3. 卡西尔：《语词魔力》
   (Ernst Cassirer, "Word Magic," 1925) ························· 57

4. The Structural Study of Myth（1955）
   By Claude Lévi-Strauss ·· 65
4. 列维-斯特劳斯：《神话的结构研究》
   (Claude Lévi-Strauss, "The Structural Study of Myth," 1955) ········ 78

5. Dostoevsky and Parricide（1927）
   By Sigmund Freud ·· 82
5. 弗洛伊德：《陀思妥耶夫斯基与弑父》
   (Sigmund Freud, "Dostoevsky and Parricide," 1927) ··············· 100

18. Archetypal Criticism：Theory of Myths（1957）
   By Northrop Frye ·· 454
18. 弗莱：《原型批评：神话理论》
   （Northrop Frye, "Archetypal Criticism：Theory of Myths," 1957） ······ 473

19. An Ethics of Sexual Difference（1929）
   By Luce Irigaray ·· 479
19. 伊利格瑞：《性别差异伦理学》
   （Luce Irigaray, "An Ethics of Sexual Difference," 1929） ·············· 491

20. Towards a Poetics of Culture（1986）
   By Stephen J. Greenblatt ·· 496
20. 格林布拉特：《通向一种文化诗学》
   （Stephen J. Greenblatt, "Towards a Poetics of Culture," 1986） ······ 514

21. *Heinrich von Ofterdingen* as Data Feed（1986）
   By Friedrich A. Kittler ·· 518
21. 基特勒：《〈亨利希·奥夫特丁根〉作为数据传输记录》
   （Friedrich A. Kittler, "*Heinrich von Ofterdingen* as Data
   Feed," 1986） ·· 551

编者后记 ·· 559

1. The Resurrection of the Word (1914)
By Viktor Shklovsky

The word—the image and its fossilisation. The epithet as a means of renewal of the word. The history of the epithet—the history of poetic style. The fate of works of old artists of the word is of the same nature as the fate of the word itself: they complete the journey from poetry to prose. The death of things. The aim of Futurism is the resurrection of things. —the return to man of sensation of the world. The connection of the devices of the Futurists' poetry with the devices of general linguistic thought-processes. The semi-comprehensible language of ancient poetry. The language of the Futurists.

The most ancient poetic creation of man was the creation of words. Now words are dead, and language is like a graveyard, but an image was once alive in the newly-born word. Every word is basically—a trope. For example *mesyats*('moon'; 'month'): the original meaning of this word was 'measurer' (Russ. *meritel'*); grief (Russ. *gore*, *pechal'*; cf. *goret'* = to burn, *pech'* = to bake) and sorrow mean that which burns and scorches; the word '*enfant*' (just like the Old Russian '*otrok*' ['boy'; 'child'] as well) in a literal translation means 'not speaking'. As many such examples as there are words in language could be adduced. And often enough, when you get through to the image which is now lost and effaced, but once embedded at the basis of the word, then you are struck by its beauty—by a beauty which existed once and is now gone.

When words are being used by our thought-processes in place of general concepts, and serve, so to speak, as algebraic symbols, and must needs be devoid of imagery, when they are used in everyday speech and are not completely enunciated or completely heard, then they have become familiar, and their internal (image) and external (sound) forms have ceased to be sensed. We do not sense the familiar, we do not see it, but recognise it. We do not see the walls of our rooms, it is so hard for us to spot a misprint in a proof—particularly if it is written in a language well known to us, because we cannot make ourselves see and read through, and not 'recognise' the familiar word.

If we should wish to make a definition of 'poetic' and 'artistic' perception in general, then doubtless we would hit upon the definition: 'artistic' perception is perception in which form is sensed (perhaps not only form, but form as an essential part). It is easy to demonstrate the correctness of this 'working' definition in those instances when some expression or other, having been poetic, becomes prosaic. For example, it is evident that the expressions—the 'foot' (Russ. *podoshva*) of a mountain or the 'chapter' (Russ. *glava*) of a book, in their passage from poetry to prose, have not changed their meaning, but have only lost their form (in the given instance—internal form). The experiment proposed by A. Gornfel'd in the article 'Torments of the Word'— to transpose the words in the poem:

Stikh, kak monetu, chekan',
Strogo, otchetlivo, chestno.
Pravilu sledui uporno:
Chtoby slovam bylo tesno,
Myslyam—prostorno, —

(Verse, like coins, mint
Strictly, precisely, honestly.
Follow the rule stubbornly:
So that words may be compact,
Thoughts—expansive…)

in order to satisfy himself that with the loss of form (in the given instance—external form) the poem changes into a 'commonplace didactic aphorism,'—this experiment confirms the correctness of the proposed definition.

Therefore: the word, as it loses 'form', completes the irrevocable journey from poetry to prose. (Potebnya: *Lectures on the Theory of Literature*).

This loss of the form of the word represents a great easement for the thought-processes and may be a necessary condition for the existence of science, but art could never be satisfied with this eroded word. It could hardly be said that poetry has made up the damage it has suffered through the loss of the figurativeness of words by replacing this figurativeness with a higher type of creation—for example by the creation of character-types, because in such a case poetry would not have held on so avidly to the figurative word even at such high stages of its evolution as in the era of epic chronicles. In art, material must be alive and precious. And this is where there appeared the epithet, which does not introduce anything new into the word, but simply renews its dead figurativeness; for example: the bright sun, (Russ. *solntse yasnoe* = literally 'clear sun'), the bold warrior, the wide world, (Russ. *belyi svet* = literally 'white world'), miry mud, rain shower ... the very word '*dozhd*', ('rain'), contains the concept of scattering, but the image has died, and the thirst for concreteness, which constitutes the soul of art (Carlyle), demanded its renewal. The word, revitalised by the epithet, became poetic once more. Time passed— and the epithet ceased to be sensed—again because of its familiarity. And the epithet began to be handled through habit, by virtue of scholastic traditions and not through living poetic feeling. Moreover, the epithet is by now sensed so little that quite often its application cuts right across the general situation and colouring of the picture; for example:

> Burn, burn, you tallow candle,
> Tallow candle of ardent wax ...
>
> (Folk-song)

or the 'white hands' of the blackmoor (the Serbian epos), 'my true love' of the Old English ballads, a term applied in them indiscriminately—whether it is a case of either true or untrue love, or Nestor, raising his hands to the starry sky in broad daylight, and so on.

Constant epithets have worn smooth, no longer evoke a figurative impression and do not satisfy its demands. Within their limits new epithets are created, they accumulate, and definitions become diversified through descriptive terms borrowed from the material of the saga or legend (Alexander Veselovsky: *The*

History of the Epithet). Complex epithets too relate to most recent times.

'The history of the epithet—is the history of poetic style in an abridged edition.' (A. Veselovsky: *Collected Works*, Vol. 1, p. 58). This history shows us how all forms of art always recede from life, forms which, just like the epithet, live, fossilise and finally die.

People pay too little attention to the death of forms in art, they all too flippantly contrast the old with the new without thinking whether the old is alive or has already vanished, as the sound of the sea vanishes for those who live by its shores, as the thousand-voiced roar of the town has vanished for us, as everything familiar, too well known, disappears from our consciousness.

Not only words and epithets fossilise, whole situations can fossilise too. Thus, for example, in the Baghdad edition of the Arabian Nights a traveller, whom robbers have stripped naked, ascended a mountain and in desperation 'tore his clothes to shreds'. In this extract the whole picture has become congealed to the point of unconsciousness.

The fate of the works of old artists of the word is exactly the same as the fate of the word itself. They are completing the journey from poetry to prose. They cease to seen and begin to be recognised. Classical works have for us become covered with the glassy armour of familiarity—we remember them too well, we have heard them from childhood, we have read them in books, thrown out quotations from them in the course of conversation, and now we have callouses on our souls—we longer sense them. I am speaking about the masses. Many people think that the masses sense all art. But how easy it is to make mistakes here! Goncharov not without reason sceptically compared the sensation of the classicist when reading a Greek drama with the sensations of Gogol's Petrushka. It is often quite impossible to assimilate old art. Look at the books of the renowned connoisseurs of classicism—see what trite vignettes and photos of broken down sculptures they put on the covers. Rodin, having copied Greek sculptures for years on end, had to resort to measuring them in order, eventually, to transmit their forms; it turned out that he had been carving them too thin all the time. So a genius could not simply repeat the forms of another age. And the raptures of the profane in the museums can be explained only by their flippancy and undemanding attitude towards their own assimilation of antiquity.

The illusion that old art is sensed is supported by the fact that elements alien to art are often present in it. Such elements are in fact found above all in literature; therefore literature now has hegemony in art and the largest number of connoisseurs. What is typical for artistic perception is our material disinterestedness in it. Exhilaration at the speech of one's defence counsel in the law court is not an artistic sensation, and, if we sense the nobility and humanity of the thoughts of the most humane poets in the world, then these sensations have nothing in common with art. They were never poetry, and therefore have not completed the journey from poetry to prose either. The existence of people who place Nadson higher than Tyutchev also shows that writers are often valued from the point of view of the quantity of noble thoughts contained in their works, a yardstick very widespread, by the way, amongst the young in Russia. The apotheosis of the sensing of 'art' from the point of view of its 'nobility' is the case of the two students in Chekhov's *The Old Teacher*, one of whom asks the other in the theatre: 'What is he saying there? Something noble?'—'Yes, something noble'. 'Bravo!'.

Here we have the outline of the attitude of the critics to new tendencies in art.

Go out into the street, look at the houses: how are the forms of old art applied in them? You will see quite nightmarish things. For example, (a house on Nevsky Prospekt opposite Konyushennaya Street, a building of the architect Lyalevich) semi-circular arches rest on columns, and between their abutments are inserted crosspieces, of rough-faced stone, like flat arches. This whole system has thrust at the edges—there are no supports at the actual sides; so the entire impression created is that the house is crumbling and falling.

This architectural absurdity (not noticed by the general public and critics) cannot be due, in the given instance, to the ignorance or lack of talent of the architect.

The fault is obviously that the form and meaning of the arch (and the form of the column too, which can also be demonstrated) are not sensed, and are therefore applied as nonsensically as the application of the epithet 'tallow' to the wax candle.

Let us now see how people make quotations from the old authors.

Unfortunately no-one has yet collected incorrectly and inaptly applied quotations; but the material is interesting. At performances of the Futurists' drama the public shouted 'eleventh verst', 'madness' and 'Ward 6', and the newspapers reported these howls with some satisfaction—whereas surely in 'Ward 6' there weren't any madmen, but just a doctor sitting in it through ignorance, surrounded by idiots, along with some sort of philosopher-sufferer figure. So this work of Chekhov was dragged in (from the point of view of those who shouted) completely irrelevantly. We observe here, so to speak, a fossilised quotation, which signifies the same thing as the fossilised epithet— lack of sensation (in the example given the whole work has become fossilised).

The broad masses are satisfied with market-place art, but market-place art shows the death of art. At one time people said to each other when they met: '*zdravstvui*' ('Hello')—now the word has died—and we say to each other '*aste*'. The legs of our chairs, the design of materials, the decoration of houses, the pictures of the 'Petersburg Society of Artists', the sculptures of Gintsburg—all these say to us '*aste*'. Here the decoration is not made, it is 'narrated' and relies on people not seeing it, but on their recognising it and saying—'it's the same'. The golden ages of art did not know the meaning of 'bazaar furniture'. In Assyria—the pole of a soldier's tent, in Greece—the statue of Hecuba, the guardian of the rubbish tip, in the Middle Ages—decorations placed so high up that they couldn't even be seen very well—all these were made, they were all designed for admiring scrutiny. In eras when the forms of art were alive no-one would have brought bazaar monstrosities into the house. When artisan icon-painting spread in Russia in the 17th century, and 'in the icons there appeared such violence and absurdities as were not fitting for a Christian even to look at', this meant that the old forms were already superseded. Nowadays the old art has already died, the new has not yet been born; and things have died—we have lost our awareness of the world; we are like a violinist who has ceased to feel the bow and the strings, we have ceased to be artists in everyday life, we do not love our houses and clothes, and easily part from a life of which we are not aware. Only the creation of new forms of art can restore to man sensation of the world, can resurrect things and kill pessimism.

When we wish, through a surge of tenderness or malice, to caress or insult a person, then we have but a few worn-out, bare words for this, and we then crumple up and break up words to make them strike the ear, so that they should be seen and not recognised. We say, for example, to a man—'silly old woman', (Russ. *dura*['fool'], feminine gender, instead of masculine form *durak*) to make the word grate; or, among the common folk ('The Office' by Turgenev) they use the feminine gender instead of the masculine to express tenderness. Also in this category come all the countless words that are simply mutilated, so many of which all of us use when speaking in moments of passion and which are so hard to remember.

And now, today, when the artist wishes to deal with living form and with the living, not the dead, word, and wishes to give the word features, he has broken it down and mangled it up. The 'arbitrary' and 'derived' words of the Futurists have been born. They either create the new word from an old root (Khlebnikov, Guro, Kamensky, Gnedov) or split it up by rhyme, like Mayakovsky, or give it incorrect stress by use of the rhythm of verse (Kruchenykh). New, living words are created. The ancient diamonds of words recover their former brilliance. This new language is incomprehensible, difficult, and cannot be read like the *Stock Exchange Bulletin*. It is not even like Russian, but we have become too used to setting up comprehensibility as a necessary requirement of poetic language. The history of art shows us that (at least very often) the language of poetry is not a comprehensible language, but a semi-comprehensible one. Thus, savages often sing in an archaic or alien tongue, sometimes so incomprehensible that the singer (or, more correctly, the lead singer) must translate and explain to the choir and audience the meaning of the song he has just composed. (Veselovsky, *Three Chapters from Historical*

Poetics; Grosse, *The Beginnings of Art.*)

The religious poetry of almost all peoples is written in just such a semi-comprehensible language. Church-Slavonic, Latin, Sumerian, which died out in the 20th century B. C. and was used as a religious language until the 3rd Century, the German language of the Russian Stundists (the Russian Stundists preferred for a long time not to translate the German religious hymns into Russian, but to learn German. Dostoïevsky: 'Diary of a Writer').

Jakob Grimm, Hoffmann, Hebel, point out that the ordinary folk often sing not in dialect, but in an elevated language, close to the literary one: 'the incanted Yakut language is differentiated from the everyday language just as our Slavonic is from the present-day conversational language'. (Korolenko: '*At-Davan*'). Arnaut Daniel with his dark style, impeded forms of art (*Schwere Kunstmanier*), cruel (*harte*) forms (Diez: *Leben und Werke der Troubadour*, p. 285), which present difficulties in pronunciation, the *dolce stil nuovo* (13th Century) of the Italians——all these are semi-comprehensible languages, while Aristotle in *Poetics* (Chapter 23) advises giving language a foreign aspect. The explanation of these facts is that this sort of semi-comprehensible language seems to the reader, by reason of its unfamiliarity, more figurative (a fact noted, by the way, by D. N. Ovsyanniko-Kulikovsky).

The writers of past times wrote too smoothly, too sweetly. Their things were reminiscent of that polished surface of which Korolenko spoke: 'across it runs the plane of thought, touching nothing. ' The creation of a new, 'tight' (Russ. *tugoi*-Kruchenykh's term) language is necessary, directed at seeing, and not at recognition. And this necessity is unconsciously felt by many people.

The paths of the new art have only been indicated. It is not theoreticians, but artists who will travel those paths ahead of all others. Whether those who will create the new forms will be the Futurists, or whether this achievement is destined for others—at any rate the Futurist (Translator's Note: In these instances the term used for 'Futurists' *is Budetlyane*; elsewhere the term used is *Futuristy*) poets are on the right path: they have correctly evaluated the old forms. Their poetic devices are the devices of general linguistic thoughtprocesses, simply introduced by them into poetry, just as, in the first centuries of Christianity, rhyme was introduced into poetry, rhyme which had probably always existed in language.

The realisation of new creative devices, which were also met with in poets of the past—for example in the Symbolists—but just by accident—is by itself a great undertaking. And it has been accomplished by the Futurists.

1. 什克洛夫斯基：《语词的复活》

(Viktor Shklovsky, "The Resurrection of the Word," 1914)

作者小识

什克洛夫斯基(Viktor Shklovsky, 1893—1984)，苏联小说家、散文作家和文学理论家，出生于传统知识分子家庭，求学于彼得堡大学，修习古典语文学，对文学语言和修辞手法着迷，与俄国未来主义作家和艺术家交往甚密。《语词的复活》(1914)，为俄国形式主义运动制定了源始纲领。什克洛夫斯基反思赫列勃尼科夫、马雅可夫斯基的艺术实践，构建了形式主义诗学与美学。他的名言是："艺术永远是独立于生活的，它的颜色从不反映飘扬在城堡上空的旗帜的颜色。"[①]1916年，俄国"诗歌语言研究会"(The Society for the Study of Poetic Language)在彼得堡成立，简称"奥波亚兹"(Opoyaz)。什克洛夫斯基为这个诗学团体的核心成员，被誉为"形式主义的斗士"。

他撰写的《作为程序的艺术》(1917)，成为形式主义运动的宣言。其理论代表作是《散文理论》(1925)，书中提出文学技巧至上、形式优先以及"陌生化"原则。"陌生化"原则对文学理论与文学批评影响最为深刻、深远。这一命题的基本含义是：艺术，尤其是诗歌，必须通过艺术上的务求新奇，激活人类心灵对于世界的敏感性，保持对物自身的常新体验。

什克洛夫斯基于1917年至1922年撰写了自传体散文作品《感伤的旅程》。20世纪30年代以后，什克洛夫斯基宣布放弃形式主义诗学与美学，转向历史小说创作与研究，这方面的代表作是《托尔斯泰》《赞成与反对：陀思妥耶夫斯基评论》。

背景略说

俄国形式主义诗歌文化运动不是一夜之间生成的思想奇葩，而是复杂的

---

① 什克洛夫斯基等：《俄国形式主义文论选》，方珊等译，前言11页，北京，生活·读书·新知三联书店，1989。

因缘际会促成的历史成就。首先，俄国平民阶层向文化人的地位跃迁，自然牵动了一场对贵族"斯文"传统的反叛。直到 19 世纪中期，俄国文学批评大体上处在贵族"斯文"传统的影响之下，有闲阶层及其生活方式主导着文学批评话语，社会思想及实用主义成为思想的习性和话语的模式。在这种传统话语的笼罩下，文学被视为社会思想的表现，批评话语则普遍偏离文学形式本身。19 世纪末，俄国文学批评深化对"迫切"社会问题的探索，向前迈出了可贵的一步：开始注重文学技巧问题。而对于文学形式的关注，贯穿在比较文学、民间文学和语言哲学研究中。语言学家亚历山大·波捷勃尼亚（1835—1891）提出，诗歌是最富有创造性的语言，每个字词均具诗意美质。俄国比较文学的奠基人、文学文化史家亚历山大·维谢洛夫斯基（1838—1906）给文学史下了一个经典定义，即"文学史是体现于形象—诗意体验及其表现形式之中的社会思想史"①。这一定义与形式主义文论纲领高度契合。维谢洛夫斯基开创了文学体裁学，注重"诗歌媒介研究"。20 世纪初，文学技巧、形式媒介、艺术手法等美学本体问题跃升到了俄国批评话语的中心。象征主义诗学、未来主义运动风云涌动。在复杂的国际文化语境及残酷的冲突中，在同俄国传统诗学的对抗与传承中，文学形式主义经历着昙花一现而又暴风骤雨般的存在过程，迎来了俄国诗歌与诗学的灿烂复兴。

俄国象征主义旨在将诗歌变成一种幽深玄远的世界观，致力于解决"终极问题"，摆脱"世纪末"精神困境。对于存在境遇的敏感，以及对于"如影随形、相伴始终的灾难"的预感，决定了象征主义诗学的一项根本志业，即"将对诗歌技巧的真知灼见与对诗歌幽深玄远意境的执着有机地融为一体"。20 世纪第二个十年，阿克梅诗学运动的兴起，使象征主义面临着严峻的挑战。阿克梅诗学拒绝象征主义的幽深玄远的世界观及音乐精神。反象征主义之道而行之，阿克梅派追求阿波罗式的清澈明净，刻意营造一种结构上的粗犷凌厉。俄国未来派艺术运动不仅拒绝象征诗学的世界观，而且还要拒绝俄国全部文学遗产，主张诗歌语言的使命是创造新神话。随着"象征的词语丛林"发展出"词语的价值自足"，俄国 20 世纪头二十年的诗学便开启了通往"文学形式主义"的通途。

同时，日内瓦语言学派和现象学哲学运动也策应着这场文学形式主义的转向，且为文学形式主义提供了方法论引领。瑞士语言学家索绪尔（Ferdinand de Saussure，1857—1913）的划时代著作《普通语言学教程》（*Cours de linguis-*

---

① 维谢洛夫斯基：《历史诗学》，刘宁译，30 页，天津，百花文艺出版社，2003。

tique générale，1916)区分语言与言语、能指与所指、内部与外部、共时性与历时性，为文学自律性研究提供了语言学的方法论。援索绪尔语言学入诗学研究，形式主义文学批评便在诗学与语言结构之间建立了紧密联系，从而为诗学规定了探索语言形式审美特质的使命。与索绪尔一样，形式主义者也致力于分离文学的内部要素，即诗学特质(雅可布森称之为"文学性")。[①] 另一方面，由胡塞尔(Edmund Husserl，1859—1938)开创的现象学致力于运用本质还原的方法，将哲学变成严格的科学，也就是以纯粹的直观来穷究认识的开端，抵达认识的终极基础。胡塞尔认为，为了把握认识的开端，必须悬搁一切自然意识和人为设定，面对纯粹意识本身(他称之为"事情本身")。"原初给与的直观都是认识的合法源泉"[②]。俄国形式主义也同样要求，悬搁一切社会思想、文化史、神秘世界观，面对诗学的结构、形式与技巧，即面对文学性本身，建构形式自律的美学。

形式主义理论与批评以"文学性"为重心，因而在三个维度上彰显出其自律美学的关怀。第一，将文学(诗)视为一个独立自足的存在，反对艺术模仿论，也反对"形象思维"论。依据阿布拉姆斯文学要素论，我们不妨说，形式主义批评专注于作品(文本)的形式与结构，而不太关心作者与世界、读者与作品的关系。因为形式主义理论的前提，是将艺术视为一种"体验事物创造之方式"。至于创造的主体和被创造物，在艺术之中已经无关紧要。第二，将文学(诗)的形式和结构分析设定为批评的中心，反对机械区分内容与形式，而主张形式与内容在审美对象上的有机统一。分析艺术的形式与结构，目的是探索感知的规律。什克洛夫斯基力举诗歌技法的"陌生化"，其宗旨就在于从陈腐流俗的正常状态下解救出审美的敏感，让人通过创新的形式去感知艺术，通过艺术去感知世界。第三，将诗学和语言学融合起来，探索艺术的结构方式。结构主义语言学将语言系统视为一个与实在世界无关的封闭系统，形式主义理论也将文学(诗)视为一个与社会、文化、历史无关的封闭系统。诗学

---

① 詹姆逊指出，受索绪尔语言学的启发，形式主义者提出了三大否定：第一，针对象征主义，否定将文学视为世界观或哲学的载体；第二，针对文学文化史方法，否定对文学进行发生学或历时性的分析；第三，针对别林斯基的"形象思维"，否定将文学归结为一种技巧、一种心理机制。参见詹姆逊：《语言的牢笼——结构主义及俄国形式主义述评》，钱佼汝译，35页，南昌，百花洲文艺出版社，1995。

② 胡塞尔：《纯粹现象学通论 纯粹现象学和现象学哲学的观念(第一卷)》，李幼蒸译，84页，北京，商务印书馆，1992。

系统遵循艺术原则，服从美学标准，表现创造规律。

按照 V. 厄利希的研究，俄国形式主义运动大体可以分为三个阶段：斗争与论战（1916—1920）、狂飙突进（1921—1926）、危机与溃退（1926—1930）。① 形式主义与 20 世纪先锋派艺术的兴亡息息相关，在同传统艺术观、社会批评观、象征主义诗学的残酷争论之中脱颖而出，建构了艺术自律、形式优先的美学，却也因为形式主义的孤立境界和结构分析方法的贫瘠而衰落。20 世纪 30 年代后，形式主义融入了马克思主义，经过布拉格诗学而融入结构主义批评，最后为德国接受美学所改造，而成就了一种艺术形式进化的动力观。

基本内容

写作《语词的复活》时，什克洛夫斯基还是一名大学生。1913 年，在未来派艺术家的一场集会上，他做了关于词语创造、诗意凋敝和词语复活的讲演。以这个讲演为蓝本，他写作了《语词的复活》。该文集中表达了一个基本思想：随着时间的推移，词语会僵化，形象会丧失生命力，诗歌会丧失生命之美。诗学的使命就是将人的感性生命从僵化的智性结构之中解放出来，将词语的生命力从僵化的代数符号之中解放出来。具体的论证逻辑大体可以概括为：（1）人类最古老的诗性创造是词语的创造。（2）诗学的形象本来元气弥漫、生机盎然，然而随着时间的流逝，词语已经死亡，语言就像墓地，形象曾经活在再生的词语中。这就是"诗的危机"，即词语成为化石（fossilization）。（3）远溯古希腊诗人荷马，属性形容词（epithet）就已经成为复活词语、激活形象的手段。"长足的阿喀琉斯""鹰眼的雅典娜""见多识广的奥德修斯""长着翅膀飞翔的言语"，如此等等，读来畅快淋漓，形象栩栩如生，传达出活跃的生命，指点出视像的起源。因而，一部属性形容词的历史，也就是诗学风格进化的写照。（4）古老词语艺术家之作品，与词语本身分享着同样的命运。他们完成了从诗歌到散文的进化。什克洛夫斯基说："我们的思想程序不是运用普遍概念而是运用词语，让词语充当代数符号，而铁定必要抽空意象，被运用于日常话语之中，既没有被充分表述，又没有被充分理解，词语便落入俗套，习以为常，而它们的内在形象和外在声音的形式也就再也不为人所感触了。"一旦落入俗套，变得让人们习以为常，词语和事物也就寿终正寝了。（5）未来主

---

① 厄利希：《俄国形式主义　历史与学说》，张冰译，四、五、七章，北京，商务印书馆，2017。

义的目标，是复活万物，也就是将感性世界的生机活力归还给人类。复活词语的具体做法，是将未来主义诗学的技巧与普通语言学思想程序的技巧融为一体，即诗学和语言学的紧密结合。（6）实现崭新的创造技巧本身就是一项伟业，而未来主义自觉地担负起了这一伟业。

《语词的复活》是形式主义的纲领性文献。虽未正式命名，但"陌生化"形式主义原则已经隐含在字里行间。词语变得熟悉、司空见惯，仿佛太阳底下无新事。"我们感受不到熟悉之物，也看不到熟悉之物，但认识到熟悉之物。"极度的熟悉，就是极度的流俗、极度的堕落、极度的平庸。超越流俗，阻止堕落，反抗平庸，端赖于以艺术新技巧消解熟悉之物，进入陌生化境界。

> 那种被称为艺术的东西的存在，正是为了唤回人对生活的感受，使人感受到事物，使石头更成其为石头。艺术的目的，就是使你对事物的感觉如同你所见的视像那样，而不是如同你所认知的那样。艺术的手法，是事物的"陌生化"手法，是复杂化形式的手法，它增加了感受的难度和时延。①

诗学之本质，在于"陌生化"，即让事物变得陌生，让感知再度变得敏锐。"陌生化"是创造心理学法则，但具有深刻的伦理含义，什克洛夫斯基甚至还赋予其一种形而上的意味，表示一种源始的道德立场。他引用托尔斯泰的一段创作手记来支撑这一艺术原则：

> 我在清洁房间，四下打扫之时，来到长沙发面前，但我已经记不清是否曾经掸过它。既然我的这些举动都是习惯性的、无意识的，我记不清并感到也不可能记得清——这样，要是我已经掸过了，但却把这事给忘了——也就是说，要是我无意识地掸过它，那么这也就和我未曾掸过它一样。如果有一位有意识的旁观者一直在注意着我，那么，这事就可以说得清了。但如果没人在一旁观察，或只是无意识地观看，如果许多

---

① Viktor Shklovsky, "Art as Device"（1917/1919）, in Alexandra Berlina（ed.）, *Viktor Shklovsky：A Reader*, New York/London, Bloomsbury, 2017, p. 80.

人都是无意识地过着复杂的一生，那么，这种生命就犹如从未存在过一样。①

通过"陌生化"程序，托尔斯泰恢复了自觉的体验，打破了机械的行为习惯，让感觉从清新而又恐怖的世界中获得新生。

拓展讨论

詹姆逊在马克思主义辩证批评的视角下，看到了"陌生化"原则的独特之处：它适用于所有文学的一种过程，绝不暗示一种特殊的文学成分（比如隐喻）或某个特殊的文学类型优于其他文学成分或类型。詹姆逊具体地论列"陌生化"纯形式概念的三个优势：第一，将文学（纯诗学系统）与其他语言形式区分开来，为文学理论的建立预设了一个先决条件。第二，在文学作品内部确立一种等级关系，突出"更新感知""新的眼光""观察世界的新方式"的优先性。第三，启示了一种新文学史观，将文学史视为一系列的突变，即与过去断裂，与主导前代的艺术准则决裂。

什克洛夫斯基的"陌生化"原则，被钱锺书拿来与梅尧臣（1002—1060）的"以故为新，以俗为雅"命题进行互释：

近世俄国形式主义文评家希克洛夫斯基（Victor Shklovsky）等以为文词最易袭故蹈常，落套刻板（habitualization, automatization），故作者手眼须使熟者生（defamiliarization），或亦曰使文者野（rebarbarization）。窃谓圣俞二语，夙悟先觉。夫以故为新，即使熟者生也；而使文者野，亦可谓之使野者文，驱使野言，俾入文语，纳俗于雅尔。②

《六一诗话》记圣俞论诗所谓"状难写之境，含不尽之意"，数百年来已熟挂谈艺者口角。而山谷、后山祖述圣俞论诗语，迄无过问者，故拈出而稍拂拭之。抑不独修词为然，选材取境，亦复如是。歌德、诺瓦利斯、华兹华斯、柯尔律治、雪莱、狄更斯、福楼拜、尼采、巴斯可里等

---

① 托尔斯泰 1897 年 2 月 29 日杂记，转引自 Viktor Shklovsky, "Art as Device" (1917/1919), in Alexandra Berlina (ed.), *Viktor Shklovsky：A Reader*, New York/London, Bloomsbury, 2017, p. 80。

② 钱锺书：《谈艺录》，42～43 页，北京，生活·读书·新知三联书店，2001。

cessful poems; yet most students have the greatest difficulty in accounting for its goodness. The attempt to account for it on the grounds of nobility of sentiment soon breaks down. On this level, the poem merely says: that the city in the morning light presents a picture which is majestic and touching to all but the most dull of soul; but the poem says very little more about the sight: the city is beautiful in the morning light and it is awfully still. The attempt to make a case for the poem in terms of the brilliance of its images also quickly breaks down: the student searches for graphic details in vain; there are next to no realistic touches. In fact, the poet simply huddles the details together:

> *silent, bare,*
> *Ships, towers, domes, theatres, and temples lie*
> *Open unto the fields …*

We get a blurred impression—points of roofs and pinnacles along the skyline, all twinkling in the morning light. More than that, the sonnet as a whole contains some very flat writing and some well-worn comparisons.

The reader may ask: Where, then, does the poem get its power? It gets it, it seems to me, from the paradoxical situation out of which the poem arises. The speaker is honestly surprised, and he manages to get some sense of awed surprise into the poem. It is odd to the poet that the city should be able to "wear the beauty of the morning" at all. Mount Snowden, Skiddaw, Mont Blanc—these wear it by natural right, but surely not grimy, feverish London. This is the point of the almost shocked exclamation:

> *Never did sun more beautifully steep*
> *In his first splendour,* valley, rock, *or* hill …

The "smokeless air" reveals a city which the poet did not know existed: man-made London is a part of nature too, is lighted by the sun of nature, and lighted to as beautiful effect.

The river glideth at his own sweet will ...

A river is the most "natural" thing that one can imagine; it has the elasticity, the curved line of nature itself. The poet had never been able to regard this one as a real river—now, uncluttered by barges, the river reveals itself as a natural thing, not at all disciplined into a rigid and mechanical pattern: it is like the daffodils, or the mountain brooks, artless, and whimsical, and "natural" as they. The poem closes, you will remember, as follows:

> *Dear God! the very houses seem asleep;*
> *And all that mighty heart is lying still!*

The city, in the poet's insight of the morning, has earned its right to be considered organic, not merely mechanical. That is why the stale metaphor of the sleeping houses is strangely renewed. The most exciting thing that the poet can say about the houses is that they are *asleep*. He has been in the habit of counting them dead—as just mechanical and inanimate; to say they are "asleep" is to say that they are alive, that they participate in the life of nature. In the same way, the tired old metaphor which sees a great city as a pulsating heart of empire becomes revivified. It is only when the poet sees the city under the semblance of death that he can see it as actually alive—quick with the only life which he can accept, the organic life of "nature."

It is not my intention to exaggerate Wordsworth's own consciousness of the paradox involved. In this poem, he prefers, as is usual with him, the frontal attack. But the situation is paradoxical here as in so many of his poems. In his preface to the second edition of the *Lyrical Ballads* Wordsworth stated that his general purpose was "to choose incidents and situations from common life" but so to treat them that "ordinary things should be presented to the mind in an unusual aspect." Coleridge was to state the purpose for him later, in terms which make even more evident Wordsworth's exploitation of the paradoxical: "Mr. Wordsworth ... was to propose to himself as his object, to give the charm of novelty to things of every day, and to excite a feeling analogous to the super-

nalogies, but the metaphors do not lie in the same plane or fit neatly edge to edge. There is a continual tilting of the planes; necessary overlappings, discrepancies, contradictions. Even the most direct and simple poet is forced into paradoxes far more often than we think, if we are sufficiently alive to what he is doing.

But in dilating on the difficulties of the poet's task, I do not want to leave the impression that it is a task which necessarily defeats him, or even that with his method he may not win to a fine precision. To use Shakespeare's figure, he can

> *with assays of bias*
> *By indirections find directions out.*

Shakespeare had in mind the game of lawnbowls in which the bowl is distorted, a distortion which allows the skillful player to bowl a curve. To elaborate the figure, science makes use of the perfect sphere and its attack can be direct. The method of art can, I believe, never be direct—is always indirect. But that does not mean that the master of the game cannot place the bowl where he wants it. The serious difficulties will only occur when he confuses his game with that of science and mistakes the nature of his appropriate instrument. Mr. Stuart Chase a few years ago, with a touching naïveté, urged us to take the distortion out of the bowl—to treat language like notation.

I have said that even the apparently simple and straightforward poet is forced into paradoxes by the nature of his instrument. Seeing this, we should not be surprised to find poets who consciously employ it to gain a compression and precision otherwise unobtainable. Such a method, like any other, carries with it its own perils. But the danger are not overpowering; the poem is not predetermined to a shallow and glittering sophistry. The method is an extension of the normal language of poetry, not a perversion of it.

I should like to refer the reader to a concrete case. Donne's "Canonization" ought to provide a sufficiently extreme instance. The basic metaphor which underlies the poem (and which is reflected in the title) involves a sort of paradox.

For the poet daringly treats profane love as if it were divine love. The canonization is not that of a pair of holy anchorites who have renounced the world and the flesh. The hermitage of each is the other's body; but they do renounce the world, and so their title to sainthood is cunningly argued. The poem then is a parody of Christian sainthood; but it is an intensely serious parody of a sort that modern man, habituated as he is to an easy yes or no, can hardly understand. He refuses to accept the paradox as a serious rhetorical device; and since he is able to accept it only as a cheap trick, he is forced into this dilemma. Either: Donne does not take love seriously; here he is merely sharpening his wit as a sort of mechanical exercise. Or: Donne does not take sainthood seriously; here he is merely indulging in a cynical and bawdy parody.

Neither account is true; a reading of the poem will show that Donne takes both love and religion seriously; it will show, further, that the paradox is here his inevitable instrument. But to see this plainly will require a closer reading than most of us give to poetry.

The poem opens dramatically on a note of exasperation. The "you" whom the speaker addresses is not identified. We can imagine that it is a person, perhaps a friend, who is objecting to the speaker's love affair. At any rate, the person represents the practical world which regards love as a silly affectation. To use the metaphor on which the poem is built, the friend represents the secular world which the lovers have renounced.

Donne begins to suggest this metaphor in the first stanza by the contemptuous alternatives which he suggests to the friend:

> ... *chide my palsie, or my gout,*
> *My five gray haires, or ruin'd fortune flout* ...

The implications are: (i) All right, consider my love as an infirmity, as a disease, if you will, but confine yourself to my other infirmities, my palsy, my approaching old age, my ruined fortune. You stand a better chance of curing those; in chiding me for this one, you are simply wasting your time as well as mine. (ii) Why don't you pay attention to your own welfare—go on and get wealth and honor for yourself. What should you care if I do give these up in pursuing my love.

The two main categories of secular success are neatly, and contemptuously epitomized in the line

Or the Kings reall, or his stamped face ···

Cultivate the court and gaze at the king's face there, or, if you prefer, get into business and look at his face stamped on coins. But let me alone.

This conflict between the "real" world and the lover absorbed in the world of love runs through the poem; it dominates the second stanza in which the torments of love, so vivid to the lover, affect the real world not at all——

What merchants ships have my sighs drown'd?

It is touched on in the fourth stanza in the contrast between the word "Chronicle" which suggests secular history with its pomp and magnificence, the history of kings and princes, and the word "sonnets" with its suggestions of trivial and precious intricacy. The conflict appears again in the last stanza, only to be resolved when the unworldly lovers, love's saints who have given up the world, paradoxically achieve a more intense world. But here the paradox is still contained in, and supported by, the dominant metaphor: so does the holy anchorite win a better world by giving up this one.

But before going on to discuss this development of the theme, it is important to see what else the second stanza does. For it is in this second stanza and the third, that the poet shifts the tone of the poem, modulating from the note of irritation with which the poem opens into the quite different tone with which it closes.

Donne accomplishes the modulation of tone by what may be called an analysis of love-metaphor. Here, as in many of his poems, he shows that he is thoroughly self-conscious about what he is doing. This second stanza, he fills with the conventionalized figures of the Petrarchan tradition: the wind of lovers' sighs, the floods of lovers' tears, etc. —extravagant figures with which the contemptuous secular friend might be expected to tease the lover. The implication is that the poet himself recognizes the absurdity of the Petrarchan love metaphors. But what of it? The very absurdity of the jargon which lovers are expected to talk makes for his argument: their love, however absurd it may appear to the world, does no harm to the world. The practical friend need have no fears: there will still be wars to fight and lawsuits to argue.

The opening of the third stanza suggests that this vein of irony is to be maintained. The poet points out to his friend the infinite fund of such absurdities which can be applied to lovers:

> *Call her one, mee another flye,*
> *We'are Tapers too, and at our owne cost die …*

For that matter, the lovers can conjure up for themselves plenty of such fantastic comparisons: *they* know what the world thinks of them. But these figures of the third stanza are no longer the threadbare Petrarchan conventionalities; they have sharpness and bite. The last one, the likening of the lovers to the phoenix, is fully serious, and with it, the tone has shifted from ironic banter into a defiant but controlled tenderness.

The effect of the poet's implied awareness of the lovers' apparent madness is to cleanse and revivify metaphor; to indicate the sense in which the poet accepts it, and thus to prepare us for accepting seriously the fine and seriously intended metaphors which dominate the last two stanzas of the poem.

The opening line of the fourth stanza,

> *Wee can dye by it, if not live by love,*

achieves an effect of tenderness and deliberate resolution. The lovers are ready to die to the world; they are committed; they are not callow but confident. (The basic metaphor of the saint, one notices, is being carried on; the lovers in their renunciation of the world, have something of the confident resolution of the saint. By the bye, the word "legend"—

> *... if unfit for tombes and hearse*
> *Our legend bee—*

in Donne's time meant "the life of a saint.") The lovers are willing to forego the ponderous and stately chronicle and to accept the trifling and insubstantial "sonnet" instead; but then if the urn be well wrought, it provides a finer memorial for one's ashes than does the pompous and grotesque monument. With the finely contemptuous, yet quiet phrase, "halfe-acre tombes," the world which the lovers reject expands into something gross and vulgar. But the figure works further; the pretty sonnets will not merely hold their ashes as a decent earthly memorial. Their legend, their story, will gain them canonization; and approved as love's saints, other lovers will invoke them.

In this last stanza, the theme receives a final complication. The lovers in rejecting life actually win to the most intense life. This paradox has been hinted at earlier in the phoenix metaphor. Here it receives a powerful dramatization. The lovers in becoming hermits, find that they have not lost the world, but have gained the world in each other, now a more intense, more meaningful world. Donne is not content to treat the lovers' discovery as something which comes to them passively, but rather as something which they actively achieve. They are like the saint, God's athlete:

> *Who did the whole worlds soule* contract, *and* drove
> *Into the glasses of your eyes ...*

The image is that of a violent squeezing as of a powerful hand. And what do the lovers "drive" into each other's eyes? The "Countries, Townes," and "Courtes," which they renounced in the first stanza of the poem. The unworldly lovers thus become the most "worldly" of all.

The tone with which the poem closes is one of triumphant achievement, but the tone is a development contributed to by various earlier elements. One of the more important elements which works toward our acceptance of the final paradox is the figure of the phoenix, which will bear a little further analysis.

The comparison of the lovers to the phoenix is very skillfully related to the two earlier comparisons, that in which the lovers are like burning tapers, and that in which they are like the eagle and the dove. The phoenix comparison gathers up both: the phoenix is a bird, and like the tapers, it burns. We have a selected series of items: the phoenix figure seems to come in a natural stream of association. "Call us what you will," the lover says, and rattles off in his desperation the first comparisons that occur to him. The comparison to the phoenix seems thus merely another outlandish one, the most outrageous of all. But it is this most fantastic one, stumbled over apparently in his haste, that the poet goes on to develop. It really describes the lovers best and justifies their renunciation. For the phoenix is not two but one, "we two being one, are it"; and it burns, not like the taper at its own cost, but to live again. Its death is life: "Wee dye and rise the same…" The poet literally justifies the fantastic assertion. In the sixteenth and seventeenth centuries to "die" means to experience the consummation of the act of love. The lovers after the act are the same. Their love is not exhausted in mere lust. This is their title to canonization. Their love is like the phoenix.

I hope that I do not seem to juggle the meaning of *die*. The meaning that I have cited can be abundantly justified in the literature of the period; Shakespeare uses "die" in this sense; so does Dryden. Moreover, I do not think that I give it undue emphasis. The word is in a crucial position. On it is pivoted the transition to the next stanza,

> *Wee can dye by it, if not live by love,*
> *And if unfit for tombes …*

Most important of all, the sexual submeaning of "die" does not contradict the other meanings: the poet is saying: "Our death is really a more intense life"; "We can afford to trade life (the world) for death (love), for that death is the consummation of life"; "After all, one does not expect to live *by* love, one expects, and wants, to die *by* it." But in the total passage he is also saying: "Because our love is not mundane, we can give up the world"; "Because our love is not merely lust, we can give up the other lusts, the lust for wealth and power"; "because," and this is said with an inflection of irony as by one who knows the world too well, "because our love can outlast its consummation, we are a minor miracle, we are love's saints." This passage with its ironical tenderness and its realism feeds and supports the brilliant paradox with which the poem closes.

There is one more factor in developing and sustaining the final effect. The poem is an instance of the doctrine which it asserts; it is both the assertion and the realization of the assertion. The poet has actually before our eyes built within the song the "pretty room" with which he says the lovers can be content. The poem itself is the well-wrought urn which can hold the lovers' ashes and which will not suffer in comparison with the prince's "halfe-acre tomb."

And how necessary are the paradoxes? Donne might have said directly, "Love in a cottage is enough." "The Canonization" contains this admirable thesis, but it contains a great deal more. He might have been as forthright as a later lyricist who wrote, "We'll build a sweet little nest, /Somewhere out in the West, /And let the rest of the world go by." He might even have imitated that more metaphysical lyric, which maintains, "You're the cream in my coffee." "The Canonization" touches on all these observations, but it goes beyond them, not merely in dignity, but in precision.

I submit that the only way by which the poet could say what "The Canonization" says is by paradox. More direct methods may be tempting, but all of them enfeeble and distort what is to be said. This statement may seem the less surprising when we reflect on how many of the important things which the poet has to say have to be said by means of paradox: most of the language of lovers is such—"The Canonization" is a good example; so is most of the language of religion—"He who would save his life, must lose it"; "The last shall be first." Indeed, almost any insight important enough to warrant a great poem apparently has to be stated in such terms. Deprived of the character of paradox with its twin concomitants of irony and wonder, the matter of Donne's poem unravels into "facts," biological, sociological, and economic. What happens to Donne's lovers if we consider them "scientifically," without benefit of the supernaturalism which the poet confers upon them? Well, what happens to Shakespeare's lovers, for Shakespeare uses the basic metaphor of "The Canonization" in his *Romeo and Juliet*? In their first conversation, the lovers play with the analogy between the lover and the pilgrim to the Holy Land. Juliet says:

> *For saints have hands that pilgrims' hands do touch*
> *And palm to palm is holy palmers' kiss.*

Considered scientifically, the lovers become Mr. Aldous Huxley's animals, "quietly sweating, palm to palm."

For us today, Donne's imagination seems obsessed with the problem of unity; the sense in which the lovers become one—the sense in which the soul is united with God. Frequently, as we have seen, one type of union becomes a metaphor for the other. It may not be too far-fetched to see both as instances of, and metaphors for, the union which the creative imagination itself effects. For that fusion is not logical; it apparently violates science and common sense; it welds together the discordant and the contradictory. Coleridge has of course given us the classic description of its nature and power. It "reveals itself in the balance or reconcilement of opposite or discordant qualities: of sameness, with difference; of the general, with the concrete; the idea, with the image; the individual, with the representative; the sense of novelty and freshness, with old and familiar objects; a more than usual state of emotion, with more than usual order…" It is a great and illuminating statement, but is a series of paradoxes. Apparently Coleridge could describe the effect of the imagination in no other way.

Shakespeare, in one of his poems, has given a description that oddly parallels that of Coleridge.

> *Reason in it selfe confounded,*
> *Saw Division grow together,*
> *To themselves yet either neither,*

Simple were so well compounded.

I do not know what his "The Phoenix and the Turtle" celebrates. Perhaps it *was* written to honor the marriage of Sir John Salisbury and Ursula Stanley; or perhaps the Phoenix is Lucy, Countess of Bedford; or perhaps the poem is merely an essay on Platonic love. But the scholars themselves are so uncertain, that I think we will do little violence to established habits of thinking, if we boldly pre-empt the poem for our own purposes. Certainly the poem is an instance of that magic power which Coleridge sought to describe. I propose that we take it for a moment as a poem about that power;

> *So they loved as love in twaine,*
> *Had the essence but in one,*
> *Two distincts, Division none,*
> *Number there in love was slaine.*
>
> *Hearts remote, yet not asunder;*
> *Distance and no space was seene,*
> *Twixt this* Turtle *and his* Queene;
> *But in them it were a wonder …*
>
> *Propertie was thus appalled,*
> *That the selfe was not the same;*
> *Single Natures double name,*
> *Neither two nor one was called.*

Precisely! The nature is single, one, unified. But the name is double, and today with our multiplication of sciences, it is multiple. If the poet is to be true to his poetry, he must call it neither two nor one: the paradox is his only solution. The difficulty has intensified since Shakespeare's day: the timid poet, when confronted with the problem of "Single Natures double name," has too often funked it. A history of poetry from Dryden's time to our own might bear as its subtitle "The Half-Hearted Phoenix."

In Shakespeare's poem, Reason is "in it selfe confounded" at the union of the Phoenix and the Turtle; but it recovers to admit its own bankruptcy:

> *Love hath Reason, Reason none,*
> *If what parts, can so remaine* ...

and it is Reason which goes on to utter the beautiful threnos with which the poem concludes:

> *Beautie, Truth, and Raritie,*
> *Grace in all simplicitie,*
> *Here enclosde, in cinders lie.*

> *Death is now the* Phoenix *nest,*
> *And the* Turtles *loyall brest,*
> *To eternitie doth rest* ...
> *Truth may seeme, but cannot be,*
> *Beautie bragge, but tis not she,*
> *Truth and Beautie buried be.*

> *To this urne let those repaire,*
> *That are either true or faire,*
> *For these dead Birds, sigh a prayer.*

Having pre-empted the poem for our own purposes, it may not be too outrageous to go on to make one further observation. The urn to which we are summoned, the urn which holds the ashes of the phoenix, is like the well-wrought urn of Donne's "Canonization" which holds the phoenix-lovers' ashes: it is the poem itself. One is reminded of still another urn, Keats's Grecian urn, which contained for Keats, Truth and Beauty, as Shakespeare's urn encloses "Beautie, Truth, and Raritie." But there is a sense in which all such well-wrought urns contain the ashes of a phoenix. The urns are not meant for memorial purposes only, though that often seems to be their chief significance to the professors of literature. The phoenix rises from its ashes; or ought to rise; but it will not arise for all our mere sifting and measuring the ashes, or testing them for their chemical content. We must be prepared to accept the paradox of the imagination itself; else "Beautie, Truth, and Raritie" remain enclosed in their cinders and we shall end with essential cinders, for all our pains.

2. 布鲁克斯：《悖论的语言》

(Cleanth Brooks, "The Language of Paradox," 1947)

作者小识

布鲁克斯(Cleanth Brooks，1906—1994)，美国南方文学批评的代表人物。20世纪中期，他以自己的批评活动将新批评的文本细读方法经典化，为美国高等学校文学教育做出了贡献。1935年至1942年，他与皮普金(Charles W. Pipkin)、沃伦(Robert Penn Warren)合作编辑《南方评论》(*The Southern Review*)。这份杂志成为美国新批评运动的阵地，主要刊发美国新生一代南方作家和批评家的作品。布鲁克斯深受早期新批评运动主将兰瑟姆、泰特和沃伦的影响，几乎全盘接受20世纪30年代美国南方农业平均主义运动的哲学观念与政治纲领。

布鲁克斯文学批评的代表作包括《现代诗歌与传统》(*Modern Poetry and the Tradition*，1939)和《精致的瓮》(*The Well Wrought Urn*，1947)。其《理解诗歌》(*Understanding Poetry*，1938)、《理解小说》(*Understanding Fiction*，1943，与沃伦合著)，以及《理解戏剧》(*Understanding Drama*，1945，与罗伯特·海尔曼合著)，现在已经是高等学校文学教育的经典教科书，普及了新批评的文本细读方法。

布鲁克斯1953年获得美国和加拿大古根海姆人文教席(Guggenheim Fellowship for Humanities US & Canada)，1985年获得杰弗逊人文教席(Jefferson Lecture in the Humanities)。

布鲁克斯的批评思想之核心，是将反讽、歧义与悖论确立为诗歌结构的基本原则，以及理解诗歌含义的修辞切入点。而他以文本细读为主要方法的批评实践，体现了新批评的基本主张，即把诗歌当作诗歌来考察，强化"诗歌的内在生命力"。

背景略说

"新批评"是一个充满歧义的术语。它第一次出现，是作为斯平加恩(Joel

Elias Spingarn)的书名(*The New Criticism*)，意指黑格尔后学，尤其是指克罗齐的美学。第二次出现，则是指 20 世纪 20 年代酝酿于英国、30 年代发展于美国、50 年代盛极一时、60 年代衰落的现代文学批评思潮，史称"英美新批评"。"新批评"的第二种含义是指一种反实证主义和反社会学传统的文学理论、批评实践，主张以文本细读为手段，将文学作品作为独立的审美存在来研究，透过文本的肌理、词语的歧异，烛照幽微，理解文本的意义。它第三次出现，则与法国结构主义、后结构主义文学批评合流。第三种含义的新批评，又被称为"新新批评"。作为一种新近的文学理论和批评实践，新新批评致力于提示阅读策略，探索书写的自主性以及能指与所指的矛盾关系，揭示再现世界和表现主体的诸种困境。

就"英美新批评"而言，不仅这个术语之所指相当庞杂，而且也根本就不存在一个自诩为"新批评"的团体和流派，其松散的批评实践也很难说形成了一场文学运动。没有固定的批评团体，没有火热的文学运动，但"英美新批评"分享着俄国形式主义的原则：艺术作品，特别是文学性或诗性的存在物应该自主自律，人们不应该将它们还原为社会要素、文化要素、作者意向或读者反应，不应该拿非艺术非诗性的标准来评价艺术和诗。

新批评的活动历时近半个世纪，其发展历史大致可分为奠基期(1915—1930)、形成期(1930—1945)、极盛期(1945—1957)以及衰落期(20 世纪 60 年代以后)。

(1)奠基期。英美新批评的渊源可以追溯到晚古时代希腊罗马的修辞批评，以及浪漫主义时代的有机艺术整体结构观。然而，新批评的直接先驱则是 T. S. 艾略特(T. S. Eliot，1888—1965)、I. A. 理查兹(I. A. Richards，1893—1979)以及 F. R. 利维斯(F. R. Leaves，1895—1978)。艾略特为新批评奠定了思想基础，理查兹为新批评开拓了理论视野，而利维斯为新批评预备了精读方法。

诗人艾略特是保守的传统主义者，他一面哀叹现代社会沉疴遍地，一面要求诗人泯灭个性、皈依传统秩序。其名作《传统与个人才能》确立了历史秩序的原则：诗人必须意识到历史的秩序，诗人或作家不仅要理解"过去的过去性"，还要理解"过去的现存性"；不仅要呈现自己的时代背景，还要感知"从荷马以来欧洲的整个文学及本国的整个文学是一种同时的存在"。在艾略特看来，诗学批评的历史原则同时也是美学原则，它要求将艺术作品之诞生视为一个新的事件，而现存的艺术经典本身就构成了一种理想的秩序。①

理查兹独步20世纪20年代的剑桥文坛，30年代在中国传道授业，后来开启回归"基础英语"运动，并在哈佛大学酿造了文学课爆棚的奇观。在同奥登合著的《意义的意义》中，他尝试"废黜形而上学"，反其道而行之，通过语言过程的种种局限和混乱来探索意义。在《文学批评原理》中，他力举科学与诗歌的互补，甚至试图将两种文化融为一体，让诗歌担负起宗教的使命，拯救已经在现代社会沦丧的"卓越自我"。在《实用批评》中，他将文学批评诉诸情感，因为情感是审美活动的中心。理查兹以古典人文主义的"卓越自我"为基础，重构了一套将科学与诗学融为一体的文学理论及批评方法，并建构了一套以拯救为使命的教育哲学。这种"经纬天地的古典人文主义"，是新批评话语之中隐而不现的思想纲维。②

利维斯在剑桥大学主编《细察》(Scrutiny)，培养了在此求学问道的学者和学生，让他们的思想和情感走向成熟。这份杂志堪称文学批评圣经，而利维斯被奉为先知。《细察》撇开"图书馆里的批评著作"，致力于为公众提供"有用的分析"，培育公众对语言的微妙敏感力，帮助读者自己去理解作品。利维斯提出英国文学的"伟大的传统"这一概念，表现了一位批评家的责任感，以及一位文学史家高瞻远瞩的胸襟。"伟大的传统"是指"英国小说的伟大之处构成其特征属性的那个传统"③，其核心是天才的方法、独创的技巧和永恒的形式。

（2）形成期。1921年，美国范德比尔特大学教师兰塞姆(John Crowe Ransom)发起并创办小众诗刊《逃亡者》。以兰塞姆为核心，在20世纪30年代形成了"美国南方批评家"群体，主要成员有泰特(Allen Tate)、沃伦和布鲁克斯。他们以《南方评论》为主要阵地，表达具有浓郁保守气息和贵族色彩的文化历史观，以及以艺术存在为本体、以文本精读为方法、以修辞和结构为切入点的文学批评观念。同时，他们还编撰大学文学教材，将新批评方法经典化，推崇从诗歌结构出发阐释意义的分析技巧。

---

① 艾略特：《传统与个人才能：艾略特文集·论文》，卞之琳、李赋宁等译，2～3页，上海，上海译文出版社，2012。

② 参见斯潘诺斯：《现代人文教育中阿波罗的威权——阿诺德、白璧德和瑞恰慈文学思想论略（上）》，胡继华译，见曹卫东：《跨文化研究》，2016年第1辑，164页，北京，社会科学文献出版社，2016。

③ 利维斯：《伟大的传统》，袁伟译，12页，北京，生活·读书·新知三联书店，2002。

（3）极盛期。第二次世界大战之后，新批评在美国大学被体制化，其代表性批评家控制了大学文科和主要的文学刊物，文学家、美学家和批评家对"美国南方批评学派"望风归顺。韦勒克和沃伦合著《文学理论》，布鲁克斯和维姆萨特合著《文学批评简史》，这两部作品一经一纬，合纵连横，将新批评理论和实践体系化了。特别值得一提的是，韦勒克自觉地将新批评理论运用于比较文学研究，致力于克服比较文学法国学派实证主义方法的偏差。韦勒克指出，艺术作品绝不仅仅是来源和影响的总和，而是"由自由想象构思而成的整体"，所以文学批评必须"把握住艺术与诗的本质，看到它战胜命运、超越人类短促的生命而长存的力量，看到它创造出一个想象的新世界"。他还主张，文学研究必须像艺术本身一样，"成为一种想象的活动，从而也成为人类最高价值的保存者和创造者"。[1]

（4）衰落期。20 世纪 60 年代以后，新批评衰落了。为何衰落？一些批评家称，新批评"死于其巨大的成功"。具体说来，曲高和寡的唯美主义、隔离文学与现实的反历史主义，以及保守主义的文化立场，让新批评难以为继，只能成为少数知识分子逃避现代性的精神避难所。斯潘诺斯甚至断言，隐含在新批评形式至上观念之中的古典人文主义，对现代多元文化和个体立场具有一种规训、抑制的威权。韦勒克却认为，新批评衰落之原因，主要有三个：第一，其代表人物的保守政治文化与宗教立场令人生疑；第二，解构论的崛起让新批评成为虚无主义的牺牲品；第三，地方中心主义倾向明显，即不是以英格兰为中心，就是以美国南方为堡垒，而抗拒"世界文学"的开放视野。[2]

基本内容

《悖论的语言》是布鲁克斯名作《精致的瓮》之开篇。作者贯彻文本细读方法，研究英国诗歌的经典之作，以编年史的办法对论文集中的十一篇文章进行排列，大体覆盖了从伊丽莎白时代的玄学诗人到现代主义诗人叶芝。全书以《悖论的语言》开篇，以《释义异说》作结，致力于揭示诗歌共同的结构特性，并将经典之作置于文化基质（cultural matrix）中予以审视。《精致的瓮》象征永

---

[1] 韦勒克：《比较文学的危机》，见《批评的概念》，张金言译，270～271 页、279 页，杭州，中国美术学院出版社，1999。

[2] 韦勒克：《近代文学批评史》(1750—1950)，第六卷，杨自伍译，262～263 页，上海，上海译文出版社，2005。

恒的人文价值，全书却在伸张一种以语境化为基础的审美相对主义。"任何一种从永恒角度审视诗歌的尝试都将导致一种虚无缥缈的幻觉。"布鲁克斯在撰写这本书时表现出犀利的问题意识，那就是对甚嚣尘上的"人文学科的衰微"做出回应。他写道："文学不仅需要人文学科的复兴，而且指出了如何才能实现人文学科的复兴。"他呼吁文学研究者尊重、相信"交流的奇迹"，对诗歌传递信息的方式和意义生成结构做出贴近的考察，从而捍卫传统的人文主义。

论文开宗明义："诗歌语言即悖论语言。"悖论，在古典修辞学和逻辑学中是指这么一种言语行为：一个陈述、一个命题看起来自相矛盾、荒诞不经，但经过深入思考和详尽解释，它却理据十足、近乎真理。庄子《齐物论》所言"吊诡"，义近"悖论"：

> 君乎，牧乎，固哉！丘也与汝皆梦也，予谓汝梦亦梦也。是其言也，其名为吊诡。万世之后而一遇大圣知其解者，是旦暮遇之也。

意思是说，你在做梦，我也在做梦，你我互相说对方在做梦，这就是"吊诡"。自相矛盾和荒诞言语隐含着颠扑不破的真理，这同样也是"悖论"的力量。布鲁克斯说，"悖论适合于诗，并且是无法规避的诗歌语言"。科学的真理要求肃清悖论的痕迹，但诗人表现真理却只能依靠悖论。华兹华斯的诗歌语言看似简单自然，但蕴含着潜在的悖论，揭示"平凡之事不平凡，猥琐之物蕴含诗意"。诗人在运用悖论语言之时，不仅强化了反讽，而且凸显了类比，赋予日常事物以神奇魔力。布鲁克斯说服我们相信，即便是最为朴素的诗人，也会频繁地运用悖论。

将悖论语言普遍化为一条诗学原则之后，布鲁克斯对玄学诗人邓恩（John Donne，1572—1631）的名篇《封圣》（"Canonization"）进行了逐字逐句的文本细读，揭示诗的基本隐喻所涉及的种种悖论。(1)现实世界与爱欲世界之间的冲突贯穿诗的始终，生与死的对峙赋予诗歌结构以强大的张力。(2)诗的第二、第三节完成了从愤怒到叹息的变调，悖论推动着爱欲向神圣的境界上升。精致的瓮，一如"优美的十四行诗，不仅像一件体面的世俗纪念物那样存放恋人们的骨灰"，而且还将他们的传奇神圣化。(3)在诗歌主题趋向于复杂化的时刻，凤凰作为一个基本的隐喻，暗示着一个元次级的悖论：恋人们舍弃尘世，却赢得了最热切的生活。凤凰涅槃，意味着死就是生，出死入生，抵达永恒。(4)因为圣爱在圆满之后仍然还在延续，有情人和钟情者都是小小的奇迹，是爱的圣者。伴随着这个精妙的反讽，邓恩暗示一首诗就是盛放恋人骨灰的精致之瓮，包容着济慈的"真与美"，包含着"真实、美好和珍贵的情感"，承载着永恒。

拓展讨论

在这篇论文中，布鲁克斯详细论述"悖论的语言"，大有通过文本细读将"悖论"提升为一项诗学原则的架势。那么，能否有一种悖论诗学，逾越古今，涵濡中外，经纬天地，堪称通则呢？苏格拉底"自知无知"，老子说"信言不美""美言不信"（《道德经》），庄子言"道隐于小成，言隐于荣华"（《庄子·齐物论》），甚至到王国维感叹"可爱者不可信，可信者不可爱"（《三十自序》），悖论俨然是人类生存的普遍境遇。诗人以语言悖论，迂回曲折地双关出真理，而诗学的真理又关涉着人类的深刻悲剧。

中国古代诗人深知"悖论"（"吊诡"）之秘密，也自觉地运用"悖论"（"吊诡"）去加强诗歌的表达力与感染力。诗人修辞，奇情幻想，翻新旧说，更生新意。一如莎士比亚《凤凰与斑鸠》所咏叹的："单一的本质，双重的名字，既非是一，亦非是二。"天理、人情、物象，无不蕴含二义，以至于歧义丛生，含糊暧昧。诗人之唯一解决办法，自然是悖论。

《国风·周南·兔罝》乃名篇，其中的悖论尤其醒人耳目：

> 肃肃兔罝，椓之丁丁。赳赳武夫，公侯干城。肃肃兔罝，施于中逵。赳赳武夫，公侯好仇。肃肃兔罝，施于中林。赳赳武夫，公侯腹心。

将打桩设网捕兔的狩猎者和捍卫公侯的赳赳武夫相提并论，似乎充满了反讽意味，但细想却是诗人呈现人类普遍悖论境遇的方式。初读觉得滑稽可笑，沉思冥想之后读者会幡然领悟，表面上的讽刺隐含着真诚的赞美：王侯将相，勿论出生，狩猎者和国家卫士享有同等的尊严。"肃肃兔罝""赳赳武夫"，本无高低贵贱之分，这是诗经所传递的古典人文主义信息。方玉润《诗经原始》云："窃意此必羽林卫士，扈跸游猎，英姿伟抱，奇杰魁梧，遥而望之，无非公侯妙选。识者于此有以知西伯异世之必昌，如后世刘基赴临淮，见人人皆英雄，屠贩者气宇亦异，知为天子所在，而叹其从龙者之众也。诗人咏之，亦以为王气钟灵特盛乎此耳。"

悖论诗学建立在悖论的语言上，将语言的工具性和本体性融为一体。悖论诗学源于"立象以尽意"传统，尝试解决言、象、意之间的矛盾。"意翻空而易奇，言征实而难巧"，"至精而后阐其妙，至变而后通其数"（《文心雕龙·神思》），这就暂时摆脱了"方其搦翰，气倍辞前，暨乎篇成，半折心始"的困境。悖论诗学的原则是"言少而意多"，其极端形式是拈花微笑、"无言而言尽"。①总之，悖论诗学驱动着诗歌意象的流转、境界的开拓，以至于"境生象外"，"言外重旨"。

延伸阅读

1. 兰色姆：《新批评》，王腊宝、张哲译，南京，江苏教育出版社，2006。该书清晰地描述了理查兹、艾略特、温特斯这三位新批评的代表人物，分别称他们为"心理学批评家""历史学批评家""逻辑学批评家"，最后呼唤本体论批评。

2. 赵毅衡：《"新批评"文集》，卞之琳等译，天津，百花文艺出版社，2001。该书选编的论文涵盖了新批评理论与方法论、新批评派的细读式评论、新批评派自辩等内容。

① 参见周发祥：《西方文论与中国文学》，164～168页，南京，江苏教育出版社，1997。

3. Word Magic (1925)
By Ernst Cassirer

So far we have sought to discover the common root of linguistic and mythic conception; now arises the question, how this relationship is reflected in the structure of the "world" that is given by speech and by myth. Here we encounter a law that holds equally for all symbolic forms, and bears essentially on their evolution. None of them arise initially as separate, independently recognizable forms, but every one of them must first be emancipated from the common matrix of myth. All mental contents, no matter how truly they evince a separate systematic realm and a "principle" of their own, are actually known to us only as thus involved and grounded. Theoretical, practical and aesthetic consciousness, the world of language and of morality, the basic forms of the community and the state—they are all originally tied up with mythico-religious conceptions. This connection is so strong that where it begins to dissolve the whole intellectual world seems threatened with disruption and collapse; so vital that as the separate forms emerge from the original whole and henceforth show specific characteristics against its undifferentiated background they seem to uproot themselves and lose some of their own proper nature. Only gradually do they show that this self-imposition is part of their self-development, that the negation contains the embyro of a new assertion, that the very divorcement becomes the starting point of a new connection, which arises from extraneous postulations.

The original bond between the linguistic and the mythico-religious consciousness is primarily expressed in the fact that all verbal structures appear as also mythical entities, endowed with certain mythical powers, that the Word, in fact, becomes a sort of primary force, in which all being and doing originate. In all mythical cosmogonies, as far back as they can be traced, this supreme position of the Word is found. Among the texts which Preuss has collected among the Uitoto Indians there is one which he has adduced as a direct parallel to the opening passage of St. John, and which, in his translation, certainly seems to fall in with it perfectly: "In the beginning," it says, "the Word gave the Father his origin. "[1] Of course, striking though it may be, no one would try to argue from this coincidence to any direct relationship or even an analogy of material content between that primitive creation story and the speculations of St. John. And yet it presents us with a certain problem, it points to the fact that some indirect relationship must obtain, which covers everything from the most primitive gropings of mythico-religious thought to those highest products in which such thought seems to have already gone over into a realm of pure speculation.

A more precise insight into the foundations of this relationship can be attained only in so far as we are able to carry back the study of those examples of Word veneration, which the history of religions is always uncovering, from the mere analogy of their respective contents to the recognition of their common *form*. There must be some particular, essentially unchanging *function* that endows the Word with this extraordinary, religious character, and exalts it *ab initio* to the religious sphere, the sphere of the "holy." In the creation accounts of almost all great cultural religions, the Word appears in league with the highest Lord of creation; either as the tool which he employs or actually as the primary source from which he, like all other Being and order of Being, is derived. Thought and its verbal utterance are usually taken directly as one; for the mind that thinks and the tongue that speaks belong essentially together. Thus, in one of the earliest records of Egyptian theology, this primary force of "the heart and the tongue" is attributed to the creation-god Ptah, whereby he produces and governs all gods and men, all animals, and all that lives. Whatever is has come into being through the thought of his heart and the command of his tongue; to these two, all physical and spiritual being, the existence of the Ka as well as all properties of things, owe their origin. Here, as indeed certain scholars have pointed out, thousands of years before the Christian era, God is conceived as a spiritual Being who *thought* the world before he created it, and

---

[1] Preuss, *Religion und Mythologie der Uitoto*, I, 25f. ; II, 659.

who used the *Word* as a means of expression and an instrument of creation. ①
And as all physical and psychical Being rest in him, so do all ethical bonds and
the whole moral order.

Those religions which base their world picture and their cosmogony essentially on a fundamental ethical contrast, the dualism of good and evil, venerate
the spoken Word as the primary force by whose sole agency Chaos was transformed into an ethico-religious Cosmos. According to the Bundahish, the cosmogony and cosmography of the Parsis, the war between the power of Good
and the power of Evil, i. e. , between Ahura Mazda and Angra Mainyu, begins
with Ahura Mazda's reciting the words of the Holy Prayer (Ahuna Vairya):

---

① See Moret, *Mystères Egyptians* (Paris, 1913), pp, 118ff. , 138. Cf. esp. Erman,
"Ein Denkmal memphitischer Theologie," *Sitzungsbericht der königlich-Preussischen Akademie
der Wissenschaften*, XLIII (1911), 916ff. An exact parallel to this may be found in a creation hymn of Polynesia, which, according to Bastian's German translation (here rendered into English), reads as follows:

> In the beginning, Space and the Companion,
> Space in the height of Heaven,
> Tananaoa filled; he ruled the Heaven,
> And Mutuhei wound himself above it.
> In those days was no voice, no sound,
> No living thing yet in motion.
> No day there was as yet, no light,
> Only a gloomy, black-dark night.
> Tananaoa it was who conquered the night,
> And Mutuhei's spirit the distance pierced.
> From Tananaoa Atea was sprung,
> Mighty, filled with the power of life,
> Atea it was, who now ruled the Day,
> And drove away Tananaoa.

"The basic idea is that Tananaoa induces the process in that the original silence (Mutu-
hei) is removed through the production of Tone (Ono), and Atea (Light) is wedded with the
Red Dawn (Atanua). " See Bastian, *Die heilige Sage der Polynesier*, *Kosmogonie u. Theologie*
(Leipzig, 1881), pp. 13f. ; also Achelis, Ueber Mythologie u. Kultus von Hawaii, *Das Ausland*,
Vol. 66 (1893), p. 436.

"He spake that which has twenty-one words. The end, which is his victory, the impotence of Angra Mainyu, the decline of the Daevas, the resurrection and the future life, the ending of opposition to the (good) creation for all eternity—all these he showed to Angra Mainyu··· When a third of this prayer had been spoken, Angra Mainyu doubled up his body with terror, when two-thirds had been spoken he fell upon his knees, and when the whole had been uttered he was confounded, and powerless to abuse the creatures of Ahura Mazda, and remained confounded for three thousand years. "[1]

Here, again the words of the prayer precede the material creation, and preserve it ever against the destructive powers of the Evil One. Similarly, in India, we find the power of the Spoken Word (Vāc) exalted even above the might of the gods themselves.

"On the Spoken Word all the gods depend, all beasts and men; in the Word live all creatures··· the Word is the Imperishable, the firstborn of the eternal Law, the mother of the Veddas, the navel of the divine world. "[2]

As the Word is first in origin, it is also supreme in power. Often it is the name of the deity, rather than the god himself, that seems to be the real source of efficacy. [3] Knowledge of the name gives him who knows it mastery even over the being and will of the god. Thus a familiar Egyptian legend tells how Isis, the great sorceress, craftily persuaded the sun-god Ra to disclose his name to her, and how through possession of the name she gained power over him and

---

[1] See *Der Bundehesh*, *zum* ersten *Male* herausgegeben von *Ferdinand Justi* (Leipzig, 1868), Chap. 1, p. 3.

[2] *Taittiriya* Brahm. , 2, 8, 8, 4 (German by Gelder in his Religions-geschichtliches Lesebuch, p. 125).

[3] According to the tradition of the Maori, upon their first immigration in New Zealand they did not take along their old gods, but only their mighty prayers, by means of which they were assured the power of bending the gods to their will. Cf. Brinton, *Religions of Primitive Peoples*, pp. 103f.

over all the other gods. ① In many other ways, too, Egyptian religious life in all its phases evinces over and over again this belief in the supremacy of the name and the magic power that dwells in it. ② The ceremonies attending the anointment of kings are governed by minute prescriptions for the transference of the god's several names to the Pharaoh; each name conveys a special attribute, a new divine power. ③

Moreover, this motive plays a decisive role in the Egyptian doctrines of the soul and its immortality. The souls of the departed, starting on their journey to the land of the dead, must be given not only their physical possessions, such as food and clothing, but also a certain outfit of a magical nature: this consists chiefly of the names of the gatekeepers in the nether world, for only the knowledge of these names can unlock the doors of Death's kingdom. Even the

---

① "I am he," says Re in this story, "with many names and many shapes, and my form *is* in every god… My father and my mother have told me my name, and it has remained hidden in my body since my birth, lest some sorcerer should acquire magic power over me thereby. " Then said Isis to Re (who has been stung by a poisonous serpent of her creation, and is appealing to all the gods for help from the poison): "Tell me your name, father of gods, … that the poison may go out of you; for the man whose name is spoken, he lives. " And the poison burned hotter than fire, so that the god could no longer resist. He said to Isis: "My name shall go forth from my body and over into thine. " And he added: "Thou shalt conceal it, but to thy son Horus thou mayst reveal it as a potent spell against every poison. " See Erman, *Aegypten* u. aegyptisches *Leben im Altertum*, II, 360ff.; *Die aegyptische Religion*, Vol. 2, pp. 173f.

② Cf. the examples cited by Budge, *Egyptian Magic* (London, 1911), Vol. 2, pp. 157ff.; also Hopfner, *Griechisch-Aegyptischer Offenbarungszauber* (Leipzig, 1921), pp. 680ff.

③ Cf. esp. G. Foucart, Histoire des religions et méthode comparative (Paris, 1912), pp. 202f.: "Donner au Pharaon un 'nom' nouveau, dans lequel entrait la désignation d'un attribut ou d'une manifestation de l'Epervier, puis, plus tard, de Râ et l'ajouter aux autres noms du protocol royale, c'était pour les Egyptiens introduire dans la personne royale, et superposer aux autres éléments qui la composaient déjà, un être nouveau, exceptionnel, qui était une incarnation de Râ. Ou, plus exactement, c'était bel et bien détacher de Râ une des vibrations, une des âmes forces, dont chacune est lui tout entier; et en la faisant entrer dans la personne du Roi, c'était transformer toute celle-ci en un nouvel exemplaire, un nouveau support matériel de la divinité. "

boat in which the dead man is conveyed, and its several parts, the rudder, the mast, etc. , demand that he call them by their right names; only by virtue of this appellation can he render them willing and subservient and cause them to take him to his destination. ①

The essential identity between the word and what it denotes becomes even more patently evident if we look at it not from the objective standpoint, but from a subjective angle. For even a person's ego, his very self and personality, is indissolubly linked, in mythic thinking, with his name. Here the name is never a mere symbol, but is part of the personal property of its bearer; property which must be carefully protected, and the use of which is exclusively and jealously reserved to him. Sometimes it is not only his name, but also some other verbal denotation, that is thus treated as a physical possession, and as such may be acquired and usurped by someone else. Georg von der Gabelentz, in his book on the science of language, mentions the edict of a Chinese emperor of the third century B. C. , whereby a pronoun in the first person, that had been legitimately in popular use, was henceforth reserved to him alone. ② And the name may even acquire a status above the more or less accessory one of a personal possession, when it is taken as a truly substantial Being, an integral part of its bearer. As such it is in the same category as his body or his soul. It is said of the Eskimos that for them man consists of three elements—body, soul, and name. ③ And in Egypt, too, we find a similar conception, for there the physical body of man was thought to be accompanied, on the one hand, by his Ka, or double, and, on the other, by his name, as a sort of spiritual double. And of all these three elements it is just the last-mentioned which becomes more and more the expression of a man's "self," of his "personality."④ Even in far more advanced cultures this connection between name and personality continues to be felt. When, in Roman law, the concept of the "legal person"

---

① For further details see Budge, op. *cit.* , pp. 164ff.

② *Die Sprachwissenschaft*, p. 228.

③ See Brinton, *Religions of Primitive Peoples*, p. 93.

④ Cf. Budge, op. *cit.* , p. 157; also Moret, *Mystères Egyptiens*, p. 119.

was formally articulated, and this status was denied to certain physical subjects, those subjects were also denied official possession of a proper name. Under Roman law a slave had no legal name, because he could not function as a legal person. [1]

In other ways, too, the unity and uniqueness of the name is not only a mark of the unity and uniqueness of the person, but actually constitutes it; the name is what first makes man an individual. Where this verbal distinctiveness is not found, there the outlines of his personality tend also to be effaced. Among the Algonquins, a man who bears the same name as some given person is regarded as the latter's other self, his alter ego. [2] If, in accordance with a prevalent custom, a child is given the name of his grandfather, this expresses the belief that the grandfather is resurrected, reincarnated in the boy. As soon as a child is born, the problem arises which one of his departed ancestors is reborn in him; only after this has been determined by the priest can the ceremony be performed whereby the infant receives that progenitor's name. [3]

Furthermore, the mythic consciousness does not see human personality as something fixed and unchanging, but conceives every phase of a man's life as a new personality, a new self; and this metamorphosis is first of all made manifest in the changes which his name undergoes. At puberty a boy receives a new name, because, by virtue of the magical rites accompanying his initiation, he has ceased to exist as a boy, and has been reborn as a man, the reincarnation of one of his ancestors. [4] In other cases the change of name sometimes serves to

---

[1] Mommsen, Römisches Staatsrecht, III, 1, p. 203; cf. Rudolph Hirzel, "Der Name—ein Beitrag zu seiner Geschichte im Altertum u. besonders bei den Griechen," *Abhandlungen der sächsischen* Gesellschaft der Wissenschaften, Vol. XXVI (1918), p. 10.

[2] "The expression in the Algonkin tongue for a person of the same name is *nind owiawina*, 'He is another myself.'" (Cuoq, Lexique Algonquine, p. 113, quoted from Brinton, op. *cit.*, p. 93). Cf. esp. Giesebrecht, *Die alttestamentliche Schätzung des Gottesnamens in ihrer religionsgeschichtlichen Grundlage* (Königsberg, 1901), p. 89.

[3] See, for instance, Spieth, Die Religion der *Eweer*, p. 229.

[4] Characteristic examples may be found especially among the initiation rites of Australian native tribes; cf. esp. Howitt, *The Native Tribes of South East Australia* (London, 1904), and James, *Primitive Ritual and Belief* (London, 1917), pp. 16ff.

protect a man against impending danger; he escapes by taking on a different self, whose form makes him unrecognizable. Among the Evé it is customary to give children, and especially those whose elder brothers or sisters have died young, a name that has a frightful connotation, or attributes some non-human nature to them; the idea is that Death may be either frightened away, or deceived, and will pass them by as though they were not human at all. [1] Similarly, the name of a man laboring under disease or bloodguilt is sometimes changed, on the same principle, that Death may not find him. Even in Greek culture this custom of altering names, with its mythic motivation, still maintained itself. [2] Quite generally, in fact, the being and life of a person is so intimately connected with his name that, as long as the name is preserved and spoken, its bearer is still felt to be present and directly active. The dead may, at any moment, be literally "invoked," the moment those who survive him speak his name. As everyone knows, the fear of such visitation has led many savages to avoid not only every mention of the departed, whose name is tabooed, but even the enunciation of all assonances to his name. Often, for instance, an animal species whose name a defunct person had borne has to be given a different appellation, lest the dead man be inadvertently called upon by speaking of the beast. [3] In many cases procedures of this sort, entirely mythic in their motivation, have had a radical influence on language, and modified vocabularies considerably. [4] And the further a Being's power extends, the more mythic potency and "significance" he embodies, the greater is the sphere of influence of his name. The rule of secrecy, therefore, applies first and foremost to the Holy Name; for the mention of it would immediately release all the powers inherent

---

[1] Cf. Spieth, op. *cit.*, p. 230.

[2] Hermippos 26, 7: διὰ τοῦτο καλῶς ἡμῖν θεῖοι καὶ ἱεροὶ ἄνδρες ἐθίσπισαν ἐναλλάττειν τὰ τῶν ἀποιχομένων ὀνόματα, ὅπως τελωνοῦντας αὐτοὺς κατὰ τὸν ἐναέριον τόπον λανθάνειν ἐξῇ καὶ διέρχεσθαι.

[3] Ten Kate, "Notes ethnographiques sur les Comanches," *Revue d'Ethnographie*, IV, 131 (cited from Preuss, "Ursprung der Religion u. Kunst," *Globus*, Vol. 87, p. 395).

[4] Name taboos, I am told in a personal communication from Meinhof, play a vital part especially in Africa; among many Bantu tribes, for instance, women are not allowed to speak the names of their husbands or their fathers, so they are compelled to invent new words.

in the god himself. ①

Here, again, we are faced with one of the prime and essential motives which, rooted as it is in the deepest layers of mythical thought and feeling, maintains itself even in the highest religious formulations. Giesebrecht has traced the origin, extent and development of this motive throughout the Old Testament, in his work, *Die alttestamentliche Schätzung des Gottesnamens und ihre religionsgeschichtliche Grundlage*. But early Christianity, too, still labored entirely under the spell of this idea.

"The fact that the name functions as proxy for its bearer," says Dieterich in his *Eine Mithrasliturgie*, "and to speak the name may be equal to calling a person into being; that a name is feared because it is a real power; that knowledge of it is sought because being able to speak it bestows control of that power on the knower—all these facts indicate clearly what the early Christians were still feeling and trying to express when they said 'In God's name' instead of 'In God,' or 'In Christ's name' for 'In Christ.' ... Thus we can understand such expressions as βαπτίζειν εἰς τὸ ὄνομα Χριστοῦ instead of βαπ- τίζειν εἰς Χριστόν; the name is pronounced over the font, and thereby takes possession of the water and pervades it, so that the neophyte is quite literally immersed in the name of the Lord. The congregation, whose liturgy begins with the words: 'In the name of God,' was thought at the time to be within the bourne of the name's efficacy (no matter how figuratively and formally the phrase is taken). 'Where two or three are gathered together in my name, (εἰς τὸ ἐμὸν ὄνομα) there am I in the midst of them' (Matthew 18: 20) means simply, 'Where they pronounce my name in their assembly, there I am really present.' 'Ἁγιασθήτω τὸ ὄνομά σου once had a much more concrete sense than one would ever suspect from the her-

① For later Greek magical practices, cf. Hopfner, *Griechisch-ägyptischer Offenbarungszauber*, § 701, p. 179: "Je höher und mächtiger der Gott war, desto kräftiger und wirksamer musste auch sein wahrer Name sein. Daher ist es ganz folgerichtig anzunehmen, dass der wahre Name des einen Urgotts, des Schöpfers (ονμιουργός) für Menschen überhaupt unerträglich sei: denn dieser Name war ja zugleich auch das Göttliche an sich und zwar in seiner höchsten Potenz, daher für die schwache Natur des Sterblichen viel zu stark; daher tötet er den, der ihn hört."

meneutics of the several churches and their doctrines. '"[1]

The "special god," too, lives and acts only in the particular domain to which his name assigns and holds him. Whoever, therefore, would be assured of his protection and aid must be sure to enter his realm, i. e. , to call him by his "right" name. This need explains the phraseology of prayer, and of religious speech in general, both in Greece and in Rome—all the turns of phrase which ring a change on the several names of the god, in order to obviate the danger of missing the proper and essential appellation. Concerning the Greeks, this practice is recorded for us by a well-known passage in Plato's *Kratylos*;[2] in Rome it produced a standing formula, in which the various terms of invocation, corresponding to the several aspects of the god's nature and will, are disjoined by "either—or," "sive—sive."[3] This stereotyped mode of address must be repeated every time; for every act of devotion to the god, every appeal directed to him, commands his attention only if he is invoked by his appropriate name. The art of right address, therefore, was developed in Rome to the point of a sacerdotal technique, which produced the *indigitamenta* in the keeping of the pontifices. [4]

But here let us stop; for it is not our intention to collect theological or ethnological material, but to clarify and define the problem presented by such material. Such interweaving and interlocking as we have found between the elements of language, and the various forms of religious and mythical conception cannot be due to mere chance; it must be rooted in a common characteristic of language and myth as such. Some scholars have sought to base this intimate connection on the suggestive power of words, and especially of a spoken command, to which primitive man is supposed to be particularly subject; the magical and daemonic power which all verbal utterance has for the mythic state of consciousness seems to them to be nothing more than an objectification of that experience. But such a narrow empirical and pragmatic foundation, such a de-

---

[1] Dieterich, *Eine Mithrasliturgie*, pp. 111, 114f.

[2] Plato, *Kratylos*, 400E.

[3] For details see Norden, *Agnostos Theos*: *Untersuchungen zur Formengeschichte religiöser Rede*(Leipzig, 1913), pp. 143ff.

[4] Cf. Wissowa, *Religion und Kultus der Römer*, Vol. 2, p. 37.

tail of personal or social experience, cannot support the prime and fundamental facts of linguistic and mythic conception. More and more clearly we see ourselves faced with the question whether the close relationship of contents which certainly obtains between language and myth may not be most readily explained by the common form of their evolution, by the conditions which govern both verbal expression and mythic imagination from their earliest, unconscious beginnings. We have found these conditions given by a type of apprehension that is contrary to theoretical, discursive thinking. For, as the latter tends toward expansion, implication and systematic connection, the former tends toward concentration, telescoping, separate characterization. In discursive thought, the particular phenomenon is related to the whole pattern of being and of process; with ever-tightening, ever more elaborate bonds it is held to that totality. In mythic conception, however, things are not taken for what they mean indirectly, but for their immediate appearance; they are taken as pure presentations, and embodied in the imagination. It is easy to see that this sort of hypostatization must lead to an entirely different attitude toward the spoken word, toward its power and content, than the standpoint of discursive thought would produce. For theoretical thinking, a word is essentially a vehicle serving the fundamental aim of such ideation: the establishment of relationships between the given phenomenon and others which are "like" it or otherwise connected with it according to some co-ordinating law. The significance of discursive thought lies entirely in this function. In this sense, it is something essentially ideal, a"sign" or symbol, the object of which is not a substantial entity but lies rather in the relations it establishes. The word stands, so to speak, between actual particular impressions, as a phenomenon of a different order, a new intellectual dimension; and to this mediating position, this remoteness from the sphere of immediate data, it owes the freedom and ease with which it moves among specific objects and connects one with another.

This free ideality, which is the core of its *logical* nature, is necessarily lacking in the realm of mythic conception. For in this realm nothing has any significance or being save what is given in tangible reality. Here is no "reference" and "meaning"; every content of consciousness to which the mind is directed is immediately translated into terms of actual presence and effectiveness. Here thought does not confront its data in an attitude of free contemplation, seeking to understand their structure and their systematic connections, and analyzing them according to their parts and functions, but is simply captivated by a total impression. Such thinking does not develop the given content of experience; it does not reach backward or forward from that vantage point to find "causes" and "effects," but rests content with taking in the sheer existent. When Kant defined "reality" as any content of empirical intuition which follows general laws and thus takes its place in the "context of experience," he gave an exhaustive definition of the concept of reality in the canons of discursive thought. But mythic ideation and primitive verbal conception recognize no such "context of experience." Their function, as we have seen, is rather a process of almost violent separation and individuation. Only when this intense individuation has been consummated, when the immediate intuition has been focused and, one might say, reduced to a single point, does the mythic or linguistic form emerge, and the word or the momentary god is created. And this peculiar genesis determines the type of intellectual content that is common to language and myth; for where the process of apprehension aims not at an expansion, extension, universalizing of the content; but rather at its highest intensification, this fact cannot fail to influence human consciousness. All other things are lost to a mind thus enthralled; all bridges between the concrete datum and the systematized totality of experience are broken; only the present reality, as mythic or linguistic conception stresses and shapes it, fills the entire subjective realm. So this one content of experience must reign over practically the whole experiential world. There is nothing beside or beyond it whereby it could be measured or to which it could be compared; its mere presence is the sum of all Being. At this point, the word which denotes that thought content is not a mere conventional symbol, but is merged with its object in an indissoluble unity. The conscious experience is not merely wedded to the word, but is consumed by it. Whatever has been fixed by a name, henceforth is not only real, but is Reality. The potential between "symbol" and "meaning" is resolved; in place of a more or less adequate "expression," we find a relation of identity, of complete congruence between "image" and "object," between the name and the thing.

From another angle, too, we may observe and elucidate this substantial embodiment which the spoken word undergoes: for the same sort of hypostatization or transubstantiation occurs in other realms of mental creativity; indeed, it seems to be the typical process in all unconscious ideation. All cultural work, be it technical or purely intellectual, proceeds by the gradual shift from the direct relation between man and his environment to an indirect relation. In the beginning, sensual impulse is followed immediately by its gratification; but gradually more and more mediating terms intervene between the will and its object. It is as though the will, in order to gain its end, had to move away from the goal instead of toward it; instead of a simple reaction, almost in the nature of a reflex, to bring the object into reach, it requires a differentiation of behavior, covering a wider class of objects, so that finally the sum total of all these acts, by the use of various "means," may realize the desired end.

In the realm of technical achievement this increasing mediation may be seen in the invention and use of *tools*. But here, again, it may be observed that as soon as man employs a tool, he views it not as a mere artifact of which he is the recognized maker, but as a Being in its own right, endowed with powers of its own. Instead of being governed by his will, it becomes a god or daemon on whose will he depends—to which he feels himself subjected, and which he adores with the rites of a religious cult. Especially the ax and the hammer seem to have attained such religious significance in earliest times;[1] but the cult of other implements, too, such as the hoe or the fishhook, the spear or the sword, may be found to this day among primitive peoples. Among the Evé the smith's hammer (Zu) is deemed a mighty deity whom they worship and to whom they make sacrifices.[2] And even in Greek religion and Greek classical literature the sentiment that prompts such a cult often finds direct expression. As an example of this, Usener has drawn attention to a passage in the *Seven a-*

---

[1] Examples of this may be found, e. g., in Beth's *Einführung in die vergleichende Religionsgeschichte* (Leipzig, 1920), pp. 24ff.

[2] Spieth, *Religion der Eweer*, p. 115.

gainst Thebes of Aeschylos, in which Parthenopaeus swears by his spear, which he "honors above god, and above his eyes," to destroy Thebes. "Life and Victory depend upon direction and power, as also on the good will of the weapon; this feeling wells up irresistibly in the crucial moment of the battle; and prayer does not invoke a god from afar to guide the weapon—the weapon itself is god, the helper and deliverer. "[1]

An implement, then, is never regarded as something simply manufactured, something thought of and produced, but as a "gift from above." Its origin does not go back to man himself, but to some "culture hero," either a god or an animal. This attribution of all cultural values to a "savior" is so universal that attempts have been made to find the essence and origin of the god concept in this notion. [2] Again we are faced with a characteristic of mythic thinking which divides it sharply from the way of "discursive," or theoretical, reflection. The latter is characterized by the fact that even in apparently immediately "given" data it recognizes an element of mental creation, and stresses this active ingredient. Even in matters of fact it reveals an aspect of mental formulation; even in sheer sense data it traces the influence of a "spontaneity of thought" that goes to their making. —But while logical reflection tends, in this wise, to resolve all receptivity into spontaneity, mythic conception shows exactly the opposite tendency, namely, to regard all spontaneous action as receptive, and all human achievement as something merely bestowed. This holds for all the technical means of culture, and no less for its intellectual tools. For between these two sorts of implement there is originally no sharp dividing line, but rather a fluid distinction. Even purely mental assets and achievements, such as the words of human speech, are at first conceived entirely in the category of physical existence and the physical support of mankind. Preuss reports that, according to the Cora Indians and the Uitoto, the "Patriarch" created men and nature, but that since this creation he no longer interferes directly with the

---

[1] Usener, *Götternamen*, p. 285.

[2] Cf. Kurt Breysig, *Die Entstehung des Gottesgedankens u. der Heilbringer*, Berlin, 1905.

course of events. In lieu of such personal intervention, he gave to men his "Words," i. e. , his cult and the religious ceremonies by means of which they now control nature and attain whatever is necessary for the welfare and perpetuation of the race. Without these holy spells which were originally given into their keeping, men would be entirely helpless, for nature yields nothing merely in return for human labor. ① Among the Cherokees, too, it is an accepted belief that success in hunting or fishing is due chiefly to the use of certain words, of the proper magic formulas. ②

It was a long evolutionary course which the human mind had to traverse, to pass from the belief in a physico-magical power comprised in the Word to a realization of its spiritual power. Indeed, it is the Word, it is language, that really reveals to man that world which is closer to him than any world of natural objects and touches his weal and woe more directly than physical nature. For it is language that makes his existence in a *community* possible; and only in society, in relation to a "Thee," can his subjectivity assert itself as a "Me. " But here again the creative act, while it is in progress, is not recognized as such; all the energy of that spiritual achievement is projected into the result of it, and seems bound up in that object from which it seems to emanate as by reflection. Here, too, as in the case of tools and instruments, all spontaneity is felt as receptivity, all creativity as being, and every product of subjectivity as so much substantiality. And yet, this very hypostatization of the Word is of crucial importance in the development of human mentality. For it is the first form in which the spiritual power inherent in language can be apprehended at all; the Word has to be conceived in the mythic mode, as a substantive being and power, before it can be comprehended as an ideal instrument, an organon of the mind, and as a fundamental function in the construction and development of spiritual reality.

---

① For details see Preuss, *Die Nayarit-Expedition*, I, LXVIIIf. ; *Religion u. Mythologie der Uitoto* I, 25f. ; cf. also Preuss's article: "Die höchste Gottheit bei den kulturarmen Völkern," *Psychol. Forschungen*, II, 1922.

② Cf. Mooney, "Sacred Formulas of the Cherokee," *VIIth Annual Report of the Bureau of Ethnology* (Smithsonian Institution).

3. 卡西尔:《语词魔力》

(Ernst Cassirer,"Word Magic," 1925)

作者小识

卡西尔(Ernst Cassirer,1874—1945),德国现代哲学家,文化哲学(哲学人类学)的奠基人之一,象征形式哲学的创立者。卡西尔青年时代置身于新康德主义哲学运动中,深受马堡学派领袖人物柯亨(Hermann Cohen,1842—1918)、纳托普(Paul Natorp,1854—1924)思想的影响,随后成长为马堡学派的主将。1904年,卡西尔成为首位"库诺—费舍尔奖"(Kuno-Fischer Prize)获得者。1919年,卡西尔任汉堡大学哲学教授,1930年任汉堡大学校长。1933年1月,希特勒掌权。5月卡西尔辞去汉堡大学校长职务,离开德国,开始了漫长的流亡生涯。此后,他再也没有回到自己的故国。1919年至1933年是卡西尔创造的年代,他利用瓦堡人文图书馆的丰富藏书,展开科学认识论研究、哲学史研究,缔造象征形式哲学。流亡期间的卡西尔,先后任教于英国牛津大学、瑞典斯德哥尔摩大学、美国耶鲁大学、美国哥伦比亚大学。

卡西尔主要有三个研究领域。

(1)科学认识论,拓展逻辑经验主义的领域,延伸新康德主义的哲学方法论,甚至成为20世纪欧陆语言哲学研究的先驱。这方面的重要著作包括《现代哲学与科学中的认识论问题》(*Das Erkenntnisproblem in der Philosophie und Wissenschaft der neueren Zeit*. Berlin:Bruno Cassirer,1906,1907)、《实体概念与功能概念》(*Substanzbegriff und Funktionsbegriff:Untersuchungen über die Grundfragen der Erkenntniskritik*. Berlin:Bruno Cassirer,1910)。

(2)哲学史研究,系统研究文艺复兴哲学、新柏拉图主义、启蒙哲学、德国哲学史,这方面的主要著作包括《莱布尼茨体系及其科学基础》(*Leibniz' System in seinen wissenschaftlichen Grundlagen*. Marburg:Elwert,1902)、《启蒙哲学》(*Die Philosophie der Aufklärung*. Tübinen:Morh,1932)、《论爱因斯坦的相对论》(*Zur Einsteinschen Relativitätstheorie:Erkenntnistheoretische Betrachtungen*. Berlin:Bruno Cassirer,1921)、《文艺复兴哲学中的个人与宇宙》(*Individuum und Kosmos in der Philosophie der Renaissance*. Leipzig：Teubner，1927）。

（3）象征形式哲学，反对传统哲学的实体论统一观，主张以功能来描绘人类精神活动的整体图景，认为象征形式永远体现出一种本源性的赋予形式的力量。这方面的主要著作包括《象征形式的哲学》（*Philosophie der symbolisch-en Formen*．Berlin：Bruno Cassirer，1923，1925，1929）、《语言与神话》（*Sprache und Mythos*：*Ein Beitrag zum Problem der Götternamen*．Leipzig：Teubner，1925）、《人文科学的逻辑》（*Zur Logik der Kulturwissenschaften*．Göteborg：Göteborgs Högskolas Årsskrift，1942）、《论人》（*An Essay on Man*．New Haven：Yale University Press，1944）、《国家的神话》（*The Myth of the State*．New Haven：Yale University Press，1946）。

背景略说

要理解卡西尔的象征形式学说，宜于先略微了解三层背景。

（1）近代西方哲学认识论转向（epistemological turn）和新康德主义。近代西方哲学认识论转向始于笛卡儿的怀疑论，在康德的纯粹理性批判中臻于高潮。在这一场转向中，数学和自然科学知识得以正名，并获得了可能性的前提。康德的"哥白尼革命"，已经成为自然知识确然性的基本隐喻：知性为自然立法，知识的确定性在认知的主体而不在认知的客体。自然知识经纬天地，人文科学位置何在？显然人文科学在认识论转向中一直处在无家可归的状态。后康德时代的哲学，从狄尔泰的生命哲学到胡塞尔的现象学，其主导动机之一是为人而抗争，与自然知识争夺人文科学的地盘。新康德主义马堡学派，依然在无止境地拓展自然科学的逻辑，以至于吞噬了人文科学的空间。这一学派的代表人物坚称，纯粹认知的逻辑、精密科学的逻辑不仅是自然科学的基础，也是文化哲学的基础。他们将康德哲学或先验方法论理解为"文化哲学"，并要求用清晰的数学公式来表达人文世界。卡西尔深受马堡学派的熏染，1919 年，他在写作《实体概念与功能概念》时也依然在贯彻研究数理逻辑和科学思维结构。"仅仅在逻辑学里，哲学思想才获取了一个稳固的基础。"[①]但这种信念马上动摇了。在缔造象征形式哲学时，他发现如果将形式逻辑和科学思维应用于精神科学，传统认识论便暴露出严重的局限性。于是，他决

---

① 卡西尔：《实体与功能和爱因斯坦的相对论》，李艳会译，5 页，武汉，湖北科学技术出版社，2016。

定拓展认识论的全部计划，为文化哲学提供充足的方法论基础。卡西尔就这样偏离了新康德主义，醒悟到数理逻辑与自然科学仅仅是一种学术范式，而不是一切。认识论首要地位的衰微，构成了卡西尔象征形式哲学构建的思想背景。象征形式哲学，就是将康德的理性批判拓展为文化批判，从而建构一种系统的人类文化哲学。

(2)文化哲学。在康德哲学和新康德主义思想中，文化哲学或哲学人类学是一个边缘话题。20世纪20年代和30年代，文化哲学在德国现代思想中迅速崛起，致力于叩问人性的基本常量，为人文科学奠定人性基础。要为人性确定基本常量，首先必须回答："我能知道什么?""我能做什么?""我能希望什么?"在回答了这三个问题之后，才能尝试回答"人是什么?"这个关键问题。人类学家舍勒、普莱斯纳、盖伦分别从自己的视角对人性常量做出了有限的定义。舍勒将人与植物、动物在进化等级体系中的地位进行比较，认为唯有人能否定本能和血气，向"精神"生成。而普莱斯纳认为，与生存环境的整体断裂，是人类存在的重要特征。为了达成平衡，人类变得有意识，习得语言，且借助言语和手势进行表达。① 盖伦则断言，人类是"匮乏存在物"(Mängelwesen)。动物拥有环境，而人类需要一个世界，因而为了通达这个世界，他就必须行动，而非反应。为了站稳根基而行动，人类就必须发展出"制序"(institutions)。"制序"包括语言与习俗、行为模式与社会结构、神话、仪式以及信仰体系，其作用是为匮乏而盲目的人类导航。在这种观念博弈的语境下，卡西尔指出："唯有从一种'象征形式的哲学'出发……才能从根本上回答人类'本质概念'问题。"②

(3)文化哲学与基础存在论之争。1929年春天，在瑞士的达沃斯，卡西尔和海德格尔展开了一场论辩。论辩的主题是康德哲学和思想的起点/终点问题。这场思想交锋，可谓传统人文主义和新兴非理性主义、文化哲学和基础存在论之间的较量。海德格尔注意到了关于哲学之起点和目标的冲突观念。对于卡西尔来说，"在必须解释塑造意识之诸种形式的整全性的意义上，目标(terminus ad quem)就构成了一种文化哲学的整体"。也就是说，卡西尔哲学

---

① Helmuth Plessner, *Die Stufen des Organischen und der Mensch*, in *Gesammelte Schriften*, vol. 4, Frankfurt, Suhrkamp, 1981, pp. 181-183.

② Ernst Cassirer, *The philosophy of Symbolic Form*, vol. 4, trans. John Michael Krois, ed. John Michael Krois and Donald Verene, New Haven, Yale University Press, 1966, pp. 37-38.

的目标，是决定象征形式的逻辑（人类如何获得一种世界观，如何描述神话、语言、科学等的特殊逻辑）。海德格尔进一步指出，卡西尔所关心的，仅仅是"意识塑造力量的某个维度"，所有这一切却抛开了他的起点（terminus a quo）问题（海德格尔认为这个问题本质上关联着人类有限性），因而卡西尔的立场是"非常成问题的"。他补充说："我的立场正好相反：起点是我的中心问题，是我所发挥的问题意识。我认为，这个起点不在一种文化哲学的整体之中，而在'Τι το ον'问题之中，或者说在'什么叫作一般的存在?'的问题之中。"①在这场不对称的争论中，卡西尔居于弱势，海德格尔表现出优势。这预示着传统人文主义衰微，而存在主义冉冉上升。

基本内容

《语词魔力》为卡西尔的《语言与神话》之第三章，集中论述语言概念过程与神话思维过程之间的同源共生。《语言与神话》的基本主题是"为神命名"，旨在揭示人类思维的源始形式，为文化哲学清理出"前逻辑"的生活世界根基。语言作为人类思维的基本"器官"，并非以空灵虚白的抽象为至境，而是以元气淋漓的隐喻为根源。语言与宗教意识、神话体系相伴而生，逻辑思维建基于前逻辑思维之上，抽象概念从非理论的生活世界发展而来。于是，卡西尔真正完成了从笛卡儿到康德一直没有真正完成的"认识论转向"，甚至通过将"理性批判拓展到文化批判"而拯救了没落的认识论。揭示语言与神话、逻各斯与秘索斯的源始根基，卡西尔为认识论，甚至为整个人类文化开拓了视界，为哲学奠定了新的存在论基础，甚至从根本上改变了我们对人类心灵的全部定见。

要准确理解语言概念与神话概念这两个过程的同源共生，就必须首先理解卡西尔象征形式哲学的基本命意。象征形式哲学，就是卡西尔的文化哲学或哲学人类学。在这种思想体系中，人被定义为象征的存在物，即运用符号制作象征形式，建构理想生活境界的存在物。人的生活世界，便是一种"可能的""理想的"象征宇宙。卡西尔以一个宏大而坚执的判断结束了《人论》全书：作为一个整体的人类文化，可以被称作人不断解放自身的历程。② 象征形式便

---

① "Davos-Disptutation," in *Kant und das Problem der Metaphysik*［GA 3］，Frankfurt：Vittorio Klostermann，1973，202/GA 3，p. 288。

② 卡西尔：《人论》，甘阳译，288 页，上海，上海译文出版社，1985。

成为整个人类文化的支柱。

(1)象征形式概念。象征形式哲学标志着传统实体论向现代功能论哲学的转变。"独断的形而上学在所有特殊现存物都可以还原于斯的某个实体之中寻求绝对的统一；与之相反，批判哲学则寻求一种支配着具体多样的认识功能法则，这种法则既不否定亦不摧毁这些功能，而是将它们集合到行动的统一性，一种自足的人类努力的同一性中。"①象征形式的功能统一性构成了人类精神的特征，当然也构成了认识的特征：不是单纯地模仿，而是体现一种本源的赋予形式的力量；不是被动地表示事物存在这么一个单纯的事实，而是主动地释放一种独立的人类精神能量。借着这种精神能量，现象的单纯在场获得了确定的意义。认知、艺术、宗教、神话，便是象征形式在人类精神各个维度上的呈现。于是，一切都生活在特殊的影像世界之中。或者干脆说，生活世界便是影像世界。②象征形式或影像世界，是人类精神迈向客观化即自我显现的多条道路。通过将人定义为"象征动物"（animal symbolicum），卡西尔的文化哲学指明了人之为人的独特性，也指明了通往文化的正道。

(2)语言与神话同源。共生象征形式并不体现为千篇一律，而是体现为复杂多变。语言与神话之本质，也从象征形式建构的世界结构之中折射出来。语言意识与神话宗教意识之间的同源共生也体现为这么一个事实：所有的言语结构同时也作为赋有神话力量的神话实体而出现，词语（逻各斯）实质上是一种将全部"存在"和全部"行为"拖出深渊的源始力量。从这个角度看，自启蒙运动到新康德主义哲学一直流传的"从神话到逻各斯"的公式，就不具有解释思想史和人类精神史的效力。正确的说法应该是：神话与逻各斯同源共生，相伴到永远。

(3)神话思维与理论思维的差异。神话思维重领悟（apprehension），理论思维重推演（reasoning）。理论思维趋向于扩张、暗示和系统化的联系，而神话思维趋向于凝聚、叠缩和分辨的特征描绘。在理论思维中，特殊现象被联系到存在和过程的整体结构上；在神话思维中，事物之在场被视为纯粹的显现，并在想象中得到具体表象。

---

① Ernst Cassirer, *Philosophie der symbolischen Formen. Band I.* Berlin, Bruno Cassirer, 1923, p. 8.

② Ernst Cassirer, *Philosophie der symbolischen Formen. Band I.* Berlin, Bruno Cassirer, 1923, p. 9.

（4）从语词魔力到澄明境界的历程。人类心灵和智慧必须经过漫长的演化过程，才能走出那种对于蕴含在词语（逻各斯）中的物理—魔力之信仰，臻于认识其精神力量的境界。正是通过语言和言语，人类才能揭示和建构一个令自己惬意的世界。语词的魔力，而非物质的实在，深刻地触动了人的幸福与悲哀。卡西尔赞美人类学家乌泽纳（Hermann Usener），因为他将"瞬息神"（Augenblickgöttern）原型置于人类认知行为和象征形式建构的开端。[①] 生活世界的边缘无时不在经历着异化、恐怖、怪异、恐惧的过程。在更为强大的情境下，借助语词魔力而展开的命名活动，导致了神秘性的形成。神秘性是一种隐在未知事物之后或未知事物之中的可怕权力。而克服这种神秘性、征服这种可怕权力的途径，是赋予它们以身份，赋予它们以名称，给予它们以行为的责任，以及通过行动而让它们有彼此影响的能力。当所面对的恐怖之物化作一个名字时，生活世界的混沌便化作一派澄明。

拓展讨论

如果细察中国现代文学新传统，我们则不难发现，卡西尔的象征形式哲学参与了中国现代诗学话语的建构。具体说来，20世纪20年代初留学德国的宗白华及其他学者，受到了当时风头正劲的新康德主义哲学的影响。20世纪30年代之后，这批学者将尼采、克罗齐、卡西尔的学说转化为中国诗学和美学的建构资源。尼采的两境相入悲剧学说堪称王国维"有我之境""无我之境"诗学的底色，克罗齐的"形相直觉"学说构成了朱光潜的"情趣""意象"合一诗学的基础，而卡西尔的象征形式哲学为宗白华的意境美学提供了思想架构。[②]在此，重点讨论宗白华以"总汇菁华"的方法，主动化合卡西尔的象征形式哲学，融构出中国现代节奏论美学。

1922年至1925年，宗白华游学德国，浸润在新康德主义的思想氛围中。

---

① Ernst Cassirer，*Sprache und Mythos：Ein Beitrag zum Problem der Götternamen*，Kapital 2："通过研究神祇的名字，乌泽纳追溯了神祇概念的演化过程。他把这一过程划分为三个主要阶段。其中最古老的阶段以'瞬息神'的产生为标志。……它是某种纯粹转瞬即逝的东西，是一种一掠而过、方生方死的心灵内容，其客观化和外化便创造出了这种'瞬息神'意象。"参见 Hans Blumenberg，*Theorie der Lebenswelt*，Hsg.，Manfred Sommer，Frankfurt，Suhrkamp，2010，pp. 135-136。

② 参见罗钢：《传统的幻象：跨文化语境中的王国维诗学》，264～274页，北京，人民文学出版社，2015。

这段时间正好是卡西尔建构象征形式哲学的时期，出版了《象征形式哲学》第一、第二卷。要说宗白华对卡西尔的学说一无所知，肯定不符合事实。相反，回国之后，宗白华在中央大学哲学系主讲"美学""艺术学"过程中，多次明确提出"艺术须有象征""象征的内容越复杂越好"。他不仅非常熟悉新康德主义者朗格的唯物史论，而且还接触到了斯宾格勒以"象征"观念为基础的历史哲学。

1944 年，宗白华的《中国艺术意境之诞生》（增订稿）明显表现出卡西尔的影响。首先，"增订稿"强调，研究境界诗学是"自我认识"以及"民族文化的自省"。这一观点直接源自卡西尔。1944 年，卡西尔提炼《象征形式哲学》之精华，用英文撰写《人论》。该书开篇就论述人类自我认识的危机，主张绕开独断论，从创造符号制作象征出发把握人性与人类世界。宗白华亦强调指出，在"历史转折点"上检讨旧文化，研究艺术"意境的特构"，"以窥探中国心灵的幽情壮采"。

其次，"增订稿"将人类境界分为六种：功利境界、伦理境界、政治境界、学术境界、宗教境界和艺术境界。这一理论区分的构架也是对卡西尔文化哲学构架的化用。在其象征形式理论的建构中，卡西尔用"象征"连接文化的各个扇面，形成人类符号世界的整体，以"象征"为桥梁将科学、哲学、宗教、艺术和历史境界统一到文化理念境界。

最后，在"增订稿"以及同期的许多论文中，宗白华特别强调艺术自成境界。他认为，艺术家从"写实""传神"到"妙悟"，经过境界的创造和提升，"透过鸿蒙之理，堪留百代之奇"。艺术境界之表现于作品，就是要"透过秩序的网幕，使鸿蒙之理闪闪发光"。"这秩序的网幕是由各个艺术家的意匠组织线、点、光、色、形体、声音或文字成为有机谐和的艺术形式，以表出意境"。[1]在《论文艺的空灵与充实》里，宗白华强调，人类生命境界的广大，包括经济、政治、宗教、哲学、科学，而一切都反映在文艺里面，"然而文艺不只是一面镜子，映现着世界，且是一个独立的自足的形象创造。它凭着韵律、节奏、形式的和谐、彩色的配合，成立一个自己的有情有象的小宇宙；这宇宙是圆满的、自足的，而内部一切都是必然性的，因此是美的"。[2]"有情有象""圆满""自足"，这些说法都好像直接就是对卡西尔"象征形式""符号宇宙"的改

---

[1] 《宗白华全集》（第二卷），366 页，合肥，安徽教育出版社，1994。
[2] 《宗白华全集》（第二卷），344～345 页，合肥，安徽教育出版社，1994。

写。卡西尔说，人类的想象力具有虚构、拟人化和激发美感纯形式的力量，而艺术给我们一种新型的真实——并非经验事物的真实，而是纯形式的真实。"人类最高的心灵"被卡西尔称为"生命本质最高的活动"，"象征形式的世界就是生命自身的世界"。[1]

宗白华的"境界"诗学和卡西尔的象征形式哲学之间更深刻的同构性还在于，二者都奋力守护艺术境界的"形上学地位"。宗白华认为，艺术境界是艺术家的独创，直接地启示"宇宙真体的内部和谐节奏"，"音乐的节奏是它们的本体"。卡西尔也断定，艺术形式不是空洞的形式，它在人类经验的构造和组织中担负着塑造人类生命形式的使命。有迹象表明，宗白华不只是被动地吸收卡西尔的思想，而是已经主动融合和化合卡西尔的思想资源，展开更为宏大的哲学体系建构。落笔于20世纪40年代中后期的《形上学——中西哲学之比较》的著作残篇，就表明宗白华开创了"以中化西""自构体系"的工程。"示物法象，惟新其制"，这八个字融汇和化合了卡西尔思想的精粹：人之为人，独特之处在于创造性地使用象征形式，生生不息地通往文化世界。[2]

延伸阅读

1. 卡西尔：《人论》，甘阳译，上海，上海译文出版社，1985。这是卡西尔用英语写作的专著，堪称《象征形式哲学》的凝缩版。全书从多个维度上论述了人的独特性，即使用象征形式创造自己的世界，将人学、文化哲学和象征形式哲学合为一体。

2. 卡西尔：《神话思维》，黄龙保、周振选译，北京，中国社会科学出版社，1992。这是《象征形式哲学》的第二卷，研究神话意识在直觉思维到概念思维演化中的地位，论题涉及神话哲学、艺术哲学和宗教哲学。

---

[1] 卡西尔：《人论》，甘阳译，209页，上海，上海译文出版社，1985。
[2] 进一步的论述，可参见胡继华：《思想的制序：中国现代文论的多元取向》，305～315页，北京，北京师范大学出版社，2019。

4. The Structural Study of Myth (1955)

By Claude Lévi-Strauss

"It would seem that mythological worlds have been built up only to be shattered again, and that new worlds were built from the fragments."

—Franz Boas

Despite some recent attempts to renew them, it seems that during the past twenty years anthropology has increasingly turned from studies in the field of religion. At the same time, and precisely because the interest of professional anthropologists has withdrawn from primitive religion, all kinds of amateurs who claim to belong to other disciplines have seized this opportunity to move in, thereby turning into their private playground what we had left as a wasteland. The prospects for the scientific study of religion have thus been undermined in two ways.

The explanation for this situation lies to some extent in the fact that the anthropological study of religion was started by men like Tylor, Frazer, and Durkheim, who were psychologically oriented although not in a position to keep up with the progress of psychological research and theory. Their interpretations, therefore, soon became vitiated by the outmoded psychological approach which they used as their basis. Although they were undoubtedly right in giving their attention to intellectual processes, the way they handled these remained so crude that it discredited them altogether. This is much to be regretted, since, as Hocart so profoundly noted in his introduction to a posthumous book recently published, psychological interpretations were withdrawn from the intellectual field only to be introduced again in the field of affectivity, thus adding to "the inherent defects of the psychological school ⋯ the mistake of deriving clear-cut ideas ⋯ from vague emotions. " Instead of trying to enlarge the framework of our logic to include processes which, whatever their apparent differences, belong to the same kind of intellectual operation, a naïve attempt was made to reduce them to inarticulate emotional drives, which resulted only in hampering our studies.

Of all the chapters of religious anthropology probably none has tarried to the same extent as studies in the field of mythology. From a theoretical point of view the situation remains very much the same as it was fifty years ago, namely, chaotic. Myths are still widely interpreted in conflicting ways: as collective dreams, as the outcome of a kind of esthetic play, or as the basis of ritual. Mythological figures are considered as personified abstractions, divinized heroes, or fallen gods. Whatever the hypothesis, the choice amounts to reducing mythology cither to idle play or to a crude kind of philosophic speculation.

In order to understand what a myth really is, must we choose between platitude and sophism? Some claim that human societies merely express, through their mythology, fundamental feelings common to the whole of mankind, such as love, hate, or revenge or that they try to provide some kind of explanations for phenomena which they cannot otherwise understand—astronomical, meteorological, and the like. But why should these societies do it in such elaborate and devious ways, when all of them are also acquainted with empirical explanations? On the other hand, psychoanalysts and many anthropologists have shifted the problems away from the natural or cosmological toward the sociological and psychological fields. But then the interpretation becomes too easy: If a given mythology confers prominence on a certain figure, let us say an evil grandmother, it will be claimed that in such a society grandmothers are actually evil and that mythology reflects the social structure and the social relations; but should the actual data be conflicting, it would be as readily claimed that the purpose of mythology is to provide an outlet for repressed feelings. Whatever the situation, a clever dialectic will always find a way to pretend that a meaning has been found.

Mythology confronts the student with a situation which at first sight appears contradictory. On the one hand it would seem that in the course of a myth anything is likely to happen. There is no logic, no continuity. Any characteristic can be attributed to any subject; every conceivable relation can be found. With myth, everything becomes possible, But on the other hand, this apparent arbitrariness is belied by the astounding similarity between myths collected in widely different regions. Therefore the problem: If the content of a myth is contingent, how are we going to explain the fact that myths throughout the world are so similar?

It is precisely this awareness of a basic antinomy pertaining to the nature of myth that may lead us toward its solution. For the contradiction which we face is very similar to that which in earlier times brought considerable worry to the first philosophers concerned with linguistic problems; linguistics could only begin to evolve as a science after this contradiction had been overcome. Ancient philosophers reasoned about language the way we do about mythology. On the one hand, they did notice that in a given language certain sequences of sounds were associated with definite meanings, and they earnestly aimed at discovering a reason for the linkage between those *sounds* and that *meaning*. Their attempt, however, was thwarted from the very beginning by the fact that the same sounds were equally present in other languages although the meaning they conveyed was entirely different. The contradiction was surmounted only by the discovery that it is the combination of sounds, not the sounds themselves, which provides the significant data.

It is easy to see, moreover, that some of the more recent interpretations of mythological thought originated from the same kind of misconception under which those early linguists were laboring. Let us consider, for instance, Jung's idea that a given mythological pattern—the so-called archetype—possesses a certain meaning, This is comparable to the long-supported error that a sound may possess a certain affinity with a meaning: for instance, the "liquid" semi-vowels with water, the open vowels with things that are big, large, loud, or heavy, etc. , a theory which still has its supporters. Whatever emendations the original formulation may now call for, everybody will agree that the Saussurean principle of the *arbitrary character of linguistic signs* was a prerequisite for the accession of linguistics to the scientific level.

To invite the mythologist to compare his precarious situation with that of the linguist in the prescientific stage is not enough. As a matter of fact we may thus be led only from one difficulty to another. There is a very good reason why myth cannot simply be treated as language if its specific problems are to be solved; myth *is* language: to be known, myth has to be told; it is a part of human speech. In order to preserve its specificity we must be able to show that it is both the same thing as language, and also something different from it. Here, too, the past experience of linguists may help us. For language itself can be analyzed into things which are at the same time similar and yet different. This is precisely what is expressed in Saussure's distinction between *langue* and *parole*, one being the structural side of language, the other the statistical aspect of it, *langue* belonging to a reversible time, *parole* being non-reversible. If those two levels already exist in language, then a third one can conceivably be isolated.

We have distinguished *langue* and *parole* by the different time referents which they use. Keeping this in mind, we may notice that myth uses a third referent which combines the properties of the first two. On the one hand, a myth always refers to events alleged to have taken place long ago. But what gives the myth an operational value is that the specific pattern described is timeless; it explains the present and the past as well as the future. This can be made clear through a comparison between myth and what appears to have largely replaced it in modern societies, namely, politics. When the historian refers to the French Revolution, it is always as a sequence of past happenings, a non-reversible series of events the remote consequences of which may still be felt at present. But to the French politician, as well as to his followers, the French Revolution is both a sequence belonging to the past—as to the historian—and a timeless pattern which can be detected in the contemporary French social structure and which provides a clue for its interpretation, a lead from which to infer future developments. Michelet, for instance, was a politically minded historian. He describes the French Revolution thus: "That day ⋯ everything was possible⋯ Future became present ⋯ that is, no more time, a glimpse of eternity. " It is that double structure, altogether historical and ahistorical, which explains how myth, while pertaining to the realm of *parole* and calling for an explanation as such, as well as to that of *langue* in which it is expressed, can also be an absolute entity on a third level which, though it remains linguistic by nature, is nevertheless distinct from the other two.

A remark can be introduced at this point which will help to show the originality of myth in relation to other linguistic phenomena. Myth is the part of language where the formula *traduttore, tradittore* reaches its lowest truth value. From that point of view it should be placed in the gamut of linguistic expressions at the end opposite to that of poetry, in spite of all the claims which have been made to prove the contrary. Poetry is a kind of speech which cannot be translated except at the cost of serious distortions; whereas the mythical value of the myth is preserved even through the worst translation. Whatever our ignorance of the language and the culture of the people where it originated, a myth is still felt as a myth by any reader anywhere in the world. Its substance docs not lie in its style, its original music, or its syntax, but in the *story* which it tells. Myth is language, functioning on an especially high level where meaning succeeds practically at "taking off" from the linguistic ground on which it keeps on rolling.

To sum up the discussion at this point, we have so far made the following claims: (1) If there is a meaning to he found in mythology, it cannot reside in the isolated elements which enter into the composition of a myth, but only in the way those elements are combined. (2) Although myth belongs to the same category as language, being, as a matter of fact, only part of it, language in myth exhibits specific properties. (3) Those properties are only to be found *above* the ordinary linguistic level, that is, they exhibit more complex features than those which are to be found in any other kind of linguistic expression.

If the above three points are granted, at least as a working hypothesis, two consequences will follow: (1) Myth, like the rest of language, is made up of constituent units. (2) These constituent units presuppose the constituent units present in language when analyzed on other levels—namely, phonemes, morphemes, and sememes—but they, nevertheless, differ from the latter in the same way as the latter differ among themselves; they belong to a higher and more complex order. For this reason, we shall call them *gross constituent units*.

How shall we proceed in order to identify and isolate these gross constituent units or mythemes? We know that they cannot be found among pho-nemes, morphemes, or sememes, but only on a higher level; otherwise myth would become confused with any other kind of speech. Therefore, we should look for them on the sentence level. The only method we can suggest at this stage is to proceed tentatively, by trial and error, using as a check the princi-ples which serve as a basis for any kind of structural analysis: economy of ex-planation; unity of solution; and ability to reconstruct the whole from a frag-ment, as well as later stages from previous ones.

The technique which has been applied so far by this writer consists in ana-lyzing each myth individually, breaking down its story into the shortest possi-ble sentences, and writing each sentence on an index card bearing a number cor-responding to the unfolding of the story.

Practically each card will thus show that a certain function is, at a given time, linked to a given subject. Or, to put it otherwise, each gross constituent unit will consist of a *relation*.

However, the above definition remains highly unsatisfactory for two dif-ferent reasons. First, it is well known to structural linguists that constituent units on all levels are made up of relations, and the true difference between our *gross* units and the others remains unexplained; second, we still find ourselves in the realm of a non-reversible time, since the numbers of the cards correspond to the unfolding of the narrative. Thus the specific character of mythological time, which as we have seen is both reversible and non-reversible, synchronic and diachronic, remains unaccounted for. From this springs a new hypothesis, which constitutes the very core of our argument: The true constituent units of a myth are not the isolated relations but *bundles of such relations*, and it is only as bundles that these relations can be put to use and combined so as to produce a meaning. Relations pertaining to the same bundle may appear diachronically at remote intervals, but when we have succeeded in grouping them together we have reorganized our myth according to a time referent of a new nature, corre-sponding to the prerequisite of the initial hypothesis, namely a two-dimensional time referent which is simultaneously diachronic and synchronic, and which ac-cordingly integrates the characteristics of *langue* on the one hand, and those of *parole* on the other. To put it in even more linguistic terms, it is as though a phoneme were always made up of all its variants.

Two comparisons may help to explain what we have in mind.

Let us first suppose that archaeologists of the future coming from another planet would one day, when all human life had disappeared from the earth, excavate one of our libraries. Even if they were at first ignorant of our writing, they might succeed in deciphering it—an undertaking which would require, at some early stage, the discovery that the alphabet, as we are in the habit of printing it, should be read from left to right and from top to bottom. However, they would soon discover that a whole category of books did not fit the usual pattern—these would be the orchestra scores on the shelves of the music division. But after trying, without success, to decipher staffs one after the other, from the upper down to the lower, they would probably notice that the same patterns of notes recurred at intervals, either in full or in part, or that some patterns were strongly reminiscent of earlier ones. Hence the hypothesis: What if patterns showing affinity, instead of being considered in succession, were to be treated as one complex pattern and read as a whole? By getting at what we call *harmony*, they would then see that an orchestra score, to be meaningful, must be read diachronically along one axis—that is, page after page, and from left to right—and synchronically along the other axis, all the notes written vertically making up one gross constituent unit, that is, one bundle of relations.

The other comparison is somewhat different. Let us take an observer ignorant of our playing cards, sitting for a long time with a fortune-teller. He would know something of the visitors: sex, age, physical appearance, social situation, etc. , in the same way as we know something of the different cultures whose myths we try to study. He would also listen to the séances and record them so as to be able to go over them and make comparisons—as we do when we listen to myth-telling and record it. Mathematicians to whom I have put the problem agree that if the man is bright and if the material available to him is sufficient, he may be able to reconstruct the nature of the deck of cards being used, that is, fifty-two or thirty-two cards according to the case, made up of four homologous sets consisting of the same units (the individual cards) with only one varying feature, the suit.

Now for a concrete example of the method we propose. We shall use the Oedipus myth, which is well known to everyone. I am well aware that the Oedipus myth has only reached us under late forms and through literary transmutations concerned more with esthetic and moral preoccupations than with religious or ritual ones, whatever these may have been. But we shall not interpret the Oedipus myth in literal terms, much less offer an explanation acceptable to the specialist. We simply wish to illustrate and without reaching any conclusions with respect to it—a certain technique, whose use is probably not legitimate in this particular instance, owing to the problematic elements indicated above. The "demonstration" should therefore be conceived, not in terms of what the scientist means by this term, but at best in terms of what is meant by the street peddler, whose aim is not to achieve a concrete result, but to explain, as succinctly as possible, the functioning of the mechanical toy which he is trying to sell to the onlookers.

The myth will be treated as an orchestra score would be if it were unwittingly considered as a unilinear series; our task is to reestablish the correct arrangement. Say, for instance, we were confronted with a sequence of the type: 1, 2, 4, 7, 8, 2, 3, 4, 6, 8, 1, 4, 5, 7, 8, 1, 2, 5, 7, 3, 4, 5, 6, 8 ⋯ , the assignment being to put all the 1's together, all the 2's, the 3's, etc. ; the result is a chart:

1	2		4			7	8
	2	3	4		6		8
1			4	5		7	8
1	2			5		7	
		3	4	5	6		8

We shall attempt to perform the same kind of operation on the Oedipus myth, trying out several arrangements of the mythemes until we find one which is in harmony with the principles enumerated above. Let us suppose, for the sake of argument, that the best arrangement is the following (although it might certainly be improved with the help of a specialist in Greek mythology):

1	2	3	4
Cadmos seeks his sister Europa, ravished by Zeus			
		Cadmos kills the dragon	
	The Spartoi kill one another		
			Labdacos (Laios' father) = *lame* (?)
	Oedipus kills his father, Laios		Laios (Oedipus' father) =*left-sided*(?)
		Oedipus kills the Sphinx	
			Oedipus = *swollen-foot*(?)
Oedipus marries his mother, Jocasta			
	Eteocles kills his brother, Polynices		
Antigone buries her brother, Polynices, despite prohibition			

We thus find ourselves confronted with four vertical columns, each of which includes several relations belonging to the same bundle. Were we to *tell* the myth, we would disregard the columns and read the rows from left to right and from top to bottom. But if we want to *understand* the myth, then we will have to disregard one half of the diachronic dimension (top to bottom) and read from left to right, column after column, each one being considered as a unit.

All the relations belonging to the same column exhibit one common feature which it is our task to discover. For instance, all the events grouped in the first column on the left have something to do with blood relations which are overemphasized, that is, are more intimate than they should be. Let us say, then, that the first column has as its common feature the *overrating of blood relations*. It is obvious that the second column expresses the same thing, but inverted: *underrating of blood relations*. The third column refers to monsters being slain. As to the fourth, a few words of clarification are needed. The remarkable connotation of the surnames in Oedipus' father-line has often been noticed. However, linguists usually disregard it, since to them the only way to define the meaning of a term is to investigate all the contexts in which it appears, and personal names, precisely because they are used as such, are not accompanied by any context. With the method we propose to follow the objection disappears, since the myth itself provides its own context. The significance is no longer to be sought in the eventual meaning of each name, but in the fact that all the names have a common feature: All the hypothetical meanings (which may well remain hypothetical) refer to *difficulties in walking straight and standing upright.*

What then is the relationship between the two columns on the right? Column three refers to monsters. The dragon is a chthonian being which has to be killed in order that mankind be born from the Earth; the Sphinx is a monster unwilling to permit men to live. The last unit reproduces the first one, which has to do with the *autochthonous origin* of mankind. Since the monsters are overcome by men, we may thus say that the common feature of the third column is *denial of the autochthonous origin of man.*

This immediately helps us to understand the meaning of the fourth column. In mythology it is a universal characteristic of men born from the Earth that at the moment they emerge from the depth they either cannot walk or they walk clumsily. This is the case of the chthonian beings in the mythology of the Pueblo: Muyingwu, who leads the emergence, and the chthonian Shumaikoli are lame ("bleeding-foot," "sore-foot"). The same happens to the Koskimo of the Kwakiutl after they have been swallowed by the chthonian monster, Tsiakish: When they returned to the surface of the earth "they limped forward or tripped sideways. " Thus the common feature of the fourth column is *the persistence of the autochthonous origin of man.* It follows that column four is to column three as column one is to column two. The inability to connect two kinds of relationships is overcome (or rather replaced) by the assertion that contradictory relationships are identical inasmuch as they are both self-contradictory in a similar way. Although this is still a provisional formulation of the structure of mythical thought, it is sufficient at this stage.

Turning back to the Oedipus myth, we may now see what it means. The myth has to do with the inability, for a culture which holds the belief that mankind is autochthonous (see, for instance, Pausanias, VIII, xxix, 4: plants provide a *model* for humans), to find a satisfactory transition between this theory and the knowledge that human beings are actually born from the union of man and woman. Although the problem obviously cannot be solved, the Oedipus myth provides a kind of logical tool which relates the original problem—born from one or born from two? —to the derivative problem: born from different or born from same? By a correlation of this type, the overrating of blood relations is to the underrating of blood relations as the attempt to escape autochthony is to the impossibility to succeed in it. Although experience contradicts theory, social life validates cosmology by its similarity of structure. Hence cosmology is true.

Two remarks should be made at this stage.

In order to interpret the myth, we left aside a point which has worried the specialists until now, namely, that in the earlier (Homeric) versions of the Oedipus myth, some basic elements are lacking, such as Jocasta killing herself and Oedipus piercing his own eyes. These events do not alter the substance of the myth although they can easily be integrated, the first one as a new case of autodestruction (column three) and the second as another case of crippledness (column four). At the same time there is something significant in these additions, since the shift from foot to head is to be correlated with the shift from autochthonous origin to self-destruction.

Our method thus eliminates a problem which has, so far, been one of the main obstacles to the progress of mythological studies, namely, the quest for the *true* version, or the *earlier* one. On the contrary, we define the myth as consisting of all its versions; or to put it otherwise, a myth remains the same as long as it is felt as such. A striking example is offered by the fact that our interpretation may take into account the Freudian use of the Oedipus myth and is certainly applicable to it. Although the Freudian problem has ceased to be that of autochthony *versus* bisexual reproduction, it is still the problem of understanding how *one* can be born from *two*: How is it that we do not have only one procreator, but a mother plus a father? Therefore, not only Sophocles, but Freud himself, should be included among the recorded versions of the Oedipus myth on a par with earlier or seemingly more "authentic" versions.

An important consequence follows. If a myth is made up of all its variants, structural analysis should take all of them into account. After analyzing all the known variants of the Theban version, we should thus treat the others in the same way: first, the tales about Labdacos' collateral line including Agave, Pentheus' and Jocasta herself; the Theban variant about Lycos with Am-phion and Zetos as the city founders; more remote variants concerning Dionysus (Oedipus' matrilateral cousin); and Athenian legends where Cecrops takes the place of Cadmos, etc. For each of them a similar chart should be drawn and then compared and reorganized according to the findings: Cecrops killing the serpent with the parallel episode of Cadmos; abandonment of Dionysus with a-bandonment of Oedipus; "Swollen Foot" with Dionysus' *loxias*, that is, walking obliquely; Europa's quest with Antiope's; the founding of Thebes by the Spartoi or by the brothers Amphion and Zetos; Zeus kidnapping Europa and Antiope and the same with Semele; the Theban Oedipus and the Argian Per-seus, etc. We shall then have several two-dimensional charts, each dealing with a variant, to be organized in a three-dimensional order, as shown in Figure 16, so that three different readings become possible: left to right, top to bottom, front to back (or vice versa). All of these charts cannot be expected to be iden-tical; but experience shows that any difference to be observed may be correlated with other differences, so that a logical treatment of the whole will allow sim-plifications, the final outcome being the structural law of the myth.

At this point the objection may be raised that the task is impossible to per-form, since we can only work with known versions. Is it not possible that a new version might alter the picture? This is true enough if only one or two ver-sions are available, but the objection becomes theoretical as soon as a reasona-bly large number have been recorded. Let us make this point clear by a comparison. If the furniture of a room and its arrangement were known to us only through its reflection in two mirrors placed on opposite walls, we should

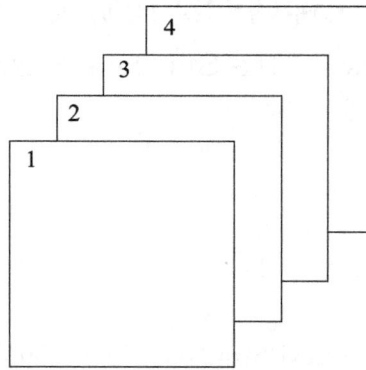

FIGURE 16

theoretically dispose of an almost infinite number of mirror images which would provide us with a complete knowledge. However, should the two mirrors be obliquely set, the number of mirror images would become very small; nevertheless, four or five such images would very likely give us, if not complete information, at least a sufficient coverage so that we would feel sure that no large piece of furniture is missing in our description.

On the other hand, it cannot be too strongly emphasized that all available variants should be taken into account. If Freudian comments on the Oedipus complex are a part of the Oedipus myth, then questions such as whether Cushing's version of the Zuni origin myth should be retained or discarded become irrelevant. There is no single "true" version of which all the others are but copies or distortions. Every version belongs to the myth.

4. 列维-斯特劳斯:《神话的结构研究》

(Claude Lévi-Strauss，"The Structural Study of Myth，" 1955)

作者小识

列维-斯特劳斯(Claude Lévi-Strauss，1908—2009)，法国人类学家。他将社会学、语言学和古典学研究融于人类学研究，分析亲属结构，解析古典神话，探究人类思维的本质。代表作包括《野性的思维》(*The Savage Mind*，1962)、《结构人类学》(*Structural Anthropology*，1961)、《遥远的目光》(*The View from Afar*，1983)，以及让他赢得世界性文学声誉的传记式学术著作《忧郁的热带》(*Tristes Tropiques*，1955)。列维-斯特劳斯对于文学理论和批评实践的贡献在于，将结构主义语言学引入神话研究，确立了文学结构主义研究的经典范式。

背景略说

结构主义的兴起，源自对存在主义主体精神的质疑与解构。列维-斯特劳斯青年时代浸润在卢梭传统中，并受到马克思主义的深刻影响。作为社会学家和人类学家的列维-斯特劳斯意识到，历史与辩证法之间存在着一种有意义的张力。站在人类学家的立场上，列维-斯特劳斯以历史反对"理性的辩证法"。在他看来，在人文科学当中，那种兼有"叙事性"和"几何性"的思想，并不能一言以蔽之地被称为"辩证法思想"。尤其是当人类学家将眼光转向"野性思维"时就会发现，"野性思维"并非辩证的，而是历史的、结构的、整合的(totalisante)。于是，人类学家要想追溯人类思维的起源，就必须超越萨特的"辩证理性"架构。辩证理性让"纯粹的系列性"(sérialité pure)逃逸了人类学的分类系统，并排除了使系统臻于完善的图式化(schématisme)的可能。反之，列维-斯特劳斯坚持人文科学的历史方法，认为"真实的辩证理性原则应当从野性的思维顽固地拒绝使任何关于人的(甚至是关于有生命的)东西与自己疏离的态度中去寻找"。他认为这种真正的辩证理性原则之使命，在于"把人类的事物分解为非人类的事物"。列维-斯特劳斯在理论上预示了人类纪向后人类纪的转向：人文科学的最终目的不是去构成人，而是去分解人。①

20世纪50年代到60年代，一些文学批评家将瑞士语言学家索绪尔的学说运用于叙述话语分析。列维-斯特劳斯就是其中卓有建树的一位。他被神话之中丰富的象征吸引，开始研究世界各地的经典神话。他发现，神话，就像亲属关系的基本结构一样，也具有一种类似的语言结构。神话遵循语言学法则。个别神话便是言语（parole）的范例，而神话的象征总体便是语言（langue）的范式。神话研究的目标，就是要找到这个象征总体，即语言系统或总体结构。正是语言系统让个别神话发生作用、生产意义。

在阅读了大量的神话之后，列维-斯特劳斯辨识出了一些贯穿在神话之中并反复出现的主题。这些主题超越时空，不受文化传统的制约，对一切民族都有效，直指本心，塑造人性。他将这些基本主题视为一些结构，并称之为"神话素"（mythemes）。神话素，类似于音素（phonemes），是语言结构的基本元素。像音素一样，神话素也通过神话结构之中的内在关系而生产意义。同时，像音素一样，这么一些神话素的内在关系也常常引发对立，甚至导致冲突。举个例子来说，/b/和/p/，这两个音素有些类似，因为它们的发音方式都是用舌头突然堵死气流。它们彼此不同甚至互相对立，原因只有一个：通过气管的气流是否振动声带。在实际说话过程中，振动声带就发出了/b/，而不振动声带则发出了/p/。同理，神话素也是通过对立而获得意义的。神话素的对立体现在这么一些例子中：爱恨情仇、悲欢离合、远游复归、兴衰沉浮。决定神话素连接方式的规则，便构成了神话的结构，或神话的语法。所以，一切个别神话的意义，便取决于故事之中神话素的相互作用及其秩序，而神话的意义便源自这种结构模型。

我们无意识地控制着语言体系。同样，我们也无意识地控制着神话结构。列维-斯特劳斯指出，人类理解神话结构的能力是天生的。神话一如语言，亦是我们区分和建构世界的一种方式。

基本内容

《神话的结构研究》节选自列维-斯特劳斯的《结构人类学》，这部作品是他将现代语言学运用于人类学的典范。在文章的开篇，他就抱怨神话研究观念

---

① 列维-斯特劳斯：《野性的思维》，李幼蒸译，279～281页，北京，商务印书馆，1987。

陈旧、方法老套、停滞不前，紧接着指出神话的自相矛盾，建议将神话当作语言来研究。"神话是语言：神话要让人知道，就必须讲述；神话是人类言语的一部分。"以索绪尔"语言符号的任意性"为基本原则，他区分了神话结构的非历史性、历史性和绝对统一性三个层面。依据这种区分，列维-斯特劳斯提供了神话研究的三个工作假说：(1)神话意义在整体方式中；(2)神话语言显示出独特性；(3)神话独特性在超越语言的层次上。基于这些假说，他做出三点推论：(1)神话与语言一样，具有构成单位；(2)神话与语言结构具有类似的构成单位，即音素、词素和义素；(3)神话具有更高级、更复杂的构成单位。最后，列维-斯特劳斯神话研究的核心假设便是：神话的真正构成单位不是一些孤立的关系，而是一束关系，既具有时间可逆性又具有时间不可逆性，既具有共时特征又具有历时特征。

带着这些工作假设，列维-斯特劳斯进入了古典神话世界，以严格的结构主义方法解读"俄狄浦斯神话"。这种解读的程序如下：(1)将神话中的故事分离为一个非线性的序列，仿佛是一个共时的音乐总谱世界，于是得到四个栏目，每一栏都包括几种属于同一束的关系。(2)我们可以从上到下，再从左至右，以历时的方式阅读这个系列，更应该从左至右，以共时的方式阅读这些独立的故事，将每一栏都看作一个独立的单元。(3)于是我们发现，每一个独立单元都有一个共同特点，如第一、第二栏分别表现过分重视血缘关系或过分低估血缘关系，第三、第四栏分别表现对大地的排斥或对大地的依赖。(4)对立关系是人类普遍经验之中矛盾的写照，神话结构则是人类经验悖论的投射，或人类经验矛盾的暂时解决。神话思维也就是人类的源始思维，或者"野性思维"，其本质是"非时间性"，它试图在同一时间中将这个世界理解为一个整体。

拓展讨论

列维-斯特劳斯在其思想传记《忧郁的热带》之中以悲剧笔调描述人类纪的宇宙学历史与前景："这个世界开始的时候，人类并不存在，这个世界结束的时候，人类也不会存在……人类的角色并没有使人类具有一个独立于整个衰败过程之外的特殊地位，人类的一切作为，即使都避免不了失败的命运，也并没有能扭转整个宇宙性的衰亡程序，相反的，人类自己似乎成为整个世界事物秩序瓦解过程最强有力的催化剂。"年高德劭的人类学家甚至表示很不喜欢他所生活的这个世界，想要逃离人类纪，到前人类纪的南美土著民族那里去享受素朴的宇宙秩序，挥洒智性灵魂的诗情画意。他特别注意到现代传播给人类带来的困境："每一句对话，每一句印出来的文字，都使人与人得以沟通，沟通的结果就是创造出平等的层次"，沟通导致的信息平均化导致了组织的瓦解、秩序的衰落、无序的增长。如果说，人类纪是"熵纪"，是熵大规模增长而将宇宙驱向无序的世纪，那么列维-斯特劳斯的话可谓昏世警钟："人类学实际上可以改成为'熵类学'（entropology），改成为研究最高层次的解体过程的学问。"[1]安德森的预言如出一辙：大数据如同大洪水，将人类再次带向洪荒。在这么一个洪荒的宇宙，"无产阶级化"臻于峰极，超个体化导致了精神的衰微，知识已经死亡，理论寿终正寝。星球肃杀，万物枯萎，灵魂陨落，熵趋极值——如果这种描述属实，那就真的没有未来，没有出路，没有弥赛亚降临的空隙，没有自救的力量，也没有他救的代理。然而，果真如此吗?[2]

延伸阅读

1. 列维-斯特劳斯：《结构人类学——巫术·宗教·艺术·神话》，陆晓禾、黄锡光等译，北京，文化艺术出版社，1989。此书精选并翻译了《结构人类学》中论述巫术、宗教、艺术、神话、仪式的部分，让人一窥结构主义之堂奥。

2. 列维-斯特劳斯：《忧郁的热带》，王志明译，北京，生活·读书·新知三联书店，2000。此书为列维-斯特劳斯赢得了文学声誉，将人类学的基本观点传记化，并对人类未来进行了展望。

---

[1]　列维-斯特劳斯：《忧郁的热带》，王志明译，543～544 页，北京，生活·读书·新知三联书店，2000。

[2]　参见胡继华：《负人类纪对美学的挑战——一则读书与思考札记》，载《广州大学学报（社会科学版）》，2019(2)。

5. Dostoevsky and Parricide (1927)

By Sigmund Freud

Four facets may be distinguished in the rich personality of Dostoevsky: the creative artist, the neurotic, the moralist and the sinner. How is one to find one's way in this bewildering complexity?

The creative artist is the least doubtful: Dostoevsky's place is not far behind Shakespeare. *The Brothers Kamarazov* is the most magnificent novel ever written; the episode of the Grand Inquisitor, one of the peaks in the literature of the world, can hardly be valued too highly. Before the problem of the creative artist analysis must, alas, lay down its arms.

The moralist in Dostoevsky is the most readily assailable. If we seek to rank him high as a moralist on the plea that only a man who has gone through the depths of sin can reach the highest summit of morality, we are neglecting a doubt that arises. A moral man is one who reacts to temptation as soon as he feels it in his heart, without yielding to it. A man who alternately sins and then in his remorse erects high moral standards lays himself open to the reproach that he has made things too easy for himself. He has not achieved the essence of morality, renunciation, for the moral conduct of life is a practical human interest. He reminds one of the barbarians of the great migrations, who murdered and did penance for it, till penance became an actual technique for enabling murder to be done. Ivan the Terrible behaved in exactly this way; indeed this compromise with morality is a characteristic Russian trait. Nor was the final outcome of Dostoevsky's moral strivings anything very glorious. After the most violent struggles to reconcile the instinctual demands of the individual with the claims of the community, he landed in the retrograde position of submission both to temporal and spiritual authority, of veneration both for the Tsar and for the God of the Christians, and of a narrow Russian nationalism—a position which lesser minds have reached with smaller effort. This is the weak point in that great personality. Dostoevsky threw away the chance of becoming a teacher and liberator of humanity and made himself one with their gaolers. The future of human civilization will have little to thank him for. It seems probable that he was condemned to this failure by his neurosis. The greatness of his intelligence and the strength of his love for humanity might have opened to him another, an apostolic, way of life.

To consider Dostoevsky as a sinner or a criminal rouses violent opposition, which need not be based upon a philistine assessment of criminals. The real motive for this opposition soon becomes apparent. Two traits are essential in a criminal: boundless egoism and a strong destructive urge. Common to both of these, and a necessary condition for their expression, is absence of love, lack of an emotional appreciation of (human) objects. One at once recalls the contrast to this presented by Dostoevsky—his great need of love and his enormous capacity for love, which is to be seen in manifestations of exaggerated kindness and caused him to love and to help where he had a right to hate and to be revengeful, as, for example, in his relations with his first wife and her lover. That being so, it must be asked why there is any temptation to reckon Dostoevsky among the criminals. The answer is that it comes from his choice of material, which singles out from all others violent, murderous and egoistic characters, thus pointing to the existence of similar tendencies within himself, and also from certain facts in his life, like his passion for gambling and his possible confession to a sexual assault upon a young girl. ① The contradiction is resolved by the realization that Dostoevsky's very strong destructive instinct, which might easily have made him a criminal, was in his actual life directed mainly against his own person (inward instead of outward) and thus found expression as masochism and a sense of guilt. Nevertheless, his personality retained sadistic traits in plenty, which show themselves in his irritability, his love of tormenting and his

---

① See the discussion of this in Fülöp-Miller and Eckstein (1926). Stefan Zweig (1920) writes: 'He was not halted by the barriers of bourgeois morality; and no one can say exactly how far he transgressed the bounds of law in his own life or how much of the criminal instincts of his heroes was realized in himself.' For the intimate connection between Dostoevsky's characters and his own experiences, see René Fülöp Miller's remarks in the introductory section of Fülöp-Miller and Eckstein (1925), which are based upon N. Strakhov.

intolerance even towards people he loved, and which appear also in the way in which, as an author, he treats his readers. Thus in little things he was a sadist towards others, and in bigger things a sadist towards himself, in fact a masochist—that is to say the mildest, kindliest, most helpful person possible.

We have selected three factors from Dostoevsky's complex personality, one quantitative and two qualitative: the extraordinary intensity of his emotional life, his perverse innate instinctual disposition, which inevitably marked him out to be a sado-masochist or a criminal, and his unanalysable artistic gift. This combination might very well exist without neurosis; there are people who are complete masochists without being neurotic. Nevertheless, the balance of forces between his instinctual demands and the inhibitions opposing them (plus the available methods of sublimation) would even so make it necessary to classify Dostoevsky as what is known as an 'instinctual character'. But the position is obscured by the simultaneous presence of neurosis, which, as we have said, was not in the circumstances inevitable, but which comes into being the more readily, the richer the complication which has to be mastered by the ego. For neurosis is after all only a sign that the ego has not succeeded in making a synthesis, that in attempting to do so it has forfeited its unity.

How then, strictly speaking, does his neurosis show itself? Dostoevsky called himself an epileptic, and was regarded as such by other people, on account of his severe attacks, which were accompanied by loss of consciousness, muscular convulsions and subsequent depression. Now it is highly probable that this so-called epilepsy was only a symptom of his neurosis and must accordingly be classified as hystero-epilepsy—that is, as severe hysteria. We cannot be completely certain on this point for two reasons—firstly, because the anamnestic data on Dostoevsky's alleged epilepsy are defective and untrustworthy, and secondly, because our understanding of pathological states combined with epileptiform attacks is imperfect.

To take the second point first. It is unnecessary here to reproduce the whole pathology of epilepsy, for it would throw no decisive light on the problem. But this may be said. The old *morbus sacer* is still in evidence as an ostensible clinical entity, the uncanny disease with its incalculable, apparently unprovoked convulsive attacks, its changing of the character into irritability and aggressiveness, and its progressive lowering of all the mental faculties. But the outlines of this picture are quite lacking in precision. The attacks, so savage in their onset, accompanied by biting of the tongue and incontinence of urine and working up to the dangerous *status epilepticus* with its risk of severe self-injuries, may, nevertheless, be reduced to brief periods of *absence*, or rapidly passing fits of vertigo or may be replaced by short spaces of time during which the patient does something out of character, as though he were under the control of his unconscious. These attacks, though as a rule determined, in a way we do not understand, by purely physical causes, may nevertheless owe their first appearance to some purely mental cause (a fright, for instance) or may react in other respects to mental excitations. However characteristic intellectual impairment may be in the overwhelming majority of cases, at least *one* case is known to us (that of Helmholtz) in which the affliction did not interfere with the highest intellectual achievement. (Other cases of which the same assertion has been made are either disputable or open to the same doubts as the case of Dostoevsky himself.) People who are victims of epilepsy may give an impression of dullness and arrested development just as the disease often accompanies the most palpable idiocy and the grossest cerebral defects, even though not as a necessary component of the clinical picture. But these attacks, with all their variations, also occur in other people who display complete mental development and, if anything, an excessive and as a rule insufficiently controlled emotional life. It is no wonder in these circumstances that it has been found impossible to maintain that 'epilepsy' is a single clinical entity. The similarity that we find in the manifest symptoms seems to call for a functional view of them. It is as though a mechanism for abnormal instinctual discharge had been laid down organically, which could be made use of in quite different circumstances—both in the case of disturbances of cerebral activity due to severe histolytic or toxic affections, and also in the case of inadequate control over the mental economy and at times when the activity of the energy operating in the mind reaches crisis-pitch. Behind this dichotomy we have a glimpse of the identity of the underlying mechanism of instinctual discharge. Nor can that mechanism stand remote from the sexual processes, which are fundamentally of toxic origin: the earliest phy-sicians described coition as a minor epilepsy, and thus recognized in the sexual act a mitigation and adaptation of the epileptic method of discharging stimuli.

The 'epileptic reaction', as this common element may be called, is also undoubtedly at the disposal of the neurosis whose essence it is to get rid by so-matic means of amounts of excitation which it cannot deal with psychically. Thus the epileptic attack becomes a symptom of hysteria and is adapted and modified by it just as it is by the normal sexual process of discharge. It is there-fore quite right to distinguish between an organic and an 'affective' epilepsy. The practical significance of this is that a person who suffers from the first kind has a dis-ease of the brain, while a person who suffers from the second kind is a neurotic. In the first case his mental life is subjected to an alien disturbance from without, in the second case the disturbance is an expression of his mental life itself.

It is extremely probable that Dostoevsky's epilepsy was of the second kind. This cannot, strictly speaking, be proved. To do so we should have to be in a position to insert the first appearance of the attacks and their subsequent fluctuations into the thread of his mental life; and for that we know too little. The descriptions of the attacks themselves teach us nothing and our information about the relations between them and Dostoevsky's experiences is defective and often contradictory. The most probable assumption is that the attacks went back far into his childhood, that their place was taken to begin with by milder symptoms and that they did not assume an epileptic form until after the shattering experience of his eighteenth year—the murder of his father. [1] It

---

[1] See René Fülöp-Miller (1924). Of especial interest is the information that in the novelist's childhood 'something terrible, unforgettable and agonizing' happened, to which the first signs of his illness were to be traced (from an article by Suvorin in the newspaper *Novoe Vremya*, 1881, quoted in the introduction to Fülöp-Miller and Eckstein, 1925, xlv). See also Orest Miller (1921, 140): 'There is, however, another special piece of evidence about Fyodor Mikhailovich's illness, which relates to his earliest youth and brings the illness into connection with a tragic event in the family life of his parents. But, although this piece of evidence was given to me orally by one who was a close friend of Fyodor Mikhailovich, I cannot bring myself to reproduce it fully and pre-cisely since I have had no confirmation of this rumour from any other quarter. ' Biographers and scientific research workers cannot feel grateful for this discretion.

would be very much to the point if it could be established that they ceased completely during his exile in Siberia, but other accounts contradict this. ① The unmistakable connection between the murder of the father in *The Brothers Kamarazov* and the fate of Dostoevsky's own father has struck more than one of his biographers, and has led them to refer to 'a certain modern school of psychology'. From the standpoint of psycho-analysis (for that is what is meant), we are tempted to see in that event the severest trauma and to regard Dostoevsky's reaction to it as the turning-point of his neurosis. But if I undertake to substantiate this view psycho-analytically, I shall have to risk the danger of being unintelligible to all those readers who are unfamiliar with the language and theories of psycho-analysis.

We have one certain starting-point. We know the meaning of the first attacks from which Dostoevsky suffered in his early years, long before the incidence of the 'epilepsy'. These attacks had the significance of death: they were heralded by a fear of death and consisted of lethargic, somnolent states. The illness first came over him while he was still a boy, in the form of a sudden, groundless melancholy, a feeling, as he later told his friend Soloviev, as though he were going to die on the spot. And there in fact followed a state exactly similar to real death. His brother Andrey tells us that even when he was quite young Fyodor used to leave little notes about before he went to sleep, saying that he was afraid he might fall into this death-like sleep during the night and therefore begged that his burial should be postponed for five days. (Fülöp-Miller and Eckstein, 1925, lx.)

We know the meaning and intention of such deathlike attacks. They signify an identification with a dead person, either with someone who is really dead or with someone who is still alive and whom the subject wishes dead. The latter

---

① Most of the accounts, including Dostoevsky's own, assert on the contrary that the illness only assumed its final, epileptic character during the Siberian exile. Unfortunately there is reason to distrust the autobiographical statements of neurotics. Experience shows that their memories introduce falsifications which are designed to interrupt disagreeable causal connections. Nevertheless, it appears certain that Dostoevsky's detention in the Siberian prison markedly altered his pathological condition. Cf. Fülöp-Miller (1924, 1186).

case is the more significant. The attack then has the value of a punishment. One has wished another person dead, and now one *is* this other person and is dead oneself. At this point psycho-analytical theory brings in the assertion that for a boy this other person is usually his father and that the attack (which is termed hysterical) is thus a self-punishment for a death-wish against a hated father.

Parricide, according to a well-known view, is the principal and primal crime of humanity as well as of the individual. (See my *Totem and Taboo* 1912-13.) It is in any case the main source of the sense of guilt, though we do not know if it is the only one: researches have not yet been able to establish with certainty the mental origin of guilt and the need for expiation. But it is not necessary for it to be the only one. The psychological situation is complicated and requires elucidation. The relation of a boy to his father is, as we say, an 'ambivalent' one. In addition to the hate which seeks to get rid of the father as a rival, a measure of tenderness for him is also habitually present. The two attitudes of mind combine to produce identification with the father; the boy wants to be in his father's place because he admires him and wants to be like him, and also because he wants to put him out of the way. This whole development now comes up against a powerful obstacle. At a certain moment the child comes to understand that an attempt to remove his father as a rival would be punished by him with castration. So from fear of castration—that is, in the interests of preserving his masculinity—he gives up his wish to possess his mother and get rid of his father. In so far as this wish remains in the unconscious it forms the basis of the sense of guilt. We believe that what we have here been describing are normal processes, the normal fate of the so-called 'Oedipus complex'; nevertheless it requires an important amplification.

A further complication arises when the constitutional factor we call bisexuality is comparatively strongly developed in a child. For then, under the threat to the boy's masculinity by castration, his inclination becomes strengthened to diverge in the direction of femininity, to put himself instead in his mother's place and take over her role as object of his father's love. But the fear of castration makes *this* solution impossible as well. The boy understands that he must also submit to castration if he wants to be loved by his father as a woman. Thus both impulses, hatred of the father and being in love with the father, undergo repression. There is a certain psychological distinction in the fact that the hatred of the father is given up on account of fear of an *external* danger (castration), while the being in love with the father is treated as an *internal* instinctual danger, though fundamentally it goes back to the same external danger.

What makes hatred of the father unacceptable is *fear* of the father; castration is terrible, whether as a punishment or as the price of love. Of the two factors which repress hatred of the father, the first, the direct fear of punishment and castration, may be called the normal one; its pathogenic intensification seems to come only with the addition of the second factor, the fear of the feminine attitude. Thus a strong innate bisexual disposition becomes one of the preconditions or reinforcements of neurosis. Such a disposition must certainly be assumed in Dostoevsky, and it shows itself in a viable form (as latent homosexuality) in the important part played by male friendships in his life, in his strangely tender attitude towards rivals in love and in his remarkable understanding of situations which are explicable only by repressed homosexuality, as many examples from his novels show.

I am sorry, though I cannot alter the facts, if this exposition of the attitudes of hatred and love towards the father and their transformations under the influence of the threat of castration seems to readers unfamiliar with psychoanalysis unsavoury and incredible. I should myself expect that it is precisely the castration complex that would be bound to arouse the most general repudiation. But I can only insist that psychoanalytic experience has put these matters in particular beyond the reach of doubt and has taught us to recognize in them the key to every neurosis. This key, then, we must apply to our author's so-called epilepsy. So alien to our consciousness are the things by which our unconscious mental life is governed! But what has been said so far does not exhaust the consequences of the repression of the hatred of the father in the Oedipus complex. There is something fresh to be added: namely that in spite of everything the identification with the father finally makes a permanent place for itself in the ego. It is received into the ego, but establishes itself there as a separate agency in contrast to the rest of the content of the ego. We then give it the name of super-ego and ascribe to it, the inheritor of the parental influence, the most important functions. If the father was hard, violent and cruel, the super-ego takes over those attributes from him and, in the relations between the ego and it, the passivity which was supposed to have been repressed is reestablished. The super-ego has become sadistic, and the ego becomes masochistic—that is to say, at bottom passive in a feminine way. A great need for punishment develops in the ego, which in part offers itself as a victim to Fate, and in part finds satisfaction in ill-treatment by the super-ego (that is, in the sense of guilt). For every punishment is ultimately castration and, as such, *a* fulfillment of the old passive attitude towards the father. Even Fate is, in the last resort, only a later projection of the father.

The normal processes in the formation of conscience must be similar to the abnormal ones described here. We have not yet succeeded in fixing the boundary line between them. It will be observed that here the largest share in the outcome is ascribed to the passive component of repressed femininity. In addition, it must be of importance as an accidental factor whether the father, who is feared in any case, is also especially violent in reality. This was true in Dostoevsky's case, and we can trace back the fact of his extraordinary sense of guilt and of his masochistic conduct of life to a specially strong feminine component Thus the formula for Dostoevsky is as follows: a person with a specially strong innate bisexual disposition, who can defend himself with special intensity against dependence on a specially severe father. This characteristic of bisexuality comes as an addition to the components of his nature that we have already recognized. His early symptoms of death-like attacks can thus be understood as a father-identification on the part of his ego, which is permitted by his super-ego as a punishment. 'You wanted to kill your father in order to be your father yourself. Now you *are* your father, but a dead father'—the regular mechanism of hysterical symptoms. And further: 'Now your father is killing *you.*' For the ego the death symptom is a satisfaction in phantasy of the masculine wish and at the same time a masochistic satisfaction; for the super-ego it is a punitive satisfaction—that is, a sadistic satisfaction. Both of them, the ego and the super-ego, carry on the role of father.

To sum up, the relation between the subject and his father-object, while retaining its content, has been transformed into a relation between the ego and the super-ego—a new setting on a fresh stage. Infantile reactions from the Oedipus complex such as these may disappear if reality gives them no further nourishment. But the father's character remained the same, or rather, it deteriorated with the years, and thus Dostoevsky's hatred for his father and his death-wish against that wicked father were maintained. Now it is a dangerous thing if reality fulfills such repressed wishes. The phantasy has become reality and all defensive measures are thereupon reinforced. Dostoevsky's attacks now assumed an epileptic character; they still undoubtedly signified an identification with his father as a punishment, but they had become terrible, like his father's frightful death itself. What further content they had absorbed, particularly what sexual content, escapes conjecture.

One thing is remarkable: in the aura of the epileptic attack, one moment of supreme bliss is experienced. This may very well be a record of the triumph and sense of liberation felt on hearing the news of the death, to be followed immediately by an all the more cruel punishment. We have divined just such a sequence of triumph and mourning, of festive joy and mourning, in the brothers of the primal horde who murdered their father, and we find it repeated in the ceremony of the totem meal. ① If it proved to be the case that Dostoevsky was free from his attacks in Siberia, that would merely substantiate the view that they were his punishment. He did not need them any longer when he was being punished in another way. But that cannot be proved. Rather does this necessity for punishment on the part of Dostoevsky's mental economy explain the fact that he passed unbroken through these years of misery and humiliation. Dostoevsky's condemnation as a political prisoner was unjust and he must have known it, but he accepted the undeserved punishment at the hands of the Little Father, the Tsar, as a substitute for the punishment he deserved for his sin against his real father. Instead of punishing himself, he got himself punished by his father's deputy. Here we have a glimpse of the psychological justification of

---

① See *Totem and Taboo*.

the punishments inflicted by society. It is a fact that large groups of criminals want to be punished. Their super-ego demands it and so saves itself the necessity for inflicting the punishment itself.

Everyone who is familiar with the complicated transformation of meaning undergone by hysterical symptoms will understand that no attempt can be made here to follow out the meaning of Dostoevsky's attacks beyond this beginning. ① It is enough that we may assume that their original meaning remained unchanged behind all later accretions. We can safely say that Dostoevsky never got free from the feelings of guilt arising from his intention of murdering his father. They also determined his attitude in the two other spheres in which the father-relation is the decisive factor, his attitude towards the authority of the State and towards belief in God. In the first of these he ended up with complete submission to his Little Father, the Tsar, who had once performed with him in *reality* the comedy of killing which his attacks had so often represented in *play*. Here penitence gained the upper hand. In the religious sphere he retained more freedom: according to apparently trustworthy reports he wavered, up to the last moment of his life, between faith and atheism. His great intellect made it impossible for him to overlook any of the intellectual difficulties to which faith leads. By an individual recapitulation of a development in world-history he hoped to find a way out and a liberation from guilt in the Christ ideal, and even to make use of his sufferings as a claim to be playing a Christ-like role. If on the whole he did not achieve freedom and became a reactionary, that was because the filial guilt, which is present in human beings generally and on which religious feeling is built, had in him attained a super-individual intensity and remained insurmountable even to his great intelligence. In writing this we are lay-

---

① The best account of the meaning and content given by Dostoevsky himself, when he told his friend Strakhov that his irritability and depression after an epileptic attack were due to the fact that he seemed to himself a criminal and could not get rid of the feeling that he had a burden of unknown guilt upon him, that he had committed some great misdeed, which oppressed him. (Fülöp-Miller, 1924, 1188.) In self-accusations like these psycho-analysis sees signs of a recognition of 'psychical reality', and it endeavours to make the unknown guilt known to consciousness.

ing ourselves open to the charge of having abandoned the impartiality of analysis and of subjecting Dostoevsky to judgements that can only be justified from the partisan standpoint of a particular *Weltanschauung*. A conservative would take the side of the Grand Inquisitor and would judge Dostoevsky differently. The objection is just; and one can only say in extenuation that Dostoevsky's decision has every appearance of having been determined by an intellectual inhibition due to his neurosis.

It can scarcely be owing to chance that three of the masterpieces of the literature of all time—the *Oedipus Rex* of Sophocles, Shakespeare's *Hamlet* and Dostoevsky's *The Brothers Kamarazov*—should all deal with the same subject, parricide. In all three, moreover, the motive for the deed, sexual rivalry for a woman, is laid bare.

The most straightforward is certainly the representation in the drama derived from the Greek legend. In this it is still the hero himself who commits the crime. But poetic treatment is impossible without softening and disguise. The naked admission of an intention to commit parricide, as we arrive at it in analysis, seems intolerable without analytic preparation. The Greek drama, while retaining the crime, introduces the indispensable toning-down in a masterly fashion by projecting the hero's unconscious motive into reality in the form of a compulsion by a destiny which is alien to him. The hero commits the deed unintentionally and apparently uninfluenced by the woman; this latter element is however taken into account in the circumstance that the hero can only obtain possession of the queen mother after he has repeated his deed upon the monster who symbolizes the father. After his guilt has been revealed and made conscious, the hero makes no attempt to exculpate himself by appealing to the artificial expedient of the compulsion of destiny. His crime is acknowledged and punished as though it were a full and conscious one—which is bound to appear unjust to our reason, but which psychologically is perfectly correct.

In the English play the presentation is more indirect; the hero does not commit the crime himself; it is carried out by someone else, for whom it is not parricide. The forbidden motive of sexual rivalry for the woman does not need, therefore, to be disguised. Moreover, we see the hero's Oedipus complex, as it were, in a reflected light, by learning the effect upon him of the other's crime. He ought to avenge the crime, but finds himself, strangely enough, incapable of doing so. We know that it is his sense of guilt that is paralysing him; but, in a manner entirely in keeping with neurotic processes, the sense of guilt is displaced on to the perception of his inadequacy for fulfilling his task. There are signs that the hero feels this guilt as a super-individual one. He despises others no less than himself: 'Use every man after his desert, and who should 'scape whipping'?

The Russian novel goes a step further in the same direction. There also the murder is committed by someone else. This other person, however, stands to the murdered man in the same filial relation as the hero, Dmitri; in this other person's case the motive of sexual rivalry is openly admitted; he is a brother of the hero's, and it is a remarkable fact that Dostoevsky has attributed to him his own illness, the alleged epilepsy, as though he were seeking to confess that the epileptic, the neurotic, in himself was a parricide. Then, again, in the speech for the defence at the trial, there is the famous mockery of psychology—it is a 'knife that cuts both ways': a splendid piece of disguise, for we have only to reverse it in order to discover the deepest meaning of Dostoevsky's view of things. It is not psychology that deserves the mockery, but the procedure of judicial enquiry. It is a matter of indifference who actually committed the crime; psychology is only concerned to know who desired it emotionally and who welcomed it when it was done. And for that reason all of the brothers, except the contrasted figure of Alyosha, are equally guilty—the impulsive sensualist, the sceptical cynic and the epileptic criminal. In *The Brothers Karamazov* there is one particularly revealing scene. In the course of his talk with Dmitri, Father Zossima recognizes that Dmitri is prepared to commit parricide, and he bows down at his feet. It is impossible that this can be meant as an expression of admiration; it must mean that the holy man is rejecting the temptation to despise or detest the murderer and for that reason humbles himself before him. Dostoevsky's sympathy for the criminal is, in fact, boundless; it goes far beyond the pity which the unhappy wretch has a right to, and reminds us of the 'holy awe' with which epileptics and lunatics were regarded in the past. A criminal is to him almost a Redeemer, who has taken on himself the guilt which must else have been borne by others. There is no longer any need for one to murder, since *he* has already murdered; and one must be grateful to him, for, except for him, one would have been obliged oneself to murder. That is not kindly pity alone, it is identification on the basis of similar murderous impulses—in fact, a slightly displaced narcissism. (In saying this, we are not disputing the ethical value of this kindliness.) This may perhaps be quite generally the mechanism of kindly sympathy with other people, a mechanism which one can discern with especial ease in this extreme case of a guilt-ridden novelist There is no doubt that this sympathy by identification was a decisive factor in determining Dostoevsky's choice of material. He dealt first with the common criminal (whose motives are egotistical) and the political and religious criminal; and not until the end of his life did he come back to the primal criminal, the parricide, and use him, in a work of art, for making his confession.

The publication of Dostoevsky's posthumous papers and of his wife's diaries has thrown a glaring light on one episode in his life, namely the period in Germany when he was obsessed with a mania for gambling (cf. Fülöp-Miller and Eckstein, 1925), which no one could regard as anything but an unmistakable fit of pathological passion. There was no lack of rationalizations for this remarkable and unworthy behaviour. As often happens with neurotics, Dostoevsky's sense of guilt had taken a tangible shape as a burden of debt, and he was able to take refuge behind the pretext that he was trying by his winnings at the tables to make it possible for him to return to Russia without being arrested by his creditors. But this was no more than a pretext and Dostoevsky was acute enough to recognize the fact and honest enough to admit it. He knew that the chief thing was gambling for its own sake—*le jeu pour le jeu.* [1] All the details of his impulsively irrational conduct show this and something more besides. He never rested until he had lost everything. For him gambling was a

---

[1] 'The main thing is the play itself,' he writes in one of his letters. '1 swear that greed for money has nothing to do with it, although Heaven knows I am sorely in need of money.'

method of self-punishment as well. Time after time he gave his young wife his promise or his word of honour not to play any more or not to play any more on that particular day; and, as she says, he almost always broke it. When his losses had reduced himself and her to the direst need, he derived a second pathological satisfaction from that. He could then scold and humiliate himself before her, invite her to despise him and to feel sorry that she had married such an old sinner; and when he had thus unburdened his conscience, the whole business would begin again next day. His young wife accustomed herself to this cycle, for she had noticed that the one thing which offered any real hope of salvation—his literary production—never went better than when they had lost everything and pawned their last possessions. Naturally she did not understand the connection. When his sense of guilt was satisfied by the punishments he had inflicted on himself, the inhibition upon his work became less severe and he allowed himself to take a few steps along the road to success. [1]

What part of a gambler's long-buried childhood is it that forces its way to repetition in his obsession for play? The answer may be divined without difficulty from a story by one of our younger writers. Stefan Zweig, who has incidentally devoted a study to Dostoevsky himself (1920), has included in his collection of three stories *Die Verwirrung der Gefühle* (1927) one which he calls 'Vierundzwanzig Stunden aus dem Leben einer Frau'. This little masterpiece ostensibly sets out only to show what an irresponsible creature woman is, and to what excesses, surprising even to herself, an unexpected experience may drive her. But the story tells far more than this. If it is subjected to an analytical interpretation, it will be found to represent (without any apologetic intent) something quite different, something universally human, or rather something masculine. And such an interpretation is so extremely obvious that it cannot be resisted. It is characteristic of the nature of artistic creation that the author, who is a personal friend of mine, was able to assure me, when I asked him,

---

[1] 'He always remained at the gaming tables till he had lost everything and was totally ruined. It was only when the damage was quite complete that the demon at last retired from his soul and made way for the creative genius.' (Fülöp-Miller and Eckstein, 1925, ixxxvi.)

that the interpretation which I put to him had been completely strange to his knowledge and intention, although some of the details woven into the narrative seemed expressly designed to give a clue to the hidden secret.

In this story, an elderly lady of distinction tells the author about an experience she has had more than twenty years earlier. She has been left a widow when still young and is the mother of two sons, who no longer need her. In her forty-second year, expecting nothing further of life, she happens, on one of her aimless journeyings, to visit the Rooms at Monte Carlo. There, among all the remarkable impressions which the place produces, she is soon fascinated by the sight of a pair of hands which seem to betray all the feelings of the unlucky gambler with terrifying sincerity and intensity. These hands belong to a handsome young man—the author, as though unintentionally, makes him of the same age as the narrator's elder son—who, after losing everything, leaves the Rooms in the depth of despair, with the evident intention of ending his hopeless life in the Casino gardens. An inexplicable feeling of sympathy compels her to follow him and make every effort to save him. He takes her for one of the importunate women so common there and tries to shake her off; but she stays with him and finds herself obliged, in the most natural way possible, to join him in his apartment at the hotel, and finally to share his bed. After this improvised light of love, she exacts a most solemn vow from the young man, who has now apparently calmed down, that he will never play again, provides him with money for his journey home and promises to meet him at the station before the departure of his train. Now, however, she begins to feel a great tenderness for him, is ready to sacrifice all she has in order to keep him and makes up her mind to go with him instead of saying goodbye. Various mischances delay her, so that she misses the train. In her longing for the lost one she returns once more to the Rooms and there, to her horror, sees once more the hands which had first excited her sympathy: the faithless youth had gone back to his play. She reminds him of his promise, but, obsessed by his passion, he calls her a spoil-sport, tells her to go, and flings back the money with which she has tried to rescue him. She hurries away in deep mortification and learns later that she has not succeeded in saving him from suicide.

The brilliantly told, faultlessly motivated story is of course complete in itself and is certain to make a deep effect upon the reader. But analysis shows us that its invention is based fundamentally upon a wishful phantasy belonging to the period of puberty, which a number of people actually remember consciously. The phantasy embodies a boy's wish that his mother should herself initiate him into sexual life in order to save him from the dreaded injuries caused by masturbation. (The numerous creative works that deal with the theme of redemption have the same origin.) The 'vice' of masturbation is replaced by the addiction to gambling; and the emphasis laid upon the passionate activity of the hands betrays this derivation. Indeed, the passion for play is an equivalent of the old compulsion to masturbate; 'playing' is the actual word used in the nursery to describe the activity of the hands upon the genitals. The irresistible nature of the temptation, the solemn resolutions, which are nevertheless invariably broken, never to do it again, the stupefying pleasure and the bad conscience which tells the subject that he is ruining himself (committing suicide)—all these elements remain unaltered in the process of substitution. It is true that Zweig's story is told by the mother, not by the son. It must flatter the son to think: 'if my mother only knew what dangers masturbation involves me in, she would certainly save me from them by allowing me to lavish all my tenderness on her own body'. The equation of the mother with a prostitute, which is made by the young man in the story, is linked up with the same phantasy. It brings the unattainable woman within easy reach. The bad conscience which accompanies the phantasy brings about the unhappy ending of the story. It is also interesting to notice how the *façade* given to the story by its author seeks to disguise its analytic meaning. For it is extremely questionable whether the erotic life of women is dominated by sudden and mysterious impulses. On the contrary, analysis reveals an adequate motivation for the surprising behaviour of this woman who had hitherto turned away from love. Faithful to the memory of her dead husband, she had armed herself against all similar attractions; but—and here the son's phantasy is right—she did not, as a mother, escape her quite unconscious transference of love on to her son, and Fate was able to catch her at this undefended spot.

If the addiction to gambling, with the unsuccessful struggles to break the habit and the opportunities it affords for self-punishment, is a repetition of the compulsion to masturbate, we shall not be surprised to find that it occupied such a large space in Dostoevsky's life. After all, we find no cases of severe neurosis in which the auto-erotic satisfaction of early childhood and of puberty has not played a part; and the relation between efforts to suppress it and fear of the father are too well known to need more than a mention. ①

---

① Most of the views which are here expressed are also contained in an excellent book by Jolan Neufeld (1923).

5. 弗洛伊德：《陀思妥耶夫斯基与弑父》

(Sigmund Freud, "Dostoevsky and Parricide," 1927)

作者小识

弗洛伊德（Sigmund Freud，1856—1939），奥地利科学家和思想家。他所开创的心理学常常被比之于哥白尼的天文学革命、达尔文的进化论、爱因斯坦的相对论以及马克思的历史唯物主义，而他本人也被认为是一位伟大的创新者——他创建了"动力心理学"。

弗洛伊德是学医的，而且是临床医生。1876年，他展开的第一项科研工作是在鳝鱼身上找到睾丸。随后他醉心于神经系统研究，在当时医学知识和技术装备十分贫乏的情况下，他使用催眠疗法、宣泄疗法、联想疗法施展医道，治病救人。弗洛伊德志在治疗神经性疾病，但科学好奇心驱使着他去探索大脑的秘密，研究神经失常的内驱力。"我一生只追求一个目标，即推断或猜测人的心理器官是怎样构成的，是哪些力量在这一器官中互相影响、互相作用。"[①]

1900年，划时代的心理学巨著《梦的解析》出版。此书表面道幻说梦，本质上却是探寻人类灵魂的深层动力和心理构造。论著基于临床个案，为缓解神经性疾病的痛苦提供妙方，同时也让人面对潜意识的心理驱动力。20世纪头一个十年过去，孤军奋战的弗洛伊德终于得到了学界的认可，一场国际性的精神分析运动如火如荼。阿德勒、荣格、拉康等从各自的立场拓展了精神分析学说，各有卓越建树，展示了人的深层心理及其复杂维度。1930年，弗洛伊德获得了歌德奖。1933年，纳粹政权宣布他的著作为禁书。

对人性的本质和文明的命运之关怀，几乎贯穿了弗洛伊德的一生。他探索存在的焦虑和恐惧之心理渊源，否定超自然神迹的存在，但肯定宗教信仰的合法性。他还思索人性的弱点，并提出补救、救赎的办法。托马斯·曼(Thomas Mann，1875—1955)指出，弗洛伊德，一位医学心理学家，"将作为

---

① 转引自霍尔等：《弗洛伊德心理学与西方文学》，包华富、陈昭全、杨莘燊译，15页，长沙，湖南文艺出版社，1986。

我们所预见到的一种未来的人文主义的开路先驱而为人们所敬仰"，而他所开创的"精神分析学的认识具有改变世界的性质"，"一种善意的猜疑随之一起也被放进世界，这是一种与心灵的隐秘和阴谋有关的、披露性的怀疑，它一旦被唤醒，就再也不可能从世界消失"，"它渗透生命，损伤生命原生的天真，夺去它无知之激情，推行它的非激情化"。[①]

背景略说

弗洛伊德是近代科学遗产的继承人，也是理性主义的颠覆者。近代科学起码给人类精神造成了三度创伤：哥白尼颠覆"地心说"，让人经历了宇宙论的创伤，达尔文的"进化论"让人经历了生物学的创伤，而弗洛伊德的精神分析则让人刻骨铭心地体会到心理学的创伤。甚至还可以说，心理学的创伤是近代科学给人类创伤之集大成者。

《物种起源》在弗洛伊德三岁时问世，此后人们越来越明白，自己也是动物世界之成员。弗洛伊德四岁那年，费希纳（Gustav Fechner）创建心理学，主张对心灵现象进行量化分析。19世纪后半叶，病菌理论获得了开拓性发展，现代遗传学的创立让生命科学的发展登峰造极。同时，能量研究与能量理论的发展进入了历史上的黄金时代，但"热力学第二定律"（或"熵定律"）给宇宙的演化和生命的未来涂抹了一层悲剧的色彩。

在弗洛伊德创设心理分析的时代，不仅自然科学而且整个欧洲的科学文化都在经历着质的飞跃，以及科学范式的转型。X射线、放射性物质研究、遗传法则以及量子的发现，都表明科学领域思想重心的转移。马克斯·韦伯（Max Weber）的"社会学研究会"与弗洛伊德的"心理学研究所"，都是在正统学术体制外围发展起来的文化团体，其研究、运动与成果都为观察、审视现代人类的生存处境提供了人文主义的三棱镜。马克斯·韦伯本人略带揶揄地说，弗洛伊德将心理分析文化圈中持不同见解的人革出门户，"将集会变成秘密"。心理分析学派确实有密教的性质，其核心成员似乎比较相信"真理只能秘传"。弗洛伊德毕生是一位"反哲学的哲人"，并以追寻英雄命运的"英雄"自我期许，自然而然地带有马克斯·韦伯的所谓"个人神奇魅力"，以及与这种

[①] 曼：《弗洛伊德与未来——一九三六年五月八日在维也纳弗洛伊德八十华诞庆贺会上的讲话》，见《多难而伟大的十九世纪》，朱雁冰译，234页，杭州，浙江大学出版社，2013。

资质相连的贵族情怀。

托马斯·曼断言，精神分析将个体心理溯源到幼年时代，同时也将人类精神溯源至荒渺太古，总而言之就是追溯源始。精神分析与神话的邂逅便在所难免。精神分析与神话都是"深层心理学"，不仅要发掘空间的深层，而且要流连在时间的深层。从1880年到1910年，整个欧洲知识界处在一个"精神分析与神话邂逅"的时段，也就是"探索原始的人类、人类的内心、人类的深层知识的年代，也是从神话中发掘人类原始观念层的时代"。[①] 从古希腊到现代启蒙时代"神话与理性"对峙的格局，到弗洛伊德的时代似乎已经二极相通，归向神话世界，探求知识的源始，感性权力得以复位。文学现代主义远眺太古，自然科学让古典宇宙论重获生机。文学现代主义主动地承载着科学与神秘主义二重身份。而在精神分析学说中，人类的无意识与神话的邂逅仿佛是神定的约会。弗洛伊德将探索心理奥秘的眼光投向了前逻辑的无意识及其承载形式，即神话、隐喻、象征、直观的渊流，从而改变了对文学主体、作品存在方式、艺术流通过程的固有成见，导致了文学研究范式的转型。

基本内容

《陀思妥耶夫斯基与弑父》是弗洛伊德为德文版陀思妥耶夫斯基全集撰写的补充论文，写作时间为1925—1927年。这篇文章集中阐述陀思妥耶夫斯基的性格特征，包括神经病患者、创造性艺术家、道德学家和罪犯四个人格维度。文章重点探讨作家的受虐狂倾向、犯罪感、癫痫发作，及其俄狄浦斯情结中的矛盾态度。弗洛伊德在欧洲文学史的脉络中，结合俄罗斯民族精神品格，将弑父描述为人类的命运。这篇文章的后一部分，通过分析茨威格的小说《一个女人的二十四小时》，对观陀思妥耶夫斯基的"赌瘾"，论述无意识的神秘冲动对人物性格的深刻影响。

为理解弗洛伊德关于文学与人类弑父命运、无意识与性格形成的关系的理论，我们有必要简述弗洛伊德精神分析的基本理论假定。

（1）人类心灵的动力学模式。弗洛伊德认为，主宰人类行为的不是意识，而是无意识（unconsciousness）。无意识构成了人类心灵的非理性部分，隐藏着隐秘的欲望、野心、恐惧、激情以及不合理的思想。无意识往往以乔装打

[①] 　上山安敏：《神话与理性——19世纪末至20世纪初欧洲的知识界》，孙传钊译，272页，上海，上海人民出版社，1992。

扮的方式呈现为意识，隐秘的欲望和源始的冲动也会通过压缩、变形、移情、伪装的方式表现在现实的行动中。

（2）经济学模式。弗洛伊德将主宰精神生活的原则分为"快乐原则"（Pleasure Principle）和"现实原则"（Reality Principle）。快乐原则按照本能行事，要求片刻满足，拒绝社会设定的性别与道德戒律。现实原则按照规范行事，调节快乐需求，超越本能冲动。

（3）心理地形学模式。地形学是个隐喻说法，意在将无形的心理存在有形化。弗洛伊德认为，人格在心理上有三个成分，即"本我"（id）、"自我"（ego）和"超我"（superego）。本我包含着隐秘欲望、黑暗的意愿以及最强烈的恐惧，追求满足快乐原则。不仅如此，本我还是"力比多"（性力量，libido）的储蓄所。若让这种源始性力逃避了监控，它就即刻要求得到满足。自我是心灵的逻辑层面、意识领域、醒觉部分。当本我遵循快乐原则而活力乱奔之时，自我则遵循现实原则调节欲望，以合理方式释放源始性力。超我则构成心灵内在的审查机制和压抑力量，按照社会原则进行道德评判，一切负罪感和恐惧都由此而来。

（4）俄狄浦斯情结、阉割和埃勒克特拉情结。化用古希腊悲剧诗人索福克勒斯的作品《俄狄浦斯王》中的人物形象，弗洛伊德断言，在婴儿发育晚期，男性会对母亲产生一种强烈的爱欲依恋。每一个男人都有杀父娶母的隐秘愿望，但是又恐惧强权父亲的阉割。女性婴儿则是对父亲有强烈的爱欲依恋。每一个女人都有杀母嫁父的隐秘愿望。在论述陀思妥耶夫斯基的《卡拉马佐夫兄弟》的论文中，弗洛伊德发表了关于"俄狄浦斯情结"的看法，断定索福克勒斯、莎士比亚和陀思妥耶夫斯基都表现了为争夺女人而弑父这一事关人类命运的主题。

（5）梦境释义。梦境是被压抑的意愿和欲望的表现形式。心灵为本我打开一扇窗口，让被意识压抑的无意识以各种方式化妆表现，梦境就是这样的窗口之一。梦境形成的过程可以隐喻文学的创造过程，也就是通过置换、压缩、转型和升华等多道程序，曲折地将隐秘的欲望和黑暗的意愿表现出来。反之，文学理解和批评类似于释梦过程，即穿越符号形式的表象，烛照幽微，把握艺术家或作家的无意识冲动。文学艺术，是源始欲望的升华，因而是作家的白日梦。

（6）文学与精神分析。论述陀思妥耶夫斯基的论文表明，心灵深层难以调解的冲突导致了神经官能症，而这些冲突便是文学的素材。文学作品是作家无意识心灵的外在表现。既然可以把文学作品当作一个梦境来处理，因而也就应该运用精神分析的技术去分析文本，以便揭示作家隐秘的动机、压抑的欲望、黑暗的希望。

拓展讨论

早在 1925 年，弗洛伊德就写作了《抑制、症状和焦虑》，论述焦虑和恐惧的起源及其生存论意义。在他看来，焦虑是一种对于危险做出的紧迫心理反应。弗洛伊德将焦虑追溯到女性分娩时刻，暗示焦虑是人类与生俱来的，具有生存论意义。尤其是阉割焦虑，必然发展出一种道德焦虑，以及对于父权所象征的超我之愤怒。对超我的愤怒连接着对死亡的恐惧，因而焦虑伴随着向死而生的历程。

在生存论意义上，焦虑无处不在，没有确定的对象，却引起实在的恐惧。布鲁门伯格在研究神话的起源时，将这种生存论焦虑称为"实在专制主义"（Absolutismus der Wirklichkeit）。布鲁门伯格写道：实在专制主义，"是指人类几乎控制不了生存处境，而且尤其自以为他们完全无法控制生存处境"①。从个体发育转向种系进化，布鲁门伯格断定这种生存论的焦虑发生在人类直立行走以及走出森林、迁徙到平原的时刻。只要有情境的飞跃，人类就一定有生存焦虑。实在专制主义，是伴随着情境的飞跃而发生的事件之总体。纯粹不确定的心灵状态，就是生存论的焦虑状态。"焦虑是一种没有对象的意识的意向性。因此，整个地平线就等于所有方向的整体，从任何一个方向开始，'它都可能临近'。"②而弗洛伊德将自我面对巨大的危险时油然而生的恐惧感、孤独感、无助感描述为一种核心的创伤情境，又从婴儿在早期发育阶段对爱的渴望中看到了这种匮乏心灵状态的补偿。在神经科学研究中，焦虑被描述为一种在种类和个体历史上反复发生的对于无名恐惧的体验。为了克服这种阴郁而强大的焦虑，原始巫术、宗教、神话、仪式就出现了。

这最初并不是借助于知识经验而是通过种种心智谋略（Kunstgriffe）而造成的转化，即以熟悉代替陌生，以解释代替神秘，以命名代替无名。某些东西被"推向前台"（Überschoben），以便使隐而不显的东西成为某些

---

① 布鲁门伯格：《神话研究（上）》，胡继华译，4 页，上海，上海人民出版社，2012。
② 布鲁门伯格：《神话研究（上）》，胡继华译，5 页，上海，上海人民出版社，2012。

行为的对象——规避行为，驱魔行为，慰藉行为，以及去势行为（depo-tenzierenden Handlung）的对象。通过命名来证明和接近这些特殊要素，并把那些与诸如此类要素相周旋的一种对等关系普遍化了。通过一个命名而得以辨识的东西，就是通过隐喻的手法让它从神秘之物里脱颖而出，进而通过讲故事的办法按照其意蕴而得以领悟。恐慌与麻痹，焦虑行为的二极，就随着那些必须被应付的可以预测的巨大事物之出现而被那种协调的应付方式化解了，即使巫术礼仪替代作用的结果还偶然嘲讽那种以人类名义获得权力保护的意图。①

无论我们选取什么样的起点，削弱实在专制主义的工作都已经起步了。在那些不仅主宰着我们对早期人类的猜想而且将早期人类描画为"工具制造者"的陈年旧迹当中，我们无法勘察：究竟必须完成什么样的劳作，方可将一个陌生的世界变成一个熟知的世界，使一团混沌的经验数据可被分析探查。这包括那些超越于地平线之外而无法为经验所企及的东西。为了充实这条作为神话"世界边缘"的最后地平线，就只需期望陌生之物的萌芽与衰败。"人类画师"（Homo pictor）不仅是洞穴壁画的创造者，这些壁画与狩猎的巫术实践紧密关联，而且还是那些靠投射形象来隐藏世界稳靠性的匮乏的特殊生物。

实在专制主义遭遇到了其对立面——形象专制主义和意志专制主义。②

人类凭着命名的能力、隐喻的策略和神话创作的壮举走出了自然状态。神话、理性、教义以及现代乌托邦社会理想，都是人类借以克服"实在专制主义"，即生存论焦虑的手段。

延伸阅读

1. 弗洛伊德：《释梦》，孙名之译，北京，商务印书馆，1996。此书为弗洛伊德学说的"奠基之作"，将释梦过程描述为进入无意识、理解人类深层心理的冒险旅程。

---

① 布鲁门伯格：《神话研究（上）》，胡继华译，6页，上海，上海人民出版社，2012。
② 布鲁门伯格：《神话研究（上）》，胡继华译，8～9页，上海，上海人民出版社，2012。

2. 霍尔等：《弗洛伊德心理学与西方文学》，包华富、陈昭全、杨莘燊译，长沙，湖南文艺出版社，1986。此书为弗洛伊德心理分析的基础读本，含弗洛伊德学术要义阐发、论著选译，收入了特里林、黑塞的论文，以及部分中国学者的研究论文。

6. Archetypes of the Collective Unconscious①(1934)
By Carl G. Jung

The hypothesis of a collective unconscious belongs to the class of ideas that people at first find strange but soon come to possess and use as familiar conceptions. This has been the case with the concept of the unconscious in general. After the philosophical idea of the unconscious, in the form presented chiefly by Carus and von Hartmann, had gone down under the overwhelming wave of materialism and empiricism, leaving hardly a ripple behind it, it gradually reappeared in the scientific domain of medical psychology.

At first the concept of the unconscious was limited *to* denoting the state of repressed or forgotten contents. Even with Freud, who makes the unconscious—at least metaphorically—take the stage as the acting subject, it is really nothing but the gathering place of forgotten and repressed contents, and has a functional significance thanks only to these. For Freud, accordingly, the unconscious is of an exclusively personal nature,② although he was aware of its archaic and mythological thoughtforms.

A more or less superficial layer of the unconscious is undoubtedly personal. I call it the *personal unconscious*. But this personal unconscious rests upon a deeper layer, which does not derive from personal experience and is not a personal acquisition but is inborn. This deeper layer I call the *collective unconscious*. I have chosen the term "collective" because this part of the unconscious is not individual but universal; in contrast to the personal psyche, it has contents

---

① [First published in the *Eranos-Jahrbuch* 1934, and later revised and published in *Von den Wurzeln des Bewusstseins* (Zurich, 1954), from which version the present translation is made. The translation of the original version, by Stanley Dell, in *The Integration of the Personality* (New York, 1939; London, 1940), has been freely consulted. —EDITORS.]

② In his later works Freud differentiated the basic view mentioned here. He called the instinctual psyche the "id," and his "super-ego" denotes the collective consciousness, of which the individual is partly conscious and partly unconscious (because it is repressed).

and modes of behaviour that are more or less the same everywhere and in all individuals. It is, in other words, identical in all men and thus constitutes a common psychic substrate of a suprapersonal nature which is present in every one of us.

Psychic existence can be recognized only by the presence *of* contents that are *capable of consciousness*. We can therefore speak of an unconscious only in so far as we are able to demonstrate its contents. The contents of the personal unconscious are chiefly the *feeling-toned complexes*, as they are called; they constitute the personal and private side of psychic life. The contents of the collective unconscious, on the other hand, are known as *archetypes*.

The term "archetype" occurs as early as Philo Judaeus,[1] with reference to the *Imago Dei*(God-image) in man. It can also be found in Irenaeus, who says: "The creator of the world did not fashion these things directly from himself but copied them from archetypes outside himself. "[2] In the *Corpus Hermeticum*,[3] God is called τὸ ἀρχέτυπον φῶς (archetypal light). The term occurs several times in Dionysius the Areopagite, as for instance in *De caelesti hierarchia*, II, 4: "immaterial Archetypes,"[4] and in *De divinis nominibus*, I, 6: "Archetypal stone. "[5] The term "archetype" is not found in St. Augustine, but the idea of it is. Thus in *De diversis quaestionibus LXXXIII* he speaks of "*ideae principales*, 'which are themselves not formed … but are contained in the divine understanding. '"[6]"Archetype" is an explanatory paraphrase of the Platonic εἶδος.

---

[1]　*De opificio mundi*, I, 69. Cf. Colson/Whitaker trans. , I, p. 55.

[2]　*Adversus haereses* II, 7, 5: "Mundi fabricator non a semetipso fecit haec, sed de alienis archetypis transtulit. " (Cf. Roberts/Rambaut trans. , I, p. 139.)

[3]　Scott, *Hermetica*, I, p. 140.

[4]　In Migne, P. G, , vol. 3, col. 144.

[5]　Ibid. , col. 595. Cf. *The Divine Names*(trans. by Rolt), pp. 62, 72.

[6]　Migne, P. L. , vol. 40, col. 30. "Archetype" is used in the same way by the alchemists, as in the "Tractatus aureus" of Hermes Trismegistus (*Theatrum chemicum*, IV, 1613, p. 718): "As God [contains] all the treasure of his godhead … hidden in himself as in an archetype [*in se tanquam archetypo absconditum*] … in like manner Saturn carries the similitudes of metallic bodies hiddenly in himself. " In the "Tractatus de igne et sale" of Vigenerus (*Theatr. chem.* , VI, 1661, p. 3), the world is "ad archetypi sui similitudinem factus" (made after the likeness of its archetype) and is therefore called the "magnus homo" (the "homo maximus" of Swedenborg).

For our purposes this term is apposite and helpful, because it tells us that so far as the collective unconscious contents are concerned we are dealing with archaic or—I would say—primordial types, that is, with universal images that have existed since the remotest times. The term "representations collectives," used by Lévy-Bruhl to denote the symbolic figures in the primitive view of the world, could easily be applied to unconscious contents as well, since it means practically the same thing. Primitive tribal lore is concerned with archetypes that have been modified in a special way. They are no longer contents of the unconscious, but have already been changed into conscious formulae taught according to tradition, generally in the form of esoteric teaching. This last is a typical means of expression for the transmission of collective contents originally derived from the unconscious.

Another well-known expression of the archetypes is myth and fairytale. But here too we are dealing with forms that have received a specific stamp and have been handed down through long periods of time. The term "archetype" thus applies only indirectly to the "representations collectives," since it designates only those psychic contents which have not yet been submitted to conscious elaboration and are therefore an immediate datum of psychic experience. In this sense there is a considerable difference between the archetype and the historical formula that has evolved. Especially on the higher levels of esoteric teaching the archetypes appear in a form that reveals quite unmistakably the critical and evaluating influence of conscious elaboration. Their immediate manifestation, as we encounter it in dreams and visions, is much more individual, less understandable, and more naïve than in myths, for example. The archetype is essentially an unconscious content that is altered by becoming conscious and by being perceived, and it takes its colour from the individual consciousness in which it happens to appear. ①

What the word "archetype" means in the nominal sense is clear enough,

---

① One must, for the sake of accuracy, distinguish between "archetype" and "archetypal ideas." The archetype as such is a hypothetical and irrepresentable model, something like the "pattern of behaviour" in biology. Cf. "On the Nature of the Psyche," sec. 7.

then, from its relations with myth, esoteric teaching, and fairytale. But if we try to establish what an archetype is *psychologically*, the matter becomes more complicated. So far mythologists have always helped themselves out with solar, lunar, meteorological, vegetal, and other ideas of the kind. The fact that myths are first and foremost psychic phenomena that reveal the nature of the soul is something they have absolutely refused to see until now. Primitive man is not much interested in objective explanations of the obvious, but he has an imperative need—or rather, his unconscious psyche has an irresistible urge—to assimilate all outer sense experiences to inner, psychic events. It is not enough for the primitive to see the sun rise and set; this external observation must at the same time be a psychic happening: the sun in its course must represent the fate of a god or hero who, in the last analysis, dwells nowhere except in the soul of man. All the mythologized processes of nature, such as summer and winter, the phases of the moon, the rainy seasons, and so forth, are in no sense allegories ① of these objective occurrences; rather they are symbolic expressions of the inner, unconscious drama of the psyche which becomes accessible to man's consciousness by way of projection—that is, mirrored in the events of nature. The projection is so fundamental that it has taken several thousand years of civilization to detach it in some measure from its outer object. In the case of astrology, for instance, this age-old "scientia intuitiva" came to be branded as rank heresy because man had not yet succeeded in making the psychological description of character independent of the stars. Even today, people who still believe in astrology fall almost without exception for the old superstitious assumption of the influence of the stars. And yet anyone who can calculate a horoscope should know that, since the days of Hipparchus of Alexandria, the spring-point has been fixed at $0°$ Aries, and that the zodiac on which every horoscope is based is therefore quite arbitrary, the spring-point having gradually advanced, since then, into the first degrees of Pisces, owing to the precession

---

① An allegory is a paraphrase of a conscious content, whereas a symbol is the best possible expression for an unconscious content whose nature can only be guessed, because it is still unknown.

of the equinoxes.

Primitive man impresses us so strongly with his subjectivity that we should really have guessed long ago that myths refer to something psychic. His knowledge of nature is essentially the language and outer dress of an unconscious psychic process. But the very fact that this process is unconscious gives us the reason why man has thought of everything except the psyche in his attempts to explain myths. He simply didn't know that the psyche contains all the images that have ever given rise to myths, and that our unconscious is an acting and suffering subject with an inner drama which primitive man rediscovers, by means of analogy, in the processes of nature both great and small?[1]

* * * * * * * * * * * *

The unconscious is commonly regarded as a sort of incapsulated fragment of our most personal and intimate life—something like what the Bible calls the "heart" and considers the source of all evil thoughts. In the chambers of the heart dwell the wicked blood-spirits, swift anger and sensual weakness. This is how the unconscious looks when seen from the conscious side. But consciousness appears to be essentially an affair of the cerebrum, which sees everything separately and in isolation, and therefore sees the unconscious in this way too, regarding it outright as *my* unconscious. Hence it is generally believed that anyone who descends into the unconscious gets into a suffocating atmosphere of egocentric subjectivity, and in this blind alley is exposed to the attack of all the ferocious beasts which the caverns of the psychic underworld are supposed to harbour.

True, whoever looks into the mirror of the water will see first of all his own face. Whoever goes to himself risks a confrontation with himself. The mirror does not flatter, it faithfully shows whatever looks into it; namely, the face we never show to the world because we cover it with the *persona*, the mask of the actor. But the mirror lies behind the mask and shows the true face.

This confrontation is the first test of courage on the inner way, a test suffi-

---

[1] Cf. my papers on the divine child and the Kore in the present volume, and Kerényi's complementary essays in *Essays on* [or *Introduction to*] *a Science of Mythology*.

cient to frighten off most people, for the meeting with ourselves belongs to the more unpleasant things that can be avoided so long as we can project everything negative into the environment. But if we are able to see our own shadow and can bear knowing about it, then a small part of the problem has already been solved: we have at least brought up the personal unconscious. The shadow is a living part of the personality and therefore wants to live with it in some form. It cannot be argued out of existence or rationalized into harmlessness. This problem is exceedingly difficult, because it not only challenges the whole man, but reminds him at the same time of his helplessness and ineffectuality. Strong natures—or should one rather call them weak? —do not like to be reminded of this, but prefer to think of themselves as heroes who are beyond good and evil, and to cut the Gordian knot instead of untying it. Nevertheless, the account has to be settled sooner or later. In the end one has to admit that there are problems which one simply cannot solve on one's own resources. Such an admission has the advantage of being honest, truthful, and in accord with reality, and this prepares the ground for a compensatory reaction from the collective unconscious: you are now more inclined to give heed to a helpful idea or intuition, or to notice thoughts which had not been allowed to voice themselves before. Perhaps you will pay attention to the dreams that visit you at such moments, or will reflect on certain inner and outer occurrences that take place just at this time. If you have an attitude of this kind, then the helpful powers slumbering in the deeper strata of man's nature can come awake and intervene, for helplessness and weakness are the eternal experience and the eternal problem of mankind. To this problem there is also an eternal answer, otherwise it would have been all up with humanity long ago. When you have done everything that could possibly be done, the only thing that remains is what you could still do if only you knew it. But how much do we know of ourselves? Precious little, to judge by experience. Hence there is still a great deal of room left for the unconscious. Prayer, as we know, calls for a very similar attitude and therefore has much the same effect.

The necessary and needful reaction from the collective unconscious expresses itself in archetypally formed ideas. The meeting with oneself is, at first, the meeting with one's own shadow. The shadow is a tight passage, a narrow door, whose painful constriction no one is spared who goes down to the deep well. But one must learn to know oneself in order to know who one is. For what comes after the door is, surprisingly enough, a boundless expanse full of unprecedented uncertainty, with apparently no inside and no outside, no above and no below, no here and no there, no mine and no thine, no good and no bad. It is the world of water, where all life floats in suspension; where the realm of the sympathetic system, the soul of everything living, begins; where I am indivisibly this and that; where I experience the other in myself and the other-than-myself experiences me.

No, the collective unconscious is anything but an incapsulated personal system; it is sheer objectivity, as wide as the world and open to all the world. There I am the object of every subject, in complete reversal of my ordinary consciousness, where I am always the subject that has an object. There I am utterly one with the world, so much a part of it that I forget all too easily who I really am. "Lost in oneself" is a good way of describing this state. But this self is the world, if only a consciousness could see it. That is why we must know who we are.

The unconscious no sooner touches us than we *are* it—we become unconscious of ourselves. That is the age-old danger, instinctively known and feared by primitive man, who himself stands so very close to this pleroma. His consciousness is still uncertain, wobbling on its feet. It is still childish, having just emerged from the primal waters. A wave of the unconscious may easily roll over it, and then he forgets who he was and does things that are strange to him. Hence primitives are afraid of uncontrolled emotions, because consciousness breaks down under them and gives way to possession. All man's strivings have therefore been directed towards the consolidation of consciousness. This was the purpose of rite and dogma; they were dams and walls to keep back the dangers of the unconscious, the "perils of the soul." Primitive rites consist accordingly in the exorcizing of spirits, the lifting of spells, the averting of the evil omen, propitiation, purification, and the production by sympathetic magic of helpful occurrences.

It is these barriers, erected in primitive times, that later became the foundations of the Church. It is also these barriers that collapse when the symbols become weak with age. Then the waters rise and boundless catastrophes break over mankind. The religious leader of the Taos pueblo, known as the Loco Tenente Gobernador, once said to me: "The Americans should stop meddling with our religion, for when it dies and we can no longer help the sun our Father to cross the sky, the Americans and the whole world will learn something in ten years' time, for then the sun won't rise any more. " In other words, night will fall, the light of consciousness is extinguished, and the dark sea of the unconscious breaks in.

Whether primitive or not, mankind always stands on the brink of actions it performs itself but does not control. The whole world wants peace and the whole world prepares for war, to take but one example. Mankind is powerless against mankind, and the gods, as ever, show it the ways of fate. Today we call the gods "factors," which comes from *facere*, 'to make. ' The makers stand behind the wings of the world-theatre. It is so in great things as in small. In the realm of consciousness we are our own masters; we seem to be the "factors" themselves. But if we step through the door of the shadow we discover with terror that we are the objects of unseen factors. To know this is decidedly unpleasant, for nothing is more disillusioning than the discovery of our own inadequacy. It can even give rise to primitive panic, because, instead of being believed in, the anxiously guarded supremacy of consciousness—which is in truth one of the secrets of human success—is questioned in the most dangerous way. But since ignorance is no guarantee of security, and in fact only makes our insecurity still worse, it is probably better despite our fear to know where the danger lies. To ask the right question is already half the solution of a problem. At any rate we then know that the greatest danger threatening us comes from the unpredictability of the psyche's reactions. Discerning persons have realized for some time that external historical conditions, of whatever kind, are only occasions, jumping-off grounds, for the real dangers that threaten our lives. These are the present politico-social delusional systems. We should not regard them causally, as necessary consequences of external conditions, but as decisions precipitated by the collective unconscious.

This is a new problem. All ages before us have believed in gods in some form or other. Only an unparalleled impoverishment of symbolism could enable us to rediscover the gods as psychic factors, that is, as archetypes of the unconscious. No doubt this discovery is hardly credible at present. To be convinced, we need to have the experience pictured in the dream of the theologian, for only then do we experience the self-activity of the spirit moving over the waters. Since the stars have fallen from heaven and our highest symbols have paled, a secret life holds sway in the unconscious. That is why we have a psychology today, and why we speak of the unconscious. All this would be quite superfluous in an age or culture that possessed symbols. Symbols are spirit from above, and under those conditions the spirit is above too. Therefore it would be a foolish and senseless undertaking for such people to wish to experience or investigate an unconscious that contains nothing but the silent, undisturbed sway of nature. Our unconscious, on the other hand, hides living water, spirit that has become nature, and that is why it is disturbed. Heaven has become for us the cosmic space of the physicists, and the divine empyrean a fair memory of things that once were. But "the heart glows," and a secret unrest gnaws at the roots of our being. In the words of the *Völuspa* we may ask:

What murmurs Wotan over Mimir's head?
Already the spring boils ...

Our concern with the unconscious has become a vital question for us—a question of spiritual being or non-being. All those who have had an experience like that mentioned in the dream know that the treasure lies in the depths of the water and will try to salvage it. As they must never forget who they are, they must on no account imperil their consciousness. They will keep their standpoint firmly anchored to the earth, and will thus—to preserve the metaphor—become fishers who catch with hook and net what swims in the water. There may be consummate fools who do not understand what fishermen do, but the latter will not mistake the timeless meaning of their action, for the symbol of their craft is many centuries older than the still unfaded story of the Grail. But not every man is a fisherman. Sometimes this figure remains arrested at an early, instinctive level, and then it is an otter, as we know from Oskar Schmitz's fairytales. ①

Whoever looks into the water sees his own image, but behind it living creatures soon loom up; fishes, presumably, harmless dwellers of the deep—harmless, if only the lake were not haunted. They are water-beings of a peculiar sort. Sometimes a nixie gets into the fisherman's net, a female, half-human fish. ②

Nixies are entrancing creatures:

> Half drew she him,
> Half sank he down
> And nevermore was seen.

The nixie is an even more instinctive version of a magical feminine being whom I call the *anima*. She can also be a siren, *melusina* (mermaid), ③ woodnymph, Grace, or Erlking's daughter, or a lamia or succubus, who infatuates young men and sucks the life out of them. Moralizing critics will say that these figures are projections of soulful emotional states and are nothing but worthless fantasies. One must admit that there is a certain amount of truth in this. But is it the whole truth? Is the nixie really nothing but a product of moral laxity? Were there not such beings long ago, in an age when dawning human con-

---

① [The "Fischottermärchen" in *Märchen aus dem Unbewussten*, pp. 14ff. , 43ff. — EDITORS.]

② Cf. Paracelsus, *De vita longa* (1562), and my commentary in "Paracelsus as a Spiritual Phenomenon" (concerning Melusina, pars. 179ff. , 215ff.

③ Cf. the picture of the adept in *Liber mutus* (1677) (fig. 13 in *The Practice of Psychotherapy*, p. 320). He is fishing, and has caught a nixie. His *soror mystica*, however, catches birds in her net, symbolizing the animus. The idea of the anima often turns up in the literature of the 16th and 17th cent. , for instance in Richardus Vitus, Aldrovandus, and the commentator of the *Tractatus aureus*. Cf. "The Enigma of Bologna" in my *Mysterium Coniunctionis*, pars. 51ff.

sciousness was still wholly bound to nature? Surely there were spirits of forest, field, and stream long before the question of moral conscience ever existed. What is more, these beings were as much dreaded as adored, so that their rather peculiar erotic charms were only one of their characteristics. Man's consciousness was then far simpler, and his possession of it absurdly small. An unlimited amount of what we now feel to be an integral part of our psychic being disports itself merrily for the primitive in projections ranging far and wide.

The word "projection" is not really appropriate, for nothing has been cast out of the psyche; rather, the psyche has attained its present complexity by a series of acts of introjection. Its complexity has increased in proportion to the despiritualization of nature. An alluring nixie from the dim bygone is today called an "erotic fantasy," and she may complicate our psychic life in a most painful way. She comes upon us just as a nixie might; she sits on top of us like a succubus; she changes into all sorts of shapes like a witch, and in general displays an unbearable independence that does not seem at all proper in a psychic content. Occasionally she causes states of fascination that rival the best bewitchment, or unleashes terrors in us not to be outdone by any manifestation of the devil. She is a mischievous being who crosses our path in numerous transformations and disguises, playing all kinds of tricks on us, causing happy and unhappy delusions, depressions and ecstasies, outbursts of affect, etc. Even in a state of reasonable introjection the nixie has not laid aside her roguery. The witch has not ceased to mix her vile potions of love and death; her magic poison has been refined into intrigue and self-deception, unseen though none the less dangerous for that.

But how do we dare to call this elfin being the "anima"? Anima means soul and should designate something very wonderful and immortal. Yet this was not always so. We should not forget that this kind of soul is a dogmatic conception whose purpose it is to pin down and capture something uncannily alive and active. The German word *Seele* is closely related, via the Gothic form *saiwalô* to the Greek word αἰόλος, which means "quick-moving," "changeful of hue," "twinkling," something like a butterfly— ψυχή in Greek—which reels drunkenly from flower to flower and lives on honey and love. In Gnostic typology the ἄνθρωπος ψυχικός, "psychic man," is inferior to the πνευματικός, "spiritual man" and finally there are wicked souls who must roast in hell for all eternity. Even the quite innocent soul of the unbaptized newborn babe is deprived of the contemplation of God. Among primitives, the soul is the magic breath of life (hence the term "anima"), or a flame. An uncanonical saying of our Lord's aptly declares: "Whoso is near unto me is near to the fire." For Heraclitus the soul at the highest level is fiery and dry, because ψυχή as such is closely akin to "cool breath"—ψύχειν means "to breathe," "to blow"; ψυχρός and ψῦχος mean "cold,"" chill," "damp."

Being that has soul is living being. Soul is the living thing in man, that which lives of itself and causes life. Therefore God breathed into Adam a living breath, that he might live. With her cunning play of illusions the soul lures into life the inertness of matter that does not want to live. She makes us believe incredible things, that life may be lived. She is full of snares and traps, in order that man should fall, should reach the earth, entangle himself there, and stay caught, so that life should be lived; as Eve in the garden of Eden could not rest content until she had convinced Adam of the goodness of the forbidden apple. Were it not for the leaping and twinkling of the soul, man would rot away in his greatest passion, idleness. ① A certain kind of reasonableness is its advocate, and a certain kind of morality adds its blessing. But to have soul is the whole venture of life, for soul is a life-giving daemon who plays his elfin game above and below human existence, for which reason—in the realm of dogma—he is threatened and propitiated with superhuman punishments and blessings that go far beyond the possible deserts of human beings. Heaven and hell are the fates meted out to the soul and not to civilized man, who in his nakedness and timidity would have no idea of what to do with himself in a heavenly Jerusalem.

The anima is not the soul in the dogmatic sense, not an *anima rationalis*, which is a philosophical conception, but a natural archetype that satisfactorily sums up all the statements of the unconscious, of the primitive mind, of the history of language and religion. It is a "factor" in the proper sense of the

---

① La Rochefoucauld, Pensées DLX. Quoted in *Symbols of Transformation*, p. 174.

word. Man cannot make it; on the contrary, it is always the *a priori* element in his moods, reactions, impulses, and whatever else is spontaneous in psychic life. It is something that lives of itself, that makes us live; it is a life behind consciousness that cannot be completely integrated with it, but from which, on the contrary, consciousness arises. For, in the last analysis, psychic life is for the greater part an unconscious life that surrounds consciousness on all sides— a notion that is sufficiently obvious when one considers how much unconscious preparation is needed, for instance, to register a sense-impression.

Although it seems as if the whole of our unconscious psychic life could be ascribed to the anima, she is yet only one archetype among many. Therefore, she is not characteristic of the unconscious in its entirety. She is only one of its aspects. This is shown by the very fact of her femininity. What is not-I, not masculine, is most probably feminine, and because the not-I is felt as not belonging to me and therefore as outside me, the anima-image is usually projected upon women. Either sex is inhabited by the opposite sex up to a point, for, biologically speaking, it is simply the greater number of masculine genes that tips the scales in favour of masculinity. The smaller number of feminine genes seems to form a feminine character, which usually remains unconscious because of its subordinate position.

With the archetype of the anima we enter the realm of the gods, or rather, the realm that metaphysics has reserved for itself. Everything the anima touches becomes numinous—unconditional, dangerous, taboo, magical. She is the serpent in the paradise of the harmless man with good resolutions and still better intentions. She affords the most convincing reasons for not prying into the unconscious, an occupation that would break down our moral inhibitions and unleash forces that had better been left unconscious and undisturbed. As usual, there is something in what the anima says; for life in itself is not good only, it is also bad. Because the anima wants life, she wants both good and bad. These categories do not exist in the elfin realm. Bodily life as well as psychic life have the impudence to get along much better without conventional morality, and they often remain the healthier for it,

The anima believes in the καλὸν κἀγαθόν,, the 'beautiful and the good,' a primitive conception that antedates the discovery of the conflict between aesthetics and morals. It took more than a thousand years of Christian differentiation to make it clear that the good is not always the beautiful and the beautiful not necessarily good. The paradox of this marriage of ideas troubled the ancients as little as it does the primitives. The anima is conservative and clings in the most exasperating fashion to the ways of earlier humanity. She likes to appear in historic dress, with a predilection for Greece and Egypt. In this connection we would mention the classic anima stories of Rider Haggard and Pierre Benoît. The Renaissance dream known as the *Ipneroto-machia* of Poliphilo,[1] and Goethe's *Faust*, likewise reach deep into antiquity in order to find "le vrai mot" for the situation. Poliphilo conjured up Queen Venus; Goethe, Helen of Troy. Aniela Jaffé[2] has sketched a lively picture of the anima in the age of Biedermeier and the Romantics. If you want to know what happens when the anima appears in modern society, I can warmly recommend John Erskine's *Private Life of Helen of Troy*. She is not a shallow creation, for the breath of eternity lies over everything that is really alive. The anima lives beyond all categories, and can therefore dispense with blame as well as with praise. Since the beginning of time man, with his wholesome animal instinct, has been engaged in combat with his soul and its daemonism. If the soul were uniformly dark it would be a simple matter. Unfortunately this is not so, for the anima can appear also as an angel of light, a psychopomp who points the way to the highest meaning, as we know from *Faust*.

If the encounter with the shadow is the "apprentice-piece" in the individual's development, then that with the anima is the "master-piece." The relation with the anima is again a test of courage, an ordeal by fire for the spiritual and moral forces of man. We should never forget that in dealing with the anima we are dealing with psychic facts which have never been in man's possession before, since they were always found "outside" his psychic territory, so

---

① Cf. *The Dream of Poliphilo*, ed. by Linda Fierz-David. [For Haggard and Benoît, see the bibliography. —EDITORS.]

② "Bilder und Symbole aus E. T. A. Hoffmanns Märchen, 'Der Goldne Topf.'"

to speak, in the form of projections. For the son, the anima is hidden in the dominating power of the mother, and sometimes she leaves him with a sentimental attachment that lasts throughout life and seriously impairs the fate of the adult. On the other hand, she may spur him on to the highest flights. To the men of antiquity the anima appeared as a goddess or a witch, while for medieval man the goddess was replaced by the Queen of Heaven and Mother Church. The desymbolized world of the Protestant produced first an unhealthy sentimentality and then a sharpening of the moral conflict, which, because it was so unbearable, led logically to Nietzsche's "beyond good and evil." In centres of civilization this state shows itself in the increasing insecurity of marriage. The American divorce rate has been reached, if not exceeded, in many European countries, which proves that the anima projects herself by preference on the opposite sex, thus giving rise to magically complicated relationships. This fact, largely because of its pathological consequences, has led to the growth of modern psychology, which in its Freudian form cherishes the belief that the essential cause of all disturbances is sexuality—a view that only exacerbates the already existing conflict. ① There is a confusion here between cause and effect. The sexual disturbance is by no means the cause of neurotic difficulties, but is, like these, one of the pathological effects of a maladaptation of consciousness, as when consciousness is faced with situations and tasks to which it is not equal. Such a person simply does not understand how the world has altered, and what his attitude would have to be in order to adapt to it.

In dealing with the shadow or anima it is not sufficient just to know about these concepts and to reflect on them. Nor can we ever experience their content by feeling our way into them or by appropriating other people's feelings. It is no use at all to learn a list of archetypes by heart. Archetypes are complexes of experience that come upon us like fate, and their effects are felt in our most personal life. The anima no longer crosses our path as a goddess, but, it may be, as an intimately personal misadventure, or perhaps as our best venture. When, for instance, a highly esteemed professor in his seventies abandons his

---

① I have expounded my views at some length in "Psychology of the Transference."

family and runs off with a young red-headed actress, we know that the gods have claimed another victim. This is how daemonic power reveals itself to us. Until not so long ago it would have been an easy matter to do away with the young woman as a witch.

In my experience there are very many people of intelligence and education who have no trouble in grasping the idea of the anima and her relative autonomy, and can also understand the phenomenology of the animus in women. Psychologists have more difficulties to overcome in this respect, probably because they are under no compulsion to grapple with the complex facts peculiar to the psychology of the unconscious. If they are doctors as well, their somato-psychological thinking gets in the way, with its assumption that psychological processes can be expressed in intellectual, biological, or physiological terms. Psychology, however, is neither biology nor physiology nor any other science than just this knowledge of the psyche.

The picture I have drawn of the anima so far is not complete, Although she may be the chaotic urge to life, something strangely meaningful clings to her, a secret knowledge or hidden wisdom, which contrasts most curiously with her irrational elfin nature. Here I would like to refer again to the authors already cited. Rider Haggard calls She "Wisdom's Daughter"; Benoît's Queen of Atlantis has an excellent library that even contains a lost book of Plato. Helen of Troy, in her reincarnation, is rescued from a Tyrian brothel by the wise Simon Magus and accompanies him on his travels. I purposely refrained from mentioning this thoroughly characteristic aspect of the anima earlier, because the first encounter with her usually leads one to infer anything rather than wisdom. ① This aspect appears only to the person who gets to grips with her seriously. Only then, when this hard task has been faced,② does he come to realize more and more that behind all her cruel sporting with human fate there lies some-

---

① I am referring here to literary examples that are generally accessible and not to clinical material. These are quite sufficient for our purpose.

② I. e., coming to terms with the contents of the collective unconscious in general. This is *the* great task of the integration process.

thing like a hidden purpose which seems to reflect a superior knowledge of life's laws. It is just the most unexpected, the most terrifyingly chaotic things which reveal a deeper meaning. And the more this meaning is recognized, the more the anima loses her impetuous and compulsive character. Gradually breakwaters are built against the surging of chaos, and the meaningful divides itself from the meaningless. When sense and nonsense are no longer identical, the force of chaos is weakened by their subtraction; sense is then endued with the force of meaning, and nonsense with the force of meaninglessness. In this way a new cosmos arises. This is not a new discovery in the realm of medical psychology, but the age-old truth that out of the richness of a man's experience there comes a teaching which the father can pass on to the son. ①

In elfin nature wisdom and folly appear as one and the same; and they *are* one and the same as long as they are acted out by the anima. Life is crazy and meaningful at once. And when we do not laugh over the one aspect and speculate about the other, life is exceedingly drab, and everything is reduced to the littlest scale. There is then little sense and little nonsense either. When you come to think about it, nothing has any meaning, for when there was nobody to think, there was nobody to interpret what happened. Interpretations are only for those who don't understand; it is only the things we don't understand that have any meaning. Man woke up in a world he did not understand, and that is why he tries to interpret it.

Thus the anima and life itself are meaningless in so far as they offer no interpretation. Yet they have a nature that can be interpreted, for in all chaos there is a cosmos, in all disorder a secret order, in all caprice a fixed law, for everything that works is grounded on its opposite. It takes man's discriminating understanding, which breaks everything down into antinomial judgments, to recognize this. Once he comes to grips with the anima, her chaotic capriciousness will give him cause to suspect a secret order, to sense a plan, a meaning, a purpose over and above her nature, or even—we might almost be tempted to

---

① A good example is the little book by Gustav Schmaltz, *Östliche Weisheit und Westliche Psychotherapie*.

say—to "postulate" such a thing, though this would not be in accord with the truth. For in actual reality we do not have at our command any power of cool reflection, nor does any science or philosophy help us, and the traditional teachings of religion do so only to a limited degree. We are caught and entangled in aimless experience, and the judging intellect with its categories proves itself powerless. Human interpretation fails, for a turbulent life-situation has arisen that refuses to fit any of the traditional meanings assigned to it. It is a moment of collapse. We sink into a final depth—Apuleius calls it "a kind of voluntary death." It is a surrender of our own powers, not artificially willed but forced upon us by nature; not a voluntary submission and humiliation decked in moral garb but an utter and unmistakable defeat crowned with the panic fear of demoralization. Only when all props and crutches are broken, and no cover from the rear offers even the slightest hope of security, does it become possible for us to experience an archetype that up till then had lain hidden behind the meaningful nonsense played out by the anima. This is the *archetype of meaning*, just as the anima is the *archetype of life itself*.

It always seems to us as if meaning—compared with life—were the younger event, because we assume, with some justification, that we assign it of ourselves, and because we believe, equally rightly no doubt, that the great world can get along without being interpreted. But how do we assign meaning? From what source, in the last analysis, do we derive meaning? The forms we use for assigning meaning are historical categories that reach back into the mists of time—a fact we do not take sufficiently into account. Interpretations make use of certain linguistic matrices that are themselves derived from primordial images. From whatever side we approach this question, everywhere we find ourselves confronted with the history of language, with images and motifs that lead straight back to the primitive wonder-world.

Take, for instance, the word "idea." It goes back to the εἶδος concept of Plato, and the eternal ideas are primordial images stored up ἐν ὑπερουρανίῳ τόπῳ (in a supracelestial place) as eternal, transcendent forms. The eye of the seer perceives them as "imagines et lares," or as images in dreams and revelatory visions. Or let us take the concept of energy, which is an interpretation of physical events. In earlier times it was the secret fire of the alchemists, or phlogiston, or the heat-force inherent in matter, like the "primal warmth" of the Stoics, or the Hera-clitean πῦρ ἀεὶ ζῶον (ever-living fire), which borders on the primitive notion of an all-pervading vital force, a power of growth and magic healing that is generally called *mana*,

I will not go on needlessly giving examples. It is sufficient to know that there is not a single important idea or view that does not possess historical antecedents. Ultimately they are all founded on primordial archetypal forms whose concreteness dates from a time when consciousness did not *think*, but only *perceived*. "Thoughts" were objects of inner perception, not thought at all, but sensed as external phenomena—seen or heard, so to speak. Thought was essentially revelation, not invented but forced upon us or bringing conviction through its immediacy and actuality. Thinking of this kind precedes the primitive ego-consciousness, and the latter is more its object than its subject. But we ourselves have not yet climbed the last peak of consciousness, so we also have a pre-existent thinking, of which we are not aware so long as we are supported by traditional symbols—or, to put it in the language of dreams, so long as the father or the king is not dead.

I would like to give you an example of how the unconscious "thinks" and paves the way for solutions. It is the case of a young theological student, whom I did not know personally. He was in great straits because of his religious beliefs, and about this time he dreamed the following dream: ①

He was standing in the presence of a handsome old man dressed entirely in black. *He knew it was the* white *magician. This personage had just addressed him at considerable length, but the dreamer could no longer remember what it was about. He had only retained the closing words:* "And for this we need the help of the black *magician.*" *At that moment the door opened and in came another old man exactly like the first, except that he was dressed in*

---

① I have already used this dream in "The Phenomenology of the Spirit in Fairytales," par. 398, infra, and in "Psychology and Education," pp. 117ff. , as an example of a "big" dream, without commenting on it more closely.

white. *He said to the white magician, "I need your advice," but threw a side-long, questioning look at the dreamer, whereupon the white magician answered: "You can speak freely, he is an innocent." The black magician then began to relate his story. He had come from a distant land where something extraordinary had happened. The country was ruled by an old king who felt his death near. He—the king—had sought out a tomb for himself. For there were in that land a great number of tombs from ancient times, and the king had chosen the finest for himself. According to legend, a virgin had been buried in it. The king caused the tomb to be opened, in order to get it ready for use. But when the bones it contained were exposed to the light of day, they suddenly took on life and changed into a black horse, which at once fled into the desert and there vanished. The black magician had heard of this story and immediately set forth in pursuit of the horse. After a journey of many days, always on the tracks of the horse, he came to the desert and crossed to the other side, where the grasslands began again. There he met the horse grazing, and there also he came upon the find on whose account he now needed the advice of the white magician. For he had found the lost* keys of paradise, *and he did not know what to do with them.* At this exciting moment the dreamer awoke.

In the light of our earlier remarks the meaning of the dream is not hard to guess: the old king is the ruling symbol that wants to go to its eternal rest, and in the very place where similar "dominants" lie buried. His choice falls, fittingly enough, on the grave of anima, who lies in the death trance of a Sleeping Beauty so long as the king is alive—that is, so long as a valid principle (Prince or *princeps*) regulates and expresses life. But when the king draws to his end,[①] she comes to life again and changes into a black horse, which in Plato's parable stands for the unruliness of the passions. Anyone who follows this horse comes into the desert, into a wild land remote from men—an image of spiritual and moral isolation. But there lie the keys of paradise.

Now what is paradise? Clearly, the Garden of Eden with its two-faced tree of life and knowledge and its four streams. In the Christian version it is also the

---

① Cf. the motif of the "old king" in alchemy, *Psychology and Alchemy*, pars. 434ff.

heavenly city of the Apocalypse, which, like the Garden of Eden, is conceived as a mandala. But the mandala is a symbol of individuation. So it is the *black* magician who finds the keys to the solution of the problems of belief weighing on the dreamer, the keys that open the way of individuation. The contrast between desert and paradise therefore signifies isolation as contrasted with individuation, or the becoming of the self.

This part of the dream is a remarkable paraphrase of the Oxyrhynchus sayings of Jesus,[1] in which the way to the kingdom of heaven is pointed out by animals, and where we find the admonition: "Therefore know yourselves, for you are the city, and the city is the kingdom." It is also a paraphrase of the serpent of paradise who persuaded our first parents to sin, and who finally leads to the redemption of mankind through the Son of God. As we know, this causal nexus gave rise to the Ophitic identification of the serpent with the εἶδος (Saviour). The black horse and the black magician are half-evil elements whose relativity with respect to good is hinted at in the exchange of garments. The two magicians are, indeed, two aspects of the *wise old man*, the superior master and teacher, the archetype of the spirit, who symbolizes the pre-existent meaning hidden in the chaos of life. He is the father of the soul, and yet the soul, in some miraculous manner, is also his virgin mother, for which reason he was called by the alchemists the "first son of the mother." The black magician and the black horse correspond to the descent into darkness in the dreams mentioned earlier.

What an unbearably hard lesson for a young student of theology! Fortunately he was not in the least aware that the father of all prophets had spoken to him in the dream and placed a great secret almost within his grasp. One marvels at the inappropriateness of such occurrences. Why this prodigality? But I have to admit that we do not know how this dream affected the student in the long run, and I must emphasize that to me, at least, the dream had a very great deal to say. It was not allowed to get lost, even though the dreamer did not understand it.

---

[1] Cf. James, *The Apocryphal New Testament*, pp. 27f.

The old man in this dream is obviously trying to show how good and evil function together, presumably as an answer to the still unresolved moral conflict in the Christian psyche. With this peculiar relativization of opposites we find ourselves approaching nearer to the ideas of the East, to the *nirdvandva* of Hindu philosophy, the freedom from opposites, which is shown as a possible way of solving the conflict through reconciliation. How perilously fraught with meaning this Eastern relativity of good and evil is, can be seen from the Indian aphoristic question: "Who takes longer to reach perfection, the man who loves God, or the man who hates him?" And the answer is: "He who loves God takes seven reincarnations to reach perfection, and he who hates God takes only three, for he who hates God will think of him more than he who loves him." Freedom from opposites presupposes their functional equivalence, and this offends our Christian feelings. Nonetheless, as our dream example shows, the balanced co-operation of moral opposites is a natural truth which has been recognized just as naturally by the East. The clearest example of this is to be found in Taoist philosophy. But in the Christian tradition, too, there are various sayings that come very close to this standpoint. I need only remind you of the parable of the unjust steward.

Our dream is by no means unique in this respect, for the tendency to relativize opposites is a notable peculiarity of the unconscious. One must immediately add, however, that this is true only in cases of exaggerated moral sensibility; in other cases the unconscious can insist just as inexorably on the irreconcilability of the opposites. As a rule, the standpoint of the unconscious is relative to the conscious attitude. We can probably say, therefore, that our dream presupposes the specific beliefs and doubts of a theological consciousness of Protestant persuasion. This limits the statement of the dream to a definite set of problems. But even with this paring down of its validity the dream clearly demonstrates the superiority of its standpoint. Fittingly enough, it expresses its meaning in the opinion and voice of a wise magician, who goes back in direct line to the figure of the medicine man in primitive society. He is, like the anima, an immortal daemon that pierces the chaotic darknesses of brute life with the light of meaning. He is the enlightener, the master and teacher, a psychopomp whose personification even Nietzsche, that breaker of tablets, could not escape—for he had called up his reincarnation in Zarathustra, the lofty spirit of an almost Homeric age, as the carrier and mouthpiece of his own "Dionysian" enlightenment and ecstasy. For him God was dead, but the driving daemon of wisdom became as it were his bodily double. He himself says:

> Then one was changed to two
> And Zarathustra passed me by.

Zarathustra is more for Nietzsche than a poetic figure; he is an involuntary confession, a testament. Nietzsche too had lost his way in the darknesses of a life that turned its back upon God and Christianity, and that is why there came to him the revealer and enlightener, the speaking fountainhead of his soul. Here is the source of the hieratic language of *Zarathustra*, for that is the style of this archetype.

Modern man, in experiencing this archetype, comes to know that most ancient form of thinking as an autonomous activity whose object he is. Hermes Trismegistus or the Thoth of Hermetic literature, Orpheus, the Poimandres (shepherd of men) and his near relation the Poimen of Hermes,[1] are other formulations of the same experience. If the name "Lucifer" were not prejudicial, it would be a very suitable one for this archetype. But I have been content to call it the *archetype of the wise old man*, or *of meaning*. Like all archetypes it has a positive and a negative aspect, though I don't want to enter into this here. The reader will find a detailed exposition of the two-facedness of the wise old man in "The Phenomenology of the Spirit in Fairytales."

The three archetypes so far discussed—the shadow, the anima, and the wise old man—are of a kind that can be directly experienced in personified form. In the foregoing I tried to indicate the general psychological conditions in which such an experience arises. But what I conveyed were only abstract

---

[1] Reitzenstein interprets the "Shepherd" of Hermas as a Christian rejoinder to the Poimandres writings.

generalizations. One could, or rather should, really give a description of the process as it occurs in immediate experience. In the course of this process the archetypes appear as active personalities in dreams and fantasies. But the process itself involves another class of archetypes which one could call the *archetypes of transformation*. They are not personalities, but are typical situations, places, ways and means, that symbolize the kind of transformation in question. Like the personalities, these archetypes are true and genuine symbols that cannot be exhaustively interpreted, either as signs or as allegories. They are genuine symbols precisely because they are ambiguous, full of half-glimpsed meanings, and in the last resort inexhaustible. The ground principles, the ἀρχαί, of the unconscious are indescribable because of their wealth of reference, although in themselves recognizable. The discriminating intellect naturally keeps on trying to establish their singleness of meaning and thus misses the essential point; for what we can above all establish as the one thing consistent with their nature is their *manifold meaning*, their almost limitless wealth of reference, which makes any unilateral formulation impossible. Besides this, they are in principle paradoxical, just as for the alchemists the spirit was conceived as "senex et iuvenis simul"—an old man and a youth at once.

If one wants to form a picture of the symbolic process, the series of pictures found in alchemy are good examples, though the symbols they contain are for the most part traditional despite their often obscure origin and significance. An excellent Eastern example is the Tantric *chakra* system,[1] or the mystical nerve system of Chinese yoga.[2] It also seems as if the set of pictures in the Tarot cards were distantly descended from the archetypes of transformation, a view that has been confirmed for me in a very enlightening lecture by Professor Bernoulli.[3]

The symbolic process is an experience *in images and of images*. Its development usually shows an enantiodromian structure like the text of the *I*

---

[1] Arthur Avalon, *The Serpent Power*.

[2] Erwin Rousselle, "Spiritual Guidance in Contemporary Taoism."

[3] R. Bernoulli, "Zur Symbolik geometrischer Figuren und Zahlen," pp. 397ff.

Ching, and so presents a rhythm of negative and positive, loss and gain, dark and light. Its beginning is almost invariably characterized by one's getting stuck in a blind alley or in some impossible situation; and its goal is, broadly speaking, illumination or higher consciousness, by means of which the initial situation is overcome on a higher level. As regards the time factor, the process may be compressed into a single dream or into a short moment of experience, or it may extend over months and years, depending on the nature of the initial situation, the person involved in the process, and the goal to be reached. The wealth of symbols naturally varies enormously from case to case. Although everything is experienced in image form, i. e. , symbolically, it is by no means a question of fictitious dangers but of very real risks upon which the fate of a whole life may depend. The chief danger is that of succumbing to the fascinating influence of the archetypes, and this is most likely to happen when the archetypal images are not made conscious. If there is already a predisposition to psychosis, it may even happen that the archetypal figures, which are endowed with a certain autonomy anyway on account of their natural numinosity, will escape from conscious control altogether and become completely independent, thus producing the phenomena of possession. In the case of an anima-possession, for instance, the patient will want to change himself into a woman through self-castration, or he is afraid that something of the sort will be done to him by force. The best-known example of this is Schreber's *Memoirs of My Nervous Illness*. Patients often discover a whole anima mythology with numerous archaic motifs. A case of this kind was published some time ago by Nelken. [1] Another patient has described his experiences himself and commented on them in a book. [2] I mention these examples because there are still people who think that the archetypes are subjective chimeras of my own brain.

The things that come to light brutally in insanity remain hidden in the background in neurosis, but they continue to influence consciousness nonetheless. When, therefore, the analysis penetrates the background of conscious

---

[1] "Analytische Beobachtungen über Phantasien eines Schizophrenen," pp. 504ff.

[2] John Custance, *Wisdom, Madness, and Folly*.

phenomena, it discovers the same archetypal figures that activate the deliriums of psychotics. Finally, there is any amount of literary and historical evidence to prove that in the case of these archetypes we are dealing with normal types of fantasy that occur practically everywhere and not with the monstrous products of insanity. The pathological element does not lie in the existence of these ideas, but in the dissociation of consciousness that can no longer control the unconscious. In all cases of dissociation it is therefore necessary to integrate the unconscious into consciousness. This is a synthetic process which I have termed the "individuation process."

As a matter of fact, this process follows the natural course of life—a life in which the individual becomes what he always was. Because man has consciousness, a development of this kind does not run very smoothly; often it is varied and disturbed, because consciousness deviates again and again from its archetypal, instinctual foundation and finds itself in opposition to it. There then arises the need for a synthesis of the two positions. This amounts to psychotherapy even on the primitive level, where it takes the form of restitution ceremonies. As examples I would mention the identification of the Australian aborigines with their ancestors in the *alcheringa* period, identification with the "sons of the sun" among the Pueblos of Taos, the Helios apotheosis in the Isis mysteries, and so on. Accordingly, the therapeutic method of complex psychology consists on the one hand in making as fully conscious as possible the constellated unconscious contents, and on the other hand in synthetizing them with consciousness through the act of recognition. Since, however, civilized man possesses a high degree of dissociability and makes continual use of it in order to avoid every possible risk, it is by no means a foregone conclusion that recognition will be followed by the appropriate action. On the contrary, we have to reckon with the singular ineffectiveness of recognition and must therefore insist on a meaningful application of it. Recognition by itself does not as a rule do this, nor does it imply, as such, any moral strength. In these cases it becomes very clear how much the cure of neurosis is a moral problem.

As the archetypes, like all numinous contents, are relatively autonomous, they cannot be integrated simply by rational means, but require a dialectical procedure, a real coming to terms with them, often conducted by the patient in dialogue form, so that, without knowing it, he puts into effect the alchemical definition of the *meditatio*: "an inner colloquy with one's good angel."[1] Usually the process runs a dramatic course, with many ups and downs. It expresses itself in, or is accompanied by, dream symbols that are related to the "representations collectives," which in the form of mythological motifs have portrayed psychic processes of transformation since the earliest times. [2]

---

[1] Ruland, *Lexicon alchemiae* (1612).
[2] Cf. *Symbols of Transformation*.

6. 荣格：《集体无意识原型》

(Carl G. Jung, "Archetypes of the Collective Unconscious," 1934)

作者小识

荣格(Carl G. Jung，1875—1961)，瑞士心理学家，精神分析运动的代表人物之一。荣格出身于一个新教牧师家庭，是这个不幸家庭里唯一存活下来的男孩。少年时代的荣格，性格内倾，孤独忧郁。19 世纪和 20 世纪之交，普遍的精神危机日趋紧逼，欧洲人的心智生活遇到了不可解决的难题。青年荣格任职于苏黎世大学的波古尔兹利精神病院(Burghölzli Asylum)，拜师精神病理学家布勒雷(Eugen Bleuler)。运用联想测试，荣格研究病人对语言刺激的非逻辑反应，将精神病源溯至无意识的情感联想。1907 年与弗洛伊德交往，对其心理动力学的观点产生了强烈的共鸣，一度为弗洛伊德的忠实合作者，并出任首届世界精神分析学会主席。但对于弗洛伊德用生物学的性来解决神经官能症问题的立场，荣格并不照单全收，尤其反对弗洛伊德将无意识的压抑局限于个体心理发育史。

1912 年，他发表《无意识心理学》(*The Psychology of the Unconscious*)，这标志着他与弗洛伊德的分道扬镳。他将人格类型一分为二，并判定东方人具有典型的内倾气质(introverted，inward-looking attitude)，而西方人具有典型的外倾气质(extraverted，outward-looking attitude)。1921 年，他发表《心理类型》(*Psychological Types*)，挪用希波克拉底的"血型四分说"，描述人类心智的四种功能：思想、感觉、情感与直观。

荣格远游印度、斯里兰卡、墨西哥和非洲各国，尝试进入原始部落的内心世界。他迷恋中国文化，为德文版《易经》作序，还向西方人介绍老子和孔子的学说。他熟悉古希腊罗马神话，沉潜于基督教神秘主义和灵知主义的研究。这方面的代表作有《伊雍：自性现象学研究》(*Aion：Researches into the Phenomenology of the Self*，1951)。1944 年，他发表《心理学与炼金术》(*Psychology and Alchemy*)，这是他关联神话与心理学而建构象征文化学的重要著作之一。荣格晚年隐居乡野，在苏黎世湖畔美丽的家园中度过余生。有英文版《荣格文集》(Herbert Read and Gerhard Adler eds. , *The Collected Works of C. G. Jung*,1966-1979)20 卷传世,他自己选编的《寻找灵魂的现代人》(*Modern Man in Search of a Soul*,1933)则集中表现了对现代人灵魂困境的忧思。

背景略说

弗洛伊德的精神分析学说自身具有相当的局限性,更兼其学派的组织形式机械刻板,导致了学说的教条化和模型化。正统与异端随之立马分明,内部分裂在所难免,弗洛伊德本人也被新生者视为落伍人物。精神分析运动之内在裂变,自弗洛伊德与其弟子的学理分歧开始,然后显"蝴蝶效应",引发宗教运动、政治运动和文化研究种种连锁振荡。

荣格曾为精神分析运动之中坚力量。然而,随着运动的扩大,荣格的人格和学理所蕴含的异质性要素也渐渐发酵,终于异端崛起,加剧了精神分析运动的分裂。荣格发表《无意识心理学》,好似向弗洛伊德下战书,大有别立新宗之势。于是,维也纳学派和苏黎世学派双峰对峙,犹太传统与非犹太传统之间的亘古冲突也得到了象征性的呈现。弗洛伊德圈内,精神分析的精英皆为犹太人,甚至酝酿着一场犹太种族主义运动。对非犹太主义、反犹太主义异常敏感的维也纳学派,在荣格发出的反犹太主义信号以及随后的亲纳粹主义言论中,嗅出了欧洲文化和政治的危机。

所以,毫不奇怪,当托马斯·曼在弗洛伊德寿开八序庆祝会上发表讲话,将弗洛伊德的学说解释为"神话与心理学之邂逅"之时,弗洛伊德怒不可遏。因为,托马斯·曼执着地将荣格的理论纳入精神分析的框架下,并且用他自己小说的神话意境僭越弗洛伊德的学说,甚至把精神分析强行拉入荣格的文化无意识范畴之中。维也纳学派和苏黎世学派之分歧,是生命与神话的分野、生物与文明的对峙,甚至是科学与诗歌的对抗。弗洛伊德讲生物个体的发育史,荣格重文化群体的种族进化,一个要求人们相信重视分析心理的自然科学家,一个呼召人们对"活生生的神话"顶礼膜拜。故而,弗洛伊德与荣格的对立,是 20 世纪欧洲思想整体景观裂变的缩影,也是欧洲精神危机的征兆之一。

荣格与弗洛伊德学说的分歧表现在如下几点。第一,在阐释人类心理动力上,弗洛伊德重视生物学因素,而荣格重视文化人类学因素。第二,在对无意识的理解上,弗洛伊德集中于个体无意识,而荣格凸显集体无意识;弗洛伊德将无意识看作被压抑物的储存器，而荣格认为无意识是一个巨大的历史仓库。第三，在心理学方法论上，弗洛伊德主张科学的分析，荣格则主张哲学和神秘主义的思辨。第四，在对源始性力的理解上，弗洛伊德将力比多理解为纯粹的性爱之力，而荣格认为力比多是普通的生命冲动。

荣格对弗洛伊德的批判表现在两个方面：一方面，他认为弗洛伊德的学说建立在一种未加批判的世界观上，从而极大地限制甚至缩减了人类经验的理解领域；另一方面，他认为弗洛伊德将无意识局限于性领域，完全漠视了人类心灵的文化要素。

基本内容

《集体无意识原型》建基于荣格精神分析学的基本假说：精神自在自为，独立自足，构成了个体灵魂独立存在的必要条件。精神分析学必须成为一种"有灵魂的心理学"，即建立一种以自主精神原则为终极基础的心理理论。灵魂本质上是肉体的生命，是生命的气息，一种瞬间被直觉到的生命力。无意识构成了灵魂的源始生命，容纳着所有祖先遗传下来的生活和行为模式，个体一出生就潜在地具有一套能够适应环境的心理机制。所以，无意识是一种巨大的经验体系，不是幻觉，而是实在，其整体运转具有目的性，即确保个体的生存。"无意识作为从原始时代遗传下来的心理功能的体系，总是先于意识而存在。意识不过是无意识的后裔而已。"①

在《集体无意识原型》中，荣格阐述了自己与弗洛伊德的区别、原型概念的思想史渊源、原型的表现领域和形式、原型的诸种重要类型、象征过程。

（1）与弗洛伊德的区别。弗洛伊德看到了无意识的源始性及其具有神话色彩的思想形式，却仍然赋予无意识以个体特性，看不到无意识的超个体心理基础。个体无意识的内容是"情感色彩情结"，而集体无意识的内容则是"原型"。

（2）原型概念的思想史渊源。在犹太人斐洛（Philo Judaeus）、早期教父思想家伊里奈乌（Irenaeus）、（托名）狄奥尼修斯（Dionysius the Areopagite）等人的著作中，原型概念指向了上帝形象、宇宙形象，表征世界、人类和上帝的关系。在柏拉图、奥古斯丁的著作中，原型暗示了非物质的形式，以及某些

---

① 荣格：《分析心理学的基本假设》，见《心理学与文学》，冯川、苏克译，43～44页，北京，生活·读书·新知三联书店，1987。

集体无意识内容。在现代人类学中，原型暗指"集体表现"，与原始部落的传说、神话、童话相关。

（3）原型的表现领域和形式。原型概念表现在部族学问、秘传仪式之中，包含着启示的要素，呈现灵魂的秘密。原型也呈现在基督教世界观及其象征体系中，呈现在东方象征主义的魔力之中，融于一个普遍的思想体系，赋予世界以秩序，并借着教会机构而世代相传。新教改革的反传统运动，导致基督教象征秩序的瓦解，以及古典世界诸神的死亡。现代人寻求灵验的形象，以满足心灵的渴求，安抚不安的灵魂。为了治愈象征的贫困所带来的灵魂干枯，现代人必须到集体无意识和原型之中寻找古老的活性智慧。

（4）原型的诸种重要类型。玛纳（mana），即超自然的神秘力量，特指精灵、魔鬼、诸神，他们同人类命运休戚相关，常常化身为国王和父亲。母亲，即无意识、本能和自然生命的象征。母亲原型的化身有时善良有时邪恶，有时美丽有时丑陋。阴影，即个体在外化过程中的阻力，象征着灵魂的沉睡、生命的险境以及幸福与不幸的幻觉。阿尼玛（anima），即男性之中的女性气质，一个自然形象，引领着个体走进神圣的王国。个体与"阴影"相遇，那是一件"习作"，而与阿尼玛融为一体，便是生命的"杰作"。智慧老人，就像阿尼玛一样，用意义之光穿透混沌与黑暗，作为启蒙者、统治者与教导者，完成了精神的仪式。

（5）象征过程。这是一种"形象的经验"和"在形象之中的经验"，发展出两极对称的结构，呈现得与失、光明与黑暗、肯定与否定的节奏。疗治精神疾病，也是将无意识融入意识的综合性"个体化"过程。

拓展讨论

"集体无意识"是深层心理学的一个关键概念，或可引来解释民族精神和文化传统。在中国民族传统中，圣贤"发愤抒情"，堪称中华美学所蕴含的"集体无意识"。

《史记·太史公自序》曰：

> 夫《诗》、《书》隐约者，欲遂其志之思也。昔西伯拘羑里，演《周易》；孔子厄陈蔡，作《春秋》；屈原放逐，著《离骚》；左丘失明，厥有《国语》；孙子膑脚，而论兵法；不韦迁蜀，世传《吕览》；韩非囚秦，《说难》、《孤愤》；《诗》三百篇，大抵贤圣发愤之所为作也。此人皆意有所郁结，不得

通其道也，故述往事，思来者。

《屈原贾生列传》又云："屈平之作《离骚》，盖自怨生也。"屈原自己表达《离骚》之宗旨——"惜诵以致愍兮，发愤以抒情"。从"风雨如晦""杨柳依依"到"正声何微茫，哀怨起骚人"，中国文学始终在表现一种普遍的忧患，而诗人似乎永远是为忧患而生、为忧患而死的。对此，美学家高尔泰先生写道：

> 所谓诗人，是那种对忧患特别敏感的人们，他们能透过生活中暂时的和表面上的圆满看到它内在的和更深刻的不圆满，所以他们总是在欢乐中体验到忧伤，紧接着"我有嘉宾，鼓瑟吹笙"之后，便是"忧从中来，不可断绝"，紧接着"今日良宴会，欢乐难俱陈，弹筝奋逸响，新声妙入神"之后，便是"齐心同所愿，含意俱未伸，人生寄一世，奄忽若飙尘"。这种沉重的情绪环境，这种忧愁的心理氛围，正是中国诗歌音乐由之而生的肥沃的土壤。
>
> 读中国诗、文，多听中国词、曲，实际上也就是间接地体验愁绪。梧桐夜雨，芳草斜阳，断鸿声里，烟波江上，处处都可以感觉到一个"愁"字。出了门是"鸡声茅店月，人迹板桥霜"；在家里是"梨花小院月黄昏"，"一曲栏干一断魂"，真的是"出亦愁，入亦愁，座中何人，谁不怀忧?"以致人们觉得，写诗写词，无非就是写愁。即使是"少年不识愁滋味"，也还要"为赋新词强说愁"。浩大而又深沉的忧患意识，作为在相对不变的中国社会历史条件下代代相继的深层心理动力，决定了中国诗、词的这种调子，以至于它在诗、词中的出现，好像是不以作者的主观意志为转移似的。"愁极本凭诗遣兴，诗成吟诵转凄凉"，即使杜甫那样的大诗人，也不免于受这种"集体无意识"的支配。[①]

用"集体无意识"来阐释中国古典美学精神，应该是一条可取的思路。在这个意义上，集体无意识支配着中华民族精神深处的"伦理意识"和"美学意识"，构成了古典解释学和文化批评的概念硬核。沿着集体无意识这条幽微之

---

① 高尔泰：《中国艺术与中国哲学》，见李天道：《古代文论与美学研究》，59～60页，北京，商务印书馆，2005。

路，或许可以探入中国美学精神的内脉。

早在西周初年就已经成熟的"五行论"，是中国文化的基础论述之一。它尝试对五类"物"给出完整的解释。将中国文明的"五行"（金、木、水、火、土）与印度文明的四元素（地、水、风、火）、古希腊的四根（水、火、气、土）予以比较，人们似乎很难不从人类"集体无意识"及其原型入手探幽穷赜，解释这些文明论述元素的意义。杨儒宾教授撰成《五行原论》，从集体无意识和原型入手，辅之以伊利亚德（M. Eliade）的"圣显"及其根基隐喻，对"五行"的"原物理性"展开了富有创意的阐释。

> "五行"说可视为筑基于"圣显"（hierophany）之上的五种喻根。由比较宗教学提供的视角，可以很放心地将这些因素上推到文明早期的宗教象征，亦即在文明初期，中国的五行就像希腊或印度的四元素，也像普见于世界各民族对水、火、山、天、土等等自然意象的理解一样，这些"自然"因素都被视为具有超自然的因素，都是神圣的载体。正因这些"自然"因素是如此的超自然，它们的性质是如此的重要，范围又是那么普遍，所以很自然而然地，五行的施用范围不能不广，它们这些天生异禀的神圣因素串连起各种异质性的质素，熔为一炉。五行相连，相生，相克，复杂勾连，最后布下天罗地网般的知识体系，构成了原初的一种世界秩序。①

于是，哲人说"太初存有"。这个世界是力动而又律动的世界，声息形气一体化生，原物与自体若即若离，不即不离。整个世界属于非逻辑的境界，唯有以隐喻表达其普遍流行。荣格在讨论无意识的本质时，特别强调无意识世界万物生命充盈、灵性盎然的状态。而在以"五行"论述中华早期文明的时候，先哲将"金、木、水、火、土"五种重要的自然意象提升到超验的原型层面，以解释天理、人情、物象的本源。原型蕴含原力，所以是生命的象征。以五行为原型建构的世界秩序，是物活论、泛灵论的秩序。原型意象指向本源，又超越本源，离合引生。同样，"五行的世界是整体流动应化的世界，云

---

① 杨儒宾：《五行原论：先秦思想的太初存有论》，12～13页，上海，上海古籍出版社，2020。

行雨施，品物流形"①。

延伸阅读

1. 荣格：《寻求灵魂的现代人》，黄奇铭译，上海，上海译文出版社，2013。围绕现代人的精神困境，荣格论述集体无意识、梦、象征、人格，广泛涉猎宗教、哲学和文学，为现代人自我理解提供指引。

2. 霍尔、诺德拜：《荣格心理学纲要》，张月译，郑州，黄河文艺出版社，1987。该书对荣格的人格理论、深层心理学、象征理论、心理类型理论进行了纲要式呈现，并附录了荣格的几篇重要论文。

---

① 杨儒宾：《五行原论：先秦思想的太初存有论》，43页，上海，上海古籍出版社，2020。

7. Seminar on "The Purloined Letter" (1955)

By Jacques Lacan

> Und wenn es uns glückt,
> Und wenn es sich schickt,
> So sind es Gedanken.

Our inquiry has led us to the point of recognizing that the repetition automatism (*Wiederholungszwang*) finds its basis in what we have called the *insistence* of the signifying chain. ① We have elaborated that notion itself as a correlate of the *ex-sistence* (or: eccentric place) in which we must necessarily locate the subject of the unconscious if we are to take Freud's discovery serious- ly. ② As is known, it is in the realm of experience inaugurated by psychoanaly- sis that we may grasp along what imaginary lines the human organism, in the most intimate recesses of its being, manifests its capture in a *symbolic* dimension. ③

The lesson of this seminar is intended to maintain that these imaginary in- cidences, far from representing the essence of our experience, reveal only what in it remains inconsistent unless they are related to the symbolic chain which binds and orients them.

We realize, of course, the importance of these imaginary impregnations (*Prägung*) in those partializations of the symbolic alternative which give the

---

① The translation of repetition *automatism*—rather than *compulsion*—is indicative of Lacan's speculative effort to reinterpret Freudian "overdetermination" in terms of the laws of probability. (Chance is *automaton*, a "cause not revealed to human thought," in Aristotle's *Physics.*) Whence the importance assumed by the Minister's passion for gambling later in Lacan's analysis. Cf. *Ecrits*, pp. 41-61). —Ed.

② Cf. Heidegger, *Vom Wesen dar Wahrheit*. Freedom, in this essay, is perceived as an "ex-posure." *Dasein* ex-sists, stands out "into the disclosure of what is." It is *Dasein*'s "ex-sistent in-sistence" which preserves the disclosure of beings. —Ed.

③ For the meanings Lacan attributes to the terms *imaginary* and *symbolic*, see entries from the *Vocabulaire de la Psychanalyse* (Laplanche and Pontalis) reproduced below. —Ed.

symbolic chain its appearance. But we maintain that it is the specific law of that chain which governs those psychoanalytic effects that are decisive for the subject: such as foreclosure (*Verwerfung*), repression (*Verdrängung*), denial (*Verneinung*) itself—specifying with appropriate emphasis that these effects follow so faithfully the displacement (*Entstellung*) of the signifier that imaginary factors, despite their inertia, figure only as shadows and reflections in the process. ①

But this emphasis would be lavished in vain, if it served, in your opinion, only to abstract a general type from phenomena whose particularity in our work would remain the essential thing for you, and whose original arrangement could be broken up only artificially.

Which is why we have decided to illustrate for you today the truth which may be drawn from that moment in Freud's thought under study—namely, that it is the symbolic order which is constitutive for the subject—by demonstrating in a story the decisive orientation which the subject receives from the itinerary of a signifier. ②

It is that truth, let us note, which makes the very existence of fiction possible. And in that case, a fable is as appropriate as any other narrative for bringing it to light—at the risk of having the fable's coherence put to the test in the process. Aside from that reservation, a fictive tale even has the advantage of manifesting symbolic necessity more purely to the extent that we may believe its conception arbitrary.

Which is why, without seeking any further, we have chosen our example from the very story in which the dialectic of the game of even or odd—from whose study we have but recently profited—occurs. ③ It is, no doubt, no acci-

---

① For the notion of *foreclosure*, the defence mechanism specific to psychosis, see entry from the *Vocabulaire* below.

② For the notion of the signifier (and its relation to the Freudian "memory trace,") see previous essay. —Ed.

③ Lacan's analysis of the guessing game in Poe's tale entails demonstrating the insufficiency of an *imaginary* identification with the opponent as opposed to the *symbolic* process of an identification with his "reasoning." See *Ecrits*, p. 59. —Ed.

dent that this tale revealed itself propitious to pursuing a course of inquiry which had already found support in it.

As you know, we are talking about the tale which Baudelaire translated under the title: *La lettre volée*. At first reading, we may distinguish a drama, its narration, and the conditions of that narration.

We see quickly enough, moreover, that these components are necessary and that they could not have escaped the intentions of whoever composed them.

The narration, in fact, doubles the drama with a commentary without which no *mise en scène* would be possible. Let us say that the action would remain, properly speaking, invisible from the pit—aside from the fact that the dialogue would be expressly and by dramatic necessity devoid of whatever meaning it might have for an audience: —in other words, nothing of the drama could be grasped, neither seen nor heard, without, dare we say, the twilighting which the narration, in each scene, casts on the point of view that one of the actors had while performing it.

There are two scenes, the first of which we shall straightway designate the primal scene, and by no means inadvertently, since the second may be considered its repetition in the very sense we are considering today.

The primal scene is thus performed, we are told, in the royal *boudoir*, so that we suspect that the person of the highest rank, called the "exalted personage," who is alone there when she receives a letter, is the Queen. This feeling is confirmed by the embarrassment into which she is plunged by the entry of the other exalted personage, of whom we have already been told prior to this account that the knowledge he might have of the letter in question would jeopardize for the lady nothing less than her honor and safety. Any doubt that he is in fact the King is promptly dissipated in the course of the scene which begins with the entry of the Minister D... At that moment, in fact, the Queen can do no better than to play on the King's inattentiveness by leaving the letter on the table "face down, address uppermost." It does not, however, escape the Minister's lynx eye, nor does he fail to notice the Queen's distress and thus to fathom her secret. From then on everything transpires like clockwork. After dealing in his customary manner with the business of the day, the Minister draws from is pocket a letter similar in appearance to the one in his view, and, having pretended to read it, he places it next to the other. A bit more conversation to amuse the royal company, whereupon, without flinching once, he seizes the embarrassing letter, making off with it, as the Queen, on whom none of his maneuver has been lost, remains unable to intervene for fear of attracting the attention of her royal spouse, close at her side at that very moment.

Everything might then have transpired unseen by a hypothetical spectator of an operation in which nobody falters, and whose *quotient* is that the Minister has filched from the Queen her letter and that—an even more important result than the first—the Queen knows that he now has it, and by no means innocently.

A *remainder* that no analyst will neglect, trained as he is to retain whatever is significant, without always knowing what to do with it: the letter, abandoned by the Minister, and which the Queen's hand is now free to roll into a ball.

Second scene: in the Minister's office. It is in his hotel, and we know— from the account the Prefect of police has given Dupin, whose specific genius for solving enigmas Poe introduces here for the second time—that the police, returning there as soon as the Minister's habitual, nightly absences allow them to, have searched the hotel and its surroundings from top to bottom for the last eighteen months. In vain, —although everyone can deduce from the situation that the Minister keeps the letter within reach.

Dupin calls on the Minister. The latter receives him with studied nonchalance, affecting in his conversation romantic *ennui*. Meanwhile Dupin, whom this pretense does not deceive, his eyes protected by green glasses, proceeds to inspect the premises. When his glance catches a rather crumpled piece of paper—apparently thrust carelessly in a division of an ugly pasteboard card-rack, hanging gaudily from the middle of the mantelpiece—he already knows that he's found what he's looking for. His conviction is re-enforced by the very details which seem to contradict the description he has of the stolen letter, with the exception of the format, which remains the same.

Whereupon he has but to withdraw, after "forgetting" his snuff-box on the table, in order to return the following day to reclaim it—armed with a facsimile of the letter in its present state. As an incident in the street, prepared for the proper moment, draws the Minister to the window, Dupin in turn seizes the opportunity to snatch the letter while substituting the imitation, and has only to maintain the appearances of a normal exit.

Here as well all has transpired, if not without noise, at least without all commotion. The quotient of the operation is that the Minister no longer has the letter, but, far from suspecting that Dupin is the culprit who has ravished it from him, knows nothing of it. Moreover, what he is left with is far from insignificant for what follows. We shall return to what brought Dupin to inscribe a message on his counterfeit letter. Whatever the case, the Minister, when he tries to make use of it, will be able to read these words, written so that he may recognize Dupin's hand: "...*Un dessein si funeste/S'il n'est digne d'Atreé est digne de Thyeste*," whose source, Dupin tells us, is Crébillon's *Atreé*. [1]

Need we emphasize the similarity of these two sequence? Yes, for the resemblance we have in mind is not a simple collection of traits chosen only in order to delete their difference. And it would not be enough to retain those common traits at the expense of the others for the slightest truth to result. It is rather the intersubjectivity in which the two actions are motivated that we wish to bring into relief, as well as the three terms through which it structures them. [2]

The special status of these terms results from their corresponding simultaneously to the three logical moments through which the decision is precipitated and the three places it assigns to the sujects among whom it constitutes a choice.

---

[1] "So infamous a scheme, /If not worthy of Atreus, is worthy of Thyestes." The lines from Atreus's monologue in Act V, Scene V of Crébillon's play refer to his plan to avenge himself by serving his brother the blood of the latter's own son to drink. —Ed.

[2] This intersubjective setting which coordinates three terms is plainly the Oedipal situation. The illusory security of the initial *dyad* (King and Queen in the first sequence) will be shattered be the introduction of a third term. —Ed.

That decision is reached in a glance's time. ① For the maneuvers which follow, however stealthily they prolong it, add nothing to that glance, nor does the deferring of the deed in the second scene break the unity of that moment.

This glance presupposes two others, which it embraces in its vision of the breach left in their fallacious complementarity, anticipating in it the occasion for larceny afforded by that exposure. Thus three moments, structuring three glances, borne by three subjects, incarnated each time by different characters.

The first is a glance that sees nothing: the King and the police.

The second, a glance which sees that the first sees nothing and deludes itself as to the secrecy of what it hides: the Queen, then the Minister.

The third sees that the first two glances leave what should be hidden exposed to whomever would seize it: the Minister, and finally Dupin.

In order to grasp in its unity the intersubjective complex thus described, we would willingly seek a model in the technique legend-arily attributed to the ostrich attempting to shield itself from danger; for that technique might ultimately be qualified as political, divided as it here is among three partners: the second believing itself invisible because the first has its head stuck in the ground, and all the while letting the third calmly pluck its rear; we need only enrich its proverbial denomination by a letter, producing *la politique de l'autruiche*, for the ostrich itself to take on forever a new meaning. ②

Given the intersubjective modulus of the repetitive action, it remains to recognize in it a *repetition automatism* in the sense that interests us in Freud's text.

The plurality of subjects, of course, can be no objection for those who are long accustomed to the perspectives summarized by our formula: *the unconscious is the discourse of the Other.* ③ And we will not recall now what the no-

---

① The necessary reference here may be found in "Le Temps logique et l'Assertion de la certitude anticipée," Ecrits, p. 197.

② *La politique de l'autruiche* condenses ostrich (*autruche*), other people (*autrui*), and (the politics of) Austria (*Autriche*). —Ed.

③ Such would be the crux of the Oedipus complex: the assumption of a desire which is originally another's, and which, in its displacements, is perpetually other than "itself." —Ed.

tion of the *immixture of subjects*, recently introduced in our re-analysis of the dream of Irma's injection, adds to the discussion.

What interests us today is the manner in which the subjects relay each other in their displacement during the intersubjective repetition.

We shall see that their displacement is determined by the place which a pure signifer—the purloined letter—comes to occupy in their trio. And that is what will confirm for us its status as repetition automatism.

It does not, however, seem excessive, before pursuing this line of inquiry, to ask whether the thrust of the tale and the interest we bring to it—to the extent that they coincide—do not lie elsewhere.

May we view as simply a rationalization (in our gruff jargon) the fact that the story is told to us as a police mystery?

In truth, we should be right in judging that fact highly dubious as soon as we note that everything which warrants such mystery concerning a crime or offense—its nature and motives, instruments and execution; the procedure used to discover the author, and the means employed to convict him—is carefully eliminated here at the start of each episode.

The act of deceit is, in fact, from the beginning as clearly known as the intrigues of the culprit and their effects on his victim. The problem, as exposed to us, is limited to the search for and restitution of the object of that deceit, and it seems rather intentional that the solution is already obtained when it is explained to us. Is *that* how we are kept in suspense? Whatever credit we may accord the conventions of a genre for provoking a specific interest in the reader, we should not forget that "the Dupin tale," this the second to appear, is a prototype, and that even if the genre were established in the first, it is still a little early for the author to play on a convention. ①

It would, however, be equally excessive to reduce the whole thing to a fable whose moral would be that in order to shield from inquisitive eyes one of those correspondences whose secrecy is sometimes necessary to conjugal peace, it suffices to leave the crucial letters lying about on one's table, even though the

---

① The first "Dupin tale" was "The Murders in the Rue Morgue. "—Ed.

meaningful side be turned face down. For that would be a hoax which, for out part, we would never recommend anyone try, lest he be gravely disappointed in his hopes.

Might there then be no mystery other than, concerning the Prefect, an incompetence issuing in failure—were it not perhaps, concerning Dupin, a certain dissonance we hesitate to acknowledge between, on the one hand, the admittedly penetrating, though, in their generality, not always quite relevant remarks with which he introduces us to his method and, on the other, the manner in which he in fact intervenes.

Were we to pursue this sense of mystification a bit further we might soon begin to wonder whether, from that initial scene which only the rank of the protagonists saves from vaudeville, to the fall into ridicule which seems to await the Minister at the end, it is not this impression that everyone is being duped which makes for our pleasure.

And we would be all the more inclined to think so in that we would recognize in that surmise, along with those of you who read us, the definition we once gave in passing of the modern hero, "whom ludicrous exploits exalt in circumstances of utter confusion. "①

But are we ourselves not taken in by the imposing presence of the amateur detective, prototype of a latter-day swashbuckler, as yet safe from the insipidity of our contemporary *superman*?

A trick… sufficient for us to discern in this tale, on the contrary, so perfect a verisimilitude that it may be said that truth here reveals its fictive arrangement.

For such indeed is the direction in which the principles of that verisimilitude lead us. Entering into its strategy, we indeed perceive a new drama we may call complementary to the first, in so far as the latter was what is termed a play without words whereas the interest of the second plays on the properties of

---

① Cf. "Fonction et champ de la parole et du langage" in *Ecrits*. Translated by A. Wilden, *The Language of the Self* (Baltimore, 1968).

speech. ①

If it is indeed clear that each of the two scenes of the real drama is narrated in the course of a different dialogue, it is only through access to those notions set forth in our teaching that one may recognize that it is not thus simply to augment the charm of the exposition, but that the dialogues themselves, in the opposite use they make of the powers of speech, take on a tension which makes of them a different drama, one which our vocabulary will distinguish from the first as persisting in the symbolic order.

The first dialogue—between the Prefect of police and Dupin—is played as between a deaf man and one who hears. That is, it presents the real complexity of what is ordinarily simplified, with the most confused results, in the notion of communication.

This example demonstrates indeed how an act of communication may give the impression at which theorists too often stop: of allowing in its transmission but a single meaning, as though the highly significant commentary into which he who understands integrates it, could, because unperceived by him who does not understand, be considered null.

It remains that if only the dialogue's meaning as a report is retained, its verisimilitude may appear to depend on a guarantee of exactitude. But here dialogue may be more fertile than seems, if we demonstrate its tactics: as shall be seen by focusing on the recounting of our first scene.

For the double and even triple subjective filter through which that scene comes to us: a narration by Dupin's friend and associate (henceforth to be called the general narrator of the story)—of the account by which the Prefect reveals to Dupin—the report the Queen gave him of it, is not merely the consequence of a fortuitous arrangement.

If indeed the extremity to which the original narrator is reduced precludes her altering any of the events, it would be wrong to believe that the Prefect is empowered to lend her his voice in this case only by that lack of imagination on

---

① The complete understanding of what follows presupposes a rereading of the short and easily available text of "The Purloined Letter."

which he has, dare we say, the patent.

The fact that the message is thus retransmitted assures us of what may by no means be taken for granted: that it belongs to the dimension of language.

Those who are here know our remarks on the subject, specifically those illustrated by the counter case of the so-called language of bees: in which a linguist[①] can see only a simple signaling of the location of objects, in other words: only an imaginary function more differentiated than others.

We emphasize that such a form of communication is not absent in man, however evanescent a naturally given object may be for him, split as it is in its submission to symbols.

Something equivalent may no doubt be grasped in the communion established between two persons in their hatred of a common object: except that the meeting is possible only over a single object, defined by those traits in the individual each of the two resist.

But such communication is not transmissible in symbolic form. It may be maintained only in the relation with the object. In such a manner it may bring together an indefinite number of subjects in a common "ideal": the communication of one subject with another within the crowd thus constituted will nonetheless remain irreducibly mediated by an ineffable relation. [②]

This digression is not only a recollection of principles distantly addressed to those who impute to us a neglect of non-verbal communication: in determining the scope of what speech repeats, it prepares the question of what symptoms repeat.

Thus the indirect telling sifts out the linguistic dimension, and the general narrator, by duplicating it, "hypothetically" adds nothing to it. But its role in the second dialogue is entirely different.

For the latter will be opposed to the first like those poles we have distin-

---

① Cf. Emile Benveniste, "Communication animale et langage humain," *Diogène*, No. 1, and our address in Rome, *Ecrits*, p. 178.

② For the notion of *ego ideal*, see Freud, *Group Psychology and the Analysis of the Ego*. —Ed.

guished elsewhere in language and which are opposed like word to speech.

Which is to say that a transition is made here from the domain of exactitude to the register of truth. Now that register, we dare think we needn't come back to this, is situated entirely elsewhere, strictly speaking at the very foundation of intersubjectivity. It is located there where the subject can grasp nothing but the very subjectivity which constitutes an Other as absolute. We shall be satisfied here to indicate its place by evoking the dialogue which seems to us to merit its attribution as a Jewish joke by that state of privation through which the relation of signifier to speech appears in the entreaty which brings the dialogue to a close: "Why are you lying to me?" one character shouts breathlessly. "Yes, why do you lie to me saying you're going to Cracow so I should believe you're going to Lemberg, when in reality you *are* going to Cracow?" ①

We might be prompted to ask a similar question by the torrent of logical impasses, eristic enigmas, paradoxes and even jests presented to us as an introduction to Dupin's method if the fact that they were confided to us by a would-be disciple did not endow them with a new dimension through that act of delegation. Such is the unmistakable magic of legacies: the witness's fidelity is the cowl which blinds and lays to rest all criticism of his testimony.

What could be more convincing, moreover, than the gesture of laying one's cards face up on the table? So much so that we are momentarily persuaded that the magician has in fact demonstrated, as he promised, how his trick was performed, whereas he has only renewed it in still purer form: at which point we fathom the measure of the supremacy of the signifier in the subject.

---

① Freud comments on this joke in *Jokes and Their Relation to the Unconscious*, New York, 1960, p. 115: "But the more serious substance of the joke is what determines the truth… Is it the truth if we describe things as they are without troubling to consider how our hearer will understand what we say? … I think that jokes of that kind are sufficiently different from the rest to be given a special position: What they are attacking is not a person or an institution but the certainty of our knowledge itself, one of our speculative possessions." Lacan's text may be regarded as a commentary on Freud's statement, an examination of the corrosive effect of the demands of an intersubjective communicative situation on any naive notion of "truth."—Ed.

Such is Dupin's maneuver when he starts with the story of the child prodigy who takes in all his friends at the game of even and odd with his trick of identifying with the opponent, concerning which we have nevertheless shown that it cannot reach the first level of theoretical elaboration, namely: intersubjective alternation, without immediately stumbling on the buttress of its recurrence. [1]

We are all the same treated—so much smoke in our eyes—to the names of La Rochefoucauld, La Bruyère, Machiavelli and Campanella, whose renown, by this time, would seem but futile when confronted with the child's prowess.

Followed by Chamfort, whose maxim that "it is a safe wager that every public idea, every accepted convention is foolish, since it suits the greatest number," will no doubt satisfy all who think they escape its law, that is, precisely, the greatest number. That Dupin accuses the French of deception for applying the word *analysis* to algebra will hardly threaten our pride since, moreover, the freeing of that term for other uses ought by no means to provoke a psychoanalyst to intervene and claim his rights. And there he goes making philological remarks which should positively delight any lovers of Latin: when he recalls without deigning to say any more that "*ambitus* doesn't mean ambition, *religio*, religion, *homines honesti*, honest men," who among you would not take pleasure in remembering… what those words mean to anyone familiar with Cicero and Lucretius. No doubt Poe is having a good time…

But a suspicion occurs to us: might not this parade of erudition be destined to reveal to us the key words of our drama? Is not the magician repeating his trick before our eyes, without deceiving us this time about divulging his secret, but pressing his wager to the point of really explaining it to us without us seeing a thing. *That* would be the summit of the illusionist's art: through one of his fictive creations to *truly delude us*.

And is it not such effects which justify our referring, without malice, to a

---

① Cf. *Ecrits*, p. 58. "But what will happen at the following step (of the game) when the opponent, realizing that I am sufficiently clever to follow him in his move, will show his own cleverness by realizing that it is by playing the fool that he has the best chance to deceive me? From then on my reasoning is invalidated, since it can only be repeated in an indefinite oscillation…"

number of imaginary heroes as real characters?

As well, when we are open to hearing the way in which Martin Heidegger discloses to us in the word *aletheia* the play of truth, we rediscover a secret to which truth has always initiated her lovers, and through which they learn that it is in hiding that she offers herself to them *most truly*.

Thus even if Dupin's comments did not defy us so blatantly to believe in them, we should still have to make that attempt against the opposite temptation.

Let us track down [*dépistons*] his footprints there where they elude [*dépiste*] us. ① And first of all in the criticism by which he explains the Prefect's lack of success. We already saw it surface in those furtive gibes the Prefect, in the first conversation, failed to heed, seeing in them only a pretext for hilarity. That it is, as Dupin insinuates, because a problem is too simple, indeed too evident, that it may appear obscure, will never have any more bearing for him than a vigorous rub of the rib cage.

Everything is arranged to induce in us a sense of the character's imbecility. Which is powerfully articulated by the fact that he and his confederates never conceive of anything beyond what an ordinary rogue might imagine for hiding an object—that is, precisely the all too well known series of extraordinary hiding places: which are promptly catalogued for us, from hidden desk draws to removable table tops, from the detachable cushions of chairs to their hollowed out legs, from the reverse side of mirrors to the "thickness" of book bindings.

After which, a moment of derision at the Prefect's error in deducing that because the Minister is a poet, he is not far from being mad, an error, it is argued, which would consist, but this is hardly negligible, simply in a false distribution of the middle term, since it is far from following from the fact that all madmen are poets.

---

① We should like to present again to M. Benveniste the question of the antithetical sense of (primal or other) words after the magisterial rectification he brought to the erroneous philological path on which Freud engaged it (cf. *La Psychanalyse*, vol. 1, pp. 5-16). For we think that the problem remains intact once the instance of the signifier has been evolved. Bloch and Von Wartburg date at 1875 the first appearance of the meaning of the verb *dépister* in the second use we make of it in our sentence.

Yes indeed. But we ourselves are left in the dark as to the poet's superiority in the art of concealment—even if he be a mathematician to boot—since our pursuit is suddenly thwarted, dragged as we are into a thicket of bad arguments directed against the reasoning of mathematicians, who never, so far as I know, showed such devotion to their formulae as to identify them with reason itself. At least, let us testify that unlike what seems to be Poe's experience, it occasionally befalls us—with our friend Riguet, whose presence here is a guarantee that our incursions into combinatory analysis are not leading us astray—to hazard such serious deviations (virtual blasphemies, according to Poe) as to cast into doubt that "x^2 plus px is perhaps not absolutely equal to q," without ever—here we give the lie to Poe—having had to fend off any unexpected attack.

Is not so much intelligence being exercised then simply to divert our own from what had been indicated earlier as given, namely, that the police have looked *everywhere*: which we were to understand—vis-à-vis the area in which the police, not without reason, assumed the letter might be found—in terms of a (no doubt theoretical) exhaustion of space, but concerning which the tale's piquancy depends on our accepting it literally: the division of the entire volume into numbered "compartments," which was the principle governing the operation, being presented to us as so precise that "the fiftieth part of a line," it is said, could not escape the probing of the investigators. Have we not then the right to ask how it happened that the letter was not found *anywhere*, or rather to observe that all we have been told of a more far-ranging conception of concealment does not explain, in all rigor, that the letter escaped detection, since the area combed did in fact contain it, as Dupin's discovery eventually proves.

Must a letter then, of all objects, be endowed with the property of *nullibiety*: to use a term which the thesaurus known as *Roget* picks up from the semiotic utopia of Bishop Wilkins? [1]

---

[1] The very one to which Jorge Luis Borges, in works which harmonize so well with the phylum of our subject, has accorded an importance which others have reduced to its proper proportions. Cf. *Les Temps modernes*, June-July 1955, pp. 2135-36 and Oct. 1955, pp. 574-75.

It is evident ("a little *too* self-evident")① that between *letter* and *place* exist relations for which no French word has quite the extension of the English adjective: *odd*. *Bizarre*, by which Baudelaire regularly translates it, is only approximate. Let us say that these relations are… *singuliers*, for they are the very ones maintained with place by the *signifier*.

You realize, of course, that our intention is not to turn them into "subtle" relations, nor is our aim to confuse letter with spirit, even if we receive the former by pneumatic dispatch, and that we readily admit that one kills whereas the other quickens, insofar as the signifier—you perhaps begin to understand—materializes the agency of death. ② But if it is first of all on the materiality of the signifier that we have insisted, that materiality is *odd* [*singulière*] in many ways, the first of which is not to admit partition. Cut a letter in small pieces, and it remains the letter it is—and this in a completely different sense than *Gestalttheorie* would account for which the dormant vitalism informing its notion of the whole. ③

Language delivers its judgment to whomever knows how to hear it: through the usage of the article as partitive particle. It is there that spirit—if spirit be living meaning—appears, no less oddly, as more available for quantification than its letter. To begin with meaning itself, which bears our saying: a speech rich with meaning ["plein *de* signification"], just as we recognize a measure of intention ["*de* l'intention"] in an act, or deplore that there is no more love ["plus *d'amour*"]; or store up hatred ["*de la* haine"] and expend devotion ["*du* dévouemenf"], and so much infatuation ["taut *d'*infatuation"] is

---

① Underlined by the author.

② The reference is to the "death instinct," whose "death," we should note, lies entirely in its diacritical opposition to the "life" of a naive vitalism or naturalism. As such, it may be compared with the logical moment in Lévi-Strauss's thought whereby "nature" exceeds, supplements, and symbolizes itself: the prohibition of incest. —Ed.

③ This is so true that philosophers, in those hackneyed examples with which they argue on the basis of the single and the multiple, will not use to the same purpose a simple sheet of white paper ripped in the middle and a broken circle, indeed a shattered vase, not to mention a cut worm.

easily reconciled to the fact that there will always be ass ["*de la* cuisse"] for sale and brawling ["*du* rififi"] among men.

But as for the letter—be it taken as typographical character, epistle, or what makes a man of letters—we will say that what is said is to be understood *to the letter* [*à la lettre*], that *a letter* [*une lettre*] awaits you at the post office, or even that you are acquainted with *letters* [*que vous avez des lettres*]—never that there is *letter* [*de la lettre*] anywhere, whatever the context, even to designate overdue mail.

For the signifier is a unit in its very uniqueness, being by nature symbol only of an absence. Which is why we cannot say of the purloined letter that, like other objects, it must be *or* not be in a particular place but that unlike them it will be *and* not be where it is, wherever it goes. [①]

Let us, in fact, look more closely at what happens to the police. We are spared nothing concerning the procedures used in searching the area submitted to their investigation: from the division of that space into compartments from which the slightest bulk could not escape detection, to needles probing upholstery, and, in the impossibility of sounding wood with a tap, to a microscope exposing the waste of any drilling at the surface of its hollow, indeed the infinitesimal gaping of the slightest abyss. As the network tightens to the point that, not satisfied with shaking the pages of books, the police take to counting them, do we not see space itself shed its leaves like a letter?

But the detectives have so immutable a notion of the real that they fail to notice that their search tends to transform it into its object. A trait by which they would be able to distinguish that object from all others.

This would no doubt be too much to ask them, not because of their lack of insight but rather because of ours. For their imbecility is neither of the individual nor the corporative variety; its source is subjective. It is the realist's

---

① Cf. Saussure, *Cours de linguistique générale*, Paris, 1969, p. 166: "The preceding amounts to saying that *in language there are only differences*. Even more: a difference presupposes in general positive terms between which it is established, but in language there are only differences *without positive terms*."—Ed.

imbecility, which does not pause to observe that nothing, however deep in the bowels of the earth a hand may seek to ensconce it, will ever be hidden there, since another hand can always retrieve it, and that what is hidden is never but what is *missing from its place*, as the call slip puts it when speaking of a volume lost in a library. And even if the book be on an adjacent shelf or in the next slot, it would be hidden there, however visibly it may appear. For it can *literally* be said that something is missing from its place only of what can change it: the symbolic. For the real, whatever upheaval we subject it to, is always in its place; it carries it glued to its heel, ignorant of what might exile it from it.

And, to return to our cops, who took the letter from the place where it was hidden, how could they have seized the letter? In what they turned between their fingers what did they hold but what *did not answer* to their description. "A letter, a litter": in Joyce's circle, they played on the homophony of the two words in English. ① Nor does the seeming bit of refuse the police are now handling reveal its other nature for being but half torn. A different seal on a stamp of another color, the mark of a different handwriting in the superscription are here the most inviolable modes of concealment. And if they stop at the reverse side of the letter, on which, as is known, the recipient's address was written in that period, it is because the letter has for them no other side but its reverse.

What indeed might they find on its observe? Its message, as is often said to our cybernetic joy? ⋯ But does it not occur to us that this message has already reached its recipient and has even been left with her, since the insignificant scrap of paper now represents it no less well than the original note.

If we could admit that a letter has completed its destiny after fulfilling its function, the ceremony of returning letters would be a less common close to the extinction of the fires of love's feasts. The signifier is not functional. And the mobilization of the elegant society whose frolics we are following would as well have no meaning if the letter itself were content with having one. For it would hardly be an adequate means of keeping it secret to inform a squad of cops of its

---

① Cf. *Our Examination Round his Factification for Incamination of Work in Progress*, Shakespeare & Co., 12 rue de l'Odéon, Paris, 1929.

existence.

We might even admit that the letter has an entirely different (if no more urgent) meaning for the Queen than the one understood by the Minister. The sequence of events would not be noticeably affected, not even if it were strictly incomprehensible to an uninformed reader.

For it is certainly not so for everybody, since, as the Prefect pompously assures us, to everyone's derision, "the disclosure of the document to a third person, who shall be nameless," (that name which leaps to the eye like the pig's tail twixt the teeth of old Ubu) "would bring in question the honor of a personage of most exalted station, indeed that the honor and peace of the illustrious personage are so jeopardized."

In that case, it is not only the meaning but the text of the message which it would be dangerous to place in circulation, and all the more so to the extent that it might appear harmless, since the risks of an indiscretion unintentionally committed by one of the letter's holders would thus be increased.

Nothing then can redeem the police's position, and nothing would be changed by improving their "culture." *Scripta manent*: in vain would they learn from a *de luxe*-edition humanism the proverbial lesson which *verba volant* concludes. May it but please heaven that writings remain, as is rather the case with spoken words: for the indelible debt of the latter impregnates our acts with its transferences.

Writings scatter to the winds blank checks in an insane charge. [1] And were they not such flying leaves, there would be no purloined letters. [2]

---

[1] The original sentence presents an exemplary difficulty in translation: "Les écrits emportent au vent les traites en blanc d'une cavalerie folle." The blank (bank) drafts (or transfers) are not delivered to their rightful recipients (the sense of *de cavalerie*, *de complaisance*). That is: in analysis, one finds absurd symbolic debts being paid to the "wrong" persons. At the same time, the mad, driven quality of the payment is latent in *traite*, which might also refer to the day's trip of an insane cavalry. In our translation, we have displaced the "switch-word"—joining the financial and equestrian series—from *traite* to *charge*. —Ed.

[2] *Flying leaves* (also fly-sheets) and *purloined letters*—*feuilles volantes* and *lettres volées*—employ different meanings of the same word in French. —Ed.

But what of it? For a purloined letter to exist, we may ask, to whom does a letter belong? We stressed a moment ago the oddity implicit in returning a letter to him who had but recently given wing to its burning pledge. And we generally deem unbecoming such premature publications as the one by which the Chevalier d'Eon put several of his correspondents in a rather pitiful position.

Might a letter on which the sender retains certain rights then not quite belong to the person to whom it is addressed? or might it be that the latter was never the real receiver?

Let's take a look: we shall find illumination in what at first seems to obscure matters: the fact that the tale leaves us in virtually total ignorance of the sender, no less than of the contents, of the letter. We are told only that the Minister immediately recognized the handwriting of the address and only incidentally, in a discussion of the Minister's camouflage, is it said that the original seal bore the ducal arms of the S... family. As for the letter's bearing, we know only the dangers it entails should it come into the hands of a specific third party, and that its possession has allowed the Minister to "wield, to a very dangerous extent, for political purposes," the power it assures him over the interested party. But all this tells us nothing of the message it conveys.

Love letter or conspiratorial letter, letter of betrayal or letter of mission, letter of summons or letter of distress, we are assured of but one thing: the Queen must not bring it to the knowledge of her lord and master.

Now these terms, far from bearing the nuance of discredit they have in *bourgeois* comedy, take on a certain prominence through allusion to her sovereign, to whom she is bound by pledge of faith, and doubly so, since her role as spouse does not relieve her of her duties as subject, but rather elevates her to the guardianship of what royalty according to law incarnates of power: and which is called legitimacy.

From then on, to whatever vicissitudes the Queen may choose to subject the letter, it remains that the letter is the symbol of a pact, and that, even should the recipient not assume the pact, the existence of the letter situates her in a symbolic chain foreign to the one which constitutes her faith. This incompatibility is proven by the fact that the possession of the letter is impossible to bring forward publicly as legitimate, and that in order to have that possession respected, the Queen can invoke but her right to privacy, whose privilege is based on the honor that possession violates.

For she who incarnates the figure of grace and sovereignty cannot welcome even a private communication without power being concerned, and she cannot avail herself of secrecy in relation to the sovereign without becoming clandestine.

From then on, the responsibility of the author of the letter takes second place to that of its holder: for the offense to majesty is compounded by *high treason*.

We say: the *holder* and not the *possessor*. For it becomes clear that the addressee's proprietorship of the letter may be no less debatable than that of anyone else into whose hands it comes, for nothing concerning the existence of the letter can return to good order without the person whose prerogatives it infringes upon having to pronounce judgment on it.

All of this, however, does not imply that because the letter's secrecy is indefensible, the betrayal of that secret would in any sense be honorable. The *honesti homines*, decent people, will not get off so easily. There is more than one *religio*, and it is not slated for tomorrow that sacred ties shall cease to rend us in two. As for *ambitus*: a detour, we see, is not always inspired by ambition. For if we are taking one here, by no means is it stolen (the word is apt), since, to lay our cards on the table, we have borrowed Baudelaire's title in order to stress not, as is incorrectly claimed, the conventional nature of the signifier, but rather its priority in relation to the signified. ① It remains, nevertheless, that Baudelaire, despite his devotion, betrayed Poe by translating as "la lettre volée" (the stolen letter) his title: the purloined letter, a title containing a word rare enough for us to find it easier to define its etymology than its usage.

To purloin, says the Oxford dictionary, is an Anglo-French word, that is: composed of the prefix *pur-*, found in *purpose*, *purchase*, *purport*, and of the

---

① See our discussion of Lévi-Strauss's statement—"the signifier precedes and determines the signified"—in the previous essay. —Ed.

Old French word: *loing*, *loigner*, *longé*. We recognize in the first element the Latin *pro-*, as opposed to *ante*, in so far as it presupposes a rear in front of which it is borne, possibly as its warrant, indeed even as its pledge (whereas *ante* goes forth to confront what it encounters). As for the second, an old French word: *loigner*, a verb attributing place *au loing* (or, still in use, *longé*), it does not mean *au loin* (far off), but *au long de* (alongside); it is a question then of *putting aside*, or, to invoke a familiar expression which plays on the two meanings: *mettre à gauche* (to put to the left; to put amiss).

Thus we are confirmed in our detour by the very object which draws us on into it: for we are quite simply dealing with a letter which has been diverted from its path; one whose course has been *prolonged* (etymologically, the word of the title), or, to revert to the language of the post office, a *letter in sufferance*. ①

Here then, *simple and odd*, as we are told on the very first page, reduced to its simplest expression, is the singularity of the letter, which as the title indicates, is the *true subject* of the tale: since it can be diverted, it must have a course *which is proper to it*: the trait by which its incidence as signifier is affirmed. For we have learned to conceive of the signifier as sustaining itself only in a displacement comparable to that found in electric news strips or in the rotating memories of our machines-that-think-like men, this because of the alternating operation which is its principle, requiring it to leave its place, even though it returns to it by a circular path. ②

This is indeed what happens in the repetition automatism. What Freud teaches us in the text we are commenting on is that the subject must pass through the channels of the symbolic, but what is illustrated here is more gripping still: it is not only the subject, but the subjects, grasped in their intersubjectivity, who line up, in other words our ostriches, to whom we here return,

---

① We revive this archaism (for the French: *lettre en souffrance*). The sense is a letter held up in the course of delivery. In French, of course, *en souffrance* means in a state of suffering as well. —Ed.

② See *Ecrits*, p. 59: "… it is not unthinkable that a modern computer, by discovering the sentence which modulates without his knowing it and over a long period of time the choices of a subject, would win beyond any normal proportion at the game of even and odd…"

and who, more docile than sheep, model their very being on the moment of the signifying chain which traverses them.

If what Freud discovered and rediscovers with a perpetually increasing sense of shock has a meaning, it is that the displacement of the signifier determines the subjects in their acts, in their destiny, in their refusals, in their blindnesses, in their end and in their fate, their innate gifts and social acquisitions notwithstanding, without regard for character or sex, and that, willingly or not, everything that might be considered the stuff of psychology, kit and caboodle, will follow the path of the signifier.

Here we are, in fact, yet again at the crossroads at which we had left our drama and its round with the question of the way in which the subjects replace each other in it. Our fable is so constructed as to show that it is the letter and its diversion which governs their entries and roles. If *it* be "in sufferance," *they* shall endure the pain. Should they pass beneath its shadow, they become its reflection. Falling in possession of the letter—admirable ambiguity of language— its meaning possesses them.

So we are shown by the hero of the drama in the repetition of the very situation which his daring brought to a head, a first time, to his triumph. If he now succumbs to it, it is because he has shifted to the second position in the triad in which he was initially third, as well as the thief—and this by virtue of the object of his theft.

For if it is, now as before, a question of protecting the letter from inquisitive eyes, he can do nothing but employ the same technique he himself has already foiled: leave it in the open? And we may properly doubt that he knows what he is thus doing, when we see him immediately captivated by a dual relationship in which we find all the traits of a mimetic lure or of an animal feigning death, and, trapped in the typically imaginary situation of seeing that he is not seen, misconstrue the real situation in which he is seen not seeing. ①

And what does he fail to see? Precisely the symbolic situation which he himself was so well able to see, and in which he is now seen seeing himself not

---

① See *Vocabulaire* entry on the *imaginary* below.

being seen.

The Minister acts as a man who realizes that the police's search is his own defence, since we are told he allows them total access by his absences: he nonetheless fails to recognize that outside of that search he is no longer defended.

This is the very *autruicherie* whose artisan he was, if we may allow our monster to proliferate, but it cannot be by sheer stupidity that he now comes to be its dupe. ①

For in playing the part of the one who hides, he is obliged to don the role of the Queen, and even the attributes of femininity and shadow, so propitious to the act of concealing.

Not that we are reducing the hoary couple of *Yin* and *Yang* to the elementary opposition of dark and light. For its precise use involves what is blinding in a flash of light, no less than the shimmering shadows exploit in order not to lose their prey.

Here sign and being, marvelously asunder, reveal which is victorious when they come into conflict. A man man enough to defy to the point of scorn a lady's fearsome ire undergoes to the point of metamorphosis the curse of the sign he has dispossessed her of.

For this sign is indeed that of woman, in so far as she invests her very being therein, founding it outside the law, which subsumes her nevertheless, originarily, in a position of signifier, nay, of fetish. ② In order to be worthy of the power of that sign she has but to remain immobile in its shadow, thus finding, moreover, like the Queen, that simulation of mastery in inactivity that the Minister's "lynx eye" alone was able to penetrate.

---

① *Autruicherie* condenses, in addition to the previous terms, deception (*tricherie*). Do we not find in Lacan's proliferating "monster" something of the *proton pseudos*, the "first lie" of Freud's 1895 *Project*: the persistent illusion which seems to structure the mental life of the patient? —Ed.

② The fetish, as replacement for the missing maternal phallus, at once masks and reveals the scandal of sexual difference. As such it is the analytic object *par excellence*. The female temptation to exhibitionism, understood as a desire to be the (maternal) phallus, is thus tantamount to being a fetish. —Ed.

This stolen sign—here then is man in its possession: sinister in that such possession may be sustained only through the honor it defies, cursed in calling him who sustains it to punishment or crime, each of which shatters his vassalage to the Law.

There must be in this sign a singular *noli me tangere* for its possession, like the Socratic sting ray, to benumb its man to the point of making him fall into what appears clearly in his case to be a state of idleness. ①

For in noting, as the narrator does as early as the first dialogue, that with the letter's use its power disappears, we perceive that this remark, strictly speaking, concerns precisely its use for ends of power—and at the same time that such a use is obligatory for the Minister.

To be unable to rid himself of it, the Minister indeed must not know what else to do with the letter. For that use places him in so total a dependence on the letter as such, that in the long run it no longer involves the letter at all.

We mean that for that use truly to involve the letter, the Minister, who, after all, would be so authorized by his service to his master the King, might present to the Queen respectful admonitions, even were he to assure their sequel by appropriate precautions, —or initiate an action against the author of the letter, concerning whom, the fact that he remains outside the story's focus reveals the extent to which it is not guilt and blame which are in question here, but rather that sign of contradiction and scandal constituted by the letter, in the sense in which the Gospel says that it must come regardless of the anguish of whomever serves as its bearer, —or even submit the letter as evalone concerns us; it suffices for us to know that the way in which he will have it issue in a Star Chamber for the Queen or the Minister's disgrace.

We will not know why the Minister does not resort to any of these uses,

---

① See Plato's *Meno*: "Socrates, ... at this moment I feel you are exercising magic and witchcraft upon me and positively laying me under your spell until I am just a mass of helplessness. If I may be flippant, I think that not only in outward appearance but in other respects as well you are like the flat sting ray that one meets in the sea. Whenever anyone comes into contact with it, it numbs him, and that is the sort of thing you are doing to me now ... "—Ed.

and it is fitting that we don't, since the effect of this non-use alone concerns us; it suffices for us to know that the way in which the letter was acquired would pose no obstacle to any of them.

For it is clear that if the use of the letter, independent of its meaning, is obligatory for the Minister, its use for ends of power can only be potential, since it cannot become actual without vanishing in the process, —but in that case the letter exists as a means of power only through the final assignations of the pure signifier, namely: by prolonging its diversion, making it reach whomever it may concern through a supplementary transfer, that is, by an additional act of treason whose effects the letter's gravity makes it difficult to predict, —or indeed by destroying the letter, the only sure means, as Dupin divulges at the start, of being rid of what is destined by nature to signify the annulment of what it signifies.

The ascendancy which the Minister derives from the situation is thus not a function of the letter, but, whether he knows it or not, of the role it constitutes for him. And the Prefect's remarks indeed present him as someone "who dares all things," which is commented upon significantly: "those unbecoming as well as those becoming a man," words whose pungency escapes Baudelaire when he translates: "ce qui est indigne d'un homme aussi bien que ce qui est digne de lui" (those unbecoming a man as well as those becoming him). For in its original form, the appraisal is far more appropriate to what might concern a woman.

This allows us to see the imaginary import of the character, that is, the narcissistic relation in which the Minister is engaged, this time, no doubt, without knowing it. It is indicated as well as early as the second page of the English text by one of the narrator's remarks, whose form is worth savoring: the Minister's ascendancy, we are told, "would depend upon the robber's knowledge of the loser's knowledge of the robber." Words whose importance the author underscores by having Dupin repeat them literally after the narration of the scene of the theft of the letter. Here again we may say that Baudelaire is imprecise in his language in having one ask, the other confirm, in these words: "Le voleur sait-il? …"(Does the robber know?), then: "Le voleur sait…"(the robber knows). What? "que la personne volée connaît son voleur" (that the loser knows his robber).

For what matters to the robber is not only that the said person knows who robbed her, but rather with what kind of a robber she is dealing; for she believes him capable of anything, which should be understood as her having conferred upon him the position that no one is in fact capable of assuming, since it is imaginary, that of absolute master.

In truth, it is a position of absolute weakness, but not for the person of whom we are expected to believe so. The proof is not only that the Queen dares to call the police. For she is only conforming to her displacement to the next slot in the arrangement of the initial triad in trusting to the very blindness required to occupy that place: "No more sagacious agent could, I suppose," Dupin notes ironically, "be desired or even imagined." No, if she has taken that step, it is less out of being "driven to despair," as we are told, than in assuming the charge of an impatience best imputed to a specular mirage.

For the Minister is kept quite busy confining himself to the idleness which is presently his lot. The Minister, in point of fact, is not *altogether* mad. ① That's a remark made by the Prefect, whose every word is gold: it is true that the gold of his words flows only for Dupin and will continue to flow to the amount of the fifty thousand francs worth it will cost him by the metal standard of the day, though not without leaving him a margin of profit. The Minister then is not *altogether* mad in his insane stagnation, and that is why he will behave according to the mode of neurosis. Like the man who withdrew to an island to forget, what? he forgot, —so the Minister, through not making use of the letter, comes to forget it. As is expressed by the persistence of his conduct. But the letter, no more than the neurotic's unconscious, does not forget him. It forgets him so little that it transforms him more and more in the image of her who offered it to his capture, so that he now will surrender it, following her example, to a similar capture.

The features of that transformation are noted, and in a form so characteris-

---

① Baudelaire translates Poe's "*altogether* a fool" as "*absolument* fou." In opting for Baudelaire, Lacan is enabled to allude to the realm of psychosis. —Ed.

tic in their apparent gratuitousness that they might validly be compared to the return of the repressed.

Thus we first learn that the Minister in turn has *turned the letter over*, not, of course, as in the Queen's hasty gesture, but, more assiduously, as one turns a garment inside out. So he must procede, according to the methods of the day for folding and sealing a letter, in order to free the virgin space on which to inscribe a new address. ①

That address becomes his own. Whether it be in his hand or another, it will appear in an extremely delicate feminine script, and, the seal changing from the red of passion to the black of its mirrors, he will imprint his stamp upon it. This oddity of a letter marked with the recipient's stamp is all the more striking in its conception, since, though forcefully articulated in the text, it is not even mentioned by Dupin in the discussion he devotes to the identification of the letter.

Whether that omission be intentional or involuntary, it will surprise in the economy of a work whose meticulous rigor is evident. But in either case it is significant that the letter which the Minister, in point of fact, addresses to himself is a letter from a woman: as though this were a phase he had to pass through out of a natural affinity of the signifier.

Thus the aura of apathy, verging at times on an affectation of effeminacy; the display of an *ennui* bordering on disgust in his conversation; the mood the author of the philosophy of furniture② can elicit from virtually impalpable details (like that of the musical instrument on the table), everything seems intended for a character, all of whose utterances have revealed the most virile

---

① We felt obliged to demonstrate the procedure to an audience with a letter from the period concerning M. de Chateaubriand and his search for a secretary. We were amused to find that M. de Chateaubriand completed the first version of his recently restored memoirs in the very month of November 1841 in which the purloined letter appeared in *Chamber's Journal*. Might M. de Chateaubriand's devotion to the power he decries and the honor which that devotion bespeaks in him (*the gift* had not yet been invented), place him in the category to which we will later see the Minister assigned: among men of genius with or without principles?

② Poe is the author of an essay with this title.

traits, to exude the oddest *odor di femina* when he appears.

Dupin does not fail to stress that this is an artifice, describing behind the bogus finery the vigilance of a beast of prey ready to spring. But that this is the very effect of the unconscious in the precise sense that we teach that the unconscious means that man is inhabited by the signifier: could we find a more beautiful image of it than the one Poe himself forges to help us appreciate Dupin's exploit? For with this aim in mind, he refers to those toponymical inscriptions which a geographical map, lest it remain mute, superimposes on its design, and which may become the object of a guessing game: who can find the name chosen by a partner? —noting immediately that the name most likely to foil a beginner will be one which, in large letters spaced out widely across the map, discloses, often without an eye pausing to notice it, the name of an entire country…

Just so does the purloined letter, like an immense female body, stretch out across the Minister's office when Dupin enters. But just so does he already expect to find it, and has only, with his eyes veiled by green lenses, to undress that huge body.

And that is why without needing any more than being able to listen in at the door of Professor Freud, he will go straight to the spot in which lies and lives what that body is designed to hide, in a gorgeous center caught in a glimpse, nay, to the very place seducers name Sant' Angelo's Castle in their innocent illusion of controlling the City from within it. Look! between the cheeks of the fireplace, there's the object already in reach of a hand the ravisher has but to extend… The question of deciding whether he seizes it above the mantelpiece as Baudelaire translates, or beneath it, as in the original text, may be abandoned without harm to the inferences of those whose profession is grilling. ①

----

① And even to the cook herself. —J. L.

The paragraph might be read as follows: analysis, in its violation of the imaginary integrity of the ego, finds its fantasmatic equivalent in rape (or castration, as in the passage analyzed in the previous essay). But whether that "rape" takes place from in front or from behind (above or below the mantelpiece) is, in fact, a question of interest for policemen and not analysts. Implicit in the statement is an attack on those who have become wed to the ideology of "maturational development" (libidinal stages *et al*) in Freud (i. e., the ego psychologists). —Ed.

Were the effectiveness of symbols[①] to cease there, would it mean that the symbolic debt would as well be extinguished? Even if we could believe so, we would be advised of the contrary by two episodes which we may all the less dismiss as secondary in that they seem, at first sight, to clash with the rest of the work.

First of all, there's the business of Dupin's remuneration, which, far from being a closing *pirouette*, has been present from the beginning in the rather unselfconscious question he asks the Prefect about the amount of the reward promised him, and whose enormousness, the Prefect, however reticent he may be about the precise figure, does not dream of hiding from him, even returning later on to refer to its increase.

The fact that Dupin had been previously presented to us as a virtual pauper in his ethereal shelter ought rather to lead us to reflect on the deal he makes out of delivering the letter, promptly assured as it is by the check-book he produces. We do not regard it as negligible that the unequivocal hint through which he introduces the matter is a "story attributed to the character, as famous as it was excentric," Baudelaire tells us, of an English doctor named Abernethy, in which a rich miser, hoping to sponge upon him for a medical opinion, is sharply told not to take medicine, but to take advice.

Do we not in fact feel concerned with good reason when for Dupin what is perhaps at stake is his withdrawal from the symbolic circuit of the letter—we who become the emissaries of all the purloined letters which at least for a time remain in sufferance with us in the transference. And is it not the responsibility their transference entails which we neutralize by equating it with the signifier most destructive of all signification, namely: money.

But that's not all. The profit Dupin so nimbly extracts from his exploit, if its purpose is to allow him to withdraw his stakes from the game, makes all the more paradoxical, even shocking, the partisan attack, the underhanded blow, he suddenly permits himself to launch against the Minister, whose insolent

---

① The allusion is to Lévi-Strauss's article of the same title ("L'efficacité symbolique") in *L'Anthropologie structurale*. —Ed.

prestige, after all, would seem to have been sufficiently deflated by the trick Dupin has just played on him.

We have already quoted the atrocious lines Dupin claims he could not help dedicating, in his counterfeit letter, to the moment in which the Minister, enraged by the inevitable defiance of the Queen, will think he is demolishing her and will plunge into the abyss: *facilis descensus Averni*,[①] he waxes sententious, adding that the Minister cannot fail to recognize his handwriting, all of which, since depriving of any danger a merciless act of infamy, would seem, concerning a figure who is not without merit, a triumph without glory, and the rancor he invokes, stemming from an evil turn done him at Vienna (at the Congress?) only adds an additional bit of blackness to the whole.[②]

Let us consider, however, more closely this explosion of feeling, and more specifically the moment it occurs in a sequence of acts whose success depends on so cool a head.

It comes just after the moment in which the decisive act of identifying the letter having been accomplished, it may be said that Dupin already *has* the letter as much as if he had seized it, without, however, as yet being in a position to rid himself of it.

He is thus, in fact, fully participant in the intersubjective triad, and, as such, in the median position previously occupied by the Queen and the Minister. Will he, in showing himself to be above it, reveal to us at the same time the author's intentions?

If he has succeeded in returning the letter to its proper course, it remains for him to make it arrive at its address. And that address is in the place previously occupied by the King, since it is there that it would re-enter the order of the Law.

As we have seen, neither the King nor the Police who replaced him in that position were able to read the letter because that *place entailed blindness*.

----

① Virgil's line reads: *facilis descensus Averno*.

② Cf. Corneille, *Le Cid* (II, 2): "A vaincre sans péril, on triomphe sans gloire." (To vanquish without danger is to triumph without glory). —Ed.

Rex et augur, the legendary, archaic quality of the words seems to resound only to impress us with the absurdity of applying them to a man. And the figures of history, for some time now, hardly encourage us to do so. It is not natural for man to bear alone the weight of the highest of signifiers. And the place he occupies as soon as he dons it may be equally apt to become the symbol of the most outrageous imbecility. ①

Let us say that the King here is invested with the equivocation natural to the sacred, with the imbecility which prizes none other than the Subject. ②

That is what will give their meaning to the characters who will follow him in his place. Not that the police should be regarded as constitutionally illiterate, and we know the role of pikes planted on the *campus* in the birth of the State. But the police who exercise their functions here are plainly marked by the forms of liberalism, that is, by those imposed on them by masters on the whole indifferent to eliminating their indiscreet tendencies. Which is why on occasion words are not minced as to what is expected of them: "*Sutor ne ultra crepidam*, just take care of your crooks. ③ We'll even give you scientific means to do it with. That will help you not to think of truths you'd be better off leaving in the dark. " ④

We know that the relief which results from such prudent principles shall have lasted in history but a morning's time, that already the march of destiny is everywhere bringing back—a sequel to a just aspiration to freedom's reign—an

---

① We recall the witty couplet attributed before his fall to the most recent in date to have rallied Candide's meeting in Venice:

"Il n'est plus aujourd'hui que cinq rois sur la terre,

Les quatre rois des cartes et le roi d'Angleterre. "

(There are only five kings left on earth: four kings of cards and the king of England.)

② For the antithesis of the "sacred," see Freud's "The Antithetical Sense of Primal Words. " The idiom *tenir à* in this sentence means both to prize and to be a function of. The two senses—King and/as Subject—are implicit in Freud's frequent allusions to "His Majesty the Ego. "—Ed.

③ From Pliny, 35, 10, 35: "A cobbler not beyond his sole…"—Ed.

④ This proposal was openly presented by a noble Lord speaking to the Upper Chamber in which his dignity earned him a place.

interest in those who trouble it with their crimes, which occasionally goes so far as to forge its proofs. It may even be observed that this practice, which was always well received to the extent that it was exercised only in favor of the greatest number, comes to authenticated in public confessions of forgery by the very ones who might very well object to it: the most recent manifestation of the preeminence of the signifier over the subject.

It remains, nevertheless, that a police record has always been the object of a certain reserve, of which we have difficulty understanding that it amply transcends the guild of historians.

It is by dint of this vanishing credit that Dupin's intended delivery of the letter to the Prefect of police will diminish its import. What now remains of the signifier when, already relieved of its message for the Queen, it is now invalidated in its text as soon as it leaves the Minister's hands?

It remains for it now only to answer that very question, of what remains of a signifier when it has no more signification. But this is the same question asked of it by the person Dupin now finds in the spot marked by blindness.

For that is indeed the question which has led the Minister there, if he be the gambler we are told and which his act sufficiently indicates. For the gambler's passion is nothing but that question asked of the signifier, figured by the automaton of chance.

"What are you, figure of the die I turn over in your encounter (*tychē*) with my fortune? ① Nothing, if not that presence of death which makes of human life a reprieve obtained from morning to morning in the name of meanings whose sign is your crook. Thus did Scheherazade for a thousand and one nights, and thus have I done for eighteen months, suffering the ascendancy of this sign at the cost of a dizzying series of fraudulent turns at the game of even or odd."

So it is that Dupin, *from the place he now occupies*, cannot help feeling a

---

① We note the fundamental opposition Aristotle makes between the two terms recalled here in the conceptual analysis of chance he gives in his *Physics*. Many discussions would be illuminated by a knowledge of it.

rage of manifestly feminine nature against him who poses such a question. The prestigious image in which the poet's inventiveness and the mathematician's rigor joined up with the serenity of the dandy and the elegance of the cheat suddenly becomes, for the very person who invited us to savor it, the true *monstrum horrendum*, for such are his words, "an unprincipled man of genius."

It is here that the origin of that horror betrays itself, and he who experiences it has no need to declare himself (in a most unexpected manner) "a partisan of the lady" in order to reveal it to us: it is known that ladies detest calling principles into question, for their charms owe much to the mystery of the signifier.

Which is why Dupin will at last turn toward us the medusoid face of the signifier nothing but whose obverse anyone except the Queen has been able to read. The commonplace of the quotation is fitting for the oracle that face bears in its grimace, as is also its source in tragedy: "...*Un destin si funeste*, /*S'il n'est digne d'Atrée, est digne de Thyeste.*"[1]

So runs the signifier's answer, above and beyond all significations: "You think you act when I stir you at the mercy of the bonds through which I knot your desires. Thus do they grow in force and multiply in objects, bringing you back to the fragmentation of your shattered childhood. So be it: such will be your feast until the return of the stone guest I shall be for you since you call me forth."

Or, to return to a more moderate tone, let us say, as in the quip with which—along with some of you who had followed us to the Zurich Congress last year—we rendered homage to the local password, the signifier's answer to whomever interrogates it is: "Eat your Dasein."

Is that then what awaits the Minister at a rendez-vous with destiny? Dupin assures us of it, but we have already learned not to be too credulous of his diversions.

---

[1] Lacan misquotes Crébillon (as well as Poe and Baudelaire) here by writing *destin* (destiny) instead of *dessein* (scheme). As a result he is free to pursue his remarkable development on the tragic Don Juan ("multiply in objects ··· stone guest). —Ed.

No doubt the brazen creature is here reduced to the state of blindness which is man's in relation to the letters on the wall that dictate his destiny. But what effect, in calling him to confront them, may we expect from the sole provocations of the Queen, on a man like him? Love or hatred. The former is blind and will make him lay down his arms. The latter is lucid, but will awaken his suspicions, But if he is truly the gambler we are told he is, he will consult his cards a final time before laying them down and, upon reading his hand, will leave the table in time to avoid disgrace. ①

Is that all, and shall we believe we have deciphered Dupin's real strategy above and beyond the imaginary tricks with which he was obliged to deceive us? No doubt, yes, for if "any point requiring reflection," as Dupin states at the start, is "examined to best purpose in the dark," we may now easily read its solution in broad daylight. It was already implicit and easy to derive from the title of our tale, according to the very formula we have long submitted to your discretion: in which the sender, we tell you, receives from the receiver his own message in reverse form. Thus it is that what the "purloined letter," nay, the "letter in sufferance" means is that a letter always arrives at its destination.

---

① Thus nothing shall (have) happen(ed)—the final turn in Lacan's theatre of lack. Yet within the simplicity of that empty present the most violent of (pre-)Oedipal dramas—Atreus, Thyestes—shall silently have played itself out. —Ed.

7. 拉康：《关于〈被窃的信〉的研讨》

(Jacques Lacan, "Seminar on 'The Purloined Letter'," 1955)

作者小识

拉康(Jacques Lacan, 1901—1981)，法国哲学家、精神分析学家，以"返回弗洛伊德"的策略创造性地阐释弗洛伊德，将精神分析发展为一门自成一体的独立科学。1966 年，《拉康文集》(*Écrits*)出版，以"镜像期""心理三界""无意识—语言结构论"发展和补正弗洛伊德的学说。拉康博学多识，学理精微，但其语言晦涩，逻辑跳跃，思维发散。他喜欢讲演，主持研讨会，有多卷本演讲集传世。

深受拉康影响的文化批评家齐泽克，对他的著作做出了这么一种论说：穿透外观，直达精神分析的核心，重新定义其基本概念，发掘其伦理内涵；将精神分析技术提升到哲学和宗教反思的至境，主动与圣经传统、希腊悲剧诗人和哲人、近代哲学家对话；烛照当代政治和思想形式的困境；以清晰简单的古典风格，表达 20 世纪人类的精神诉求。

背景略说

精神分析运动有四个主要支脉：以弗洛伊德为代表的维也纳学派，以生物学的原力来解释人类行为；以荣格为代表的苏黎世学派，将个体无意识发展为集体无意识，将集体无意识追溯到神话和原型；以阿德勒为代表的北美学派，集中关注个体人格心理学；以拉康为代表的法国学派，将精神分析理论结构化，与巴黎结构主义运动合流，建构了一种语言论心理分析理论。

语言论心理分析理论是指后期心理分析学家在对弗洛伊德进行批判的基础上，通过无意识心理的结构化而建构语言模式的心理学理论，以拉康和德里达为代表。

弗洛伊德将无意识领域描画为融合激情、欲望和被抑制的意志之复杂情结，一道黑暗而强大的渊流，既没有结构，也没有秩序。拉康却认为，"无意识的结构有如语言的结构"(the unconscious is structured, much like the structure of language)，可以用语言学的方法进行系统分析。拉康的基本假设是：

语言塑造，最后型构了我们的意识——无意识心理，形成了自我认同的精神机制。于是，拉康从主体、语言、欲望和他者的复杂关系中去透视无意识。这就将隐含在弗洛伊德学说中的语言论发掘了出来。拉康作为后期精神分析的代表人物，更加突出语言对无意识的构成作用及对文化的制约作用。要具体说明这一点，我们就有必要理解拉康的"镜像说"和"心理三界论"。

"镜像"(mirror image)，或者"镜像期"(mirror-image phase)是人的个体发育史上的重大转折，指从婴儿出生后第六个月到第十八个月这段时间。在这期间，婴儿首先在镜子中认出了自己的形象，发现自己的肢体原来是一个整体。从此，"镜像反射"就引导着主体走上了个体形式化发展的道路。"镜像阶段是一出戏剧"：首先，婴儿通过镜中的视觉形象进行自我认同；其次，与"他人"的对照，造成了自我的永恒分裂。所以，镜像阶段的自我，就已经蕴含着分裂，致使一切整体自我都成为一种幻觉。脆弱的自我必须借着形式化的语言符号进入社会文化历史的世界。[①]

"心理三界论"，指"想象界"(the imaginary order)、"象征界"(the symbolic order)和"实在界"(the real order)。这是拉康设计的三种互相涵摄和彼此映射的心理秩序，或者相继发生、彼此交错的生存境界。

想象界，是镜像阶段自我认同的精神秩序或生存境界。当人们在经历想象界时，压倒一切的巨大激情主宰着生存，这种激情就是对母亲的欲望。在这种生存境界，视觉形象成为主体关注的中心，主体通过自身的认同镜像而走上了形式化发展的道路。当激情所渴求的对象不在场时，主体所面对的客体就成为缺乏的符号。因而，想象界总是和肖像、形象、幻想等直接关联在一起，其中的主体依然有一种脆弱的幻觉，必须通过语言进入象征界。

象征界，是语言符号之中的规范的心理秩序或生存境界。如果说，母亲统治着想象界，那么，父亲则统治着象征界。在这个世界之中，我们学会了语言。语言作为文化历史的媒介，不仅塑造了独立的主体，而且还让主体借助语言和他者建立了联系。如果说，在想象界我们因为母亲的在场而快乐，那么，在象征界是父亲代表了文化规范和法律秩序。父亲介入了我们和母亲之间，父亲通过阉割的威胁迫使我们遵纪守法。

实在界，是令人迷惘的心理秩序或生存境界。拉康暗示，实在界是不可

---

① 拉康：《助成"我"的功能形成的镜子阶段——精神分析经验所揭示的一个阶段》，见《拉康选集》，褚孝泉译，89～96页，上海，上海三联书店，2001。

能通过象征和想象来把握的东西，是不可言说和不可命名的东西。一方面，实在界由物质世界构成，包括物理宇宙以及存在于其中的一切；另一方面，实在界是人的非存在、人的一切缺乏的象征。作为拉康的概念符号之一，实在界"作为人间文化的和语言的表现并非是为了直接表达世界中之事物，而是为了'暗示'人生存在之'本质'—— 物本体之真实"。① 但是，到哪里去寻求这种实在界？拉康常常在爱伦·坡、莎士比亚和乔伊斯的文本之中发现这种生存境界。如此可见，"实在界"可能是拉康的一种修辞用法，是一个滑动的能指符号，空灵而又飘逸。只有在对它的解释之中，或者说对它的散播之中，实在界才获得其意蕴。这就和德里达的解构观相趋近了。

心理分析学说对于德里达（Jacques Derrida，1930—2004）的解构思想，几乎起到了引擎对于汽车的作用。德里达认为，弗洛伊德对心理活动之无意识起源的考察，已经超越了神经病理学，而成为"书写语言学"（grammatology）了。一种书写的隐喻支配着弗洛伊德对人类心理结构的描述：弗洛伊德再现心灵事件的起源，就是开荒拓路，呼唤差异，留下踪迹。这样，弗洛伊德就通过心理分析表演了"书写戏剧"，从而对压抑书写的西方形而上学传统摆出了挑战姿态。② 德里达还将弗洛伊德、尼采和海德格尔相提并论，明确指出弗洛伊德对自我的批判是一种瓦解性的话语，导致了"结构概念的整个历史"的断裂。③ 最后，德里达明确地指出，弗洛伊德的理论已经将"延异"（differance）的各种不同含义捆绑在一起："差异""破裂""延宕""踪迹"等，都是无意识生产的基本要素，引起了"在场"的自我分裂，以及符号意义的统一体的瓦解。④

拉康将心理分析的重心从无意识转移到语言结构上，德里达则从弗洛伊德的文本之中读出了心灵活动的起源就是书写的表演。拉康认为无意识是语言的产物，德里达则暗示无意识生产就是书写活动。

---

① 李幼蒸：《形上逻辑和本体虚无——现代德法伦理学认识论研究》，211 页，北京，商务印书馆，2000。

② 德里达：《弗洛伊德与书写舞台》，见《书写与差异》，张宁译，362、372 页，北京，生活·读书·新知三联书店，2001。

③ 德里达：《人文科学话语中的结构、符号与游戏》，见《书写与差异》，张宁译，505～506 页，北京，生活·读书·新知三联书店，2001。

④ 德里达：《延异》，见汪民安、陈永国、马海良：《后现代性的哲学话语——从福柯到赛义德》，82～83 页，杭州，浙江人民出版社，2000。

基本内容

19 世纪美国作家爱伦·坡的《被窃的信》(*The Purloined Letter*)是文学历史上较早的推理故事(或者侦探故事)之一。1955 年,拉康在一次讲座中对《被窃的信》进行了创造性的解读。① 这篇小说的故事梗概是这样的:王后收到了一封暧昧的信,它的内容不得而知。就在她读信的时刻,国王进入了卧室。她便把已经启封了的信摊在桌子上,以"障眼法"蒙过了国王的眼睛。但在场的大臣看穿了这一切,便用"调包之计"将信窃走。因为国王在场,王后只能眼睁睁地看着大臣窃走了信,而不敢声张。王后命令探长寻找被窃的信。探长经多番努力却无功而返,只好求助于业余侦探杜宾。杜宾认为,大臣也会如法炮制地使用"障眼法",将信藏在明处。根据如此推理,杜宾从大臣官邸的壁炉架上的公文包中窃回了这封信。②

拉康对这个故事的解读是心理分析和结构主义珠联璧合的思想成果。首先,从心理分析角度看,拉康表明了如下见解。第一,书信是无意识的隐喻,是王后的缺乏之象征。这种缺乏激起了王后对"他者"的激情,这是一种权力主体的占有欲望。王后究竟缺乏什么呢?按照心理分析理论,她缺乏"阳物"(phallus)。如前所述,"阳物"并不等同于生殖器,它不是一个生理器官,而是一个绝对权力的符号,一种"超验的所指"。在这个故事中,"阳物"有如这封暧昧的信,成为王后的无意识欲望的象征。这种无意识欲望指向了王权、夫权和父权。第二,书信是一个漂浮的能指(fleeting signifier)。所谓"漂浮的能指",即同所指断裂、没有实在表征的能指符号,它不具有确定性,自由漂浮。在坡的故事中,被窃的信就是这种"漂浮的能指",它从一个场景转移到另一个场景,从一个人手上转移到另一个人手上,在一张复杂的主体关系网络中周旋。

其次,从结构主义的角度,拉康从这个故事之中辨认出了一种重复的场景。第一个场景发生在王后的卧室,出场人物是国王、王后和大臣,三者构成了代表实在界、想象界和象征界的三角形。其中,国王目空一切,对书信

---

① 拉康:《关于〈被窃的信〉的研讨会》,见《拉康选集》,褚孝泉译,1~56 页,上海,上海三联书店,2001。

② 坡的小说也被译为《被窃之信》,见奎恩:《爱伦·坡集 诗歌与故事(下)》,曹明伦译,北京,生活·读书·新知三联书店,1995。

视而不见，他代表了实在界的无能；王后自作聪明，沉湎于自恋性的幻觉中，她代表了想象界的脆弱；大臣则看透了国王的无能和王后的幻想，他代表着象征界的灵见。第二个场景发生在大臣的官邸，它是对第一个场景的重复。其中探长取代了国王的位置，他同样也是自恃侦探技术高超，却对所要搜寻之物视而不见，现在他代表了实在界的无能；大臣取代了王后的位置，他是诗人又是数学家，但他和傻瓜只有一步之遥，完全沉湎在自己的小伎俩中，代表了想象界的脆弱；杜宾则能洞悉一切秘密，一眼看穿了大臣的障眼法，找到了本该善藏的书信，他代表着象征界的灵见。通过两个场景的重复，主体颠覆和权力易位的地形图就清楚地呈现出来了（见图 7-1、图 7-2）。

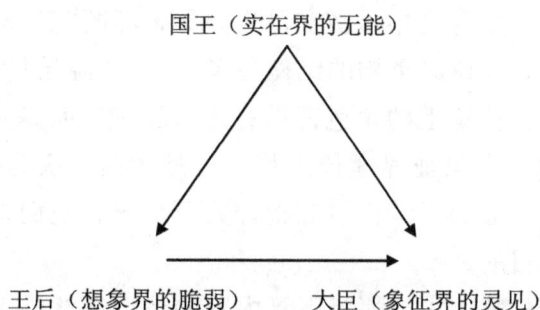

图 7-1

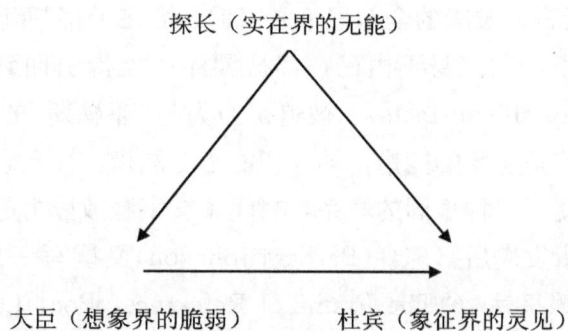

图 7-2

　　这里运用的三角结构及其重复模式，尽管遭遇了德里达等的质疑，但对于文学和艺术批评来说毕竟具有一定的合理性和可操作性，因而受到重视。拉康解读这篇小说的要点最后落在一个基本观念上：被窃的信所象征的能指及其漂浮运动就是意义所在。唯有寄寓在文本关系中，意义方可存活。而要从能指的漂浮之中劫夺出意义就必须有像杜宾侦探这样目光犀利的读者。

拓展讨论

拉康研讨爱伦·坡小说的文章一出，立即成为被解构的对象。在一篇题为"真理的转换站"的文章中，德里达首先肯定了拉康的"漂浮的能指"说，并将拉康引为自己的解构同道。但德里达对拉康的"心理三界"和"菲勒斯中心主义"展开了进一步的解构。

首先，《被窃的信》的关键是"文字"（écriture）而非"心理三界"所代表的三种视觉形式。小说中的王后将信（文字）传给大臣，大臣传给警长，警长传给杜宾，杜宾传给叙述人，叙述人传给读者。于是，文字的一切都被叙述过和解释过了。在叙述和解释之中，文字再生差异，不断"延异"，永远找不到目的地，总是在漂浮。在拉康重构的结构三场景中，"源始场景"被无休止地重复，每个处在象征界位置上的角色都没有占有真理，而是真理的转换站。在这个真理转换过程中，象征界虚位以待，先是大臣，次为警长，再为杜宾，后为拉康所取代，还会为后续读者和批评家所填充。他们将文字无限地散播开来，而文字终无目的。

其次，在拉康的解读中，那封不具内容的信，显然是王后"菲勒斯匮乏"的象征。于是，拉康沦落为一名"菲勒斯—逻各斯中心主义者"（phallogocentrism）。德里达断言，拉康的全部理论之宗旨，恰在于将"菲勒斯"确立为能指之极致。也就是说，我们身不由己，都被漂浮的能指引回到那个"最高的契约"（the contract of all contracts），被迫奋力去与"菲勒斯"的在场合一，而这个在场的"菲勒斯"是超验的能指，即一切能指之能指。[①]于是，拉康在菲勒斯与逻各斯之间确立了一种稳固的联系，封闭了文字释放能力的"闸口"。

德里达的文章发表后，琼森（Barbara Johnson）又撰写一文——《指涉的框架：坡、拉康、德里达》（"The Frame of Reference：Poe，Lacan，Derrida"），对德里达的解构展开了进一步的解构。琼森断定，德里达和拉康一样，不自觉地将自己放置在象征界，自以为具有获得真理的灵见，其实都落入指涉构

---

① Jacques Derrida，"Le facteur de la vérité," in *The Postcard：From Socrates to Freud and Beyond*，trans. with an Introduction and Additional Notes，by Alan Bass，Chicago and London，The University of Chicago Press，1987，pp. 411-476.

架当中，而堵死了文本散播的空间。①

批评家霍兰德（Norman Holland）从读者的精神动力学和阅读反应出发，撰写《寻回〈被窃的信〉》，对拉康的解读、德里达的解构进一步予以解构。霍兰德认为，拉康重构信件漂浮的场景，突出了一种"虚无境界"。德里达解构拉康，则证明了一种怀疑的律令。他提出交互批评模式，站在读者的立场上，要求文学批评更加接近文学反应，更加凸显人的活力。②

21世纪，数字技术崛起，人工智能成为文学、哲学和文化批评的重要反思对象。刘禾（Lydia H. Liu）发表论文《控制论阴影下的无意识——对拉康、坡和法国理论的再思考》（"The Cybernetic Unconscious：Rethinking Lacan，Poe，and French Theory"），提出通过反思拉康和法国理论，重读爱伦·坡，深入研究控制论的人类无意识。③

延伸阅读

1. 拉康：《拉康选集》，褚孝泉译，上海，上海三联书店，2001。该书汇集了拉康的主要论文，可一览"结构化精神分析""心理三界论""菲勒斯的意义"等主要观点，把握拉康思想的核心。

2. Jacques Lacan，*The Ethics of Psychoanalysis 1959-1960：The Seminar of Jacques Lacan*，Book Ⅶ，ed. Jacques-Alain Miller，trans. with notes by Dennis Porter，London and New York，Routledge，1992. 该书紧扣"物"的范畴，论述升华的难题，解释快乐的吊诡，解构悲剧的本质，呈现精神分析的悲剧之维。

---

① Barbara Johnson，"The Frame of Reference：Poe，Lacan，Derrida，" in *Yale French Studies*，1977，No. 55/56，Literature and Psychoanalysis. The Question of Reading：Otherwise (1977)，pp. 457-505.

② 霍兰德：《寻回〈被窃的信〉：作为个人交往活动的阅读》，见王逢振、盛宁、李自修：《最新西方文论选》，97～98页，桂林，漓江出版社，1991。

③ Lydia H. Liu，"The Cybernetic Unconscious：Rethinking Lacan，Poe，and French Theory，" in *Critical Inquiry*，Vol. 36，No. 2 (Winter 2010)，pp. 288-320.

8. "Homecoming/To Kindred Ones" (1943)
By Martin Heidegger

"HOMECOMING/TO KINDRED ONES"

1

Drinn in den Alpen ists noch helle Nacht und die Wolke,

Freudiges dichtend, sie dekt drinnen das gähnende Thal.

Dahin, dorthin toset und stürzt die scherzende Bergluft,

Schroff durch Tannen herab glänzet und schwindet ein Stral.

Langsam eilt und kämpft das freudigschauernde Chaos,

Jung an Gestalt, doch stark, feiert es liebenden Streit

Unter den Felsen, es gährt und wankt in den ewigen Schranken,

Denn bacchantischer zieht drinnen der Morgan herauf.

Denn es wächst unendlicher dort das Jahr und die heilgen

Stunden, die Tage, sie sind kühner geordnet, gemischt.

Dennoch merket die Zeit der Gewittervogel und zwischen

Bergen, hoch in der Luft weilt er und rufet den Tag.

Jezt auch wachet und schaut in der Tiefe drinnen das Dörflein,

Furchtlos, Hohem vertraut, unter den Gipfeln hinauf.

Wachstum ahnend, denn schon, wie Blize, fallen die alten

Wasserquellen, der Grund unter den Stürzenden dampft,

Echo tönet umher, und die unermessliche Werkstatt

Reget bei Tag und Nacht, Gaaben versendend, den Arm.

2

Ruhig glänzen indess die silbernen Höhen darüber,

Voll mit Rosen ist schon droben der leuchtende Schnee.

Und noch höher hinauf wohnt über dem Lichte der reine
Seelige Gott vom Spiel heiliger Stralen erfreut.
Stille wohnt er allein, und hell erscheinet sein Antliz,
Der ätherische scheint Leben zu geben geneigt,
Freude zu schaffen, mit uns, wie oft, wenn, kundig des Maases,
Kundig der Athmenden auch zögernd und schonend der Gott
Wohlgediegenes Glük den Städten und Häussern und milde
Reegen, zu öffnen das Land, brütende Wolken, und euch,
Trauteste Lüfte dann, euch, sanfte Frühlinge, sendet,
Und mit langsamer Hand Traurige wieder erfreut,
Wenn er die Zeiten erneut, der Schöpferische, die stillen
Herzen der alternden Menschen erfrischt und ergreifft,
Und hinab in die Tiefe wirkt, und öffnet und aufhellt,
Wie ers liebet, und jezt wieder ein Leben beginnt,
Anmuth blühet, wie einst, und gegenwärtiger Geist kömmt,
Und ein freudiger Muth wieder die Fittige schwellt.

3

Vieles sprach ich zu ihm, denn, was auch Dichtende sinnen
Oder singen, es gilt meistens den Engeln und ihm;
Vieles bat ich, zu lieb dem Vaterlande, damit nicht
Ungebeten uns einst plözlich befiele der Geist;
Vieles für euch auch, die im Vaterlande besorgt sind,
Denen der heilige Dank lächelnd die Flüchtlinge bringt,
Landesleute! für euch, indessen wiegte der See mich,
Und der Ruderer sass ruhig und lobte die Fahrt.
Weit in des Sees Ebene wars Ein freudiges Wallen
Unter den Seegeln und jezt blühet und hellet die Stadt
Dort in der Frühe sich auf, wohl her von schattigen Alpen
Kommt geleitet und ruht nun in dem Hafen das Schiff.
Warm ist das Ufer hier und freundlich offene Thale,
Schön von Pfaden erhellt, grünen und schimmern mich an.

Gärten stehen gesellt und die glänzende Knospe beginnt schon,

Und des Vogels Gesang ladet den Wanderer ein.

Alles scheinet vertraut, der vorübereilende Gruss auch

Scheint von Freunden, es scheint jegliche Miene verwandt.

4

Freilich wohl! das Geburtsland ists, der Boden der Heimath,

Was du suchest, es ist nahe, begegnet dir schon.

Und umsonst nicht steht, wie ein Sohn, am wellenumrauschten

Thor' und siehet und sucht liebende Nahmen für dich,

Mit Gesang ein wandernder Mann, glükseeliges Lindau!

Eine der gastlichen Pforten des Landes ist diss,

Reizend hinauszugehn in die vielversprechende Ferne,

Dort, wo die Wunder sind, dort, wo das göttliche Wild,

Hoch in die Ebnen herab der Rhein die verwegene Bahn bricht,

Und aus Felsen hervor ziehet das jauchzende Thal,

Dort hinein, durchs helle Gebirg, nach Komo zu wandern,

Oder hinab, wie der Tag wandelt, den offenen See;

Aber reizender mir bist du, geweihete Pforte!

Heimzugehn, wo bekannt blühende Wege mir sind,

Dort zu besuchen das Land und die schönen Thale des Nekars,

Und die Wälder, das Grün heiliger Bäume, wo gern

Sich die Eiche gesellt mit stillen Birken und Buchen,

Und in Bergen ein Ort freundlich gefangen mich nimmt.

5

Dort empfangen sie mich. O Stimme der Stadt, der Mutter!

O du triffest, du regst Langegelerntes mir auf!

Dennoch sind sie es noch! noch blühet die Sonn' und die Freud' euch,

O ihr Liebsten! und fast heller im Auge, wie sonst.

Ja! das Alte noch ists! Es gedeihet und reifet, doch keines

Was da lebet und liebt, lässet die Treue zurük.

Aber das Beste, der Fund, der unter des heiligen Friedens

Bogen lieget, er ist Jungen und Alten gespart.

Thörig red ich. Es ist die Freude. Doch morgen und künftig

Wenn wir gehen und schaun draussen das lebende Feld,

Unter den Blüthen des Baums, in den Feiertagen des Frühlings

Red' und hoff' ich mit euch vieles, ihr Lieben! davon.

Vieles hab' ich gehört von grossen Vater und habe

Lange geschwiegen von ihm, welcher die wandernde Zeit

Droben in Höhen erfrischt und waltet über Gebirgen,

Der gewährhet uns bald himmlische Gaaben und ruft

Hellern Gesang und schikt viel gute Geister. O säumt nicht,

Kommt, Erhaltenden ihr! Engel des Jahres! und ihr,

6

Engel des Hausses, kommt! in die Adern alle des Lebens,

Alle freuend zugleich, theile das Himmlische sich!

Adle! verjünge! damit nichts Menschlichgutes, damit nicht

Eine Stunde des Tags ohne die Frohen und auch

Solche Freude, wie jezt, wenn Liebende wieder sich finden,

Wie es gehört fur sie, schiklich geheiliget sei.

Wenn wir seegnen das Mahl, wen darf ich nennen und wenn wir

Ruhn von Leben des Tags, saget, wie bring' ich den Dank?

Nenn' ich den Hohen dabei? Unschikliches liebet ein Gott nicht,

Ihn zu fassen, ist fast unsere Freude zu klein.

Schweigen müssen wir oft; es fehlen heilige Nahmen,

Herzen schlagen und doch bleibet die Rede zurük?

Aber ein Saitenspiel leiht jeder Stunde die Töne,

Und erfreuet vieleicht Himmlische, welche sich nahn.

Das bereitet und so ist auch beinahe die Sorge

Schon befriediget, die unter das Freudige kam.

Sorgen, wie diese, muss, gern oder nicht, in der Seele

Tragen ein Sänger und oft, aber die anderen nicht.

1

Within the Alps it is still bright night and the cloud,

Composing poems full of joy, covers the yawning valley within.

This way, that way, roars and rushes the playful mountain breeze,

Steep down through the fir trees a ray of light gleams and vanishes.

Chaos, trembling with joy, slowly hurries and struggles,

Young in form, yet strong, it celebrates loving strife

Amidst the rocks, it seethes and shakes in its eternal bounds,

For more bacchantically morning rises within.

For the year grows more endlessly there and the holy

Hours, the days, are more boldly ordered and mingled.

Yet the bird of the thunderstorm notes the time and between

Mountains, high in the air he hovers and calls out the day.

Now in the depths within, the little village also awakens and

Fearless, familiar with the high, looks up from under the peaks.

Divining growth, for already, like lightning flashes, the ancient

Waterfalls crash, the ground steaming beneath the falls,

Echo resounds all about, and the immeasurable workshop,

Dispensing gifts, actively moves its arm by day and night.

2

Meanwhile the silvery heights gleam peacefully above,

Up there the luminous snow is already full of roses.

And still higher up, above the light, dwells the pure

Blissful god rejoicing in the play of holy rays.

Silently he dwells alone, and brightly shines his countenance,

The aetherial one seems inclined to give life

To create joy, with us, as often, when, knowing the measure,

Also knowing those who breathe, hesitant and sparing, the god

Sends true good fortune to towns and houses and gentle

Rain to open the land, brooding clouds, and then you,

Dearest breezes, you gentle springtimes,

And with patient hand brings joy again to those who mourn,

When he renews the seasons, the creative one, refreshes

And seizes the silent hearts of aging men,

And works down to the depths, and opens and brightens up,

As he loves to do, and now once again a life begins,

Grace blooms, as once, and present spirit comes,

And a joyous courage spreads its wings once more.

3

Much I spoke to him, for whatever poets meditate

Or sing, it mostly concerns the angels and him;

Much I asked for, for love of the fatherland, lest

Unbidden one day the spirit might suddenly fall upon us;

Much also for you, who have cares in the fatherland,

To whom holy thanks, smiling, brings the fugitives,

Countrymen! for you, meanwhile the lake rocked me,

And the boatman sat calmly and praised the journey.

Far out on the surface of the lake was One joyous swell

Beneath the sails, and now the town blooms and brightens

There in the dawn, and the boat is safely guided

From the shady Alps and now rests in the harbor.

Warm is the shore here and friendly the open valleys,

Beautifully lit up with paths, gleam verdantly toward me.

Gardens stand together and already the glistening bud is beginning,

And the bird's song invites the wanderer.

All seems familiar, even the hurried greetings

Seem those of friends, every face seems a kindred one.

4

But of course! It is the land of your birth, the soil of your homeland,

What you seek, it is near, already comes to meet you.

And not in vain does he stand, like a son, at the wave-washed
Gate, and sees and seeks loving names for you,
With his song, a wandering man, blessed Lindau!
This is one of the land's hospitable portals,
Enticing us to go out into the much-promising distance,
There, where the wonders are, there, where the divine wild game,
High up the Rhine breaks his daring path down to the plains,
And forth from the rocks the jubilant valley emerges,
In there, through bright mountains, to wander to Como,
Or down, as the day changes, to the open lake;
But you are more enticing to me, you consecrated portal!
To go home, where the blossoming paths are known to me,
There to visit the land and the beautiful valleys of the Neckar,
And the forests, the green of holy trees, where the oak
Likes to stand amidst silent birches and beeches,
And in the mountains a place, friendly, takes me captive.

5

There they welcome me. O voice of the town, of my mother!
O you touch me, you stir up what I learned long ago!
Yet they are still the same! Still the sun and joy blossom for you,
O you dearest ones! And almost more brightly in your eyes than before.
Yes! Old things are still the same! They thrive and ripen, yet nothing
Which lives and loves there abandons its faithfulness.
But the best, the real find, which lies beneath the rainbow
Of holy peace, is reserved for young and old.
I talk like a fool. It is joy. Yet tomorrow and in the future
When we go outside and look at the living fields.
Beneath the tree's blossoms, in the holidays of spring,
Much shall I talk and hope with you about this, dear ones!
Much have I heard about the great father and have
Long kept silent about him, who refreshes wandering time

In the heights above, and reigns over mountain ranges,
Who will soon grant us heavenly gifts and call
For brighter song and send many good spirits. O do not delay,
Come, you preservers! Angels of the year, and you.

6

Angels of the house, come! Into all the veins of life,
Rejoicing all at once, let the heavenly share itself!
Ennoble! Renew! So that nothing that's humanly good, so that not a
Single hour of the day may be without the joyful ones and that also
Such joy, as now, when lovers are reunited,
As it should be, may be fittingly hallowed.
When we bless the meal, whom shall I name and when we
Rest from the life of day, tell me, how shall I give thanks?
Shall I name the high one then? A god does not love what is unfitting,
To grasp him, our joy is almost too small.
Often we must be silent; holy names are lacking,
Hearts beat and yet talk holds back?
But string-music lends its tones to every hour,
And perhaps brings joy to the heavenly who draw near.
This makes ready, and care too will almost be
Appeased, which came into our joy.
Cares like these, whether he likes it or not, a singer
Must bear in his soul, and often, but the others not.

> To know little, but of joy much
> Is given to mortals…
>
> (IV, 240)

According to its title, Hölderlin's poem speaks of homecoming. This makes us think of arrival on one's native soil, and meeting one's countrymen in the homeland. The poem tells of a trip across the lake "from the shady Alps" to

Lindau. In the spring of 1801, Hölderlin, then a private tutor, left the Thurgau village of Hauptwil near Constance and traveled back across Lake Constance to his Swabian homeland. So the poem "Homecoming" might represent a piece of poetry about a joyful trip home. Yet the last stanza, whose tone is set by the word "care," suggests nothing of the joyful mood of someone who returns home care-free. The last word of the poem is an abrupt "not." The first stanza, which describes the Alpine mountains, stands directly before us as though it too were a mountain range consisting of verses. It reveals nothing of the pleasures suggestive of home. The "echo" of the "immeasurable workshop" of what is rather unhomelike "resounds all about." When stanzas such as these enclose it, this "homecoming" is hardly accomplished just by an arrival on the shore of the "land of one's birth." Indeed, even the arrival on the home shore is already strange:

> All seems familiar, even the hurried greetings
> Seem those of friends, every face seems a kindred one.

The people and things of the homeland seem pleasantly familiar. Yet they are not so. They have shut away what is most proper to them. That is why the homeland addresses a line to the newcomer immediately upon his arrival:

> What you seek, it is near, already comes to meet you.

The one returning home has not yet reached his homeland simply by arriving there. And so the homeland is "difficult to win, what is self-reserved" ("The Journey," IV, 170). For that reason the one who arrives is still seeking something. What is sought, however, does come to meet him. It is near. But that which is sought is not yet found if "find" means to appropriate what is found, make it one's own, and to live with it as though it were a possession.

> But the best, the real find, which lies beneath the rainbow
> Of holy peace, is reserved for young and old.

Hölderlin later changed a second fair copy of this poem, and instead of "but the best, the real find … ," he wrote the words "But the treasure, the German … is still reserved. " All that is most unique to the homeland was prepared long ago, and apportioned to those who lived in the land of one's birth. The homeland's own special nature was a gift of destiny, or what we today call history. Nevertheless, this destiny has not yet conveyed what is most distinct about it. That is still held back. And that is why whatever pertains to this destiny itself, what is becoming to it, has yet to be found. What has been granted, and yet is still denied, is, we say, reserved. And so this real find that we meet is still reserved and still being sought. Why? Because those who "have cares in the fatherland" are not yet ready to receive the homeland's very own peculiar character, "the German," as their own possession. Therefore what constitutes the homecoming is that the countrymen must first become at home in the still withheld essence of their homeland—indeed; even prior to this, that the "dear ones" at home must first learn how to become at home. For this it is necessary to know in advance what is the homeland's own specific nature and what is best in it. But how should we ever find this, unless a seeker is there for us, and the sought-for essence of the homeland shows itself to him?

What you seek, it is near, already comes to meet you.

The friendly openness of the homeland, and everything there that is brightened up, and glows and gleams, and casts forth its light, comes forth in one single gracious appearance upon one's arrival at the door of the homeland. The door is

> Enticing to go out into the much-promising distance
> … …
> But you are more enticing (to the poet) …
> To go home, where the blossoming paths are known to me,
> There to visit the land and the beautiful valleys of the Neckar
> And the forests, the green of holy trees, where the oak

Likes to stand amidst silent birches and beeches,
And in the mountains a place, friendly, takes me captive.

What should we call the silent shining appearance in which everything—things and persons alike—send their greeting to the seeker? What is most inviting in the homeland, and what comes to meet him half-way, is called "full of joy," the joyful. This name outshines all others in the entire poem "Homecoming." The second stanza abounds with references to the "joyful" and to "joy," almost as much as in the last stanza. The words are found less frequently in the other stanzas. They are missing only in the fourth stanza, the one which offers an immediate vision of the joyful. But the joyful is named at the very start of the poem in connection with the composition of poetry:

Within the Alps it is still bright night and the cloud,
Composing poems full of joy, covers the yawning valley within.

Joyfulness is composed into a poem. The joyful is tuned by joy into joy. In this way it is what is rejoiced in, and equally what rejoices. And this again can bring joy to others. So the joyful is at the same time that which brings joy. The cloud "within the Alps" drifts upward toward the "silvery heights." It opens itself up to the lofty brightness of the heavens, while at the same time it "covers" "the yawning valley." The cloud lets itself be seen from the open brightness. The cloud composes poetry. Because it looks straight into that which gazes upon it in return, its poem is not idly invented or contrived. To compose is to find. Accordingly, the cloud must reach out beyond itself toward something other than itself. It does not generate the theme of its poem. The theme does not come out of the cloud. It comes over the cloud, as something that the cloud awaits. The cloud waits in an open brightness that gladdens the waiting. The cloud is cheered in this gladness. What it composes, the joyful, is gaiety. We also call it the cheerful, but from now on we have to use this word in a strict sense: what has been cleared and brightened up. What has been cleared in this way has had a space freely made for it, illuminated and put in order. Only gaiety, that which has been cleared and brightened up in this manner, is able to place everything in its proper place. The joyful has its being in the gaiety that brightens. But gaiety itself appears only in that which gives joy, that which delights. As this brightening makes everything clear, gaiety grants to each thing its essential space, where everything, according to its kind, belongs, in order to stand there in the brightness of gaiety, like a quiet light, contented in its own being. The rejoicing shines forth toward the homecoming poet,

> ... where the oak
>
> Likes to stand amidst silent birches and beeches,
>
> And in the mountains a place, friendly, takes me captive.

Near is the gentle spell of well-known things and their simple relations. But nearer still and becoming ever nearer, though less apparent than birches and mountains and therefore mostly overlooked and passed by, is the gaiety itself in which people and things appear. Gaiety lingers in its inconspicuous appearance. It demands nothing for itself, is not an object, and nevertheless it is not "nothing." In the joyful, however, which first comes to meet the poet, the greeting of that which brightens already holds sway. Those who offer the greeting of gaiety are the messengers, ἄγγελοι, the "angels." That is why the poet, while greeting what is joyful in the homeland and comes to meet him, invokes in "Homecoming" the "angels of the house" and the "angels of the year."

Here "the house" means the space opened up for a people as a place in which they can be "at home," and thereby fulfill their proper destiny. This space is bestowed by the inviolate earth. The earth houses the peoples in their historical space. The earth brightens up "the house." Thus the brightening earth is the first angel "of the house."

"The year" houses those times that we call the seasons. In the "mingled" play of fiery brightness and frosty darkness which the seasons grant, things blossom and close up again. The seasons "of the year" bestow upon man, in the changes of gaiety, the stay which has been allotted for his historical sojourn in the "house." "The year" extends its greeting in the play of light. The brightening light is the first "angel of the year. "

Both, earth and light, the "angels of the house," and "the angels of the year," are called "preservers," because as the greeting ones they bring to light the gaiety in whose clarity the "nature" of things and people is safely preserved. What remains preserved, safe and sound, is "homelike" in its essence. The messengers' greeting comes out of the gaiety that allows everything to be at home. The granting of this feeling of being-at-home is the essence of the homeland. It is already approaching—namely, in the joyful, where gaiety first comes to appearance.

Yet what is already approaching still remains what is sought. Since the joyful is only encountered where a composer of poems comes to greet it, so too the angels, messengers of gaiety, can appear only if there are poets. That is why in the poem "Homecoming," we find this verse:

> … for whatever poets meditate,
> Or sing, it mostly concerns the angels and him.

The song of the poetic word concerns "mostly the angels," because as the messengers of gaiety, they are the first "who draw near. " "And him"—the poetic saying is intended for "him. " The "and" here actually signifies "and above all"—"him. "

Who is He? If the poesis concerns "him" above all, and if the poesis composes the joyful, then He dwells within the most joyful. But what is this and where is this?

The cloud, "composing poems full of joy," gives us the sign. The cloud hovers between the peaks of the Alps, and covers the mountain ravines, down into whose unlit depths plunges the brightening ray of light. That is why the young Chaos "celebrates" "loving strife" there "amidst the rocks," and "celebrates" it "trembling with joy. " But the cloud, "a hill of the heavens" (IV, 71), dreams its way between the heights and into the joyful. While composing, the cloud points upward toward gaiety.

Meanwhile, the silvery heights gleam peacefully above,
Up there the luminous snow is already full of roses.
And still higher up, above the light, dwells the pure
Blissful god rejoicing in the play of holy rays.

In the Alps there comes to pass an increasingly tranquil self-surmounting of the high up to the highest. The peaks of the mountain range, which is the highest messenger of the earth, emerge into the light to meet the "angel of the year." That is why they are called "the peaks of time." Yet still higher up, above the light, gaiety itself opens up into its pure brightening, without which even the light would never be allowed its brightness. What is highest, "above the light," is the very opening for any stream of light. This pure opening which first "imparts," that is, grants, the open to every "space" and to every "temporal space," we call gaiety [*die Heitere*] according to an old word of our mother tongue. At one and the same time, it is the clarity (*claritas*) in whose brightness everything clear rests, and the grandeur (*serenitas*) in whose strength everythinghigh stands, and the merriment (*hilaritas*) in whose play everything liberated sways. Gaiety preserves and holds everything within what is safe and sound. Gaiety heals fundamentally. It is the holy. "The highest" and "the holy" are the same for the poet: gaiety. As the source for everything joyful, it remains the most joyful, and it lets the pure brightening come to pass. Here in the highest dwells "the high one," who is who he is insofar as he has re-joiced "in the play of holy rays": *the joyful one* [*der Freudige*]. If He is one of us, he seems inclined "to create joy, with us." Since his being is the brightening, "he loves" "to open up" and "to illuminate." Through a clear gaiety, he "opens" things into the rejoicing of their presence. Through a merry gaiety, he illuminates the heart of men, so that they may open their hearts to what is genuine in their fields, towns, and houses. Through a grand gaiety, he first lets the dark depth gape open in its illumination. What would depth be without lighting?

Even the "mourning ones" are gladdened again by "the joyful one," although "with a patient hand." He does not take away their mourning, but he changes it by letting those who mourn divine that mourning itself only springs from "old joys." The joyful one is the "father" of all that rejoices. He, who dwells in gaiety, only now allows himself to be named after his dwelling place. The high one is called "aether," Αἰθήρ. The wafting "air" and the lightening "light" and the "earth" which blossoms with them are the "three in one," in which gaiety brightens up and lets the joyful emerge and greet men in joy.

Yet how does gaiety come down from its height to men? The joyful one and the joyful messengers of the brightening, father aether, and the angel of the house (the earth), and the angel of the year (light), cannot accomplish anything by themselves. Indeed, among all those who dwell within the orbit of gaiety, these three-in-one are loved the most by those who rejoice; and yet—nevertheless—in their "essence," that is to say, in their brightening, the three would have become virtually exhausted if it were not for the poets who, occasionally, have come composing, and approaching near to the joyful one because they belong to him. That is why the elegy "The Wanderer," whose title already testifies to its relation to the later elegy "Homecoming," says (IV 105ff.):

> And so I am alone. But you, above the clouds,
> Father of the fatherland! Mighty aether! And you,
> Earth and Light! You three in one, who reign and love,
> Eternal gods! My bonds with you shall never break.
> Parting with you, with you too have I wandered,
> You, O joyous ones, more experienced now, I bring you back.

In "The Journey," earth and light, the angels of the house and of the year, are called "gods." And in the first fair copy of the elegy "Homecoming," Hölderlin still said "gods of the year" and "gods of the house." Likewise, in the first fair copy of the last stanza of "Homecoming" (line 94), instead of "without the happy ones," it reads: "without the gods." In the later version, then, have the gods been reduced to mere angels? Or have angels also been introduced along with the gods? Neither—but now with the name "angels" the being of those who were previously called "gods" is said more purely. For the gods are the brightening ones, whose brightening offers the greeting sent by gaiety. Gaiety is the essential ground of the greeting, that is, of the angelic, in which the very being of the gods consists. By using the word "gods" sparingly, and hesitating to say the name, the poet has brought to light the proper element of the gods, that they are the greeting ones through whom gaiety extends its offering.

The returning wanderer has become more experienced in the being of the gods, that is, of the joyful ones.

What you seek, it is near, already comes to meet you.

The poet has a clearer view of gaiety. The joyful which comes to meet him in the sight of the homeland he now sees as that which is brightened up only by the most joyful and can remain near only by coming from this alone. But now if "whatever poets meditate or sing" is above all intended for "him," the high father aether, then must not the poet who seeks the most joyful take up his stay where the joyful ones dwell, namely (according to the first stanza of the hymn "The Rhine" [IV, 172]), the place of the

> ... Steps of the Alpine range,
> Which I call the divinely built,
> Fortress of the heavenly ones,
> As in ancient belief but where
> Much still decided in secret
> Reaches men; ... ?

But now the "homecoming" manifestly leads the poet away from the "Alpine range" and over the waters of the lake to the shore of his native country. His sojourn "beneath the Alps," the nearness to the most joyful, is now sacrificed precisely for the return home. Even stranger is the fact that still above the waters which lead the poet away from the Alpine range, beneath the winds of the vessel that bears him away, the joyful appears:

Far out on the surface of the lake was One joyous swell

Beneath the sails…

Joyfulness starts to bloom upon the farewell to the "fortress of the heavenly ones." If we represent Lake Constance, which is also called "the Swabian Sea," in a geographic or tourist-like or even folkloric sense, then we mean the lake which lies between the Alps and the upper Danube, through which the young Rhine also flows. Yet we would still be thinking of this water unpoetically. How much longer shall we continue to do so? How much longer are we still going to suppose that there is first of all a nature in itself and then a landscape for itself which with the help of "poetic experiences" becomes mythically colored? How much longer are we going to prevent ourselves from experiencing beings as beings? How long will Germans continue to ignore the words which Hölderlin sang in the first stanza of the "Patmos" hymn (IV, 199 and 227)?

Near and

Hard to grasp is the god.

But where the danger is,

There also grows our saving grace.

In the darkness dwell

The eagles and fearless over

The abyss walk the sons of the Alps

On lightly built bridges.

Therefore, since amassed all around are

The peaks of time,

And the dearest dwell near, languishing on

Mountains farthest apart,

Thus give us innocent water,

O give us wings, most faithful in heart

To cross over and to return.

The poet must "cross over" to the "Alpine range"; but "most faithful in heart" means that out of faithfulness to his homeland, he will return to it, where according to the words of "Homecoming," what is sought "is near." Therefore, the nearness to the most joyful, and that means nearness to the origin of all that is joyful, cannot be found there "beneath the Alps." The nearness to the origin, therefore, is something quite mysterious. The Swabian homeland, separated from the Alpine range, must be the very place of nearness to the origin. Yes, so it is. The first stanzas of the hymn "The Journey" say so. Hölderlin published this hymn in 1802, together with the elegy "Homecoming," in an issue of the almanac *Flora*. This enigmatic hymn begins by invoking the homeland. The poet deliberately gives it the old name "Suevien." He thereby names the oldest, most proper, still concealed essence of the homeland—which was already prepared from the beginning (IV, 167).

The hymn "The Journey" begins:

> Blissful Suevien, my mother,
> You too, like the more shining, your sister
> Lombardy on the other side,
> Traversed by a hundred brooks!
> And trees enough, white-flowering and reddish,
> And darker ones, wild, full of deeply greening foliage,
> And the Alpine range of Switzerland, too, casts its shade
> On you, the neighboring; for near the hearth of the house
> You dwell, and hear how within,
> From silver vessels of sacrifice
> The source murmurs, poured out
> By pure hands, when touched
>
> By warm rays
> Crystalline ice and overturned
> By gently quickening light
> The snowy summit floods the earth

With purest water. That is why
Faithfulness is inborn in you. For whatever dwells
Near the origin is loathe to leave the place.
And your children, the towns
By the distantly glimmering lake,
By the Neckar's willows, by the Rhine,
They all believe there could be
No better place to dwell.

Suevien, the mother, dwells near "the hearth of the house." The hearth watches over the ever-reserved glow of the fire, which, when it bursts into flame, gives air and light to gaiety. Around the fire of the hearth is the workshop, where what is decided in secret is forged. The "hearth of the house," that is, of the maternal earth, is the origin of that brightening, whose light pours forth in streams over the earth. Suevien dwells near the origin. This nearness is mentioned twice. The homeland itself dwells near. It is the place of nearness to the hearth and to the origin. Suevien, the mother's voice, points toward the essence of the fatherland. It is in this nearness to the origin that the neighborhood to the most joyful is grounded. What is most characteristic of the homeland, what is best in it, consists solely in its being this nearness to the origin—and nothing else besides this. That is why in this homeland, too, faithfulness to the origin is inborn. That is why anyone who has to, is loathe to leave this place of nearness. But now, if the homeland's being a place of nearness to the most joyful is what is most unique about it, what, then, is homecoming?

Homecoming is the return to the nearness to the origin.

Only he can return home who previously, and perhaps for a long time, has wandered as a traveler and borne upon himself the burden of the journey upon his shoulders, and has crossed over into the origin, so that there he might experience what that is which was to be sought, in order then, as the seeker, to come back more experienced.

What you seek, it is near, already comes to meet you.

The nearness that now prevails lets what is near be near, and yet at the same time lets it remain what is sought, and thus not near. We usually understand nearness as the smallest possible measurement of the distance between two places. Now, on the contrary, the essence of nearness appears to be that it brings near that which is near, yet keeping it at a distance. This nearness to the origin is a mystery.

But now, if homecoming signifies becoming at home in nearness to the origin, then must not the return home consist first of all, and perhaps for a long time, in knowing the mystery of this nearness, or even prior to this, in learning to know it? Yet we never know a mystery by unveiling or analyzing it to death, but only in such a way that we preserve the mystery *as* mystery. But how can we preserve it—this mystery of nearness—without our knowing it? For the sake of this knowledge there must always be one who first returns home and says the mystery again and again:

> But the best, the real find, which lies beneath the rainbow
> Of holy peace, is reserved for young and old.

"The treasure," which is most proper to the homeland, "the German," is reserved. The nearness to the origin is a nearness which still holds something back in reserve. It withholds the most joyful. It preserves and saves it for those who are coming; but this nearness does not take away the most joyful, it only lets it appear precisely as saved. In the essence of nearness there comes to pass a concealed reserving. That it reserves the near is the secret of the nearness to the most joyful. The poet knows that when he calls the reserved "the real find," that is, something he has found, he says something that runs counter to common sense. To say that something is near while it remains distant means, after all, either violating a fundamental rule of ordinary thought, the principle of contradiction, or else playing with empty words, or else making an outrageous statement. That is why the poet, almost as soon as he has brought himself to say his words about the mystery of the reserving nearness, interrupts himself:

I talk like a fool.

But he talks nevertheless. The poet must talk, for

It is joy.

Is it just any indefinite joy over something or other, or is it the joy which is joy only because in it the essence of all joy unfolds itself? What is joy? The original essence of joy is learning to become at home within a nearness to the origin. For in this nearness there draws near in greeting that brightening in which gaiety appears. The poet comes home by entering into nearness to the origin. He enters into this nearness by saying the mystery of the nearness to the near. He says it insofar as he composes poems full of joy, that is, by putting the most joyful into a poem. Poesis does not merely bring joy to the poet, but rather it *is* the joy, the brightening, because it is in poesis first of all that the homecoming takes place. The elegy "Homecoming" is not a poem about homecoming; rather, the elegy, the poetic activity which it is, is the homecoming itself and still it comes to pass as long as its words ring like a bell in the language of the German people. Poesis means to be in the joy which preserves in words the mystery of nearness to the most joyful. Joy is *the joy* of the poet, as he puts it when he says "our joy" (line 100). The poetic joy is the knowledge that in everything joyful, which already comes to meet us, the joyful greets us while reserving itself. In order therefore that the reserving nearness to the most joyful may remain protected, the poetic word must take care not to hasten by or to lose that which sends its greeting out of the joyful, which sends its greeting as the self-reserving. Thus it is that, since care must be taken to protect the self-reserving nearness of the most joyful, care enters into the joyful.

Therefore, the joy of the poet is in truth the care of the singer, whose singing protects the most joyful as the reserved, and lets what is sought be near in its reserving nearness.

But now that care has entered into the most joyful, how then must the poet say the most joyful? At the time of the elegy "Homecoming" and the hymn

"The Journey," Hölderlin noted in an "epigram" how the song of the most joyful, i. e. , of the reserved, how therefore the "German Song" should be sung; the epigram bears the title "Sophocles" and reads (IV, 3):

> Many have sought in vain to joyfully say the most joyful,
> Here at last it is expressed to me, here in mourning.

Now we know why, at the time when he returned home to the homeland, to the place of the reserving nearness to the origin, the poet had to translate "The Tragedies of Sophocles." Separated from mere sadness by an abyss, mourning is the joy which is brightened up for the most joyful, insofar as it still reserves itself and hesitates. From where else could come the far-reaching inner light of mourning, if in its concealed ground, it were not a joy about the most joyful?

Hölderlin's poetic dialogtue with Sophocles in his "Translations" and "Commentaries" does indeed belong to the poetic homecoming, but it does not exhaust its full meaning. That is why the dedication with which Hölderlin launched his translation of "The Tragedies of Sophocles," closes with the confession (V, 91):

> For the rest, I wish, if there is time, to sing of
> the parents of our princes, their thrones and the
> angels of the holy fatherland.

"For the rest," so read the timid words for "in truth." For now and in the future the song concerns "mostly the angels and him." The high one, the one who inhabits the gaiety of the holy, is most of all the one who draws near within the reserving nearness, where the reserving joy of the poet has become at home. But

> To grasp him our joy is almost too small.

"To grasp" means to name the high one himself. To name poetically means to let the high one himself appear in words, not merely to say his dwelling-place, gaiety, the holy, not merely to name him only with respect to his dwelling-place. To name him himself, even mourning joy will not yet suffice for that, even though it abides in a fitting nearness to the high one.

Indeed, at times "the holy" can be named and the word spoken out of its brightening light. But these "holy" words are not naming "names":

> ... holy names are lacking.

To say who He himself is who dwells in the holy, and in saying this to let him appear as himself—for this the naming word is lacking. This is why poetic "singing," because it lacks the genuine, naming word, still remains a song without words—"lyre-music." To be sure, the "song" of the stringplayer follows the high one everywhere. The "soul" of the singer does indeed glance into gaiety, but the singer does not see the high one himself. The singer is blind. In the poem "The Blind Singer," which is prefaced by a line from Sophocles, Hölderlin says (IV, 58):

> After him, O my strings! With him lives
> My song, and as the source follows the stream,
> There where he thinks, there I must go and
> Follow the sure one on the stray path.

"Lyre-music"—this is the most timid name for the hesitant singing of the singer who cares:

> But lyre-music lends to each hour its tones,
> And perhaps gladdens the heavenly ones, who draw near.
> This makes ready...

To prepare joyfully for the greeting messengers, who bring the greeting of the still-reserved treasure, is to prepare for the fitting nearness for their approach—this is what determines the vocation of the home-coming poet. The holy does indeed appear. But the god remains distant. The time of the reserved discovery is the age when the god is absent. The "absence" of the god is the ground for the lack of "holy names." However, since the find is near, although in a reserved manner, the absent god extends his greeting in the nearing of the heavenly ones. Thereby "god's absence" is also not a deficiency. Therefore, the countrymen, too, may not try to make themselves a god by cunning, and thus eliminate by force the presumed deficiency. But they must also not comfort themselves by merely calling on an accustomed god. True, on such paths the presence of the absence would go unnoticed. But if the nearness were not determined by the absence, and thus were not a reserving nearness, the precious find could not be near in the way in which it is near. Thus for the poet's care there is only one possibility: without fear of appearing godless, he must remain near to the god's absence, and wait long enough in this prepared nearness to the absence till out of the nearness to the absent god there is granted an originative word to name the high one.

In the same annual in which the elegy "Homecoming" and the hymn "The Journey" appeared, Hölderlin also published a poem entitled "The Poet's Vocation." This poem culminates in the stanza (IV, 147):

> But fearless man remains, as he must,
> Alone before God, simplicity protects him,
> And he needs no weapons and no
> Cunning, till God's absence helps.

The poet's vocation is homecoming, by which the homeland is first prepared as the land of the nearness to the origin. To preserve the mystery of the reserving nearness to the most joyful, and thus to unfold it while preserving it, that is the care of homecoming. That is why the poem ends with the words:

> Cares like these, whether he likes it or not, a singer

Must bear in his soul, and often, but the others not.

Who are "the others" to whom the abrupt "not" is spoken? The poem which closes in this way begins with the ambiguous dedication "To Kindred Ones." But why should the "homecoming" first be spoken to the countrymen, who have been in the homeland forever? The homecoming poet is met by the hurried greeting of his countrymen. They *seem* to be kindred to him, but they are not yet so—i. e. , not related to him, the poet. But assuming that the "others" named at the end are those who are first to become the poet's kindred ones, why does the poet explicitly exclude them from the singer's care?

The abrupt "not" does indeed release "the others" from the care of the poetic saying, but it in no way releases them from the care of listening to what "the poets meditate or sing" here in "Homecoming." The "not" is the mysterious call "to" the others in the fatherland, to become listeners, so that for the first time they may learn to know the essence of the homeland. "The others" must first learn to reflect upon the mystery of the reserving nearness. Such thinking first forms the thoughtful ones, who do not hasten by that precious find which has been reserved and committed into the words of the poem. Out of these thoughtful ones will come the patient ones of a lasting spirit, which itself again learns to persist in the still-enduring absence of the god. Only the thoughtful ones and the patient ones are the careful ones. Because they think of what is composed in the poem, they are turned with the singer's care toward the mystery of the reserving nearness. Through this single devotion to the same theme, the careful listeners are related to the speaker's care; they are "the others," the poet's true "kindred spirits."

Assuming then that those who are merely residents on the soil of the native land are those who have not yet come home to the homeland's very own; and assuming, too, that it belongs to the *poetic* essence of homecoming, over and above the merely casual possession of domestic things and one's personal life, to be open to the origin of the joyful; assuming *both* of these things, then are not the sons of the homeland, who though far distant from its soil, still gaze into the gaiety of the homeland shining toward them, and devote and sacrifice their life for the still reserved find, are not these sons of the homeland the poet's closest kin? Their sacrifice shelters in itself the poetic call to the dearest in the homeland, so that the reserved find may remain reserved.

So it will remain, if those who "have cares in the fatherland" become the careful ones. Then there will be a kinship with the poet. Then there will be a homecoming. But this homecoming is the future of the historical being of the German people.

They are the people of poetry *and* of thought. For now there must first be thinkers so that the poet's word may be perceptible. By thinking again of the composed mystery of the reserving nearness, the thinking of the careful ones alone is the "remembrance of the poet." In this remembrance there is a first beginning, which will in time become a far-reaching kinship with the homecoming poet.

But now, if through remembrance "the others" become akin, are they not then turned *toward* the poet? Does the abrupt "not" with which "Homecoming" ends, concern them? Yes, it does. But not only them. If they have become akin, "the others" are also the "others" in still another sense. By heeding the spoken word and thinking of it, so that it may be properly interpreted and preserved, they help the poet. This help corresponds to the essence of the reserving nearness, in which the most joyful draws near. For just as the greeting messengers must help, in order that gaiety may reach people in its brightening, so, too, there must be a first one who poetically rejoices before the greeting messengers, in order that he, alone and in advance, may first shelter the greeting in the word.

But because the word, once it is spoken, slips out of the protection of the caring poet, he alone cannot easily hold fast in all its truth the spoken knowledge of the reserving find and of the reserving nearness. That is why the poet turns to others, so that their remembrance may help in understanding the poetic word, so that in understanding each may have come to pass a homecoming appropriate for him.

Because of the protection in which the spoken word must remain for the poet and his kindred spirits, the singer of "Homecoming" names at the same

time in "The Poet's Vocation" the other relation of the poet to the "others."
Here Hölderlin speaks of the poet and his knowledge of the reserving nearness
(IV, 147):

  ... But alone he cannot easily preserve it,
  And a poet gladly joins with others,
  So that they may understand how to help.

8. 海德格尔：《荷尔德林〈还乡——致亲人〉释读》

(Martin Heidegger, "Homecoming/To Kindred Ones," 1943)

作者小识

海德格尔(Martin Heidegger，1889—1976)，德国哲学家，在现象学的基础上开创了"基础存在论"(Fundamental Ontology，又译"基础本体论")，致力于在"时间"和"历史"之中的活跃而又具体的生存中把握"存在的意义"，因而将解释学发展为哲学解释学。海德格尔对 20 世纪欧洲哲学的发展产生了深刻的影响：一方面，其存在论思想催生了存在主义哲学运动，人生在世的忧烦、焦虑和异化成为存在主义哲学关注的中心；另一方面，其基础存在论对于传统形而上学的解析，又为解构的兴起预备了思想资源和文本策略。20 世纪 30 年代到 40 年代，海德格尔完成了两重转向：从存在论哲学建构转向荷尔德林(Friedrich Hölderlin，1770—1843)及德国诗歌的释读，从当代语境开启"回归的脚步"，致力于归向古希腊甚至前苏格拉底时代，探索思想之本源。

《海德格尔全集》有 80 多卷传世，迄今尚未编辑完成。其代表作有《存在与时间》(*Sein und Zeit*，1927)及其续篇《康德与形而上学问题》(*Kant und das Problem der Metaphysik*，1929)，后期转向的代表作有《荷尔德林诗歌的释读》(*Erläuterungen zu Hölderlins Dichtung*，1936—1968)，多卷本《尼采》(*Nietzsche* I，II，1936—1946)。

背景略说

20 世纪 30 年代后期，海德格尔中断"基础存在论"的建构，转而吟诵和释读德意志高古诗人荷尔德林的诗歌。这一思想史事件释放出两重信号。第一，哲学家对诗人实施"易容术"，海德格尔要把荷尔德林装扮为神言的信使(Hermes of Words)。第二，柏拉图在公元前 5 世纪断言，"诗哲之争"由来已久，到了海德格尔的时代，这场争论仍然未曾平息。在现代人的自我伸张臻于紧迫的时代，海德格尔触摸荷尔德林的诗篇，又是一场如履薄冰、如临深渊的尝试——再次启动和解"哲学与诗"的大业。对此，海德格尔告白说：他对荷尔德林的一系列释读，无意成为文学史研究论文和美学论文。

这些释读"出自一种思的必然"，是"思"与"诗"的对话。海德格尔想要在对话中确立"诗的唯一性"。"诗的唯一性"与文学史无关，却只能通过荷尔德林来运思，进而见证"存在的意义"。于是，海德格尔的释读首先悬置了文学批评和美学的圭臬，而通过"思—诗对话"进入"存在史"，直逼存在的意义本身。通过转向诗，海德格尔在存在问题上另辟蹊径。从哲学转向诗歌，从现代欧洲转向古代希腊，荷尔德林成为海德格尔"双重转向"的一个醒目的路标。这就宜于对诗人荷尔德林略作了解。

荷尔德林，德国高古诗文的经典作家，海德格尔赞美他是"诗人之中的诗人"。荷尔德林之诗风所系，乃远去的故乡、淡灭的幻美、忧叹的人群，以及流连徘徊、正在降临的"神圣"。乡恋、哀歌、赞歌、诗剧，是荷尔德林诗体建构的成就。(1)其乡恋之诗，情系大地，而家园让灵魂憔悴。(2)其哀歌之作，有五部传世，书写天地人神，吟诵斜阳路影，歌咏帝国兴衰，将罗马世界之后衰落的哀歌升华到了 19 世纪的道德空间，铺展了千禧年主义灵知向废墟世界的回归之路。(3)其赞歌之作，尽是同古圣先贤和梦中靓影对话的呢喃，尤其将现代人对"黄金时代"的追忆投射到被进化飓风扫荡的苍白心空。(4)其诗剧之作，是一位生不逢时的高古诗人对现代性的逆反省察。诗人决意归向古希腊，将荷马的灵泉、品达的花瓣、第俄提玛的神谕、索福克勒斯的悲剧情愫、恩培多克勒的救赎灵知融为一种隐微的诗学，对神性隐蚀、英雄远逝、俗世嚣张、群氓张狂的现代做出绝望的回应。

"只有断肠花，那有长生药"。救世之志愈疾，悲剧之情愈烈，而心灵迷乱和人格分裂愈盛。荷尔德林在迷暗和疯狂之中度过了惨淡的三十六年，幽居内卡河畔的塔楼，他还在沉思："当新的生命重生于人性，岁月就这般汩没于沉寂。"荷尔德林生之默默，而身后被尊为诗神，被追封为诗圣。保罗·策兰、曼德尔斯塔姆都奉他为师，自觉传递其诗风灵韵，在 20 世纪道德空白的时空中抒写爱意和情殇、惊险与惊艳。

海德格尔借着荷尔德林完成了思想的转向——从冷酷的生存论逻辑分析，转向温馨的神话学诗意栖居。他还借着荷尔德林开启了希腊之旅，踏上了重访前苏格拉底世界的"归向之路"。在海德格尔眼里，荷尔德林的诗不仅是艺术，而且是对艺术的反思、对存在的建构。这种反思与建构取决于"存在的意义"问题。艺术不是文化成就，不是人类的伟业丰功，不是精神的表象，艺术属于源始事件(Ereignis)。唯有借着这种源始事件，"存在的意义"方可得到规定，得以澄明。

写完《存在与时间》，海德格尔就陷入思想的困境，无奈地转向了"时间与存在"，从而延宕了基础存在论的建构。他意识到，笛卡儿式的"思"完全不适合接近存在的意义，传统形而上学的语言也无法表述这种转向。他以为，当务之急，便在于转向诗，归向希腊，去复活被遗忘的存在，复活诗性语言。以诗性语言揭开"被遗忘的存在"，言说"存在的真理"，表述"理性"（logos）与"自然"（phusis）的源始总汇体。phusis，汉语通译为"自然"，其实是指这么一种状态："通过一种基本的诗性之思的存在体验，早期希腊人发现了万物竞相涌现。"于是，我们不妨说，phusis 几乎可以相通于庄子描写的自然境界："天地有大美而不言，四时有明法而不议，万物有成理而不说。"（《庄子·外篇·知北游》）在这种境界中，思与诗、哲学与诗歌合一。海德格尔既是哲人也是诗人，荷尔德林既是诗人也是哲人，20 世纪支离破碎的灵魂与 19 世纪高古悲壮分裂的"诗魂"互为镜像。

基本内容

这篇释读是 1943 年 6 月 6 日海德格尔在弗莱堡大学纪念荷尔德林逝世一百周年的聚会上所做的讲演。同年 6 月 21 日，他在弗莱堡大学再次做同题讲演。海德格尔将荷尔德林诗的释读结集出版时，这篇讲演被置于卷首，作为全部释读讲演的开场白。

海德格尔抱怨过，仅知"哀歌""颂歌"这些体裁之名，而不知诗意创造物，就是"在无诗意的语言的喧嚣之中，诗歌像悬于旷野里的钟，已然为轻飘的降雪覆盖而荒腔走板"。他的诗歌释读所关注的是哲学，诗歌为道具，演示哲学的秘意，即见证"存在之真理"。于是，在他的释读中，几个关切着"存在意义"的问题坚执地自我凸显出来：（1）喜悦和忧伤——心灵为何憔悴？（2）形式与生命——金字塔为何颠转？（3）创建与劫毁——历史如何可能？（4）架构与灵知——人生何处栖居？（5）家园与荒原——回归更待何时？

海德格尔与荷尔德林倾心交谈、悉心对话，触摸到诗人的一颗破碎的心及其所负载的悖论情感。（1）乡愁，既是喜悦，又是忧心。"在阿尔卑斯山上，夜色微明，云／创作着喜悦，遮盖着空荡的山谷。"（2）家园，既熟悉又陌生。"一切都显得亲切熟悉，连那匆忙而过的问候，也仿佛亲人的问候，每一张面孔都显露亲近。""但那最美好的，在神圣和平彩虹下的发现物，却已经对少年们和老人们隐匿起来。"（3）光亮，既让人臻于极乐，又让灵魂憔悴。在阿尔卑斯山脉，发生着一种愈来愈寂静的自我攀高，在光明之上的更高处，明朗者首先自行澄明而为纯粹的朗照；一切纯净之物都沉浸于明澈的光华之中，一切高空之物都矗立于高超之威严中，一切自由之物都回荡于欢悦之运作中。欢悦之中，悲哀不绝；还乡途中，灵魂憔悴。返乡者孤身一人。"素衣莫起风尘叹，犹及清明可到家。"荷尔德林见证了灵魂从憔悴到阳刚的坚挺过程：

> 于是，我寂然一人。而你，高居云霄的
> 祖国之父！强大的天穹！还有你，
> 大地和光明！你们统一的三方，主宰又热爱，
> 永恒的诸神！我与你们的纽带永不断裂。
> 我从你们那里出发，也与你们一道漫游，
> 经历渐丰，我把喜悦的你们带回故园。

家园天使和年岁天使，是存在意义的象征。"家园"，意指这样一个空间，它赋予人一个处所，人唯在其中才能有"在家"之感，因而才能在其命运的本己要素中存在。这一空间由完好无损的大地所赠予。大地为民众设置了他们的历史空间。大地朗照着家园。如此这般被朗照着的大地，乃第一个家园天使。"年岁"，为我们称之为季节的时间设置空间。在季节所允许的火热的光华与寒冷的黑暗的"混合"游戏中，万物欣荣开放又幽闭含藏。在明朗者的交替变化中，"年岁"的季节赠予人以片刻之时，那是人在"家园"的历史性居留所分得的片刻之时。"年岁"在光明的游戏中致以它的问候。这种朗照着的光明就是第一个"年岁天使"。

诗人的天职是返乡。唯有通过返乡，故乡才能作为达乎本源的切近国度而得到准备。守护那达乎极乐的有所隐匿的切近之神秘，并且在守护之际把神秘展开出来，此乃返乡的忧心。因此，《还乡——致亲人》之结句是："歌者的灵魂必得常常承受，这般忧心，不论他是否乐意，而他人却忧心全无。"

拓展讨论

在海德格尔看来，荷尔德林比希腊人更本真地体验到了希腊性，因而最为遥远地体验到了德国人的历史使命感。在其划时代的哲学巨著《存在与时间》出版十年之后，大约也就是在纳粹覆灭，以及海德格尔本人的政治生涯无

疾而终之后，海德格尔写作了一部怪异的著作——《哲学献词》[Beiträge zur Philosophie（vom Ereignis）]。这部作品开启了海德格尔的所谓"思想转向"——从前期的"基础存在论"转向了"（此在）诗性解释学"（Poetic Hermeneutics of Dasein or Existence）。在论说"德国观念论"和西方历史命运的语境中，海德格尔将荷尔德林、克尔凯郭尔和尼采三人相提并论，凸显出事关西方历史未来的四个问题。这段晦涩的论说值得全文照录：

> 荷尔德林—克尔凯郭尔—尼采
>
> 当今之士，谁也不可肆心骄妄地认为他们三人是个纯粹的巧合。他们三个，都以自己独一无二的方式，最终体验到西方历史被抛入其中的那种深邃无比的连根拔起的痛苦，同时又以最亲密的方式暗示他们的诸神。这三位都必须告别各自未成熟岁月的明澈状态。
>
> 正在预备着什么呢？
>
> 荷尔德林位居三者之首，在思想再度渴望绝对地认知迄今为止的全部历史之特殊纪元，同时成为将最遥远的未来诗化的诗人。这意味着什么呢？
>
> 在此，被强烈祈祷的19世纪之隐秘历史发生了什么？那些思属未来的人又被预期了何等激动人心的原则？
>
> 为了变成那些依然属于当今敞开的必然性的人，我们是否必须将思想转向全然不同的领域，遵循全然不同的标准，以及选择全然不同的生存方式？不是因为历史属于过去，而是因为历史仍然在距离我们太遥远的未来。作为此在根基的历史是否一如既往地不为我们所知？①

海德格尔对荷尔德林的阐释事关西方历史的命运，其话题包括体验西方历史被抛入连根拔起状态的生存痛苦、以亲密的方式暗示隐微的诸神、憧憬最为遥远的未来。也就是在写作《哲学献词》的同时，海德格尔从1934年到1944年选择荷尔德林作为思想史形象展开系统的解释，对荷尔德林的《日耳曼尼亚》《面包与葡萄酒》《如当节日的时候……》《莱茵河》《伊斯特尔河》《追忆》

---

① Martin Heidegger, *Contributions to Philosophy（From Enowning）*, trans. Parvis Emad and Kenneth Maly, Bloomington & Indianapolis, Indiana University Press, 1999, pp. 142-143.

《还乡——致亲人》《希腊》等诗篇进行系统的解释，并在大大小小的讲演中反复演示。这些讲演与论文被收入《海德格尔全集》第 75 卷，名曰"希腊之旅"。也就是说，海德格尔在荷尔德林的引领下走上了希腊朝圣之途。海德格尔对荷尔德林的解释有一个思想预设和诗学逻辑，那就是"这些解释乃出自一种思的必然性"。这些解释确实没有文献学依据，并不遵循文本的客观原则，甚至是断章取义，将单文孤证从文章脉络之中活剥出来，将诗人之文当作演示哲人之思的道具。海德格尔的理由在于，"这些解释是一种思（Denken）与一种诗（Dichten）的对话；这种诗的历史唯一性是绝不能在文学史上得到证明的，而是通过运思的对话进入这种唯一性的"。在解释荷尔德林的《追忆》一诗时，海德格尔将诗人的世界与德国人的命运联系起来，将"作诗"等同于"创建"现代城邦——民族国家。满堂诗韵，漫天野心，海德格尔动情地讲道："追忆乃是在适宜的诗人世界之本质中的诗意持存，而这个适宜的诗人世界在德国人未来历史的壮丽命运中节日般地显示着它的创建基础。命运把诗人发送到这个诗人世界的本质之中，并且选定他为初生的祭品。"[①]海德格尔把话说到这个份上，我们就不能不明白，海德格尔解释荷尔德林，是春秋笔法、微言大义，言在谈诗论文，意在治国安邦。海德格尔心中的荷尔德林，正如诺瓦利斯笔下的游吟诗人，他们不只是舞文弄墨，吟诵雪月风花，而且是担负着更重大的使命：扶持君王，匡扶正义，洁净城邦，升华情欲，化育臣民。恰如中国古典诗文，不出言志与载道二端，既有益身心，又事关家国。荷尔德林的诗在海德格尔眼里，便是"志在《春秋》"的城邦法意。正如中国近代经学家廖平所言："《诗》乃志之本，盖《春秋》名分之书，不能任意轩轾；《诗》则言无方物，可以便文起义。"言下之意，《诗经》与《春秋》体例虽有不同，但其宗旨都关乎国家命运。海德格尔对荷尔德林的解释论域宽广，历史意识深厚，政治诉求激越，但过分执迷于微言大义，而将一位羸弱、安静的浪漫诗人漫画化了，更主要的是让诗学丧失了审美的自律性。

延伸阅读

1. 海德格尔：《形而上学导论》，熊伟、王庆节译，北京，商务印书馆，2011。此书以 1935 年海德格尔在弗莱堡大学夏季学期的课程为蓝本，发展《存在与时间》中被延宕的难题：不去追问"存在者的存在"，而是追问"存在的

---

① 海德格尔：《荷尔德林诗的阐释》，孙周兴译，181 页，北京，商务印书馆，2000。

意义"，即追问存在本身。

2. Marc Froment-Meurice，*That Is to Say：Heidegger's Poetics*，trans.，Jan Plug，Stanford，California，Stanford University Press，1998. 该书从"基础存在论"的视角解读语言的意义，对海德格尔的诗学进行了分析，指向了诗学的限度，即超越艺术与文学，为解读艺术与文学提供新的视角。

9. Hölderlin and Antiquity (1943)

By Hans Georg-Gadamer

It is the distinction of classical antiquity in its effect on German culture that it is able, in a mysterious fashion, to keep pace with the constant changes appearing on our cultural horizon. Even if our view of history and the values it posits otherwise change with the changing spirit of the times, antiquity nevertheless remains, within the ever-shifting contours of our cultural life, the guarantee that it is always possible to rise above ourselves. Today we simply cannot find a more accurate test of this proposition than to inquire into Hölderlin's relationship to antiquity. For this is an authentic and still unfinished event in our cultural life, which began in our century with the reawakening of Hölderlin's poetic works. This contemporary of Schiller and Goethe proves ever more to be the contemporary of our own future, a poet who in particular has inspired in our youth a passionate and unreserved following an utterly unique event in the cultural history of modern times: the history of a poet's work delayed in its reception for more than a century. If the changing image of Greece from Winckelmann to Nietzsche seems to probe the outer limits of the nature of Greek humanity, there is no doubt that, following the humanist and the political views of Greece, our own view of antiquity is being reshaped anew by coming into contact with the world of Hölderlin. The gods of Greece are acquiring a new seriousness.

But the real importance about the question of Hölderlin and antiquity lies in the fact that the poetic existence of Hölderlin is determined by his relation to antiquity; and that to such an extent, that it even singles him out in the period of German Classicism. His poetic works as well as his theoretical reflections on art are, as a whole, both an intense probing of this question and its fateful answer. Therefore, it is not just any arbitrary relationship, one among others, as it was in the case of Goethe or Schiller or Kleist or Jean Paul, when we investigate Hölderlin's relationship to antiquity. On the contrary, this question goes to the very heart of his nature and the totality of his work. For this reason, a purely literary-aesthetic investigation, pursuing the influence of the classical poets and thinkers on Hölderlin, on his world-view, his poetic language, his style, and the images of his poetic world would be entirely inappropriate. It is certainly true that Pindar's hymns are an essential presupposition of Hölderlin's late hymns, just as his constant preoccupation with Greek tragedy is essential for his entire work. And yet, Hölderlin's art cannot be understood proceeding simply from the influence that the classical tradition had on his work. Precisely that is what distinguishes him from classical Weimar, that he encounters the world of antiquity not simply as one of the disciplines of the school curriculum, but rather as a force demanding from him an exclusive commitment. Hölderlin's stout heart claims as its own the territory between the Greek and the German, between the Greek gods and Christ, the master of the Hesperian-Germanic age.

Today it has become a habit of thought to transform the transcendent scope of spiritual Being into phases of spiritual development that are then, as such, accessible to our understanding. We must therefore consider as a matter of considerable fortune the fact that the creator of the first great edition, Norbert von Hellingrath, already opposed the idea of viewing the Germanic hymns of Hölderlin as an abandonment of the Greek model, as a "Hesperian turn" that would correspond to the rejection by German Romanticism of the classic ideal. ①
In this way, Hellingrath contributed to preserving the actual range of Hölderlin's poetic geniusor better, he understood the tension between the Greek and Germanic elements as a expression of Hölderlin's authentic self and as the secret of his Greeklike greatness. I think, then, that it is appropriate to direct our attention to the actual high point of this tension, to the great hymns of the final years of the poet's creative work. According to the reports, Hölderlin appears to have continued to suffer the reverberations of this tension even in the first years of his insanity. On the other hand, the novel *Hyperion*, which has its setting entirely in Greece, mirrors the Germanic yearning of the poet in a borrowed garment and in the terrible reversal that took the form of the

---

① In the preface published by him as the fourth volume of his edition, p. xii.

great philippic addressed to the Germans. In the great hymns of the late period, however, this tension finds both its poetic expression and its resolution in the continually renewed attempt to fuse poetically all the forces that he experienced so acutely.

Included in these late works is a hymn that is the perfect artistic formation of this discord, the hymn "Der Einzige. " ①

> What is it that chains me to these old
>
> blessed shores? that I love them even
>
> more than my Fatherland? ...

When we hear this so-called hymn to Christ, we are obviously confronted by a puzzle: it is not at all the excessive love for the old gods, which the poet confesses early in the poem and he repeats this confession in numerous other poems that is responsible for Christ's absence. On the contrary, the fault lies in the excessive love for Christ(v. 48ff.). Not that the heavenly powers would exclude one another in jealousy the inclination of the poet's own heart, his love for the Unique Divinity, is the fault that prevents the union of Christ with the old gods. "Never do I strike, as I would, the proper measure" (v. 77).

Indeed, this is precisely what Hölderlin realized and to which he gave creative form more deeply than any of the other great Hellas-explorers of the German soul: that the problem of German classicism is not that its preference for classical Greece cannot be fulfilled. Quite the reverse, this preference refuses to be reconciled with the inclination of the heart, which is unable to perfect its Western-Christian and Germanic nature on the "blessed shores of Ionia. " Using this poem as a guiding thread, we want to attempt to trace the contours of Hölderlin's thinking and thus learn to understand Hölderlin's, as well as our own, attitude toward antiquity. In regard to the fragmentary character of the hymn, we will supplement our interpretation with motifs of the later version, which remained a sketch.

---

① Volume 4, pp. 186ff. (All quotations are taken from the first historical-critical edition, begun by von Hellingrath.) [In the meantime we can compare them with the great Stuttgart Edition for which we are indebted to Friedrich Beissner.]

The poet begins with his preference for Hellas, and we know on the basis of both his poetry and his philosophical writings what for him was the distinguishing feature of Greek life in contrast to life in his Fatherland. In Hellas, the gods appear in the midst of humanity, are united with them in marriage, so that god's image "lives among the people." The lament over the end of this divinely fulfilled Day of the Greeks is for us the most characteristic tone of Hölderlin's poetry, a tone that permeates the *Hyperion* and conjured into being the splendid images of yearning in the great elegies, like "Archipelagus" and "Brot und Wein." But even the constant philosophical reflections of the poet tell us clearly what and why he loved Greek life so deeply: there everyone belonged to the world with sense and soul, and precisely because of that, there developed in characters and relationships a particular interiority; whereas in the case of modern peoples, there prevails an insensitivity for the honor and peculiar character of the community, a narrow-mindedness that paralyses them all from within, especially the Germans (vol. 3, p. 366). Coming from this general insight, Hölderlin gains a basically positive relationship to the philosophy of his time. He views the task of Kant's and Fichte's Idealism and its wakening of the "vital self-activity of human nature" as an education toward universality and although he sees in this an admittedly one-sided emphasis, still, as a "philosophy of the time," it is the correct kind of influence (vol. 3, p. 367). He certainly feels that it is still a giant step from this universality, binding in duty and justice, to the ancients' way of life. "But then, how much is still to be done to achieve human harmony" (vol. 3, p. 370). The ancients did not need what philosophy must achieve for our contemporaries today. In their case the circle of life, in which they experienced common activity and common suffering, was broad enough so that each one received from it an increase of vital growth. Hölderlin clarifies this by a comparison with the warrior who, fighting together with the army, feels more courageous and more powerful, and in actuality is so. This surpassing excellence, transcending the individual not only in his own feeling, but as an actual power of Being, this sphere in which all people live simultaneously is the divinity of their community. A marginal note to one of the poems actually says, "This sphere which is higher than that of the human being, that is precisely the God" (vol. 4, p. 355). It is of course a matter of general knowledge that among the Greeks all relationships were of a religious nature, all those "finer infinite bonds of life" as Hölderlin calls them, which we with our enlightened morality and etiquette regulate with our "iron-clad concepts" (vol. 3, pp. 262f.). What are here called *religious relationships* Hölderlin defines as "those that one must consider not so much in and for themselves but rather from the viewpoint of that spirit which prevails in the sphere where those relations occur." This life, experienced by the Greeks as openness to the presence of divine forces and interpreted in their name, is, according to Hölderlin, eminently justified in comparison to the life of the modern "snail" who is exclusively concerned with order and security; in other words, it is the more authentic experience of the vital energy of life.

Now the poet refers to this divine Day of the Greeks in the hymn "Der Einzige" as a submission (or a being sold) into the "prison of the gods." Imprisonment, however, means enduring the suffering of alienation. What kind of suffering is that? Again we are supported by a theoretical study of Hölderlin's entitled: "The Angle from Which We Ought to View Antiquity" (vol. 3, pp. 257-259). Here Hölderlin speaks of servitude as the mark of our conduct toward antiquity, a servitude so all-encompassing and oppressive that all our talk about education and piety, about originality and independence is just a dream, a reaction, a mild revenge, so to speak, against this servitude. In a letter to his brother, Hölderlin once used a grotesque image: "Even I, with all good will, grope blindly in my activity and thinking to catch a glimpse of these unique human beings in the world, and find myself, in everything I do and say, all the clumsier and more absurd because I, like flat-footed geese, stand around in modern water impotently struggling to lift myself up into the Greek sky" (vol. 3, p. 371). For the oppressive character of this servitude he offers here as solid an argumentation as found in the philosophy of Idealism itself. The human desire for education, in any case already weak in modern times, appears vital only in the souls of independent thinkers (an expression of Fichte's). It finds in the educational material provided by antiquity all too much that is premodeled. The near boundless world of antiquity, of which we become aware either through schooling or through experience, is an oppressive burden that threatens us with disaster in no way less than the positive forms, the luxury that their fathers had produced, had brought disaster to earlier peoples. What Hölderlin is obviously describing here is the specter of classicism, an artificial humanism of the schools and the straitjacket of an alien style.

But in this heightened danger, intensified by historical consciousness, he sees also an advantageous moment for being able to determine our own direction, because we know all the essential directions that the impulse toward education can take. When we consider this reversal of attitude, which Hölderlin only hints at, we then suddenly recognize it in the goal and meaning of all his efforts at theoretical reflection on art that we find in the prose studies and the so-called philosophical writings. Almost all of the essayistic projects, elaborated on the model of antiquity, have the same subject matter: the difference between literary genres, which is, as everyone knows, a principle strictly observed by the ancients. For him, the classical poets are models of artistic practice. And it is precisely this strictness of the ancient poets from which Hölderlin expects a rich blessing for the success of his own work. [1] In their practical procedures, the ancient poets become ideal models for him. Quite characteristic is the comment in the Preface to his translation of Sophocles to the effect that this is an enterprise regulated by foreign but still strict and historical laws (v. 91). [2] As a matter of fact, the *Notes to Oedipus* begin with the demand for a poetics according to the Greek model (v. 175). There is an echo of this in a letter to a young poet where he says, "And for that reason I have come more and more to honor the thorough, free, and unprejudiced practice of art,

---

[1]   See, for example, vol. 3, p. 463.

[2]   See vol. 5, p. 335. In the first printing of this essay I falsely cited this passage as proof that Hölderlin took the Greek conception of art as model. I should have followed Beissner's interpretation of "gegen" (*Hölderlin's Translations from the Greek*, p. 168). Not only does linguistic usage demand that "gegen" here signifies direction, but also in its context the passage from the letter confirms that Hölderlin thought he had achieved Greek simplicity by the very fact that he had achieved real freedom from the Greek letter. He wants to indicate this goal with the expression *gegen die exzentrische Begeisterung* [toward eccentric enthusiasm].

because I consider it to be the aegis that protects genius from the ephermeral. "

However, the fact that Hölderlin takes Greek artistic practice as a model in no way implies a confession of Classicism. On the contrary, it was in his study of the ancients that he realized, as he writes in the famous letter to Boehlendorff from December 4, 1801 (vol. 5, pp. 318ff.).

> ... besides that which among both the Greeks and us must occupy the highest place, namely a vital sense of relationship and destiny, we doubtless have nothing otherwise in common with them. But that which is one's own must be mastered just as well as that which is foreign. For that very reason the Greeks are indispensable to us. It is simply that in what is our very own, in our national character, we cannot imitate them, because ... the free use of what is specifically one's own is the most difficult thing to achieve.

It is quite clear: the theory of art is more than it seems; it is the essential form of the poet's self-emancipation from servitude to the ancients. We hear the very same thing in the last letter to Schiller, where, concerning the study of Greek literature, he says he had continued to study it until it had given him back the freedom it so easily takes away at the beginning. The "liberation from the 'letter' of the Greeks," of which he boasts at the end, leads to a fundamental subordination of what is Greek to what is German, something he also asserts in that profound contrast in the *Notes to Antigone* (vol. 5, pp. 257ff.).

This path of Hölderlin's reflection on art is actually a way of liberation from servitude to the ancients. But are this servitude and this liberation the same as those spoken of in our hymn? Is not the breaking out of the stylistic prison of a classicistic aesthetic something different from the overcoming of that all too great love for the divinely fulfilled life of the Greeks? And if intellectual discernment is considered to be the holy aegis, then certainly not only poetic reflection is meant by this. The poetic word is the word as such, and the word is the effect and the experience of the very divine itself in the way it is grasped and "distributed." The binding of the spirit to the earth is not only the task of the poet for which he receives the aid of artistic discretion by uniting Junonian sobriety with enthusiasm. The enthusiastic violence of the human heart is always in need of the holy aegis of quiet understanding to protect itself from the offences of the world (vol. 3, pp. 36-40). Therefore, Hölderlin, in the face of the "ardent riches" of the human heart, can say of man in general, "that he is to guard the spirit, just as the priestess guards the heavenly flame; that is, his understanding (vol. 4, p. 246). But should that supreme love for Greece that the poet confesses in his poetry be overcome at all? It is certainly not a submission to classicistic moderation, but rather is itself already an expression of a poetically won freedom. The lament, which yearns to return to Greece and celebrates the departed gods in song, bears in itself a poetically transformed meaning. Precisely by refusing to call back the departed gods and to reanimate the dead past,[1] it becomes clear in what way the gods are still present.

> And yet we do receive much of the divine.
> The flame was given into our hands and
> Earth and the flood of the sea. (vol. 5, p. 164, "Versöhnender" vv. 63ff.)

Thus the language of the native landscape, its fateful signs, mountain and stream, in which earth and sky meet, becomes the object of a new, German hymn. Those are the angels of the Fatherland that the poets intend to proclaim, the mediators and messengers of the divine. This turn to the Fatherland is however not at all a retreat from the ancient journey of the soul to the East; it is the same journey of the heart:

> Not them, the blessed ones, who have appeared,
> The images of the Gods in the ancient land,
> Of course I may no longer call to them; but if
> You waters of my home, if the love of my heart
> Can lament with you, what otherwise does it desire
> To accomplish, that holy mourning? ... (vol. 4, p. 181, "Germanien")

---

[1] See the beginning of "Germanien," vol. 4, p. 181.

This profession of love for Greece and the lament for its vanished glory belong essentially to the poetic experience of a vigorous and lively present in the new freedom of the German hymn. To this experience the lament owes the fact that its proclamation of the old gods is more than a display of classicistic pomp, that it really does call forth vital images.

It is precisely here, however, in the divine freedom of this imprisonment in what is past and what is present, that there arises a different lament, that Christ remains far distant, that he refuses his presence. To whom does he refuse it? To the hymn of God's image; in other words, the poetic invocation. The poet expressly rejects the idea that this refusal rests on an irreconcilable jealousy among the heavenly beings. In his opinion, the fault lies with the poet who adheres too exclusively to Christ in order to be able to compare him with others, in order to be able to celebrate him as the Present One, as World.

> A certain sense of shame
> Prevents me from comparing
> To you those world-bound men.

If any comparison at all seems well founded, then that perhaps with Heracles and Dionysus (vv. 41ff.). For all three of them are the harbingers of a new and better order: Heracles as the liberator of the world from monsters; Dionysus as the donor of the grape, the tamer of wild animals, and he who joins men in ecstasy; Christ is the mediator, he who makes peace between God and men.

The poet himself has tried more and more to support this comparison in the later version of the hymn. And yet the word *diesesmal* [this time] with which the sketch of the expanded version breaks off, shows that even now a return to the two final strophes was still intended; in other words, that the failure of the comparison between the world-bound gods of antiquity and Christ has remained the unchanged basic theme of the poem. ①

---

① What was said then remains correct, even after the great Stuttgart Edition presents the tradition more exactly. In the final analysis, the second version of the hymn that, precisely as far as content is concerned, still needs considerable decoding, seems to have a different ending. But from verse 54 on, it seems even to have a different theme.

Seen in detail, the newly added part presents a number of difficulties, but at the same time brings such an important development of the comparison, that its interpretation must be attempted. Christ is accorded an equal status with the "world-bound men" to the extent that he too had his hour, his mission of destiny from God, and thus "stood alone" just as the others did. His constellation, that is, his mission, was to rule freely "over what was appointed." What was appointed was the positive aspect of the law in which the actual spirit no longer lives which is of course the main theme of Hegel's early theological writings. That is explained here in such a way that the constant and enduring aspect of the living spirit is overgrown with the bustle of business, thus preventing experience from being understood. But even that is the office of each and everyone of these religious heroes, to dispense fire and life anew when the "holy fire is exhausted" ("Versöhnender," v. 78). And so here we also read:

> Of course the world ever rejoices turning
> Away from this earth, that it lays it bare;
> Where what is human cannot hold it.

But they have all appeared precisely to hold and to bind, particularly those who bring a new order, like Heracles and Dionysus. For this reason the poem states: "thus those are like one another." Similarly the poet shows in an earlier sketch of the later version that he insists on this equality of Christ with the others against the Christian claim: "Indeed even Christ had one thing which enraptured him ..." Namely, each one has a destiny, that is (it?) (vol. 4, p. 379). Now in a rather mysterious way, the story of the temptation (Matthew 4) is connected with those who bring and maintain the fire. Obviously it is the desert, that is, the earth denuded of the divine presence, that is conjured up here by the temptation story, and again its purpose is not to distinguish him, but rather to equate him with the other orderers of the chaotic earth, with Heracles and Dionysus. Even in the time when the gods are absent there still remains "a trace of a word": so Christ knows how to withstand temptation

by the Devil, because for him what is written has still not been extinguished. ①
He is a man who, appearing in the desert of an ossified religious life, still has
the knack of catching the trace of a word, and precisely because of that rejects
the tempter and takes upon himself the office of the suffering savior. ②

Also in what follows the poet endeavors to show Christ in his comparability with the others. By equating him, for example, not with Apollo or Zeus, but
with those who are truly comparable, with Heracles and Dionysus, who are
themselves different from "other Heroes," he pursues a genuine context of religious history. Particularly Dionysus is for him a truly fraternal companion to
Christ; he had already dared in "Brot und Wein" to fuse the two Syrian
dispensers of joy and wine. Indeed, these three seem to be like each other, "a
clover leaf." In contrast to the other "great ones," they do not exclude one another. Rather, they form a unity, and this makes it "beautiful and lovely to …
compare,"

> … that they are under the sun like
> Hunters of the chase, or a tiller of the
> Soil who, his breath exhausted from his
> Work, bares his head, or beggar.

Which is to say, they are all three what they are, withholding nothing of
themselves in fulfilling their mission ("hunters of the chase"). They all three
suffer, thus do not insist on making themselves the center, and for that reason
are God: we need only think of Heracles's labors and his end; Dionysus is the
dying and rising God of the ancient cult; this above all connects them with
Christ who died "with a victorious glance" ("Patmos," v. 89). Therefore the
poet now says: "Hercules is like the kings. Dionysus is a public spirit. But
Christ is the End"; that is, he "fulfills" what the others lack of the presence of

---

① Compare the three repetitions of "It is written" in the text of the Gospel.

② On the word *Spuren* (traces) compare the "traces of ancient discipline" in the first
Pindar fragment (vol. 5, p. 271).

the "divine."

Nevertheless, even when making this comparison, he is continually aware of the inequality: "But there is a struggle that tempts me …" That is precisely the "sense of shame" that comes over him when he wants to assimilate Christ to the others. It obviously rests on the fact that Christ is not presence in the same sense as those "world-bound men." Those, "as sons of God," have their signs on them out of necessity.

> For the Thunderer has provided
> Quite differently, expediently.
> But Christ is modestly humble.

The nature of Christ is obviously not exhausted in simply completing the "heavenly choir" ("Brot und Wein," strophe 8); that is, in being simply the last in a series of equal gods whose activity is presence. What distinguishes him is his humility. Those others are what they are, fending off present distress the Thunderer has always provided quite differently. That is, they fulfill only their limited mission for the present. Christ, on the other hand, exercises humility and, because of that, reaches out beyond his own present moment. He even knew about that of which he was silent ("Versöhnender," vv. 86ff.), and precisely because he does not just passively suffer the death he was sent to undergo, but rather freely takes it upon himself (and one should no doubt consider that this is the critical meaning of the temptation story), he is the End. But that means that he exercises dominion over all future time (for which no other provision could be made). He is the God, whose annunciation and promise of return rules as a quiet reality over the whole final age of the world. So it becomes ever clearer that he is of a different nature.

But does that not really mean that the divinities are precluding one another and that there is here no fault of the poet? In other words, does the actual claim of Christ to be the only God not defeat all attempts of the poet at reconciliation? Is this not precisely the place where the powerful religious authority of Christianity overwhelms the poet? However, any attempt at such a biasedly

Christian interpretation① is fundamentally contradicted by Hölderlin's basic conception of the nature of God. Hölderlin never makes any concession to this Christian claim to uniqueness. In our hymn it is clearly stated that this supreme God has not one, but numerous mediators.

> For he never rules alone.
> And does not know all things. There ever
> stands someone or other between men and him. (vv. 65f.)

And

> For many are the high thoughts
> That have sprung from the Father's head … (vv. 13f.)

The hymn "Patmos," dedicated to the Christian Landgrave of Hamburg, must actually justify its Christian piety before the god-imbued soul of the poet: "For Christ still lives." But this very certainty of the poet himself states that he is not the only one:

> But all the Heroes, his sons, have come
> from him, as well as the Holy Scriptures,
> And until now the deeds of the earth
> Explain the sudden lightning,
> A competitive race unstoppable … ("Patmos," vv. 204ff.)

What does it mean then to say that the poet's love clings too much to the Single One? He is called *Master* and *Lord*; he is called *Teacher* ("Der Einzige," v. 36), that is, the teacher of the poet and of the age of the Western world to which the poet belongs. Actually then, the poet's tie to his own age blocks the path to the desired conciliation. For it is simply a fact that Christ is the God of

---

① Compare Romano Guardini, *Hölderlin*, pp. 557f.

this Christian-Western age; and he is so precisely as the one who is invisible and absent. With amazing insight, Hölderlin has described in the Patmos hymn (vv. 113ff.) the new nature of Christian piety:

> ... The joy of the eyes
> Was extinguished with him.
> From now on it was joy to live
> In a loving night and to sustain
> The abysses of Wisdom in
> Simplicity of heart ...

The eye cast down and inner illumination are the new forms of mediation where

> ... Modestly glancing
> From swelling eyebrows there
> Falls only quietly burning power ... ("Patmos," vv. 192 f.) [1]

It is then really in opposition to his own religious reality that the poet attempts, with the richness of his treasures,

> To form an image and similarly
> To see how he was, the Christ ... ("Patmos," vv. 164 f.)

Here lies the answer the poet gives to himself: it is not that the divinities themselves, all present for one another, would exclude each other in jealousy, but rather that the poet cannot strike a balance of their divine being, since Christ is of a different nature than presence. However, it is precisely this other reality of Christ that rules the world hour of the poet, in such a way that he is

---

[1] Compare Max Kommerell, *Geist und Buchstabe in der Dichtung* [Spirit and Letter in Literature], p. 287.

unable to celebrate him, as he would celebrate the Greek gods, as the worldly presence of "Nature." What the poet above all admits to be his guilt, "But I know; it's my own fault" ("Der Einzige," v. 48); what he laments as a failure for which he must make amends, "Never do I strike, as I would, the proper measure," ("Der Einzige," v. 77) he finally recognizes as the poet's peculiar way of having a destiny.

So the conclusion of the hymn deals with the imprisonment of the spirit in his human-historical situation. But only "a God knows when the best that I desire will come." Everyone else has a destiny in which his soul is caught. Even Christ was such a prisoner on the earth and "much afflicted," until he became free for his unearthly-spiritual destiny, "until he rose to heaven on the winds." "In the same way the souls of the heroes are imprisoned," even the unconditioned nature of the hero suffers the fate of imprisonment in time. They too are not free, are not masters of their fate. And now those who are all spiritual, and yet imprisoned, are joined in the final, all-disposing conclusion by

> The poets must also, the
> Spiritual ones, be of the world.

The poets are by nature "spiritual," that is, they are related to the presence of the divine as a whole, including all the heavenly beings. But even they suffer an irrevocable imprisonment in time. That is precisely what the poet has discovered by his own experience. They too cannot procure the best that they desire simply by force of will it remains at the discretion of "a God."

The poets, then, must be of this world, because they can sing only of the present in which they are imprisoned. It is part and parcel of Hölderlin's present that Christ is not accessible to poetic form. The Greek gods are the present time of legend that becomes reinterpreted for the poet in the light of "ever-present" nature. Christ, on the other hand, is he who lives in faith and whose worship is "in the spirit." "For Christ still lives." The poet knows what a transgression it would be if he wanted to gain by force something that is denied him. "But suppose one spurred oneself on … "("Patmos," vv. 166ff.), or

For anyone who gains it by deception

It becomes a dream and punishes

Him who wants to equal him in power ⋯ ("Die Wanderung," vv. 133ff.)

The fact of the matter is that the poet belongs to the otherworldly inferiority of the West, which holds him, as poet, captive, sold into the heavenly imprisonment of the world-bound gods, the only ones who offer themselves as subject for his song, and prevent him from achieving the desired conciliation. This tension, readily confessed and painfully endured by the poet, finds its resolution in this insight. But the surprising thing about this resolution is that the renunciation of the desired conciliation, this insight into the fact of inequality, sets him free to pursue the great new task of the Germanic hymn. Christ is, indeed, different from the others. ① Because the presence of Christ is not that of his short life on earth alone. He is presence in the historical destiny of the Western world. Thus the renunciation is transformed into a mission.

I'd like to sing to him,

---

① There seems to be a contradiction between this attempt to interpret the inequality of the Unique One and the "worldly" gods and a passage of the other Christ hymn, "Versöhnender ⋯ ," where it is stated of course with reference to Christ, but in an even more general sense: "For ever greater is his realm, like the God of Gods, he himself must also be one of the others" (vv. 89 f.). This, stated in such general terms, seems to annul the primacy of the Unique One. But the question is whether it is not precisely the Christian promise that, maintained in gratitude, makes this proposition true even for the other gods. Compare the role of the Comforter in "Brot und Wein" and also here in an earlier sketch: "No one, like you, has validity in the place of all the others" (vol. 4, p. 335). F. Beissner, *Friedensfeier*, p. 36, points to the fact that a variant of the passage "übrigen alle" (all the others) reads *Menschen* [human beings]. Precisely that confirms Christ's distinction, but understood of course as being within the divinity of all of them.

In the meantime, through the discovery of the "Friedensfeier," the hymn has found a highly significant parallel to the extent that also there the figure of Christ is particularly emphasized and yet, despite the emphasis, is articulated into the general worship of the gods. It is probably recognized today that Christ in the "Friedensfeier" is not to be understood as the "Fürst des Festes" [Prince of the feast].

Just as I sing to Hercules ...
But that is not allowed. A
Destiny is different. More Wonderful.
To sing more richly. Since his coming,
Beyond eyes' reach, the story ... ①

In this act of renunciation there opens up to the poet's view the panorama of Western history through a genuinely historical logic. History, "the story beyond eyes' reach," appears along side the poetic present of Greek myth.

We have to consider these connections more closely to see how, from this double imprisonment, both in that of his love for the Greeks as well as that of the world-hour of the Christian West, the poet gains a unique depth of knowledge about both of them, the Greek gods as well as the "Angel of the Fatherland." What the poem "Der Einzige," the starting point of our investigation, tells us is in a way more hidden than revealed, but remains the key we need for our understanding.

The world-boundness of the ancients and the interiority of the Christian-Western soul constitute, of course, the incomprehensible burden we ourselves are working out.

The poet experiences this in the elegiac form of the gods' departure, their turning away, their flight, as the advent of evening and night. The Greek landscape now lies like a giant, abandoned table ("Brot und Wein," strophe 4), the "honor" of the heavenly beings has become invisible.

Only as if coming from the flames of a grave,
There moves across the sky
A golden cloud, the legend of them, and
Now disappears around our doubting heads
Into the twilight. ("Germanien," vv. 24ff.)

---

① "Patmos," fragments of a later version, vol. 4, p. 229.

So the poet, called to be the prophet of the divine presence in the word, lives like one rejected by men. "And what purpose have poets in a paltry age?" ("Brot und Wein," v. 122)

The answer that the poet continually finds to the painful doubt about his vocation grows right out of his affirmation of this night. Already in the splendid beginning of "Brot und Wein," the twofold nature of this night becomes visible: by allowing the bustle of the day's activities and its noisy uproar to die down, its previously hidden life is awakened, the night's own voices; but above all, it grants the waking person encouragement to live a "bolder life" that makes it possible to express the mystery of the soul; and thus, by preserving the memory of the day, assures a return to one who stands in the darkness of Western history ("Brot und Wein," strophe 2). Here the Christian liturgical form of the Last Supper finds an interpretation quite peculiar to Hölderlin. Christ, the quiet Genius, the last God to be actually present among men, bequeathed, to those abandoned in the night, comfort and a promise of return; and, as their sign, the Last Supper. Bread and Wine. But Hölderlin does not see this as a mystical communion, nor as an act of "transsubstantiation," nor even as the memorial meal founded by the departing savior, as taught in the Reformed Church. He sees it in the holiness of the elements, of earth and sun, from which come both bread and wine. Hölderlin assumes that these two, bread and wine, even in our godless age, are still regarded differently than anything else; they are not there only to be used, but are still honored with thanksgiving, "there still quietly exists some modicum of gratitude"; that is, when using them, one still commemorates the divine beings. Thus, the elements of bread and wine, being of this world and yet considered holy, are the guarantee that the gods will return in fullness of life.

> Bread is the fruit of the earth, yet it's blessed by the light
> And from the thundering God comes the joy of wine.

Memory is the presence of an absent one in his absence; bread and wine are such presence, a pledge for what is absent, the fullness of the gods' gifts and the divine reality. Their holiness lives not from the legend (for instance, its institution by Christ), but rather the legend, God's image, lives in these symbols, in the presence of these elements and in the gratitude that preserves them.

This reversal and foundation of the myth on the present is the decisive shift from abandonment to expectation, giving the night of Western history its peculiar meaning, rich in hope for both present and future. Because memory has a present, it can become expectation. To cultivate the memory is from time immemorial the office of the poet. In this context, this office assumes the significance of the reawakening and calling into presence of what is absent. "Signs in the heavens" stir up our courage. The lament becomes the hymn, the purpose of which is to invoke what lies "before one's eyes" ("Germanien," v. 83). But that is not all: the night itself, the absence of the gods and the suffering caused by it, are not just a matter of emptiness and deprivation in these very things. There is a historical necessity. This night is the night of protective care. "Only occasionally can man now endure the fullness of divinity" ("Brot und Wein," v. 114). But it is also the night of gathering strength in preparation for a new day. Thus the poet poses the question and himself gives the answer:

> ... when honor for the
> Demigod and for his companions
> dissolves, and even the highest God
> Turns away his countenance, so that
> Nowhere in the heavens or on the green
> Earth is an immortal to be seen. What is this?
> It is the cast of the sower, when, with the ladle
> He takes the wheat, and throwing it into the
> Clear air, spreads it over the threshing floor.
> The chaff falls before his feet; but then
> Appears the grain. ("Patmos," vv. 145ff.)

The anticipated future is interpreted as the fruit of Hesperia ("Brot und

Wein," v. 150). Precisely that which has long been hidden and reserved in silence, that for which there was no word, because the general sense of it was not yet present, will be the truth of a new day. For "the power of the word grows in sleep" ("Brot und Wein," v. 68). But precisely with this insight, the poet has taken his office and his destiny upon himself. He must be alone because he is the first to invoke and call by name a divinity common to all, just as the organ prelude introduces the chorale, the song of the congregation ("AM Quell der Donau," strophe 1; "Der Mutter Erde," strophe 1).

This turning round of memory into the invocation of what lies in the future, as the poet succeeds in doing, is the naming of a very specific presence; not that of the ancient, well-known gods, not even that of the Genius of Christ who reigns over all absence. It is the invocation and interpretation of pure signs and hints, above all the significant figures of the mountains and streams of the Fatherland that, as runes of history, fuse antiquity and the Western world. We need but think of the symbolic course of the Danube. Here nature becomes history; the course of the river, in which heaven and earth are joined in marriage, becomes a symbol of the time and the course of Western history. In the presence of such richly hopeful figures, the legend of the departed gods becomes a prophecy of their eventual return. The presence of expectation is the medium in which the sorely missed harmony of the divine world can now be brought about. Expectation is, like memory, the presence of what is absent. In this expectation, the God of the West, he who reconciles all things, can now be called reconciled. For his reality, like that of no other God, is the presence of promise and expectation. Now the poet can say that he unknowingly has always served mother earth and the light of the sun ("Patmos," final verse). For what he did, what carried his song beyond the invocation of classical specters into a new future, was precisely that his hymn had a vision of what was present.

> The Father, he who reigns over all,
> desires most that the firm letter
> Be cultivated, and that what is
> Traditional be well interpreted.

Such is the law of the German hymn.

The letter and the tradition are not simply the teaching and practice of Christianity alone; it is the "languages of heaven" ("Unter den Alpen gesungen," v. 27) that is the poet's task to interpret. "Many have been written by men; nature wrote the others" (Am Quell der Donau, prose version, vol. 4, p. 338).

Now the Hesperian poet, because even he sings of the present even though not that of fullness and of the commonly shared Day can take up the ancient form used for the celebration of the present Gods, the hymn, in the shape given to it by Pindar. And yet, a quite different language, the language of Luther, and a quite different spirit transforms and fulfills these poetic forms of antiquity. It is the present of urgent expectation, not that of a secure and artfully woven possession, characteristic of Pindar's piety. It is the present of the Open into which are transformed the ancient images of the gods and that even the Christian God does not deny himself who, more than all of the others, is the "coming God" ("Brot und Wein," v. 54).

> ... one is always for all.
> Be like the light of sun. ("Versödhnender," vv. 102 f.)

Here, too, we must refer to Hölderlin's theoretical ideas to contrast with the ancient model what is peculiar to Hölderlin's poetic practice. Indeed, Hölderlin exercised this new freedom, witnessed by his German hymns, even in his work on the poetic documents of antiquity themselves, above all in his translation of Sophocles, as we have learned from the investigations of Beissner. There, ① in explicit reflections, he has shown the reason why the Western-Germanic type of representation is different, why it is superior to the Greek type, and why it is related to the Greek type as its opposite. The tragic Word among the Greeks he finds "more mediately factual because it moves the

---

① *Anmerkungen zur "Antigonä"* [Notes to Antigone], 3, vol. 5, p. 257.

more sensual body": the tragic catastrophe actually occurs in the form of bodily destruction. "In contrast," Hölderlin continues, "the tragic Word is, for our time and way of representation, more immediately effective because it moves the more spiritual body. It kills by annihilating what is internal." We would like to apply these reflections on the tragic Word of the drama to the new style of the hymns and to his Pindaric model. But what we read in his studies on the tragic ode does not even begin to reflect on this contrast with reference to the Greek model. It simply shows that Hölderlin also here, as in the case of the drama, quite in contrast to Romanticism, followed the artistic practice of the classical poet just as his own hymns obey the strict laws of architectonic structure. Nevertheless, what he thinks through in such general terms on the occasion of the Sophocles translation was undoubtedly clear to him here, too. The lyric word of the Germanic hymn is also more immediate than that of Pindar, for whom the context lay in a pregiven set of circumstances: in the family and the stature of the hero being celebrated and in a firm order of religious reality. Even to some aspects of this too Hölderlin holds fast by weaving into his verse address and dedication; but precisely this seal of dedication makes obvious that the one who is addressed in them belongs to a different ontological order of poetic reality. Particularly if one looks at the religious context of the Word, it is absolutely clear why Hölderlin subordinates the Greek art form to the Germanic. For what Pindar says about the divine is rooted in a firm religious present, whose untainted cultivation is the office of the poet; what Hölderlin says, on the other hand, is exposed to such unreconciled forces as Greek world-boundness and Western inferiority. Even in the case of the classical poets, in Pindar, words are chosen very economically out of the abundance of what deserves to be said. But when Hölderlin says: "Many things could be told about it" ("Patmos," v. 88) or "Many are the views" ("Der Einzige," späte, Fassung, v. 68), what treasures become apparent! not of what is unspoken, but of what is ineffable.

The lament of the individual, "Never do I strike, as I would, the proper measure," has thus proven its significance for Hölderlin's artistic practice in all of his works. It is not the admission of an unmastered task and a failure that would limit the poet's otherwise consistent excellence at one particular spot. On the contrary, the fact that he stands at this extreme boundary constitutes the mystery of the suggestively prophetic nature of Hölderlin's poetic power. Not "striking the proper measure" is the constant expression of his unique intensity. "I wanted to sing a carefree song, but I never succeed" (vol. 4, p. 315). It is the "fullness of happiness," the "burden of joy" ("Der Rhein," v. 158), that brings this intimate immediacy into Hölderlin's final poetic tone, a discourse both foolish and divine, continuing to resound even in the silence:

> But now my song, weeping in soul,
> Is finished, like a legend of love, and
> so it has proven to be from the beginning,
> Blushing and paling. ("Am Quell der Donau," vv. 89ff.)

9. 伽达默尔：《荷尔德林与古代世界》

(Hans Georg-Gadamer，"Hölderlin and Antiquity，" 1943)

作者小识

伽达默尔（Hans Georg-Gadamer，1900—2002），20世纪德国哲学家，解释学发展史上的决定性人物。在影响与声望上，伽达默尔与胡塞尔、海德格尔、哈贝马斯齐名。在解释学领域，其哲学解释学与海德格尔的"存在解释学"（ontological Hermeneutics）、利科（Paul Ricouer）的"怀疑解释学"（sceptical Hermeneutics）、瓦蒂莫（Gianni Vattimo）的"现代性解释学"（Hermeneutics of modernity）一起构成了现代解释学的基本格局。在20世纪人文学科领域，其哲学解释学与法兰克福学派的批判理论、法国解构论不仅关联，而且有直接互动，一起推进了现代与后现代以解释伦理为中心的新人文主义转向。

伽达默尔的《真理与方法——哲学诠释学的基本特征》（*Wahrheit und Methode：Grundzüge einer philosophischen Hermeneutik*，1960）堪称20世纪欧洲新人文主义思潮中脱颖而出的经典之作。在这部详论"哲学解释学"的专著中，伽达默尔将解释学从经验描述提升为哲学规范：第一，以"教化""共通感""判断力""趣味"四个人文主义传统之核心概念为基础，论述艺术体验之中真理的展现；第二，传承和更新浪漫主义解释学，将"真理问题"扩大到精神科学的理解问题；第三，以语言为主线，推进并完成解释学的"存在论转向"（"本体论转向"）。

在其哲学自述中，伽达默尔坦诚告白：他的哲学解释学的起点，是复活德国观念论和浪漫主义的失败。[①] 也就是说，复活古典世界科学观念的努力失败之处，就是哲学解释学崛起之地。其哲学解释学则可以被理解为一种通过谈话而复活过去、建构传统的努力。每一次谈话，就是要克服历史间距，力图寻找"我们的"语言。

---

① 加达默尔：《真理与方法——哲学诠释学的基本特征（下卷）》，洪汉鼎译，778页，上海，上海译文出版社，1999。

背景略说

解释学，即研究解释技艺的学问。从词源来看，hermeneutics 源出希腊信使之神"赫耳墨斯"（Hermes）。相传赫耳墨斯统治着道路，故而被称为"道路之神"。在多条道路交叉的地方，人们发现了成堆的石头，赫耳墨斯因之而得名。凡是路过的人，都向他扔石头。他有懂得和翻译神言的天赋，因而又被称为神的信使，常常给过路的人带来幸运。但有时他也被称为"高速公路上的强盗之神"。在当代，一项远程通信项目以及一颗人造卫星也被命名为"赫耳墨斯"。在一场思想游戏之中，海德格尔称赫耳墨斯为当代解释学的守护天使。在古希腊，神的信使是长着翅膀飞翔的天使，而且据说还有着"灿烂的外观"。他长着翅膀，可以瞬间穿过惊涛骇浪，直抵世界末日之岛，而那里就是卡吕索普女神软禁特洛伊战争英雄奥德修斯之地。假如不是奥林匹斯神主宙斯派遣赫耳墨斯去传信，就不会有奥德修斯的海上历险，也就不会有乔伊斯笔下的巨著《尤利西斯》。换言之，没有赫耳墨斯，就没有神谕的传递，也就没有英雄史诗之中壮怀激烈的故事，甚至没有人们津津乐道的文化、传统、风俗、礼仪等。

早期的解释学主要关注神学解释的技艺，即如何正确地解释《圣经》，如何正确地理解神言。在晚古时代，古希腊哲学与希伯来宗教融合，对《圣经》的理解有三种竞争的理路，一是将《旧约》理解为犹太民族的特殊历史记录，二是将《新约》中耶稣的遗训上升为普世的宗教信仰，三是融合希腊哲学文化将《圣经》教义理性化。为了为《圣经》解释确立规范，统一宗教信仰，神学解释学应运而生，担负着建立经学技术学的使命。

将《圣经》解释技术运用于对法律条文、法律证据的解释，便产生了法律解释学。现代解释学兴起于浪漫主义文化语境中，与之相联系的重要人物是施莱尔马赫（Friedrich Schleiermacher，1768—1834）。他将解释学发展为一种关于"理解"（Verstehen）与"解释"（Auslegung）的技艺学，认为解释学的使命不是回避误解，断定误解可能是解释的起点。施莱尔马赫的普遍解释学认定，陌生的经验、时间的间距和误解的可能是一些普遍的现象。文本或者话语越陌生，时间的间距越巨大，误解的可能性也就越大。因而，解释学的使命就是拓展"有意义的对话"（das bedeutsam Gespräch），在对话中克服陌生的经验和时间的间距。狄尔泰（Wilhelm Dilthey，1833—1911）推进施莱尔马赫的"普遍解释学"谋划，以精神科学为规范为解释学奠定方法论基础，从而完成了向历史意识的转向。海德格尔的"基础存在论"通过对时间之中的存在进行生存论分析,将"理解"视为一种生存的技艺,一种对于"存在意义"的领悟,从而将解释学从认识论转化为存在论,催生了伽达默尔的"哲学解释学"。

伽达默尔的解释学是哲学的沉思,更是文化实践的智慧。他从海德格尔那里接过"人类此在的时间性分析",将解释活动当作此在本身的存在方式。所以,哲学解释学标志着此在的根本运动性,而这种运动性既构成了此在的有限性与历史性,又构成了全部世界经验的无限性和永恒性。《真理与方法——哲学诠释学的基本特征》始于审美意识的批判,捍卫艺术体验之中获得的真理概念,将真理问题拓展到精神科学,完成语言论转向,而将解释学提升为存在论。在《真理与方法——哲学诠释学的基本特征》中,伽达默尔重点论述了三个命题:(1)在艺术经验维度上,真理的呈现方式是游戏,游戏让游戏者在游戏过程之中得以自我表现。"游戏的存在方式,就是自我表现。"(2)在精神科学的历史维度上,理解就是一种效果历史事件。在他看来,解释学的真正历史对象,不是他者,而是自我与他者在对话之中的统一,是自我与他者克服历史间距而建立的一种关系。在这种关系之中,历史的实在是被理解的实在,是一种历史建构的效果。(3)在理解的自我实现维度上,能被理解的存在就是语言。语言不是人生在世的装备,而是人类所拥有的整个世界。世界本身在语言之中得以表现,所以唯有通过语言呈现者方可获得理解。

基本内容

像海德格尔关于荷尔德林《还乡——致亲人》的讲座一样,伽达默尔的讲座也是 1943 年弗莱堡大学纪念荷尔德林逝世一百周年的系列学术事件之一。海德格尔以荷尔德林为向导,奋力归向古希腊,寻觅思想的源头,切近存在的意义。伽达默尔则以荷尔德林为对话伙伴,通过诗歌(艺术)的经验而切近真理,探索正确理解和解释的技术。海德格尔褒扬荷尔德林,而对黑格尔极尽贬低,将艺术作品解释为一种源始的真理事件。伽达默尔则从自己的思想轨道出发,反思自己的解释学指向,从对话出发思考语言,通过对话超越每一种语言的固定用法。于是,荷尔德林的诗歌,就是"一种新含义上的'构成物'","一种卓越的'本文'","自为存在并自己存在,而语词则可以被它们所抛弃的话语的意向所超越"。[①] 伽

---

① 加达默尔:《真理与方法——哲学诠释学的基本特征(下卷)》,洪汉鼎译,806 页,上海,上海译文出版社,1999。

达默尔在哲学解释学而非基础存在论视域下透视荷尔德林的诗篇，揭示了现代、荷尔德林、古典世界以及人类未来的复杂构成关系。

首先，现代通过荷尔德林闯入古代世界，而重新塑造了古希腊世界图像。荷尔德林与古代世界的关联，不是随意的关联，而是现代与古代的命定关联。现代为古代所笼罩，而古代为现代所重铸。荷尔德林带着一种现代的异质闯入古代世界，以强大的意志与古希腊较量，将古希腊塑造为一幅可望而不可即的神话图景。于是，伽达默尔断言，"希腊与父国之间、希腊群神和西方-日耳曼(Hesperia-Germania)的圣者基督之间，巍然屹立着诗人荷尔德林的心"。通过解读荷尔德林的颂诗《唯一者》，伽达默尔揭示了德意志灵魂与古希腊灵魂之间不可和解的深刻张力：荷尔德林挚爱希腊之心无法与自己的心灵倾向统一，而在"天堂一般的爱奥尼亚海岸"，其心灵又无法以基督教的和父国的方式得以完美实现。于是，我们不妨将荷尔德林与古代世界的遭遇，解读为一种绝对的现代悲剧。现代人分裂的生命也将一种不圆满的悲剧阴影投射到古代世界的幻美图景中。

其次，荷尔德林以反古典的方式模仿古代世界。古希腊艺术与诗是后世不可超越的典范，荷尔德林所代表的现代人、西方人和德意志人，也只能模仿这些不可超越的典范。可是，荷尔德林虽然将希腊艺术的理解力视为楷模，却并不意味着他完全认同古代世界。荷尔德林诗学，为走出古人奴役指出了一条艰难的自由之路。"承认对希腊的爱，哀诉消逝的古希腊辉煌，在本质上都属于德意志歌咏的新自由中'充满生机的当代'诗学经验。"

最后，最为引人注目的是荷尔德林诗文中呈现的三个神圣超越者及其悲剧性的诱惑史。这三位神圣超越者，便是赫拉克勒斯、狄奥尼索斯和基督，他们都是新的崇高秩序的缔造者。赫拉克勒斯扫荡妖魔鬼怪；狄奥尼索斯授种植之艺，传畜牧之术，显酒神精神；而基督致力于和解，给人类和神界带来和平。诗人荷尔德林将这三位神圣超越者予以对比，追寻一种真正的宗教历史关联。通过对荷尔德林诗文中所呈现的复杂关联展开反思，伽达默尔揭示了诗人的归属性：诗人归属于西方非俗世的内在性，而构成了"西方历史性命运中的当下"。"古代希腊世界的俗世性和西方-基督教灵魂的内在性，也是我们自己所承担的不可把握的重负。"

拓展讨论

1981 年 4 月，福格特教授(Prof. Philippe Forget)组织了一场"文本与解

释"的学术研讨会，邀请伽达默尔和德里达参加。这是解释学和解构论、德国学派和法国学派第一次面对面的对质和论辩，史称"巴黎论辩"或"德法之争"。在研讨会上，伽达默尔和德里达分别做了主题发言。

伽达默尔的发言题目为"文本与解释"（"Text and Interpretation"）。他通过简略追溯解释学的历史而声明自己扎根于浪漫主义和人文主义传统之中。然后话锋一转，他将法国同行的学说视为对自己的真正挑战。他指出，不是海德格尔，而是尼采，将哲学从关于存在与真理的形而上学概念的束缚之中解放出来，造就了解释的逻辑，展现了揭示文本意义的过程。伽达默尔支持海德格尔将尼采解读为"形而上思想家"，但批评尼采为了克服形而上语言的局限性而转向诗性语言。他特别指出，哲学解释学以谈话为理想空间寻求理解和解释的技艺，而独立于"在场的哲学"。

德里达的发言题目为"解释签名（尼采/海德格尔）：两个问题"（"Interpreting Signatures（Nietzsche/Heidegger）：Two Questions"）。他集中探讨了海德格尔对于尼采的解释，不过并非为了推进自己与伽达默尔的对话，甚至一次也没有直接提到伽达默尔的名字。他认为，海德格尔从思想而非生命出发理解尼采的努力，即为"善良意志"所驱动而拯救尼采于心-生理误读的努力，本身就是以误读为中心组织起来的。这就赋予了尼采这个专名以整体的签名，认为"永恒轮回"的思想就是关于存在整体的思想。

在主题发言次日的圆桌会议上，德里达以即兴形式向伽达默尔提出了三方面的问题。这些问题都围绕着对话与理解之中的"善良意志"。第一，伽达默尔诉诸"善良意志"及其对理解一致的承诺，康德赋予对话者以"尊严"，视之为无条件的公理。于是，德里达追问，这是否属于"意志形而上学的时代"？这个无条件的公理岂不预先假定了意志便是那种无条件的形式、最后归宿和最终规定？第二，涉及精神分析及其对话而至理解的程序，那就必须追问：精神分析中的"善良意志"意味着什么？理解单靠扩大语境能否实现？理解是不是一种突破？一种对语境以及全部语境概念的完全重构？对话是连续拓展，还是非连续重构？第三，与"善良意志"的基本结构有关，即理解的前提是和谐关系的延续，还是和谐关系的中断，以及全部协调活动的中止？德里达的问题隐含着对哲学解释学基本前提的质疑，以及对整个西方传统形而上学传统的解构。第一方面的问题隐含着对"善良意志"的质疑，暗示"意志形而上学时代"仍然属于"逻各斯中心主义时代"。第二方面的问题质疑"语境"概念，暗示对话过程和理解程序不是语境的平展延伸，而是语境的扭曲和断裂，意义

10. The Functional Structure of the Blank (1976)
By Wolfgang Iser

We shall now have a closer look at the basic function of the blank as regards the guidance it exercises in the process of communication. As blanks
mark the suspension of connectability between textual segments, they simultaneously form a condition for the connection to be established. By definition,
however, they can clearly have no determinate content of their own. How,
then, is one to describe them? As an empty space they are nothing in themselves, and yet as a "nothing" they are a vital propellant for initiating communication. Wherever there is an abrupt juxtaposition of segments, there must automatically be a blank, breaking the expected order of the text. "The division
of the text," writes Lotman, "into segments of equal value endows the text
with a certain order. But it seems to be of vital importance that this order
should not be completely followed through. This prevents it from becoming automatic and, in relation to the structure, redundant. The orderly sequence of
the text always appears as an organizing force which builds the heterogeneous
material into series of equivalences but, at the same time, does not eliminate its
heterogeneity. " Indeed, as a matter of principle this *cannot* be eliminated by the
text, as the segments, and the equivalences to be formed from them, have no
basis and do not refer to any given object, so that only their relations to one
another make it possible for the "object" or world of the text to be constituted.

But how can the equivalences to be formed from the heterogeneous segments be sufficiently controlled to prevent this world—at least structurally—
from being constituted according to purely arbitrary subjectivity? Our starting-
point must be the fact that each textual segment does not carry its own determi-
nacy within itself, but will gain this in relation to other segments. Here literature may join hands with other media, such as the cinema. Balazs says of film
sequences: "… even the most meaningful take is not sufficient to give the picture its total meaning. This is ultimately decided by the position of the picture

between other pictures… In every case and unavoidably the picture takes on its meaning by way of its place in the series of associations… the pictures are, as it were, loaded with a tendency toward a meaning, and this is fulfilled at the moment when it makes contact with other pictures. "

The segments of the literary text follow precisely the same pattern. Between segments and cuts there is an empty space, giving rise to a whole network of possible connections which will endow each segment or picture with its determinate meaning. Whatever regulates this meaning cannot itself be determinate, for, as we have pointed out before, it is the relationship that gives significance to the segments—there is no *tertium comparationis*. Now, if blanks open up this network of possible connections, there must be an underlying structure regulating the way in which segments determine each other.

If we are to grasp the unseen structure that regulates but does not formulate the connection or even the meaning, we must bear in mind the various forms in which the textual segments are presented to the reader's viewpoint. Their most elementary form is to be seen on the level of the story. The threads of the plot are suddenly broken off, or continued in unexpected directions. One narrative section centers on a particular character and is then continued by the abrupt introduction of new characters. These sudden changes are often denoted by new chapters and so are clearly distinguished; the object of this distinction, however, is not separation so much as a tacit invitation to find the missing link. Furthermore, in each articulated reading moment, only segments of textual perspectives are present to the reader's wandering viewpoint and their connection to each other is more often than not suspended. An increase of blanks is bound to occur through the frequent subdivisions of each of the textual perspectives: thus the narrator's perspective is often split into that of the implied author set against that of the author as narrator; the hero's perspective may be set against that of the minor characters; the fictitious reader's perspective may be divided between the explicit position ascribed to him and the implicit attitude he must adopt to that position.

As the reader's wandering viewpoint travels between all these segments, its constant switching during the time-flow of reading intertwines them, thus bringing forth a network of perspectives, within which each perspective opens up a view not only of others but also of the intended imaginary object. Hence no single textual perspective can be equated with this imaginary object, of which it only forms one aspect. The object itself is a product of interconnections, the structuring of which is to a great extent regulated and controlled by blanks. In order to explain this operation, we shall first give a schematic description of how the blanks function and then we shall try to illustrate this function with an example.

In the time-flow of reading, segments of the various perspectives move into focus and take on their actuality by being set off against preceding segments. Thus the segments of characters narrator, plot and fictitious reader perspectives are not only marshaled into a graduated sequence, but are also transformed into reciprocal reflectors. The blank as an empty space between segments enables them to be joined together thus constituting a field of vision for the wandering viewpoint. A referential field is always formed when there are at least two positions related to and influencing one another—it is the minimal organizational unit in all processes of comprehension, and it is also the basic organizational unit of the wandering viewpoint. Gurwitsch, with his modification of the gestalt theory, has clearly demonstrated the extent to which the conscious mind organizes external data into "fields" and thereby creates the precondition for all comprehension. The first structural quality of the blank, then, is that it makes possible the organization of a referential field of interacting projections.

Now the segments present in the field are structurally of equal value, and the fact that they are brought together highlights their affinities and their differences. This relationship gives rise to a tension that has to be resolved, for, as Arnheim has observed in a more general context: "It is one of the functions of the third dimension to come to the rescue when things get uncomfortable in the second. " The third dimension comes about, when the segments of the referential field are given a common framework which allows the reader to relate affinities and differences and so to grasp the pattern underlying the connections. But this framework is also a blank, which requires an act of ideation in order to be filled. It is as if the blank in the field of the reader's viewpoint has changed its position. It began as the empty space between segments, indicating what we have called their "connectability," and so organizing them into projections of reciprocal influence. But with the establishment of this "connectability" the blank, as the unformulated framework of these interacting segments, now enables the reader to produce a determinate relationship between them. We may infer already from this change in position that the blank exercises significant control over all the operations that occur within the referential field of the wandering viewpoint.

We now come to the third and most decisive function of the blank. Once the segments have been connected and a determinate relationship established, a referential field is formed, which constitutes a particular reading moment, which in turn has a discernible structure. The grouping of segments within the referential field comes about, as we have seen, by making the viewpoint switch between the perspective segments. The segment on which the viewpoint focuses at each particular moment becomes the theme. The theme of one moment becomes the horizon against which the next segment takes on its actuality, and so on. Whenever a segment becomes a theme, the previous one must lose its thematic relevance and be turned into a marginal, thematically vacant position, which can be and usually is occupied by the reader, so that he may focus on the new thematic segment. In this sense it might be more appropriate to designate the marginal or horizontal position as a vacancy and not as a blank; blanks refer to suspended connectability in the text, vacancies refer to nonthematic segments within the referential field of the wandering viewpoint. Vacancies, then, are important guiding devices for building up the aesthetic object, because they condition the reader's view of the new theme, which in turn conditions his view of previous themes. These modifications, however, are not formulated in the text—they are to be implemented by the reader's ideational activity. And so these vacancies enable the reader to combine segments into a field by reciprocal modification, to form positions from those fields, and then to adapt each position to its successor and predecessors in a process that ultimately transforms the textual perspectives, through a whole range of alternating themes and horizons, into the aesthetic object of the text.

Let us turn now to an example, in order to illustrate the operations sparked and governed by the vacancies in the referential field of the wandering viewpoint. The example may also help us to describe how the various structural qualities of blanks and vacancies interlock. If we consider *Tom Jones* again, we shall see how this process works. Fielding's novel is an excellent example to choose, because it makes maximum use of the theme-and-horizon structure to convey its intended picture of human nature. For our present purpose, it will be sufficient to single out the characters' perspective; that of the hero and that of the minor characters, who in turn split up this central textual perspective in accordance with their different starting-points and intentions. The aim of depicting human nature is fulfilled by way of a repertoire that incorporates the prevailing norms of eighteenth-century thought systems and social systems and represents them as governing the conduct of the most important characters. In general, these norms are arranged in more or less explicitly, contrasting, patterns: Allworthy (*benevolence*) is set against, Squire Western (*ruling passion*) ; the same applies to the two pedagogues, Square(*the eternal fitness of things*) and Thwackum (*the human mind as a sink of iniquity*), who in turn are also contrasted with Allworthy. There are various other sets of opposites—the view of love, for instance, as shown in Sophia (the ideality of natural inclinations), Molly Seagrim (seduction), and Lady Bellaston (depravity). All these serve as contrasts to the position of the hero, so that the relationship between his perspective and theirs is transformed into a tension, which is most strikingly represented by the Tom—Blifil contrast: Blifil follows the norms of his mentor and is corrupted; Tom acts against them and gains in human qualities.

Thus in the individual situations, the hero is linked with the norms of latitudinarian morality, orthodox theology, deistic philosophy, eighteenth-century anthropology, and eighteenth-century aristocracy. Contrasts and discrepancies within the perspective of the characters give rise to the missing links, which enable the hero and the norms to shed light upon one another, and through which the individual situations may combine into a referential field. The hero's conduct cannot be subsumed, under the norms, and through the sequence of situations the norms shrink to a reified manifestation of human nature. This, however, is already an observation which the reader must make for himself, because such syntheses are rarely given in the text, even though they are prefigured in the theme-and-horizon structure. The discrepancies continually arising between the perspectives of hero and minor characters bring about a series of changing positions, with each theme losing its relevance but remaining in the background to influence and condition its successor.

Whenever the hero violates the norms—as he does most of the time—the resultant situation may be judged in one of two different ways: either the norm appears as a drastic reduction of human nature, in which case we view the theme from the standpoint of the hero; or the violation shows the imperfections of human nature, in which case it is the norm that conditions our view. In both cases, we have the same structure of interacting positions being transformed into a determinate meaning. For those characters that incorporate a norm—in particular, Allworthy, Squire Western, Square, and Thwackum—human nature is defined in terms of one principle, so that all the possibilities which are not in harmony with the principle are given a negative slant. This applies even to Allworthy, whose allegorical name indicates his moral integrity, which, however, frequently tends to cloud his judgment. But when these negated possibilities exert their influence upon the course of events, and so show up the limitations of the principle concerned, the norms begin to appear in a different light. The apparently negative aspects of human nature fight back, as it were, against the principle itself and cast doubt upon it in proportion to its limitations. In this way, the negation of other possibilities by the norm in question gives rise to a virtual diversification of human nature, which takes on a definite form to the extent that the norm is revealed as a restriction on human nature.

The reader's attention is now fixed not upon what the norms represent, but upon what their representation excludes, and so the aesthetic object— which is the whole spectrum of human nature—begins to arise out of what is adumbrated by the negated possibilities. In this way, the function of the norms themselves has changed: they no longer represent the social regulators prevalent in the thought systems of the eighteenth century, but instead they indicate the amount of human experience which they suppress because, as rigid princi-ples, they cannot tolerate any modifications. Transformations of this kind take place whenever the norms are the foregrounded theme and the perspective of the hero remains the background, conditioning the reader's viewpoint. But whenever the hero becomes the theme, and the norms of the minor characters shape the viewpoint his well-intentioned spontaneity turns into the depravity of an impulsive nature. Thus the position of the hero is also transformed, for it is no longer the standpoint from which we are to judge the repertoire of norms; instead, we see that even the best of intentions may come to nought if they are not guided by *circumspection*, and spontaneity must be controlled by *pru-dence*, if it is to allow a possibility of self-preservation.

The transformations brought about by the theme-and-horizon interaction are closely connected with the changing position of the vacancy within the referential field. Once a theme has been grasped, conditioned by the marginal position of the preceding segment, a feed-back is bound to occur, thus retroactively modifying the shaping influence of the reader's viewpoint. This reciprocal transformation is hermeneutic by nature, even though we may not be aware of the processes of interpretation resulting from the switching and reciprocal conditioning of our viewpoints. In this sense, the vacancy transforms the referential field of the moving viewpoint into a self-regulating structure, which proves to be one of the most important links in the interaction between text and reader, and which prevents the reciprocal transformation of textual segments from being arbitrary. This is even borne out by the variegated history of responses that a novel like *Tom Jones* has elicited. The differences in interpretation do not spring so much from the structure described, but rather from the different ideas and experiences evoked by the repertoire.

Thus it is that even in the eighteenth century different readers formed dif-ferent concepts of Thwackum, the orthodox, theologian, depending upon their own attitude toward orthodox Anglicanism. This fact, however, has no bearing upon the structure of theme and horizon. The structure is only upset when the reader refuses to allow the change of viewpoint laid down for him—in other words, when he is not prepared to view Thwackum from the standpoint of the hero, because for him the norms of orthodoxy embody a system that covers all aspects of life and must therefore not be questioned. There are examples of this, too, in the history of Fielding criticism. The fact that many readers regarded the novel as blasphemous is an indication of the potential effectiveness of the theme-and-horizon structure: by setting the hallowed norm against an unfamiliar background, the text illuminates those aspects of the norm that had hitherto remained hidden, thereby arousing an explosive reaction from the faithful followers of that norm.

From this fact we may extrapolate a general observation. The more committed the reader is to an ideological position, the less inclined he will be to accept the basic theme-and-horizon structure of comprehension which regulates the text-reader interaction. He will not allow his norms to become a theme, because as such they are automatically open to the critical view inherent in the virtualized positions that form the background. And if he is induced to participate in the events of the text, only to find that he is then supposed to adopt a negative attitude toward values he does not wish to question, the result will often be open rejection of the book and its author. Even this reaction still testifies to the undiminished validity of this structure, which brings about an involuntary self-diagnosis in its irritated recipients.

To sum up, then, the blank in the fictional text induces and guides the reader's constitutive activity. As a suspension of connectability between perspective segments, it marks the need for an equivalence, thus transforming the segments into reciprocal projections, which, in turn, organize the reader's wandering viewpoint as a referential field. The tension which occurs within the field between heterogeneous perspective segments is resolved by the theme-and-horizon structure, which makes the viewpoint focus on one segment as the theme, to be grasped from the thematically vacant position now occupied by the reader as his standpoint. Thematically vacant positions remain present in the background against, which new themes occur; they condition and influence those themes and are also retroactively influenced by them, for as each theme recedes into the background of its successor, the vacancy shifts, allowing for a reciprocal transformation to take place. As the vacancy is structured by the sequence of positions in the time-flow of reading, the reader's viewpoint cannot proceed arbitrarily; the thematically vacant position always acts as the angle from which a selective interpretation is to be made.

Two points need to be emphasized. 1. We have described the structure of the blank in an abstract, somewhat idealized way in order to explain the pivot on which the interaction between text and reader turns. 2. The blank has different structural qualities, which appear to dovetail. The reader fills in the blank in the text, thereby bringing about a referential field; the blank arising, in turn, out of the referential field is filled in by way of the theme-and-horizon structure; and the vacancy arising from juxtaposed themes and horizons is occupied by the reader's standpoint, from which the various reciprocal transformations lead to the emergence of the aesthetic object. The structural qualities outlined make the blank shift, so that the changing positions of the empty space mark a definite need for determination, which the constitutive activity of the reader is to fulfill. In this sense, the shifting blank maps out the path along which the wandering viewpoint is to travel, guided by the self-regulatory sequence in which the structural qualities of the blank interlock.

Now we are in a position to qualify more precisely what is actually meant by reader participation in the text. If the blank is largely responsible for the activities described then participation means that the reader is not simply called upon to "internalize" the positions given in the text, but he is induced to make them act upon and so transform each other, as a result of which the aesthetic object begins to emerge. The structure of the blank organizes this participation, revealing simultaneously the intimate connection between this structure and the reading subject. This interconnection completely conforms to a remark, made by Piaget: "In a word, the subject is there and alive, because the basic quality of each structure is the structuring process itself."

The blank in the fictional text appears to be a paradigmatic structure; its function consists in initiating structured operations in the reader, the execution of which transmits the reciprocal interaction of textual positions into consciousness. The shifting blank is responsible for a sequence of colliding images which condition each other in the time-flow of reading. The discarded image imprints itself on its successor, even though the latter is meant to resolve the deficiencies of the former. In this respect, the images hang together in a sequence, and it is by this sequence that the meaning of the text comes alive in the reader's imagination.

10. 伊瑟尔:《文本空白的功能结构》

(Wolfgang Iser, "The Functional Structure of the Blank," 1976)

作者小识

伊瑟尔(Wolfgang Iser,1926—2007),德国美学家、文学批评家、接受美学创始人,出生于马林贝格(Marienberg)。他先后在莱比锡大学和蒂宾根大学学习文学,1950 年在海德堡获得英语博士学位。1952 年在格拉斯哥大学担任助理讲师,由此开始了探索当代哲学和文学的生涯,同时加深了对跨文化交流的兴趣。1967 年,伊瑟尔在康斯坦茨大学工作,与姚斯一起建立了接受美学。他的重要著作有《文本的召唤结构》(*Text's Response-Inviting Structure*,1970)、《隐在读者》(*Implied Reader*,1974)、《阅读行为》(*The Act of Reading*,1976)。

背景略说

接受美学产生于 20 世纪 60 年代后期并在 70 年代达到高潮,其主要代表是德国南部康斯坦茨大学的五位教授,分别是姚斯、伊瑟尔、福尔曼、普莱斯丹茨、斯特里德,他们被称为"康斯坦茨学派"。作为创始人之一,姚斯主要受伽达默尔的解释学的影响,关注文学接受的历史性。伊瑟尔的理论则源于现象学,受英伽登的现象学文学理论的影响,主要致力于研究文本结构内部的阅读反应机制。在《阅读行为》的序言中,伊瑟尔称姚斯的理论研究为"接受研究",而称自己的理论研究为"反应研究"。他认为姚斯关注的是"历史学—社会学的方法",而自己突出"文本分析的方法",只有将两种研究结合起来,接受美学才是完整的学科。

伊瑟尔的"反应研究"强调文学作品是文本与读者交流的形式,因此阅读的研究不能脱离文本。于是伊瑟尔提出"文本召唤结构"这一概念,认为文本具有一种召唤读者阅读的机制。在此伊瑟尔改造了英伽登和伽达默尔的理论。英伽登认为作品布满了不定点和空白(blank),读者应该在阅读的过程中对空白进行填充。伊瑟尔接受了这一理论,强调空白就是召唤读者的机制。之后,伊瑟尔结合伽达默尔的视域融合理论，认为阅读就是唤起读者的视域，并且打破它，使读者获得新的视域，然后再填补空白，生成新的视域，继续填补空白……从而达到对作品的接受。选文就是选取了《阅读行为》中讨论空白功能的部分，详细分析了空白与读者之间的互动和其产生效果的过程。

基本内容

空白的前提是文本各部分结构存在一定的秩序。这种秩序并不是一种连续的秩序，其中存在的许多中断被称为"空白"。空白本身虽不具有任何意义，就像文本中间存在的一个空间，但它是文本交流不可缺少的部分，只有存在空白，才能促进读者对文本进一步阅读和探究。伊瑟尔将文本的联结模式与电影中的"蒙太奇"手法相类比，把文本看作利用空白将各部分联结在一起的整体。每一部分的意义在于它在文本中的位置以及它与上、下两部分之间的关系。读者在阅读过程中将文本的各部分联结起来，形成自己的观念网（network of perspective），而空白在构成观念的过程中起着调节和制约作用。

空白在阅读中的调节和制约作用有哪些？第一，在阅读过程中，读者利用空白将文本各部分联结在一起时，就会对文本形成一种视野（field of vision）。当至少两种互相关联的视野存在时，读者就会产生一种具有参考意义的视野——这是理解过程中最小的单位。第二，阅读过程中出现的对文本理解的不同视野在结构上具有相同的价值，它们交织在一起形成一种张力，而空白作为文本中存在却未被描述出来的结构，促使读者利用想象填补空白，在填补的过程中消除视野间的张力。第三，一旦文本各部分联结起来，文本就会具有明确的结构。在阅读过程中，读者在某一时刻只会关注某一主题，此刻的主题又成为下一部分的视野。每当一个主题失去与上一主题的关联，就成为处于边缘的空白点。处于边缘的空白点被称为"空缺"（vacancy）。空缺功能的实现是通过读者想象完成的。

伊瑟尔对阅读过程的描述如下：读者通过填补文本的空白形成视野，视野中的空白又被主题填充，并列的主题和视野中产生的空缺被读者接受，并通过转变进而导致审美对象的产生。

文章所涉及的思考如下：首先，要了解空白与空缺之间的关系，同时进一步思考在阅读中读者是如何跟随空白所给予的召唤进行阅读的。其次，伊瑟尔所分析的是超验的、可能的阅读条件，是一种现象学的文本理论，这种阅读分析方法是否具有局限性，需要我们进一步思考。

拓展讨论

正如上文所提到的，空白理论来源于英伽登文学层次说中的"不定点"（places of indeterminacy）概念。英伽登将文学作品视为由四种层次构成的"纯意向客体"，认为正是语音构造层、意义单元层、图式化观相层以及再现客体层的结合创造了"复调和声"的状态并让文学作品得以形成。其中，图式化观相层中存在着许多不完整或者不明确的点，这些点需要由读者通过阅读这一行动来填补，英伽登称之为不定点。正是不定点的出现，使得读者对文学作品的阅读变得不定型，读者作为阅读主体的地位被提升了上来。将文学作品视作"不可拆散的、不可肢解的、不可解构的"的观点消解，文学在现象学视野内获得了新的阐释空间。伊瑟尔的空白理论便是由不定点理论深化发展而来的。伊瑟尔将"空白"定义为文学作品中非确定的凝固表现，是联结作品与读者的基础结构。因此，若要进一步探索空白理论的逻辑生成和前进方向，回首英伽登《论文学作品》中对于"不定点"与"图式化观相层"的定义是必要的。

"空白"的问题并非一个简单的近代西方哲学概念或是理论问题。我国的理论传统中也有着类似的观点。例如，道家在很早的时候便阐述了关于"无"的存在和作用，并将其融入其他领域中。魏晋时期，玄学的"贵无"思想也使得创作者与理论家对于所谓"不存在"的地方进行思考与创作。例如，王弼言道："言者所以明象，得象而忘言；象者所以存意，得意而忘象。"（《周易略例·明象》）在此之后，不论是严羽的"妙语说"还是钟嵘的"直寻说"都承认言语之外存在着可以被感受和追求的地方。相关的观点与思想也渗透到了艺术领域。"留白"作为我国绘画艺术中的一个独特之处，承载着不同人的不同意志与品位。直到现在，我们依然可以从八大山人的留白中感受到"残山剩水"的凄凉，这是中国空白的独特影响力。中西方文论是两种截然不同的话语体系。植根于现象学的空白理论是基于西方叙事文学传统而产生的文学理论。中国文学的抒情传统是不容忽视的，因此我国的理论或创作讨论都是基于抒情方式的探讨，这也就导致了我们对空白的认识常常停留在一种方法的层面上，并且完全是从作者立场出发的。

总之，"空白"作为文学理论概念，不仅有着西方传统的哲学背景，而且有着中国传统文化中的独特阐释，具有充足的理论学习价值。

延伸阅读

1. 姚斯、霍拉勃：《接受美学与接受理论》，周宁、金元浦译，沈阳，辽宁人民出版社，1987。本书分为两部分，前半部分是姚斯的思想，后半部分是霍拉勃对接受理论的概述以及对接受美学史的梳理。

2. 伽达默尔：《诠释学Ⅰ 真理与方法——哲学诠释学的基本特征（修订译本）》，洪汉鼎译，北京，商务印书馆，2017。本书探究的是在对艺术真理进行辩护的基础上去发展一种与整个诠释学经验相适应的认知和真理的概念。

3. 伊格尔顿：《二十世纪西方文学理论》，伍晓明译，北京，北京大学出版社，2007。作者梳理出起自俄国形式主义的纷繁复杂的20世纪西方文学理论革命的三条发展脉络——从形式主义、结构主义到后结构主义，从现象学、解释学到接受美学，以及精神分析理论，并对其产生和流变、问题和局限性进行了深入分析。

4. 朱立元：《接受美学导论》，合肥，安徽教育出版社，2004。本书介绍了接受美学的理论来源、发展历史，以及接受美学理论下的文学本体论、作品论、创作论等问题。

11. On the Romantic Philosophy of Life: Novalis (1907)
By Georg Lukács

Das Leben eines wahrhaft kanonischen Menschen muss durchgehends
symbolisch sein. ①

Novalis: Blütenstaub

THE background is the dying eighteenth century: the century of rationalism, of
the fighting, victorious bourgeoisie conscious of its triumph. In Paris, dreamy
doctrinaires were thinking through every possibility of rationalism with their
cruel and bloodthirsty logic, while at German universities one book after
another undermined and destroyed the proud hope of rationalism—the hope that
nothing was ultimately out of reason's reach, Napoleon and the intellectual
reaction were already frighteningly near; after a new anarchy that was already
on the point of collapse, the old order was looming up once more.

Jena at the end of the eighteenth century. An episode in the lives of a few
human beings, of no more than episodic significance for the world at large.
Everywhere the earth resounds with battles, whole worlds are collapsing, but
here, in a small German town, a few young people come together for the purpose of creating a new, harmonious, all-embracing culture out of the chaos.
They rush at it with that inconceivable, reckless naïvety that is given only to
people whose degree of consciousness is morbidly high, and to these only for a
single cause in their lives and then again only for a few moments. It was a dance
on a glowing volcano, it was a radiantly improbable dream; after many years
the memory of it still lives on in the observer's soul as something bewilderingly
paradoxical. For despite all the wealth of what they dreamed and scattered,
"still there was something unhealthy about the whole thing. " A spiritual tower
of Babel was to be erected, with nothing but air for its infrastructure; it had to

---

① "The life of a truly canonical person must be symbolic throughout. " (Trans.)

collapse, but when it did, its builders broke down too.

1

Friedrich Schlegel once wrote that the French Revolution, Fichte's doctrine of science and Goethe's *Wilhelm Meister* represented the greatest events of the age. This juxtaposition is characteristic of the tragedy and greatness of the German cultural movement. For Germany, there was only one way to culture: the inner way, the way of revolution of the spirit; no one could seriously envisage a real revolution. Men destined for action had to fall silent and wither away, or else they became mere utopians and played games with bold possibilities in the mind; men who, on the other side of the Rhine, would have become tragic heroes could, in Germany, live out their destinies only in poetic works. Thus Schlegel's observation, if we properly evaluate the time and the circumstances, is surprisingly just and objective; it is astonishing that he places the French Revolution as high as he does, for in the minds of German intellectuals Fichte and Goethe represented real events in real life, whereas the Revolution could have little concrete meaning. Since outward progress could not be thought of, every energy turned inwards and soon "the land of poets and thinkers" surpassed all others by the depth, subtlety and power of its interiority. But this made the gap between the peaks and the plains ever greater; if those who arrived at the top became dizzy at the depth of the abysses, if the thinness of the Alpine air took their breath away, it was all in vain, for the descent had already become impossible: all those below lived in centuries long past. To take them higher, so that life on the mountain-tops might become less isolated and more secure for those who dwelt there, was just as impossible. The only path led still higher, towards a deadly solitude.

Everything seemed out of joint Every summit projected into empty space. The effects of rationalism had been dangerous and destructive enough: rationalism had dethroned all existing values, at least theoretically, and those who had the courage to oppose it had nothing to guide them but an atomistic, anarchic emotional reaction. But when Kant appeared on the scene to destroy the proud armouries of both warring parties, there seemed to be nothing any longer capable of creating order in the ever-increasing mass of new knowledge or in the opaque depths below.

Goethe alone achieved it. In that sea of moody, untamed individualisms, his tyrannically conscious cult of the self is an island resplendent with flowers. All around him individualism was going to rack and ruin, was becoming an anarchy of instincts, a triviality that lost itself in a welter of moods and details, a pathetic renunciation; he alone was able to find order for himself. He had the strength to wait quietly until good fortune brought him fulfillment—and also the strength to reject, with cold equanimity, everything that spelt danger for him. He had the art of fighting in such a way that he never staked his innermost essence nor ever sacrificed any of it on compromises and arrangements. His conquests were of such a kind that newly discovered deserts turned into gardens at his mere glance, and when he renounced something, the power and harmony of possession was only heightened by the loss.

Yet all the forces unleashed in that century stormed within him too, and his flashes of lightning had to tame titans who raged within him more fiercely, perhaps, than those who, through their own unrestraint, were hurled into the depths of Tartarus. He faced all dangers, but he crushed every one of them underfoot; he suffered all the torments of loneliness, but he prepared himself always to stand alone. Every echo was for him a surprise, a happy, happiness creating accident; but the whole of his life was a great, cruel and glorious necessity where every loss had to bring as much enrichment as every gain.

The truest way of speaking of the early Romantics would surely be to describe in the utmost detail what Goethe meant to each of them at each moment of their lives. Then one would see jubilant victory and speechless tragedy, great hopes, daring adventures, long voyages, and would hear two war-cries merging into a single shout of battle: to reach him! to surpass him!

2

Jena at the end of the eighteenth century. A few steeply rising trajectories cross here for a moment; men who have always lived in loneliness discover with intoxicating joy that others are thinking in accordance with the same rhythm as their own and feeling in a way which seems to fit into the same system. They were as different from one another as can be conceived, and it sounds like a romantic fairytale that they were able to love one another—that, even if for a short time, they could believe in the possibility of continuing their ascent together.

Of course the whole thing was really no more than a big literary salon, even if scattered over the whole of Germany. It was the founding of a new literary group on a social basis. Germany's most independent and headstrong personalities came together in it. Each of them climbed his own long, hard path to reach the point from where he could at last see sunlight and a wide view opening up before him; each suffered all the torments of a man driven out into the wilderness, thirsting for culture and intellectual communion, and the tragic, ecstatic pain of an idealism stretched to breaking-point. They felt that the way they had gone, the way that each young generation of the newly-awakened Germany had gone before them, led into nothingness; and almost simultaneously they saw the possibility of coming from the nothing into a something, of freeing themselves from the anarchy of living as mere litterati—a necessity forced upon them by outward circumstances—and hastening towards fruitful, culture-creating new goals.

Not so long before, Goethe had finally arrived at such a goal. Perhaps it was this that rescued the new generation from the constant, aimless, energy-devouring, energy-destroying agitation which for half a century had been the undoing of Germany's greatest men. Today we should probably call the thing they were striving for "culture"; but they, when for the first time it stood before their eyes as a redeeming, a possible goal, had a thousand poetic formulae to describe it and saw a thousand ways of coming nearer to it. They knew that each of their paths must lead to it, they felt that every conceivable experience had to be accepted and lived through in order that the "invisible church" which it was their mission to build should be all-embracing and full of riches. It looked as though a new religion were about to be created, a pantheistic, monistic religion which worshipped progress, a religion born of the new truths and discoveries of the new science. Friedrich Schlegel believed that in the allpenetrating force of idealism which revealed itself in the natural sciences before it became conscious as a philosophy, before it united the consciousness of the age, there lay concealed a myth-engendering force which only needed to be awakened into life in order to provide a ground which would be as strong and as collective as that of the Greeks for poetry, art and every life-expression. This mythology was not simply an ideal demand of those whose highest aspiration was to create a new style; it also became the infrastructure of a new religion. For they often called this goal of theirs a religion, and indeed it was with a purely religious exclusivity and single-mindedness that their questing spirit subordinated every other aim to it. Hardly anyone at the time could put in clear language what that goal was, and even today it is not easy to compress its meaning into any formula. The question, of course, was put to them quite clearly and unambiguously by life itself. A new world seemed to be in process of creation, bringing forth human beings with new life-possibilities; but the old, still persisting life was so constituted, and the new life, too, developed in such a way that no place could be found in it for its best sons. It was becoming more and more difficult and problematic for the great men of the age simply to exist, to belong to life, to occupy a place, to take up a stand. Everywhere and in every work of art, the question asked was: how can one, how ought one to live today? They looked for an ethic of genius ("genius is the natural condition of man," said Novalis) and, beyond it, for a religion of genius—since even ethics could only be a means of attaining that distant goal, that final harmony. The old religions, the Middle Ages, Goethe's Greece, Catholicism, all were no more than makeshift symbols for this new longing which, in their passionate will for unity, elevated every feeling into a religion: everything small and everything great, friendship and philosophy, poetry and life.

And the apostles of this new religion gathered in their salons in Berlin and Jena and discussed in passionate paradoxes the programme of the new conquest of the world. Then they started a review, a very clever, very bizarre one, very profound and completely esoteric, whose every line betrayed the impossibility of its having any practical effect whatsoever. And if it had had one nevertheless…? "Still there was something unhealthy about the whole thing…"

Goethe and Romanticism. I think that what has been said already makes it clear where the connection between them lies—and perhaps still more clear where their ways part. Of course the Romantics, too, were aware of both; every point at which they came near to Goethe was a source of proud joy to them, and most of them dared only to hint, timidly and stealthily, at what it was that divided them from him. *Wilhelm Meister* was the decisive experience for them all, yet only Karoline① remained faithful to the Goethean way of life and only Novalis had the courage to say openly that it had to be abandoned. He was the one who most clearly saw Goethe's superiority to himself and his friends: he saw that everything which remained mere method and idea with them was turned into action by Goethe; that in trying to cope with their own problems, they could only produce reflections which were in turn problematic, whereas Goethe actually transcended his; that they sought to create a new world where the genius, the poet of that world, might find a home, whereas Goethe found his home in the life of his own time.

Yet he saw just as clearly what Goethe had had to sacrifice in order to find that home, and his whole being rebelled against the idea that this solution was the only possible one. He too dreamed of the ultimate harmony of *Wilheim Meister* as his life's goal, and with the same clarity as Goethe he saw how fraught with danger were the beginnings and the paths of that journey. Yet he believed that Goethe had reached his goal a poorer man than the reaching of it demanded.

Here the way of Romanticism and Goethe's way part. Both seek a balance of the same opposing forces, but Romanticism wants a balance in which its intensity can remain unimpaired. Its individualism is tougher, more self-willed, more conscious, more uncompromising than Goethe's, but by stretching this individualism to its uttermost limits, Romanticism wants to achieve the ultimate harmony.

---

① See footnote on p. 33. (*Trans.*)

Poetry is its ethic, morality its poetry. Novalis once said that morality was, at root, poetry; Friedrich Schlegel thought that all genuine and spontaneous originality was morally valuable in itself. Yet the Romantics' individualism was not meant to isolate them, "Our thinking is a dialogue, our feeling sympathy," said Novalis. The aphorisms and fragments of the *Athenaeum*—the most characteristic and lyrically truest expression of their programme—were not one work of any single individual; in many cases it is not even possible to identify their originator. In writing these aphorisms and fragments, the Romantics were concerned with emphasizing the directions and lines of thought common to them all; sometimes they synthesized the most widely differing ideas in the form of an aphorism simply in order to produce the effect of homogeneity and to avoid a single personality coming too strongly to the fore.

They wanted to create a culture, to make art learnable, to organize genius. They wanted—as in the great epochs of the past—every newly created value to become an inalienable possession, they wanted progress no longer to be subject to accident. They clearly saw that the only possible basis for such a culture was an art born of technology and the spirit of matter. They wanted to dedicate themselves to the art of putting words together just as goldsmiths had once given their lives to studying gold ore. But to produce a work of art, even a perfect one, could not be an ultimate goal for them; if anything possessed real value, it had that value only as a formative means. "To become a god, to be a man, to educate oneself—all these are different ways of expressing the same meaning," says Friedrich Schlegel, and Novalis adds: "Poetry is the specific mode of action of the human mind." This is not art for art's sake, it is pan-poetism.

It is the ancient dream of a golden age. But their golden age is not a refuge in a past that has been lost forever, only to be glimpsed from time to time in beautiful old legends—it is a goal whose attainment is the central duty of everyone. It is the "blue flower" which dreaming knights have to seek everywhere and always; it is the Middle Ages which they romantically worship, it is the Christianity they embrace; nothing is unattainable; a time must come when the impossible will be unknown. "People accuse poets of exaggeration," writes Novalis. "But it seems to me that poets do not exaggerate nearly enough… They do not know what forces they have under their control, what worlds belong to them. " This is why *Wilhelm Meister* disappointed him, this is why he said that it was essentially an anti-poetic work, "a *Candide* levelled at poetry. "

By saying this he pronounced his death-sentence upon the book, for to the Romantics poetry was the centre of the entire world. The world-view of Romanticism is the most authentic pan-poetism: everything is poetry and poetry is "the one and the all. " Never and for no one was the word "poet" so full of meaning, so holy, so all-embracing as for the German Romantics. It is true that in later times, too, many men and many poets have been ready to offer sacrifices at the altar of poetry; but what made Romanticism unique was that it extended to the whole of life: it was not a renunciation of life, nor a refusal of its riches; Romanticism seemed to offer the only possibility of achieving the goal without renouncing anything along the way. The goal of the Romantics was a world in which men could lead real lives. They spoke, with Fichte, of the "I. " In this sense they were egoists: servants and fanatics of their own development, to whom everything mattered and had value only in so far as it contributed to their growth. "We are not yet 'I'," wrote Novalis. "But we can and must become 'I,' we are the buds of becoming-'I'. " The poet is the only human being who corresponds to the norms, he alone has the full possibility of "becoming-'I'. " Why is this so?

An epoch which longs for culture will find its centre only in the arts; the less culture there is and the more intensely it is missed, the stronger the desire for it. But here what mattered was a passive capacity for experiencing life. The Romantics' philosophy of life was based—even if never quite consciously so—on their passive life-experiencing capacity. For them the art of living was one of self-adaptation, carried through with genius, to all the events of life. They exploited to the full and raised to the status of necessity everything that fate put in their path; they poeticized fate, but did not mould or conquer it. The path they took could only lead to an organic fusion of all given facts, only to a beautiful harmony of images of life, but not to controlling life.

Yet this path was the only possibility open to their longing for the great synthesis of unity and universality. They looked for order, but for an order that comprised everything, an order for the sake of which no renunciation was needed; they tried to embrace the whole world in such a way that out of the unison of all dissonances might come a symphony. To combine this unity and this universality is possible only in poetry, and that is why poetry for the Romantics became the centre of the world. In poetry alone they found a natural possibility of resolving all contradictions and bringing them together into higher harmony; in poetry alone was it possible to allocate to every separate thing its appointed place, simply by giving it a little more or a little less emphasis. Everything becomes a symbol in poetry, but then everything, in poetry, is only a symbol; everything has a meaning but nothing can claim value for itself and in itself. The Romantics' art of living was poetry as action; they transformed the deepest and most inward laws of poetic art into imperatives for life.

Where everything is properly understood and deeply lived, there can be no real contradictions. Whatever other roads they appeared to travel, the Romantics looked for their own "I," and the rhythm of their seeking created friendships and kinships, but not an identity of direction. At the root of their agreements and their differences lay only words; even their opinions were, at best, only ways towards the real values—generally imperfect and provisional expressions of feelings not yet mature enough to be given form. A sense of rhythm and social tact (the two concepts mean the same) were what made all the unresolved dissonances disappear. If Goethe had not intervened, the Schlegels would have printed Schelling's *Heinz Widerporst* and Novalis' *Christendom* side by side in the same issue of the *Athenaeum*. Convictions could not separate anyone from anyone else—their life-value was considered to be far too small. Every endeavour, whatever its goal, was received with irony but, viewed symbolically, it was—if it so deserved—acknowledged as a religion.

The egoism of the Romantics is strongly coloured with social feeling. They hoped that the intense unfolding of the personality would in the end bring human beings really close to one another; in that unfolding they themselves sought their salvation from loneliness and chaos. They were deeply convinced that their uncompromising, self-willed manner of writing would produce the right and necessary communion between writers and readers and would ensure that popularity which was one of the highest aims of all Romantics. They dearly saw that the absence of such communion was the sole reason why the glorious development of individual forces characteristic of their time never ripened into cultural deeds. They hoped to develop such communion out of their small, closed circle, and they succeeded—within that circle and for a few years. So long as they, who came from the most different directions and followed the most different paths, appeared to be travelling along the same great road, they wanted to regard every divergence as something merely external, to consider only what they had in common as important; and this harmony was meant to be no more than the modest prelude to a greater, truer harmony to come. Yet it was enough for a few values to become slightly displaced in the minds of a few of them, and the "Hansa" disintegrated, the harmony became a deafening sequence of cacophonous sounds.

A seemingly deliberate withdrawal from life was the price of the Romantic art of living, but this was conscious only at the surface, only within the realm of psychology. The deep nature of this withdrawal and its complex relations were never understood by the Romantics themselves and therefore remained unresolved and devoid of any life-redeeming force. The actual reality of life vanished before their eyes and was replaced by another reality, the reality of poetry, of pure psyche. They created a homogeneous, organic world unified within itself and identified it with the real world. This gave their world the quality of something angelic, suspended between heaven and earth, incorporeally luminous; but the tremendous tension that exists between poetry and life and gives both their real, value-creating powers was lost as a result. And they did not even look for it, they simply left it behind on their heroically frivolous flight towards heaven; they were scarcely aware any longer that it existed. Only in this way could they achieve their universality, but because of this they could not recognize its limitations. These limitations were for them neither a tragedy—as they are for men who live life through to its end—nor ways towards a real, authentic *ceuvre* whose greatness and strength would reside, precisely, in that it kept heterogeneous things apart and created a new, unified stratification of the world finally cut loose from reality. These limitations meant for them a collapse, an awakening from a beautiful, feverish dream a melancholy end without enrichment, without the promise of a new beginning. Because they identified the cosmos they had created in their dreams with the real world, they could not arrive at a clear division anywhere; because of this they could believe that action is possible without renunciation and that poetry-making is possible within reality. Yet all action, every deed, every act of creation is limiting. No action can be performed without renouncing something, and he who performs an action can never possess universality. This is why, almost imperceptibly, the ground slipped away under their feet and their monumental, powerful constructions were gradually transformed into sandcastles and finally dissolved into thin air. The dream of advancing side by side dissolved like a fine mist, too, and a few years later scarcely a single one of them could understand the other's language; and the deepest dream of all, the hope of the culture to come, went the same way. But by now they had enjoyed the intoxication of belonging to a community and could no longer continue their ascent by solitary, separate paths. Many became mere imitators of their own youth; some, worn out by the comfortless search for a new religion and the dismal sight of increasing anarchy—a sight which merely helped to intensify their desire for order—returned with resignation into the quiet waters of the old religions. And so it happened that men who had once set out to remould and re-create an entire world became pious converts. "Still there was something unhealthy about the whole thing."

4

So far we have not said very much about Novalis, and yet he has been our central subject throughout. No one emphasized the exclusive importance of the ultimate goals more stubbornly than this delicate youth doomed to an early death; no one was more at the mercy of all the hazards of the Romantic way of life—and yet he was the only one among all these great theoreticians of the art of living who succeeded in leading a harmonious life. Each of the others became dizzy at the sight of the abyss which spread before their feet even on the brightest days, and each fell from the heights into that abyss; only Novalis succeeded in wresting a life-enhancing strength from the ever-present danger. The danger which threatened him was more brutal, more physical than that of the others, and yet (or perhaps just because of this) he was able to draw the greatest life-energy from it.

The danger which threatened him was death—his own and that of the people who were closest to his soul. The programme of his life could take only one form: to find the proper rhymes for these deaths in the poem into which he made his life—and to fit his life harmoniously, as an unassailable fact, in between these deaths. To live in such a way that death would come in answer to a cue, not as an interruption; but for this to be possible, the inner laws and beauty of everything he did had to demand that it remain a fragment forever. To survive the death of his beloved, but in such a way that the melody of his pain was never wholly hushed, and that a new time-reckoning began with that death; in such a way that his own certain death should stand in a deep inner relation to the beloved's death, and that the short life fitted in between the two deaths should nevertheless be rich and full of lived experience.

In Novalis the tendencies of Romanticism find their most intense expression. Romanticism always consciously refused to recognize tragedy as a form of life (though not, of course, as a form of literary creation). The highest aspiration of Romanticism was to make tragedy disappear completely from the world, to resolve tragic situations in an untragic way. Here, too, Novalis' life was the most Romantic: his destiny always placed him in situations from which another man would have drawn nothing but suffering or tragic ecstasy, yet whatever his hand touched turned into gold and nothing could come his way that did not enrich him. He was always face to face with pain, he was forced again and again to sink to the very depths of despair, yet he smiled and was happy.

The young Friedrich Schlegel noted down the first conversation that ever took place between them. Both were twenty years old. Novalis asserted with fiery vehemence that "there is nothing evil in the world, and everything is bringing us closer to another golden age. " Many years later, at the end of his life, the hero of Novalis' only novel expressed the same feeling when he said that "fate and soul are but two different names for a single concept."

Fate struck him more than once, brutally and ruthlessly. But he surrendered everything to fate and became richer than before. After a troubled youth it seemed as though a young girl were to become the fulfillment of all his dreams; she died, and nothing was left to him but his belief that he too would soon follow her into the grave. He did not think of suicide nor of being consumed by his sorrow; he was unshakeably convinced that he could devote himself serenely and calmly to what was left of his life, and that it would not be for long. He wanted to die, did he not? Surely his will was strong enough to call for death, to make death come?

But life came instead and stood in his way. It showed him unwritten poems, radiant and soaring; luminous paths that led further than the whole of Goethe. It spread before him all the innumerable wonders of the new sciences, their perspectives pointing into infinity, their possibilities destined to create new worlds. It led him into the world of action and he had to recognize that nothing could be dry or sterile for him, that everything turned into harmony at his approach; even a government official's existence was transformed into a song of triumph. Yet he still wanted death.

But life refused him this gift. It would not grant him this, the only thing he asked from fate. Instead it offered him new happiness and a new love—the love of a woman who was superior to his first and only beloved; but he would not accept it. He wanted only to keep faith. In the end he could resist no longer. He re-entered life, he who had been calling for death only a little earlier, he who eternally proclaimed that nothing is impossible for man, yet who, in reality, wanted only one thing—to achieve the very opposite of what he wanted. Even when the whole edifice of his life collapsed, nothing broke within him; he went forward to happiness as serene and resolute as he had previously been in readiness for death.

And when, at last, he stretched out his hand for life, when at last he overcame his cult of death, then the saviour he had once longed for came at last: death, which only a little while before would have been the jubilant crowning of his life, struck like a discordant blow. But, even now, how he died! His friends could not believe that death had really been so close at hand; later, they were convinced that he had no idea it was so near. Yet he drew up a new life-programme for the period of his dying; he carefully avoided anything that a sick man could not do to perfection or with absolute intensity; he lived only for what his illness could actually advance. Once he wrote: "Disease is certainly a most important subject for humanity⋯ We have as yet a very imperfect knowledge of the art of utilizing it." When, a few months before his death, he wrote to his friend Tieck describing his life, he said: "⋯so you see, it was a troubled time. I have mostly been serene." And Friedrich Schlegel, who sat at his deathbed, speaks of Novalis' "indescribable serenity" when dying.

5

Novalis is the only true poet of the Romantic school. In him alone the whole soul of Romanticism turned to song, and only he expressed nothing but that soul. The others, if they were poets at all, were merely Romantic poets; Romanticism supplied them with new motifs, it altered the direction of their development or enriched it, but they were poets before they recognized Romantic feelings in themselves and remained poets after they had completely abandoned Romanticism. Novalis' art and work—there is no help for it, it is a platitude but it is the only way of saying it—form an indivisible whole, and as such they are a symbol of the whole of Romanticism. It is as though, redeemed by his life, Romantic poetry became pure and authentic poetry once more after venturing forth into life and going astray there. In his work, all the tentative approaches of Romanticism remained mere approaches; the Romantic will for unity, a will which always, of necessity, remained fragmentary, was nowhere so fragmentary as in Novalis who had to die just as he was beginning to create his real works. Yet he was the only one whose life left something more behind it than a picturesque heap of rubble from which one can dig up a few glorious fragments and wonder what the edifice of which they were part was once like. All his paths led to a goal, all his questions were answered. Every ghost, every *fata morgana* of Romanticism acquired solid flesh in him, he alone refused to be lured into the bottomless quagmire by the will-o'-the-wisps of Romanticism;

his eyes saw every will-o'-the-wisp as a star, and he had wings to follow it. He met the most cruel fate of all, but only he was capable of growing as a result of his struggle. Of all the Romantic seekers for mastery over life, he was the only practical artist of the art of living.

Yet even he received no answer to his question: he put the question to life, and death brought the answer. To sing the praises of death *is* perhaps something more and something greater than to sing the praises of life: but it was not to find such songs that the Romantics set out.

The tragedy of Romanticism was that only Novalis' life could turn to poetry. His victory is a death sentence passed on the Romantic school as a whole. Everything the Romantics wanted to conquer sufficed for no more than a beautiful death. Their life-philosophy was one of death; their art of living, an art of dying. They strove to embrace the world, and this made them into slaves of fate. Perhaps Novalis seems so great and so complete to us today only because he became the slave of an unconquerable master.

11. 卢卡奇：《浪漫的生命哲学：诺瓦利斯》

(Georg Lukács, "On the Romantic Philosophy of Life: Novalis," 1907)

作者小识

卢卡奇(Georg Lukács, 1885—1971)，匈牙利无产阶级革命家，西方马克思主义的创始人之一。他以第二次世界大战之前的美学与文学批评著作闻名于世，对法兰克福学派产生了深刻的影响。即便在当今晚期资本主义时代，或者说后现代，卢卡奇的《小说理论》(*Theory of the Novel*，1916)和《历史与阶级意识》(*History and Class Consciousness*，1923)仍然广为流传，被奉为马克思主义理论发展史上的经典之作。"总体性""历史主体性""物化"等重要概念，显示了经典马克思主义理论与时俱进的巨大潜能，以及自我转型的思想品格，但最能吸引欧洲现代文人的是他早期的那些文学批评著作。这些作品上承浪漫主义流风余韵，下开反主流文化批判的先声，尤其是他的多卷本论述社会和美学存在论(或本体论)的巨著，给予了现代性反思和理论再度建构以深远的启示。

卢卡奇也是活跃的政治家，身体力行反对将马克思主义教条化。于他而言，理论不仅就是实践，而且也只有作为实践才能获得生命力。

背景略说

要把握卢卡奇的思想，首先应该了解他将哲学建构与文化批判融为一体的特征。其哲学建构基于德国古典哲学，尤其是康德、黑格尔哲学及其后学，当然马克思主义哲学起主导作用。其文化批判犀利敏感、强大有力，灵感源自马克斯·韦伯(Max Weber, 1864—1920)和格奥尔格·齐美尔(Georg Simmel, 1858—1918)对于现代理性化过程的社会学分析。

马克斯·韦伯倡导在社会学中展开"与价值无涉"的中立研究，提出资本主义发展的原动力是新教伦理，即一种"斯多葛主义的禁欲伦理"，从中发展出一种工于算计的工具理性，而这便是现代理性化进程的精神基础。理性化进程的结果，首先是自然脱除神秘魅力，"世界不再迷人"(disenchantment of the world），其次是非人化管理的科层制形成，从而颠覆了神权、王权，建立了法权在现代的主导地位。齐美尔为社会学在人文学科之中争得一席之地而苦斗，力求将社会学置于生命哲学的基础上，以研究社会关系为对象，分析社会化过程。但齐美尔最终发现，人与文化之间发展出了严酷的对峙，最终酿成了"文化的悲剧"（cultural tragedy）。韦伯的社会学、齐美尔的文化哲学所得出的结论，偏执而又深刻，甚至提出了救赎世界的可能性问题，从而将一种启示录式的语调渗透到了人文学科中。

深思韦伯的"理性化"（rationalization），卢卡奇以"物化"（reification）为回应，提出了历史的主体以及存在论问题。回味齐美尔"生命与形式"（life and form）分裂的文化悲剧，卢卡奇通过反思浪漫传统，展开了对"灵魂与形式"（soul and form）的辩证分析。"理性化""形式论"两脉思想源远流长，远溯柏拉图的哲学，近缘启蒙思想及其所引发的现代进程，在卢卡奇的思想体系之中一直延伸，甚至构成了其"理性的毁灭"之叙述架构。

《灵魂与形式》（*Soul and Form*）一书，内含 10 篇杂文，从柏拉图到浪漫主义诗人诺瓦利斯，以及存在主义的先驱克尔凯郭尔，集中论说"随笔"与现代碎片之间的映射关系、形式与生命的辩证法，凸显现代人的精神贫困及其悲剧性存在方式。这本小册子或许受到新康德主义者克拉格斯（Ludwig Klages，1872—1956）的《精神作为灵魂之敌人》（*Der Geist als Widersacher der Seele*）的影响。特别值得一提的是，卢卡奇写作这些文章不仅受到"爱欲"的驱动，而且直接献给了"爱欲"：1908 年，卢卡奇与画家伊尔玛一见钟情，但卢卡奇优柔寡断，害怕为爱而承担责任，致使伊尔玛绝望而另嫁他人，婚姻痛苦不堪，一日纵身跳入多瑙河。卢卡奇哀悼这段毁灭的恋情，而这批作品中"灵魂""形式"两个范畴的张力或许正来源于爱欲的体验。灵魂漫溢爱欲，但形式要求收敛，二者之间不解的冲突，终于酿成个体悲剧。书中关键一篇是论述"悲剧的形而上学"，自是叔本华、尼采、克尔凯郭尔最为钟爱的主题。卢卡奇借着古希腊悲剧淋漓尽致地发挥道：真正的生命表现为否定形式，而死亡凸显了生命的意义，揭示了现实生命之中"伟大的瞬间"。戈德曼断言，卢卡奇的生命悲剧观预兆着海德格尔的《存在与时间》。

1918 年，卢卡奇从浪漫主义者转向布尔什维克。他阅读陀思妥耶夫斯基，奋力在小说中发现超越"实在强暴力量"的动机。《小说理论》一书在黑格尔历史哲学的框架下探索现代文类的生成，展开了对现代文明的批判，寻求精神危机的解救之道。深受席勒思想的影响，卢卡奇将人性圆满的境界以及人与世界的和谐状态投射到了古希腊，而与现代机械化碎片生活构成了令人忧伤的对立。在古今对立的图景中，以及在人类精神的张力下，卢卡奇认为史诗与小说之诗学形式折射了时代之差异。"小说是上帝遗弃世界的史诗"，但它刻画了最为广博的总体，比其他形式更能让作者展示自由的想象力。形式，依然是卢卡奇美学思想的重心："一切形式都是对生活的根本不和谐状态的化解。"这一命题意味着他赋予了小说以建构外延总体性和实施审美救赎的神圣使命。他断言，"犯罪与疯癫，是超验的无家可归之客观化，意味着社会关系之中人类秩序里某一行动的无家可归之客观化，以及在超越个人的价值体系之应然秩序里某一心灵的无家可归之客观化"。要克服这种超验和内在的双重无家可归，文学形式就担负着这样一种使命：在一个无意义取代了生活恰当位置的世界，决然化解根本不和谐状态，将之表现为意义的必要条件。①

基本内容

《灵魂与形式》是卢卡奇早期美学和文学批评的代表作，字里行间渗透着他对现代文明危机的深切忧虑。这种忧虑在他的思想生涯一以贯之，并且转化到了他成熟的马克思主义思想当中。在这些文章中，他发挥出一套成熟的美学理论，还表现了批判现代文明的敏锐意识。在他看来，齐美尔"文化与形式"的悲剧就是现代文明的悲剧：客观文化形式与真正丰富的生命之间，横亘着一道悲剧性的深渊。直面这一文化悲剧，卢卡奇首先必须沉思形式与生命的关系，而这就是《灵魂与形式》一书的基本主题。巴特勒对这个主题进行了精到的概述："形式、文学形式，以及在松散随意的柏拉图主义意义上的'形式'——它们的使命都是将每一种生命之中的偶然理性化。若非有人创造，形式就根本不存在。那些创造如此极端脆弱而飘忽无定的形式之人将会发现：无论多么偶然，生命的一切方面都将成为必然，成为本质。"②

分散在《灵魂与形式》一书中的基本观点可以归纳如下：（1）散文形式的美学意义。散文或者随笔（essay）是源始形态的书写方式，它通过形式媒介凸显生命意识，将艺术形式严肃地视为独立存在的现实。（2）现代艺术的进退两

① 参见卢卡奇：《小说理论》，燕宏远、李怀涛译，54～55 页，北京，商务印书馆，2012。译文略有调整。

② 参见 Judith Butler，"Introduction to *Soul and Form*，" in Georg Lukács，*Soul and Form*，trans. Anna Bostock，New York，Columbia University Press，2010，p. 8。

难。现代艺术，要么牺牲生命的强度与潜能，要么在纯粹象征与想象维度上实现生命与形式的和解，即从生命之中退出，逃向虚幻境界。无论采取哪种方式，艺术与生命都背道而驰。相反，如果要真正地努力赋予"实在"或"绝对生命"以独一无二的形式，就必须拒绝经验生命之中无意义的偶然。这么一种努力必须认可一种不可融入日常生活的奇特生命形式，这就是浪漫主义的意义。(3)悲剧形而上学。当自然和命运"可怕地丧失了灵魂"，而一切对于"爱欲秩序"的期盼都烟消云散，悲剧的使命就是形而上学的使命——拒绝日常生活，寻求"在悲剧外围生活"的机会。(4)精神的贫困。克尔凯郭尔的恋爱与婚姻的故事表明，存在论的伦理立场陷入困境——根本就不可能以绝对的生命形式来超越日常生活，以悲剧生活代替日常生活。由于一种内在的歧义，以及同形式的绝然对立，悲剧的日常生活是一种"不可能的诗学想象"。卢卡奇最后克服异化(物化)的构想暴露出其早期立场的僵局，代价是赞同伦理决断论(ethical decisionism)，以及审美的弥赛亚主义(aesthetic messianism)。

卢卡奇不仅叙述了浪漫主义向现实主义的转型，而且还力求在一种不可还原为实证主义的现实主义领域发掘浪漫主义的残像余韵。在卢卡奇看来，诺瓦利斯具体地代表着浪漫主义的力竭神枯，即浪漫主义处处承认其自身的不可能。他的生命方案仅仅获得了一种形式，即在他生命转换而成的诗歌之中去寻找死亡的真正节奏。卢卡奇认为，浪漫主义的生活方式力求将死亡从一场"中断"转化为一种诗意的必要特征，而要完成这一使命，就唯有全然从生命之中退出。所以在他看来，浪漫主义之本质，就在于将生命变成必要的诗意，从而彻底否定生命。于是，浪漫主义的生命哲学就是"不可能的诗学"(poetics for the impossible)。

拓展讨论

在《小说理论》论述"史诗与小说"的部分，卢卡奇提出了"存在的根本不和谐"这么一个激进命题。他认为，艺术形式的使命，就是化解这种不和谐。审美救赎论在此采取了乌托邦主义的形式。但是，在卢卡奇的思想中，唯物主义和形式主义互相对峙，现实主义和乌托邦主义彼此成全，存在论和先知论复杂纠结，好战主义和反抗主义锋芒直指现代文明。这些显著的矛盾均可追溯到"存在的根本不和谐"，也让卢卡奇成为一个令人困惑的矛盾体，不仅必须被反复地解释，而且必须被策略性地转换。"存在的根本不和谐"成为"物化""理性毁灭"的动因，也意味着现代文化批评必须烛照幽微，揭示现代文明的悖论，重构"总体性原则"，从根本上超越、颠覆资本主义异化社会。

早期卢卡奇认为，"根本"并非"整体"，而是"和谐的缺失"。因为他的全部幻想指向了一个世界："心灵之中燃烧的烈火，与星体具有同一的本质。"于是，每一种形式、人类的每一造物、每一个理智的概念、每一种理解世界的努力，以及每一种行动和每一个表达，都见证着发生在根本分裂僵局之中的斗争。卢卡奇的论述并不限于史诗和小说等艺术形式，还延伸到了20世纪20年代的全部政治著作之中，甚至决定了其政治实践和哲学介入。

以资本主义为例，足以说明问题之实质。如果说，资本主义是一个"总体"，那么卢卡奇的命题就不具有存在论含义，但暗示着一切形式的出现，必然导致巨大的斗争。资本主义也是一种形式。同样，理解也就不是穿透形式，而是作为形式的进化形态。资本主义系统之"总体性"只不过是资本主义之可理解性原则。像"无产阶级"范畴一样，总体性范畴也具有"归责性"，它是一套公理体系，而非体系的产物。在《历史与阶级意识》中，卢卡奇提出，克服物化的努力必然消灭"形式对于内容的冷漠"。他力求探寻一种形式概念，这一概念之基础和效用并不依赖于纯粹理性以及免于一切内容规定的自由。在《灵魂与形式》和《小说理论》中，卢卡奇构想了一种对偶然性敞开，以至于将偶然性提升为建构原则的概念。在他看来，思考"偶然"便是实践的特殊意义。"唯有在历史之中，在历史进程之中，在新质事物的不断涌流之中，我们才能在物质王国发现必要的典范秩序。"于是，卢卡奇认为，当务之急是从黑格尔的迷暗之中走出来，避免将历史交付给哲学体系。梅洛-庞蒂写道：被赋予历史的形式，必须被认为源自历史本身。正是我们赋予历史以意义，而非在历史暗示我们赋予其意味之前。①

20世纪30年代末期，卢卡奇与布洛赫的对话，最为生动地证明了卢卡奇关于"总体性"思想的连续性。二人对于表现主义艺术的关心，开启了这场争论。卢卡奇蔑视表现主义。在布洛赫看来，那是一种征兆，表明他无能适应"一切奋力在表面相互关联之中发掘现实裂缝的艺术"，无能"在断裂之中发现新生事物"。布洛赫用明知故问的方式来废黜卢卡奇对于现实主义的承诺："如果卢卡奇的现实，一种和谐有致、无限中介的现实最终并非客观存在，那

---

① Maurice Merleau-Ponty, *Phenomenology of Perception*, trans. Colin Smith, London and New York, Routledge, 2002, p. 522.

12. The Image of Proust (1929)

By Walter Benjamin

I

The thirteen volumes of Marcel Proust's *A la Recherche du temps perdu* are the result of an unconstruable synthesis in which the absorption of a mystic, the art of a prose writer, the verve of a satirist, the erudition of a scholar, and the self-consciousness of a monomaniac have combined in an autobiographical work. It has rightly been said that all great works of literature found a genre or dissolve one—that they are, in other words, special cases. Among these cases this is one of the most unfathomable. From its structure, which is fiction, autobiography, and commentary in one, to the syntax of endless sentences (the Nile of language, which here overflows and fructifies the regions of truth), everything transcends the norm. The first revealing observation that strikes one is that this great special case of literature at the same time constitutes its greatest achievement of recent decades. The conditions under which it was created were extremely unhealthy: an unusual malady, extraordinary wealth, and an abnormal disposition. This is not a model life in every respect, but everything about it is exemplary. The outstanding literary achievement of our time is assigned a place in the heart of the impossible, at the center—and also at the point of indifference—of all dangers, and it marks this great realization of a "lifework" as the last for a long time. The image of Proust is the highest physiognomic expression which the irresistibly growing discrepancy between literature and life was able to assume. This is the lesson which justifies the attempt to evoke this image.

We know that in his work Proust did not describe a life as it actually was, but a life as it was remembered by the one who had lived it. And yet even this statement is imprecise and far too crude. For the important thing for the remembering author is not what he experienced, but the weaving of his memory, the Penelope work of recollection. Or should one call it, rather, a Penelope work of forgetting? Is not the involuntary recollection, Proust's *mémoire involontaire*, much closer to forgetting than what is usually called memory? And is not this work of spontaneous recollection, in which remembrance is the woof and forgetting the warf, a counterpart to Penelope's work rather than its likeness? For here the day unravels what the night was woven. When we awake each morning, we hold in our hands, usually weakly and loosely, but a few fringes of the tapestry of lived life, as loomed for us by forgetting. However, with our purposeful activity and, even more, our purposive remembering each day unravels the web and the ornaments of forgetting. This is why Proust finally turned his days into nights, devoting all his hours to undisturbed work in his darkened room with artificial illumination, so that none of those intricate arabesques might escape him.

The Latin word *textum* means "web." No one's text is more tightly woven than Marcel Proust's; to him nothing was tight or durable enough. From his publisher Gallimard we know that Proust's proofreading habits were the despair of the typesetters. The galleys always went back covered with marginal notes, but not a single misprint had been corrected; all available space had been used for fresh text. Thus the laws of remembrance were operative even within the confines of the work. For an experienced event is finite—at any rate, confined to one sphere of experience; a remembered event is infinite, because it is only a key to everything that happened before it and after it. There is yet another sense in which memory issues strict weaving regulations. Only the *actus purus* of recollection itself, not the author or the plot, constitutes the unity of the text. One may even say that the intermittence of author and plot is only the reverse of the continuum of memory, the pattern on the back side of the tapestry. This is what Proust meant, and this is how he must be understood, when he said that he would prefer to see his entire work printed in one volume in two columns and without any paragraphs.

What was it that Proust sought so frenetically? What was at the bottom of these infinite efforts? Can we say that all lives, works, and deeds that matter were never anything but the undisturbed unfolding of the most banal, most fleeting, most sentimental, weakest hour in the life of the one to whom they pertain? When Proust in a well-known passage described the hour that was most his own, he did it in such a way that everyone can find it in his own existence. We might almost call it an everyday hour; it comes with the night, a lost twittering of birds, or a breath drawn at the sill of an open window. And there is no telling what encounters would be in store for us if we were less inclined to give in to sleep. Proust did not give in to sleep. And yet—or, rather, precisely for this reason—Jean Cocteau was able to say in a beautiful essay that the intonation of Proust's voice obeyed the laws of night and honey. By submitting to these laws he conquered the hopeless sadness within him (what he once called *"l'imperfection incurable dans l'essence même du prêsent"*)[1], and from the honeycombs of memory he built a house for the swarm of his thoughts. Cocteau recognized what really should have been the major concern of all readers of Proust and yet has served no one as the pivotal point of his reflections or his affection. He recognized Proust's blind, senseless, frenzied quest for happiness. It shone from his eyes; they were not happy, but in them there lay fortune as it lies in gambling or in love. Nor is it hard to say why this paralyzing, explosive will to happiness which pervades Proust's writings is so seldom comprehended by his readers. In many places Proust himself made it easy for them to view this *oeuvre*, too, from the time-tested, comfortable perspective of resignation, heroism, asceticism. After all, nothing makes more sense to the model pupils of life than the notion that a great achievement is the fruit of toil, misery, and disappointment. The idea that happiness could have a share in beauty would be too much of a good thing, something that their *ressentiment* would never get over.

There is a dual will to happiness, a dialectics of happiness: a hymnic and an elegiac form. The one is the unheard-of, the unprecedented, the height of bliss; the other, the eternal repetition, the eternal restoration of the original, the first happiness. It is this elegiac idea of happiness—it could also be called

---

① " … the incurable imperfection in the very essence of the present moment. "

Eleatic—which for Proust transforms existence into a preserve of memory. To it he sacrificed in his life friends and companionship, in his works plot, unity of characters, the flow of the narration, the play of the imagination. Max Unold, one of Proust's more discerning readers, fastened on the "boredom" thus created in Proust's writings and likened it to "pointless stories." "Proust managed to make the pointless story interesting. He says: 'imagine, dear reader, yesterday I was dunking a cookie in my tea when it occurred to me that as a child I spent some time in the country.' For this he uses eighty pages, and it is so fascinating that you think you are no longer the listener but the daydreamer himself." In such stories—"all ordinary dreams turn into pointless stories as soon as one tells them to someone"—Unold has discovered the bridge to the dream. No synthetic interpretation of Proust can disregard it. Enough inconspicuous gates lead into it—Proust's frenetically studying resemblances, his impassioned cult of similarity. The true signs of its hegemony do not become obvious where he suddenly and startlingly uncovers similarities in actions, physiognomies, or speech mannerisms. The similarity of one thing to another which we are used to, which occupies us in a wakeful state, reflects only vaguely the deeper resemblance of the dream world in which everything that happens appears not in identical but in similar guise, opaquely similar one to another. Children know a symbol of this world: the stocking which has the structure of this dream world when, rolled up in the laundry hamper, it is a "bag" and a "present" at the same time. And just as children do not tire of quickly changing the bag and its contents into a third thing—namely, a stocking—Proust could not get his fill of emptying the dummy, his self, at one stroke in order to keep garnering that third thing, the image which satisfied his curiosity—indeed, assuaged his homesickness. He lay on his bed racked with homesickness, homesick for the world distorted in the state of resemblance, a world in which the true surrealist face of existence breaks through. To this world belongs what happens in Proust, and the deliberate and fastidious way in which it appears. It is never isolated, rhetorical, or visionary; carefully heralded and securely supported, it bears a fragile, precious reality: the image. It detaches itself from the structure of Proust's sentences as that summer day at Balbec—old, immemorial, mummified—emerged from the lace curtains under Françoise's hands.

II

We do not always proclaim loudly the most important thing we have to say. Nor do we always privately share it with those closest to us, our intimate friends, those who have been most devotedly ready to receive our confession. If it is true that not only people but also ages have such a chaste—that is, such a devious and frivolous—way of communicating what is most their own to a passing acquaintance, then the nineteenth century did not reveal itself to Zola or Anatole France, but to the young Proust, the insignificant snob, the playboy and socialite who snatched in passing the most astounding confidences from a declining age as from another, bone-weary Swann. It took Proust to make the nineteenth century ripe for memoirs. What before him had been a period devoid of tension now became a field of force in which later writers aroused multifarious currents. Nor is it accidental that the two most significant works of this kind were written by authors who were personally close to Proust as admirers and friends: the memoirs of Princess Clermont-Tonnerre and the autobiographical work of Léon Daudet; the first volumes of both works were published recently. An eminently Proustian inspiration led Léon Daudet, whose political folly is too gross and too obtuse to do much harm to his admirable talent, to turn his life into a city. *Paris vécu*, the projection of a biography onto the city map, in more than one place is touched by the shadows of Proustian characters. And the very title of Princess Clermont-Tonnerre's book, *Au Temps des équipages*, would have been unthinkable prior to Proust. This book is the echo which softly answers Proust's ambiguous, loving, challenging call from the Faubourg Saint-Germain. In addition, this melodious performance is shot through with direct and indirect references to Proust in its tenor and its characters, which include him and some of his favorite objects of study from the Ritz. There is no denying, of course, that this puts us in a very aristocratic milieu, and, with figures like Robert de Montesquiou, whom Princess Clermont-Tonnerre depicts masterfully, in a very special one at that. But this is true of Proust as well, and in his writings Montesquiou has a counterpart. All this would not be worth discussing, especially since the question of models would be secondary and unimportant for Germany, if German criticism were not so fond of taking the easy way out. Above all, it could not resist the opportunity to descend to the level of the lending-library crowd. Hack critics were tempted to draw conclusions about the author from the snobbish milieu of his writings, to characterize Proust's works as an internal affair of the French, a literary supplement to the *Almanach de Gotha*. [1] It is obvious that the problems of Proust's characters are those of a satiated society. But there is not one which would be identical with those of the author, which are subversive. To reduce this to a formula, it was to be Proust's aim to design the entire inner structure of society as a physiology of chatter. In the treasury of its prejudices and maxims there is not one that is not annihilated by a dangerous comic element. Pierre-Quint was the first to draw attention to it. "When humorous works are mentioned," he wrote, "one usually thinks of short, amusing books in illustrated jackets. One forgets about *Don Quixote*, *Pantagruel*, and *Gil Blas*—fat, ungainly tomes in small print." These comparisons, of course, do not do full justice to the explosive power of Proust's critique of society. His style is comedy, not humor; his laughter does not toss the world up but flings it down—at the risk that it will be smashed to pieces, which will then make him burst into tears. And unity of family and personality, of sexual morality and professional honor, are indeed smashed to bits. The pretensions of the bourgeoisie are shattered by laughter. Their return and reassimilation by the aristocracy is the sociological theme of the work.

Proust did not tire of the training which moving in aristocratic circles required. Assiduously and without much constraint, he conditioned his personality, making it as impenetrable and resourceful, as submissive and difficult, as it had to be for the sake of his mission. Later on this mystification and ceremoniousness became so much part of him that his letters sometimes constitute whole systems of parentheses, and not just in the grammatical sense—let-

---

[1] *The Almanach de Gotha* is a journal that chronicles the social activities of the French aristocracy.

ters which despite their infinitely ingenious, flexible composition occasionally call to mind the specimen of a letter writer's handbook: "My dear Madam, I just noticed that I forgot my cane at your house yesterday; please be good enough to give it to the bearer of this letter. P. S. Kindly pardon me for disturbing you; I just found my cane. " Proust was most resourceful in creating complications. Once, late at night, he dropped in on Princess Clermont-Tonnerre and made his staying dependent on someone bringing him his medicine from his house. He sent a valet for it, giving him a lengthy description of the neighborhood and of the house. Finally he said: "You cannot miss it. It is the only window on the Boulevard Haussmann in which there still is a light burning!" Everything but the house number! Anyone who has tried to get the address of a brothel in a strange city and has received the most long-winded directions, everything but the name of the street and the house number, will understand what is meant here and what the connection is with Proust's love of ceremony, his admiration of the Duc de Saint-Simon, and, last but not least, his intransigent French spirit. Is it not the quintessence of experience to find out how very difficult it is to learn many things which apparently could be told in very few words? It is simply that such words are part of a language established along lines of caste and class and unintelligible to outsiders. No wonder that the secret language of the salons excited Proust. When he later embarked on his merciless depiction of the *petit clan*, the Courvoisiers, the "esprit d'Oriane," he had through his association with the Bibescos become conversant with the improvisations of a code language to which we too have recently been introduced.

In his years of life in the salons Proust developed not only the vice of flattery to an eminent—one is tempted to say, to a theological—degree, but the vice of curiosity as well. We detect in him the reflection of the laughter which like a flash fire curls the lips of the Foolish Virgins represented on the intrados of many of the cathedrals which Proust loved. It is the smile of curiosity. Was it curiosity that made him such a great parodist? If so, we would know how to evaluate the term "parodist" in this context. Not very highly. For though it does justice to his abysmal malice, it skirts the bitterness, savagery, and grimness of the magnificent pieces which he wrote in the style of Balzac, Flaubert,

Sainte-Beuve, Henri de Régnier, the Goncourts, Michelet, Renan, and his favorite Saint-Simon, and which are collected in the volume *Pastiches et mélanges*. ① The mimicry of a man of curiosity is the brilliant device of this series, as it is also a feature of his entire creativity in which his passion for vegetative life cannot be taken seriously enough. Ortega y Gasset was the first to draw attention to the vegetative existence of Proust's characters, which are planted so firmly in their social habitat, influenced by the position of the sun of aristocratic favor, stirred by the wind that blows from Guermantes or Méséglise, and inextricably intertwined in the thicket of their fate. This is the environment that gave rise to the poet's mimicry. Proust's most accurate, most convincing insights fasten on their objects as insects fasten on leaves, blossoms, branches, betraying nothing of their existence until a leap, a beating of wings, a vault, show the startled observer that some incalculable individual life has imperceptibly crept into an alien world. The true reader of Proust is constantly jarred by small shocks. In the parodies he finds again, in the guise of a play with "styles," what affected him in an altogether different way as this spirit's struggle for survival under the leafy canopy of society. At this point we must say something about the close and fructifying interpenetration of these two vices, curiosity and flattery. There is a revealing passage in the writings of Princess Clermont-Tonnerre. "And finally we cannot suppress the fact that Proust became enraptured with the study of domestic servants—whether it be that an element which he encountered nowhere else intrigued his investigative faculties or that he envied servants their greater opportunities for observing the intimate details of things that aroused his interest. In any case, domestic servants in their various embodiments and types were his passion." In the exotic shadings of a Jupien, a Monsieur Aimé, a Célestine Albalat, their ranks extend from François, a figure with the coarse, angular features of St. Martha that

① Henri de Régnier (1864-1936) was a prominent French poet. Ernest Renan (1823-1892) was a French philosopher, historian, and scholar of religion. Louis de Rouvroy, duc de Saint-Simon (1675-1755), was a soldier, statesman, and writer, whose *Mémoire* depicted the French court under Louis XIV and Louis XV.

seems to be straight out of a Book of Hours, to those grooms and *chasseurs* who are paid for loafing rather than working. And perhaps the greatest concentration of this connoisseur of ceremonies was reserved for the depiction of these lower ranks. Who can tell how much servant curiosity became part of Proust's flattery, how much servant flattery became mixed with his curiosity, and where this artful copy of the role of the servant on the heights of the social scale had its limits? Proust presented such a copy, and he could not help doing so, for, as he once admitted, "*voir*" and "*désirer imiter*" were one and the same thing to him. This attitude, which was both sovereign and obsequious, has been preserved by Maurice Barrès in the most apposite words that have ever been written about Proust: "*Un poète persan dans une loge de portière.*"[1]

There was something of the detective in Proust's curiosity. The upper ten thousand were to him a clan of criminals, a band of conspirators beyond compare: the Camorra of consumers.[2] It excludes from its world everything that has a part in production, or at least demands that this part be gracefully and bashfully concealed behind the kind of manner that is sported by the polished professionals of consumption. Proust's analysis of snobbery, which is far more important than his apotheosis of art, constitutes the apogee of his criticism of society. For the attitude of the snob is nothing but the consistent, organized, steely view of life from the chemically pure standpoint of the consumer. And because even the remotest as well as the most primitive memory of nature's productive forces was to be banished from this satanic magic world, Proust found a perverted relationship more serviceable than a normal one even in love. But the pure consumer is the pure exploiter—logically and theoretically—and in Proust he is that in the full concreteness of his actual historical existence. He is concrete because he is impenetrable and elusive. Proust describes a class which is everywhere pledged to camouflage its material basis and for this very reason is

---

[1]   Maurice Barrès (1862-1923) was a French writer and politician whose individualism and nationalism were influential in the early twentieth century. The phrase means: "A Persian poet in a porter's lodge."

[2]   The *Camorra* was a secret Italian criminal society that arose in Naples in the nineteenth century.

attached to a feudalism which has no intrinsic economic significance but is all the more serviceable as a mask of the upper middle class. This disillusioned, merciless deglamorizer of the ego, of love, of morals—for this is how Proust liked to view himself—turns his whole limitless art into a veil for this one most vital mystery of his class: the economic aspect. He did not mean to do it a service. Here speaks Marcel Proust, the hardness of his work, the intransigence of a man who is ahead of his class. What he accomplishes he accomplishes as its master. And much of the greatness of this work will remain inaccessible or undiscovered until this class has revealed its most pronounced features in the final struggle.

III

In the last century there was an inn by the name of "Au Temps Perdu" at Grenoble; I do not know whether it still exists. In Proust, too, we are guests who enter through a door underneath a suspended sign that sways in the breeze, a door behind which eternity and rapture await us. Fernandez rightly distinguished between a *thème de l'éternité* and a *thème du temps* in Proust. But his eternity is by no means a platonic or a utopian one; it is rapturous. Therefore, if "time reveals a new and hitherto unknown kind of eternity to anyone who becomes engrossed in its passing," this certainly does not enable an individual to approach "the higher regions which a Plato or Spinoza reached with one beat of the wings." It is true that in Proust we find rudiments of an enduring idealism, but it would be a mistake to make these the basis of an interpretation, as Benoist-Méchin has done most glaringly. The eternity which Proust opens to view is convoluted time, not boundless time. His true interest is in the passage of time in its most real—that is, space-bound—form, and this passage nowhere holds sway more openly than in remembrance within and aging without. To observe the interaction of aging and remembering means to penetrate to the heart of Proust's world, to the universe of convolution. It is the world in a state of resemblances, the domain of the *correspondances*; the Romanticists were the first to comprehend them and Baudelaire embraced them most fervently, but Proust was the only one who managed to reveal them in our lived life. This is the work of the *mémoire involontaire*, the rejuvenating force which is a match for the inexorable process of aging. When the past is reflected in the dewy fresh "instant," a painful shock of rejuvenation pulls it together once more as irresistibly as the Guermantes way and Swann's way become intertwined for Proust when, in the thirteenth volume, he roams about the Combray area for the last time and discovers the intertwining of the roads. In a trice the landscape jumps about like a child. *"Ah! que le monde est grand à la clarté des lampes! Aux yeux du souvenir que le monde est petit!"*[1] Proust has brought off the tremendous feat of letting the whole world age by a lifetime in an instant. But this very concentration in which things that normally just fade and slumber consume themselves in a flash is called rejuvenation. *À la Recherche du temps perdu* is the constant attempt to charge an entire lifetime with the utmost awareness. Proust's method is actualization, not reflection. He is filled with the insight that none of us has time to live the true dramas of the life that we are destined for. This is what ages us—this and nothing else. The wrinkles and creases on our faces are the registration of the great passions, vices, insights that called on us; but we, the masters, were not home.

Since the spiritual exercises of Loyola there has hardly been a more radical attempt at self-absorption. Proust's, too, has as its center a loneliness which pulls the world down into its vortex with the force of a maelstrom. And the overloud and inconceivably hollow chatter which comes roaring out of Proust's novels is the sound of society plunging down into the abyss of this loneliness. This is the location of Proust's invectives against friendship. It was a matter of perceiving the silence at the bottom of this crater, whose eyes are the quietest and most absorbing. Something that is manifested irritatingly and capriciously in so many anecdotes is the combination of an unparalleled intensity of conversation with an unsurpassable aloofness from his partner. There has never been anyone else with Proust's ability to show us things; Proust's pointing finger is unequaled. But there is another gesture in amicable togetherness, in conversa-

---

[1]　"Oh, how large the world is in the brightness of the lamps. How small the world is in the eyes of recollection." Charles Baudelaire, "Le Voyage."

tion: physical contact. To no one is this gesture more alien than to Proust. He cannot touch his reader either; he could not do so for anything in the world. If one wanted to group literature around these poles, dividing it into the directive and the touching kind, the core of the former would be the work of Proust, the core of the latter, the work of Péguy. [1] This is basically what Fernandez has formulated so well: "Depth, or, rather, intensity, is always on his side, never on that of his partner." This is demonstrated brilliantly and with a touch of cynicism in Proust's literary criticism, the most significant document of which is an essay that came into being on the high level of his fame and the low level of his deathbed: "À Propos de Baudelaire." The essay is Jesuitic in its acquiescence in his own maladies, immoderate in the garrulousness of a man who is resting, frightening in the indifference of a man marked by death who wants to speak out once more, no matter on what subject. What inspired Proust here in the face of death also shaped him in his intercourse with his contemporaries: so spasmodic and harsh an alternation of sarcasm and tenderness that its recipients threatened to break down in exhaustion.

The provocative, unsteady quality of the man affects even the reader of his works. Suffice it to recall the endless succession of "*soit que* ...," by means of which an action is shown in an exhaustive, depressing way in the light of the countless motives upon which it may have been based. And yet these paratactic sequences reveal the point at which weakness and genius coincide in Proust: the intellectual renunciation, the tested skepticism with which he approached things. After the self-satisfied inwardness of Romanticism Proust came along, determined, as Jacques Rivière puts it, not to give the least credence to the "*Sirènes intérieures.*" "Proust approaches experience without the slightest metaphysical interest, without the slightest penchant for construction, without the slightest tendency to console." Nothing is truer than that. And thus the basic feature of this work, too, which Proust kept proclaiming as being planned, is anything but the result of construction. But it is as planned as the

---

[1]   Charles Péguy (1873-1914) was a French poet and philosopher whose work brought together Christianity, socialism, and French nationalism.

lines on the palm of our hand or the arrangement of the stamen in a calyx. Completely worn out, Proust, that aged child, fell back on the bosom of nature—not to drink from it, but to dream to its heartbeat. One must picture him in this state of weakness to understand how felicitously Jacques Rivière interpreted the weakness when he wrote: "Marcel Proust died of the same inexperience which permitted him to write his works. He died of ignorance of the world and because he did not know how to change the conditions of his life which had begun to crash him. He died because he did not know how to make a fire or open a window. " And, to be sure, of his psychogenic asthma.

The doctors were powerless in the face of this malady; not so the writer, who very systematically placed it in his service. To begin with the most external aspect, he was a perfect stage director of his sickness. For months he connected, with devastating irony, the image of an admirer who had sent him flowers with their odor, which he found unbearable. Depending on the ups and downs of his malady he alarmed his friends, who dreaded and longed for the moment when the writer would suddenly appear in their drawing rooms long after midnight—*brisé de fatigue* and for just five minutes, as he said—only to stay till the gray of dawn, too tired to get out of his chair or interrupt his conversation. Even as a writer of letters he extracted the most singular effects from his malady. "The wheezing of my breath is drowning out the sounds of my pen and of a bath which is being drawn on the floor below. " But that is not all, nor is it the fact that his sickness removed him from fashionable living. This asthma became part of his art—if indeed his art did not create it. Proust's syntax rhythmically and step by step reproduces his fear of suffocating. And his ironic, philosophical, didactic reflections invariably are the deep breath with which he shakes off the weight of memories. On a larger scale, however, the threatening, suffocating crisis was death, which he was constantly aware of, most of all while he was writing. This is how death confronted Proust, and long before his malady assumed critical dimensions—not as a hypochondriacal whim, but as a *"réalité nouvelle,"* that new reality whose reflections on things and people are the marks of aging. A physiology of style would take us into the innermost core of this creativeness. No one who knows with what great tenacity memories are preserved by the sense of smell, and smells not at all in the memory, will be able to call Proust's sensitivity to smells accidental. To be sure, most memories that we search for come to us as visual images. Even the free-floating forms of the *mémoire involontaire* are still in large part isolated, though enigmatically present, visual images. For this very reason, anyone who wishes to surrender knowingly to the innermost overtones in this work must place himself in a special stratum—the bottommost—of this involuntary memory, one in which the materials of memory no longer appear singly, as images, but tell us about a whole, amorphously and formlessly indefinitely and weightily, in the same way as the weight of his net tells a fisherman about his catch. Smell—that is the sense of weight of someone who casts his nets into the sea of the *temps perdu*. And his sentences are the entire muscular activity of the intelligible body; they contain the whole enormous effort to raise this catch.

For the rest, the closeness of the symbiosis between this particular creativity and this particular malady is demonstrated most clearly by the fact that in Proust there never was a breakthrough of that heroic defiance with which other creative people have risen up against their infirmities. And therefore one can say, from another point of view, that so close a complicity with life and the course of the world as Proust's would inevitably have led to ordinary, indolent contentment on any basis but that of such great and constant suffering. As it was. however, this malady was destined to have its place in the great work process assigned to it by a furor devoid of desires or regrets. For the second time there rose a scaffold like Michelangelo's on which the artist, his head thrown back, painted the Creation on the ceiling of the Sistine Chapel: the sickbed on which Marcel Proust consecrates the countless pages which he covered with his handwriting, holding them up in the air, to the creation of his microcosm.

12. 本雅明：《普鲁斯特的形象》

(Walter Benjamin, "The Image of Proust," 1929)

作者小识

本雅明（Walter Benjamin, 1892—1940），西方马克思主义美学家和批评家之代表。在马克思主义的发展史上，他与卢卡奇、布洛赫、布莱希特齐名，对法兰克福学派的社会批判理论产生了深刻的影响。在其学术生涯早期，本雅明集中研究德国浪漫主义批评理论和观念论哲学。20 世纪 30 年代，本雅明发展出一套以政治为导向的唯物主义美学理论，并杂糅了卡巴拉神秘主义、弥赛亚主义，建构出一套现代性批判话语。

本雅明有七卷德文版《文集》（*Gesammelte Schriften* ed. Tiedemann and Schweppenhauser, Frankfurt, Suhrkamp Verlag, forthcoming）、四卷英文版《选集》（*Selected Writings*, ed. Howard Eiland & Michael W. Jennings, Cambridge, MA. & London, Harvard University Press, 1991-1999）传世。《德国浪漫派的批评概念》（*The Concept of Criticism in German Romanticism*）引发了 20 世纪学者对浪漫时代的回访和对浪漫遗产的重估。《论翻译者的使命》（"On the Task of Translator"）等代表性著述为翻译理论和语言哲学的发展注入了灵感。《机械复制时代的艺术作品》（"The Work of Art in the Age of Its Technical Reproducibility"）则直接推动了文化研究的兴起，作为一项原创性电影理论可谓当之无愧。他那项庞大的 19 世纪研究计划《拱廊计划》（*The Arcades Project*）最终未能完成，其断简残篇《单向街》（*One-Way Street*）为文化理论和现代性哲学概念提供了活的个案。本雅明的"救世论历史观"让许多理论家，甚至哲学家感到无比着迷同时又万分绝望，影响所及还包括德里达、阿甘本和哈贝马斯。特别值得提及的是，本雅明的《暴力批判》（"The Critique of Violence"）和《历史哲学论纲》（"On the Concept of History"）是德里达讨论的"弥赛亚性"（或"救世精神"）的重要文本。它们为解构的伦理转向提供了强大的动力，而德里达对于本雅明的解读，连同保罗·德·曼关于寓言与象征的讨论，改变了本雅明历史接受的流向，即从批判理论转向了宗教回归，而这表明本雅明的思想中蕴含着神学维度。

背景略说

本雅明思想生涯起步于浪漫主义美学和德国悲剧（或悲悼剧）巴洛克风格研究，但他的犹太人血统以及"最后一波欧洲犹太精英"的身份，却让他别无选择地成为"解放"的先知。在卢卡奇等人"奠基"了西方马克思主义之后，本雅明用"救赎"思想浸润着马克思主义批评传统。马克思批评"神圣家族"，心系"人类解放"，像启示录一般照亮了本雅明以政治审美化为导向的批判意识。犹太人的苦难，在马克思和本雅明那里，已经从群族的苦难升华为人类的苦难，犹太人的救赎也由此转换成了人类"解放"的诉求。"任何一种解放都是把人的世界和人的关系还给人自己。"可是，救赎也好，解放也好，在本雅明那里都不是经纬天地的宏大"象征"（symbol），而是历史废墟上支离破碎的隐微"寓言"（allegory）。

第一，在德国古典思想哺育下成长的本雅明，竟然反出"康德传统"。康德哲学的伟大之处在于，为理性标明界限，给信仰留下地盘，终归将自由的人视为终极目的。在本雅明看来，康德思想过于先验化，缺少基于体验的"乌托邦精神"，特别是将自我确定性作为知识的基础，而不能跳出笛卡儿"我思"的窠臼。于是，本雅明提出"认识论批判"的任务，以体验来涵盖人、世界、神圣、自我四元关系，反对将任何一元工具化，以便整体理解生存的意义（真理）。

第二，反对犹太复国主义，本雅明却领悟了"卡巴拉神秘传统"和"弥赛亚精神"。卡巴拉（Kabbalah）是古代希伯来人的灵修智慧，其教义是陈述苦难体验，开启创造潜能，奋力逼近生命的自由境界。弥赛亚（Messiah）是卡巴拉传统中的"救赎者"。他受膏为圣，传递神意，掌握正义尺度，救助苦难者于悲惨境遇，预言终极平等的社会终会到来。有鉴于此，在学术史上本雅明视其为"救赎批评家"，因为他们弘扬了审美救赎的希望。

第三，与世界政治的虚无主义抗争，本雅明提出了一种反抗现代性的历史观。本雅明的史观漫溢悲情。在他看来，苦难、灾难是永恒规律，历史的节奏便摆动在悲剧和整体偿还之间。但是在悲剧的历史意识之中，本雅明还是吐露出"绝望的希望"。在他看来，"历史时间"如同一潭死水，而"弥赛亚时间"却涌动巨澜。弥赛亚时间终结了历史时间，打碎了"进步""永恒轮回"等神话，而守护着更为古老的存在真理。存在真理，即"知识树"，凋零之后，"生命树"绚丽开放，呼唤人类重返天堂。那里的一切都舒叶吐花、灵性盎然，尤其是超越了人的语言、物的语言而忆起了神圣且纯洁的语言。

第四，置身艺术复制时代，沐浴在"灵韵"消逝后的凄艳之美中，重构 19 世纪的文化景观。在可以复制的境遇下，艺术的膜拜价值荡然无存。在大量的摹本和赝品中"灵韵"淡灭，于是艺术成为政治，成为商业，艺术家成为帮忙与帮闲之徒。灵韵淡灭，呼应了马克斯·韦伯的"世界祛魅"。但本雅明有所不甘，他从超现实主义作家阿拉贡的《巴黎乡下人》中发现了灵感，发誓要重构 19 世纪"世界再次附魅"的景观，借着《拱廊计划》而书写一部"唯物主义的文化史"。而这部未竟之作，同瓦堡的《记忆图谱》一起，竟然催生了 20 世纪的"媒介考古学"。

第五，贯穿在本雅明美学批评之中的一个核心概念是"辩证意象"（dialectic image）。理解"辩证意象"是洞察历史的关键，因为"真理时代"标志着"世俗时代"的连续性瞬间破裂。"辩证意象"便是过去与未来的复杂纠缠、寓言与象征的互相颠覆。"辩证意象"之光不是从过去投射到当下，也不是将当下之光投射到过去，而是进入复杂的星丛，从而实现了对历史的拯救。"辩证意象"注定"在下一瞬间永远失落"，但它会在特定的历史时代再现，让人擦亮双眼，认出梦幻之中的意象。19 世纪的文化，就是那一庞大的梦幻意象。

基本内容

《普鲁斯特的形象》或可被理解为本雅明对于"辩证意象"的策略性运用。本雅明将普鲁斯特的 13 卷本《追忆逝水年华》读作一种"不可解释的综合之产物"、一部自传式的百科全书风格之写照，其中渗透着神秘主义的专注、散文作家的灵性、现代思想者的震惊，以及作家偏执狂一般的自我反省意识。普鲁斯特的文本深不可测，要烛照幽微，势必从"形象"（或"意象"）开始。

首先，普鲁斯特的意象是"观相术"之最高表现形式（the highest physiognomic expression），呈现出生命与文学、个体与群族之间不可遏制的差异，以及不可和解的冲突。普鲁斯特不是按照"如实样貌"来模仿生活，而是通过编织记忆来建构生活。所以，普鲁斯特的意象是辩证意象的典型形式。本雅明断定，重要的不是书中人物或者作家所经历的事情，而是"回忆的编织"。记忆为纬，遗忘是经，经纬交织，经天纬地，让普鲁斯特成为现代的帕涅罗佩——黑夜中编织，光明中拆解。最后呈现在文本之中者，乃记忆统一体的反面，即"挂毯背面的图案"。在普鲁斯特的故事中，所有意象都是通往梦境的桥梁，平常的梦境立即转化为无意义的事件。

其次，普鲁斯特的风格是喜剧而非幽默。遥远地回应"荷马式的笑声"（homeric laughter），普鲁斯特笔下的现代英雄也用笑声将世界高高托举，又让世界沉重地堕落，令一个堕落的世界备受诅咒。普鲁斯特的形象摧毁了资产阶级的虚伪作秀，从而让布尔乔亚读者感到震惊。"普鲁斯特作品的坚实，以及他和走在其所属阶层前面的人之不妥协"，决定了他自己便是其所创造的一切的主人，其伟大无与伦比，其奥妙也不能轻易知之。

最后，普鲁斯特及其《追忆逝水年华》的意义便在于以现实化的方式将自我意识注入整整一生的时间中，再将整体的时间融入瞬间。观察衰老的进程，与记忆交互作用，便进入了普鲁斯特世界错综复杂的中心。"这是相似状态的世界，这是相称对应的领地。"诗人波德莱尔热切地拥抱了这个"应和"的宇宙，但唯有普鲁斯特才与所有读者一起体验并再现这个世界。这是无意识记忆或"非自愿记忆"（mémoire involontaire）的成果：更新的力量与势不可挡的衰老过程互相较量，过去在露水般清新的"瞬间"映射出来，"更新的痛楚震惊"，一再将过去势不可挡地拉在一起，通往盖尔芒特家的路和通往斯旺家的路可能就是同一条。迷恋阴暗并长期忍受失眠困扰的普鲁斯特在病榻上累积着厚厚的书稿，风险给了他所创生的微型宇宙。

拓展讨论

从浪漫主义者到本雅明，现代人分享着席勒所说的"人与自然"分裂的感伤体验。人在宇宙之间占有一个非常尴尬的位置：万物在神，神在万物，可是人根本体验不到神的存在，因而感到极端的孤独。一如帕斯卡尔所言，人是一根偶尔会思考的芦苇，随时随地都可能遭到巨大盲目的宇宙力量的碾压。会思考却被碾压的芦苇，在被碾压的时刻，也会爆发出"受造物的叹息"。人类自以为优越于一切自然的东西。人类较之于鸟兽虫鱼而自为中心的意识，不再导致他与宇宙万物之更高存在融合，反而标志着他与其他存在物之间有不可逾越而且越来越大的鸿沟。从一个整体宇宙之共同体中疏离出来的人，感到此生非所有，故乡是异乡，既而产生某种严酷的陌生感。在这种人类共同的现代境遇中，"人的理性可以对内在于宇宙的逻各斯感到亲近，而这个宇宙已经消逝了；人在整体秩序占一席之地，而这个整体秩序也消逝了。人的地位现在看来只是一个纯粹的、无情的偶然"。① 这种境遇不仅意味着无家可归、孤苦伶仃和万分焦虑，而且意味着自然本身并不指向一个目的。目的论的消逝、终末论的审判在所难免。正如布洛赫以自己与一只来自莱茵河地区的"巴特曼罐子"的遭遇，来象征自我与黑暗的遭遇，本雅明与自然的遭遇也是一场与自我的悲剧性遭遇。面对"受造物之叹息"，我们也在叹息，被碾压甚至构成了一脉传统，我们生活于其中的例外状态，或许正是一种常态。

在本雅明的思想中，这种与黑暗遭遇的灵知却首先是呈现在对语言的沉思中。与造物的关系最为紧密、和人类生命最为融洽，并且最后本源于神意之中的语言，也最能体现"弥赛亚的自然节奏"。存在向世俗秩序的沉沦和向神圣秩序的复命，都和语言的纯洁与污染有直接的关联。在本雅明那里，堕落首先是语言的堕落。什么是语言的堕落？就是具有神圣气息的名称降格为单纯交流的符号，这样的堕落开始于"人类语言的诞生"。从本源的存在状态到占有状态的降格，使语言成为必须有所负载、有所交流和有所意指的媒介。当神圣的名字堕落为世俗的媒介，"抽象"、"判断"和"意义"也就随之出现了。如果说，在神圣乐园之中，被命名的世界是一个自我封闭的纯洁世界，没有外在性，只有内在性，那么，语言的堕落则开创了一个外在的深渊。当人类在知识之树上偷食禁果时，人类就废黜了纯洁语言的神圣禁忌和完美状态。这种犯罪招致了巨大的惩罚：自我放逐于纯洁语言境界之外，也就意味着要被驱逐于乐园之外了。一旦语言堕落，一切罪孽、一切灾难、一切悲苦都可以溯源于语言了。以语言制定的法律，使人永远离弃了自然权利，其中肯定包含着一种神秘的暴力，而这种暴力在世俗的秩序之中竟然是一切权威的基础。公开的邪恶和绝对的虚无，都通过语言的堕落而肆行于世间。本雅明把这一切看作全部基础失落、一切形而上学真理丧失的标记。他带着暗淡乡愁而轻叹的在机械复制时代消失的艺术"灵韵"，也是只有在隐而不显的神学背景下才能正确地得到理解的东西：灵韵也许是神圣命名之中流泻在大地上的气息，当神圣命名降格成纯粹符号，这气息就是在一瞬间消逝的美丽，会不可挽回地成为神圣的"余象"。

---

① 约纳斯：《诺斯替宗教 异乡神的信息与基督教的开端》，张新樟译，297 页，上海，上海三联书店，2006。

延伸阅读

1. 本雅明：《德国悲剧的起源》，陈永国译，北京，文化艺术出版社，2001。该书是本雅明对17世纪巴洛克悲剧的深入研究，辨析巴洛克悲悼剧与古希腊悲剧，阐述"象征"与"寓言"，在浪漫主义的语境下展开"认识论的元批判"。

2. 本雅明：《巴黎，19世纪的首都》，刘北成译，上海，上海人民出版社，2006。该书是《拱廊计划》的残篇，包含两份提纲、两篇论述诗人波德莱尔的文章。

13. On Lyric Poetry and Society (1957)
By Theodor Adorno

The announcement of a lecture on lyric poetry and society will make many of you uncomfortable. You will expect a sociological analysis of the kind that can be made of any object, just as fifty years ago people came up with psychologies, and thirty years ago with phenomenologies, of everything conceivable. You will suspect that examination of the conditions under which works are created and their effect will try to usurp the place of experience of the works as they are and that the process of categorizing and relating will suppress insight into the truth or falsity of the object itself. You will suspect that an intellectual will be guilty of what Hegel accused the "formal understanding" of doing, namely that in surveying the whole it stands above the individual existence it is talking about, that is, it does not see it at all but only labels it. This approach will seem especially distressing to you in the case of lyric poetry. The most delicate, the most fragile thing that exists is to be encroached upon and brought into conjunction with bustle and commotion, when part of the ideal of lyric poetry, at least in its traditional sense, is to remain unaffected by bustle and commotion. A sphere of expression whose very essence lies in either not acknowledging the power of socialization or overcoming it through the pathos of detachment, as in Baudelaire or Nietzsche, is to be arrogantly turned into the opposite of what it conceives itself to be through the way it is examined. Can anyone, you will ask, but a man who is insensitive to the Muse talk about lyric poetry and society?

Clearly your suspicions will be allayed only if lyric works are not abused by being made objects with which to demonstrate sociological theses but if instead the social element in them is shown to reveal something essential about the basis of their quality. This relationship should lead not away from the work of art but deeper into it. But the most elementary reflection shows that this is to be expected. For the substance of a poem is not merely an expression of individual impulses and experiences. Those become a matter of art only when they come to participate in something universal by virtue of the specificity they acquire in being given aesthetic form. Not that what the lyric poem expresses must be immediately equivalent to what everyone experiences. Its universality is no *volonté de tous*, not the universality of simply communicating what others are unable to communicate. Rather, immersion in what has taken individual form elevates the lyric poem to the status of something universal by making manifest something not distorted, not grasped, not yet subsumed. It thereby anticipates, spiritually, a situation in which no false universality, that is, nothing profoundly particular, continues to fetter what is other than itself, the human. The lyric work hopes to attain universality through unrestrained individuation. The danger peculiar to the lyric, however, lies in the fact that its principle of individuation never guarantees that something binding and authentic will be produced. It has no say over whether the poem remains within the contingency of mere separate existence.

The universality of the lyric's substance, however, is social in nature. Only one who hears the voice of humankind in the poem's solitude can understand what the poem is saying; indeed, even the solitariness of lyrical language itself is prescribed by an individualistic and ultimately atomistic society, just as conversely its general cognecy depends on the intensity of its individuation. For that reason, however, reflection on the work of art is justified in inquiring, and obligated to inquire concretely into its social content and not content itself with a vague feeling of something universal and inclusive. This kind of specification through thought is not some external reflection alien to art; on the contrary, all linguistic works of art demand it. The material proper to them, concepts, does not exhaust itself in mere contemplation. In order to be susceptible of aesthetic contemplation, works of art must always be thought through as well, and once thought has been called into play by the poem it does not let itself be stopped at the poem's behest.

Such thought, however—the social interpretation of lyric poetry as of all works of art—may not focus directly on the so-called social perspective or the social interests of the works or their authors. Instead, it must discover how the entirety of a society, conceived as an internally contradictory unity, is manifested in the work of art, in what way the work of art remains subject to society and in what way it transcends it. In philosophical terms, the approach must be an immanent one. Social concepts should not be applied to the works from without but rather drawn from an exacting examination of the works themselves. Goethe's statement in his *Maxims and Reflections* that what you do not understand you do not possess holds not only for the aesthetic attitude to works of art but for aesthetic theory as well; nothing that is not in the works, not part of their own form, can legitimate a determination of what their substance, that which has entered into their poetry, represents in social terms. To determine that, of course, requires both knowledge of the interior of the works of art and knowledge of the society outside. But this knowledge is binding only if it is rediscovered through complete submission to the matter at hand. Special vigilance is required when it comes to the concept of ideology, which these days is belabored to the point of intolerability. For ideology is untruth, false consciousness, deceit. It manifests itself in the failure of works of art, in their inherent falseness, and it is countered by criticism. To repeat mechanically, however, that great works of art, whose essence consists in giving form to the crucial contradictions in real existence, and only in that sense in a tendency to reconcile them, are ideology, not only does an injustice to their truth content but also misrepresents the concept of ideology. That concept does not maintain that all spirit serves only for some human beings to falsely present some particular values as general ones; rather, it is intended to unmask spirit that is specifically false and at the same time to grasp it in its necessity. The greatness of works of art, however, consists solely in the fact that they give voice to what ideology hides. Their very success moves beyond false consciousness, whether intentionally or not.

Let me take your own misgivings as a starting point. You experience lyric poetry as something opposed to society, something wholly individual. Your feelings insist that it remain so, that lyric expression, having escaped from the weight of material existence, evoke the image of a life free from the coercion of reigning practices, of utility, of the relentless pressures of self-preservation.

This demand, however, the demand that the lyric word be virginal, is itself social in nature. It implies a protest against a social situation that every individual experiences as hostile, alien, cold, oppressive, and this situation is imprinted in reverse on the poetic work: the more heavily the situation weighs upon it, the more firmly the work resists it by refusing to submit to anything heteronomous and constituting itself solely in accordance with its own laws. The work's distance from mere existence becomes the measure of what is false and bad in the latter. In its protest the poem expresses the dream of a world in which things would be different. The lyric spirit's idiosyncratic opposition to the superior power of material things is a form of reaction to the reification of the world, to the domination of human beings by commodities that has developed since the beginning of the modern area, since the industrial revolution became the dominant force in life. Rilke's cult of the thing [as in his *Dinggedichte* or "thing poems"] is part of this idiosyncratic opposition; it attempts to assimilate even alien objects to pure subjective expression and to dissolve them, to give them metaphysical credit for their alienness. The aesthetic weakness of this cult of the thing, its obscurantist demeanor and its blending of religion with arts and crafts, reveals the real power of reification, which can no longer be gilded with a lyrical halo and brought back within the sphere of meaning.

To say that the concept of lyric poetry that is in some sense second nature to us is a completely modern one is only to express this insight into the social nature of the lyric in different form. Analogously, landscape painting and its idea of "nature" have had an autonomous development only in the modern period. I know that I exaggerate in saying this, that you could adduce many counterexamples. The most compelling would be Sappho. I will not discuss the Chinese, Japanese, and Arabic lyric, since I cannot read them in the original and I suspect that translation involves them in an adaptive mechanism that makes adequate understanding completely impossible. But the manifestations in earlier periods of the specifically lyric spirit familiar to us are only isolated flashes, just as the backgrounds in older painting occasionally anticipate the idea of landscape painting. They do not establish it as a form. The great poets of the distant past—Pindar and Alcaeus, for instance, but the greater part of Walther von der Vogelweide's work as well—whom literary history classifies as lyric poets are uncommonly far from our primary conception of the lyric. They lack the quality of immediacy, of immateriality, which we are accustomed, rightly or not, to consider the criterion of the lyric and which we transcend only through rigorous education.

Until we have either broadened it historically or turned it critically against the sphere of individualism, however, our conception of lyric poetry has a moment of discontinuity in it—all the more so, the more pure it claims to be. The "I" whose voice is heard in the lyric is an "I" that defines and expresses itself as something opposed to the collective, to objectivity; it is not immediately at one with the nature to which its expression refers. It has lost it, as it were, and attempts to restore it through animation, through immersion in the "I" itself. It is only through humanization that nature is to be restored the rights that human domination took from it. Even lyric works in which no trace of conventional and concrete existence, no crude materiality remains, the greatest lyric works in our language, owe their quality to the force with which the "I" creates the illusion of nature emerging from alienation. Their pure subjectivity, the aspect of them that appears seamless and harmonious, bears witness to its opposite, to suffering in an existence alien to the subject and to love for it as well—indeed, their harmoniousness is actually nothing but the mutual accord of this suffering and this love. Even the line from Goethe's "Wanderers Nachtlied" ["Wanderer's Night-Song"], "Warte nur, balde/ruhest du auch" ["Only wait, soon/you too shall rest"] has an air of consolation: its unfathomable beauty cannot be separated from something it makes no reference to, the notion of a world that withholds peace. Only in resonating with sadness about that withholding does the poem maintain that there is peace nevertheless. One is tempted to use the line "Ach, ich bin des Treibens müde" ["1 am weary of restless activity"] from the companion poem of the same title to interpret the "Wanderers Nachtlied." To be sure, the greatness of the latter poem derives from the fact that it does not speak about what is alienated and disturbing, from the fact that within the poem the restlessness of the object is not opposed to the subject; instead, the subject's own restlessness echoes it. A second immediacy is promised: what is human, language itself, seems to become creation again, while everything external dies away in the echo of the soul. This becomes more than an illusion, however; it becomes full truth, because through the expression in language of a good kind of tiredness, the shadow of yearning and even of death continues to fall across the reconciliation. In the line "Warte nur, balde" the whole of life, with an enigmatic smile of sorrow, turns into the brief moment before one falls asleep. The note of peacefulness attests to the fact that peace cannot be a-chieved without the dream disintegrating. The shadow has no power over the image of life come back into its own, but as a last reminder of life's deformation it gives the dream its profound depths beneath the surface of the song. In the face of nature at rest, a nature from which all traces of anything resembling the human have been eradicated, the subject becomes aware of its own insignifi-cance. Imperceptibly, silently, irony tinges the poem's consolation: the seconds before the bliss of sleep are the same seconds that separate our brief life from death. After Goethe, this sublime irony became a debased and spiteful irony. But it was always bourgeois: the shadow-side of the elevation of the liberated subject is its degradation to something exchangeable, to something that exists merely for something else; the shadow-side of personality is the "So who are you?" The authenticity of the "Nachtlied," however, lies in its moment in time: the background of that destructive force removes it from the sphere of play, while the destructive force has no power over the peaceable power of con-solation. It is commonly said that a perfect lyric poem must possess totality or universality, must provide the whole within the bounds of the poem and the in-finite within the poem's finitude. If that is to be more than a platitude of an aes-thetics that is always ready to use the concept of the symbolic as a panacea, it indicates that in every lyric poem the historical relationship of the subject to ob-jectivity, of the individual to society, must have found its precipitate in the me-dium of a subjective spirit thrown back upon itself. The less the work thematizes the relationship of "I" and society, the more spontaneously it crystallizes of its own accord in the poem, the more complete this process of precipitation will be.

You may accuse me of so sublimating the relationship of lyric and society in this definition out of fear of a crude sociologism that there is really nothing left of it; it is precisely what is not social in the lyric poem that is now to become its social aspect. You could call my attention to Gustav Doré's caricature of the arch-reactionary deputy whose praise of the *ancien régime* culminated in the exclamation, "And to whom, gentlemen, do we owe the revolution of 1789 if not to Louis XVI!" You could apply that to my view of lyric poetry and society: in my view, you could say, society plays the role of the executed king and the lyric the role of his opponents; but lyric poetry, you say, can no more be explained on the basis of society than the revolution can be made the achievement of the monarch it deposed and without whose inanities it might not have occurred at that time. We will leave it an open question whether Doré's deputy was truly only the stupid, cynical propagandist the artist derided him for being or whether there might be more truth in his unintentional joke than common sense admits; Hegel's philosophy of history would have a lot to say in his defense. In any case, the comparison does not really work. I am not trying to deduce lyric poetry form society; its social substance is precisely what is spontaneous in it, what does not simply follow from the existing conditions at the time. But philosophy—Hegel's again——is familiar with the speculative proposition that the individual is mediated by the universal and vice versa. That means that even resistance to social pressure is not something absolutely individual; the artistic forces in that resistance, which operate in and through the individual and his spontaneity, are objective forces that impel a constricted and constricting social condition to transcend itself and become worthy of human beings; forces, that is, that are part of the constitution of the whole and not at all merely forces of a rigid individuality blindly opposing society. If, by virtue of its own subjectivity, the substance of the lyric can in fact be addressed as an objective substance—and otherwise one could not explain the very simple fact that grounds the possibility of the lyric as an artistic genre, its effect on people other than the poet speaking his monologue—then it is only because the lyric work of art's withdrawal into itself, its self-absorption, its detachment from the social surface, is socially motivated behind the author's back. But the medium of this is language. The paradox specific to the lyric work, a subjectivity that turns into objectivity, is tied to the priority of linguistic form in the lyric; it is that priority from which the primacy of language in literature in general (even in prose forms) is derived. For language is itself something double. Through its configurations it assimilates itself completely into subjective impulses; one would almost think it had produced them. But at the same time language remains the medium of concepts, remains that which establishes an inescapable relationship to the universal and to society. Hence the highest lyric works are those in which the subject, with no remaining trace of mere matter, sounds forth in language until language itself acquires a voice. The unself-consciousness of the subject submitting itself to language as to something objective, and the immediacy and spontaneity of that subject's expression are one and the same: thus language mediates lyric poetry and society in their innermost core. This is why the lyric reveals itself to be most deeply grounded in society when it does not chime in with society, when it communicates nothing, when, instead, the subject whose expression is successful reaches an accord with language itself, with the inherent tendency of language.

On the other hand, however, language should also not be absolutized as the voice of Being as opposed to the lyric subject, as many of the current ontological theories of language would have it. The subject, whose expression—as opposed to mere signification of objective contents——is necessary to attain to that level of linguistic objectivity, is not something added to the contents proper to that layer, not something external to it. The moment of unself-consciousness in which the subject submerges itself in language is not a sacrifice of the subject to Being. It is a moment not of violence, nor of violence against the subject, but reconciliation: language itself speaks only when it speaks not as something alien to the subject but as the subject's own voice. When the "I" becomes oblivious to itself in language it is fully present nevertheless; if it were not, language would become a consecrated abracadabra and succumb to reification, as it does in communicative discourse. But that brings us back to the actual relationship between the individual and society. It is not only that the individual is inherently socially mediated, not only that its contents are always social as well. Conversely, society is formed and continues to live only by virtue of the individuals whose quintessence it is. Classical philosophy once formulated a truth now disdained by scientific logic: subject and object are not rigid and isolated poles but can be defined only in the process in which they distinguish themselves from one another and change. The lyric is the aesthetic test of that dialectical philosophical proposition. In the lyric poem the subject, through its identification with language, negates both its opposition to society as something merely monadological and its mere functioning within a wholly socialized society [*vergesellschaftete Gesellschaft*]. But the more the latter's ascendancy over the subject increases, the more precarious the situation of the lyric becomes. Baudelaire's work was the first to record this; his work, the ultimate consequence of European *Weltschmerz*, did not stop with the sufferings of the individual but chose the modern itself, as the antilyrical pure and simple, for its theme and struck a poetic spark in it by dint of a heroically stylized language. In Baudelaire a note of despair already makes itself felt, a note that barely maintains its balance on the tip of its own paradoxicalness. As the contradiction between poetic and communicative language reached an extreme, lyric poetry became a game in which one goes for broke; not, as philistine opinion would have it, because it had become incomprehensible but because in acquiring selfconsciousness as a literary language, in striving for an absolute objectivity unrestricted by any considerations of communication, language both distances itself from the objectivity of spirit, of living language, and substitutes a poetic event for a language that is no longer present. The elevated, poeticizing, subjectively violent moment in weak later lyric poetry is the price it has to pay for its attempt to keep itself undisfigured, immaculate, objective; its false glitter is the complement to the disenchanted world from which it extricates itself.

Everything I have said needs to be qualified if it is to avoid misinterpretation. My thesis is that the lyric work is always the subjective expression of a social antagonism. But since the objective world that produces the lyric is an inherently antagonistic world, the concept of the lyric is not simply that of the expression of a subjectivity to which language grants objectivity. Not only does the lyric subject embody the whole all the more cogently, the more it expresses itself; in addition, poetic subjectivity is itself indebted to privilege: the pres-

sures of the struggle for survival allow only a few human beings to grasp the u-
niversal through immersion in the self or to develop as autonomous subjects capable of freely expressing themselves. The others, however, those who not only stand alienated, as though they were objects, facing the disconcerted poetic
subject but who have also literally been degraded to objects of history, have the
same right, or a greater right, to grope for the sounds in which sufferings and
dreams are welded. This inalienable right has asserted itself again and again, in
forms however impure, mutilated, fragmentary, and intermittent—the only
forms possible for those who have to bear the burden.

A collective undercurrent provides the foundation for all individual lyric
poetry. When that poetry actually bears the whole in mind and is not simply an
expression of the privilege, refinement, and gentility of those who can afford to
be gentle, participation in this undercurrent is an essential part of the substantiality of the individual lyric as well: it is this undercurrent that makes language
the medium in which the subject becomes more than a mere subject.
Romanticism's link to the folksong is only the most obvious, certainly not the
most compelling example of this. For Romanticism practices a kind of program-
matic transfusion of the collective into the individual through which the
individual lyric poem indulged in a technical illusion of universal cogency without that cogency characterizing it inherently. Often, in contrast, poets who ab-
jure any borrowing from the collective language participate in that collective undercurrent by virtue of their historical experience. Let me mention Baudelaire
again, whose lyric poetry is a slap in the face not only to the *juste milieu* but
also to all bourgeois social sentiment, and who nevertheless, in poems like the
"Petites vieilles" or the poem about the servant woman with the generous heart
in the *Tableaux Parisiens*, was truer to the masses toward whom he turned his
tragic, arrogant mask than any "poor people's" poetry. Today, when individual
expression, which is the precondition for the conception of lyric poetry that is
my point of departure, seems shaken to its very core in the crisis of the individual,
the collective undercurrent in the lyric surfaces in the most diverse places:
first merely as the ferment of individual expression and then perhaps also as an
anticipation of a situation that transcends mere individuality in a positive way.

If the translations can be trusted, García Lorca, whom Franco's henchmen murdered and whom no totalitarian regime could have tolerated, was the bearer of a force of this kind; and Brecht's name comes to mind as a lyric poet who was granted linguistic integrity without having to pay the price of esotericism. I will forgo making a judgment about whether the poetic principle of individuation was in fact sublated to a higher level here, or whether its basis lies in regression, a weakening of the ego. The collective power of contemporary lyric poetry may be largely due to the linguistic and psychic residues of a condition that is not yet fully individuated, a state of affairs that is prebourgeois in the broadest sense—dialect. Until now, however, the traditional lyric, as the most rigorous aesthetic negation of bourgeois convention, has by that very token been tied to bourgeois society.

Because considerations of principle are not sufficient. I would like to use a few poems to concretize the relationship of the poetic subject, which always stands for a far more general collective subject, to the social reality that is its antithesis. In this process the thematic elements, which no linguistic work, even *poésie pure*, can completely divest itself of, will need interpretation just as the so-called formal elements will. The way the two interpenetrate will require special emphasis, for it is only by virtue of such interpenetration that the lyric poem actually captures the historical moment within its bounds. I want to choose not poems like Goethe's, aspects of which I commented on without analyzing, but later ones, poems which do not have the unqualified authenticity of the "Nachtlied." The two poems I will be talking about do indeed share in the collective undercurrent. But I would like to call your attention especially to the way in which in them different levels of a contradictory fundamental condition of society are represented in the medium of the poetic subject. Permit me to repeat that we are concerned not with the poet as a private person, not with his psychology or his so-called social perspective, but with the poem as a philosophical sundial telling the time of history.

Let me begin by reading you Eduard Mörike's "Auf einer Wanderung" ["On a Walking Tour"]:

In ein freundliches Städtchen tret' ich ein

In den Strassen liegt roter Abendschein,

Aus einem offenen Fenster eben,

Über den reichsten Blumenflor

Hinweg, hört man Goldglockentöne schweben,

Und *eine* Stimme scheint ein Nachtigallenchor,

Daß die Blüen beben,

Daß die Lüfte leben,

Daß in höherem Rot die Rosen leuchten vor.

Lang' hielt ich stauneind, lustbeklommen.

Wie ich hinaus vors Tor gekommen,

Ich weiss es wahrlich selber nicht,

Ach hier, wie liegt die Welt so licht!

Der Himmel wogt in purpurnem Gewühle,

Rückwärts die Stadt in goldnem Rauch;

Wie rauscht der Erlenbach, wie rauscht im Grund die Mühle!

Ich bin wie trunken, irrgeführt—

O Muse, du hast mein Herz berührt

Mit einem Liebeshauch!

[I enter a friendly little town,

On the streets lies the red evening light,

From an open window,

Across the richest profusion of flowers

One hears golden bell-tones hover.

And *one* voice seems to be a choir of nightingales,

So that the blossoms quaver,

So that the breezes are lively,

So that the roses glow forth in a higher red.

I stood a long while marvelling, oppressed with pleasure.

How I got out beyond the city gate,

I really do not know myself,

Oh, how bright the world is here!

The sky surges in purple turbulence,

At my back the town in a golden haze;

How the alder stream murmurs, how the mill roars below!

I am as if drunken, led astray—

Oh muse, you have touched my heart,

With a breath of love!]

Up surges the image of the promise of happiness which the small south German town still grants its guests on the right day, but not the slightest concession is made to the pseudo-Gothic small-town idyll. The poem gives the feeling of warmth and security in a confined space, yet at the same time it is a work in the elevated style, not disfigured by *Gemütlichkeit* and coziness, not sentimentally praising narrowness in opposition to the wide world, not happiness in one's own little corner. Language and the rudimentary plot both aid in skillfully equating the utopia of what is close at hand with that of the utmost distance. The town appears in the narrative only as a fleeting scene, not as a place of lingering. The magnitude of the feeling that results from the speaker's delight in the girl's voice, and not that voice alone but the voice of all of nature, the choir, emerges only outside the confined arena of the town, under the open purple-billowing sky, where the golden town and the rushing brook come together in the *imago*. Linguistically, this is aided by an inestimably subtle, scarcely definable *classical*, ode-like element. As if from afar, the free rhythms call to mind unrhymed Greek stanzas, as does the sudden pathos of the closing line of the first stanza, which is effected with the most discreet devices of transposition of word order: "Daβ in höherem Rot die Rosen leuchten vor. " The single word "Muse" at the end of the poem is decisive. It is as if this word, one of the most overused in German classicism, gleamed once again, truly as if in the light of the setting sun, by being bestowed upon the *genius loci* of the friendly little town, and as though even in the process of disappearing it were possessed of all the power to enrapture which an invocation of the muse in the modern idiom, comically inept, usually fails to capture. The poem's inspiration proves itself perhaps more fully in this than in any of its other features: that the choice of this most objectionable word at a critical point, carefully prepared by the latent Greek linguistic demeanor, resolves the urgent dynamic of the whole like a musical *Abgesang*. ① In the briefest of spaces, the lyric succeeds in doing what the German epic attempted in vain, even in such projects as Goethe's *Hermann und Dorothea*.

The social interpretation of a success like this is concerned with the stage of historical experience evidenced in the poem. In the name of humanity, of the universality of the human, German classicism had undertaken to release subjective impulses from the contingency that threatens them in a society where relationships between human beings are no longer direct but instead mediated solely by the market. It strove to objectify the subjective as Hegel did in philosophy and tried to overcome the contradictions of men's real lives by reconciling them in spirit, in the idea. The continued existence of these contradictions in reality, however, had compromised the spiritual solution: in the face of a life not grounded in meaning, a life lived painstakingly amid the bustle of competing interests, a prosaic life, as artistic experience sees it; in the face of a world in which the fate of individual human beings works itself out in accordance with blind laws, art, whose form gives the impression of speaking from the point of view of a realized humanity, becomes an empty word. Hence classicism's concept of the human being withdrew into private, individual existence and its images; only there did humanness seem secure. Of necessity, the idea of humankind as something whole, something self-determining, was renounced by the bourgeoisie, in aesthetic form as in politics. It is the stubborn clinging to one's own restricted sphere, which itself obeys a compulsion, that makes ideals like comfort and *Gemütlichkeit* so suspect. Meaning itself is linked to the contingencies of human happiness; through a kind of usurpation, individual happiness is ascribed a dignity it would attain only along with the happiness of the whole.

---

① The *Abgesang* was the closing portion of a stanza in medieval lyric poetry.

The social force of Mörike's genius, however, consists in the fact that he combined the two experiences——that of the classicistic elevated style and that of the romantic private miniature—and that in doing so he recognized the limits of both possibilities and balanced them against one another with incomparable tact. In none of his expressive impulses does he go beyond what could be genuinely attained in his time. The much-invoked organic quality of his work is probably nothing other than this tact, which is philosophically sensitive to history and which scarcely any other poet in the German language possessed to the same degree. The alleged pathological traits in Mörike reported by psychologists and the drying up of his production in later years are the negative aspect of his very highly developed understanding of what is possible. The poems of the hypochondriacal clergyman from Cleversulzbach, who is considered one of our naive artists, are virtuoso pieces unsurpassed by the masters of *l'art pour l'art*. He is as aware of the empty and ideological aspects of elevated style as of the mediocrity, petit-bourgeois dullness, and obliviousness to totality of the Biedermeier period, in which the greater part of his lyric work falls. The spirit in him is driven to create, for the last time, images that would betray themselves neither by their classical drapery nor by local color, neither by their manly tones nor by their lip-smacking. As if walking a fine line, the residues of the elevated style that survive in memory echo in him, together with the signs of an immediate life that promised fulfillment precisely at the time when they were already condemned by the direction history was taking; and both greet the poet on his wandering only as they are about to vanish. He already shares in the paradox of lyric poetry in the ascending industrial age. As indeterminate and fragile as his solutions are the solutions of all the great lyric poets who come afterwards, even those who seem to be separated from him by an abyss—like Baudelaire, of whom Claudel said that his style was a mixture of Racine's and that of the journalists of his time. In industrial society the lyric idea of a self-restoring immediacy becomes—where it does not impotently evoke a romantic past—more and more something that flashes out abruptly, something in which what is possible transcends its own impossibility.

The short poem by Stefan George I would now like to discuss derives from a much later phase in this development. It is one of the celebrated songs from the *Seventh Ring*, a cycle of extremely condensed works which for all their lightness of rhythm are over-heavy with substance and wholly without *Jugendstil* ornament. Their eccentric boldness was rescued from the frightful cultural conservativism of the George circle only when the great composer Anton von Webern set them to music; in George, ideology and social substance are very far apart. The song reads:

> Im windes-weben
> War meine frage
> Nur träumerei.
> Nur lächeln war
> Was du gegeben.
> Aus nasser nacht
> Ein glanz entfacht—
> Nun drängt der mai
> Nun muss ich gar
> Um dein aug und haar
> Alle tage
> In sehnen leben.

> [In the winds-weaving
> My question was
> Only daydreaming.
> Only a smile was
> What you gave.
> From a moist night
> A gleam ignites—
> Now May urges
> Now I must
> For your eyes and hair
> Every day

Live in yearning.]

Unquestionably, this is elevated style. Delight in things close at hand, something that still colors Mörike's much earlier poem, has fallen under a prohibition. It has been banished by the Nietzschean pathos of detached reserve which George conceives himself to be carrying on. The remains of Romanticism lie, a deterrent, between him and Mörike; the remains of the idyll are hopelessly outdated and have degenerated to heartwarmers. While George's poetry, the poetry of an imperious individual, presupposes individualistic bourgeois society and the autonomous individual as its preconditions, a curse is put on the bourgeois element of conventional form no less than on the bourgeois contents. But because this poetry can speak from no overarching framework other than the bourgeois, which it rejects not only tacitly and a priori but also expressly, it becomes obstructed: on its own initiative and its own authority, it simulates a feudal condition. Socially this is hidden behind what the cliché refers to as George's aristocratic stance. This stance is not the pose that the bourgeois, who cannot reduce these poems to objects of fondling, waxes indignant about. Rather, despite its demeanor of hostility to society, it is the product of the social dialectic that denies the lyric subject identification with what exists and its world of forms, while that subject is nevertheless allied with the status quo in its innermost core: it has no other locus from which to speak but that of a past seigneurial society. The ideal of nobility, which dictates the choice of every word, image, and sound in the poem, is derived from that locus, and the form is medieval in an almost undefinable way, a way that has been virtually imported into the linguistic configuration. To this extent the poem, like George altogether, is neoromantic. But it is not real things and not sounds that are evoked but rather a vanished condition of the soul. The artistically effected latency of the ideal, the absence of any crude archaicism, raises the song above the hopeless fiction it nonetheless offers. It no more resembles the medieval imitations used on wall plaques than it does the repertoire of the modern lyric; the poem's stylistic principle saves it from conformity. There is no more room in it for organic reconciliation of conflicting elements than there was for their pacification in the reality of George's time; they are mastered only through selection, through omission. Where things close at hand, the things one commonly calls concrete immediate experiences, are admitted into George's lyric poetry at all, they are allowed only at the price of mythologization: none may remain what it is. Thus in one of the landscapes of the *Seventh Ring* the child picking berries is transformed, wordlessly, as if with a magic wand, through a magical act of violence, into a fairy-tale child. The harmony of the song is wrested from an extreme of dissonance: it rests on what Valéry called *refus*, on an unyielding renunciation of everything through which the conventions of lyric poetry imagine that they have captured the aura of things. The method retains only the patterns, the pure formal ideas and schemata of lyric poetry itself, which speak with an intensity of expression once again in divesting themselves of all contingency. In the midst of Wilhelmine Germany the elevated style from which that lyric poetry emerged as polemic has no tradition at all to which it may appeal, least of all the legacy of classicism. It is achieved not by making a show of rhetorical figures and rhythms but by an ascetic omission of whatever might diminish its distance from a language sullied by commerce. If the subject is to genuinely resist reification in solitude here, it may no longer even try to withdraw into what is its own as though that were its property; the traces of an individualism that has in the meantime delivered itself over to the market in the form of the feuilleton are alarming. Instead, the subject has to step outside itself by keeping quiet about itself; it has to make itself a vessel, so to speak, for the idea of a pure language. George's greatest poems are aimed at rescuing that language. Formed by the Romance languages, and especially by the extreme simplification of the lyric through which Verlaine made it an instrument of what is most differentiated, the ear of George, the German student of Mallarmé, hears his own language as though it were a foreign tongue. He overcomes its alienation, which is an alienation of use, by intensifying it until it becomes the alienation of a language no longer actually spoken, even an imaginary language, and in that imaginary language he perceives what would be possible, but never took place, in its composition. The four lines "Nun muss ich gar/Um dein aug und haar/Alle tage/In sehnen leben," which I consider some of the most irresistible lines in German poetry, are like a quotation, but a quotation not from another poet but from something language has irrevocably failed to a-chieve: the medieval German poetry of the *Minnesang* would have succeeded in achieving it if it, if a tradition of the German language—if the German language itself, one is tempted to say—had succeeded. It was in this spirit that Borchardt tried to translate Dante. Subtle ears have taken umbrage at the elliptical "gar," which is probably used in place of "ganz und gar" [completely] and to some ex-tent for the sake of the rhyme. One can concede the justice of this criticism and the fact that as used in the line the word has no proper meaning. But great works of art are the ones that succeed precisely where they are most problematic. Just as the greatest works of music may not be completely reduced to their structure but shoot out beyond it with a few superfluous notes or measures, so it is with the "gar," a Goethean "residue of the absurd" in which language es-capes the subjective intention that occasioned the use of the word. It is probably this very "gar" that establishes the poem's status with the force of a déjà vu: through it the melody of the poem's language extends beyond mere significa-tion. In the age of its decline George sees in language the idea that the course of history has denied it and constructs lines that sound as though they were not written by him but had been there from the beginning of time and would remain as they were forever. The quixotism of this enterprise, however, the impossi-bility of this kind of restorative writing, the danger of falling into arts and crafts, enriches the poem's substance: language's chimerical yearning for the impossible becomes an expression of the subject's insatiable erotic longing, which finds relief from the self in the other. This transformation of an individu-ality intensified to an extreme into self-annihilation—and what was the Maximin cult in the late George but a desperate renunciation of individuality construing itself as something positive—was necessary in creating the phantasmagoria of the folksong, something the German language had been groping for in vain in its greatest masters. Only by virtue of a differentiation taken so far that it can no longer bear its own difference, can no longer bear anything but the universal, freed from the humiliation of isolation, in the particular does lyrical language represent language's intrinsic being as opposed to its service in the realm of ends. But it thereby represents the idea of a free humankind, even if the George School concealed this idea from itself through a base cult of the heights. The truth of George lies in the fact that his poetry breaks down the walls of individuality through its consummation of the particular, through its sensitive opposition both to the banal and ultimately also to the select. The expression of his poetry may have been condensed into an individual expression which his lyrics saturate with substance and with the experience of its own solitude; but this very lyric speech becomes the voice of human beings between whom the barriers have fallen.

13. 阿多诺:《论抒情诗与社会》

(Theodor Adorno,"On Lyric Poetry and Society,"1957)

作者小识

阿多诺(Theodor Adorno, 1903—1969),德国哲学家、文学批评家和音乐评论家,"法兰克福学派"第一代学术领袖。他以碎片方式写作,揭示启蒙自毁的逻辑,建构瓦解一切的否定辩证法,捍卫美学自律,以"无调性哲学"完成了西方马克思主义的转向,将理性批判转化为文化批判。

阿多诺的哲学代表作有《启蒙辩证法》(*Dialectic of Enlightenment*,1947,与霍克海姆合著)和《否定辩证法》(*Negative Dialectics*,1966),美学代表作有《美学理论》(*Aesthetic Theory*,1970),文学批评代表作有《文学札记》(*Notes to Literature*,1966—1969),音乐批评代表作有《现代音乐哲学》(*Philosophy of Modern Music*,1949),文化批评代表作有《多棱镜》(*Prisms*,1955)。他有23卷本《阿多诺全集》(*Gesammelte Schriften*,Suhrkamp,1980)传世。

背景略说

阿多诺的思想源自欧洲现代性的三重危机。第一,奥斯维辛之后,西方的古典和现代人文主义陷入空前的困境,连柏拉图、康德、歌德、荷尔德林、马赫、贝多芬、勋伯格等文化英雄都束手无策,西方似乎走上了一条通往荒原的现代之路;第二,近代哲学日趋与实践紧密结合,然而在20世纪哲学实践遭到了空前的挫折,欧洲政治运动走向了一种霸权,但霸权建立在虚无主义基础之上;第三,法兰克福学派主要成员和欧洲文化精英被迫流亡美国,他们发现美国式文化工业主宰世界,招致了同样的失败。本雅明的说法,"文化史无不是野蛮的记录",被阿多诺改写为"文化史是一部人类牺牲的内化史"。在他看来,文化形式变了:古希腊时代有荷马史诗,文艺复兴时代有人文主义,现代欧洲有希特勒主义,现代美国有文化工业。但是,野蛮没有变,只不过从旧野蛮格局发展出了新野蛮格局:惨绝人寰的奥斯维辛之于现代欧洲,受虐—施虐的文化工业之于现代美国,恰如暴力血腥荷马史诗之于古代希腊，是欧洲文化的登峰造极之意象。于是，阿多诺的传世之作，也是觉世之书，其根本却深植在对人类文化败绩的反思中，所以我们不妨称之为"失败之书"。

阿多诺和霍克海姆发现，"启蒙"便是理性的慧黠，它教会了人类盲目乐观，却没有引导人类真的走向自由，而是将人类抛向了灾难的深渊。从但丁的地狱走向了人间炼狱，便是启蒙赐予人类的"恩典"。比如说，"二战"、屠杀犹太人、奥斯维辛等，都并非太古的野蛮，而是现代的野蛮，甚至还建基于精致的逻辑思维，还标榜着道德义务。理性主宰下的暴力、野蛮与邪恶，阿伦特一言以蔽之，即彻底的恶（radical evil），就是平庸的恶（banality of evil）。启蒙之初心，是醒觉世界，驱逐神话，以知识取代蒙昧。可是，启蒙背离了初心，将自己变为神话，从而自我中毒，万劫不复。启蒙唤醒了理性，可是理性中混杂了欲望与野心，最后蜕变为"肆心"（hubris）。众所周知，古代雅典人的肆心，导致了帝国的烟消云散，一场悲剧在所难免。于是，关于启蒙与神话的经典表述便是"启蒙的辩证法"：启蒙祛除了神话，但神话即启蒙，启蒙将自己变成神话而毁于神话。阿多诺和霍克海姆用荷马史诗《奥德修斯》中的思想意象来坐实这一辩证逻辑：被启蒙的特洛伊战争幸存者"见多识广""足智多谋"，一路巧妙应对风险，抗拒魑魅魍魉的诱惑和天地人神的干扰，历经磨难终得荣耀，即还乡之后作为独立的政治主体重整伊塔卡秩序，但立即变成一个暴戾的主体，斩杀异端，甚至伤及无辜。他射杀了所有向帕涅罗珀求婚的人，虐杀了无辜的女仆。于是，野蛮成为文明的主旋律，而启蒙也毁于神话。

文化工业也是启蒙的骄子，但它以消费社会为基础，以大众媒介为工具，以资本盈利为鹄的。好莱坞明星是施虐者，而追星族是受虐者，施虐—受虐的关系，与纳粹政治的统治—被统治关系，便完美地同型同构。深受本雅明的影响，阿多诺也转换立场，站在文化大众的立场上重新考虑文化工业。文化工业尊重买方市场，根据消费来组织生产；文化工业假借现代技术，延伸消费欲望；文化工业驱逐美学"灵韵"，解构高雅与低俗的秩序；文化工业以消费大众为神圣，对之进行精致的盘算。阿多诺从主宰与被主宰两个侧面反思文化工业，近似于将文化工业视为一场"幻象的瘟疫"，一场"商品拜物教"仪式，与资本主义的全面管理之总体性异曲同工。在幻象传播的过程中，在拜物教仪式上，"大众媒体"作用最为关键，因为它蛊惑大众，为消费者量身定制，打开了原子化个体进入法西斯集体的魅惑之路。

阿多诺的思想基础，是"否定的辩证法"。这一思想的要义在于"瓦解的逻辑"，就像勋伯格颠覆音乐调性。依据这一思想原则，他历数"第一哲学"的原罪，说它崇拜权威、讲求秩序、拘泥逻各斯，进而要求破除同一性的神话，描绘"星丛式哲学"图景。将这种思想应用于美学，阿多诺主张，"唯有通过具体的否定，艺术品才获得其真理性"。于是，一方面，阿多诺强调艺术的美学自律性；另一方面，他又强调艺术具有拯救人性于堕落的使命。艺术及其所持存之真理的不确定性，构成了阿多诺与解构论对话的基础。不妨说，阿多诺身陷"双重约束"：既要证明艺术是瞬息万变的星丛，又要坚持在艺术之中去寻找真理性。在不确定的艺术之中去寻找确定的真理，这就注定了阿多诺美学的悖论性。

基本内容

　　《论抒情诗与社会》选自阿多诺的《文学札记》第一卷。阿多诺的文学批评是其"反调性"的哲学即"否定辩证法"的具体演示。否定辩证法锋芒所向，是传统哲学的总体化逻辑。在他看来，任何认知对象都不可能完全被认识，所以总体认识一定是幻象体系。总体性或者同一性的哲学抹杀了个体的感性动力。总体性幻象在艺术之中的表现，将是在艺术之中排斥异质，用苍白的概念、僵化的观念压制艺术品的独特个性。"有多少意志的自由，就有多少想自由的人。"这么一个绝对否定的瓦解性逻辑，也自然而然地贯注在阿多诺的文学批评中。

　　他的文学批评有两个独特的取向。第一，关注语言与形式的关系。在他看来，艺术的生命和形式的命运"生死与共"。阿多诺认为，语言既具有逻辑制约力，又具有超越逻辑的时刻及其乌托邦的虚幻性，这就构成了语言与生命之间的悖论、经验与反经验之间的矛盾。第二，解放随笔写作的自由潜能。随笔或称杂论，虽然在文学史上备受压制，但它唤醒了"智性的自由"（intellectual freedom）。写作随笔的作家或行神如风，行气如虹，或戛然而止，余韵悠长，总之是以一切可能的形式道说一切内容。于是，随笔如同醉拳，形醉意不醉，外散而内聚，法无定法，无法即有法。随笔作为一种书写风格，将语言的悖论呈现到极致。一方面，语言具有将个体解放出来的潜力；另一方面，语言的使用又具有政治性，就像帝国主义对待其臣民那般。个体对于自由的自觉，体现为随笔写作对于集体政治无意识的质疑、颠覆与解构。而这一否定辩证法及其对总体性幻象的解构，直接体现在阿多诺关于"抒情诗与社会"的讨论中。

首先，抒情诗的悖论性在于，唯有从彻底的个体化之中，诗歌才能赢得普遍性。唯有能够在诗歌之中领悟到人类孤独声音的人，才是诗人的知音。个体化，以至于最终原子化的社会，却导致了抒情诗语言本身的孤独，而语言的普遍联系又依赖于个体的聚集。为了化解这个悖论，诗人就必须让一个社会总体以自身充满矛盾的统一体的形式出现在作品之中。

其次，抒情诗的否定性在于，它反对虚假普遍性，抗拒人的世界被物化。虚假意识是意识形态体系的别称，或者说是幻象体系，其本质是虚假。只要艺术有染虚假意识，艺术就难免失败。"伟大的艺术作品之本质就在于它的形象，以及通过形象来反映现实生活中那些蕴含着调和趋势的社会冲突。……而艺术作品的伟大之处正在于，它让那些被意识形态掩盖了的东西得以表露出来。"社会对人压抑得越厉害，抒情诗对社会的反抗也就越强烈。在对社会的强烈抗议中，抒情诗坚守艺术的自律性，即完全根据自己的法则来构建自身。"抒情诗与现实的距离，便成了衡量客观实在的荒诞和恶劣的尺度。在这种对社会的抗议之中，抒情诗表达了人对于与现实不同的另一个世界的想象。抒情诗对物的超暴力的强烈憎恶和反感，是对人的世界被物化的一种反抗形式。"

再次，抒情诗的现代性在于，它比其他艺术品更为纯粹，是内心灵感的瞬间产物。通过分析歌德的《浪游者的夜歌》，阿多诺展示了抒情现代性的基本维度。（1）抒情之"我"与集体之"我"以及客观外在形象之间的对立。自我丧失了自然，又渴望通过赋予其灵魂和沉迷于自我来重建自然。（2）抒情的和谐是苦恼与爱恋的掺和。《浪游者的夜歌》之中那种难以言传之美，就在于渴望和平与拒绝和平的世界之间那种不可克服的张力。诗人歌德的高明之处就在于只字不提"异化"，只字不提摧毁世界的不安。抒情诗所表达的，不是主体—客体之间的对立与不安，而是心灵内部的不安与颤栗。（3）抒情的宇宙就是在外在一切都消逝之后的语言宇宙。这是一个象征的世界，我们于其中看到了"整个生命由于充满悲戚的神秘微笑，都浓缩在人睡前的时间里"。（4）抒情的完美在于，在有限之中蕴含无限，在无限之中伸张有限，在有限的时空之中表现万物的生机与活力。在每一首抒情诗里，主体与客体、个人与社会的历史关系都必然会通过主体的回复和自我的精神中介而留下自己的痕迹。

【附】

浪游者的夜歌

歌德 作　钱春绮 译

群峰一片
沉寂，
树梢微风
敛迹。
林中栖鸟
缄默，
稍待你也
安息。

最后，阿多诺反复论证抒情诗同社会的对抗性。抒情诗反抗社会所采取的独特方式是退回自我，发掘自我，远离社会的表层，然后经过诗人之大脑，将社会的东西变成创造的灵感。语言就是这一过程的媒介：一方面，语言通过形象的营构来模拟主体的情感律动；另一方面，语言作为逻辑的媒介与普遍性相连，而指向了社会交流境界。不过，阿多诺警告，我们不能将语言绝对化，将之变成海德格尔的"存在"之声，而对立于抒情的主体。以波德莱尔为例，在现代性视野下，阿多诺论述了以语言为中介消解抒情诗与社会对立之可能性。

　　在抒情诗中，主体通过认同语言而实现了双重否定：否定了其作为纯粹单子存在的同社会之对立，也否定了它在一个彻底社会化的社会之内的作用。然而，社会对主体的压制越强，抒情诗的处境越脆弱。波德莱尔第一个将这种处境落墨成文，记录在案。因为它的主题，以及它通过一种崇高的风格化语言而点燃的诗性火花，波德莱尔的作品可谓欧洲人痛苦的终极后果之写照。他并未止步于个体的苦难，而是选取现代性本身作为纯而又纯的反抒情性之表征。在波德莱尔那里，一种绝望的气息已经自我预示，而几乎只能在其悖论的巅峰保持其勉为其难的平衡。当抒情语言和交流语言之间的矛盾发展到极致，抒情诗就成为一场人人拼死拼命想要赢得的赌博。这不是像世俗庸见所认为的那样，因为它已经变得晦涩难解，而是因为它在作为一种文学语言而获得自我意识的过程中，在为一种不受任何交流意图所制约的绝对客观性而奋斗的过程中，语言一方面远离了精神的客观性以及活的语言，另一方面又以一场诗意的事件取代了不复存在的语言。晚期抒情诗衰落，在那个崇高、诗化和主观暴力纵横的时刻，它必须为其自我修持、不变本色、纯真质朴和客观实在的努力付出惨痛的代价。虚无缥缈的光亮，是对其自我异化的祛魅世界所做出的补偿。

"抒情诗永远是一种社会对抗精神的主体表达"，这是阿多诺反复论述的主题。他同时也指出："滋生抒情诗的客观世界也是一个本质上对立的世界，所以抒情概念不仅仅意味着表现一种为语言赋予客观性的主体性。不仅要说，抒情主体越是有效地体现整体，主体也越是强有力地表现自身，而且还要指出，诗性主体本身受益于这么一种特权——唯有极少数人才能在为生存而斗争的压力下通过浸润于自我而把握普遍性，或者作为能够自由表达自我的自律主体而发展。然而，另外一些人，面对迷惘的诗歌主体仿佛置身事外，就像他们是一些客体，不仅感到陌生，而且还明显地被降格为历史的对象，但他们同样有权或者更有权利寻找将痛苦与梦想和盘托出的声音。"社会性成为一道永恒的暗流，驱动着抒情诗不断地逼近本真，完成抒情主体自我建构的使命。

拓展讨论

1957 年，也就是阿多诺发表《论抒情诗与社会》的那一年，捷克汉学家普实克(Jaroslav Prusek，1906—1980)发表了《中国现代文学中的主观主义和个人主义》一文。文中提出，清代到第一次世界大战期间的中国文学之基本特征是"主观主义和个人主义"。在世界文学的背景下，参照欧洲文学发展史，普实克断定，中国现代艺术家不注重记录现实，而注重心灵表现，而这是社会历史发生巨大变革的表征。这就表明"个人从传统的哲学、宗教或伦理观念中解放，甚至表明对因袭的社会秩序的现实反抗"①。普实克这一论断，暗示着中国现代文学反社会性抒情意识的崛起，在史诗时代还有抒情的声音。这一论

①　普实克：《抒情与史诗——中国现代文学论集》，郭建玲译，1 页，上海，上海三联书店，2010。

断，直接提出了中国现代文学史中"抒情与史诗"的论辩：究竟是抒情衰微史诗崛起，还是抒情贯穿在史诗之中，抒情与史诗辩证互动，两境相入，气象宏大？但看古典诗文体制变革，似乎抒情式微毋庸置疑。但从古典抒情美典的创造性转换来看，史诗时代抒情的声音自成一脉，甚至波澜涌动，蔚为壮观。①

从中国现代文学发生的源始场景看，林纾翻译《茶花女》，"以华人之典料，写欧人之性情"，哀艳感染时人，抒情直达"情教"。王国维援引叔本华学说解读《红楼梦》，为化解"欲望"之情而教化"主观之诗人"，可谓用心良苦。20世纪20年代被史家视为"抒情主义"年代，一时间"扩张""解放""自由"成为艺术家甚至普通人的基本诉求。最值得重视的是，美学家宗白华所提出的"普遍同情"的"新抒情主义"。1921年，宗白华在一位景仰东方文明的德国教授家里体验到一个"浪漫之夜"。舞阑人散，柔情萦绕，万籁俱静，星月无声，宗白华感到："无限凄凉之感里，夹着无限热爱之感。似乎这微渺的心和那遥远的自然，和那茫茫的广大的人类，打通了一道地下的深沉的神秘的暗道，在绝对的静寂里获得自然人生最亲密的接触。"②美学家写诗，自然是抒情，但那是一种情到深处人孤独的"情"，对自然物象、宇宙人生最深刻的同情。窗内的人心，遥领着世界深秘的回音。生命的悲壮、存在的卑微、情怀的波动，与宇宙万象神秘相契，于是个体与永恒同在，生命与宇宙同流，心灵与神圣相依，自我与他人相望相守。宗白华还把同情的目光投向了"最混乱、最苦痛"的晋代，更认为这是一个极自由、极解放、最富于智慧、最浓于热情的时代。晋人向外发现了自然，向内发现了自己的深情。"晋人虽超，未能忘情，所谓'情之所钟，正在我辈'！"宗白华以晋人之情为典范，诠释"宇宙的深情"，即"审美的同情"："深于情者，不仅对宇宙人生体会到至深的无名的哀感，扩而充之，可以成为耶稣、释迦的悲天悯人；就是快乐的体验也是深入肺腑，惊心动魄；浅俗薄情的人，不仅不能深哀，且不知所谓真乐。"③宗白华在现代性境遇下，将"抒情"提升为审美的同情，情感便获得了史诗的韵味。通过将"抒情史诗化"，宗白华解构了古典境界美学，以情感为中心建构了中国现代艺术心灵模式，这一模式具有史诗气象。

---

①　参见王德威：《抒情传统与中国现代性　在北大的八堂课》，序论，北京，生活·读书·新知三联书店，2010。

②　宗白华：《美学散步》，285页，上海，上海人民出版社，1981。

③　宗白华：《美学漫步》，299～300页，武汉，长江文艺出版社，2019。

延伸阅读

1. 阿多诺：《美学理论（修订译本）》，王柯平译，上海，上海人民出版社，2020。该书对美学、艺术、文化工业展开了"否定辩证法"的批判研究，凸显了艺术真理性与审美自律性。

2. 阿多诺：《最低限度的道德　对受损生活的反思》，丛子钰译，上海，上海人民出版社，2020。该书是以碎片式书写结构呈现宏大叙事衰落的典范，从否定辩证法的角度，将日常生活的细微体验与 20 世纪的灾难性事件的隐微联系揭示出来。

14. The Concept of Reality and the Possibility of the Novel (1964) [①]

By Hans Blumenberg

The history of Western literary theory can be summed up as a continuous debate on the classical dictum that poets are liars. [②] Even Nietzsche was still

---

① Originally published as "Wirklichkeitsbegriff und Möglichkeit des Romans," in *Nachahmung und Illusion: Kolloquium Gießen, Juni* 1963. *Vorlagen und Verhandlungen* (*Poetik und Hermeneutik I*), ed. Hans Robert Jauß (Munich: Eidos), 9-27; from Hans Blumenberg, *Ästhetische und metaphorologische Schriften*, ed. Anselm Haverkamp (Frankfurt am Main: Suhrkamp, 2001), 47-73. English-language version published in *New Perspectives in German Literary Criticism: A Collection of Essays*, ed. Richard E. Amacher and Victor Lange (Princeton, NJ: Princeton University Press, 1979), 29-48.

② For the history of its influence, the origin of this dictum is scarcely relevant, but for a proper understanding of the matter, it is worth noting that at first there was no general devaluation but a critical reminder that the epic is obliged to be truthful—it should not bring up the unprofitable writings of earlier times, but ought to reveal noble deeds through the power of memory (*esthlà anaphaínei*) (Xenophanes, fr. B i, 19-23, Diels). The reproach of untruthfulness is therefore based on the premise that the epic should communicate truth. As Bruno Snell has shown in *The Discovery of the Mind: The Greek Origins of European Thought* (Cambridge, MA: Harvard University Press, 1953), 90-112, the reproach takes on a general significance only through problems connected with dramatic illusion in the theater; here the technique of actualization, arising from the mythical significance of the lyric and tragic chorus, no longer coincides with the consciousness of reality underlying the epic. The transition from ecstatic identification in the cult of Dionysos to technical accomplishments of *representation* tears open the differences between reality and art, a split which, typically, is thought out to its ultimate theoretical consequences by the Greeks; even for Aeschylus, Agatharchos not only painted a decor in perspective but also left behind a treatise on it (Diels, 59 A, 39; 1: 14 et seq.). There has also survived a piece by Gorgias (fr. B 23, Diels), with a moralizing justification of illusion in tragedy which is apparently excused by its effect on the spectator. And so in classical times, as in the eighteenth century with Diderot, the starting point for these reflections on poetic illusion was provided by the drama. But in both eras, this starting point was soon abandoned. For the tradition of this saying—that poets are liars—two points became significant: Plato's critique of the truth content of art in general and the Stoic-Christian habit of allegorizing, which depended on defending a *relic of truth* in literature in order to be able to *rescue* it from dispersal or concealment.

under the influence of this assertion, when, claiming a metaphysical dignity for art, he had to invert it, contrasting the *truthfulness of art* to the *falseness of nature*. ① Halfway between the classical topos and the modern antithesis stands the scholastic concession to literature of a *minimum veritatis* [the least truth].

If we are to consider the pros and cons of the classical dictum, we must first decide what is meant by its antithesis—i. e. , that poets "tell the truth. " There are, I believe, two sorts of truth involved: first, when it is claimed that literature refers to a given outside reality—whatever that reality may be; second, when literature is said to create a reality of its own. We must also bear in mind the purely logical possibility that both thesis and antithesis may be ignored, and art may be regarded as totally divorced from such considerations as truth and falseness or any criterion connected with "reality. " However, this logical scheme does not necessarily coincide with the historical possibilities.

At no time in the history of Western aesthetic theory has there been any serious departure from the tendency to legitimize the work of art in terms of its relation to reality, and so any critical assessment of the foundation of traditional aesthetics must begin with a clarification of what is meant by "reality. " This is difficult, for generally in our dealings with what we regard as real, we never get down to the predicative stage of defining exactly what it is that constitutes the reality. And yet the moment a doubt is cast on the reality of an action or a proposition, our attention is drawn to the specific conditions which have led us to regard it as real. The very fact that the "truth" of literature has always been

---

① *Der Philosoph*: *Betrachtungen über den Kampf von Kunst und Erkenntnis* (Entwürfe von 1872) (WW, Musarion-Ausg. , vi, 31). Now the concept of *nature* is completely oriented toward scientific objectification and its command over the concept of truth, which fulfills itself in the destruction of anthropomorphic immanence. But the "taming of science" offers a questionable justification for "the need for illusion" (WW, vi, 12); ultimately, this kind of truth cannot escape from the tradition of *imitation* but is committed only to a world interpreted as an *appearance* that liberates the desire for cognition: "Art therefore treats appearance as appearance, and so does not seek to deceive at all, but is true" (WW, vi, 98). This interpretation of "art as a true appearance" remains bound to the metaphysical tradition of art theory, for it pins art down to the character of given reality, even if this is called *incognizability*. As regards the function intended for art in this reversal of history, it cannot be anything different: such efforts always assume the premises of that which they set out to *repeat*.

contested has made literary theory a focus for the critical assessment of concepts of reality and for the unmasking of implicit preconceptions. Ultimately, we shall have to recognize what at a given time has been taken for granted as most obvious and trivial, i. e. , not even worth stating—and hence never specifically formulated. Our immediate task, then, must be to define the *various* historical concepts of reality.

The first historical concept that I should like to discuss here is what we might call the "reality of *instantaneous evidence*. " This concept is not explicitly propounded but is presupposed when, for instance, Plato unhesitatingly proceeds from the assumption that at the first sight of ideas the human mind immediately and with total confidence realizes that it is confronted with the ultimate and unsurpassable reality and, at the same time, is aware that the sphere of the empirical and the sensual is not and could never be such a reality. However, it is by no means taken for granted that anyone could view the duality of the empirical world and the ideal world without risking a corresponding split in his own consciousness of reality—a risk we should certainly apprehend the moment we tried to imagine our minds transferred from the world around us to one that was completely different. The classical concept of reality that gave rise to Plato's doctrine of ideas—though not identical to it—presumes that reality presented itself as such and of its own accord, and that at the moment of its presence it was there and totally incontrovertible. [1] For these formal charac-

---

[1] Although I should not maintain that the Platonic world of ideas is representative of the classical concept of reality, I do believe that it would be virtually unthinkable without the implication of that concept. It has been said often enough that the Greeks' access to their world was not just through their eyes but also through their thoughts. This may need elaborating: the Greeks preferred *seeing in repose* and the seeing of *given realities in repose*—*horan* [to see] is leaving the eyes at rest on the outside appearance of something, on a shape or a picture, as I have learned from Bruno Snell's lectures "Homerische Bedeutungslehre. " Aristotle referred to the momentariness of sight as an analogy to pleasure (*Eth. Nic.* , x, 3; 1174 a, 13 et seq.); *horasis* [the act of seeing] is at all moments complete and has no need of additional integration in time, like *hēdonē* [enjoyment]. Reality for sight does not constitute itself within time; although of course objects accumulate, the course of experience does not endow them with anything that could increase their given character. In the here and now, seeing, without any reference to *genesis* [creation], is a whole (1174 b, 9-13). The direct consequence of this is the concept of any *aisthēsis* [perception] (x, 4; 1174 b, 14-17). The fact that sight takes place in a series of aspects, that it is a process which essentially takes in *events*, relations, and representations, causes no difficulties and has no bearing on the formation of concepts.

teristics, the metaphor of light is particularly apt. This concept of reality also gave sustenance to a way of thinking that saw nothing problematic in biblical and other accounts of the appearance of God or of a god, who could present himself as such in a moment of direct revelation, leaving absolutely no room for the suspicion or the fear that he was illusory. ① "Instantaneous evidence" is a concept that involves the instant recognition of ultimate reality and can be identified precisely through this implication.

A second concept of reality, basic to the Middle Ages and after, may be called *guaranteed reality*. The length of time philosophy took to grasp and express the implications behind man's understanding of an attitude to the world may be gauged from the fact that the history of modern philosophy had its starting point in the systematic formulation of this particular concept. For Descartes, there is no instantaneous evidence of the ultimate reality, either for the self comprehending itself in a quasi-syllogism (*cogito, ergo sum* [I think therefore I am]), or for God, whose existence is deduced from the concept of God. The given reality becomes certain only by virtue of a guarantee which has to be secured by thought in a complex metaphysical process, because only by means of this process can the suspicion of a world as gigantic hoax be eliminated. The idea of God as the guarantor of the reliability of human knowledge—the schema

---

① A late, ironic reflection of such instantaneous evidence is to be found in a novel whose theme is the interweaving of fiction and reality, their equivalence as far as human destiny is concerned, and the consequent irrelevance of their identity. This novel is Andre Gide's *Caves du Vatican*. After the funeral of the poor crusader Amadeus, who had failed in his attempt to prove the alleged exchange of popes, there is a conversation in the coach between Count Julius Baraghoul and Anthimos, who is told by the count that the present pope in fact is not the real one. Anthimos, the one-time atheist, who has been as totally converted as he has been totally cured of lameness, thinks over this revelation and returns instantly to his atheism; who can reassure him now that Amadeus Fleunssoire, as he enters Paradise, will not have to recognize that his God is also not "the real one"? The count's answer implies an unclouded faith, for in such a case there can be nothing but momentary evidence; for him, it is a bizarre idea that there could be a false presentation of God, a mix-up "as if one could imagine another God being there. " But, typically, this argument makes not the slightest impression on Anthimos. Undoubtedly, he no longer shares this concept of reality, stops the coach, gets out, and—limps again.

of the third instance—of the absolute witness, had been emerging throughout the history of the medieval concept of the human mind ever since Augustine. This schema precludes the possibility of any one characteristic that might pinpoint the total reality of a given object. The characteristic of clarity and distinctness which Descartes attributes to evidence can only be explained in terms of the metaphysical assumptions arising from his philosophical doubts; otherwise, as has rightly been observed, there would be no difference between this sort of clarity and that found in a state of paranoia. The schema of guaranteed reality, with a third instance mediating in the relationship between subject and object, has had a considerable impact on modern theory of art. It is still to be seen in the attempt to guarantee the truth of the artistic product by referring to the underlying experiences of the artist and the psychological integrity with which he has transformed these experiences.

A third concept of reality may be defined as the *actualization of a context in itself*. ① This concept differs from the others through its time component: reality as "evidence" makes itself felt in the present moment; guaranteed reality refers back to the instance that creates and mediates between the world and human reason—in other words, to what scholasticism called *veritas ontologica* [ontological truth] that has its place in the past. The third concept takes reality as the result of an actualization, a progressive certainty which can never reach a total, final consistency, as it always looks forward to a future that might con-

---

① It has rightly been pointed out that this is the concept of reality of Husserl's phenomenology. Perhaps I should have insisted on being more precise—it is the concept of reality *presented* [*expliziert*] by phenomenology. But I doubt whether this description of the constitution of reality could have been possible at any time; this is why it was important for me to determine what such a phenomenological thematization presupposes, and since when it could have been written and understood. Precisely in this context, it becomes clear that concepts of reality do not simply *take over* from one another, but that the exhaustion of their implications and the excessive strain on their capacity to answer questions inspire a search for a new basis. The fact that *here* I am confining myself to an enumeration of concept-types is due to the thematic interest in the *vertical* foundation structure. More *recent* discussion on the connection of the concepts of reality is contained in my "Preliminary Remarks on the Concept of Reality" [in this volume].

tain elements which could shatter previous consistency and so render previous "realities" unreal. Even when a person's life-space is complete, we can only say that *his* reality has been continuous, and that such and such constituted *his* illusions, delusions, and imaginings—in other words, "his" reality. It is typical of this particular concept that the possessive adjective is linked with the word *reality*. The transcendency of time either invalidates the self's concept of "its" reality, or, at best, allows it the quasi-justification that it is nothing but a single perspectivistic topographical view. Reality as a self-constituting context is a *boundary concept* of the *ideal totality* of all selves—it is a confirmative value for the experience and interpretation of the world that take place in *intersubjectivity*. Obviously, this concept of reality has a sort of "epic" structure, relating to the totality of a world that can never be completed or grasped in its entirety—a world that can be only partially experienced and so can never exclude different contexts of experience which in themselves constitute different *worlds*. ①

① The concept of reality of the "open" context legitimizes the aesthetic quality of the *novitas* [novelty], the element of surprise and unfamiliarity, whereas "guaranteed" reality does not allow anything new or unfamiliar to become *real*, ascribes to tradition and authority a world that is already mastered and rounded off as the sum total of all that is knowable, and so leads inevitably to the postulate of *nihil novum dicere* [to say nothing new] (e. g. , Petrarch, *Epist. fam.* , vi, 2; cf. x, 1). The change in the concept of reality removes the dubiousness from what is new, and so *terra incognita* [unknown soil], or the *mundus novus* [new world], becomes possible and effective as a *stimulus* to human activity; if one might phrase the process as a paradox, surprise is something to be expected. This is also relevant to the history of the "falseness" of poetry: aesthetic pleasure in *falseness* becomes legitimate so long as it can be regarded as *newness* as well (i. e. , as something possible, a reality lying just beyond the horizon). Julius Caesar Scaliger, author of an oft-quoted poetics (1561), discusses in his even more interesting work *De subtilitate ad Hieronymum Cardanum* (1557; I use the edition of 1582), Cardanum's dictum: "Falsa delectant quia admirabilia" [fictions delight because they are marvellous] (*Exerc.* 307, 11; p. 936 et seq.). Scaliger protests against his commentary that it is only children and fools that could have such pleasure in the untrue, because they assume that there is *plus veritatis* [more truth] in it, so that ultimately it would actually *be* a (supposed) form of truth, which gives rise to pleasure. However, art can give far more satisfaction than nature to a naturally infinite, reasoning mind; those falsehoods in which even *sapientes* [the wise] find pleasure (e. g. , the *Homerica phasmata* [Homeric inventions]) are revealed as the rich overflow by which art exceeds the (still) constant (转下页注)

The last concept of reality that we shall discuss here is based on the experience of *resistance*. Here illusion is understood as the desires entertained by the self: unreality as the threat to and seduction of the self through the projection of its own wishes; the consequent antithesis is *reality as that which cannot be mastered by the self.*, i. e. , which resists it not merely as an experience of contact with an inert mass but also—most radically—in the logical form of the *paradox*. This would explain why paradox has become the favorite form of testimony in theology, which in the very frustrations and vexations of its logically inconsistent contents sees the proof of an ultimate reality that overwhelms the self and demands that it subjugate itself. Reality here is that which is totally unavailable, which cannot be relegated simply to the level of material for manipulation, but can only occasionally appear to be processed by one technique or another, then to reveal itself in the full potency of its overwhelming autonomy as a *factum brutum* [brute fact] of which it may afterwards be said, though not conceived, that it might have emanated from a free and constructive process of creative thinking. The significant feature of this concept is that which cannot be further analyzed—the basic constant, the "atomic fact"; it is typified by such claims as Heisenberg's, that playing off two mutually exclusive images against each other can ultimately convey the correct impression of a particular reality— or George Thomson's, that a "complicated section of mathematics is just as representative of reality as 'mass,' 'energy,' etc. " The beginnings of this

---

（接上页注）quantity of nature. "At quare delectant admirabilia? Quia movent. Cur movent? Quoniam nova. Nova sane sunt, quae nunquam fuere neque dum existunt… Mentem nostram esse natura sua infinitam. Quamobrem et quod ad potentiam attinet aliena appetere, et quod spectat ad intellectionem, etiam e falsis ac monstrorum picturis capere voluptatem. Propterea quod exsuperant vulgares limites veritatis… Mavultque pulchram imaginem, quam naturali similem designatae. Naturam enim in eo superat ars" [And why do marvellous fictions delight? Because they are moving. Why are they moving? Because they are new. Indeed, new things are things that have never been done and that do not yet exist… Our mind is infinite in nature. That is why it can, in accordance with its ability, strive for strange things, and, insofar as knowledge is concerned, gain pleasure from the depiction of false and even monstrous things. And this is so because these things transcend the ordinary boundaries of truth… (The wise man) prefers a beautiful picture to one that resembles a natural thing. For art surpasses nature in this respect].

concept are perhaps to be found where awareness of reality is supposed to involve an *instinct*, the practical workings of which need not necessarily exclude or remove theoretical doubts but make them irrelevant to our assertions concerning our existence or that of the self in general. D'Alembert suggests this in the introduction to the *Encyclopédie*. One might perhaps also cite Lessing's letter to Mendelssohn—written more or less at the same time—in which he states, "with every violent desire or detestation, we are aware to a larger extent of our reality"[1]—an idea that separates awareness of reality from thought and removes this awareness of reality to the sphere of experiences unavailable to the mind with itself. Clearly, then, we must face the possibility that the modern era is one in which there is no longer any one homogeneous concept of reality, or that if one particular form of awareness predominates, it does so through confrontation with another fully developed or developing experience of reality.

This historical sequence of concepts of reality and the different ways of understanding works of art are dependent on each other. Without doubt, the theory of imitation[2]—the concept that is dominant in our aesthetic tradition—is based on the notion of *instantaneous evidence*. The theory of imitation depends upon two ontological premises:

1. a realm of actual, self-evident *exemplary* reality that is given or may be assumed;

2. the *completeness* of this realm as regards all possible contents and forms of reality.

---

[1] Lessing, *Gesammelte Werke* (Berlin: Aufbau, 1957), ix, 105 (letter of February 2, 1757).

[2] The following description of the origin and historical role of the mimesis theory not only refers to but also partly corrects the corresponding section of my study " 'Imitation of Nature': Toward a Prehistory of the Idea of the Creative Being" [in this volume]. Above all, I am no longer satisfied with establishing the ambivalence of the Platonic schema but would like to show that positive and negative evaluation, and emphasis on participation or deficiency, belong to different levels of reference, which might be labelled real and merely relational imitation. This will clarify what takes place in the Aristotelian theory of art, which cannot make this difference and is open only to the positive evaluation of mimesis, and also what Neoplatonism and Platonic Gnosis have "left out."

It follows from these premises that an artist can only *repeat* nature, because there is no scope for him to transcend it. Furthermore, it is a fundamental feature of this exemplary given reality that not only *can* it be repeated, but indeed it *should* be repeated: it demands imitation of itself because if, in its exemplariness, it failed to instigate such images of itself, it would remain totally sterile. Thus, Platonic idealism demonstrates why there are such things as works of artifice and art, but also why nothing essential can be "achieved" by them. Herein lies the peculiar *ambivalence of Platonism* in the history of aesthetics: it has always been at one and the same time a justification and a devaluation of artistic activity. Plato himself verifies this in the tenth book of his *Republic*, where he attacks literature and the pictorial arts in general, arguing that in depicting given objects the artist is already creating something second-hand, insofar as whatever he is basing his work on is not itself the true and ultimate reality, but merely an imitation of it by nature or by a craftsman. The work of art, then, is an imitation of an imitation. The fact that the image of an image demands a completely different evaluation from that of the image of the original is also based on the concept of instantaneous evidence: in the unsurpassable evidence of the "original," reality can be experienced as something reliable, and the image of this original is legitimized by the *fact* that it has to be, and not by *what* it has to be (a definition applicable only to the original). This is confirmed by Plato's example of artistic representation of elementary household objects through the art of painting. There is no such thing in nature as a table or a bed; also, for Plato there can be no question of the craftsman's having *invented* such objects for a particular practical purpose, for this would mean that the craftsman was the originator of the idea. According to Plato, for every meaningful human design there must already be "originals" in the world of ideas, and it is upon these that the craftsman bases his work. And so the copy of the original is accomplished by the man who manufactures the table or bed. The painter, however, who in turn reproduces such objects, bases his work on something that has already been produced—in other words, he creates a copy of what is already a copy.

But why does Plato not concede that the painter—just like the craftsman—

may himself see the idea, when depicting such objects, thus fulfilling the requirements for producing a copy of the original? The tenth book of the *Republic* offers no answer to this question. But the problem is not unimportant if one wishes to understand the ambivalence of Platonism in aesthetic theory. It also plays a significant role in justifying the thesis that the Platonic residue within our aesthetic tradition is what denies the *novel* a legitimate place in the traditional system of aesthetics, making it a *genre of the bad aesthetic conscience* that has constantly had to be transcended or assimilated into other legitimate genres.

Platonic ideas fix a canon of what is both demanded of and permitted to the copier. They were, first of all, the basis of our abstract concepts, not yet themselves the primal images of forms, but norms for the accomplishments of reason, say, for establishing relations between objects, for comprehending geometrical proportions, and, finally, for evaluating actions. In all these spheres, ideas had the prescriptive character of rules; they were representative not of reality as it ought to be, but of the actual obligation. The fact that the original, preexistent experience of the ideas had to be visualized in the imagination led to their eidetic character's becoming more and more clearly defined, so that they formed primal images of all the vague copies we see in the visible world around us. But these ideas were not only images of pure essences—they were primal images with the true exemplary character that demands and compels imitation. The terms "primal image" and "copy" are not just relational concepts arising out of the completed imitation but they themselves have an ideal quality, corresponding to the origin of the doctrine of ideas: i. e. , the primal image is independent of the actual imitation and preceded it as a norm that could be substantiated only through the actuality and the faithfulness of the copy. This consequence of the doctrine of ideas, which had already come to the fore in the *Republic* through the singling out of goodness as an idea of ideas, is revealed in its full significance in the dialogue *Timaeus*: here the fact *of* the creation of the world is shown to need no further motivation than that of a mere glimpse of the ideas by a craftsman who is considered capable of performing this task, and who only requires affirmation of the truthfulness of his work, but not of any particular disposition of his will to take on and execute such a work. The visible world is, accordingly, a fulfillment of the compulsive implications of the primal images, which demand imitation as the correlative that completes their meaning. However, it is clear that in this system only the first, direct copy can be the legitimate fulfillment of the demands of the original, and this first copy therefore represents the end of the process of imitation; its imitative nature, though accepted itself as real predication, precludes the possibility of its becoming a binding model in its own right. The artist therefore only copies something which itself is *already* a copy and can be nothing but a copy, and he thereby raises it to the level of an original—a level which intrinsically it is not qualified to occupy. It is not every copy, or copies as such, that Plato derogates, but only those that did not directly imitate the original—i. e. , the "unreal" copies, the indirect secondhand imitations that are based on what is already an imitation. One of the misunderstandings of Neoplatonism is that it gives a totally negative evaluation to all imitations, so that even the creating of the world itself, and not just that of the copies worked by the artist, becomes a dubious event. However, this Neoplatonic misconception of Plato's criticism of imitation at the same time clarifies the curious fact that Platonic elements had a part in a development which led eventually to the liquidation of imitation as a basis for the artistic creativity.

We must not forget that the aesthetic theory of imitation is part of the *Aristotelian* tradition. [1] With Aristotle, ideas became formal principles of nature itself, so that actuality and necessity merged in the world to such an extent that the artist's function was to extract from the external world what ought to be and the way it ought to be. Artistic representation therefore became a direct copy, and was not, so to speak, a copy once removed. The dignity of imitation as the essence of artistic activity was thus established, not by revaluing mimesis itself, but simply by reducing the number of levels of reference: art now took

---

[1] We must also bear in mind that in this tradition the general metaphysical interpretation of *art* (*technē*) in the broadest sense was predominant, before what we would call Aristotelian *aesthetics* could take effect with the rediscovery of his *Poetics*. Medieval criticism resulted in Aristotelianism minus the *Poetics* (which only follows Arabic lines of tradition); the consequences of this are something that urgently require closer study.

over the position which in Plato had been occupied by nature itself or by the de-miurge that created it, a position in which artistic activity had been essentially superfluous and even inconsistent with the system.

It is true that this is but a residue of Platonism in Aristotelism, explaining why a work of art may be possible, but endowing it with neither justification nor necessity. This is why the Aristotelian tradition in aesthetics, even though it sets out to define artistic activity as an imitation of nature, accounts for it and evaluates it almost exclusively in terms of man's emotional needs and its effect on these needs. In Aristotelian aesthetics, the basic concept of *man* is more important than that of reality; it is a system conceived from the standpoint of the viewer or listener. Against such a background, the original, angry dictum that artists, and particularly poets, are liars is deprived of its negatively critical substance, insofar as the Aristotelian definition of art as imitation does not concern what *ought* to be done, but only what *can* be done.

The revival of Platonism during the Renaissance① did not signify a reversal

---

① It is difficult to define in detail what is really "Platonic" about this revival. In studying the history of concepts, we must not forget that the "Platonism" of the Renaissance after Petrarch originated from Cicero criticism and its capacity for comprehension was determined by this. As a result, a guideline such as the *idea* is unsuited to the discovery of Platonisms, as can be seen from Erwin Panofsky's "Idea" (*Studien der Bibl. Warburg*, 1924; 2nd ed., 1960); by choosing *species* as the Latin equivalent, Cicero had removed all precision from the term (even though he also left it in Greek), out of which humanism made an all-round word. When Panofsky refers, for instance, to Melanchthon's express equation of *idea* with *notitia*[knowledge; notion] for the "pulcherrima imago humani corporis" [most beautiful image of the human body] included in the *in animo* [in the mind] of Apelles, in order to demonstrate the immanence of Platonism, he is contradicted by Melanchthon's own embarrassment, who, when compelled, at one stage, to reproduce an authentic Platonic idea, uses, for instance, *imitatio*, which is scarcely compatible with *notitia*, and so the *statuarius* [sculptor] has in himself a *certa notitia* [certain notion] of his work, which guides his hand: "donec efficiatur similitudo eius archetypi quem imitatur" [until it becomes a likeness of the archetype he imitates] (*Corp. Ref.*, XIII, 305). If *idea* were really taken here "almost as a specifically aesthetic" concept, *archetypus* would not need to be smuggled in in this way, but *idea* is, of course, the nice academic term which in fact can be used for anything except something Platonic.

of the original derivation—Aristotelian concept arising from Platonian; the critique of the ideal of imitation was now based on a shift in metaphysical interest. In the late Middle Ages, man's interest in himself and in his position in the world became the overriding consideration, and the answer to his questions lay first and foremost in man's own works and achievements. Together with the dignity of man's works, the dignity of art itself became the central theme of the Renaissance. An aesthetic system concerned principally with the observer's reactions scarcely fitted in with such an approach. The comparability of man's creations with those of God was implicit or even explicit in this newly developing concept of the artist; this meant returning directly to the question of art's relationship to reality, and the extent to which this relationship was inevitable or contingent, necessary or dispensable. If this reinterpretation of the early symptoms of the modern view of art is correct, then the result of such an approach is not only a new definition of the difference between physical and aesthetic objects but also an inherent rivalry between the artist and the outside world as a whole—in other words, the artist offers not only a transformation, idealization, or variation of the world, but works that are, so to speak, of *equal rank* to it. Both in terms of the classical concept of instantaneous evidence and the medieval concept of reality guaranteed by God, this idea of the artist's competing with given reality would have been senseless and groundless. Only a new concept, bestowing upon the intersubjective consistency of the given in space and time the sole right to recognition through a mind conscious of reality, could give substance, and even intelligibility, to the artist's claim to totality as against the claim of the factual world.

The same concept of creation, now involving the possibility of totality in a single work—without this possibility's being systematically made explicit—removed the very foundations of the Aristotelian concept of the artificial and the artistic. While nature appeared as the expression of an omnipotent, divine will, idealization as the task of the artist had become something not only dubious but demonic by the implication that nature was perhaps not what it ought to be; the artist had, as it were, to "catch up" with its possibilities and make up for its deficiencies in relation to what it ought to be. What, according to the Aristotelian definition, could it mean that art and technology completed what nature could not finish? For the medieval view of the world, nature had lost its specific, authentic evidence as reality. The fact, now constituted and guaranteed by an absolute will, was a great new element of ambiguity: it allowed the reassurance of not having to ask questions, and at the same time gave rise to the annoyance that anything factual is bound to arouse in man's reason. The fact that no aesthetics came forth from the premises and postulates of Cartesian philosophy was clearly due to this philosophy's being—in respect of its concept of reality—"medieval," clinging to the guaranteed schema of reality. Cartesian aesthetics could not have been anything but, at best, a theory of medieval art. We should not be surprised or misled by this historical phenomenon; it is quite natural that the most deeply hidden implication of an era—namely, its concept of reality—should become explicit only when the awareness of that reality has already been broken.

If the question of the *possibility* of the novel is put as an ontological one, searching out the foundations of the concept of reality, this means that one is also inquiring into the origin of a new claim of art—its claim, not merely to represent *objects* of the world, or even to imitate *the* world, but to actualize *a* world. A world—nothing less—is the theme and postulate of the novel. ① It is

---

① There is a certain affinity between Georg Lukács's comment that "The novel is the epic of a world that has been abandoned by God" (*The Theory of the Novel* [Cambridge, MA: MIT Press, 1971], 88), that is to say, the epic under the conditions of the modern view of the world—and the arguments developed here. The longed-for revival of the Greek epic, and the claim that it set the absolute standard, foundered against a view of reality that took the world for *a* world, the *cosmos* for a *universe*. The ultimate failure of Leibniz and Wolff to ensure the *ratio sufficiens* [sufficient reason] of the factual world opened the gates for a critique of the factual from the standpoint of the rational and the possible—a critique which was bound to work on the imagination and stimulate it into testing out the meaning of its own "worlds." The uniqueness of the cosmos and the Greeks' commitment to the epic as an interpretation of the world were just two aspects of the reality given by *instantaneous evidence*. The novel could not be a "secularization" of the epic after the world's loss of religion; on the contrary, the contingency, the factualness of the indefinite article, the inrush of *possibilia* all go back to the theologizing of the world. The "worlds" which the aesthetically minded self is willing to belong to only provisionally, in the accessible finiteness of a context, are the quintessence of the novel's thematization of reality and the irony essential to it.

odd that the premise underlying this approach was created by the renewal of Platonism, for, in this context, Platonism took on a historical function that was quite extraneous to it. Its inherent negative evaluation of imitation was, at the beginning of the modern age, more or less the "desired" effect, whose genuine *premises* certainly were not to be renewed: the difference between what is and what ought to be, as the scope of art, was a possibility that had in the meantime been excluded. Art was rather to concern itself with that sphere which had not been actualized by God or by nature, and so there was no longer any duality of existent reality and formative art. Instead, every work, measured against the new concept of reality, was the *reality of the possible*, whose unreality had to be the premise for the relevance of its actualization.

If our original thesis is correct—namely, that the history of aesthetics is one long debate on the classical dictum that poets are liars—this history must always be intimately related to concepts of the human capacity to "tell the truth." It is *the change in the concept of truth* which opens up new possibilities for art to be "true." The classical concept of truth, valid throughout most of the Middle Ages, maintained that in cognition, ontologically, there were present and effective the same constituent factors that made objects themselves what they were—in Aristotelian terms, their essential form. Between the object and the act of perception there exists a causal link of clearly *imitative* representation. Connected with the medieval concept of a *transcendently guaranteed reality*, there arose a new possibility of abandoning this direct causal link and, instead, viewing the sphere of cognition as a heterogeneous, individual world of mere *signs for objects*—a world whose internal order needed only to correspond precisely to the internal order of the elements of things for truth to be attained. The concept of *nonimitative cognition*, in which words and figures and their correlations can stand for objects and their correlations, has its metaphysical foundation in the premise of a *third instance*, which guarantees the strict coherence even of that which is totally heterogeneous. The Aristotelian claim that the soul is everything of the possible—a view that gave the most abstract definition to the age-old principle of cognition through similarity and affinity—takes on a new meaning: the cognitive mind, with its capacity for putting symbols in place of things and their correlations, is capable of *every* formulation of objective facts. The late Middle Ages had to abandon the concept of cognition through similarity and imitation mainly because it seemed to set the human spirit up too close to the divine. The new *concept of cognition*, however, radically separates the divine spirit, which sees all things directly and in their essence, from the human spirit, which can only represent them symbolically; the human spirit thus loses its receptive openness to things, and becomes instead a creative principle employing its own symbolic tools. ① The enhanced *transcendency* of the divine rule over things forcibly gives rise to the *immanence* of the new concept of human mastery over these things. The correspondence between cognition and its objects is no longer *material* but *functional*. The immanent consistency of the symbolic system of concepts remains the only—though adequate—approximation to the given reality. The concept of the image is released from its hitherto inescapable confinement between the original and the copy. ② Truth, in the strict sense of *adaequatio*, remains possible only for what man himself has created and of which he can therefore be completely aware without any symbolic mediation: this includes the structural laws governing his symbolic tools of cognition—laws that are formulated by logic—mathematics, history, language, and, last but not least, art. No longer is absolute truth to be seen somewhere in the relation between the representational work of art and nature; it now lies between the subjective mind perceiving the work and the product which is viewed as a possible piece of reality created by the artist. It is no longer through his relationship to nature, as a form of creation from which he is

---

① For the *similitudo divini intellectus in creando* [the similarity of the human intellect to the divine lies in its creative activity], see my book *The Legitimacy of the Modern Age*, trans. Robert M. Wallace (Cambridge, MA: MIT Press, 1983), 530.

② Already in the (disputed) Platonic 7th letter, *eídōlon* [image] and *ónoma* [word] are put on a level as regards their distance from truth (342 et seq.), but in a derogatory sense, as provisional measures for what is then an unsurpassable immediacy. The modern levelling out of the difference between *image* and *concepts* as suppositions which are free of any similarity relation to reality knows no greater approximation or immediate access to reality *as such*. It is, in fact, one of the features of the modern concept of reality that it excludes the "ontological comparative" (Walter Bröcker).

alienated, but through his cultural works, that man can match God's direct contact with his own works both as creator and as observer. This hitherto unknown metaphysical dignity of the work of art has its foundation in what is, at one and the same time, a limiting and an intensifying transformation and dissolution of the concept of truth. The consequences of this new view of man's spiritual achievements are far-reaching. Reality can no longer be considered an inherent quality of an object but is the embodiment of a consistently applied *syntax of elements*. Reality presents itself now as ever before as a sort of text which takes on its particular form by obeying certain rules of internal consistency. Reality is for modern times a context; even such an important phenomenon in the history of ideas as criticism of the theological interpretation of miracles as testifying to the divine, is totally compelled to maintain this concept of reality. Now, if aesthetic objects can have such a thing as a specific reality, they, too, are not only bound by the criterion of context as proof of their reality but are also constrained, as regards their scope and the wealth of elements they incorporate, to compete with the context of *nature*, i. e. , to become *secondary worlds*: they no longer extract, by imitation, realities from the one reality, but imitate the fact of being real.

Ultimately, art claims as its subject matter the formal proof of reality and not the material content that presents itself with this proof. Without doubt, the *nonpossible* would represent the fulfillment of this claim—namely, the infinite context, which alone could be counted as the normal equivalent to the open-endedness of physical experience. This is the starting point from which modern literature—and the aesthetics appropriate to it—proceeded toward the novel as the most comprehensively "realistic" genre, representing a context which, though finite in itself, presumes and indicates infinity. The *potential infinity* of the novel represents its *ideality*, arising out of the concept of reality, as well as the aesthetic *irritation* inevitable in view of the fact that its task of representing an infinite context can be fulfilled only by aesthetically binding principles of form. Perhaps the clearest embodiment of the problems of the genre is to be seen in the humorous novel: already in Sterne's *Tristram Shandy*, the subject is the possibility as well as the impossibility of the novel. The increasing incongruity between the real and the represented existence brings out the novel's implication of infinity, and shows the dilemma created when a finite text tries to evoke an infinite context. As a finite and discontinuous work, the novel thwarts the reader's expectations of the "et cetera," and so focuses his attention on its true theme: that it is ultimately not concerned with proving its own validity as a work of art through a sequence of edited events, but with the conflict between the imaginary reality of a context and the reality of the existing world. Another such humorous novel that is not only in fact incomplete but also incompletable, and that has reality itself as its subject matter, is Jean Paul's *Der Komet* [*The Comet*]. ① Here the theme is the "experimental" presentation of the illusory world of the supposed crown prince Nikolaus Marggraf, interwoven with the real, or supposedly real, world of the German petty principality; as the two worlds act upon each other, the predicates of illusion and reality appear to be interchangeable. This very fact shows that what we tend to call "representation" in a novel is in fact "asemantic"—i. e. , it represents nothing but itself; it removes the boundaries between being and meaning, matter and symbol, object and sign, destroying the correspondences that had been integral to our whole tradition of truth concepts. This destruction, nevertheless, involves continuing dependence on the tradition it negates, indirectly creating the uncreatable by removing the hitherto unchallenged function: the sign no longer purports to represent a "thing," and so itself takes on the substantiality of a thing. This, of course, is an approach that ranges beyond the novel and its basic concept of reality, to an awareness of reality that is determined by resistance, and to a corresponding and confirmatory art form that is made up of means of expression

---

① Jean Paul himself, in his introductory *investiture* of the reader with the story, points out this thematization by so projecting history and novel onto one another that to convey this *given historical* subject he wishes for himself the capacity of the novelist, so that with "one mighty stroke" he could complete the creation of his hero: "and I shall reach my *goal if I can set out the historical truths* of this story in such a way that they seem to the reader like successful fictions, with the result that, raised above the juridical law of *fictio sequitur naturam* (fiction, or appearance, follows nature), here conversely nature or history follows fiction—or, to put it in Latin, natura fictionem sequatur. "

that annihilate themselves, and use their own inconsistencies to demonstrate their own lack of meaning. ① Once more the novel takes itself as its own subject matter; by demonstrating the impossibility of the novel, a novel becomes possible. I should like to go into rather more detail concerning this problem of form. The idea of reality as context imposes on the novel the form of linear consistency within a given system of space and time. But, as I have pointed out, this concept of reality becomes valid only through an agreement among subjects that are capable of understanding one another—i. e. , through *intersubjectivity* and its various possible perspectives. So far as I am aware, the novel first took on a *perspective pattern* with Balzac, whose cycle of novels creates the illusory reality of a whole human society through the recurrence of identical characters viewed from changing perspectives. As far as the question of reality is con-

---

① Such a *substantialization* through annihilating the function of "means of meaning" has not been discovered in the immanent history of the novel; the reality that occurs in *resistance* is, from the viewpoint of the aesthetics of genre, basic to *lyric poetry*. Late nineteenth-century aesthetic experiences gained from poetry in its strictest and narrowest sense, have become prototypical—among other things, for the changing of novel aesthetics into the thematization of the "impossibility" of the novel. Perhaps I can best define this prototypical discovery of lyric poetry through the passage in Paul Valéry's letter to J. -M. Carré, February 23, 1943 (*Lettres à quelques-uns* [Paris: Gallimard, 1952], 240), in which he tries to systematize the experience of shock caused fifty years back by Rimbaud's *Illuminations*: "le système, conscient ou non, que supposent les passages les plus virulents de ces poèmes. Il me souvient d'avoir résumé ces observations—et, en somme, mes défenses—par ces termes: R. a inventé ou découvert la puissance de l'incohérence harmonique. Arrivé à ce point extrême, paroxystique de l'irritation volontaire de la fonction du langage, il ne pouvait que faire ce qu'il a fait—fuir" [the system, conscious or not, that underlay the most virulent passages of these poems. I remember having summed up these observations—and, in short, my defenses—in the following terms: R. has invented or discovered the power of harmonic incoherence. At this extreme, paroxysmal point of voluntary irritation of the function of language, he could only do what he did—flee]. The anticlimax of the "actualization," the exhaustibility of the ontological basis of this concept of reality, are preconditions for the transposition of the principle to other genres and arts (e. g. , the abandonment of tonality), but the novel (in a different way from the drama) has shown itself to be particularly resistant to the "paroxysmal" consequence of the principle, and so, as extremely flexible and productive as far as experiments are concerned.

cerned, there is a big difference between the epic-linear and the perspective recurrence of characters—the spatial consciousness is different, and the world
created is far subtler. Balzac's perspective system enables a linear series of episodes to be translated into simultaneous events. But it demands more than mere
consistency with elements already dealt with, for perspective consistency allows
a transformation of those elements as the emphasis shifts, for instance, from
one character to another, or from one aspect of character to another. The result
is a highly complex process of reconciling individual aspects to one another and
to the overall identity of the object to which they belong. This is basically quite
different from the traditional introduction of individual characters drawn in
preparation for their ultimate meeting at the climax of the plot. It is no longer
merely the characters in the novel that move through the various events contained in the plot; the reader now moves around the body of imaginary reality,
passing through all the different aspects from which it can be viewed. Balzac
himself believed, and expressly indicated as one of his most daring intentions,
that the recurrence of individual characters in his *Comédie Humaine* [*The Human Comedy*] would endow this fictitious cosmos with more life and movement, ① but in fact it is not the world of the novel that is set in motion so much
as the reader himself as he experiences the various changes of perspective. The
world of the novel itself takes on a greater degree of stability and substance,
which seems both to the author and the reader more and more to defy total mastery, compelling them to ever greater efforts, by which the imaginative reality
itself remains quite unaffected. The more the novel's reality depends on the
standpoint of the mediating self, the less it seems to depend on that *self* and

---

① "The result is what one might call a novelistic mobile, a whole formed by a certain
number of parts which we can approach in almost any order we please… Evidently, the recurrence of characters or their persistence from one novel to another has in Balzac a much greater
importance than in what is called the *roman fleuve*." Michel Butor, "Balzac and Reality," in
Inventory (New York: Simon and Schuster, 1968), 104. "But Balzac's definitive victory
over his great predecessor (Walter Scott), his liberation from him, finds its expression in an
extraordinary invention which will utterly transform the structure of his work … the recurrence of characters" (Butor, 103).

his imagination, and in fact the more he seems to depend on it.

Clearly, then, the idea of reality as an intersubjective context can lead to an idea of it as the experience of the resistance of any given object. In the novel, this transition is marked as a breaking up of connections between aspects resulting from different perspectives. The beginnings of this process are to be seen in Jean Paul's humorous novel *Der Komet*;① and it came beyond all humorous implications to full fruition, for instance, in Robert Musil's novel *Der Mann ohne Eigenschaften* [*The Man without Qualities*]. In this immense fragment, even the (existing) conclusion does not begin to bring together the different threads of the plot or to lead them toward any common end; epic perspectivism is here virtually exploded, wrecked on the consequences of its own precision. In 1932, Musil wrote of his *Mann ohne Eigenschaften*: "This book has a passion for something which nowadays is to a certain extent out of place in the field of literature: namely, correctness and precision. What the story of this novel amounts to is the fact that the story which is to be told is not told."② The increasing specificity of the narrative leads to a demonstration of the impossibility of narrative itself. But this impossibility in turn is felt to indicate the unbreakable resistance of the imaginary reality to being described, and in this sense the aesthetic principle inherent in the concept of reality of immanent consistency leads at a certain point of transition to a different concept of reality al-

---

① It is worth noting how the dialogues in Jean Paul's *Der Komet* always "function" only through misunderstandings and never allow the fictional context to be exploded. But as the structure of intersubjective communication is shown to be strong enough to reify even unreality into quasi-reality, the concept of reality is not only thematized but also used as an aesthetic element—one might almost say it is instrumentalized. Inevitably, the aesthetic instrumentalization creates, indeed even presupposes, critical awareness: suspicion as regards the malleability of reality for specific purposes is here implied; this suspicion is also contained in the unexpected, socially critical virulence of the novel, in the ceaseless *probing*, for instance, of the deformability of elements of reality, up to the discovery of the breaking point as in the solipsistic dialogues of Kafka or Beckett. The triumph (as yet not properly understood) of finally having hit upon something stable, is what marks the phrasing of this development: the functional collapse of intersubjectivity releases a new concept of reality.

② [Robert Musil, Tagebücher, ed. Adolf Frisé (Reinbek: Rowohlt, 1983), 1598.]

together. Herein lies the reason why the constantly anticipated "liquidation" of the novel has never been achieved. It also explains why irony seems to have become the authentic mode of reflection as far as the aesthetic claims of the modern novel are concerned: the novel becomes ironic through the connections with reality that it is unable to dispense with and yet incapable of forming. Thomas Mann once spoke of the *seeming accuracy* of scientific discourse used as a stylistic means of irony: in his 1942 lecture on *Josef und Seine Brüder* [*Joseph and His Brothers*], he calls this the application of the scientific to the totally unscientific—and this precisely is for him the purest expression of irony.

I should like to deal with just one more facet of the basic connection between the concept of reality and the feasibility of the novel. I have tried to show that the concept of reality as a phenomenal and immanent consistency lies at the root of the autonomous reality of the work of art. What I have not mentioned, but what actually brings together man's created works in competition with the existing reality of nature, is the strange fact that, on the one hand, man asserts himself in the actualization of his creative potential, while, on the other, he must seek to conceal the dependence of his art on his own abilities and will; he must do this, because only then can his works take on the unquestionable autonomy and individuality that will make them indistinguishable from the products of nature. It may therefore be taken as a characteristic feature of modern art and literature that they have undergone a sort of dereification; the more familiar *alienation* is only a partial phenomenon within this trend. Human art presents itself neither as an imitation of nature nor as a "piece of nature," but it is to have the same rank and dignity as natural objects; it is to be the work of man, but it is not to be characterized by the contingency of the individual will, or the actuality of the mere idea. In other words, it must be, at one and the same time, both novelty and fossil. We want to be able to disregard ourselves as the condition of the possibility of these works, because we do not want them to be a part of our conditional or our historical nature, of which we are proud despite the afflictions they cause us; we do not want our works to be *objects* dependent on subjects, but to be *things* in themselves. And these works for their part should not *represent* aspects but should *offer* us aspects of themselves.

From the perspective structure systematically prepared and laid out in the novel, there can emerge a perspective potential that is stimulated by the work and yet at the same time is not fulfilled by it; we recognize this potential when we realize the essential openness of modern art to commentary and varied interpretation which is apparent from Romanticism onward. This *hermeneutic ambiguity* is integral to the "reality" of the work of art, insofar as it is this which proves its independence of our own subjectivity. This is why we tend artificially to *historicize* the work of art, in order to strip it of its dependence on ourselves and to "reify" it. Just as archaic sculpture exists in the landscape, such as the *things* tossed on to the green grass of Otterloo, there is also the novel distanced by language or by the artifice of a narrative framework—the type of novel of which we "know too much" for it to have its desired effect of alienation on us. In the same way that we can artificially historicize, we can also artificially *naturalize*, but no longer can we do this by representing or imitating nature; we must instead claim "naturalness" for our works, erecting things which resemble the products of eruptions or erosions, like the *objet ambigu* in Paul Valery's *Eupalinos*. Corresponding to these in the novel is the artificially artless transcript of streams of consciousness and interior monologues—the "writing-the-minutes" type of novel [*Protokollroman*], which claims to create, and at the same time renounces, the creation of a whole world.

The concept of reality of the phenomena's context presents a reality that can never be assured, is constantly in the process of being actualized, and continually requires some new kind of confirmation. This idea of reality, even when transformed into the reality of an aesthetic object, remains a sort of consistency which is, so to speak, open at both ends and dependent on continuous proofs and accomplishments, without ever achieving the finality of evidence that characterized the classical concept of reality. This is one reason for the uneasiness and dissatisfaction that have been a constant critical undercurrent throughout the history of the novel. One way out of this dissatisfaction is to resist the need for an endless actualization by deliberately breaking through set patterns of formal consistency—a breaking through which shows by the way it is handled that it does not spring from any failure or exhaustion of creative powers but, on the contrary, represents a conscious effort which can afford to disregard the quasi-objective principle of formal consistency. The idea that poets are liars can be completely invalidated only if they no longer set out to prove its antithesis—namely, that poets tell the truth—but concentrate on deliberately breaking the bonds of this antithesis and indeed all the rules of the reality game itself. Commitment to reality is rejected as an unwanted limitation on form, an aesthetic heteronomy wearing the mask of authenticity. Herein lie the roots of an aesthetic concept that can now present as "true" what all previous concepts of reality would have designated as unreal: paradox, the inconsistency of dreams, deliberate nonsense, centaurian hybrids, objects placed in the most unlikely positions, the reversal of natural entropy, in which refuse can be used to make *objets d'art*, newspaper cuttings be made into novels, or the noises of technology into a musical composition.

Modern art, however, has not freed itself from the compulsion to refute its dependence on the given realities of nature; its antiphysicism is not even directed against a constant *nature* whose dimensions are known or defined. The liberation of the imagination always being proclaimed, for instance by Breton, goes so far as to dissolve even the (now merely formal) connection between the concept of reality of immanent consistency and its commitment to the reality value of *nature*, and so it is again and again compelled to make desperate efforts to actualize itself despite its extreme improbability, in what remains, when all is said and done, a type of *instantaneous evidence*.

The fact that the novel still adheres to the concept of reality of immanent consistency can be gauged from the problems that accrue to it from any heterogeneous concept of reality. It cannot actualize itself simply by contradicting whatever has hitherto been regarded as significant evidence of reality. The ideal of the *perfetta deformità* [perfect deformation] cannot be fulfilled by the novel. But it is characteristic of the novel that at this point it takes its own possibility as its subject matter, thus demonstrating its dependence on the concept of reality. I need only point to the technique of uncommunicative dialogue to explain what I mean: the failure of conversation, its hypertrophy in meaningless chatter, misunderstanding as a constituent product of language—all this remains essential to the novel, embedded in a world that is still presumed and produced with too much imagination for it ever to be said that pure absurdity can really become the subject matter. The novel has its own "realism," which has evolved from its own particular laws, and this has nothing to do with the ideal of imitation but is linked precisely to the aesthetic illusion which is essential to the genre. Fixing (or causing) a world [*Welthaftigkeit*] as a formal, overriding structure is what constitutes the novel. When the absurd was proclaimed the program of art, its function was defined as "transcending the foundations," and ultimately even architecture showed itself suited to this function of the absurd. But the novel had advanced much earlier and much more spontaneously to this transcending of the foundations—i. e. , to the resolution of the conflict between reality and fiction—and, as I have shown, it had taken as its theme its own possibility, not as a fiction of reality, but as a *fiction of the reality of realities*. The novel's preeminence in the actualization of basic modern ideas of aesthetics is comprehensible only if one realizes that it has not adopted absurdity, that new criterion of absolute poetry, because it has no need of such a stigma. The novel fulfills the aesthetic norm which, according to Boswell's diary, was first formulated by Samuel Johnson during the famous conversation in the Literary Club about the excessive price of an antique marble dog: the extension of the sphere of the *humanly* possible (April 3, 1778), [1] whereas even the broadest interpretation of the Aristotelian ideal of imitation—perhaps Johann Jakob Breitinger's—is concerned with the sphere of the *naturally* possible. [2]

Translated by David H. Wilson [3]

---

① [Blumenberg paraphrases Boswell's account, which has: "Everything that enlarges the sphere of human powers, that shows man he can do what he thought he could not do, is valuable." James Boswell, *The Life of Samuel Johnson*, LL. D (Ware, Hertfordshire, UK: Wordsworth Editions, 1999), 636.]

② The notes added subsequently to this paper have been written, with grateful acknowledgments, as a result of suggestions, doubts, and objections raised during the discussion.

③ [Minor corrections by Hannes Bajohr.]

14. 布鲁门伯格：《实在概念与小说的可能性》

(Hans Blumenberg, "The Concept of Reality and the Possibility of the Novel," 1964)

作者小识

布鲁门伯格（Hans Blumenberg，1920—1996），在尼采、海德格尔之后，应该说是和哈贝马斯齐名的哲学家。与哈贝马斯侧重于政治、法律和伦理不一样，布鲁门伯格更多地从古典学入手通过解读神话、圣经、文学文本重构西方思想史。他更加重视文学感悟与生命筹划的关系，更为关注思想历史的隐喻、象征、修辞等语言维度。

他的研究聚焦西方文化史上的宏大叙事，但缺少体系建构。其方法论是融合修辞学、哲学人类学与现象学，试图越过理性与逻辑的藩篱，而返回到前概念的生活世界。其代表作所覆盖的思想史主题如下：《哥白尼世界的起源》(*Die Geneis der kopernikanischen Welt*，Suhrkamp Verlag，Frankfurt am Main，1975)探索希腊精神、中世纪经院思想与近代科学的发生及其人文精神；《现代的正当性》(*Die Legitimatät der Neuzeit*，Suhrkamp Verlag，Frankfurt am Main，1966)检测基督教神学、中世纪神学绝对论、古代异教灵知主义同现代性的关系；《神话研究》(*Arbeit am Mythos*，Suhrkamp Verlag，Frankfurt am Main，1979)全面考量荷马以来直到 20 世纪神话创作和神话研究的传统，力求发掘其中蕴含的西方思想资源，特别重视呈现在文学与哲学之中的思想与想象的关系；《马太受难曲》(*Matthauspassion*，Suhrkamp Verlag，Frankfurt am Main，1990)通过解读古典音乐，把巴赫的作品呈现为一种深刻的悲剧事件，从而力求超越"神话研究"，将错综复杂的思想意象置放到基督教信仰的语境中，在"后神义论"视野下拓展审美文化的论域。

背景略说

20 世纪 30 年代到 40 年代，布鲁门伯格浸润于德国思辨哲学的氛围之中，深受生命哲学、现象学和哲学人类学的熏染，狄尔泰、盖兰、海德格尔、罗特哈克、弗洛伊德、恽格尔、卡西尔、罗森伯格，都为他奉献了思想资源，但真正起思想催化作用的是海德格尔和弗洛伊德。海德格尔的"存在本体论"之中的"此在""共在"概念，被转化为布鲁门伯格神话诗学体系之中的"象征化生活世界"概念。弗洛伊德的心理分析学说直接为布鲁门伯格探索神话的个体发生和种系发生提供了概念工具。布鲁门伯格 50 年代参与赖因哈德·科勒泽克主持的概念史研究工作，60 年代为尧斯、伊塞尔主政的《诗学与解释学》(*Poetik und Hermeneutik*)撰稿。在从出道学界之后近 40 年的学术生涯之中，布鲁门伯格作为哲学教授，先后任教于吉塞尔大学、波鸿大学和明斯特大学。布鲁门伯格的研究领域覆盖了思想史、科学史、人类学、古典学、修辞学、艺术学、政治哲学以及神话诗学。

在为"概念史文库"(Archiv für Begriffsgeschichte)撰写"隐喻"条目的过程中，布鲁门伯格日渐显示出自己独特的学术风格，确立了回归源始而抗拒系统化的研究取向。德国概念史学派，志在超越传统"精神史"或"思想史"研究的理论架构，将概念置放到宗教史、神话学、社会学、人类学的复杂关联体之中，对概念进行考镜源流，探幽索隐，描述思想意象的起源、知识结构的形成、词语形式的进化和概念语义的变易。布鲁门伯格受命撰写"隐喻"概念史，一头扎进了晚古、中古和早期现代，发现了一条思想借着修辞来呈现而修辞上升到存在论地位的线索。在这个过程中，布鲁门伯格陷入了隐喻概念的"非概念性"悖论之中。"隐喻是规避实在论苛刻要求的语言学形式。"[1]不仅如此，隐喻还作为神话，甚至神学的原型，参与了克服"实在绝对主义"的人类伟业。"隐喻"条目写成，却未被科勒泽克、罗特哈克等人接受，这也表明布鲁门伯格同"概念史"学派存在着根本的歧见，分道扬镳在所难免。所撰写的词条，他自己独立出版，以《一种隐喻学范式》(*Paradigmen zur einer Meta-phorologie*)刊行。这部著作堪称布鲁门伯格的出道之作，其中蕴含着他后来全部思想的萌芽及其学术方法的端倪。避开主导西方思想史的"理性逻辑"，布鲁门伯格在"幻想逻辑"上大作文章，指出"隐喻"是一切思想体系无法融化的"残余要素"。"隐喻学"，是布鲁门伯格生造的新词，其研究对象绝不仅限于修辞学上狭义的隐喻，还包括更为宽泛的比喻、象征、寓言、故事、轶事。通过对它们的分析，布鲁门伯格意在揭示这些非概念的范畴对于概念史的源

---

[1]　Hans Blumenberg, *Shipwreck with Spectator*, trans. Steven Rendall, Cambridge, The MIT Press, 1997, p. 94.

始贡献。①"隐喻"对于逻辑和体系的持久抵抗，拒绝还原为"概念"与"命题"，便证明了"神话到逻各斯"的进步是一个"伪命题"。这本书的基本主张是：同概念相比，隐喻具有更为根本的历史性，为通往一个蕴意丰富而且隐秘无形的世界指明了道路，从而让那些"以人类的生存为基础"的问题得到了解决。这种思想与方法，同海德格尔晚期哲学转向若合符契：从基础生存论退向诗学沉思，向"生活世界"索取思想的真源。但布鲁门伯格深知，通过研讨隐喻而呈现出来的，只不过是思想史的"半成品"(halbzeug)，而用以论说"存在"的圆融完美的理论，在隐喻研究领域之中仍然是可望而不可即的。② 像海德格尔一样，他也将隐喻学确定为"基础存在论"的竞争性构想，却不是以附属修辞学和文献学上训练有素的方式重述海德格尔的学说。一样关注"存在之退缩""存在之自我遮蔽"，但海德格尔和布鲁门伯格的处理方法却迥然异趣：海德格尔相信哲学可以臻于圆融完美，而布鲁门伯格却认为一切哲学努力所得到的"本真性行话"都是"半成品"而已。他似乎在警告思想史家，体系的七宝楼台、历史的宏大叙事，总是建立在断简残篇之上，显赫威仪却万分脆弱。但是他坚持认为，隐喻之所以重要，就在于它是诗性的智慧、历史的源头、思想的基础、概念的原型，不仅关涉着神话、哲学、教义的本质及其内在联系，而且蕴含着神圣、宇宙和人类的关系，尤其是象征着人类在宇宙之中的地位。

基本内容

如题目所示，这篇文章探索实在概念与小说的可能性，关联着"诗人说谎"这一旷古之争。从柏拉图《理想国》中对诗人的指责，到尼采关于艺术形而上学的论断，"诗"与"实在"的关系是一个哲学上必须反复推敲和考究的恒常论题。"诗人说谎"，全面否定了诗与实在的关系。如果颠倒过来，"诗人言真"，那就必然从逻辑上牵引出两个问题。第一，诗与何种给定的实在相关？第二，诗人要创造出什么样的独特存在？如果信任诗人还是呈现了最低限度的真理，我们就必须承认：诗人，以及广义的艺术家可以完全不受真假的约

---

① 参见 Rüdiger Campe, Jocelyn Holland, Paul Reitter, "From the Theory of Technology to the Technique of Metaphor: Blumenberg's Opening Move," in *qui parle*, 2000, 12(1), pp. 105-126。

② Hans Blumenberg, *Paradigmen zu einer Metaphorologie*, Frankfurt, Suhrkamp, 1998, p. 29.

束，独立进行形象建构。于是，要弄清诗与实在的关系，首先必须说明实在的含义。

运用"概念史"的方法，布鲁门伯格论列了四种实在概念：（1）瞬间自明的实在，以柏拉图的"理念论"为典型，且在亚里士多德的诗学中延续，主导了整个希腊至现代的模仿论传统；（2）被担保的实在，上起奥古斯丁，下至中世纪经院哲学体系，都构想出一个超验的"上帝"来担保实在的存在论地位；（3）自我实现的语境一致性实在，在此，实在被视为现实化的一个结果，被视为一种渐进发展却不能臻于整体终极一致的确定性；（4）以抗拒为导向的实在，在此，实在被视为终极神秘力量对主体的压制，乃全然不可操控之物。

从运用"概念史"的方法所梳理出的实在类型来看，建立在瞬间明证实在之基础上，模仿论传统几乎否定了"小说"在艺术体系之中的合法性。柏拉图与诗人的对立堪称这种情形的证据。在西方美学传统中，柏拉图主义的残余否定了"小说"（roman）在传统美学体系中的合法地位，使之成为一种显现美学自欺的文学类型。

文艺复兴期间，柏拉图主义的复活将艺术的尊严提升为诗学理论的核心论题。"人类的创造与上帝的创造之间的可比性或隐或显地蕴含在这种新兴的艺术家概念中。"可是，在早期现代，我们必须缔造一个新概念，赋予时空实在之主体间严整秩序以通过实在意识的心灵得以认知的特权，这样才能给予艺术家的整体性诉求以实体性和合理性。当自然作为全能神圣意志的表现时，艺术家的理想化使命就不仅变得可疑，而且还被妖魔化，因为它隐秘地表示，自然或许不是"应然存在"，而艺术家从来就必须"执握"这种可能性，弥补艺术相比于"应然存在"而显示出来的匮乏。笛卡儿式的主体精神完全依附于中世纪体系，以担保的实在概念为基础，模糊了艺术与实在的关系。

如果小说的可能性被当作一个本体论问题提出，同时我们又致力于探寻实在概念的基础，那么这就意味着我们正在探索一种新艺术诉求的起源。艺术不仅要再现世界上的客体，甚至要模仿这个世界，而且还要把这个世界变成现实。一个世界（最起码）也是小说的主题和设定。因此，小说是一种货真价实的现代文学体裁。如卢卡奇所言，小说是"上帝遗弃的世界之史诗"（Epopöe der gottverlassenen Welt），是现代世界观烛照下的史诗。不仅如此，在一种可理解的有限语境中，审美的心灵主体所纯粹地临时归属的"多元世界"，构成了小说的本质——将"实在"主题化，确立一种根本的浪漫反讽立场。

现代诗学与美学发展出小说这种最具有包容性的"现实主义风格"之文学类型，去再现一种本身有限但假设和显示着无限性的语境。小说的无限性潜能代表着源自实在概念的艺术至境，以及面对事实而不可避免地产生的审美焦虑。这种引发审美焦虑的事实在于，唯有通过形式原则的审美约束，才能完成再现一种无限语境的使命。或许，在幽默小说的滑稽叙事之中，我们能够看到这个文学类型难题之最清楚的体现。在斯泰因的《项狄传》（*Tristram Shandy*）中，小说本身的可能性与不可能性已经成为小说的主题。

从巴尔扎克开始，小说第一次获取了一种视角模式（perspektivisches Modell）。巴尔扎克小说的循环通过以变化的视角看待同一人物之轮回出场，创造了一个整体人类社会的幻象实在。就实在性问题而言，史诗的线性展开和人物的视角轮回之间存在着决定性的差异——空间意识不同，而小说中被创造的世界更为空灵。巴尔扎克小说的视角系统能够将一系列线性的事件插曲转化为同时发生的事件。

作为主体间语境，实在概念可能发展出作为一切既定事物抗拒经验的实在观念。在小说中，这种转化的标志是源自不同视角的型相关联之破裂。保尔（Jean Paul）的幽默小说《彗星》（*Der Komet*）、罗伯特·穆西尔（Robert Musil）的小说《没有个性的人》（*Der Mann ohne Eigenschaften*）都呈现出这么一种悖论：叙述准确性的增长却证明叙述本身的不可能性。就现代小说的美学主张而言，反讽显然已经成为货真价实的反思方式：通过与不可忽略又不能塑造的实在相关联，小说成为反讽文类。

拓展讨论

布鲁门伯格以隐喻为研究起点，隐喻也贯穿在他的整个思想生涯之中，构成了其学术遗产最凝重的主题词之一。从解读《马太受难曲》到研读柏拉图、奥古斯丁、海德格尔、维特根斯坦的经典文本，从探索现代思想之正当性到研究神话诗学之功能性，从发掘近代科学世界之起源到反思政治哲学的奥义，他的思想都围绕着隐喻这个轴心运转。航海、海难、书籍、洞穴、处女地、风暴、森林，这些隐喻都是引导他进入思想史辉煌门槛的线索。其煌煌大著所呈现者，是"关于万物的理念"，而非"万物自体"。浓烈的修辞学意味、坚定的古典学导向、执着的境界追求、强大的反思力度，以及博大的历史意识，决定了布鲁门伯格在当代思想史研究之中的里程碑地位。《现代的正当性》《哥白尼世界的起源》《神话研究》这三大巨著已经成为学术经典，具有高度原创性，成为当代思想史研究的标志性成果。这些著作所涉范围广大，所论内容驳杂，但杂而不越，驭术有方，一切逻辑都指向了"现代"的起源及其正当性。它们往返在不同视角之间，切换在不同视野之内，持久地回击来自各方的责难。布鲁门伯格坚守一个中心，秉持一个断制，怀藏一份激情，去检测论域之中不同的边缘，揭示其研究领域的潜在蕴意。自古至今，从启蒙到现代和后现代，人与神、科学与神话、哲学与诗歌到底是一种什么样的关系？是抗争还是包容？是冲突还是和解？是势不两立还是并存不害？在布鲁门伯格的著作中，所有这一切都交织在一起，但形成了一个聚焦：巧用古典学、修辞学、思想史和语义学的资源，去揭示"现代之谜"。故此，其多维度的研究方法只不过表现了其论题的多维性而已。

延伸阅读

1. Hans Blumenberg, *History*, *Metaphors*, *Fables*：*A Hans Blumenberg Reader*, ed., trans., and with an introduction by Hannes Bajohr, Florian Fuchs, and Joe Paul Kroll, Ithaca, NY, Cornell University Press, 2020. 该书是美国学者为纪念布鲁门伯格诞辰 100 周年而编译出版的研究读本。全书分四个部分：(1)历史、世俗化与实在性；(2)隐喻、修辞和非概念；(3)自然、技术和美学；(4)寓言、逸事与小说。

2. 布鲁门伯格：《神话研究》(上)，胡继华译，上海，上海人民出版社，2012。

15. Temporal Topographies: Tennyson's Tears (1992)
By J. Hillis Miller

Allegory signifies precisely the non-being of that which it represents.

—Walter Benjamin

We ordinarily distinguish sharply between criticism and poetry. Some poets, we say—Coleridge, Arnold, and T. S. Eliot, for example—were also great critics, but other poets—Shakespeare, Byron, Browning, or Thomas Hardy—were not critics at all or not critics of distinction. We would usually put Tennyson in the latter category. For one thing, he is supposed to have had no aptitude for reflection or for theoretical generalization. W. H. Auden said of Tennyson: "He had the finest ear of any English poet. He was also the stupidest. "Tennyson left no body of criticism. Such observations by Tennyson about poetry as exist, for example in the *Memoir* by Hallam Tennyson, are, as Gerhard Joseph shows in an admirable recent book on Tennyson,[1] a version of Victorian commonplaces about the general superiority of symbol over allegory, though he sometimes speaks of using a "sort of allegory" in the weak and conventional sense of a rationally concocted *"this* for *that"*(Joseph, p. 161). Tennyson favors latitude of subjective interpretation. He refuses to pin down definitely the meanings of his poems. He speaks of an "allegory in the distance" or of a "parabolic drift" in the *Idylls of the King*,[2] but he always refused to fix that "drift" with exact interpretations. Tennyson is committed to the idea that poetry should be socially useful. Perhaps letting his readers make what they like of it is part of that program.

In any case, no one in his right mind would claim that Tennyson is an im-

---

[1] Gerhard Joseph, *Tennyson and the Text: The Weaver's Shuttle* (Cambridge, 1992).

[2] Hallam Tennyson, *Alfred Lord Tennyson: A Memoir* (London, 1897), 2: 127.

portant critic in the sense that Arnold, Pater, Eliot, and even Gerard Manley Hopkins are important critics. Nevertheless, I shall show that one significant dimension of Tennyson's poems is the way they represent what might be called "poetic thinking" about the nature and powers of poetry. And I shall show that what Tennyson's poems obliquely say about poetry is far more interesting than the relatively conventional views about poetry expressed outside the poetry, or even inside the poetry when he makes overt assertions. If Tennyson was stupid, his poems are far from stupid about the nature of what they themselves are and what they do. As theoretical reflection about poetry they are deep, profound, as I shall show through the example of "Tears, Idle Tears." Here is the poem:

> Tears, idle tears, I know not what they mean,
> Tears from the depth of some divine despair
> Rise in the heart, and gather to the eyes,
> In looking on the happy Autumn-fields,
> And thinking of the days that are no more.
>
> Fresh as the first beam glittering on a sail,
> That brings our friends up from the underworld,
> Sad as the last which reddens over one
> That sinks with all we love below the verge;
> So sad, so fresh, the days that are no more.
>
> Ah, sad and strange as in dark summer dawns
> The earliest pipe of half-awakened birds
> To dying ears, when unto dying eyes
> The casement slowly grows a glimmering square;
> So sad, so strange, the days that are no more.
>
> Dear as remembered kisses after death,
> And sweet as those by hopeless fancy feigned
> On lips that are for others; deep as love,

Deep as first love, and wild with all regret;
O Death in Life, the days that are no more.

Much has been written about this powerful and moving poem. I shall not try to recapitulate that commentary here, but shall try to read the poem afresh. Though "Tears, Idle Tears" has its own integrity, is usually read outside its context, and was probably written without *The Princess* in mind, nevertheless the poem is inserted at a dramatic moment in *The Princess*. The singing of it by one of Princess Ida's "maids" helps precipitate the catastrophe of the poem: the revelation that Princess Ida's female college has been invaded by three men disguised as women. "Tears, Idle Tears" is therefore placed against a background of questions about gender roles and women's liberation. Like Henry James's *The Bostonians*, *The Princess* ends with the triumph of traditional marriage: "Accomplish thou my manhood and thyself; /Lay thy sweet hands in mine and trust to me," says the hero (7. 344-345). This is something a lot of men have said to women before and since. The ending of *The Princess* occurs according to a male wish fulfillment that neither the great Victorian poet nor the great modern novelist seems to have been able to resist. Both, nevertheless, allow the women in their narratives the opportunity for a full and even hyperbolic expression of their sense of wrong. The happy marriages at the end are accompanied in the case of *The Bostonians* by an anticipation that the heroine has by no means been thoroughly tamed and in the case of *The Princess* by many promises from the Prince that he will assist the Princess in her work for women's liberation.

If "Tears, Idle Tears" is, in part at least, oriented around an axis of height and depth, its immediate context reinforces that orientation, with its iteration of the word "down. " The Princess and her company have just come down from a geological expedition when the song is sung:

we

Down from the lean and wrinkled precipices,
By every coppice-feathered chasm and cleft,

Dropt through the ambrosial gloom to where below

No bigger than a glow-worm shone the tent

Lamp-lit from the inner. (4. 3-8)

After the song is sung, the Princess reproaches the maiden for singing a song "hatched/In silken-folded idleness" (4. 48-49) on the theme of "the mouldered lodges of the Past." Her reproach invokes the irresistible downward flow of time toward its utopian future: "let old bygones be, /While down the streams that float us each and all/To the issue" … (4. 52-53)

The Princess has, in a conversation with the disguised Prince before the song is sung, elegantly expressed the traditional metaphysical view of time:

For was, and is, and will be, are but is;

And all creation is one act at once,

The birth of light: but we that are not all,

As parts, can see but parts, now this, now that,

And live, perforce, from thought to thought, and make

One act a phantom of succession: thus

Our weakness somehow shapes the shadow, Time. (3. 307-313)

For the Princess, who, according to the poem, is wrong about just about everything, time is what it has been in the Western tradition since Plato and St. Augustine. For her, time is a series of presents—past present, present present, and future present. These presents are gathered into one by being all copresent from all time to the *nunc stans* of God. The Princess is right to be affronted by "Tears, Idle Tears," when a little later it is sung, since among other things it expresses a radically different view of time from the traditional one she so glibly expresses. It is impossible to know whether or not Tennyson knew this. His poem, however, speaks for him. It speaks poetically for a view of time as generated by difference, non-presence, distance, unattainability, and loss that can never be made up by a recovered presence in the bosom of God. God, in fact, suffers from a "divine despair" at not being able to recuperate and encompass all the times and places of his creation. By "speaking poetically," I mean speaking through image and rhetorical structure rather than through conceptual formulation.

Other songs from *The Princess* also move from high to low, most notably "Come down, O maid, from yonder mountain height/⋯ For Love is of the valley, come thou down/And find him" (7.177, 184-185). This adjacent poem suggests that the up/down axis of "Tears" has something to do with the issue of gender in the main narrative, as well as with the opposition between idle nostalgia for the past and work to fulfill the promise of the future. Associating time with a movement down from heights also prepares for the use of spatial images to express human temporality in "Tears." The up/down axis, however, has a different meaning in the poem: up is this present life and moment, while down is death.

As Heidegger observes in *Sein und Zeit*, the terminology available in Western languages for expressing time is remarkably impoverished. Since we lack adequate specifically temporal language, we Westerners always express time (and falsify it) in some spatial image or other, for example in the movement of the hands of a clock. In fact, however, space is the opening out of time, an opening out that is generated rather than merely registered by language. If there is no proper language for time, then time can only be expressed figuratively, that is, by one or another species of catachresis, through the importation of an improper word where there is no proper one. The project of "Tears, Idle Teats" is to find a way with spatial images to express Tennyson's peculiar apprehension of human time, especially his sense of the past. Tennyson must, that is, try to turn time into language or make time of words. This is both a poetic and a theoretical project. For Tennyson one of the major uses of poetry is to express the human sense of time. This is an example of what I mean when I say Tennyson's critical and theoretical thinking about poetry takes place in his poems, not in prose about poetry.

Temporal distance is associated with spatial distance in the first stanza of "Tears," when the theme of the poem is announced. "[L]ooking on the happy Autumn-fields/And thinking of the days that are no more" makes the speaker of the poem cry, but the tears are idle and without ascertainable meaning. Though the poem is sung by one of the Princess's maidens, no doubt it expresses Tennyson's own obsession with what he called the "passion of the past." Twice in comments about the poem he asserted that it was written at a particular "mouldered lodge" of the past, Tintern Abbey: "This song came to me on the yellowing autumn-tide at Tintern Abbey, full for me of its bygone memories. It is the sense of the abiding in the transient" (Ricks, 2: 232). Tennyson does not mention Wordsworth, but "Tears, Idle Tears" has the same theme as Wordsworth's poem and might almost be called Tennyson's "Tintern Abbey." Among the "bygone memories"① was surely this one of Wordsworth's many poems about memory, as well as the memory of the history that is inscribed materially in the ruined abbey. Tennyson insisted, however, that the tears of the poem were not generated by "real woe, as some people might suppose; 'it was rather the yearning that young people occasionally experience for that which seems to have passed away from them for ever'" (*Memoir*, 2: 73). This is an important clue. The poem, Tennyson is saying, with however much or little of denegation, does not express sorrow about separation from any real person, for example his separation by death from Hallam, who is buried not far from the ruins of Tintern Abbey. All the images in the poem about separation from friends and the woe of unfulfilled desire are just that, merely images, prosopopoeias for something that is imageless and has nothing to do with persons. They are images, that is, for human temporality.

The pattern of repeated adjectives woven and interwoven as the grammatical armature of the poem names no specific sorrow or loss. The adjectives name rather the quality that "the days that are no more" have just because they are no more: "Fresh"; "Sad"; "So sad, so fresh"; "sad and strange"; "so sad, so strange"; "Dear"; "sweet"; "deep"; "Deep"; "wild." Even a child who has had no actual loss to weep, says Tennyson, experiences this sense of loss as an intrinsic and apparently causeless feature of consciousness itself. To mourn this

---

① What is a "bygone memory"? It is an odd phrase, by no means the same in nuance as "memory of the bygone."

loss is the human condition. The problem for poetry is to find words to express what is outside specific experiences, even prior to them, something that has nothing to do with intersubjective relations. It is something, moreover, that seems even prior to language, at least the language of direct reference.

One mode of figurative expression exploited in this poem is to personify that primordial sense of loss by embodying it in something that can be put in words, that is, in a series of situations embodying loss or separation: friends returning by boat but not yet here; friends leaving by boat and disappearing over the horizon; a dying man or woman waking at dawn; the memory of kisses given a dead loved one when he or she was alive; the unassuagable desire to kiss "lips that are for others"; the desire of first love, a desire so deep that somehow it cannot be distinguished from regret for something lost. These personifications are explicitly labeled similes by the "as" that follows each adjective: "Fresh as," "Sad as," and so on. These images are systematically genderless. Just as it is impossible to know whether we should think of the speaker of the poem as male or female, since it was an autobiographical poem put by the male poet in the mouth of a female character in a narrative poem, so it is even impossible to tell whether the pain of unassuaged love in the poem is heterosexual or homosexual. Tennyson speaks in *In Memoriam* about Hallam in language not unlike that used in "Tears."

The other figurative strategy for expressing the inexpressible in the poem is the use of spatial images for time. If the up/down axis in the surrounding context in *The Princess* is appropriated in "Tears" to express the presence here and now of something that is so deep it belongs to another world, horizontal spatial figures serve a similar purpose. Tennyson's comments to James Knowles are helpful here: "It is in a way like St Paul's 'groanings which cannot be uttered.' ... It is what I have always felt even from a boy, and what as a boy I called the 'passion of the past.' And it is so always with me now; it is the distance that charms me in the landscape, the picture and the past, and not the immediate to-day in which I move."[1] Hallam's death did not generate

---

[1] Cited in Ricks, 2: 232 from *Nineteenth Century* 33 (1893): 170.

Tennyson's feeling of loss. Rather the death gave Tennyson an occasion to personify a loss he already felt. This loss finds its most immediate embodiment in distances in landscapes. Distance in the landscape is the immediate correlative of distance in time and so may be used for what has no language, the "groanings that cannot be uttered" of the feeling of temporal loss or fugacity, what Tennyson elsewhere called "a gulf that ever shuts and gapes." The tears that rise to the speaker's or singer's eyes in this poem happen when he or she is "looking on the happy Autumn-fields and thinking of the days that are no more." The one makes him or her think of the other.

I have spoken of such figures as catachreses for a temporality that has no literal names. But the primary figure in the poem is of course the tears. What can be said of them? Tears are an extraordinary phenomenon. They are not articulate speech. They are mute; but no one can doubt that they are signs. They say even more than words do. Oozing involuntarily from the intimacy of the body as it is moved by thoughts and feelings, they betray that intimacy, speak for it, whether the one who cries wishes to or not. They break down the chaste division between inside and outside. They turn the body inside out. As bodily fluids that are at the same time unmistakably signs they break down the division between spirit and body. Tears are profoundly embarrassing or shocking because they are the involuntary making material of what, we think, ought to be secret and immaterial. Much has been written recently about "the materiality of the sign." Tears are a paradigmatic example of such a sign. The tears in "Tears, Idle Tears" are particularly indiscrete and troubling just because they have no sufficient cause. Looking on the happy Autumn-fields and thinking of the days that are no more hardly seems something to cry about. But the tears rise to the singer's eyes.

If the tears have no sufficient cause, their meaning is also unknown. "I know not what they mean," says the singer. If the tears are signs, they are signs in an unknown language. They have come as messengers from beyond this world, from "the depths of some divine despair," but what message it is they have brought all this way is unreadable. As Leo Spitzer long ago argued, "divine despair," if it means anything, must mean what it says: the despair of some god. The phrase sounds like an oxymoron, since gods are not ordinarily thought of as ever needing to despair. These tears begin, it appears, in the weeping of some god in a state of despair. They rise from the depths of some divine despair. Then, after a mysterious transition from one world to another, they become the tears of the singer of the poem.

What might this God or "Sondergott" have to weep about? It may be his or her failure to dwell immanently within this world. The singer's sense of loss is also a despairing sense of loss for the god who must remain transcendence without immanence and cannot, as I have said, encompass the times and spaces of his or her creation. (The gender of the god who divinely despairs is not specified.) The god of this poem is a divinity who cannot save his or her creation or redeem it from guilt and death. Far from being the way to a resurrection in the other world, death now leads nowhere and cannot be dialectically recuperated. The dead are gone forever, or they return as ghosts to haunt this world as embodied memories, for example those personified figures of loss and unassuagable desire that inhabit the final three quarters of "Tears, Idle Tears. "

The world of Tennyson's "Tears, Idle Tears" is like the world of those baroque mourning plays that Walter Benjamin, in *Ursprung des deutschen Trauerspiels* , defines as a realm of nature (*physis*) bereft of any divine presence. Tennyson's poem, like those mourning plays, is a work of mourning not for any particular death, but for the loss of redeeming relation to transcendence. Tennyson's tears of mourning are brought back up like Eurydice from the underworld, but their function as communicating messengers is lost along the way. They connect this world with the other one, but in the mode of non-connection. The message the tears bring is lost in the transition from the depths of some divine despair to the singer's heart to her or his eyes. They are now signs in an unknown language, unreadable.

I have said the tears are paradigmatic examples of the materiality and therefore unreadability of the sign. They are this in part because they bring to the surface the aspect of language or of any other sign that is mute, obscure, opaque, if not meaningless at least without any ascertainable meaning. The tears seem somehow related to the days that are no more, but more as meaningless signs generated by thinking about the past than as signs for them that put the one who uses them in possession of what they signify. The tears signify the non-being of what they represent. They are like a word repeated so often that it loses its meaning and becomes pure meaningless sound. Tennyson used to say his own name over and over until it lost meaning. He then seemed to expand and become identified with the universe in a kind of waking trance. Try it: "Alfred, Alfred, Alfred, Alfred, Alfred." What could be a more useless and idle thing to do?

The tears are "idle" presumably because they are generated in a moment of idleness, whether "silken-folded" or not: In this moment the speaker or singer has turned away from the future-oriented work that normally occupies human beings just to look at the happy Autumn-fields and think of the days that are no more. This is an activity that is idle in the sense of accomplishing nothing, as the tears, so it seems, accomplish nothing. Nothing can be done to alter the non-being of the past. Or can it? The tears appear to be "idle" because they do not work. They do not do anything. The days that are no more are no more. No words can bring them back. If the tears are cognitively empty ("I know not what they mean"), they also appear to be performatively void. They are signs that fit the category of what is called an infelicitous speech act.

On the other hand, by a paradox that is at the center of what this poem says about poetry, the poem about the tears, the naming of the tears in poetry, is performatively efficacious. The poem is inaugural, a new start. The song brings tears to the eyes of the maid who sings it: "She ended with such passion that the tear/She sang of, shook and fell, an erring pearl/Lost in her bosom" (4. 41-43). "The tear she sang of": surely that is an odd statement! These tears are generated by the song or they are the very ones the song names, though it is not autumn and the maid has presumably not suffered the various losses or unassuaged desires that are named in the poem. Nevertheless, "the tears come to her eyes," as we say. Sing this poem and you will cry. But you will cry tears not for your own loss but for a generalized loss, loss in general, a loss that is, for Tennyson, the essential feature of the human sense of time past. To sing about these tears is to bring them up from the depths and to confront them again as signs whose meaning is unknown. If the tears rise up, they then fall. They fall in a way that is ominously suggestive of a moral as well as physical loss, a loss that has some shadow of sexual guilt about it. The tear is "an erring pearl/Lost in her bosom," erring presumably because it ought to have stayed in place on its string.

Another odd fact about these tears, or about tears in general, is that they obscure clear vision of what generated them. We speak of how someone's eyes are "misted with tears. " The weeper in this poem can no longer clearly see the happy autumn fields that brought on the tears through their association with the past. Tennyson himself was extremely near-sighted. He had to hold a book close to his eyes in order to read it. The happy autumn fields always presumably looked misty to him, as if he were crying, even when there were no tears in his eyes. When what is seen is seen obscured by tears, its deeper meaning is at the same time revealed, in the case of this poem by the crescendo of sideways displacements into one simile or another. Tears are apocalyptic. They unveil and veil at the same time. ①

Tears are ruined symbols, symbols that do not communicate that for which they stand. If this is so, a more proper name for the tears would be "allegorical sign," defining "allegorical sign" as a symbol turned inside out. I follow here not Tennyson's commonplace definition of allegory as *This* for *That* but the tradition of allegory that goes from Friedrich Schlegel through Ruskin and Pater to Proust, Benjamin, and de Man. To the latter tradition Tennyson's poetic practice and its implicit theory in "Tears, Idle Tears" belong, whatever he may have said elsewhere in casual comments about allegory. A symbol, according to the canonical definition by Coleridge cited by Gerhard Joseph for its presumed application to Tennyson, combines the individual and the general in a material image. A symbol, says Coleridge, "always partakes of the Reality which it renders intelligible; and while it enunciates the whole, abides itself as a living part

---

① On this aspect of tears see Jacques Derrida, *Mémoires d'aveugle : l'autoportrait et autres ruines* (Paris, 1990), pp. 123-130.

in that Unity, of which it is the representative. "[①]An allegorical sign, on the contrary, does not participate synecdochically, as part for a whole, in what it signifies. Nor can it be said to be of the same nature as what it symbolizes. Nor can it be defined as a making present, bringing near, or making intelligible of what is named.

Tennyson's idle tears are a paradigmatic example of an allegorical sign as opposed to a symbol. Such a sign is defined in terms of temporal distance, not spatial contiguity, by its unlikeness to what it stands for, not its similarity to the symbolized, by its opacity and lack of discernible meaning, not by its transparency. An allegorical sign is characterized by its failure to put the one who contemplates it in present possession of what it stands for, not by its cognitive efficacy. It has performative force, not a constative function. The tears work as signs through a strange efficacy of putting weeper, singer, and listener or witness in touch at a distance with what they cannot name as perspicuous meaning. This failure of the tears to express what they mean makes them function admirably as allegorical signs for temporality, the strange non-being of the days that are no more as Tennyson experienced them.

Another peculiarity of "Tears, Idle Tears" will reinforce my claim that the tears are allegorical signs in the Benjaminian or de Manian sense rather than transparent symbols sharing in what they name and transporting what they name to the beholder. The Coleridgean theory of the symbol is always associated with oxymoron and with the dialectical reconciliation of opposites: the general in the particular, the spiritual in the material, the far in the near, and so on. The symbol is the place where thesis and antithesis, death and life, past and present, this world and the other transcendent one, come together and are synthesized in a higher unity. It seems at first that Tennyson's poem fits neatly into this paradigm. "Happy Autumn-fields" is an oxymoron if there ever was one. It prepares for the seemingly "oxymoronic" juxtapositions in the image structure and chain of adjectives used in the poem to define the days that

---

① Samuel Taylor Coleridge, *Lay Sermons*, ed. R. J. White and others, Vol. 6 of *The Collected Works of Samuel Taylor Coleridge* (Princeton, 1969-), p. 30.

are no more as, so it seems, a combination of presence and absence. The days that are no more are fresh as the first beam glittering on a sail that brings our friends up from the underworld and at the same time sad as the last which reddens over one that sinks with all we love below the verge. They are like dawning to the eyes and ears of someone who is about to die, someone with "dying cars" and "dying eyes" who hears and sees but with awareness of imminent absolute loss, just as the "glimmering square" of the window at dawn is neither visible nor invisible but both at once.

The problem with this reading of the poem is that the pattern of dialectical opposition reconciled in an oxymoron breaks down in the poem. It is replaced by a cascade of adjectives and similes all describing the same absence and loss. If "fresh" and "sad," in the first stanza, seem opposites, the sort of opposites that might be dialectically synthesized in the symbol, "sad" and "strange" in stanza two are not so much opposites as differential versions of the same alienation of the days that are no more. It is as if the days that are no more were a sad and strange ghost in grave clothes come back to haunt the singer as an apparition walking those happy Autumn-fields. The words of the poem successfully raise that ghost. In the last stanza the adjectives multiply in a crescendo of shaded variations trying to evoke a single elusive entity (or non-entity), not in an alternation among opposites. The days that are no more are "dear," "sweet," "deep," and "wild with all regret." What began as a dialectical opposition potentially capable of being synthesized breaks down as the emotion of the poem intensifies in the confrontation of something that resists dialectical synthesis and therefore cannot be symbolized in the Coleridgean way.

A final peculiarity of the similes chosen to define the days that are no more will confirm that the past, for Tennyson, can be named only in allegorical sign, not in symbol. Though each of the similes is affirmed to be another approach to naming what the days that are no more are like from the point of view of someone who thinks about them in the present, they are not by any means all images of the past. Quite the contrary. The days that are no more are as fresh as the first beam that brings our friends up from the underworld. This may refer to a past separation, but it is oriented toward the reunion that will take place in the immediate future. If the days are sad as the last beam which reddens over a sail that sinks with all we love below the verge, that simile seems oriented toward a future separation. It is not an image of something past at all. The dying person who awakens at dawn to hear the half-awakened birds and see the window "slowly grow a glimmering square" is oriented toward his imminent future death. He or she is not thinking of the past. "Remembered kisses after death" belong to the past all right, but the second kind of kisses mentioned, those "by hopeless fancy feigned on lips that are for others" are longed-for future kisses that will not happen. "First love" is surely a longing for union with the beloved in the future, though Tennyson adds, characteristically, that "first love" is also "wild with all regret." It is as if in the moment of first love the lover already foresees the future loss of the beloved and the wild regret that loss will cause. To be deeply in love is to suffer a wild regret for something that has not yet happened, in a curious form of future anterior.

The strangest thing about the past, for Tennyson in this poem, is that the days that are no more seem to be as much located in the future as in the past. There is a coming and going or metaleptic reversal of past and future that might be defined by saying that in this poem we go forward in time to come back to the past or by saying that in this poem we remember the future. But this is precisely the characteristic of time that is best expressed by the allegorical sign in its emphasis on perpetual reversal and on a continual broken repetition rather than by the *nunc stans* of the symbol. The singer of "Tears, Idle Tears" mocks and contradicts the concept of time so confidently expressed by the Princess a little earlier in the poem and replaces it with an allegorical time of perpetual loss and absence.

Tennyson's final name for this perpetual loss and absence is "Death in Life." The phrase is a prosopopoeia, the culmination of the chain of images personifying the days that are no more as like one or another person or interpersonal situation. But like all prosopopoeias, this one is as much an invocation as a name. It can be read either as an exclamatory definition, a constative assertion: "'O Death in Life,' that is what the days that are no more are," or as a performative vocative or apostrophe, a prosopopoeia or trope of address to the absent, the inanimate, or the dead, that is, the days that are no more. Like Christ's "Lazarus, come forth" Tennyson's speaker implores the days that are no more to come forth and manifest themselves in the form of an allegorical personification: "O Death in Life." Like Wordsworth's "Ye knew him well, ye cliffs and islands of Winander," Tennyson's address to "Death in Life" presupposes that this being or personage might appear or answer back. But the poem ends abruptly with this line. No evidence is given that the days that are no more appear in answer to the speaker's call. "O Death in Life" is a failed prosopopoeia, the ruin of the trope of personification that has been a chief rhetorical tool in the poem for naming by one catachresis or another something that has no proper name, or for performatively invoking it. Insofar as the days that are no more are accurately described as death in life they could not manifest themselves except as an absence, as a ghost.

"Death in Life": the phrase reverses Coleridge's "Life in Death" in "The Rime of the Ancient Mariner," one of the grisly figures that dices for the soul of the mariner. What is the difference between Life in Death and Death in Life? Even though Coleridge may have thought that his "Life in Death" was an allegorical rather than symbolic figure, his distaste for allegory and failure to understand it seems to have caused his allegorical figure to be rather a defective version of symbol. Indeed that is how he defines allegory in *The Statesman's Manual*. The difference between "Life in Death" and "Death in Life" is precisely the difference between Coleridgean symbol, in which Tennyson may have thought he believed, and allegory, the ruin, the "broken grange," the idle figure without ascertainable meaning. Coleridge's "Life in Death" names the carrying over, as in symbol, of life, this present life here, into death, thereby giving us, as symbol does, possession now of the transcendent realm beyond life. "Death in Life" names the undermining of all presence and possession in this life by a principle of loss.

Tennyson here names that principle of loss, appropriately enough, "Death." This death is not a future end but a dimension of separation, loss, or difference that permeates life from childhood to old age, from birth to "death" in the usual sense. As Dylan Thomas said, "After the first death there is no other." The "first death" occurs the moment we are born. Human life thereafter is undermined by this constant presence of death.

I claim to have fulfilled the promise made at the beginning of this paper. I have shown that if Tennyson's abstract thinking was conventional and traditional, his poetic thinking went against that conventional thinking. "Tears, Idle Tears," as one example of that, expresses a profound apprehension of temporality as well as a profound sense of the way the poetic devices of allegorical sign, prosopopoeia, and catachresis can be used performatively to call forth that apprehension of temporality.

15. 米勒：《时间的地志学：丁尼生的眼泪》

(J. Hillis Miller, "Temporal Topographies: Tennyson's Tears," 1992)

作者小识

米勒(J. Hillis Miller, 1928—2021)，美国文学批评家，他将现象学、解构论等复杂的哲学运用于文学研究，对英美文学作品展开了富有新意的批评。他的学术生涯始于霍布金斯大学。他同批评家乔治·普莱(Georges Poulet)密切合作，发展现象学批评，专注于文学主题研究，潜心探索"对他人意识的意识"。他这个时期的研究聚焦于英国维多利亚时代的文学经典，发表了富有影响力的论著——《现实性的诗人》(*Poets of Reality*, 1965)。

1972年到达耶鲁之后，他的学术生涯发生了巨大的转变：参与并推进文学批评的"语言学转向"，与耶鲁的哈特曼、布卢姆、德曼密切互动，形成了美国文学研究解构学派。他们与德里达合著的《解构与批评》(*Deconstruction and Criticism*)成为这个松散但前卫的学派之强劲宣言。1976年，阿布拉姆斯(M. H. Abrams)发表《解构的天使》("The Deconstructive Angel")一文，质疑甚至对抗解构批评理论。米勒通过撰写《作为寄生者的批评家》("The Critic as Host")做出回应。在耶鲁期间，他出版了三部重要著作：《小说与重复》(*Fiction and Repetition*, 1982)、《语言学时刻》(*The Linguistic Moment*, 1985)，以及《德曼的教训》(*The Lesson of Paul de Man*, 1985)。

米勒的其他著作包括《阅读的伦理》(*The Ethics of Reading*, 2009)、《解读叙事》(*Reading Narrative*, 1998)、《文学的言语行为》(*Speech Acts in Literature*, 2002)、《小说的多元共同体》(*Communities in Fiction*, 2014)、《地志学》(*Topographies*, 1995)、《保卫德里达》(*For Derrida*, 2009)。他将解构论贯彻到人文学科的研究中，强调文化实践之中语言的"述行力量"(performative force)。其批评学说超越文学研究的范围，对比较文学产生了影响。

背景略说

德里达解构论登陆美国，米勒与之一拍即合，随后同德里达过从甚密，于学理上彼此启发，在思想上互相激荡。世人将他同哈特曼、布卢姆、德曼并称为"耶鲁学派四杰"，从此就注定了他将以"解构批评家"的名号传扬学界。在《解构与批评》的序言中，哈特曼称德里达、德曼、米勒为"蟒蛇的解构主义者"（boa-deconstructionist），而称他自己和布卢姆为"勉强的解构主义者"（barely deconstructionist）。哈特曼所言不虚：蟒蛇凶猛而又慧黠，对古今经典文本体系发起攻势，可谓势如破竹。像其他解构批评家一样，米勒善变，学无常道，理无至尊：从执着于意义的"现象学批评圆圈"逃逸而出，将修辞性置于逻辑性之上，从隐喻、转喻、寓言的修辞学体系的视角逼近文学性。而文学性究竟为何？解构论者若以古典汉语属文，一定会说"神无方而易无体"，大师与晚学一样感到无比尴尬。尴尬之余，米勒又力举"阅读的伦理"，在文学批评领域率先开启了当代人文学科的伦理转向。

米勒迷恋"地志学"，首先从德里达的"地志学"，而且是复数的"地志学"开始。在他看来，德里达与德勒兹一般无二，一个浪荡者，一个游牧人，都在自己的文本体系之中立体地描绘了一千块高原，其中根茎交织，沟壑纵横，洞穴密布，凶险难卜。德里达早就谆谆告诫，言之凿凿："关于要去探险之所，我有足够的认识，且充满恐惧地认为，那里事事不平；若是周详考虑，最好还是不要贸然前往。"凶险无所不在，一旦迈向解构之途，就会遭遇迎头棒喝：解构是非历史主义、虚无主义，是不讲道德以及不负责任的，而且解构批评根本就不是批评，而是以批评为由头展示那些怪异的哲学，而那些怪异的哲学就是"达达主义的学术版"。从德里达出道江湖，到米勒撰写这篇论文的20世纪90年代初，这些责难已经是老生常谈。主流学术讲述历史的方式可谓得心应手，其惯用的方略是拉起意识形态的旗帜，呼吁回归到一种不加反思更不加批判的文学阅读，即再现式的、主题学的以及传纪学的文学阅读，而解构论所开拓的修辞学阅读被视为不由正道、崇尚虚无、废黜责任、不讲道德。对此，米勒的辩护略见几分无奈，无奈中却有几分雅量与厚道：归向传统阅读方式的不幸后果在于，一旦视之为理所当然的圭臬，那就挫败了当今文化研究、女性研究、族裔研究以及"少数话语"研究之中奋力展开的政治与思想志业，而这种志业不仅必不可少，而且至关重要。

米勒还借着一种"述行的语言力量"，使得解构批评超越当下，指向未来。"施为性语言"（performative language）对立于"记述性语言"（constative language），是语言行为理论的一个关键概念。记述性语言报道事实，施为性语言预表行为。施为性语言具有建构力量和转换力量，表现语言的诗性维度和预言维度。米勒断定，在德里达的著述和讲演之中，所谓"解构论"对于当今文化研究、女性研究、新历史主义以及"少数话语"的前沿研究所做出的贡献，恰恰就是对"文学语言的施为力量"的推重。文学不是记述，而是施为——是呼唤、许诺、预言。呼唤归向宗教，许诺未来民主，预言弥赛亚的来临，于是解构便不是虚无主义，更不是非道德主义，而是灵知主义的当代形式。米勒还进一步建议，当今人们必须尽可能清晰地认识到文学语言、哲学语言、"实用批评语言"当中一切语言的施为性潜能，及其创造历史的权力意志。米勒引用本雅明的《历史哲学论纲》中的第十七条命题，结束了对解构批评原则的论述：历史唯物主义在为压抑的过去而战，从而在历史同质过程中炸开一个特殊的时代，并从这个特殊的时代炸开了一种特殊的生活，从毕生的劳作之中炸开了一种特殊劳作。于是，向整体性和同质性开战，保护个体性和异质性，成为解构的未竟之业。

基本内容

米勒集中解读丁尼生的《眼泪，无缘无故的眼泪》(以下简称《眼泪》)一诗，对时间的空间化诗性呈现方式进行了论述。诗篇中的"空间化"，构成了诗学地志学(poetic topographies)的核心内涵。在这篇论文中，米勒仍然依托日内瓦文学批评学派的"主题学"研究方法，首先阐述了丁尼生的"诗性思维"(poetic thinking)，即有关诗之本质与力量的思维向度，然后集中展示了丁尼生诗歌的隐微诗学，即诗人以诗的形式曲折地表现在诗篇之中的关于诗歌的理论沉思。

米勒解读的第一道程序为"再度语境化"。《眼泪》是丁尼生的叙事长诗《公主》("Princess")之中"一个戏剧性的时刻切入"，米勒便把这首将抒情美学推到极致的断章还原到《公主》的整体。爱妲公主(Princess Ida)的女仆吟诵了这首抒情诗，为叙事诗之中的灾难性情节和悲剧性结局起到了推波助澜的作用。在诗篇整体的文脉之中，公主和女仆持不同的时间观。在公主看来，柏拉图和奥古斯丁传统主导着"时间意识"，即"时间是一连串的现在——过去的现在、现在的现在、未来的现在"。所有的"现在"，由于并存于自古至今的上帝之"不朽的现实"而凝固为"太一"。然而，女仆所吟哦的《眼泪》之中所表达的时间意识与传统的时间观大相径庭。这种新型的时间观之要义在于，时间并非永恒的现在，而是由差异、缺场、间距、无法通达之物以及异化感、失落感构成的。尤其是那种失落感，使卡夫卡笔下那些卑微的人物永远处于"形而上学的异化境遇"之中。他们不仅永远在流亡，而且还必须渴望流亡，必须永恒地、一再地肯定和选择流亡。绝对的失落就是永恒的迷失，那是无法通过重返上帝之怀抱而得到慰藉的悲伤。相反，事实上，上帝创造了时空，却不能容纳一切。丁尼生以诗的方式道出了神性的绝望，也就是透过意象和修辞的结构来重构"时间的地志学"，以克服古典哲学中语言在表达时间方面的匮乏。在这个意义上，米勒是从海德格尔《存在与时间》的视角来解读丁尼生的《眼泪》的，他通过丁尼生的诗性思维来解构古典形而上学的时间观。

丁尼生不是诗学家，米勒的批评也不是为了演示时间意识的哲学。紧扣"昔日激情"这一抒情主题，米勒尤其关注诗中的修辞模式。（1）"拟人法"（prosopopoeias）。诗中所有关涉人间别离以及未能满足的渴望之悲伤意象，均为纯粹意象，即以意象替代无形象之物。这些意象虽与人无关，却都是关于人类时间的意象。诗中的文法策略都指向了拟人化，即化亘古的失落感为有生命的、类似于人的意象，用一系列的情境或事件来具体地呈现迷失和别离。（2）以空间意象来表征时间，具体地表象地志学的要义，以风景的距离来直接体现分离时刻"无法道出的呻吟"，如诗中唱道："凝望欢乐洋溢的秋野，想起韶光不再的往昔。"（3）"误用修辞"（catachresis）或"逆喻修辞"（oxymoron）。以具有物质实在性的"眼泪"来呈现无以表达的时间感及其所引发的绝望与悲哀。眼泪，其来无端，但诗人马上又说它"来自某一神性绝望的深渊"，表示这种绝对的失落感也是神性的份额，连神也会为此感到绝望。（4）"吊诡"（par-adoxes）。诗中的话语在述行意义上表示绝望是希望藏匿之所，终结乃开端兴发之地，毁损无用的眼泪却是新生的"讽喻符号"（allegorical sign）。讽喻拒绝象征的和解，将碎片留在废墟之上，辩证和解的模式在诗中瓦解。"过往只能以讽喻符号明指，而不能采用象征。"米勒认为，对于丁尼生而言，诗中有关过去的最为奇妙之事，便在于逝去的往昔同时坐落在未来和过去。过去与未来交织，产生了讽喻的逆转（metaleptic conversion）：我们在时间上向前，目的却在过去。

于是，爱妲公主和她的女仆，构成了一对述行上互为解构的镜像。《眼泪》的歌者嘲讽和反驳公主自信满满的象征时间观念，而代之以永恒失落和虚无的讽喻时间。米勒重构丁尼生"时间的地志学"的结论就在于：诗人丁尼生的抽象思维恪守传统、因袭陈规，但他的诗性思维却与传统的思维方式背道而驰。

《眼泪》表达了丁尼生对"岁月不居""人生几何"的深刻解悟与忧惧，同时也表达了他对讽喻符号、拟人法、矛盾比喻等诗学修辞的深刻洞见，而那些诗学修辞可以用"述行方式"唤起那种对"岁月不居""人生几何"的解悟与忧惧。

拓展讨论

怀着这么一泓悲愿，米勒进入了德里达"地形学"的隐秘空间，以一种全景绘图的程序，描绘这个巨大的未知领域：从词语开始，经过灰烬、犁沟、岩石、洞穴而下沉到黑暗的墓穴，追问文学与"隐秘的无场之所"(secret place without place)之间的关系。通过发掘德里达与现象学的关联，米勒梳理出一条从解构通往"文学对象之理念性"的隐秘途径。按照德里达的说法，文学是一套奇特的体制，文学对象之理念性在于"以一切可能的方式言说一切可能的对象"。乍看起来，好像文学不负责任，然而文学的"不负责任"恰恰是最紧迫责任的基础。因为，"对现存结构化的意识形态权力不负责任，是开始担负一种无限紧迫责任而走向未来民主的不二法门"。"未来民主"(democracy to come)，是德里达晚年思考的最重要的主题之一，它包括了政治民主而绝对不只是政治民主，更重要的是同宗教上的弥赛亚主义紧密关联。未来民主是用"仿佛"(as if)、"也许"(perhaps)、"可能"(might、would、could)等微弱话语表达的一种许诺、一种祈祷、一种期待、一种责任，它指向他人、面临他人以及应答他人。故此，文学的不负责任，恰恰是一种被推展到存在地平线之外的绝对正义，不可解构的正义，作为一切解构行为之可能性条件的正义。

在"文学对象的理念性"的牵引下，米勒进入了德里达思想的幽玄之境，碰到了解构批评的硬核之处，即"隐秘文字""墓穴书写""黑色的神话学体系"。"一套密码文字体系，彻底搅乱了绘图的逻辑。"密码文字体系，如同金字塔底层的无边黑暗世界，如同柏拉图"洞穴喻说"之中囚徒面对的光影幻象。墓穴，在又不在，非内非外，既内且外，像柏拉图《蒂迈欧斯篇》(Timeus)之中勉力描述的那个"场所"(khora)。它终结了一切逻辑的分封，抵达了秘密的最高境界。一条悖论、一道绝境、一个难解之谜在于：文学行为有一种对秘密的嗜好，可是最高的秘密恰恰是没有秘密。沉入墓穴，遭遇密码文字体系，而密码无解，唯有物的涌现，"物的议会"。隐含秘密是文学的本质特征，而一切文学的秘密都在文字的表面，深度即表层，幽玄之境即虚无之境。庄子"藏天下于天下"，此乃文学乃至一切文字之中最不可冒犯的秘密，这是浪漫的反讽，更是文学的灵知。在反深度之时强化深度，是以最负责任的方式言述未来。何谓文学？何谓"隐秘"？何谓"责任"？何谓"未来的民主"？一言以蔽之：一种对于不可能性的激情。文学与不确定性、不可侵犯的秘密以及作为最紧迫责任的不负责任紧密相连，所以对不可能性的激情是解构的典范。文学写在密码体系之上，建构起秘密的墓穴，而解构的运作势必超越当下，指向未来。

延伸阅读

1. 米勒：《J. 希利斯·米勒文集》，北京，中国社会科学出版社，2016。该书分别从解构/实践、阅读伦理、理论干预、言语行为、他者/异质、维多利亚英国文学、捍卫德里达七个方面呈现了米勒的学术成就。

2. J. Hillis Miller, *Tropes Parables and Performatives*, Durham, NC, Duke University Press, 1990. 该书汇聚了米勒从 1952 年到 1990 年撰写的论文。贯穿在这些论文中的基本线索是转喻修辞、比喻模式和述行话语。

16. The Law of Genre (1980)

By Jacques Derrida

Genres are not to be mixed.

I will not mix genres.

I repeat: genres are not to be mixed. I will not mix them.

Now suppose I let these utterances resonate all by themselves.

Suppose: I abandon them to their fate, I set free their random virtualities and turn them over to my audience—or, rather, to *your* audience, to your auditory grasp, to whatever mobility they retain and you bestow upon them to engender effects of all kinds without my having to stand behind them.

I merely said, and then repeated: genres are not to be mixed; I will not mix them.

As long as I release these utterances (which others might call speech acts) in a form yet scarcely determined, given the open context out of which I have just let them be grasped from "my" language—as long as I do this, you may find it difficult to choose among several interpretative options. They are legion, as I could demonstrate. They form an open and essentially unpredictable series. But you may be tempted by *at least* two types of audience, two modes of interpretation, or, if you prefer to give these words more of a chance, then you may be tempted by two different genres of hypothesis. Which ones?

On the one hand, it could be a matter of a fragmentary discourse whose propositions would be of the descriptive, constative, and neutral genre. In such a case, I would have named the operation which consists of "genres are not to be mixed. " I would have designated this operation in a neutral fashion without evaluating it, without recommending or advising against it, certainly without binding anyone to it. Without claiming to lay down the law or to make this an act of law, I merely would have summoned up, in a fragmentary utterance, the sense of a practice, an act or event, as you wish: which is what sometimes happens when we revert to "genres are not to be mixed. " With reference to the same case, and to a hypothesis of the same type, same mode, same genre—or same order: when I said, "I will not mix genres," you may have discerned a foreshadowing description—I am not saying a prescription—the descriptive designation telling in advance what will transpire, predicting it in the constative mode or genre, that is, it will happen thus, I will not mix genres. The future tense describes, then, what will surely take place, as you yourselves can judge; but for my part it does not constitute a commitment. I am not making you a promise here, nor am I issuing myself an order or invoking the authority of some law to which I am resolved to submit myself. In this case, the future tense does not set the time of a performative speech act of a promising or ordering type.

But another hypothesis, another type of audience, and another interpretation would have been no less legitimate. "Genres are not to be mixed" could strike you as a sharp order. You might have heard it resound the elliptical but all the more authoritarian summons to a law of a "do" or "do not" which, as everyone knows, occupies the concept or constitutes the value of *genre*. As soon as the word "genre" is sounded, as soon as it is heard, as soon as one attempts to conceive it, a limit is drawn. And when a limit is established, norms and interdictions are not far behind: "Do," "Do not" says "genre," the word "genre," the figure, the voice, or the law of genre. And this can be said of genre in all genres, be it a question of a generic or a general determination of what one calls "nature" or *physis* (for example, a biological *genre* in the sense of *gender*, or the human *genre*, a genre of all that is in general), or be it a question of a typology designated as nonnatural and depending on laws or orders which were once held to be opposed to *physis* according to those values associated with *technè*, *thesis*, *nomos* (for example, an artistic, poetic, or literary genre). But the whole enigma of genre springs perhaps most closely from within this limit between the two genres of genre which, neither separable nor inseparable, form an odd couple of one without the other in which each evenly serves the other a citation to appear in the figure of the other, simultaneously and indiscernibly saying "I" and "we," me the genre, we genres, without it being possible to think that the "I" is a species of the genre "we." For who would have us believe that we, we two, for example, would form a genre or belong to one? Thus, as soon as genre announces itself, one must respect a norm, one must not cross a line of demarcation, one must not risk impurity, anomaly, or monstrosity. And so it goes in all cases, whether or not this law of genre be interpreted as a determination or perhaps even as a destination of *physis*, and regardless of the weight or range imputed to *physis*. If a genre is what it is, or if it is supposed to be what it is destined to be by virtue of its *telos*, then "genres are not to be mixed"; one should not mix genres, one owes it to oneself not to get mixed up in mixing genres. Or, more rigorously: genres should not intermix. And if it should happen that they do intermix, by accident or through transgression, by mistake or through a lapse, then this should confirm, since, after all, we are speaking of "mixing," the essential purity of their identity. This purity belongs to the typical axiom: it is a law of the law of genre, whether or not the law is, as one feels justified in saying, "natural." This normative position and this evaluation are inscribed and prescribed even at the threshold of the "thing itself," if something of the genre "genre" can be so named. And so it follows that you might have taken the second sentence in the first person, "I will not mix genres," as a vow of obedience, as a docile response to the injunction emanating from the law of genre. In place of a constative description, you would then hear a promise, an oath; you would grasp the following respectful commitment: I promise you that I will not mix genres, and, through this act of pledging utter faithfulness to my commitment, I will be faithful to the law of genre, since, by its very nature, the law invites and commits me in advance not to mix genres. By publishing my response to the imperious call of the law, I would correspondingly commit myself to be responsible.

Unless, of course, I were actually implicated in a wager, a challenge, an impossible bet—in short, a situation that would exceed the matter of merely engaging a commitment from me. And suppose for a moment that it were impossible not to mix genres. What if there were, lodged within the heart of the law itself, a law of impurity or a principle of contamination? And suppose the condition for the possibility of the law were the *a priori* of a counter-law, an axiom of impossibility that would confound its sense, order, and reason?

I have just proposed an alternative between two interpretations. I did not do so, as you can imagine, in order to check myself. The line or trait that seemed to separate the two bodies of interpretation is affected *straight away* by an essential disruption that, for the time being, I shall let you name or qualify in any way you care to: as internal division of the trait, impurity, corruption, contamination, decomposition, perversion, deformation, even cancerization, generous proliferation, or degenerescence. All these disruptive "anomalies" are engendered—and this is their common law, the lot or site they share—by *repetition*. One might even say by citation or re-citation (*ré-cit*), provided that the restricted use of these two words is not a call to strict generic order. A citation in the strict sense implies all sorts of contextual conventions, precautions, and protocols in the mode of reiteration, of coded signs, such as quotation marks or other typographical devices used for writing a citation. The same holds no doubt for the *récit* as a form, mode, or genre of discourse, even—and I shall return to this—as a literary type. And yet the law that protects the usage, in *stricto sensu*, of the words "citation" and "*récit*" is threatened intimately and in advance by a counter-law that constitutes this very law, renders it possible, conditions it and thereby renders it impossible—for reasons of edges on which we shall run aground in just a moment—to edge through, to edge away from, or to hedge around the counter-law itself. The law and the counter-law serve each other citations summoning each other to appear, and each recites the other in this proceeding (*procès*). There would be no cause for concern if one were rigorously assured of being able to distinguish with rigor between a citation and a non-citation, a *récit* and a non-*récit* or a repetition within the form of one or the other.

I shall not undertake to demonstrate, assuming it is still possible, why you were unable to decide whether the sentences with which I opened this presentation and marked this context were or were not repetitions of a citational type; or whether they were or were not of the performative type; or certainly whether they were, both of them, together—and each time together—the one or the other. For perhaps someone has noticed that, from one repetition to the next, a change had insinuated itself into the relationship between the two initial utterances. The punctuation had been slightly modified, as had the content of the second independent clause. Theoretically, this barely noticeable shift could have created a mutual independency between the interpretative alternatives that might have tempted you to opt for one or the other, or for one *and* the other of these two sentences. A particularly rich combinatory of possibilities would thus ensue, which, in order not to exceed my time limit and out of respect for the law of genre and of the audience, I shall abstain from recounting. I am simply going to assume a certain relationship between what has just now happened and the origin of literature, as well as its aborigine or its abortion, to quote Philippe Lacoue-Labarthe.

Provisionally claiming for myself the authority of such an assumption, I shall let our field of vision contract as I limit myself to a sort of species of the genre "genre." I shall focus on this genre of genre which is generally supposed, and always a bit too rashly, not to be part of nature, of *physis*, but rather of *technè*, of the arts, still more narrowly of poetry, and most particularly of literature. But at the same time, I take the liberty to think that, while limiting myself thus, I exclude nothing, at least in principle and *de jure*—the relationships here no longer being those of extension, from exemplary individual to species, from species to genre as genus or from the genre of genre to genre in general; rather, as we shall see, these relationships are a whole order apart. What is at stake, in effect, is exemplarity and its whole *enigma*—in other words, as the word "enigma" indicates, exemplarity and the *récit*—which works through the logic of the example.

Before going about putting a certain example to the test, I shall attempt to formulate, in a manner as elliptical, economical, and formal as possible, what I shall call the law of the law of genre. It is precisely a principle of contamination, a law of impurity, a parasitical economy. In the code of set theories, if I may use it at least figuratively, I would speak of a sort of participation without belonging—a taking part in without being part of, without having membership in a set. With the inevitable dividing of the trait that marks membership, the boundary of the set comes to form, by invagination, an internal pocket larger than the whole; and the outcome of this division and of this abounding remains as singular as it is limitless.

To demonstrate this, I shall hold to the leanest generalities. But I should like to justify this initial indigence or asceticism as well as possible. For example, I shall not enter into the passionate debate that poetics has brought forth on the theory and the history of genre-theory, on the critical history of the concept of genre from Plato to the present. My stance is motivated by these considerations: in the first place, we now have at our disposal some remarkable and, of late, handsomely enriched works dealing either with primary texts or critical analyses. I am thinking especially of the journal Poétique, of its issue entitled "Genres" (32) and of Genette's opening essay, "Genres, 'Types,' Modes." From yet another point of view, *L'Absolu littéraire* [The literary absolute] has already created quite a stir in this context, and everything that I shall risk here should perhaps resolve itself in a modest annotation on the margins of this magistral work which I assume some of you have already read. I could further justify my abstention or my abstinence here simply by acknowledging the terminological luxury or rapture as well as the taxonomic exuberance which debates of this kind, in a manner by no means fortuitous, have sparked: I feel completely powerless to contain this fertile proliferation—and not only because of time constraints. I shall put forth, instead, *two* principal *motives*, hoping thereby to justify my keeping to scant preliminary generalities at the edge of this problematic.

To what do these two motives essentially relate? In its most recent phase—and this much is certainly clear in Genette's propositions—the most advanced critical axis has led to a rereading of the entire history of genre-theory. This rereading has been inspired by the perception—and it must be said, despite the initial denial, by the correction—of two types of misconstruing or confusion. On the one hand, and this will be the first motive or ground for my abstention, Plato and Aristotle have been subjected to considerable deformation, as Genette reminds us, insofar as they have been viewed in terms alien to their thinking, and even in terms that they themselves would have rejected; but this deformation has usually taken on the form of *naturalization*. Following a classical precedent, one has deemed natural structures or typical forms whose history is hardly natural but, rather, quite to the contrary, complex and heterogeneous. These forms have been treated as natural—and let us bear in mind the entire semantic scale of this difficult word whose span is so far-ranging and open-ended that it extends as far as the expression "natural language," by which term everyone agrees tacitly to oppose natural language only to a formal or artificial language without thereby implying that this natural language is a simple physical or biological production. Genette insists at length on this naturalization of genres: "The history of genre-theory is strewn with these fascinating outlines that *inform and deform reality*, a reality often heterogenous to the literary field, and that claim to discover a natural 'system' wherein they construct a factitious symmetry heavily reinforced by fake windows" (p. 408, italics added). In its most efficacious and legitimate aspect, this critical reading of the history (and) of genre-theory is based on an opposition between nature and history and, more generally—as the allusion to an artificial construct indicates ("... wherein they construct a factitious symmetry... ")—on an opposition between nature and what can be called the series of all its others. Such an opposition seems to go without saying; placed within this critical perspective, it is never questioned. Even if it has been tucked away discretely in some passage that has escaped my attention, this barely visible suspicion clearly had no effect on the general organization of the problematic. This does not diminish the relevance or fecundity of a reading such as Genette's. But a place remains open for some preliminary questions concerning his presuppositions, for some questions concerning the boundaries where it begins to take hold or take place. The form of these boundaries will contain me and rein me in. These general propositions whose number is always open and indeterminable for whatever critical interpretation will not be dealt with here. What however seems to me to require more urgent attention is the relationship of nature to history, of nature to its others, *precisely when genre is on the line*.

Let us consider the most general concept of genre, from the minimal trait or predicate delineating it permanently through the modulations of its types and the regimens of its history: it rends and defends itself by mustering all its energy against a simple opposition that arises from nature and from history, as from nature and the vast lineage of its others (*technè*, *nomos*, *thesis*, then *spirit*, *society*, *freedom*, *history*, etc.). Between *physis* and its others, *genos* certainly locates one of the privileged scenes of the process and, no doubt, sheds the greatest obscurity on it. One need not mobilize etymology to this end and could just as well equate *genos* with birth, and birth in turn with the generous force of engenderment or generation—*physis*, in fact—as with race, familial membership, classificatory genealogy or class, age class (generation), or social class; it comes as no surprise that, in nature and art, genre, a concept that is essentially classificatory and genealogico-taxonomic, itself engenders so many classificatory vertigines when it goes about classifying itself and situating the classificatory principle or instrument within a set. As with the class itself, the principle of genre is unclassifiable; it tolls the knell of the knell (*glas*), in other words, of classicum, of what permits one to call out (*calare*) orders and to order the manifold within a nomenclature. *Genos* thus indicates the place, the now or never of the most necessary meditation on the "fold" which is no more historical than natural in the classical sense of these two words, and which turns *phyein* over to itself across others that perhaps no longer relate to it according to that epoch-making logic which was decisory, critical, oppositional, even dialectical but rather according to the trait of an entirely different contract. *De jure*, this meditation acts as an absolute prerequisite without which any historical perspectivizing will always be difficult to legitimate. For example, the Romantic era—this powerful figure indicted by Genette (since it attempted to reinterpret the system of modes as a system of genres)—is no longer a simple era and can no longer be inscribed as a moment or a stage placeable within the trajectory of a "history" whose concept we could be certain of. Romanticism, if something of the sort can be thus identified, is also the general repetition of all the folds that in themselves gather, couple, divide *physis* as well as *genos* through the genre, and through all the genres of genre, through the mixing of genre that is "more than a genre," through the excess of genre in relation to itself, as to its abounding movement and its general assemblage which coincides, too, with its dissolution. ① Such a "moment" is no longer a simple moment *in* the history and theory of literary genres. To treat it thus would in effect implicate one as tributary—whence the strange logic—of something that has in itself constituted a certain Romantic motif, namely, the teleological ordering of history. Romanticism simultaneously obeys naturalizing and historicizing logic, and it can be shown easily enough that we have not yet been delivered from the Romantic heritage—even though we might wish it so and assuming that such a deliverance would be of compelling interest to us—as long as we persist in drawing attention to historical concerns and the truth of historical production in order to militate against abuses or confusions of naturalization. The debate, it could be argued, remains itself a part or effect of Romanticism.

A second motive detains me at the threshold or on the edge of a possible problematic of genre (as) history and theory of history and of genre-theory—another genre, in fact. For the moment, I find it impossible to decide—impossible for reasons that I do not take to be accidental, and this, precisely, is what matters to me—I find it impossible to decide whether the possibly exemplary text which I intend to put to the test does or does not lend itself to the distinction drawn between *mode* and *genre*. Now, as you may recall, Genette demonstrates the stringent necessity of this distinction; and he rests his case on "the confusion of modes and genres" (p. 417). This implies a serious charge against Romanticism, even though "the romantic reinterpretation of the system of modes as a system of genres is neither *de facto* nor *de jure* the epilogue to this long history" (p. 415). This confusion, according to Genette, has aided and abetted the naturalization of genres by projecting onto them the "privilege of naturalness, which was *legitimately* ⋯ that of three modes⋯" (p. 421). Suddenly, this naturalization "makes these arch-genres into ideal or natural types which they neither are nor can be: there are no arch-genres that can totally escape historicity *while preserving a generic definition*. There are modes, for example: the *récit*. There are genres, for example: the novel; the relation of

---

① In this respect, the second footnote *in L'Absolu littéraire* (Paris, 1978), p. 271, seems to me, let us say, a bit too equitable in its rigorous and honest prudence.

genres to modes is complex and perhaps not, as Aristotle suggests, one of simple inclusion. "

If I am inclined to poise myself on *this* side of Genette's argument, it is not only because of his ready acceptance of the distinction between nature and history but also because of its implications with regard to mode and to the distinction between mode and genre. Genette's definition of mode contains this singular and interesting characteristic: it remains, in contradistinction to genre, purely formal. Reference to a content has no pertinence. This is not the case with genre. The generic criterion and the modal criterion, Genette says, are "absolutely heterogenous": "each genre defined itself essentially by a specification of content which was not prescribed by the definition of mode ..." (p. 417). I do not believe that this recourse to the opposition of form and content, this distinction between mode and genre, need be contested, and my purpose is not to challenge isolated aspects of Genette's argument. One might just question the presuppositions for the legitimacy of such an argument. One might also question the extent to which his argument can help us read a given text when it behaves in a given way with regard to mode and genre, especially when the text does not seem to be written sensibly within their limits but rather about the very subject of those limits and with the aim of disrupting their order. The limits, for instance, of that mode which would be, according to Genette, the *récit* ("There are modes, for example: the *récit*"). Of the (possibly) exemplary text which I shall address shortly, I shall not hasten to add that it is a "*récit*," and you will soon understand why. In this text, the "*récit*" is not only a mode, and a mode put into practice or put to the test because it is deemed impossible; it is also the name of a theme. It is the nonthematizable thematic content of something of a textual form that *assumes* a point of view with respect to the genre, even though it perhaps does not come under the heading of any genre—and perhaps no longer even under the heading of literature, if it indeed wears itself out around genreless modalizations, and would confirm one of Genette's propositions: "Genres are, properly speaking, literary/or aesthetic/ categories; modes are categories that pertain to linguistics or, more precisely, to an anthropology of verbal expression" (p. 418).

In a very singular manner, the very short text which I will discuss present-ly makes the *récit* and the impossibility of the *récit* its theme, its impossible theme or content at once inaccessible, indeterminable, interminable, and inex-haustible; and it makes the word *"récit,"* under the aegis of a certain form, its titleless title, the mentionless mention of its genre. This text, as I shall try to demonstrate, seems to be made, among other things, to make light of all the tranquil categories of genre-theory and history in order to upset their taxonomic certainties, the distribution of their classes, and the presumed stability of their classical nomenclatures. It is a text destined, at the same time, to summon up these classes by conducting their proceeding, by proceeding from the proceeding to the law of genre. For if the juridical code has frequently thrust it-self upon me in order to hear this case, it has done so to call as witness a (pos-sible) exemplary text and because I am convinced fundamental rights are bound up in all of this: the law itself is at stake.

These are the two principal reasons why I shall keep to the liminal edge of (the) history (and) of genre-theory. Here now, very quickly, is the law of a-bounding, of *excess*, the law of participation without membership, of contami-nation, etc., which I mentioned earlier. It will seem meager to you, and even of staggering abstractness. It does not particularly concern either genres, or types, or modes, or any form in the strict sense of its concept. I therefore do not know under what title the field or object submitted to this law should be placed. It is perhaps the limitless field of general textuality. I can take each word of the series (genre, type, mode, form) and decide that it will hold for all the others (all genres of genres, types, modes, forms; all types of types, genres, modes, forms; all forms of forms, etc.). The trait common to these classes of classes is precisely the identifiable recurrence of a common trait by which one recognizes, or should recognize, a membership in a class. There should be a trait upon which one could rely in order to decide that a given textual event, a given "work," corresponds to a given class (genre, type, mode, form, etc.). And there should be a code enabling one to decide ques-tions of class-membership on the basis of this trait. For example—a very hum-ble axiom, but, by the same token, hardly contestable—if a genre exists (let us say the novel, since no one seems to contest its generic quality), then a code should provide an identifiable trait and one which is identical to itself, authorizing us to determine, to adjudicate whether a given text belongs to this genre or perhaps to that genre. Likewise, outside of literature or art, if one is bent on classifying, one should consult a set of identifiable and codifiable traits to determine whether this or that, such a thing or such an event belongs to this set or that class. This may seem trivial. Such a distinctive trait *qua* mark is however always *a priori* remarkable. It is always possible that a set—I have compelling reasons for calling this a text, whether it be written or oral—re-marks on this distinctive trait within itself. This can occur in texts that do not, at a given moment, assert themselves to be literary or poetic. A defense speech or newspaper editorial can indicate by means of a mark, even if it is not explicitly designated as such, "Violà! I belong, as anyone may remark, to the type of text called a defense speech or an article of the genre newspaper-editorial. " The possibility is always there. This does not constitute a text *ipso facto* as "literature," even though such a possibility, always left open and therefore eternally remarkable, situates perhaps in every text the possibility of its becoming literature. But this does not interest me at the moment. What interests me is that this re-mark— ever possible for every text, for every corpus of traces—is absolutely necessary for and constitutive of what we call art, poetry, or literature. It underwrites the eruption of *technè*, which is never long in coming. I submit this axiomatic question for your consideration: Can one identify a work of art, of whatever sort, but especially a work of discursive art, if it does not bear the mark of a genre, if it does not signal or mention it or make it remarkable in any way? Let me clarify two points on this subject. First, it is possible to have several genres, an intermixing of genres or a total genre, the genre "genre" or the poetic or literary genre as genre of genres. Second, this re-mark can take on a great number of forms and can itself pertain to highly diverse types. It need not be a designation or "mention" of the type found beneath the title of certain books (novel, *récit*, drama). The remark of belonging need not pass through the consciousness of the author or the reader, although it often does so. It can also refute this consciousness or render the explicit "mention" mendacious, false, inadequate, or ironic according to all sorts of overdetermined figures. Finally, this remarking-trait need be neither a theme nor a thematic component of the work—although of course this instance of belonging to one or several genres, not to mention all the traits that mark this belonging, often have been treated as theme, even before the advent of what we call "modernism." If I am not mistaken in saying that such a trait is remarkable, that is, noticeable, in every aesthetic, poetic, or literary corpus, then consider this paradox, consider the irony (which is irreducible to a consciousness or an attitude): this supplementary and distinctive trait, a mark of belonging or inclusion, does not properly pertain to any genre or class. The re-mark of belonging does not belong. It belongs without belonging, and the "without" (or the suffix "-less") which relates belonging to non-belonging appears only in the timeless time of the blink of an eye (*Augenblick*). The eyelid closes, but barely, an instant among instants, and what it closes is verily the eye, the view, the light of day. But without such respite, nothing would come to light. To formulate it in the scantiest manner—the simplest but most apodictic—I submit for your consideration the following hypothesis: a text cannot belong to no genre, it cannot be without or less a genre. Every text participates in one or several genres, there is no genreless text; there is always a genre and genres, yet such participation never amounts to belonging. And not because of an abundant overflowing or a free, anarchic, and unclassifiable productivity, but because of the *trait* of participation itself, because of the effect of the code and of the generic mark. Making genre its mark, a text demarcates itself. If remarks of belonging belong without belonging, participate without belonging, then genre-designations cannot be simply part of the corpus. Let us take the designation "novel" as an example. This should be marked in one way or another, even if it does not appear, as it often does in French and German texts, in the explicit form of a subtitled designation, and even if it proves deceptive or ironic. This designation is not novelistic; it does not, in whole or in part, take part in the corpus whose denomination it nonetheless imparts. Nor is it simply extraneous to the corpus. But this singular topos places within and without the work, along its boundary, an inclusion and exclusion with regard to genre in general, as to an identifiable class in general. It gathers together the corpus and, at the same time, in the same blinking of an eye, keeps it from closing, from identifying itself with itself. This axiom of non-closure or non-fulfillment enfolds within itself the condition for the possibility and the impossibility of taxonomy. This inclusion and this exclusion do not remain exterior to one another; they do not exclude each other. But neither are they immanent or identical to each other. They are neither one nor two. They form what I shall call the *genre-clause*, a clause stating at once the juridical utterance, the precedent-making designation and the law-text, but also the closure, the closing that excludes itself from what it includes (one could also speak of a floodgate [*écluse*] of genre). The clause or floodgate of genre declasses what it allows to be classed. It tolls the knell of genealogy or of genericity, which it however also brings forth to the light of day. Putting to death the very thing that it engenders, it cuts a strange figure; a formless form, it remains nearly invisible, it neither sees the day nor brings itself to light. Without it, neither genre nor literature come to light, but as soon as there is this blinking of an eye, this clause or this floodgate of genre, at the very moment that a genre or a literature is broached, at that very moment, degenerescence has begun, the end begins.

The end begins, this is a citation. Maybe a citation. I might have taken it from the text which seems to me to bring itself forth as an example, as an example of this unfigurable figure of clusion.

What I shall try to convey to you now will not be called by its generic or modal name. I shall not say this drama, this epic, this novel, this novella or this *récit*—certainly not this *récit*. All of these generic or modal names would be equally valid or equally invalid for something which is not even quite a book, but which was published in 1973 in the editorial form of a small volume of thirty-two pages. It bears the title *La Folie du jour* [approximately: The Madness of the Day]. The author's name: Maurice Blanchot. In order to speak about it, I shall call this thing *La Folie du jour*, its given name which it bears legally and which gives us the right, as of its publication date, to identify and classify it in our copyright records at the Bibliothèque Nationale. One could fashion a non-finite number of readings from *La Folie du jour*. I have attempted a few myself, and shall do so again elsewhere, from another point of view. The *topos* of view, sight, blindness, *point of view* is, moreover, inscribed and traversed in *La Folie du jour* according to a sort of permanent revolution that engenders and virtually brings to the light of day points of view, twists, versions, and re-versions of which the sum remains necessarily uncountable and the account, im-possible. The deductions, rationalizations, and warnings that I must inevitably propose will arise, then, from an act of unjustifiable violence. A brutal and mercilessly depleting selectivity will obtrude upon me, upon us, in the name of a law that *La Folie du jour* has, in its turn, already reviewed, and with the foresight that a certain kind of police brutality is perhaps an inevitable accom-plice to our concern for professional competence.

What will I ask *of La Folie du jour*? To answer, to testify, to say what it has to say with respect to the law of mode or the law of genre and, more pre-cisely, with respect to the law of the *récit*, which, as we have just been remin-ded, is a mode and not a genre.

On the cover, below the title, we find no mention of genre. In this most peculiar place that belongs neither to the title nor to the subtitle, nor even sim-ply to the corpus of the work, the author did not affix, although he has often done so elsewhere, the designation "*récit*" or "novel," maybe (but only maybe) by erroneously subsuming both of them, Genette would say, under the unique category of the genre. About this designation which figures elsewhere and which appears to be absent here, I shall say only two things:

1. On the one hand it commits one to nothing. Neither reader nor critic nor author are bound to believe that the text preceded by this designation conforms readily to the strict, normal, normed, or normative definition of the genre, to the law of the genre or of the mode. Confusion, irony, the shift in conventions toward a new definition (in what name should it be prohibited?), the search for a supplementary effect, any of these things could prompt one to entitle as *novel* or *récit* what in truth or according to yesterday's truth would be neither one nor the other. All the more so if the words "*récit*," "novel,""*ciné-roman*," "com-plete dramatic works" or, for all I know, "literature" are no longer in the place which conventionally mentions genre but, as has happened and will happen a-

gain (shortly), they are found to be holding the position and function of the title itself, of the work's given name.

2. Blanchot has often had occasion to modify the genre-designation from one version of his work to the next or from one edition to the next. Since I am unable to cover the entire spectrum of this problem, I shall simply cite the example of the "*récit*" designation effaced between one version and the next of *Death Sentence* (trans. Lydia Davis [Barrytown, N. Y. , 1978]) at the same time as a certain epilogue is removed from the end of a double *récit*, which, in a manner of speaking, constitutes this book. This effacement of "*récit*," leaving a trace that, inscribed and filed away, remains as an effect of supplementary relief which is not easily accounted for in all of its facets. I cannot arrest the course of my lecture here, no more than I can pause to consider the very scrupulous and minutely differentiated distribution of the designations "*récit*" and "novel" from one narrative work to the next, no more than I can question whether Blanchot distinguished the genre and mode designations, no more than I can discuss Blanchot's entire discourse on the difference between the narratorial voice and the narrative voice which is, to be sure, something other than a mode. I would point out only one thing: at the very moment the first version of *Death Sentence* appears, bearing mention as it does of "*récit*," the first version of *La Folie du jour* is published with another title about which I shall momentarily speak.

La Folie du jour, then, makes no mention of genre or mode. But the word "*récit*" appears at least four times in the last two pages in order to name the theme of *La Folie du jour*, its sense or its story, its content or part of its content—in any case, its decisive proceedings and stakes. It is a *récit* without a theme and without a cause entering from the outside; yet it is without interiority. It is the *récit* of an impossible *récit* whose "production" occasions what happens or, rather, what remains, but which does not relate it, nor relate to it as to an outside reference, even if everything remains foreign to it and out of bounds. It is even less feasible for me to relate to you the story of *La Folie du jour* which is staked precisely on the possibility and the impossibility of relating a story. Nonetheless, in order to create the greatest possible clarity, in the name of daylight itself, that is to say (as will become clear), in the name of the law, I shall take the calculated risk of flattening out the unfolding or coiling up of this text, its permanent revolution whose rounds are made to recoil from any kind of flattening. And this is why the one who says "I," and the one after all who speaks to us, who "recites" for us, this one who says "I" tells his inquisitors that he cannot manage to constitute himself as narrator (in the sense of the term that is not necessarily literary) and tells them that he cannot manage to identify with himself sufficiently or to remember himself well enough to gather the story and *récit* that are demanded of him—which the representatives of society and the law require of him. The one who says "I" (who does not manage to say "I") seems to relate what has happened to him or, rather, what has nearly happened to him after presenting himself in a mode that defies all norms of self-presentation: he nearly lost his sight (his facility for *viewing*) following a traumatic event—probably an assault. I say "probably" because *La Folie du jour* wholly upsets, in a discrete but terribly efficient manner, all the certainties upon which so much of discourse is constructed: the value of an event, first of all, of reality, of fiction, of appearance and so on, all this being carried away by the disseminal and mad polysemy of "day," of the word "day," which, once again, I cannot dwell upon here. Having nearly lost his sight (*vue*), having been taken in by a kind of medico-social institution, he now resides under the watchful eye of doctors, handed over to the authority of these specialists who are representatives of the law as well, legist doctors who demand that he testify—and in his own interest, or so it seems at first—about what happened to him so that remedial justice may be dispensed. His faithful *récit*—(but let me borrow for the sake of simplicity, and because it conforms fairly well to this context, the English word "account")—hence, his faithful account of events should render justice unto the law. The law demands a narrative account.

Pronounced four times in the last three pages of *La Folie du jour*, the word "account" does not seem to designate a literary genre but rather a certain type or mode of discourse. That is, in effect, the appearance of it. Everything seems to happen as if the account—the question of or rather the demand for the account, the response, and the nonresponse to the demand—found itself staged and figured as one of the themes, objects, stakes in a more bountiful text, *La Folie du jour*, whose genre would be of another order and would in any case overstep the boundaries of the account with all its generality and all its genericity. The account itself would of course not cover this generic generality of the literary corpus named *La Folie du jour*. Now we might already feel inclined to consider this appearance suspect, and we might be jolted from our certainties by an allusion that "I" will make: the one who says "I," who is not by force of necessity a narrator, nor necessarily always the same, notes that the representatives of the law, those who demand of him an account in the name of the law, consider and treat him, in his personal and civil identity, not only as an "educated" man—and an educated man, they often tell him, ought to be able to speak and recount; as a competent subject, he ought to be able to know how to piece together a story by saying "I" and "exactly" how things happened to him—they regard him not only as an "educated" man, but also as a writer. He is writer and reader, a creature of "libraries," *the* reader of this account. This is not sufficient cause, but it is, in any case, a first clue and one whose impact incites us to think that the required account does not simply remain in a relationship that is extraneous to literature or even to a literary genre. Lest we not be content with this suspicion, let us weigh the possibility of the inclusion of a modal structure within a vaster, more general corpus, whether literary or not and whether or not related to the genre. Such an inclusion raises questions concerning edge, borderline, boundary, and abounding which do not arise without a fold.

What sort of a fold? According to which fold and which figure of enfoldment?

Here are the three final paragraphs; they are of unequal length, with the last of these comprising approximately one line:

They demanded: Tell us "exactly" how things happened. —An account? I began: I am neither learned nor ignorant. I have known some joy. This is saying too little. I related the story in its entirety, to which they listened, it seems, with great interest—at least initially. But the end was a surprise for them all. "After that beginning," they said, "you should proceed to the facts. " How so? The account was over.

I should have realized that I was incapable of composing an account of these events. I had lost the sense of the story; this happens in a good many illnesses. But this explanation only made them more demanding. Then I noticed, for the first time, that they were two and that this infringement on their traditional method—even though it can be explained away by the fact that one of them was an eye doctor, the other a specialist in mental illnesses—increasingly gave our conversation the character of an authoritarian interrogation, overseen and controlled by a strict set of rules. To be sure, neither of them was the chief of police. But being two, due to that, they were three, and this third one remained firmly convinced, I am sure, that a writer, a man who speaks and reasons with distinction, is always capable of recounting the facts which he remembers.

An account? No, no account, nevermore.

In the first of the three paragraphs that I have just cited, he claims that something is to begin after the word "account" punctuated by a question mark (An account? —herein implied: they want an account, is it then an account that they want? "I began …"). This something is nothing other than the first line on the first page of *La Folie du jour*. These are the same words, in the same order, but this is not a citation in the strict sense for, stripped of quotation marks, these words commence or recommence a quasi-account that will engender anew the entire sequence comprising this new point of departure. In this way, the first words ("I am neither learned nor ignorant …") that come after the word "account" and its question mark, that broach the beginning of the account extorted by the law's representatives—these first words mark a collapse that is unthinkable, irrepresentable, unsituable within a linear order of succession, within a spatial or temporal sequentiality, within an objectifiable topology or chronology. One sees, without seeing, one reads the crumbling of an upper boundary or of the initial edge *in La Folie du jour*, uncoiled according to the "normal" order, the one regulated by common law, editorial convention, positive law, the regime of competency in our logo-alphabetical culture, etc. Suddenly, this upper or initial boundary, which is commonly called the first line of a book, is forming a pocket inside the corpus. It is taking the form of an *invagination* through which the trait of the first line, the borderline, splits while remaining the same and traverses yet also bounds the corpus. The "account" which he claims is beginning at the end and, by legal requisition, is none other than the one that has begun from the beginning of *La Folie du jour* and in which, therefore, he gets around to saying that he begins, etc. And it is without beginning or end, without content and without edge. There is only content without edge—without boundary or frame—and there is only edge without content. The inclusion (or occlusion, inocclusive invagination) is interminable: it is an analysis of the account that can only turn in circles in an unarrestable, inenarrable, and insatiably recurring manner—but one terrible for those who, in the name of the law, require that order reign in the account, for those who want to know, with all the required competence, "exactly" how this happens. For if "I" or "he" continued to tell what he has told, he would end up endlessly returning to this point and beginning again to begin, that is to say, to begin with an end that precedes the beginning. And from the viewpoint of objective space and time, the point at which he stops is absolutely unascertainable ("I have told them the entire story…"), for there is no "entire" story except for the one that interrupts itself in this way.

A lower edge of invagination will, if one can say so, respond to this "first" invagination of the upper edge by intersecting it. The "final line" resumes the question posed *before* the "I began" (An account?) and bespeaks a resolution or promises it, tells of the commitment made no longer to give an account. As if he had already given one! And yet, yes (yes and no), an account has taken place. Hence the last word: "An account? No, no account, nevermore." It has been impossible to decide whether the recounted event and the event of the account itself ever took place. Impossible to decide whether there was an account, for the one who barely manages to say "I" and to constitute himself as narrator recounts that he has not been able to recount—but what, exactly? Well, everything, including the demand for an account. And if an assured and guaranteed decision is impossible, this is because there is nothing more to be done than to commit oneself, to perform, to wager, to allow chance its chance—to make a decision that is essentially edgeless, bordering perhaps only on madness.

Yet another impossible decision follows, one which involves the promise "No, no account, nevermore": Is this promise a part of or apart from the account? Legally speaking, it is party to *La Folie du jour*, but not necessarily to the account or to the simulacrum of the account. Its trait splits again into an internal and external edge. It repeats—without citing—the question apparently posed above (An account?) of which it can be said that, in this permanent revolution of order, it follows, doubles, or reiterates it in advance. Thus another lip or invaginating loop takes shape here. This time the lower edge creates a pocket in order to come back into the corpus and to rise again on this side of the upper or initial line's line of invagination. This would form a double chiasmatic invagination of edges:

> A. "I am neither learned nor ignorant…"
> B. "An account? I began:"
> A'. "I am neither learned nor ignorant…"
> B'. "An account? No, no account, nevermore …"

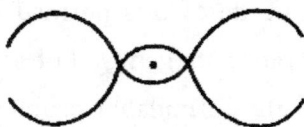

"I began …"

It is thus impossible to decide whether an event, account, account of event, or event of accounting took place. Impossible to settle upon the simple borderlines of this corpus, of this ellipse unremittingly repealing itself within its own expansion. When we fall back on the poetic consequences enfolded within this dilemma, we find that it becomes difficult indeed to speak here with conviction about an account as a determined mode included within a more general corpus or one simply related, in its determination, to other modes or, quite simply, to something other than itself. All is narrative account and nothing is; the account's outgate remains within the account in a non-inclusive mode, and this structure is itself related so remotely to a dialectical structure that it even inscribes dialectics in the account's ellipse. All is account, nothing is; and we shall not know whether the relationship between these two propositions—the strange conjunction of the account and the accountless—belongs to the account itself. What indeed happens when the edge pronounces a sentence?

Faced with this type of difficulty—the consequences or implications of which cannot be deployed here—one might be tempted to take recourse in the law or the rights which govern published texts. One might be tempted to argue as follows: all these insoluble problems of delimitation are raised "on the inside" of a book classified as a work of literature or literary fiction. Pursuant to these juridical norms, this book has a beginning and an end that leave no opening for indecision. This book has a determinable beginning and end, a title, an author, a publisher, its distinctive denomination is *La Folie du jour*. At this place, where I am pointing, on this page, right here, you can see its first word; here, its final period, perfectly situable in objective space. And all the sophisticated transgressions, all the infinitesimal subversions that may captivate you are not possible except within this enclosure for which these transgressions and subversions moreover maintain an essential need in order to take place. Furthermore, on the inside of this normed space, the word "account" does not name a literary operation or genre, but a current mode of discourse, and it does so regardless of the formidable problems of structure, edge, set theory, the part and whole, etc. , that it raises in this "literary" corpus.

That is all well and good. But in its very relevance, this objection cannot be sustained—for example, it cannot save the modal determination of the account—except by referring to extra-literary and even extra-linguistic juridical norms. The objection makes an appeal to the law and calls to mind the fact that the subversion of *La Folie du jour* needs the law in order to take place. Whereby the objection reproduces and accomplishes its staging within *La Folie du jour*: the account, mandated and prescribed by law but also, as we shall see, commanding, requiring, and producing law in turn. In short, the whole critical scene of competence in which we are engaged is *party* to and *part* of *La Folie du jour*, in whole and in part, the whole is a part.

The whole does nothing but begin. I could have begun with what resembles the absolute beginning, with the juridico-historical order of this publication. What has been lightly termed the first version *of La Folie du jour* was not a book. Published in the journal *Empédocle* (2 May 1949), it bore another title—indeed, several other titles. On the journal's cover, here it is, one reads:

Maurice Blanchot

Un récit?

[*An Account?*]

Later, the question mark disappears twice. First, when the title is reproduced within the journal in the table of contents:

Maurice Blanchot

Un récit

[*An Account*],

then below the first line:

Un récit	[*An Account* by
par	by
Maurice Blanchot	M. B.]

Could you tell whether these titles, written earlier and filed away in the archives, make up a single title, titles of the same text, titles of the account (which of course figures as an impracticable mode in the book), or the title of a genre? Even if the latter were to cause some confusion, it would be of the sort that releases questions already implemented and enacted by *La Folie du jour*. This enactment enables in turn the denaturalization and deconstitution of the oppositions nature/history and mode/genre.

Now let us turn to some of these questions. First, to what could the words "An Account" refer in their manifold occurrences and diverse punctuations? And precisely how does reference function here? In one case, the question mark can *also* serve as a supplementary remark indicating the necessity of all these questions as the insolvent character of indecision: Is this an account? Is it an account that I entitle? asks the title in entitling. Is it an account that they want? What entitles them? Is it an account as discursive mode or as literary operation, or perhaps even as literary genre whose theme would be mode or genre? Likewise, the title could excerpt, as does a metonymy, a fragment of the account without an account (to wit, the words "an account" with and without a question mark), but such an iterative excepting is not citational. For the title, guaranteed and protected by law but also making law, retains a referential structure which differs radically from the one underlying other occurrences of the "same" words in the text. Whatever the issue—title, reference, or mode and genre—the case before us always involves the law and, in particular, the relations formed around and to law. All the questions which we have just addressed can be traced to an enormous matrix that generates the non-thematizable thematic power of a simulated account: it is this inexhaustible writing which recounts without telling, and which speaks without recounting.

Account of an accountless account, an account without edge or boundary, account all of whose visible space is but some border of itself without "self," consisting of the framing edge without content, without modal or generic boundaries—such is the law of this textual event, of this text that also speaks the law, its own and that of the other as reader of this text which, speaking the law, also imposes itself as a law text, as the text of the law. What, then, is the law of the genre of this singular text? It is law, it is the figure of the law which will also be the invisible center, the themeless theme of *La Folie du jour* or, as I am now entitled to say, of "An Account?"

This law, however, as law of genre, is not exclusively binding on the genre *qua* category of art and literature. But, paradoxically, and just as impossibly, the law of genre also has a controlling influence and is binding on that which draws the genre into engendering, generations, genealogy, and degenerescence. You have already witnessed its approach often enough, with all the figures of this degenerescent self-engendering of an account, with this figure of the law which, like the day that it is, challenges the opposition between the law of nature and the law of symbolic history. The remarks that have just been made on the double chiasmatic invagination of edges should suffice to exclude any notion linking all these complications to pure form or one suggesting that they could be formalized outside the content. The question of the literary genre is not a formal one; it covers the motif of the law in general, of generation in the natural and symbolic senses, of birth in the natural and symbolic senses, of the generation difference, sexual difference between the feminine and masculine genre/gender, of the hymen between the two, of a relationless relation between the two, of an identity and difference between the feminine and masculine. The word "hymen" tells us several things. It not only points toward a paradoxical logic that is inscribed without however being formalized under this name; it should, in the first place, serve to remind the Anglo-American reader that, in French, the semantic scale of *genre* is much larger and more expansive than in English, and thus always includes within its reach the gender. Additionally, and with respect to the "hymen," let us not forget everything that Philippe Lacoue-Labarthe and Jean-Luc Nancy tell us in *L'Absolu litteraire* (especially on p. 276) about the relationship between genre (*Gattung*) and marriage, as well as about the intricate bonds of serial connections begotten by *gattieren* ("to mix,""to classify"), *gatten* ("to couple"), *Gatte/Gattin* ("husband/wife"), and so forth?

Once articulated within the precinct of Blanchot's entire discourse on the neuter, the most elliptical question would inevitably have to assume this form: What about a neutral genre/gender? Or one whose neutrality would not be *negative* (neither … nor), nor dialectical, but affirmative, and doubly affirmative (or … or)?

Here again, due to time limitations but also to more essential reasons concerning the structure of the text, I shall have to excerpt some abstract fragments. This will not occur without a supplement of violence and pain.

As first word and surely most impossible word of *La Folie du jour*, "I" presents itself as self (*moi*), me, a man. Grammatical law leaves no doubt about this subject. The first sentence, phrased in French in the masculine ("Je ne suis ni savant ni ignorant" and not "Je ne suis ni savante ni ignorante"), says, with regard to knowledge, nothing but a double negation (neither …

nor). Thus, no glint of self-presentation. But the double negation gives passage to a double affirmation (yes, yes) that enters into alignment or alliance with itself. Forging an alliance or marriage-bond ("hymen") with itself, this boundless double affirmation utters a measureless, excessive, immense *yes*: both to life and to death:

> I am neither learned nor ignorant. I have known some joy. This is saying too little: I am living, and this life gives me the greatest pleasure. And death? When I die (perhaps soon), I shall know an immense pleasure. I am not speaking of the foretaste of death, which is bland and often disagreeable. Suffering is debilitating. But this is the remarkable truth of which I am sure: I feel a boundless pleasure in living and shall be boundlessly content to die.

Now, seven paragraphs further along, the chance and probability of such an affirmation (one that is double and therefore boundless, limitless) is granted to woman. It returns to woman. Rather, not to woman or even to the feminine, to the female genre/gender, or to the generality of the feminine genre but—and this is why I spoke of chance and probability—"usually" to women. It is "usually" women who say yes, yes. To life to death. This "usually" avoids treating the feminine as a general and generic force; it makes an opening for the event, the performance, the uncertain contingencies, the encounter. And it is indeed from the contingent experience of the encounter that "I" will speak here. In the passage that I am about to cite, the expression "men" occurs twice. The second occurrence names the sexual genre, the sexual difference (*aner*, *vir*— but sexual difference does not occur between a species and a genre); in the first occurrence, "men" comes into play in an indecisive manner in order to name either the genre of human beings (the *genre humain*, named "species" in the text) or sexual difference:

> Men would like to escape death, bizarre *species* that they are. And some cry out, "die, die," because they would like to escape life. "What a

life! I'll kill myself, I'll surrender!" This is pitiful and strange; it is in error.

But I have encountered *beings* who never told life to be quiet or death to go away—usually women, beautiful creatures. As for men, terror besieges them··· [Italics added]

What has thus far transpired in these seven paragraphs? Usually women, beautiful creatures, relates "I. " As it happens, encounter, chance, affirmation of chance do not always manage to happen. There is no natural or symbolic law, universal law, or law of a genre/gender here. Only usually, usually women, (comma of apposition) beautiful creatures. Through its highly calculated logic, the comma of apposition leaves open the possibility of thinking that these women are not beautiful and then, on the other hand, as it happens, capable of saying yes, yes to life to death, of not saying be quiet, go away to life to death. The comma of apposition lets us think that they are beautiful, women and beauties, these creatures, insofar as they affirm both life and death. Beauty, the feminine beauty of these "beings," would be bound up with this double affirmation.

Now I myself, who "am neither learned nor ignorant," "I feel a boundless pleasure in living and shall be boundlessly content to die. " In this random claim that links affirmation usually to women, beautiful ones, it is then more than probable that, as long as I say yes, yes, I am a woman and beautiful. *I am a woman, and beautiful.* Grammatical sex (or anatomical as well, in any case, sex submitted to the law of objectivity): the masculine genre is thus affected by the affirmation through a random drift that could always render it other. A sort of secret coupling would take place here, forming an odd marriage ("hymen"), an odd couple, for none of this can be regulated by objective, natural, or civil law. The "usually" is a mark of this secret and odd hymen, of this coupling that is also perhaps a mixing of genres. The genres pass into each other. And we will not be barred from thinking that this mixing of genres, viewed in light of the madness of sexual difference, may bear some relation to the mixing of literary genres.

"I," then, can keep alive the chance of being a female or of changing sex. His transsexuality permits him, in a more than metaphorical and transferential way, to engender. He can give birth, and many other signs which I cannot mention here bear this out, among other things the fact that on several occasions he "brings something forth to the light of day." In the rhetoric of *La Folie du jour*, the idiomatic expression "to bring forth to the light of day" ("donner le jour") is one of the players in an exceedingly powerful polysemic and disseminal game that I shall not attempt to reproduce here. I only retain its standard and dominant meaning which the spirit of linguistics gives it: *donner le jour* is to give birth—a verb whose subject is usually maternal, that is to say, generally female. At the center, closely hugging an invisible center, a primal scene could have alerted us, if we had had the time, to *the point of view of La Folie du jour* and to *A Primal Scene*. This is also called a "short scene."

"I" can bring forth to light, can give birth. To what? Well, precisely to law or more exactly, to begin with, to the representatives of law, to those who wield authority—and let us also understand by this the authority of the author, the rights of authorship—simply by virtue of possessing an overseer's right, the right to see, the right to have everything in sight. This panoptic and this synopsis demand nothing else, but nothing less. Now herein lies the essential paradox: from where and from whom do they derive this power, this right-to-sight that permits them to have "me" at their disposal? Well, from "me," rather, from the subject who is subjected to them. It is the "I"-less "I" of the narrative voice, the I "stripped" of itself, the one that does not take place, it is he who brings them to light, who engenders these lawmen in giving them insight into what regards them and what should not regard them.

I liked the doctors well enough. I did not feel belittled by their doubts. The bother was that their authority grew with every hour. One isn't initially aware of it, but these men are kings. Showing me my rooms they said: Everything here belongs to us. They threw themselves upon the parings of my mind: This is ours. They interpellated my story: Speak! and it placed itself at their service. In haste, I stripped myself of myself. I distributed my blood, my privacy among them, I offered them the universe, I brought them forth to the light of day. Under their unblinking gaze, I became a water drop, an ink blot. I was shrinking into them, I was held entirely in their view and when, finally, I no longer had anything but my perfect nullity present and no longer had anything to see, they, too, ceased to see me, most annoyed, they rose, shouting: Well, where are you? Where are you hiding? Hiding is prohibited, it is a misdeed, etc.

Law, day. One believes it generally possible to oppose law to affirmation, and particularly to unlimited affirmation, to the immensity of yes, yes. Law—we often figure it as an instance of the interdictory limit, of the binding obligation, as the negativity of a boundary not to be crossed. Now the mightiest and most divided trait of *La Folie du jour* or of "An Account?" is the one relating birth to law, its genealogy, engenderment, generation, or genre—and here I ask you once more to be especially aware of gender—the one joining the very *genre* of the law to the process of the double affirmation. The excessiveness of *yes*, *yes* is no stranger to the genesis of law (nor to Genesis, as could be easily shown, for it also concerns an account of Genesis "in the light of seven days" [p. 20]). The double affirmation is not foreign to the genre, genius, or spirit of the law. No affirmation, and certainly no *double* affirmation without the law sighting the light of day and the daylight becoming law. Such is the madness of the day, such is an account in its "remarkable" truth, in its truthless truth.

Now the feminine, or generally affirmative gender/genre, is also the genre of this figure of law, not of its representatives, but of the law herself who, throughout an account, forms a couple with me, with the "I" of the narrative voice.

The law is in the feminine.

She is not a woman (it is only a figure, a "silhouette," and not a representative of the law) but she, *la loi*, is in the feminine, declined in the feminine; but not only as a grammatical gender/genre in my language (elsewhere Blanchot brought this genre into play for speech ["*la* parole"] and for thought ["*la* pensée"]). No, she is described as a "female element," which does not signify a female person. And the affirmative "I," the narrative voice, who has brought forth the representatives of the law to the light of day, claims to find the law seductive—sexually seductive. The law appeals to him: "The truth is that she appealed to me. In this milieu overpopulated with men, she was the only female element. One time she had me touch her knee: a bizarre impression. I declared to her: I am not the kind of man who contents himself with a knee. Her response: that would be revolting!" She pleases him and he would not like to content himself with the knee that she "had [him] touch." This contact with the knee (*genou*), as my student and friend Pierre-François Berger brought to my notice, recalls the inflectional contiguity of the I and the we, the je and the *nous*, of an I/we couple of whom we shall speak again in a moment.

The law's female element has thus always appealed to: me, I, he, we. The law is appealing: "The law appealed to me ⋯ In order to tempt her, I called softly to the law: 'Approach, so I can see you face to face' (I wanted to take her aside for a moment). Impudent appeal; what would I have done had she responded?"

He is perhaps subjected to law, but he neither attempts to escape her, nor does he shrink before her: he wishes to seduce the law to whom he gives birth (there is a hint of incest in this) and especially—this is one of the most striking and singular traits of this scene—he inspires fear in the law. He not only troubles the representatives of the law, the lawmen who are the legist doctors and the "psy-" who demand of him, but are unable to obtain, an organized account, a testimony oriented by a sense of history or his story, ordained and ordered by reason, and by the unity of an I think, or of an originally synthetic apperception accompanying all representations. That the "I" here does not always accompany itself is by no means borne lightly by the lawmen; in fact, he alarms thus the lawmen, he radically persecutes them, and, in his manner, he conceals from them without altercation the truth they demand and without which they are nothing. But he not only alarms the lawmen, he alarms the law; one would be tempted to say the law herself, if she did not remain here a silhouette and an effect of the account. And what is more, this law whom the "I" frightens is none other than "me," than the "I," effect of his desire, child of his affirmation, of the genre "I" clasped in a specular couple with "me." They are inseparable (*je/nous* and *genou*, *je/toi* and *je/toit*), and so she tells him, once more, as truth: "The truth is that we can no longer be separated. I shall follow you everywhere, I shall dwell under your roof ⌈*toit*⌉, we shall have the same sleep." We see the law, whose silhouette stands behind her representatives, frightened by "me," by "him"; she is inclined toward and declined by *je/nous*, I/we, in front of "me," in front of him, her knees marking perhaps the articulation of a gait, the flexion of the couple and sexual difference, but also the continuity without contact of the hymen and the "mixing of genres."

Behind their backs, I perceived the silhouette of the law. Not the familiar law, who is strict and not terribly agreeable: this one was different. Far from falling prey to her menace, I was the one who seemed to frighten her. According to her, my glance was lightning and my hands, grounds on which to perish. Moreover, she ridiculously attributed to me all kinds of power, she declared herself perpetually to be kneeling before me. But she let me demand nothing, and when she granted me the right to be in all places, that meant that I hadn't a place anywhere. [Elsewhere Blanchot designates the non-place and the atopical or hypertopical mobility of the narrative voice in this way.] When she placed me above the authorities, that meant: you are authorized to do nothing.

What game is the law, a law of this genre, playing? What is she playing up to when she has her knee touched? For if *La Folie du jour* plays down the law, plays at law, plays with law, it is also because the law herself plays. The law, in its female element, is a silhouette that plays. At what? At being ⋯ born, at being born like anybody and no body. She plays upon her generation and displays her genre, she plays out her nature and her history, and she makes a plaything of an account. In mock-playing herself she takes into account the account: she recites; and her birth is accountable to the account, the *récit*, one could even say to her: (to *la voix* ⋯) the narrative voice, *him*, *her*, *I*, *we*, the neuter genre that subjects and merges itself while giving birth to her, who lets himself be captivated by the law and escapes her, whom she escapes and whom she loves. She lets herself be put in motion, she lets herself be cited by him when, in the midst of her game, she says, pursuing an idiom that her disseminal polysemy conveys to the abyss, "I see day":

> Here is one of her games. [He has just recalled that she "once had (him) touch her knee."] She showed me a section of the space between the top of the window and the ceiling: "You are there," she said. I looked at this point with intensity. "Are you there?" I looked at it with all my power. "Well?" I felt the scars of my glaze leap, my sight became a wound, my head, a gap, a gutted bull. Suddenly she cried out: "Oh! I see day! Oh God!" etc. I protested that this game tired me enormously, but she was insatiable for my glory.

For the law to see the day is her madness, is what she loves madly like the glory, the emblazed illustration, the day of the writer, of the author who says "I," and who brings forth law to the light of day. He says that she is insaturable, insatiable for his glory—he, who is, too, author of the law to which he submits himself, he, who engenders her, he, her mother who no longer knows how to say "I" or to keep memory intact. I am the mother of law, behold my daughter's madness. It is also the Madness of the Day, for day, the word "day" in its disseminal abyss, is law, the law of the law. My daughter's madness is to want to be born—like anybody, whereas she remained a "silhouette," a shadow, a profile, her face never in view. He had said to her, to the law, in order to "tempt her": "Approach, so I can see you face to face."

Such would be the "remarkable truth" that clears an opening for the madness of day—and that appeals, like law, like madness, to the one who says "I" or I/we. Let us be attentive to this syntax of truth. She, the law, says: "The truth is that we can no longer be separated. I shall follow you everywhere, I shall live under your roof…" He: "The truth is that she appealed to me … ," she, law, but also—and this is always the principal theme of these sentences—

she, *la vérité*, truth. One cannot conceive truth without the madness of the law.

I have let myself be commanded by the law of our encounter, by the convention of our subject, notably the genre, the law of genre. This law, articulated as an I/we which is more or less autonomous in its movements, assigned us places and limits. Even though I have launched an appeal against this law, it was she who turned my appeal into a confirmation of her own glory. But she also desires ours insatiably. Submitting myself to the subject of our colloquium, as well as to its law, I sifted "An Account," *La Folie du jour*. I isolated a type, if not a genre, of reading from an infinite series of trajectories or possible courses. I have pointed out the generative principle of these courses, beginnings, and new beginnings in every sense: but from a certain point of view. Elsewhere—in accordance with other subjects, other colloquia and lectures, other I/we drawn together in one place—other trajectories could have, and have, come to light.

Nonetheless, it would be folly to draw any sort of general conclusion here. I could not say what exactly has happened in this scene, nor in my discourse or my account. What was perhaps seen, in the blink of time's eye, is a madness of law—and, therefore, of order, reason, sense, and meaning, of day: "But often" (said "I"), "I was dying without saying a thing. In time, I became convinced that I was seeing the madness of day face to face; such was the truth: light became mad, clarity took leave of her senses; she assailed me unreasonably, without a set of rules, without a goal. This discovery was like jaws clutching at my life. " I am woman, and beautiful; my daughter, the law, is mad about me. I speculate on my daughter. My daughter is mad about me; this is law.

The law is mad, she is mad about "me. " And across the madness of this day, I keep this in sight. There, this will have been my self-portrait of the genre.

The law is mad. The law is mad, is madness; but madness is not the predicate of law. There is no madness without the law; madness cannot be conceived before its relation to law. Madness is law, the law is madness. There is a general trait here: the madness of the law mad for me, the day madly in love with me, the silhouette of my daughter mad about me, her mother, etc. But *La Folie du jour*, *An* (accountless) *Account?*, carrying and miscarrying its titles, is not at all exemplary of this general trait. Not at all, not wholly. This is not an example of a general or generic whole. The whole, which begins by finishing and never finishes beginning apart from itself, the whole that stays at the edgeless boundary of itself, the whole greater and less than a whole and nothing, *An Account?* will not have been exemplary. Rather, with regard to the whole, it will have been wholly counter-exemplary.

The genre has always in all genres been able to play the role of order's principle: resemblance, analogy, identity and difference, taxonomic classification, organization and genealogical tree, order of reason, order of reasons, sense of sense, truth of truth, natural light and sense of history. Now, the test of *An Account?* brought to light the madness of genre. Madness has given birth to and thrown light on the genre in the most dazzling, most blinding sense of the word. And in the writing of *An Account?*, in literature, satirically practicing all genres, imbibing them but never allowing herself to be saturated with a catalog of genres, she, madness, has started spinning Peterson's genre-disc like a demented sun. And she does not only do so *in* literature, for in concealing the boundaries that sunder mode and genre, she has also inundated and divided the borders between literature and its others.

There, that is the whole of it, it is only what "I," so they say, here kneeling at the edge of literature, can see. In sum, the law. The law summoning: what "I" can sight and what "I" can say that I sight in this site of a recitation where I/we is.

Une traduction?

par

M

16. 德里达：《文类的法则》

(Jacques Derrida，"The Law of Genre，" 1980)

作者小识

德里达(Jacques Derrida，1930—2004)，20 世纪法国哲学家和文学理论家。他缔造"解构论"，质疑西方形而上学的根基——逻各斯中心主义，将索绪尔开创的现代语言学基本原则激进化。德里达的"解构论"不是一种自成体系的理论，而是一种针对具体文本的解读策略，其基本操作是从文本细节入手，凸显那些动摇系统结构之基本前提的元素，散播差异，激活矛盾，呈现冲突，展示符号自由游戏。

20 世纪 60 年代至 70 年代，德里达出版了"解构三部曲"：《书写与差异》(*Writing and Difference*，1967)、《声音与现象》(*Speech and Phenomena*，1973)、《论文字学》(*Of Grammatology*，1974)；80 年代，德里达热衷于文本实验，融哲学与文学于一炉，发表《散播》(*Dissemination*，1981)、《丧钟》(*Glas*，1986)、《明信片：从苏格拉底到弗洛伊德，甚至更多》(*The Postcard: From Socrates to Freud and Beyond*，1987)；90 年代以后，德里达开启了"伦理学转向"，呼唤"宗教回归"，将解构论贯彻到对伦理、政治、宗教的思考中。这方面的代表作包括《马克思的幽灵》(*Specters of Marx*，1994)、《友爱的政治学》(*The Politics of Friendship*，1994)、《宗教行动》(*Acts of Religion*，2002)。21 世纪初，世界政治格局的动荡，尤其是"9·11 事件"，催迫德里达思考当代世界政治，反思暴力、主权、战争、种族隔离及其形而上学前提，这方面的代表作包括《论无赖》(*Rogues*，2005)、《野兽与主权》(*The Beast and the Sovereign*，2009)。

背景略说

何谓"解构"？"解构"不是一个新词，在汉代就已经非常流行了。在古代汉语中，"解构"含义有二。一是指附会造作。《淮南子·俶真训》："孰肯解构人间之事，以物烦其性命乎？"高诱注："解构，犹合会也。"二是指离间。《后汉书·窦融传》："嚣自知失河西之助，族祸将及，欲设间离之说，乱惑真心，转相解构，以成其奸。"那么，从德里达那里舶入中国的"解构"究竟是什么意思呢？

首先，作为一种思想史的章法，"解构"就是"无法恢复源始在场的绝对明证性使我们必须涉及绝对的过去"（《论文字学》第一章）。"解构"就是追问被历史、传统遮蔽的东西。这种思想史观直接源自海德格尔："随着追问不断向前驱迫，直有一道更其源始更其浩瀚的境域展开出来，那便是或能求得存在是什么这一问题的答案的境域。"（《存在与时间》，第6节）德里达自己发挥说："解构哲学，恐怕就是以那种最忠实、最内在的方式去思考哲学概念所具有一定结构的那种谱系，同时也是从某种它无法确定、无法命名的外部着手，以求确定那被其历史所遮蔽或禁止的东西，而这种历史是通过一些对利害关系的压抑而成就的。"（《书写与差异》，"访谈代序"）

其次，作为一种文本解读策略，解构宣称"本文之外别无一物"。这个命题一旦变成公式、变成口号就相当危险、相当荒谬，仿佛它就是在明火执仗地传扬虚无主义、道德相对主义。可是不然，德里达的初衷是提醒读者，面对文本，不要轻易相信蕴含于其中的意义之权威性，不要将意义之权威性归给作者的思想、意图、情感。说到底，意义不是现存的，而是发明的、生产的，而且趋向于无限，总是被延宕在能指的无尽游戏之中。

再次，"解构"作为一种阐释路径，是指超越存在、上帝、本质、人文主义、人类学种族主义，尝试思考那种不可还原的差异及其共同渊源——"延异"。通俗地、形象地说，作为阐释方法，解构就是隐约地显现意义历史形态的受精、孕育、成型和分娩的全部生命化过程而已。

然后，"解构"作为一种独特的书写风格，是指同时写作多种文本，多层次解构文本，文本之上叠加文本，在踪迹之上再留踪迹。偶然之际，德里达从自己卷轶浩繁的文字之中拈出"灰烬"，而"灰烬"令人联想到"二战"期间纳粹对犹太种族的"最后解决"。灭绝、驱赶、焚尸和献祭，"灰烬"便与这些惨痛的记忆和无辜的苦难紧密相连。解构用"灰烬"喻指"文本"，呈现出一种典型的启示录式的书写风格，它是一种要为人类的万种苦难立言的终极诉求。在"灰烬"上书写，就是将灵性贯注于生命的残存踪迹，从而让这些踪迹为那些绝对销毁的证据提供坚实的证据，为那些完全消逝的爱留下忧伤的剪影。总之，作为写作风格的解构，那是一种守护着思想尊严的疯狂，而不是一种临水鉴影的无聊自恋。

最后，解构作为一种语言文化景观，是"一种以上的语言"（more than one language）。哪里有"一种以上的语言"的体验，哪里就有解构。世界上每天都有物种在灭绝，都有泰古冰川在消融，都有原始森林在萎缩，同样都有部落及其语言在消逝。然而，世界上毕竟存在着"一种以上的语言"，一种语言内部也存在着"一种以上的语言"。这就是庄子所说的"夫吹万不同，而使其自己也，咸其自取，怒者其谁邪？"（《齐物论》）。此等"天籁"境界，即语言的多样性，恰恰是"解构"尤为关切的"大道"。

基本内容

在《文类的法则》中，德里达解构了文类区分的法则，从而动摇了文类的稳定性。讨论文类及其法则，被德里达看作一种"文学行为"，即在文学建制之内，探讨文学空间秩序及其边界的模糊性。那么，文学是一种什么样的建制呢？德里达说，那是一种游弋在哲学与诗歌之间的奇特建制。"文学是一种允许人们以任何方式讲述任何事情的建制。"文学的空间不仅是建制的虚构，而且是虚构的建制。它不仅要求讲述一切，而且允许任何人以一切可能的方式讲述一切。于是，文学建制天然就是规避、质疑、侵蚀和解构任何禁令的建制。讲述一切，就必须逃脱禁令。文类之法则，具有无视法则和取消法则的特权。"文类之法，法无定法，然后知非法，法也。"诗人与哲人，在文学上达成共识，那就是要在"讲述一切"的经验之中去思考"文类的法则"及其本质，意识到"文学建制是一种没有建制的建制"。

一旦论涉"类型"，即讨论到文学风格、文学门类，以及种族、性别与阶级，就一定涉及法则问题。法则赋予某种规范化和标准化以正当性，也就是说，必须首先假设这种类型的区分具可操作性，并且在互不交叉、互不矛盾的前提下进行。可是，文本的现实是能指符号的漂移游戏，文类的法则在从一个语境到另一个语境的转换中自我解构了。德里达就此提出一种"关于类型法则的法则"，这一法则是指类型之间的交叉重叠，文类彼此混杂，法则互相寄生。没有任何一个类型是纯洁的，也没有任何一种法则是确定的。用数学术语说，就是任何一种类型都不属于某种集合，但参与了这种集合，不属于该集合的子集合也同时是该集合内部的函项。

所以，德里达认为，一旦我们说出"文类"，就意味着一种界限，以及超越界限的潜在欲望。正如我们说到"法律"，就意味着一种禁令，以及僭越禁令的潜在意志。德里达举出一些极端作家的难以分类的作品，证明文类互相渗透，彼此污染，界限越来越模糊，禁令越来越微弱。"谈到文类，谈到法律，我们实际上是在参与一场赌博，发出一种挑战，或者下了一次根本不可能赢的赌注。"通过解读法国作家布朗肖(Maurice Blanchot)的作品《白日的疯狂》(*La Folie du jour*)，德里达要证明文类会变异、裂变、解体、扩散，一句话，文类系统会自我解构。布朗肖的作品描述了一个女人："在慌乱中，我拆卸了自身，把自己撕成碎片。我把自己的血液和隐私统统分给了他们。我把整个宇宙都给了他们，我将把自己的心声暴露在光天化日之下。"德里达为这个女人着迷，认为她/阴性/女性就是法律/文类法则的化身。"她就是一条法则，法律，属于女性，在女性之中化为乌有。"她的疯狂迷乱，就是阅读行为的特征。这是一种文类的疯狂，"疯狂以其最令人眼花缭乱、最使人目瞪口呆的方式生成并显露了文类"。

在《白日的疯狂》中，布朗肖展示了叙述者"我"与"法"之间的悲剧性冲突。其实，这种冲突既是男性之法与女性之法的冲突，又是女性之法的内在冲突。法非自然，亦非习俗，而是一种伪装成习俗的自然，或伪装成自然的习俗。质言之，法就是双重伪装：法律的代言人(小说中的医学专家)所执行的法律，以及神秘女人所代表的灵魂大法。在一个由极端"菲勒斯中心主义"主导的传统中，这两种法则必然冲突，冲突的结果是"法律疯狂"：

> 法律彻底疯狂了。法律彻底疯狂了，法律就是疯狂，但疯狂并非法律的源始意义。没有法律，就没有疯狂，疯狂必须和法律结合在一起才可以理解。这就是法律，法律就是疯狂。

平心而论，德里达的观点诗意盎然、飘逸潇洒，但他夸大了文类的变异性和断裂性，而忽视了文类系统的稳定性和连续性。

拓展讨论

谈到文类及其法则，宜于引入时间维度，在历史进化中去省察文类系统。归岸(Claudio Guillen)的观点是，文类与系统互相强化，使对方固定以致永恒。一方面，像悲剧、喜剧这么一些概念一样，系统支撑着文类，文类归属于系统；另一方面，以新模子和现存文类的结构关系为基础，一个系统主动吸收新的作品，赋予其作为一个新规范模子的合法性，使之成为一个文类。这段话比较晦涩，意思是文类系统既具有稳定性又具有开放性，而开放性尤其值得注意。从历史进化角度说，相对于一个文类系统，新出现的作品代表着一个新模子，一个新模子引发出新文类，新文类要求合法性，而这对现存文类系统不啻是一种挑战。现存系统会吸收和同化这种新模子，赋予其作为文类的合法性。这里特别值得注意的是"新模子"和"规范模子"之间的辩证关系。新模子挑战规范模子，而规范模子反过来吸收新模子，赋予其作为文类的合法性，而使新文类也成为规范模子。文类是一个引发新系统的模子，这表明文类系统具有开放性。①

比较文学家叶维廉改造归岸（Claudio Guillen）的文类理论，将"模子"概念延伸到文类系统之外，应用于文化系统之间，而提出了"东西方比较文学中模子的运用"问题。首先，在文化系统中，一个模子就是一种结构化系统化的思维方式，一种习焉不察的文化无意识。有多少种文化传统，就有多少种模子。从一个模子去看非我族类的文化，则可能导致井蛙之见，将自己的偏见强加于他者身上，而歪曲他者的形象。比如西方人以欧洲为中心想象中国和远东，从而建立起了作为偏见系统的东方学（Orientalism），其中隐含着文化帝国主义的霸道意识。其次，"模子"所采取的样式繁多，有观念模子、美学模子、伦理模子、语言模子、修辞模子。从比较文学的角度看，一个民族的文学均有其独特的模子系统，如文类、主题、母题、制度、神话原型、人物典范、修辞套式等。如果一个模子不适合于另一个文化传统下的文学，那么，如何去发现跨文化的共同诗学（common poetics）呢？在三个以上的不同文化系统中，能否找到一组共同的模子呢？最后，在比较研究中，当务之急是放弃从一个模子看世界的立场。文化的交流正是要开拓更大的视野，互相调整，互相包容。文化交流不是以一个既定的形态去征服另一种文化的形态，而是在相互尊重的态度下，对双方本身的形态做寻根的了解。

延伸阅读

1. 德里达：《书写与差异》，张宁译，北京，生活·读书·新知三联书店，2001。该书是德里达草创"解构论"时期的代表作。其中汇聚的论文，用德里达自己的话说，"它们的共同特征是将我同时导向差异极大的哲学与文学领域的

---

① 参见胡继华：《比较文学经典导读》，154～192 页，北京，北京师范大学出版社，2015。

某种方式，我在阅读不同的哲学与文学文本，也就是福柯、勒维纳斯、阿尔托或巴塔耶等的文本的同时，开始展开某种一般的哲学阅读与解释策略"。

2. 德里达：《〈友爱的政治学〉及其他》，胡继华等译，长春，吉林人民出版社，2006。德里达解构了以"友爱"为基础的政治哲学传统，同时也回应了施米特的"政治神学"，展现了"未来民族"的可能景观。

17. Three Women's Texts and a Critique of Imperialism (1985)
By Gayatri C. Spivak

It should not be possible to read nineteenth-century British literature without remembering that imperialism, understood as England's social mission, was a crucial part of the cultural representation of England to the English. The role of literature in the production of cultural representation should not be ignored. These two obvious "facts" continue to be disregarded in the reading of nineteenth-century British literature. This itself attests to the continuing success of the imperialist project, displaced and dispersed into more modern forms.

If these "facts" were remembered, not only in the study of British literature but in the study of the literatures of the European colonizing cultures of the great age of imperialism, we would produce a narrative, in literary history, of the "worlding" of what is now called "the Third World." To consider the Third World as distant cultures, exploited but with rich intact literary heritages waiting to be recovered, interpreted, and curricularized in English translation fosters the emergence of "the Third World" as a signifier that allows us to forget that "worlding," even as it expands the empire of the literary discipline. ①

It seems particularly unfortunate when the emergent perspective of feminist criticism reproduces the axioms of imperialism. A basically isolationist admiration for the literature of the female subject in Europe and Anglo-America establishes the high feminist norm. It is supported and operated by an information-retrieval approach to "Third World" literature which often employs a deliberately "nontheoretical" methodology with self-conscious rectitude.

In this essay, I will attempt to examine the operation of the "worlding" of

---

① My notion of the "worlding of a world" upon what must be assumed to be uninscribed earth is a vulgarization of Martin Heidegger's idea; see "The Origin of the Work of Art," *Poetry, Language, Thought, trans.* Albert Hofstadter (New York, 1977), pp. 17-87.

what is today "the Third World" by what has become a cult text of feminism: *Jane Eyre*. ① I plot the novel's reach and grasp, and locate its structural motors. I read *Wide Sargasso Sea* as *Jane Eyre*'s reinscription and *Frankenstein* as an analysis—even a deconstruction—of a "worlding" such as *Jane Eyre*'s. ②

I need hardly mention that the object of my investigation is the printed book, not its "author." To make such a distinction is, of course to ignore the lessons of deconstruction. A deconstructive critical approach would loosen the binding of the book, undo the opposition between verbal text and the biography of the named subject "Charlotte Brontë," and see the two as each other's "scene of writing." In such a reading, the life that writes itself as "my life" is as much a production in psychosocial space (other names can be found) as the book that is written by the holder of that named life—a book that is then consigned to what is most often recognized as genuinely "social": the world of publication and distribution. ③ To touch Brontë's "life" in such a way, however, would be too risky here. We must rather strategically take shelter in an essentialism which, not wishing to lose the important advantages won by U. S. mainstream feminism, will continue to honor the suspect binary oppositions—book and author, individual and history—and start with an assurance of the following sort: my readings here do not seek to undermine the excellence of the individual artist. If even minimally successful, the readings will incite a degree of rage against the imperialist narrativization of history, that it should produce so abject a script for her. I provide these assurances to allow myself some room to situate feminist individualism in its historical determination rather than simply to

_____

① See Charlotte Brontë, *Jane Eyre* (New York, 1960); all further references to this work, abbreviated *JE*, will be included in the text.

② See Jean Rhys, *Wide Sargasso Sea* (Harmondsworth, 1966); all further references to this work, abbreviated *WSS*, will be included in the text. And see Mary Shelley, *Frankenstein; or, The Modern Prometheus* (New York, 1965); all further references to this work, abbreviated *F*, will be included in the text.

③ I have tried to do this in my essay "Unmaking and Making in *To the Lighthouse*," in *Women and Language in Literature and Society*, ed. Sally McConnell-Ginet, Ruth Borker, and Nelly Furman (New York, 1980), pp. 310-327.

canonize it as feminism as such.

Sympathetic U. S. feminists have remarked that I do not do justice to Jane Eyre's subjectivity. A word of explanation is perhaps in order. The broad strokes of my presuppositions are that what is at stake, for feminist individualism in the age of imperialism, is precisely the making of human beings, the constitution and "interpellation" of the subject not only as individual but as "individualist."[①] This stake is represented on two registers: childbearing and soul making. The first is domestic-society-through-sexual-reproduction cathected as "companionate love"; the second is the imperialist project cathected as civil-society-through-social-mission. As the female individualist, not-quite/not-male, articulates herself in shifting relationship to what is at stake, the "native female" as such (*within* discourse, *as* a signifier) is excluded from any share in this emerging norm.[②] If we read this account from an isolationist perspective in a "metropolitan" context, we see nothing there but the psychobiography of the militant female subject. In a reading such as mine, in contrast, the effort is to wrench oneself away from the mesmerizing focus of the "subject-constitution" of the female individualist.

To develop further the notion that my stance need not be an accusing one, I will

---

① As always, I take my formula from Louis Althusser, "Ideology an Ideological State Apparatuses (Notes towards an Investigation)," "*Lenin and Philosophy" and Other Essays*, trans. Ben Brewster (New York, 1971), pp. 127-186. For an acute differentiation between the individual and individualism, see V. N. Vološinov, *Marxism and the Philosophy of Language*, trans. Ladislav Matejka and I. R. Titunik, Studies in Language, vol. 1 (New York, 1973), pp. 93-94 and 152-153. For a "straight" analysis of the roots and ramifications of English "individualism," see C. B. MacPherson, *The Political Theory of Possessive Individualism: Hobbes to Locke* (Oxford, 1962). I am grateful to Jonathan Rée for bringing this book to my attention and for giving a careful reading of all but the very end of the present essay.

② I am constructing an analogy with Homi Bhabha's powerful notion of "not-quite/ not-white" in his "Of Mimicry and Man: The Ambiguity of Colonial Discourse," October 28 (Spring 1984): 132. I should also add that I use the word "native" here in reaction to the term "Third World Woman." It cannot, of course, apply with equal historical justice to both the West Indian and the Indian contexts nor to contexts of imperialism by transportation.

refer to a passage from Roberto Fernández Retamar's "Caliban."[1] José Enrique Rodó had argued in 1900 that the model for the Latin American intellectual in relationship to Europe could be Shakespeare's Ariel.[2] In 1971 Retamar, denying the possibility of an identifiable "Latin American Culture," recast the model as Caliban. Not surprisingly, this powerful exchange still excludes any specific consideration of the civilizations of the Maya, the Aztecs, the Incas, or the smaller nations of what is now called Latin America. Let us note carefully that, at this stage of my argument, this "conversation" between Europe and Latin America (without a specific consideration of the political economy of the "worlding" of the "native") provides a sufficient thematic description of our attempt to confront the ethnocentric and reverse-ethnocentric benevolent double bind (that is, considering the "native" as object for enthusiastic information-retrieval and thus denying its own "worlding") that I sketched in my opening paragraphs.

In a moving passage in "Caliban," Retamar locates both Caliban and Ariel in the postcolonial intellectual:

> There is no real Ariel-Caliban polarity: both are slaves in the hands of Prospero, the foreign magician. But Caliban is the rude and unconquerable master of the island, while Ariel, a creature of the air, although also a child of the isle, is the intellectual.
>
> The deformed Caliban—enslaved, robbed of his island, and taught the language by Prospero-rebukes him thus: "You taught me language, and my profit on't/Is, I know how to curse." ["C," pp. 28, 11]

As we attempt to unlearn our so-called privilege as Ariel and "seek from [a certain] Caliban the honor of a place in his rebellious and glorious ranks," we do not ask that our students and colleagues should emulate us but that they

---

① See Roberto Fernández Retamar, "Caliban: Notes towards a Discussion of Culture in Our America," trans. Lynn Garafola, David Arthur McMurray, and Robert Márquez, *Massachusetts Review* 15 (Winter-Spring 1974): 7-72; all further references to this work, abbreviated "C," will be included in the text.

② See José Enrique Rodó, *Ariel*, ed. Gordon Brotherston (Cambridge, 1967).

should attend to us ("C," p. 72). If, however, we are driven by a nostalgia for lost origins, we too run the risk of effacing the "native" and stepping forth as "the real Caliban," of forgetting that he is a name in a play, an inaccessible blankness circumscribed by an interpretable text. ① The stagings of Caliban work alongside the narrativization of history: claiming to *be* Caliban legitimizes the very individualism that we must persistently attempt to undermine from within.

Elizabeth Fox-Genovese, in an article on history and women's history, shows us how to define the historical moment of feminism in the West in terms of female access to individualism. ② The battle for female individualism plays itself out within the larger theater of the establishment of meritocratic individualism, indexed in the aesthetic field by the ideology of "the creative imagination." Fox-Genovese's presupposition will guide us into the beautifully orchestrated opening of *Jane Eyre*.

It is a scene of the marginalization and privatization of the protagonist: "There was no possibility of taking a walk that day ... Out-door exercise was now out of the question. I was glad of it," Brontë writes (*JE*, p. 9). The movement continues as Jane breaks the rules of the appropriate topography of withdrawal. The family at the center withdraws into the sanctioned architectural space of the withdrawing room or drawing room; Jane inserts herself—"I slipped in"—into the margin—"A small breakfast-room *adjoined* the drawing room" (*JE*, p. 9; my emphasis).

The manipulation of the domestic inscription of space within the upwardly mobilizing currents of the eighteenth- and nineteenth-century bourgeoisie in England and France is well known. It seems fitting that the place to which Jane withdraws is not only not the withdrawing room but also not the dining room, the sanctioned place of family meals. Nor is it the library, the appropriate place for reading. The breakfast room "contained a book-case" (*JE*, p. 9). As

----

① For an elaboration of "an inaccessible blankness circumscribed by an interpretable text," see my "Can the Subaltern Speak?" *Marxist Interpretations of Culture*, ed. Cary Nelson (Urbana, Ill. , forthcoming).

② See Elizabeth Fox-Genovese, "Placing Women's History in History," *New Left Review* 133 (May-June 1982): 5-29.

Rudolph Ackerman wrote in his *Repository* (1823), one of the many manuals of taste in circulation in nineteenth-century England, these low bookcases and stands were designed to "contain all the books that may be desired for a sitting-room without reference to the library."① Even in this already triply off-center place, "having drawn the red moreen curtain nearly close, I [Jane] was shrined in double retirement" (*JE*, pp. 9-10).

Here in Jane's self-marginalized uniqueness, the reader becomes her accomplice: the reader and Jane are united—both are reading. Yet Jane still preserves her odd privilege, for she continues never quite doing the proper thing in its proper place. She cares little for reading what is *meant* to be read: the "letter-press." *She* reads the pictures. The power of this singular hermeneutics is precisely that it can make the outside inside. "At intervals, while turning over the leaves of my book, I studied the aspect of that winter afternoon." Under "the clear panes of glass," the rain no longer penetrates, "the drear November day" is rather a one-dimensional "aspect" to be "studied," not decoded like the "letter-press" but, like pictures, deciphered by the unique creative imagination of the marginal individualist (*JE*, p. 10).

Before following the track of this unique imagination, let us consider the suggestion that the progress of *Jane Eyre* can be charted through a sequential arrangement of the family/counter-family dyad. In the novel, we encounter, first, the Reeds as the legal family and Jane, the late Mr. Reed's sister's daughter, as the representative of a near incestuous counter-family; second, the Brocklehursts, who run the school Jane is sent to, as the legal family and Jane, Miss Temple, and Helen Burns as a counter-family that falls short because it is only a community of women; third, Rochester and the mad Mrs. Rochester as the legal family and Jane and Rochester as the illicit counter-family. Other items may be added to the thematic chain in this sequence: Rochester and Céline Varens as structurally functional counter-family; Rochester and Blanche Ingram as dissimulation of legality—and so on. It is during this sequence that

① Rudolph Ackerman, *The Repository of Arts, Literature, Commerce, Manufactures Fashions, and Politics*, (London, 1823), p. 310.

Jane is moved from the counter-family to the family-in-law. In the next sequence, it is Jane who restores full family status to the as-yet-incomplete community of siblings, the Riverses. The final sequence of the book is a *community of families*, with Jane, Rochester, and their children at the center.

In terms of the narrative energy of the novel, how is Jane moved from the place of the counter-family to the family-in-law? It is the active ideology of imperialism that provides the discursive field.

(My working definition of "discursive field" must assume the existence of discrete "systems of signs" at hand in the socius, each based on a specific axiomatics. I am identifying these systems as discursive fields. "Imperialism as social mission" generates the possibility of one such axiomatics. How the individual artist taps the discursive field at hand with a sure touch, if not with transhistorical clairvoyance, in order to make the narrative structure move I hope to demonstrate through the following example. It is crucial that we extend our analysis of this example beyond the minimal diagnosis of "racism.")

Let us consider the figure of Bertha Mason, a figure produced by the axiomatics of imperialism. Through Bertha Mason, the white Jamaican Creole, Brontë renders the human/animal frontier as acceptably indeterminate, so that a good greater than the letter of the Law can be broached. Here is the celebrated passage, given in the voice of Jane:

> In the deep shade, at the further end of the room, a figure ran backwards and forwards. What it was, whether beast or human being, one could not ... tell: it grovelled, seemingly, on all fours; it snatched and growled like some strange wild animal: but it was covered with clothing, and a quantity of dark, grizzled hair, wild as a mane, hid its head and face. [*JE*, p. 295]

In a matching passage, given in the voice of Rochester speaking to Jane, Brontë presents the imperative for a shift beyond the Law as divine injunction rather than human motive. In the terms of my essay, we might say that this is the register not of mere marriage or sexual reproduction but of Europe and its not-yet-human Other, of soul making. The field of imperial conquest is here inscribed as Hell:

> "One night I had been awakened by her yells … it was a fiery West Indian night…
>
> "'This life,' said I at last, 'is hell! —this is the air—those are the sounds of the bottomless pit! I *have a right* to deliver myself from it if I can… Let me break away, and go home to God!' …
>
> "A wind fresh from Europe blew over the ocean and rushed through the open casement: the storm broke, streamed, thundered, blazed, and the air grew pure … It was true Wisdom that consoled me in that hour, and showed me the right path…
>
> "The sweet wind from Europe was still whispering in the refreshed leaves, and the Atlantic was thundering in glorious liberty…
>
> "'Go,' said Hope, 'and live again in Europe… You have done all that God and Humanity require of you. '"[*JE*, pp. 310-311; my emphasis]

It is the unquestioned ideology of imperialist axiomatics, then, that conditions Jane's move from the counter-family set to the set of the family-in-law. Marxist critics such as Terry Eagleton have seen this only in terms of the ambiguous *class* position of the governess. ① Sandra Gilbert and Susan Gubar, on the other hand, have seen Bertha Mason only in psychological terms, as Jane's dark double. ②

I will not enter the critical debates that offer themselves here. Instead, I will develop the suggestion that nineteenth-century feminist individualism could conceive of a "greater" project than access to the closed circle of the nuclear family. This is the project of soul making beyond "mere" sexual reproduction. Here the native "subject" is not almost an animal but rather the object of what

---

① See Terry Eagleton, *Myths of Power: A Marxist Study of the Brontës* (London, 1975); this is one of the general presuppositions of his book.

② See Sandra M. Gilbert and Susan Gubar, *The Madwoman in the Attic: The Woman Writer and the Nineteenth-Century Literary Imagination* (New Haven, Conn. , 1979), pp. 360-362.

might be termed the terrorism of the categorical imperative.

I am using "Kant" in this essay as a metonym for the most flexible ethical moment in the European eighteenth century. Kant words the categorical imperative, conceived as the universal moral law given by pure reason, in this way: "In all creation every thing one chooses and over which one has any power, may be used *merely as means*; man alone, and with him every rational creature, is an *end in himself*." It is thus a moving displacement of Christian ethics from religion to philosophy. As Kant writes: "With this agrees very well the possibility of such a command as: *Love God above everything*, *and thy neighbor as thy self*. For as a command it requires respect for a law which *commands love* and does not leave it to our own arbitrary choice to make this our principle."①

The "categorical" in Kant cannot be adequately represented in determinately grounded action. The dangerous transformative power of philosophy, however, is that its formal subtlety can be travestied in the service of the state. Such a travesty in the case of the categorical imperative can justify the imperialist project by producing the following formula: *make* the heathen into a human so that he can be treated as an end in himself. ② This project is presented as a sort of tangent in *Jane Eyre*, a tangent that escapes the closed circle of the *narrative* conclusion. The tangent narrative is the story of St. John Rivers, who is granted the important task of concluding the *text*.

At the novel's end, the *allegorical* language of Christian psychobiography—rather than the textually constituted and seemingly *private* grammar of

---

① Immanuel Kant, *Critique of Practical Reason*, The *"Critique of Pure Reason*," the *"Critique of Practical Reason"* and Other Ethical Treatises, the *"Critique of Judgement*," trans. J. M. D. Meiklejohn et al. (Chicago, 1952), pp. 328, 326.

② I have tried to justify the reduction of sociohistorical problems to formulas or propositions in my essay "Can the Subaltern Speak?" The "travesty" I speak of does not befall the Kantian ethic in its purity as an accident but rather exists within its lineaments as a possible supplement. On the register of the human being as child rather than heathen, my formula can be found, for example, in "What Is Enlightenment?" in Kant, *"Foundations of the Metaphysics of Morals*," *"What Is Enlightenment?"* and a Passage from *"The Metaphysics of Morals*," trans. and ed. Lewis White Beck (Chicago, 1950). I have profited from discussing Kant with Jonathan Rée.

the creative imagination which we noted in the novel's opening—marks the inaccessibility of the imperialist project as such to the nascent "feminist" scenario. The concluding passage of *Jane Eyre* places St. John Rivers within the fold of *Pilgrim's Progress*. Eagleton pays no attention to this but accepts the novel's ideological lexicon, which establishes St. John Rivers' heroism by identifying a life in Calcutta with an unquestioning choice of death. Gilbert and Gubar, by calling *Jane Eyre* "Plain Jane's progress," see the novel as simply replacing the male protagonist with the female. They do not notice the distance between sexual reproduction and soul making, both actualized by the unquestioned idiom of imperialist presuppositions evident in the last part of *Jane Eyre*:

> Firm, faithful, and devoted, full of energy, and zeal, and truth, [St. John Rivers] labours for his race … His is the sternness of the warrior Greatheart, who guards his pilgrim convoy from the onslaught of Apollyon… His is the ambition of the high master-spirit[s] … who stand without fault before the throne of God; who share the last mighty victories of the Lamb; who are called, and chosen, and faithful. [*JE*, p. 455]

Earlier in the novel, St. John Rivers himself justifies the project: "My vocation? My great work? … My hopes of being numbered in the band who have merged all ambitions in the glorious one of bettering their race—of carrying knowledge into the realms of ignorance—of substituting peace for war—freedom for bondage—religion for superstition—the hope of heaven for the fear of hell?" (*JE*, p. 376). Imperialism and its territorial and subject-constituting project are a violent deconstruction of these oppositions.

When Jean Rhys, born on the Caribbean island of Dominica, read *Jane Eyre* as a child, she was moved by Bertha Mason: "I thought I'd try to write her a life."[①] *Wide Sargasso Sea*, the slim novel published in 1965, at the end of Rhys' long

---

① Jean Rhys, in an interview with Elizabeth Vreeland, quoted in Nancy Harrison, *An Introduction to the Writing Practice of Jean Rhys: The Novel as Women's Text* (Rutherford, N. J., forthcoming). This is an excellent, detailed study of Rhys.

career, is that "life. "

I have suggested that Bertha's function in *Jane Eyre* is to render indeterminate the boundary between human and animal and thereby to weaken her entitlement under the spirit if not the letter of the Law. When Rhys rewrites the scene in *Jane Eyre* where Jane hears "a snarling, snatching sound, almost like a dog quarrelling" and then encounters a bleeding Richard Mason (*JE*, p. 210), she keeps Bertha's humanity, indeed her sanity as critic of imperialism, intact. Grace Poole, another character originally in *Jane Eyre*, describes the incident to Bertha in *Wide Sargasso Sea*: "So you don't remember that you attacked this gentleman with a knife? ⋯ I didn't hear all he said except 'I cannot interfere legally between yourself and your husband'. It was when he said 'legally' that you flew at him" (*WSS*, p. 150). In Rhys' retelling, it is the dissimulation that Bertha discerns in the word "legally"—not an innate bestiality—that prompts her violent reaction.

In the figure of Antoinette, whom in *Wide Sargasso Sea* Rochester violently renames Bertha, Rhys suggests that so intimate a thing as personal and human identity might be determined by the politics of imperialism. Antoinette, as a white Creole child growing up at the time of emancipation in Jamaica, is caught between the English imperialist and the black native. In recounting Antoinette's development, Rhys reinscribes some thematics of Narcissus.

There are, noticeably, many images of mirroring in the text. I will quote one from the first section. In this passage, Tia is the little black servant girl who is Antoinette's close companion: "We had eaten the same food, slept side by side, bathed in the same river. As I ran, I thought, I will live with Tia and I will be like her⋯ When I was close I saw the jagged stone in her hand but I did not see her throw it⋯ We stared at each other, blood on my face, tears on hers. It was as if I saw myself. Like in a looking glass" (*WSS*, p. 38).

A progressive sequence of dreams reinforces this mirror imagery. In its second occurrence, the dream is partially set in a *hortus conclusus*, or "enclosed garden"—Rhys uses the phrase (*WSS*, p. 50)—a Romance rewriting of the

Narcissus topos as the place of encounter with Love. [1] In the enclosed garden, Antoinette encounters not Love but a strange threatening voice that says merely "in here," inviting her into a prison which masquerades as the legalization of love (*WSS*, p. 50).

In Ovid's *Metamorphoses*, Narcissus' madness is disclosed when he recognizes his Other as his self: "Iste ego sum."[2] Rhys makes Antoinette see her *self* as her Other, Brontë's Bertha. In the last section of *Wide Sargasso Sea*, Antoinette acts out *Jane Eyre*'s conclusion and recognizes herself as the so-called ghost in Thornfield Hall: "I went into the hall again with the tall candle in my hand. It was then that I saw her—the ghost. The woman with streaming hair. She was surrounded by a gilt frame but I knew her" (*WSS*, p. 154). The gilt frame encloses a mirror: as Narcissus' pool reflects the selfed Other, so this "pool" reflects the Othered self. Here the dream sequence ends, with an invocation of none other than Tia, the Other that could not be selfed, because the fracture of imperialism rather than the Ovidian pool intervened. (I will return to this difficult point.) "That was the third time I had my dream, and it ended … I called 'Tia' and jumped and woke" (*WSS*, p. 155). It is now, at the very end of the book, that Antoinette/Bertha can say: "Now at last I know why I was brought here and what I have to do" (*WSS*, pp. 155-156). We can read this as her having been brought into the England of Brontë's novel: "This cardboard house"—a book between cardboard covers—"where I walk at night is not England" (*WSS*, p. 148). In this fictive England, she must play out her role, act out the transformation of her "self" into that fictive Other, set fire to the house and kill herself, so that Jane Eyre can become the feminist individualist heroine of British fiction. I must read this as an allegory of the general epistemic violence of imperialism, the construction of a self-immolating colonial subject for the glorification of the social mission of the colonizer. At least Rhys

---

[1]   See Louise Vinge, *The Narcissus Theme in Western European Literature Up to the Early Nineteenth Century*, trans. Robert Dewsnap et al. (Lund, 1967), chap. 5.

[2]   For a detailed study of this text, see John Brenkman, "Narcissus in the Text," *Georgia Review* 30 (Summer 1976): 293-327.

sees to it that the woman from the colonies is not sacrificed as an insane animal for her sister's consolation.

Critics have remarked that *Wide Sargasso Sea* treats the Rochester character with understanding and sympathy. Indeed, he narrates the entire middle section of the book. Rhys makes it clear that he is a victim of the patriarchal inheritance law of entailment rather than of a father's natural preference for the firstborn: in *Wide Sargasso Sea*, Rochester's situation is clearly that of a younger son dispatched to the colonies to buy an heiress. If in the case of Antoinette and her identity, Rhys utilizes the thematics of Narcissus, in the case of Rochester and his patrimony, she touches on the thematics of Oedipus. (In this she has her finger on our "historical moment." If, in the nineteenth century, subject-constitution is represented as childbearing and soul making, in the twentieth century psychoanalysis allows the West to plot the itinerary of the subject from Narcissus [the "imaginary"] to Oedipus [the "symbolic"]. This subject, however, is the normative male subject. In Rhys' reinscription of these themes, divided between the female and the male protagonist, feminism and a critique of imperialism become complicit.)

In place of the "wind from Europe" scene, Rhys substitutes the scenario of a suppressed letter to a father, a letter which would be the "correct" explanation of the tragedy of the book. ① "I thought about the letter which should have been written to England a week ago. Dear Father … " (*WSS*, p. 57). This is the first instance: the letter not written. Shortly afterward:

Dear Father. The thirty thousand pounds have been paid to me without question or condition. No provision made for her (that must be seen to) … I will never be a disgrace to you or to my dear brother the son you love. No begging letters, no mean requests. None of the furtive shabby manoeuvres of a younger son. I have sold my soul or you have sold it, and

---

① See, e. g. , Thomas F. Staley, *Jean Rhys: A Critical Study* (Austin, Tex. 1979), pp. 108-116; it is interesting to note Staley's masculist discomfort with this and his consequent dissatisfaction with Rhys' novel.

after all is it such a bad bargain? The girl is thought to be beautiful, she is beautiful. And yet ··· [WSS, p. 59]

This is the second instance: the letter not sent. The formal letter is uninteresting; I will quote only a part of it:

Dear Father, we have arrived from Jamaica after an uncomfortable few days. This little estate in the Windward Islands is part of the family property and Antoinette is much attached to it ··· All is well and has gone according to your plans and wishes. I dealt of course with Richard Mason ··· He seemed to become attached to me and trusted me completely. This place is very beautiful but my illness has left me too exhausted to appreciate it fully. I will write again in a few days' time. [WSS, p. 63]

And so on.

Rhys' version of the Oedipal exchange is ironic, not a closed circle. We cannot know if the letter actually reaches its destination. "I wondered how they got their letters posted," the Rochester figure muses. "I folded mine and put it into a drawer of the desk··· There are blanks in my mind that cannot be filled up" (WSS, p. 64). It is as if the text presses us to note the analogy between letter and mind.

Rhys denies to Brontë's Rochester the one thing that is supposed to be secured in the Oedipal relay: the Name of the Father, or the patronymic. In *Wide Sargasso Sea*, the character corresponding to Rochester has no name. His writing of the final version of the letter to his father is supervised, in fact, by an image of the *loss* of the patronymic: "There was a crude bookshelf made of three shingles strung together over the desk and I looked at the books, Byron's poems, novels by Sir Walter Scott, *Confessions of an Opium Eater* ··· and on the last shelf, *Life and Letters of* ··· The rest was eaten away" (WSS, p. 63).

Wide Sargasso Sea marks with uncanny clarity the limits of its own discourse in Christophine, Antoinette's black nurse. We may perhaps surmise the distance between *Jane Eyre* and *Wide Sargasso Sea* by remarking that

Christophine's unfinished story is the tangent to the latter narrative, as St. John Rivers' story is to the former. Christophine is not a native of Jamaica; she is from Martinique. Taxonomically, she belongs to the category of the good servant rather than that of the pure native. But within these borders, Rhys creates a powerfully suggestive figure.

Christophine is the first interpreter and named speaking subject in the text. "The Jamaican ladies had never approved of my mother, 'because she pretty like pretty self' Christophine said," we read in the book's opening paragraph (*WSS*, p. 15). I have taught this book five times, once in France, once to students who had worked on the book with the well-known Caribbean novelist Wilson Harris, and once at a prestigious institute where the majority of the students were faculty from other universities. It is part of the political argument I am making that all these students blithely stepped over this paragraph without asking or knowing what Christophine's patois, so-called incorrect English, might mean.

Christophine is, of course, a commodified person. "She was your father's wedding present to me," explains Antoinette's mother, "one of his presents" (*WSS*, p. 18). Yet Rhys assigns her some crucial functions in the text. It is Christophine who judges that black ritual practices are culture-specific and cannot be used by whites as cheap remedies for social evils, such as Rochester's lack of love for Antoinette. Most important, it is Christophine alone whom Rhys allows to offer a hard analysis of Rochester's actions, to challenge him in a face-to-face encounter. The entire extended passage is worthy of comment. I quote a brief extract:

> "She is Creole girl, and she have the sun in her. Tell the truth now. She don't come to your house in this place England they tell me about, she don't come to your beautiful house to beg you to marry with her. No, it's you come all the long way to her house—it's you beg her to marry. And she love you and she give you all she have. Now you say you don't love her and you break her up. What you do with her money, eh?" [And then Rochester, the white man, comments silently to himself] Her voice was still

quiet but with a hiss in it when she said "money. " [*WSS*, p. 130]

Her analysis is powerful enough for the white man to be afraid: "I no longer felt dazed, tired, half hypnotized, but alert and wary, ready to defend myself" (*WSS*, p. 130).

Rhys does not, however, romanticize individual heroics on the part of the oppressed. When the Man refers to the forces of Law and Order, Christophine recognizes their power. This exposure of civil inequality is emphasized by the fact that, just before the Man's successful threat, Christophine had invoked the emancipation of slaves in Jamaica by pro-claiming: "No chain gang, no tread machine, no dark jail either. This is free country and I am free woman" (*WSS*, p. 131).

As I mentioned above, Christophine is tangential to this narrative. She cannot be contained by a novel which rewrites a canonical English text within the European novelistic tradition in the interest of the white Creole rather than the native. No perspective *critical* of imperialism can turn the Other into a self, because the project of imperialism has always already historically refracted what might have been the absolutely Other into a domesticated Other that consolidates the imperialist self. ① The Caliban of Retamar, caught between Europe and Latin America, reflects this predicament. We can read Rhys' reinscription of Narcissus as a thematization of the same problematic.

Of course, we cannot know Jean Rhys' feelings in the matter. We can, however, look at the scene of Christophine's inscription in the text. Immediately after the exchange between her and the Man, well before the conclusion, she is simply driven out of the story, with neither narrative nor characterological explanation or justice. "'Read and write I don't know. Other things I know.' She walked away without looking back"(*WSS*, p. 133).

Indeed, if Rhys rewrites the madwoman's attack on the Man by underlining

---

① I have tried to relate castration and suppressed letters in my "The Letter As Cutting Edge," in *Literature and Psychoanalysis*; *The Question of Reading: Otherwise*, ed. Shoshana Felman (New Haven, Conn. , 1981), pp. 208-226.

of the misuse of "legality," she cannot deal with the passage that corresponds to St. John Rivers' own justification of his martyrdom, for it has been displaced into the current idiom of modernization and development. Attempts to construct the "Third World Woman" as a signifier remind us that the hegemonic definition of literature is itself caught within the history of imperialism. A full literary reinscription cannot easily flourish in the imperialist fracture or discontinuity, covered over by an alien legal system masquerading as Law as such, an alien ideology established as only Truth, and a set of human sciences busy establishing the "native" as self-consolidating Other.

In the Indian case at least, it would be difficult to find an ideological clue to the planned epistemic violence of imperialism merely by rearranging curricula or syllabi within existing norms of literary pedagogy. For a later period of imperialism—when the constituted colonial subject has firmly taken hold—straightforward experiments of comparison can be undertaken, say, between the functionally witless India of *Mrs. Dalloway*, on the one hand, and literary texts produced in India in the 1920s, on the other. But the first half of the nineteenth century resists questioning through literature or literary criticism in the narrow sense, because both are implicated in the project of producing Ariel. To reopen the fracture without succumbing to a nostalgia for lost origins, the literary critic must turn to the archives of imperial governance. ①

In conclusion, I shall look briefly at Mary Shelley's *Frankenstein*, a text of nascent feminism that remains cryptic, I think, simply because it does not speak the language of feminist individualism which we have come to hail as the language of high feminism within English literature. It is interesting that Barbara Johnson's brief study tries to rescue this recalcitrant text for the service of feminist autobiography. ② Alternatively, George Levine reads *Frankenstein* in the context of the creative imagination and the nature of the hero. He sees the novel as a book about its own writing and about writing itself, a Romantic alle-

---

① This is the main argument of my "Can the Subaltern Speak?"

② See Barbara Johnson, "My Monster/My Self," *Diacritics* 12 (Summer 1982): 2-10.

gory of reading within which Jane Eyre as unself-conscious critic would fit quite nicely. ①

I propose to take *Frankenstein* out of this arena and focus on it in terms of that sense of English cultural identity which I invoked at the opening of this essay. Within that focus we are obliged to admit that, although *Frankenstein* is ostensibly about the origin and evolution of man in society, it does not deploy the axiomatics of imperialism.

Let me say at once that there is plenty of incidental imperialist sentiment in *Frankenstein*. My point, within the argument of this essay, is that the discursive field of imperialism does not produce unquestioned ideological correlatives for the narrative structuring of the book. The discourse of imperialism surfaces in a curiously powerful way in Shelley's novel, and I will later discuss the moment at which it emerges.

Frankenstein is not a battleground of male and female individualism articulated in terms of sexual reproduction (family and female) and social subject-production (race and male). That binary opposition is undone in Victor Frankenstein's laboratory—an artificial womb where both projects are undertaken simultaneously, though the terms are never openly spelled out. Frankenstein's apparent antagonist is God himself as Maker of Man, but his real competitor is also woman as the maker of children. It is not just that his dream of the death of mother and bride and the actual death of his bride are associated with the visit of his monstrous homoerotic "son" to his bed. On a much more overt level, the monster is a bodied "corpse," unnatural because bereft of a determinable childhood: "No father had watched my infant days, no mother had blessed me with smiles and caresses; or if they had, all my past was now a blot, a blind vacancy in which I distinguished nothing" (*F*, pp. 57, 115). It is Frankenstein's own ambiguous and miscued understanding of the real motive for the monster's vengefulness that reveals his own competition with woman as maker:

---

① See George Levine, *The Realistic Imagination: English Fiction from Frankenstein to Lady Chatterley* (Chicago, 1981), pp. 23-35.

I created a rational creature and was bound towards him to assure, as far as was in my power, his happiness and well-being. This was my duty, but there was another still paramount to that. My duties towards the beings of my own species had greater claims to my attention because they included a greater proportion of happiness or misery. Urged by this view, I refused, and I did right in refusing, to create a companion for the first creature. [F, p. 206]

It is impossible not to notice the accents of transgression inflecting Frankenstein's demolition of his experiment to create the future Eve. Even in the laboratory, the woman-in-the-making is not a bodied corpse but "a human being." The (il)logic of the metaphor bestows on her a prior existence which Frankenstein aborts, rather than an anterior death which he reembodies: "The remains of the half-finished creature, whom I had destroyed, lay scattered on the floor, and I almost felt as if I had mangled the living flesh of a human being" (F, p. 163).

In Shelley's view, man's hubris as soul maker both usurps the place of God and attempts—vainly—to sublate woman's physiological prerogative. ① Indeed, indulging a Freudian fantasy here, I could urge that, if to give and withhold to/from the mother a phallus is the male fetish, then to give and withhold to/from the man a womb might be the female fetish. ② The icon of the sublimated womb in man is surely his productive brain, the box in the head. In the judgment of classical psychoanalysis, the phallic mother exists only by virtue of the

---

① Consult the publications of the Feminist International Network for the best overview of the current debate on reproductive technology.

② For the male fetish, see Sigmund Freud, "Fetishism," *The Standard Edition of the Complete Psychological Works of Sigmund Freud*, ed. and trans. James Strachey et al., 24 vols. (London, 1953-1974), 21: 152-157. For a more "serious" Freudian study of Frankenstein, see Mary Jacobus, "Is There a Woman in This Text?" *New Literary History* 14 (Autumn 1982): 117-141. My "fantasy" would of course be disproved by the "fact" that it is more difficult for a woman to assume the position of fetishist than for a man; see Mary Ann Doane, "Film and the Masquerade: Theorising the Female Spectator," *Screen* 23 (Sept. - Oct. 1982): 74-87.

castration-anxious son; in *Frankenstein*'s judgment, the hysteric father (Victor Frankenstein gifted with his laboratory—the womb of theoretical reason) cannot produce a daughter. Here the language of racism—the dark side of imperialism understood as social mission—combines with the hysteria of masculism into the idiom of (the withdrawal of) sexual reproduction rather than subject-constitution. The roles of masculine and feminine individualists are hence reversed and displaced. Frankenstein cannot produce a "daughter" because "she might become ten thousand times more malignant than her mate ⋯ [and because] one of the first results of those sympathies for which the demon thirsted would be children, and a race of devils would be propagated upon the earth who might make the very existence of the species of man a condition precarious and full of terror" (*F*, p. 158). This particular narrative strand also launches a thoroughgoing critique of the eighteenth-century European discourses on the origin of society through (Western Christian) man. Should I mention that, much like Jean-Jacques Rousseau's remark in his *Confessions*, Frankenstein declares himself to be "by birth a Genevese" (*F*, p. 31)?

In this overly didactic text, Shelley's point is that social engineering should not be based on pure, theoretical, or natural-scientific reason alone, which is her implicit critique of the utilitarian vision of an engineered society. To this end, she presents in the first part of her deliberately schematic story three characters, childhood friends, who seem to represent Kant's three-part conception of the human subject: Victor Frankenstein, the forces of theoretical reason or "natural philosophy"; Henry Clerval, the forces of practical reason or "the moral relations of things"; and Elizabeth Lavenza, that aesthetic judgment—"the aerial creation of the poets"—which, according to Kant, is "a suitable mediating link connecting the realm of the concept of nature and that of the concept of freedom⋯ (which) promotes ⋯ *moral* feeling" (*F*, pp. 37, 36). [1]

This three-part subject does not operate harmoniously in *Frankenstein*. That Henry Clerval, associated as he is with practical reason, should have as his "design ⋯ to visit India, in the belief that he had in his knowledge of its va-

---

[1] Kant, *Critique of Judgement*, trans. J. H. Bernard (New York, 1951), p. 39.

rious languages, and in the views he had taken of its society, the means of materially assisting the progress of European colonization and trade" is proof of
this, as well as part of the incidental imperialist sentiment that I speak of above
(*F*, pp. 151-152). I should perhaps point out that the language here is entre-
prencurial rather than missionary:

> He came to the university with the design of making himself complete
> master of the Oriental languages, as thus he should open a field for the
> plan of life he had marked out for himself. Resolved to pursue no
> inglorious career, he turned his eyes towards the East as affording scope
> for his spirit of enterprise. The Persian, Arabic, and Sanskrit languages
> engaged his attention. [*F*, pp. 66-67]

But it is of course Victor Frankenstein, with his strange itinerary of obsession with natural philosophy, who offers the strongest demonstration that the
multiple perspectives of the three-part Kantian subject cannot co-operate harmoniously. Frankenstein creates a putative human subject out of natural philosophy
alone. According to his own miscued summation: "In a fit of enthusiastic
madness I created a rational creature" (*F*, p. 206). It is not at all farfetched to
say that Kant's categorical imperative can most easily be mistaken for the hypothetical imperative—a command to ground in cognitive comprehension what can
be apprehended only by moral will—by putting natural philosophy in the place
of practical reason.

I should hasten to add here that just as readings such as this one do not
necessarily accuse Charlotte Brontë the named individual of harboring
imperialist sentiments, so also they do not necessarily commend Mary Shelley
the named individual for writing a successful Kantian allegory. The most I can
say is that it is possible to read these texts, within the frame of imperialism and
the Kantian ethical moment, in a politically useful way. Such an approach presupposes that a "disinterested" reading attempts to render transparent the interests of the hegemonic readership. (Other "political" readings—for instance,
that the monster is the nascent working class—can also be advanced.)

Frankenstein is built in the established epistolary tradition of multiple frames. At the heart of the multiple frames, the narrative of the monster (as reported by Frankenstein to Robert Walton, who then recounts it in a letter to his sister) is of his almost learning, clandestinely, to be human. It is invariably noticed that the monster reads *Paradise Lost* as true history. What is not so often noticed is that he also reads Plutarch's *Lives*, "the histories of the first founders of the ancient republics," which he compares to "the patriarchal lives of my protectors" (*F*, pp. 123, 124). And his *education* comes through "Volney's *Ruins of Empires*," which purported to be a prefiguration of the French Revolution, published after the event and after the author had rounded off his theory with practice (*F*, p. 113). It is an attempt at an enlightened universal secular, rather than a Eurocentric Christian, history, written from the perspective of a narrator "from below," somewhat like the attempts of Eric Wolf or Peter Worsley in our own time. [1]

This Caliban's education in (universal secular) humanity takes place through the monster's eavesdropping on the instruction of an Ariel—Safie, the Christianized "Arabian" to whom "a residence in Turkey was abhorrent" (*F*, p. 121). In depicting Safie, Shelley uses some commonplaces of eighteenth-century liberalism that are shared by many today: Safie's Muslim father was a victim of (bad) Christian religious prejudice and yet was himself a wily and ungrateful man not as morally refined as her (good) Christian mother. Having

---

[1] See [Constantin François Chasseboeuf de Volney], *The Ruins; or, Meditations on the Revolutions of Empires*, trans. pub. (London, 1811). Johannes Fabian has shown us the manipulation of time in "new" secular histories of a similar kind; see *Time and the Other: How Anthropology Makes Its Object* (New York, 1983). See also Eric R. Wolf, *Europe and the People without History* (Berkeley and Los Angeles, 1982), and Peter Worsley, *The Third World*, 2d ed. (Chicago, 1973); I am grateful to Dennis Dworkin for bringing the latter book to my attention. The most striking ignoring of the monster's education through Volney is in Gilbert's otherwise brilliant "Horror's Twin: Mary Shelley's Monstrous Eve," *Feminist Studies* 4 (June 1980): 48-73. Gilbert's essay reflects the absence of race-determinations in a certain sort of feminism. Her present work has most convincingly filled in this gap; see, e. g., her recent piece on H. Rider Haggard's *She* ("Rider Haggard's Heart of Darkness," *Partisan Review* 50, no. 3 [1983]: 444-453).

tasted the emancipation of woman, Safie could not go home. The confusion between "Turk" and "Arab" has its counterpart in present-day confusion about Turkey and Iran as "Middle Eastern" but not "Arab. "

Although we are a far cry here from the unexamined and covert axiomatics of imperialism in *Jane Eyre*, we will gain nothing by celebrating the time-bound pieties that Shelley, as the daughter of two antievangelicals, produces. It is more interesting for us that Shelley differentiates the Other, works at the Caliban/Ariel distinction, and cannot make the monster identical with the proper recipient of these lessons. Although he had "heard of the discovery of the American hemisphere and *wept with Safie* over the helpless fate of its original inhabitants," Safie cannot reciprocate his attachment. When she first catches sight of him, "Safie, unable to attend to her friend [Agatha], rushed out of the cottage" (*F*, pp. 114 [my emphasis], 129).

In the taxonomy of characters, the Muslim-Christian Safie belongs with Rhys' Antoinette/Bertha. And indeed, like Christophine the good servant, the subject created by the fiat of natural philosophy is the tangential unresolved moment in *Frankenstein*. The simple suggestion that the monster is human inside but monstrous outside and only provoked into vengefulness is clearly not enough to bear the burden of so great a historical dilemma.

At one moment, in fact, Shelley's Frankenstein does try to tame the monster, to humanize him by bringing him within the circuit of the Law. He "repair[s] to a criminal judge in the town and ... relate[s his] history briefly but with firmness"—the first and disinterested version of the narrative of Frankenstein—"marking the dates with accuracy and never deviating into invective or exclamation... When I had concluded my narration I said, 'This is the being whom I accuse and for whose seizure and punishment I call upon you to exert your whole power. It is your duty as a magistrate'" (*F*, pp. 189, 190). The sheer social reasonableness of the mundane voice of Shelley's "Genevan magistrate" reminds us that the absolutely Other cannot be selfed, that the monster has "properties" which will not be contained by "proper" measures:

"I will exert myself [he says], and if it is in my power to seize the

monster, be assured that he shall suffer punishment proportionate to his crimes. But I fear, from what you have yourself described to be his properties, that this will prove impracticable; and thus, while every proper measure is pursued, you should make up your mind to disappointment."
[*F*, p. 190]

In the end, as is obvious to most readers, distinctions of human individuality themselves seem to fall away from the novel. Monster, Frankenstein, and Walton seem to become each others' relays. Frankenstein's story comes to an end in death; Walton concludes his own story within the frame of his function as letter writer. In the *narrative* conclusion, he is the natural philosopher who learns from Frankenstein's example. At the end of the *text*, the monster, having confessed his guilt toward his maker and ostensibly intending to immolate himself, is borne away on an ice raft. We do not see the conflagration of his funeral pile—the self-immolation is not consummated in the text: he too cannot be contained by the text. In terms of narrative logic, he is "lost in darkness and distance" (*F*, p. 211)—these are the last words of the novel—into an existential temporality that is coherent with neither the territorializing individual imagination (as in the opening of *Jane Eyre*) nor the authoritative scenario of Christian psychobiography (as at the end of Brontë's work). The very relationship between sexual reproduction and social subject-production—the dynamic nineteenth-century topos of feminism-in-imperialism—remains problematic within the limits of Shelley's text and, paradoxically, constitutes its strength.

Earlier, I offered a reading of woman as womb holder in *Frankenstein*. I would now suggest that there is a framing woman in the book who is neither tangential, nor encircled, nor yet encircling. "Mrs. Saville,""excellent Margaret," "beloved Sister" are her address and kinship inscriptions (*F*, pp. 15, 17, 22). She is the occasion, though not the protagonist, of the novel. She is the feminine *subject* rather than the female individualist: she is the irreducible *recipient*-function of the letters that constitute *Frankenstein*. I have commented on the singular appropriative hermeneutics of the reader reading with Jane in the opening pages of *Jane Eyre*. Here the reader must read with Margaret

Saville in the crucial sense that she must *intercept* the recipient-function, read the letters as recipient, in order for the novel to exist. ① Margaret Saville does not respond to close the text as frame. The frame is thus simultaneously not a frame, and the monster can step "beyond the text" and be "lost in darkness. " Within the allegory of our reading, the place of both the English lady and the unnamable monster are left open by this great flawed text. It is satisfying for a postcolonial reader to consider this a noble resolution for a nineteenth-century English novel. This is all the more striking because, on the anecdotal level, Shelley herself abundantly "identifies" with Victor Frankenstein. ②

I must myself close with an idea that I cannot establish within the limits of this essay. Earlier I contended that *Wide Sargasso Sea* is necessarily bound by the reach of the European novel. I suggested that, in contradistinction, to reopen the epistemic fracture of imperialism without succumbing to a nostalgia for lost origins, the critic must turn to the archives of imperialist governance. I have not turned to those archives in these pages. In my current work, by way of a modest and inexpert "reading" of "archives," I try to extend, outside of the reach of the European novelistic tradition, the most powerful suggestion in *Wide Sargasso Sea*: that *Jane Eyre* can be read as the orchestration and staging of the self-immolation of Bertha Mason as "good wife. " The power of that suggestion remains unclear if we remain insufficiently knowledgeable about

---

① "A letter is always and a *priori* intercepted, ⋯ the 'subjects' are neither the senders nor the receivers of messages⋯ The letter is constituted ⋯ by its interception" (Jacques Derrida, "Discussion," after Claude Rabant, "Il n'a aucune chance de l' entendre," in *Affranchissement: Du transfert et de la lettre*, ed. René Major [Paris, 1981], p. 106; my translation). Margaret Saville is not made to appropriate the reader's "subject" into the signature of her own "individuality. "

② The most striking "internal evidence" is the admission in the "Author's Introduction" that, after dreaming of the yet-unnamed Victor Frankenstein figure and being terrified (through, yet not quite through, him) by the monster in a scene she later reproduced in Frankenstein's story, Shelley began her tale "on the morrow ⋯ with the words 'It was on a dreary night of November'" (*F*, p. xi). Those are the opening words of chapter 5 of the finished book, where Frankenstein begins to recount the actual making of his monster (see *F*, p. 56).

the history of the legal manipulation of widow-sacrifice in the entitlement of the British government in India. I would hope that an informed critique of imperialism, granted some attention from readers in the First World, will at least expand the frontiers of the politics of reading.

17. 斯皮瓦克：《三个女性文本与对帝国主义的批评》

(Gayatri C. Spivak, "Three Women's Texts and a Critique of Imperialism," 1985)

作者小识

斯皮瓦克(Gayatri C. Spivak，1942—　)，出生于印度，是当今世界首屈一指的文学理论家和文化批评家，西方后殖民理论思潮的主要代表，与爱德华·萨义德(Edward W. Said，1935—2003)和霍米·巴巴(Homi K. Bhabha，1949—　)并称为"后殖民研究三圣"。早年师承美国解构批评大师保罗·德曼，获得康奈尔大学博士学位，20世纪70年代曾以将解构大师德里达的《论文字学》(De La Grammatologie)引入英语世界而蜚声北美理论界，后又以演讲的雄辩和批评文风的犀利而驰骋于80、90年代的英语文化理论界。斯皮瓦克现为美国哥伦比亚大学阿维龙基金会人文学科讲座教授、比较文学与社会中心主任。斯皮瓦克作为一位第三世界出身、在第一世界生活并从事研究工作的学者，积极运用西方文学理论批评话语挑战传统的西方中心主义对西方文化意识形态的巨大影响。斯皮瓦克的研究特点是领域多样化，体系多元化，带有鲜明的女性主义与解构主义色彩。她经常把自己称为"实用的马克思主义、女性主义、解构主义者"。斯皮瓦克的伦理政治关注点主要是在西方文化的话语实践和机构中，下层人物尤其是下层妇女所处的地位与扮演的角色。萨义德对斯皮瓦克的评价是："她开创了非西方女性文学理论研究的先河，并为我们提供了这一理论最早和得到最多认可的论述之一。"她的主要著作包括在解构和翻译的范畴内试图去发掘和再现底层人和妇女的话语权力的《庶民能说话吗?》("Can the Subaltern Speak?" in Marxism and the Interpretation of Culture，1988)，以及视角涵盖20世纪90年代的经济全球化、后殖民和跨文化研究，主要从哲学、文学、历史、文化四个方面建构，探讨欧洲哲学话语与帝国主义公理之共谋的《对后殖民主义理性的批判：走向消亡的历史》(A Critique of Postcolonial Reason: Toward a History of the Vanishing Present，1999)。

背景略说

20世纪80年代，后殖民主义（postcolonialism）理论思潮在西方学术理论界进入鼎盛时期。它以反传统哲学为特征，对现代文化哲学和精神价值取向进行批判和解构。后殖民主义在百花竞放的西方理论界一枝独秀，成为绵延至今的热点批评理论。后殖民主义又叫后殖民批判主义（postcolonial criticism）。后殖民主义相对于一个理论体系，更像是一个巨大的公共话语场，如福柯提出的"正是在话语结构中权利和知识得以联结在一起"。在后殖民主义的话语场中，所有的话语实践都基于这样一个历史事实，即"第二次世界大战之后冷战和后冷战时期对'落后'民族和国家在文化价值、意识形态、知识话语、主体建构等方面进行围剿和渗透的一种帝国主义干涉政策和霸权（hegemony）意识"。安东尼奥·葛兰西（Antonio Gramsci，1891—1937）的采用各种文化工具，如文化理论、文化产品、文化资源、文化人才等对社会思想意识进行支配以期达到在政治、经济、文化和社会诸方面占主导地位的效果的"文化霸权"理论与《黑皮肤，白面具》的作者弗朗茨·法农（Frantz Fanon，1925—1961）的"为了得到认同而对白人/殖民者的语言的掌握反映了黑人人性的依附"的"民族文化"理论对于后殖民主义的产生和发展都起到了巨大的促进作用。法国哲学家福柯的"话语"与"权力"理论则是后殖民主义理论的核心话题，即权力者，包括人、机构组织、意识形态等，有更多资源和能力通过"话语"去做定义和诠释，而斯皮瓦克等有着第三世界身份背景的西方理论家旨在打破传统的殖民主义二元对立局面，建立多元共生的世界文化格局。"后殖民研究三圣"中的萨义德的理论有强烈的政治批判色彩，霍米·巴巴对殖民话语的解构和颠覆往往通过模拟和戏仿来实施，而斯皮瓦克的理论则深受解构主义与女性主义的影响。

基本内容

作为一位后殖民主义女性批评家，斯皮瓦克着重于对在文学史上已有约定俗成的评价的经典文本进行重读，并从殖民主义和女性主义视角，紧密结合文本，对小说内涵与结构做出重新阐释。在这其中，她的经典论文《三个女性文本与对帝国主义的批评》奠定了其一流殖民主义批评家的地位。斯皮瓦克运用马克思主义、解构主义以及女性主义理论框架来分析三位英国女性作家的传世经典：夏洛蒂·勃朗特的小说《简·爱》、简·里斯的《藻海无边》以及玛丽·雪莱的《弗兰肯斯坦》。

第一，《简·爱》是一部对于女性主义来说举足轻重的作品，女主人公简一直被奉为女性主义英雄，斯皮瓦克却另辟蹊径，效仿德里达选取了边缘性、私人性素材，批评美国女性主义者忽视伯莎·梅森这个次要人物的做法。她主张把帝国主义和殖民主义的现实背景纳入考虑之列，同时认为小说中设置了一系列家庭与反家庭的二元对立关系，而其中最重要的就是罗彻斯特与罗彻斯特太太所组成的"合法"家庭和简与罗彻斯特所组成的"非法"家庭的对立，而小说正是围绕这些对立关系的变化展开的。随着故事的发展，简从反家庭成员变为合法家庭成员。促使简的地位发生变化的小说的叙事动力在斯皮瓦克看来，是帝国主义的意识形态所提供的有效的"话语场域"。小说中有两处描写伯莎·梅森，一处是简初见伯莎·梅森，另一处是婚礼被打断，简决心出走之前，罗彻斯特对简的独白。从这两处描写中可以看出两组对立关系：人与兽的对立、人间与地狱的对立。作者以人与兽来区分罗彻斯特和伯莎·梅森，罗彻斯特则以人间与地狱来区分欧洲（英国）和它的殖民地（西印度群岛）。斯皮瓦克认为，正是这种区分，为简的身份变化（从"非法"到"合法"）提供了基础，"这种区分无疑是基于一种帝国主义公理的意识形态"。

在著名西方女性主义研究学者桑德拉·吉尔伯特（Sandra M. Gilbert）和苏珊·古芭（Susan Gubar）所写的被誉为"20世纪女性主义文学批评的《圣经》"的《阁楼上的疯女人》中，屋中的天使与阁楼上的疯女人被视为一人，认为疯女人不过是简·爱灵魂中妖魔化的一面，或者"从心理学角度看，是她黑暗的化身"。斯皮瓦克提到的英国女作家简·里斯比这两位更早关注到了伯莎·梅森这一次要角色，创作了《藻海无边》这部以伯莎·梅森为主人公、类似于《简·爱》前传的小说，小说中主人公的名字是伯莎·梅森的本名安托瓦内特。

第二，在斯皮瓦克看来，《藻海无边》中伯莎·梅森的疯癫是"对帝国主义的批判"。"里斯有意安排让安托瓦内特把她的'自我'看作她的'他者'，即勃朗特笔下的伯莎·梅森。"斯皮瓦克进一步分析道："里斯暗示我的是即便个人及人类身份这样私人化的事情，也可能是为帝国主义政治所决定的。"斯皮瓦克还提到了里斯的小说中有许多重要的镜像隐喻，如牙买加的黑人少女蒂亚。作为殖民地女性的代表，蒂亚无法接受与白种人克里奥少女安托瓦内特成为朋友，两人之间有着牙买加土著与英国殖民者的隔阂。小说尾声在，"封闭花园"与大厅这两个"自恋场所"，安托瓦内特把自己变成了一个他者。为了演好自己的角色，成就简这样一位女性主义英雄角色，她选择了自焚。斯皮瓦克说："我必须把它读作一个带着普遍意义的帝国主义一般认知暴力的寓言，读者为了殖民者的社会传教团的光荣而构建的一个自我牺牲和献祭的殖民地的主体。"

第三，斯皮瓦克解读了《弗兰肯斯坦》。她没有采取传统的浪漫的寓言式解读，而是依据卡利班范式对英国女作家玛丽·雪莱的《弗兰肯斯坦》进行重读。她首先指出，《弗兰肯斯坦》"流露出非常强烈的帝国主义话语"，"种族主义的语言与男性的歇斯底里相结合"。接着斯皮瓦克得出概括性的结论：该小说的表面文本是关于人类起源与理性进步的神话，但小说中那个科学怪人的原型竟来自卡利班这类人，而他反抗的对象恰是维克多隐喻的启蒙理性，这是小说的隐含文本。同时斯皮瓦克提醒我们注意弗兰肯斯坦拒绝为怪物创造女性同伴时的语气变化，她认为这是对18世纪的欧洲关于人类社会起源的话语之最严厉的批判。

拓展讨论

自殖民主义出现之后，对殖民主义的批评似乎就不绝于耳。但是在早期，不论是马克思、列宁还是霍布森，一旦涉及反殖民问题，都是站在欧洲中心主义的立场上进行思考。这不仅是时代的局限，也是其自身身份的限制使然。最早具有后殖民主义批评思想的弗朗茨·法农，是一位出生于中产阶级的黑人，接受过法国的西式教育。正是这样的在经验与生活上的对立，才使得他能够思考与注意自己对民族、对国家产生的失落感，进而站在殖民地后裔的角度反思后殖民主义。在"二战"后，尽管许多被殖民的地区和国家通过武力斗争与外交运动获得了独立地位，但是在欧洲国家的军队撤走之后，这里的人们发现自己并没有摆脱殖民统治的阴霾。西方国家在结束了表面的殖民统治之后，开始了对这些独立后地区和国家新的殖民控制，也就是所谓"新殖民主义"。这个词出现在20世纪60年代初期，代指西方国家不再通过直接管理来控制殖民地，而是通过代理人、代理集团以及文化输出、意识形态灌输的方式进行一种新的殖民统治。

斯皮瓦克关注到了在殖民统治下的"庶民阶层"。实际上在西方的学术环境中，多数学者很难摆脱精英主义的观点和立场，往往将社会上的"中产阶层"作为所谓"代表形象"，这不仅脱离了"后殖民"的方向，也远离了作为其基础的马克思主义立场。斯皮瓦克在1985年发表的《庶民能说话吗？》中探讨了导致一名年轻的孟加拉妇女自杀的社会和文化环境。这名年轻的孟加拉妇女试图在男权社会发出自己的声音，但是却被周围的人孤立与排挤，最终于无助中选择自杀。实际上这就是多数庶民的状态，没有人关注或是倾听他们的声音，更不要说本就处于生理与社会弱势的女性了。斯皮瓦克关注到了很多西方小说中的非传统女性角色，即非中产阶级、非异性恋（或有疑问的）和非白人女性，这种非传统女性角色所起到的历史作用在萨义德等男性理论家那里一直是被忽视的。正是斯皮瓦克对这样角色的发掘，才使得后殖民主义文学批评在内容与方向上获得了巨大的扩充。

延伸阅读

1. Gayatri Chakravorty Spivak, "Can the Subaltern Speak?" in *Marxism and the Interpretation of Culture*, ed. Cary Nelson and Lawrence Grossberge, Urbana, University of Illinois Press, 1988, pp. 271-313.

2. Gayatri Chakravorty Spivak, A *Critique of Postcolonial Reason*, Boston, Harvard University Press, 1999.

3. Gayatri Chakravorty Spivak, "How to Teach a 'Culturally Different' Book," in *The Spivak Reader*, ed. Donna Landry and Gerald MacLean, New York & London, Routledge, 1996.

4. 萨义德：《东方学》，王宇根译，北京，生活·读书·新知三联书店，1999。

18. Archetypal Criticism: Theory of Myths (1957)

By Northrop Frye

THEORY OF ARCHETYPAL MEANING(I):
APOCALYPTIC IMAGERY

Let us proceed according to the general scheme of the game of Twenty Questions, or, if we prefer, of the Great Chain of Being, the traditional scheme for classifying sense data.

The apocalyptic world, the heaven of religion, presents, in the first place, the categories of reality in the forms of human desire, as indicated by the forms they assume under the work of human civilization. The form imposed by human work and desire on the *vegetable* world, for instance, is that of the garden, the farm, the grove, or the park. The human form of the *animal* world is a world of domesticated animals, of which the sheep has a traditional priority in both Classical and Christian metaphor. The human form of the *mineral* world, the form into which human work transforms stone, is the city. The city, the garden, and the sheepfold are the organizing metaphors of the Bible and of most Christian symbolism, and they are brought into complete metaphorical identification in the book explicitly called the Apocalypse or Revelation, which has been carefully designed to form an undisplaced mythical conclusion for the Bible as a whole. From our point of view this means that the Biblical Apocalypse is our grammar of apocalyptic imagery.

Each of these three categories, the city, the garden, and the sheepfold, is, by the principle of archetypal metaphor dealt with in the previous essay, and which we remember is the concrete universal, identical with the others and with each individual within it. Hence the *divine* and *human* worlds are, similarly, identical with the sheepfold, city and garden, and the social and individual aspects of each are identical. Thus the apocalyptic world of the Bible presents the following pattern:

divine world	= society of gods	= One God
human world	= society of men	= One Man
animal world	= sheepfold	= One Lamb
vegetable world	= garden or park	= One Tree (of Life)
mineral world	= city	= One Building, Temple, Stone

The conception "Christ" unites all these categories in identity: Christ *is* both the one God and the one Man, the Lamb of God, the tree of life, or vine of which we are the branches, the stone which the builders rejected, and the re-built temple which is identical with his risen body. The religious and poetic identifications differ in intention only, the former being existential and the latter metaphorical. In medieval criticism the difference was of little importance, and the word "figura," as applied to the identification of a symbol with Christ, usually implies both kinds.

Now let us expand this pattern a little. In Christianity the concrete univer-sal is applied to the divine world in the form of the Trinity. Christianity insists that, whatever dislocations of customary mental processes may be involved, God *is* three persons and yet one God. The conceptions of person and substance represent a few of the difficulties in extending metaphor to logic. In pure meta-phor, of course, the unity of God could apply to five or seventeen or a million divine persons as easily as three, and we may find the divine concrete universal in poetry outside the Trinitarian orbit. When Zeus remarks, at the beginning of the eighth book of the Iliad, that he can pull the whole chain of being up into himself whenever he likes, we can see that for Homer there was some concep-tion of a double perspective in Olympus, where a group of squabbling deities may at any time suddenly compose into the form of a single divine will. In Vir-gil we first meet a malicious and spoiled Juno, but the comment of Aeneas to his men a few lines later on, "deus dabit his quoque finem," indicates that a similar double perspective existed for him. We may compare perhaps the Book of Job, where Job and his friends are much too devout for it ever to occur to them that Job could have suffered so as a result of a half-jocular bet between God and Satan. There is a sense in which they are right, and the information given to the reader about Satan in heaven wrong. Satan is dropped out of the end of the poem, and whatever rewritings may be responsible for this, it is still difficult to see how the final enlightenment of Job could ever have returned completely from the conception of a single divine will to the mood of the opening scene.

As for human society, the metaphor that we are all members of one body has organized most political theory from Plato to our own day. Milton's "A Commonwealth ought to be but as one huge Christian personage, one mighty growth, and stature of an honest man" belongs to a Christianized version of this metaphor, in which, as in the doctrine of the Trinity, the full metaphorical statement "Christ *is* God and Man" is orthodox, and the Arian and Docetic statements in terms of simile or likeness condemned as heretical. Hobbes's *Leviathan*, with its original frontispiece depicting a number of mannikins inside the body of a single giant, has also some connection with the same type of identification. Plato's Republic, in which the reason, will, and desire of the individual appear as the philosopher-king, guards, and artisans of the state, is also founded on this metaphor, which in fact we still use whenever we speak of a group or aggregate of human beings as a "body."

In sexual symbolism, of course, it is still easier to employ the "one flesh" metaphor of two bodies made into the same body by love. Donne's *The Extasie* is one of the many poems organized on this image, and Shakespeare's *Phoenix and the Turtle* makes great play with the outrage done to the "reason" by such identity. Themes of loyalty, hero-worship, faithful followers, and the like also employ the same metaphor.

The animal and vegetable worlds are identified with each other, and with the divine and human worlds as well, in the Christian doctrine of transubstantiation, in which the essential human forms of the vegetable world, food and drink, the harvest and the vintage, the bread and the wine, *are* the body and blood of the Lamb who is also Man and God, and in whose body we exist as in a city or temple. Here again the orthodox doctrine insists on metaphor as against simile, and here again the conception of substance illustrates the struggles of logic to digest the metaphor. It is clear from the opening of the *Laws* that the symposium had something of the same communion symbolism for Plato. It would be hard to find a simpler or more vivid image of human civilization, where man attempts to surround nature and put it inside his (social) body, than the sacramental meal.

The conventional honors accorded the sheep in the animal world provide us with the central archetype of pastoral imagery, as well as with such metaphors as "pastor" and "flock" in religion. The metaphor of the king as the shepherd of his people goes back to ancient Egypt. Perhaps the use of this particular convention is due to the fact that, being stupid, affectionate, gregarious, and easily stampeded, the societies formed by sheep are most like human ones. But of course in poetry any other animal would do as well if the poet's audience were prepared for it: at the opening of the Brihadaranyaka Upanishad, for instance, the sacrificial horse, whose body contains the whole universe, is treated in the same way that a Christian poet would treat the Lamb of God. Of birds, too, the dove has traditionally represented the universal concord or love both of Venus and of the Christian Holy Spirit. Identifications of gods with animals or plants and of those again with human society form the basis of totemic symbolism. Certain types of etiological folk tale, the stories of how supernatural beings were turned into the animals and plants that we know, represent an attentuated form of the same type of metaphor, and survive as the "metamorphosis" archetype familiar from Ovid.

Similar flexibility is possible with vegetable images. Elsewhere in the Bible the leaves or fruit of the tree of life are used as communion symbols in place of the bread and wine. Or the concrete universal may be applied not simply to a tree but to a single fruit or flower. In the West the rose has a traditional priority among apocalyptic flowers: the use of the rose as a communion symbol in the *Paradiso* comes readily to mind, and in the first book of *The Faerie Queene* the emblem of St. George, a red cross on a white ground, is connected not only with the risen body of Christ and the sacramental symbolism which accompanies it, but with the union of the red and white roses in the Tudor dynasty. In the East the lotus or the Chinese "golden flower" often occupied the place of the rose, and in German Romanticism the blue cornflower enjoyed a brief vogue.

The identity of the human body and the vegetable world gives us the archetype of Arcadian imagery, of Marvell's green world, of Shakespeare's forest comedies, of the world of Robin Hood and other green men who lurk in the forests of romance, these last the counterparts in romance of the metaphorical myth of the tree-god. In Marvell's *The Garden* we meet a further but still conventional extension in the identification of the human soul with a bird sitting in the branches of the tree of life. The olive tree and its oil has supplied another identification in the "anointed" ruler.

The city, whether called Jerusalem or not, is apocalyptically identical with a single building or temple, a "house of many mansions," of which individuals are "lively stones," to use another New Testament phrase. The human use of the inorganic world involves the highway or road as well as the city with its streets, and the metaphor of the "way" is inseparable from all quest-literature, whether explicitly Christian as in *The Pilgrim's Progress* or not. To this category also belong geometrical and architectural images: the tower and the winding stairway of Dante and Yeats, Jacob's ladder, the ladder of the Neo-platonic love poets, the ascending spiral or cornucopia, the "stately pleasure dome" that Kubla Khan decreed, the cross and quincunx patterns which Browne sought in every corner of art and nature, the circle as the emblem of eternity, Vaughan's "ring of pure and endless light," and so on.

On the archetypal level proper, where poetry is an artifact of human civilization, nature is the container of man. On the anagogic level, man is the container of nature, and his cities and gardens are no longer little hollowings on the surface of the earth, but the forms of a human universe. Hence in apocalyptic symbolism we cannot confine man only to his two natural elements of earth and air, and, in going from one level to the other, symbolism must, like Tamino in *The Magic Flute*, pass the ordeals of water and fire. Poetic symbolism usually puts fire just above man's life in this world, and water just below it. Dante had to pass through a ring of fire and the river of Eden to go from the mountain of purgatory, which is still on the surface of our own world, to Paradise or the apocalyptic world proper. The imagery of light and fire surrounding the angels in the Bible, the tongues of flame descending at Pentecost, and the coal of fire applied to the mouth of Isaiah by the seraph, associates fire with a spiritual or angelic world midway between the human and the divine. In Classical mythology the story of Prometheus indicates a similar provenance for fire, as does the association of Zeus with the thunderbolt or fire of lightning. In short, heaven in the sense of the sky, containing the fiery bodies of sun, moon, and stars, is usually identified with, or thought of as the passage to, the heaven of the apocalyptic world.

Hence all our other categories can be identified with fire or thought of as burning. The appearance of the Judaeo-Christian deity in fire, surrounded by angels of fire (seraphim) and light (cherubim), needs only to be mentioned. The burning animal of the ritual of sacrifice, the incorporating of an animal body in a communion between divine and human worlds, modulates into all the imagery connected with the fire and smoke of the altar, ascending incense, and the like. The burning man is represented in the saint's halo and the king's crown, both of which are analogues of the sun-god: one may compare also the "burning babe" of Southwell's Christmas poem. The image of the burning bird appears in the legendary phoenix. The tree of life may also be a burning tree, the unconsumed burning bush of Moses, the candlestick of Jewish ritual, or the "rosy cross" of later occultism. In alchemy the vegetable, mineral, and water worlds are identified in its rose, stone, and elixir; flower and jewel archetypes are identified in the "jewel in the lotus" of the Buddhist prayer. The links between fire, intoxicating wine, and the hot red blood of animals are also common.

The identification of the *city* with fire explains why the city of God in the Apocalypse is presented as a glowing mass of gold and precious stones, each stone presumably burning with a hard gemlike flame. For in apocalyptic symbolism the fiery bodies of heaven, sun, moon, and stars, are all inside the universal divine and human body. The symbolism of alchemy is apocalyptic symbolism of the same type: the center of nature, the gold and jewels hidden in the earth, is eventually to be united to its circumference in the sun, moon, and stars of the heavens; the center of the spiritual world, the soul of man, is united to its circumference in God. Hence there is a close association between

mutation of act into mime, the advance from acting out a rite to playing at the rite, is one of the central features of the development from savagery into culture. It is easy to see a mimesis of conflict in tennis and football, but, precisely for that very reason, tennis and football players represent a culture superior to the culture of student duellists and gladiators. The turning of literal act into play is a fundamental form of the liberalizing of life which appears in more intellectual levels as liberal education, the release of fact into imagination. It is consistent with this that the Eucharist symbolism of the apocalyptic world, the metaphorical identification of vegetable, animal, human, and divine bodies, should have the imagery of cannibalism for its demonic parody. Dante's last vision of human hell is of Ugolino gnawing his tormentor's skull; Spenser's last major allegorical vision is of Serena stripped and prepared for a cannibal feast. The imagery of cannibalism usually includes, not only images of torture and mutilation, but of what is technically known as *sparagmos* or the tearing apart of the sacrificial body, an image found in the myths of Osiris, Orpheus, and Pentheus. The cannibal giant or ogre of folk tales, who enters literature as Polyphemus, belongs here, as does a long series of sinister dealings with flesh and blood from the story of Thyestes to Shylock's bond. Here again the form described by Frazer as the historically original form is in literary criticism the radical demonic form. Flaubert's *Salammbo* is a study of demonic imagery which was thought in its day to be archaeological but turned out to be prophetic.

The demonic erotic relation becomes a fierce destructive passion that works against loyalty or frustrates the one who possesses it. It is generally symbolized by a harlot, witch, siren, or other tantalizing female, a physical object of desire which is sought as a possession and therefore can never be possessed. The demonic parody of marriage, or the union of two souls in one flesh, may take the form of hermaphroditism, incest (the most common form), or homosexuality. The social relation is that of the mob, which is essentially human society looking for a *pharmakos*, and the mob is often identified with some sinister animal image such as the hydra, Virgil's Fama, or its development in Spenser's Blatant Beast.

The other worlds can be briefly summarized. The animal world is portrayed in terms of monsters or beasts of prey, The wolf, the traditional enemy of the sheep, the tiger, the vulture, the cold and earth-bound serpent, and the dragon are all common. In the Bible, where the demonic society is represented by Egypt and Babylon, the rulers of each are identified with monstrous beasts: Nebuchadnezzar turns into a beast in Daniel, and Pharaoh is called a riverdragon by Ezekiel. The dragon is especially appropriate because it is not only monstrous and sinister but fabulous, and so represents the paradoxical nature of evil as a moral fact and an eternal negation. In the Apocalypse the dragon is called "the beast that was, and is not, and yet is. "

The vegetable world is a sinister forest like the ones we meet in *Comus* or the opening of the *Inferno*, or a heath, which from Shakespeare to Hardy has been associated with tragic destiny, or a wilderness like that of Browning's *Childe Roland* or Eliot's *Waste Land*. Or it may be a sinister enchanted garden like that of Circe and its Renaissance descendants in Tasso and Spenser. In the Bible the waste land appears in its concrete universal form in the tree of death, the tree of forbidden knowledge in Genesis, the barren figtree of the Gospels, and the cross. The stake, with the hooded heretic, the black man or the witch attached to it, is the burning tree and body of the infernal world. Scaffolds, gallows, stocks, pillories, whips, and birch rods are or could be modulations. The contrast of the tree of life and the tree of death is beautifully expressed in Yeats's poem *The Two Trees*.

The inorganic world may remain in its unworked form of deserts, rocks, and waste land. Cities of destruction and dreadful night belong here, and the great ruins of pride, from the tower of Babel to the mighty works of Ozymandias. Images of perverted work belong here too: engines of torture, weapons of war, armor, and images of a dead mechanism which, because it does not humanize nature, is unnatural as well as inhuman. Corresponding to the temple or One Building of the apocalypse, we have the prison or dungeon, the sealed furnace of heat without light, like the City of Dis in Dante. Here too are the sinister counterparts of geometrical images: the sinister spiral (the maelstrom, whirlpool, or Charybdis), the sinister cross, and the sinister circle, the wheel of fate or fortune. The identification of the circle with the serpent, conventionally a demonic animal, gives us the ouroboros, or serpent with its tail in its mouth. Corresponding to the apocalyptic way or straight road, the highway in the desert for God prophesied by Isaiah, we have in this world the labyrinth or maze, the image of lost direction, often with a monster at its heart like the Minotaur. The labyrinthine wanderings of Israel in the desert, repeated by Jesus when in the company of the devil (or "wild beasts," according to Mark), fit the same pattern. The labyrinth can also be a sinister forest, as in *Comus*. The catacombs are effectively used in the same context in *The Marble Faun*, and of course in a further concentration of metaphor, the maze would become the winding entrails inside the sinister monster himself.

The world of fire is a world of malignant demons like the will-o'-the-wisps, or spirits broken from hell, and it appears in this world in the form of the *auto da fe*, as mentioned, or such burning cities as Sodom. It is in contrast to the purgatorial or cleansing fire, like the fiery furnace in Daniel. The world of water is the water of death, often identified with spilled blood, as in the Passion and in Dante's symbolic figure of history, and above all the "unplumbed, salt, estranging sea," which absorbs all rivers in this world, but disappears in the apocalypse in favor of a circulation of fresh water. In the Bible the sea and the animal monster are identified in the figure of the leviathan, a sea-monster also identified with the social tyrannies of Babylon and Egypt.

THEORY OF ARCHETYPAL MEANING (3):
ANALOGICAL IMAGERY

Most imagery in poetry has of course to deal with much less extreme worlds than the two which are usually projected as the eternal unchanging worlds of heaven and hell. Apocalyptic imagery is appropriate to the mythical mode, and demonic imagery to the ironic mode in the late phase in which it returns to myth. In the other three modes these two structures operate dialectically, pulling the reader toward the metaphorical and mythical undisplaced core of the work. We should therefore expect three intermediate structures of imagery, corresponding roughly to the romantic, high mimetic, and low mimetic modes. We shall give little attention to high mimetic imagery, however, in order to preserve the simpler pattern of the romantic and "realistic" tendencies within the two undisplaced structures given at the beginning of this essay.

These three structures are less rigorously metaphorical, and are rather significant constellations of images, which, when found together, make up what is often called, somewhat helplessly, "atmosphere." The mode of romance presents an idealized world: in romance heroes are brave, heroines beautiful, villains villainous, and the frustrations, ambiguities, and embarrassments of ordinary life are made little of. Hence its imagery presents a human counterpart of the apocalyptic world which we may call the *analogy of innocence*. It is best known to us, not from the age of romance itself, but from later romanticizings: *Comus*, *The Tempest*, and the third book of *The Faerie Queene* in the Renaissance; Blake's songs of innocence and "Beulah" imagery, Keats's *Endymion* and Shelley's *Epipsychidion* in the Romantic period proper.

In the analogy of innocence the divine or spiritual figures are usually parental, wise old men with magical powers like Prospero, or friendly guardian spirits like Raphael before Adam's fall. Among the human figures children are prominent, and so is the virtue most closely associated with childhood and the state of innocence—chastity, a virtue which in this structure of imagery usually includes virginity. In *Comus* the Lady's chastity is, like Prospero's wisdom, associated with magic, as is the invincible chastity of Spenser's Britomart. It is easiest to associate with young women—Dante's Matelda and Shakespeare's Miranda are examples—but male chastity is important too, as the Grail romances show. Sir Galahad's remark in Tennyson about his purity of heart giving him tenfold strength is consistent with the imagery of the world he belongs in. Fire in the innocent world is usually a purifying symbol, a world of flame that none but the perfectly chaste can pass, as in Spenser's castle of Busirane, the refining fire at the top of Dante's purgatory, and the flaming sword that keeps the fallen Adam and Eve away from Paradise. In the story of the sleeping beauty, which belongs here, the wall of flame is replaced by one of thorns and brambles: Wagner's *Die Walküre*, however, retains the fire, to the discomposure of stage managers. The moon, the coolest and hence most chaste of all the fiery heavenly bodies, has a special importance for this world.

Of animals, the most obvious are the pastoral sheep and lambs, along with the horses and hounds of romance, in their gentler aspects of fidelity and devotion. The unicorn, the traditional emblem of chastity and the lover of virgins, has an honored place here; so does the dolphin, whose association with Arion makes him the innocent contrast to the devouring leviathan; and also, for its humility and submissiveness, a very different animal—the ass. The dramatic festival of the ass, no less than that of the Boy Bishop, belongs to this structure of imagery, and when Shakespeare put an ass's head in Fairyland he was not doing something unique, as Robinson's poem implies, but following a tradition that goes back to the transformed Lucius listening to the story of Cupid and Psyche in Apuleius. Birds, butterflies (for this is Psyche's world, and Psyche means butterfly), and spirits with their qualities, like Ariel and Hudson's Rima, are other naturalized denizens.

The paradisal garden and the tree of life belong in the apocalyptic structure, as we saw, but the garden of Eden itself, as presented in the Bible and Milton, belongs rather to this one, and Dante puts it just below his Paradiso. Spenser's Gardens of Adonis, from which the attendant spirit in *Comus* comes, are parallel, along with all the medieval developments of the theme of the *locus amoenus*. Of special significance is the symbol of the body of the Virgin as a *hortus conclusus*, derived from the Song of Songs. A romantic counterpart to the tree of life appears in the magician's life-giving wand, and such parallel symbols as the blossoming rod in *Tannhaüser*.

Cities are more alien to the pastoral and rural spirit of this world, and the tower and the castle, with an occasional cottage or hermitage, are the chief images of habitation. Water symbolism features chiefly fountains and pools, fertilizing rains, and an occasional stream separating a man from a woman and so preserving the chastity of each, like the river of Lethe in Dante. The opening rose-garden episode of *Burnt Norton* gives a brief but extraordinarily complete summary of the symbols of the analogy of innocence; one may also compare the second section of Auden's *Kairos and Logos*.

The innocent world is neither totally alive, like the apocalyptic one, nor mostly dead, like ours: it is an animistic world, full of elemental spirits. All the characters of *Comus* are elemental spirits except the Lady and her brothers, and the connections of Ariel with air-spirits, of Puck with fire-spirits (Burton says of fire-spirits that "we commonly call them Pucks"), and of Caliban with earth-spirits are clear enough. In Spenser we find Florimell and Marinell, whose names indicate that they are spirits of flowers and water, a Proserpine and an Adonis. Often, too, as in *Comus* and the *Nativity Ode*, innocent or unfallen nature, nature as a divinely sanctioned order, is represented by the inaudible harmony of the music of the spheres.

Just as the organizing ideas of romance are chastity and magic, so the organizing ideas of the high mimetic area seem to be love and form. And as the field of romantic images may be called an analogy of innocence, so the field of high mimetic imagery may be called an *analogy of nature and reason*. We find here the emphasis on cynosure or centripetal gaze, and the tendency to idealize the human representatives of the divine and the spiritual world, which are characteristic of the high mimetic. Divinity hedges the king and the Courtly Love mistress is a goddess; love of both is an educating and informing power which brings one into unity with the spiritual and divine worlds. The fire of the angelic world blazes in the king's crown and the lady's eyes. The animals are those of proud beauty: the eagle and the lion stand for the vision of the royal by the loyal, the horse and falcon for "chivalry" or the aristocracy on horseback; the peacock and the swan are the birds of cynosure, and the phoenix or unique fire-bird is a favorite poetic emblem, especially, in England, for Queen Elizabeth. Garden symbolism recedes into the background, as city symbolism does in romance; there are formal gardens in close association with buildings, but the idea of a garden *world* is still a romantic one. The magician's wand is metamorphosed into the royal sceptre, and the magic tree to the fluttering banner. The city is preeminently the capital city, with the court at its center and a series of initiatory degrees of approach within the court, climaxed by the royal "presence." We note that as we go down the modes an increasing number of poetic images are taken from actual social conditions of life. Water-symbolism centers on the disciplined river, in England the Thames which runs softly in Spenser and in neo-Classical rhythms in Denham, a river whose most appropriate ornament is the royal barge.

In the low mimetic area we enter a world that we may call the *analogy of experience*, and which bears a relation to the demonic world corresponding to the relation of the romantic innocent world to the apocalyptic one. Except for this potentially ironic connection, and except for a certain number of hieratic or specially indicated symbols like Hawthorne's scarlet letter and Henry James's golden bowl and ivory tower, the images are the ordinary images of experience, and need no further explanation here beyond a few comments about some particular features that may be of use. The organizing low mimetic ideas seem to be genesis and work. Divine and spiritual beings have little functional place in low mimetic fiction, and in thematic writing they are often deliberately rediscovered or treated as aesthetic surrogates. The advice is given to the unborn in *Erewhon* (apparently close to Butler's own view, as he repeats the idea in *Life and Habit*) that if there is a spiritual world, one should turn one's back on it and find it again in immediate work. The same doctrine of the rediscovery of faith through works may be found in Carlyle, Ruskin, Morris, and Shaw. In poets, even in explicitly sacramental ones, there are parallel tendencies. From many points of view there could hardly be a greater contrast than the contrast between the "motion and a spirit" discovered by Wordsworth in Tintern Abbey and the "chevalier" discovered by Hopkins in the windhover, yet the tendency to anchor a spiritual vision in an empirical psychological experience is common to both.

The low mimetic treatment of human society reflects, of course, Wordsworth's doctrine that the essential human situations, for the poet, are the common and typical ones. Along with this goes a good deal of parody of the idealization of life in romance, a parody that extends to religious and aesthetic experience. As for the animal world, Thomas Huxley's reference to the qualities that humanity shares with the ape and the tiger is a significantly low mimetic choice. The ape has always been *par excellence* the mimetic animal, and long before evolution he was specifically the imitator of man. The rise of evolution however suggested an analogy of proportion in which present man becomes the ape of his counterpart in the future, as in Nietzsche's *Zarathustra*. Huxley's coupling of the ape and the tiger recalls the popular belief in the implacable and invariable ferocity of both apes and "cavemen," a belief for which there seems to be little more evidence than for unicorns and phoenixes, but which, like them, shows a tendency to look at natural history from within the appropriate framework of poetic metaphors. The low mimetic is not a rich field for animal symbolism, but Huxley's ape and tiger recur in Kipling's *Jungle Book*, where the monkeys chatter in the tree-tops to no purpose, like intellectuals, while the human animal learns instead the dark predatory wisdom of the panther in the jungle below.

Gardens in the low mimetic give place to farms and the painful labor of the man with the hoe, the peasant or furze cutter who stands in Hardy as an image of man himself, "slighted and enduring. " Cities take of course the shape of the labyrinthine modern metropolis, where the main emotional stress is on loneliness and lack of communication. And just as water symbolism in the world of innocence consists largely of fountains and running streams, so low mimetic imagery seeks Conrad's "destructive element" the sea, generally with some humanized leviathan or *bateau ivre* on it of any size from the Titanic in Hardy to the capsizable open boat which is, with an irony rare even in literature, a favorite image of Shelley. *Moby Dick* returns us to a more traditional form of the leviathan. The destroyer which appears at the end of H. G. Wells's *Tono-Bungay is* notable as coming from a low mimetic writer not much given to introducing hieratic symbols. Fire symbolism is often ironic and destructive, as in the fire which ends the action of *The Spoils of Poynton*. In the industrial age, however, Prometheus, who stole fire for man's use, is one of the favorite, if not the actual favorite, mythological figure among poets.

The relation of innocence and experience to apocalyptic and demonic imagery illustrates an aspect of displacement which we have so far said little about: displacement in the direction of the moral. The two dialectical structures are, radically, the desirable and the undesirable. Racks and dungeons belong in the sinister vision not because they are morally forbidden but because it is impossible to make them objects of desire. Sexual fulfilment, on the other hand, may be desired even if it is morally condemned. Civilization tends to try to make the desirable and the moral coincide. The student of comparative mythology occasionally turns up, in a primitive or ancient cult, a bit of uninhibited mythopoeia that makes him realize how completely all the higher religions have limited their apocalyptic visions to morally acceptable ones. A good deal of expurgation clearly lies behind the development of Jewish, Greek, and other mythologies; or, as Victorian students of myth used to say, a repulsive and grotesque barbarism has been purified by a growing ethical refinement. Egyptian mythology begins with a god who creates the world by masturbation—a logical enough way of symbolizing the process of creation *de Deo*, but not one that we should expect to find in Homer, to say nothing of the Old Testament. As long as poetry follows religion towards the moral, religious and poetic archetypes will be very close together, as they are in Dante. Under such influence apocalyptic sexual imagery, for instance, tends to become matrimonial or virginal; the incestuous, the homosexual, and the adulterous go on the demonic side. The quality in art that Aristotle called *spoudaios* and that Matthew Arnold translated as "high seriousness" results from this rapprochement of religion and poetry within a common moral framework.

But poetry continually tends to right its own balance, to return to the pattern of desire and away from the conventional and moral. It usually does this in satire, the genre which is furthest removed from "high seriousness," but not always. The moral and the desirable have many important and significant connections, but still morality, which comes to terms with experience and necessity, is one thing, and desire, which tries to escape from necessity, is quite another. Thus literature is as a rule less inflexible than morality, and it owes much of its status as a liberal art to that fact. The qualities that morality and religion usually call ribald, obscene, subversive, lewd, and blasphemous have an essential place in literature, but often they can achieve expression only through ingenious techniques of displacement.

The simplest of such techniques is the phenomenon that we may call "demonic modulation," or the deliberate reversal of the customary moral associations of archetypes. Any symbol at all takes its meaning primarily from its context: a dragon may be sinister in a medieval romance or friendly in a Chinese one; an island may be Prospero's island or Circe's. But because of the large amount of learned and traditional symbolism in literature, certain secondary associations become habitual. The serpent, because of its role in the garden of Eden story, usually belongs on the sinister side of our catalogue in Western literature; the revolutionary sympathies of Shelley impel him to use an innocent serpent in *The Revolt of Islam*. Or a free and equal society may be symbolized by a band of robbers, pirates, or gypsies; or true love may be symbolized by the triumph of an adulterous liaison over marriage, as in most triangle comedy; by a homosexual passion (if it *is* true love that is celebrated in Virgil's second eclogue) or an incestuous one, as in many Romantics. In the nineteenth century, with demonic myth approaching, this kind of reversed symbolism is organized into all the patterns of the "Romantic agony," chiefly sadism, Prometheanism, and diabolism, which in some of the "decadents" seem to provide all the disadvantages of superstition with none of the advantages of religion. Diabolism is not however invariably a sophisticated development: Huckleberry Finn, for example, wins our sympathy and admiration by preferring hell with his hunted friend to the heaven of the white slave-owners' god. On the other hand, imagery traditionally demonic may be used for the starting-point of a movement of redemption, like the City of Destruction in *The Pilgrim's Progress*. Alchemical symbolism takes the ouroboros and the hermaphrodite (*res bina*), as well as the traditional romantic dragon, in this redemptive context.

Apocalyptic symbolism presents the infinitely desirable, in which the lusts and ambitions of man are identified with, adapted to, or projected on the gods. The art of the analogy of innocence, which includes most of the comic (in its happy-ending aspect), the idyllic, the romantic, the reverent, the panegyrical, the idealized, and the magical, is largely concerned with an attempt to present the desirable in human, familiar, attainable, and morally allowable terms. Much the same is true of the relation of the demonic world to the analogy of experience. Tragedy, for instance, is a vision of what does happen and must be accepted. To this extent it is a moral and plausible displacement of the bitter resentments that humanity feels against all obstacles to its desires. However malignant we may feel Athene to be in Sophocles' *Ajax*, the tragedy clearly implies that we must come to terms with her possession of power, even in our thoughts. A Christian who believed the Greek gods to be nothing but devils would, if he were criticizing a tragedy of Sophocles, make an undisplaced or demonic interpretation of it. Such an interpretation would bring out everything that Sophocles was trying *not* to say; but it could be a shrewd criticism of its latent or underlying demonic structure for all that. The same kind of interpretation would be equally possible for many passages of Christian poetry dealing with the just wrath of God, the demonic content of which is often a hated father-figure. In pointing out the latent apocalyptic or demonic patterns in a literary work, we should not make the error of assuming that this latent content is the *real* content hypocritically disguised by a lying censor. It is simply one factor which is relevant to a full critical analysis. It is often, however, the factor which lifts a work of literature out of the category of the merely historical.

18. 弗莱：《原型批评：神话理论》

(Northrop Frye, "Archetypal Criticism: Theory of Myths," 1957)

作者小识

弗莱（Northrop Frye，1912—1991），加拿大人文教育家、文学理论家和文学批评家，20 世纪原型理论和批评实践的代表之一。20 世纪 40 年代到 50 年代，英美新批评几乎一统文学话语，经纬天地。弗莱挑战这种话语霸权，强调文学批评必须关注文学模式与文学体裁，而不只是分析个别作品的语言与修辞。于是，他致力于在历史维度上探索文学模式，在伦理维度上探索文学象征，在原型维度上探索文学与神话的关系，在修辞维度上研究各种文学体裁。他发现，文学具有极广大而又尽精微的想象模型，一切文学意象在结构上均可溯源到反复出现的基本原型。弗莱后期的理论研究和批评实践侧重于探索《圣经》与文学的关系，将"巨大的存在之链"(The Great Chain of Being)与"伟大的符码"(The Great Code)联系起来，在神话世界里解读"神言的力量"，致力于描述欧洲文学的整体景观。同时，他还集中研究个别作家，如莎士比亚、布莱克、艾略特、叶芝、史蒂文森，对个别作品展开实用批评，据以补正原型理论和文学体裁研究。

弗莱的主要著作包括《可怕的对称》(*Fearful Symmetry*，1947)、《批评的解剖》(*Anatomy of Criticism*，1957)、《伟大的符码》(*The Great Code*，1982)，以及《神言的力量》(*Words with Power*，1990)。

背景略说

弗莱出生于一个信奉卫斯理宗的中产阶级家庭。这一教派强调个人体验的本质，不太看重教义，将以"圣经""传统""体验""理性"四大支柱为中心的教义原理奉为圭臬。弗莱还受戒成为加拿大联合教派的一名牧师。这一层宗教背景，让他以纵深和高远的眼光来观照人类及其创造物。其视角与那些新批评家通常采用的横向结构视角完全不一样。同时，他还从基督教宇宙观中继承了万物存在层次论，并通过解读文学经典来阐述不同存在层次的特征。

当他聚焦于人类世俗生活层面时，表现出强烈的救赎意识。在他看来，世俗存在如梦如幻，充满了苦难的折磨和对死亡的恐惧，让人倍觉孤苦无告。看到物质实体之中的虚幻，又看到神奇想象之中的真实，真正意义上的人生才正式开始，而充满了神奇想象的文学经典超越了世俗存在，反映了高层次的存在。卫斯理宗信仰让弗莱将《圣经》当作故事和想象的源泉，而不是枯燥的教义。在他看来，《圣经》就是一部神圣的历史，因为它以讲故事的方式展开了对生活世界的整体观照。

斯宾格勒(Oswald Spengler，1880—1936)的《西方的没落》(*Der Untergang des Abendlandes*，1923)强化了弗莱的文学整体观。这本书让他感到，人类的思想和文化作为一个整体展现在眼前，给了他一种整体视角。新批评方法和文化类型学方法在弗莱的思想体系之中融为一体，让他既能"烛照幽微"，又能"综观全局"。斯宾格勒将文化所经历的萌芽、生长、衰落、凋零的过程看作一种有机的循环，这就给予弗莱一种理论架构，让他构造了"世界历史"(Weltgeschichte)或"作为历史的世界"(Welt als Geschichte)之统一体观念。《西方的没落》以文化有机论为基础为书写历史提供了一种"宏大的叙事"(grand recit)，其中包括人类的堕落与救赎、普遍苦难与整体偿还。这种观照文化史的视角启发弗莱，使其意识到，文学批评既要注重文本深耕，又要把文本与其他同时代的人类造物联系起来，将其作为一个文化整体来观照。

英国文化批评的现代人文主义传统也塑造了弗莱的文化观，构成了其文学批评的内隐维度。马修·阿诺德将"文化"与"无政府状态"对立起来，认为文化是人类思想与知识的精华，是甜美与光辉，同现代市侩精神的贪欲、残酷、自私、张狂完全不同。这种纯粹智性的"文化观"，旨在将"普通的自我"提升为"卓越的自我"，并激励人为"完美的自我"而努力。利维斯(F. R. Leavis)同样相信文化是人类的高等价值，但对文化的未来持一种悲观的态度，认为标准化的文明将覆盖整个世界，高雅生活的语言及其所表现的精神都已经扭曲、堕落。利维斯谴责现代技术功利主义所主宰的社会，对已经渐渐丧失的有机、和谐社会表示怀念和哀挽。

弗莱传承着英国现代人文主义传统，提出了"关怀的神话"(myth of concern)，并以此回应解构批评"影响的焦虑"(anxiety of influence)。"关怀的神话"之要义在于，文化位居神话之中心，社会是神话中衍生出的权威力量。文化，以及具体的文学作品，通过表达个人的"基本关怀"而与大众社会联系起来。以这种"关怀的神话"为基础，弗莱将文学视为社会神话，而社会神话是一个复杂的结构，其中包含着各种观念、意象、信仰、猜测、焦虑和希望，表达出对个人境遇和人类命运的思考。于是，弗莱的文学观可以被概括为"神话以隐喻和象征表达人类的基本关怀"，而他的批评观之要义是"将文学置放在一个文化整体中观照"。

基本内容

本片段选自《批评的解剖》第三章《原型批评：神话理论》。《批评的解剖》为文学批评四论，分别从历史、伦理、神话和修辞对文学的模式、象征、原型和体裁展开了整体性探讨。

第一章在历史维度上讨论文学作品的虚构型和主题型——虚构型以叙述人物及其故事为主旨，而主题型以作者向读者传递寓意为目标。然后，作者将虚构型文学分为五种基本模式或样式（modes）：神话、浪漫传奇、高度模仿、低度模仿、反讽—讽刺。它们从神话到反讽下行，又从反讽到神话上行，如此循环、回流，呈现演变周期、节奏。

第二章在伦理维度上讨论文学作品的象征，从叙事和意义两个方面对文学作品的层次进行考察。文学作品的总体是象征，即"假设性语词结构"，其根本特征在于语境改变意义，意义表现为歧义。于是，作者分辨出意义和叙述的五个层次或五个相位（phases），或者说文学作品语境化的五种方式：文字层次、描述层次、形式层次、神话形式、总体阐释层次。

第三章在神话维度上讨论文学作品的原型，是全书的重心。弗莱已经在前两章断言，神话是文学作品的基本样式，是一切模式的原型，而一切模式都是"神话的位移"或"神话的变异"；原型是文学作品所有相位的中心，是一切层次的核心。在这一章，作者具体论述了原型理论的内涵及批评原则。其核心论点是：神话体现了最根本的文学程序和结构原理，而原型研究是一种"管窥锥指""以大观小"的宏大叙事研究，其目的是从文化整体景观中把握文学的结构和意境。本章又分为两个主干部分。

第一部分（本章选文）论述原型的意义。在意义层次上，作者将原型分为三种类型：（1）神谕意象或启示意象，展现天国景象以及人类种种理想的投射；（2）魔怪意象，表现地狱以及否定性人类想象；（3）类比意象或喻像，即游弋在天界与地狱之间的意象。神谕意象和魔怪意象是源始意象，在文学模式之中呈现出种种变异形式。类比意象萌芽于神话，但主要呈现在浪漫主义和现实主义文学结构中。

第二部分论述神话、原型的叙事结构。弗莱的基本前提是：西方文学的叙事结构总体上是对自然循环过程的模仿。自然循环有春、夏、秋、冬，文学结构也有与之相应的四种基本类型，即喜剧、浪漫传奇、悲剧和反讽。四种结构形式寓于神话原型，又呈现出周期性的循环。

第四章在修辞维度上讨论文学的各种体裁之特征，如散文、戏剧、抒情诗、史诗等。运用新批评的细读方法，弗莱从修辞的角度去研究文学作品的辞章，考究各类体裁遣词造句、远近取喻、韵律节奏等方面的特征。

拓展讨论

文学原型理论有三个源头，那就是荣格的集体无意识原型说、弗莱的神话原型说以及弗雷泽的巫术原型说。詹姆斯·弗雷泽（James Frazer，1854—1941)是英国人类学派最重要的代表之一，其划时代的人类学巨著《金枝》(*The Golden Bough*)对20世纪文学批评家产生了重大的影响。弗雷泽学说影响所及，甚至包括乔伊斯、托马斯·曼以及艾略特，这些都是20世纪最具创造力的作家。弗雷泽对巫术、礼仪和神话中的宗教之始源展开了跨文化的比较研究，其著作在1890年首次以两卷本问世，随后扩充为12卷，1922年以简略一卷本出版。

弗雷泽对于原型批评之主要贡献在于，在任何时空之中，在整个世界上，人类的主要渴望都具有本质的相似性，而且这些渴望都会反射在古代神话体系之中。比如，对于阿多尼斯神话，弗雷泽解释说，人们举行各种仪式，念诵咒语，祈求天降甘霖，保佑牲畜繁殖、果实丰硕。举行这类仪式时，他们为自己描述出植物生长和衰朽、生物诞生和死亡的意象，并认为这一切都蕴含着神性，诸神也按照人类生活的方式，生，死，婚嫁，繁育。这类仪式在东地中海边境地区广为流行。埃及、西非人民以奥西里斯(Osiris)、塔穆兹(Tammuz)、阿多尼斯(Adonis)和阿提斯(Attis)等名字来表示生命(尤其是植物生命)年复一年的衰亡与复苏，将它们当作神的化身。这些仪式的名称、细节在各地有所不同，但实质上一样，都依照着最古老的原型。[①] 艾略特承认，弗雷泽的《金枝》对他创作《荒原》影响甚巨，诗中特别引用了《金枝》中关于阿多尼斯、阿提斯、奥西里斯的部分。

---

① 弗雷泽：《金枝 巫术与宗教之研究》，徐育新、汪培基、张泽石译，473～474页，北京，中国民间文艺出版社，1987。

弗雷泽所处理的中心议题是十字架上的死亡和花园中的复活之原型，尤其是描述"谋杀神王"的神话。许多原始民族相信，统治者必须是神或者半神，其生命周期等同于自然和人类生命的周期。所以，人民的平安喜乐和世界的安详和顺就仰赖神王的生命。强壮健康的统治者确保人类和自然的生殖力，病态残疾的统治者将给国土和人民带来灾难，而这就是艾略特《荒原》"火诫"中一个意象的原型："……我坐在岸边/垂钓，身后是干旱荒芜的平原/我是否至少该把我的国家整顿好？"坐在岸边钓鱼的"我"，是一个病态的帝王，而钓鱼是寻求新生、寻求拯救、寻求永恒的象征行为。弗雷泽写道："自然的进程如果有赖于人神的生命，则人神能力的逐渐衰退并最后消灭于死亡，该会带来怎样的灾祸呢？防止危险的办法只有一个。人神的能力一露衰退的迹象，就必须马上将他杀死，必须在将要来的衰退产生严重损害之前，把它的灵魂转给一个精力充沛的继承者。"①

按照这一原型，便能解释狄安娜神庙那种奇特的祭司承袭制度了。一个祭司职位的候补者只有杀死老祭司以后才能接替祭司职位，直到他自己又被另一个更强大更慧黠的人杀死为止。这种野蛮的承袭制度，一直绵延到了罗马帝国时代。按照弗雷泽的看法，太古时代的野蛮遗迹，一直传承到罗马帝国的习俗，在当今文明社会中，就像"一堵远古石崖袒露在修剪平展的草坪上那样引人注目"。通过对这些原型的解释，弗雷泽发现，早期人类就已经以与文明人基本相似的思想方式阐述了人类最初朴素的人生哲学。弗雷泽语出惊人，说原始时代的巫术仪式与宗教无关，却与现代科学同源同质。在论述巫术与科学同源的段落中，弗雷泽表现了一个人类学家的空前激情：

> 巫术与科学在认识世界的概念上，两者是相近的。二者都认定事件的演替是完全有规律的和肯定的。并且由于这些演变是由不变的规律所决定的，所以它们是可以准确地预见到和推算出来的。一切不定的、偶然的和意外的因素均被排除在自然进程之外。对那些深知事物的起因、并能接触到这部庞大复杂的宇宙自然机器运转奥秘的发条的人来说，巫术与科学这二者似乎都为他开辟了具有无限可能性的前景。于是，巫术同科学一样都在人们的头脑中产生了强烈的吸引力；强有力地刺激着对

---

① 弗雷泽：《金枝 巫术与宗教之研究》，徐育新、汪培基、张泽石译，392～393页，北京，中国民间文艺出版社，1987。

于知识的追求。它们用对于未来的无限美好的憧憬，去引诱那疲倦了的探索者、困乏了的追求者，让他穿越对当今现实感到失望的荒野。巫术与科学将他带到极高极高的山峰之巅，在那里，越过他脚下的滚滚浓雾和层层乌云，可以看到天国之都的美景，它虽然遥远，但却沐浴在理想的光辉之中，放射着超凡的灿烂光华![1]

延伸阅读

1. 弗莱：《批评的解剖》，陈慧、袁宪军、吴伟仁译，天津，百花文艺出版社，2006。要想全面了解原型批评的原理与批评实践，宜通读弗莱的这部代表作。

2. 弗莱：《伟大的代码——圣经与文学》，郝振益、攀振帼、何成洲译，北京，北京大学出版社，1998。这部著作从文学批评角度来研究圣经，认为圣经中的意象和叙事构成了一个"幻想的框架"，即一个神话世界。

---

[1] 弗雷泽：《金枝 巫术与宗教之研究》，徐育新、汪培基、张泽石译，76 页，北京，中国民间文艺出版社，1987。

19. An Ethics of Sexual Difference (1929)

By Luce Irigaray

Coming to Rotterdam to teach philosophy represents something rather special. An adventure of thought, an adventure of discovery, or rediscovery, in a country that has offered a haven to several philosophers. Offered them tolerance and encouragement in their work. Outside of any dogmatic passion. In most cases.

Astonishingly, yet correlatively, these philosophers were often interested in passion. And it is almost a tradition that Holland should be the territory where the issue of the passions is raised.

I shall not fail that history. Or rather, that history, knowingly or not, consciously or not, has chosen me, this year, to speak, in Rotterdam, in a course titled "The Ethics of the Passions." It is as if a certain necessity has led me to this part of the Netherlands to speak on this topic.

To each period corresponds a certain way of thinking. And even though the issues relating to passion and its ethics which need careful consideration today are still clearly linked to Descartes's *wonder* and Spinoza's *joy*, the perspective is no longer the same. This change in perspective is, precisely, a matter of ethics. We are no longer in an era where the subject reconstitutes the world in solitude on the basis of one fixed point: Descartes's certainty that he is a man. This is no longer the era of Spinoza, who wrote: "It is easy to see that if men and women together assumed political authority, peace would suffer great harm from the permanent probability of conflict."

Perhaps we need to reconsider Hegel's analysis of the ethical world and the interpretation of sexual difference he founds on the brother-sister couple he borrows from ancient tragedy: a couple in which sexual difference seems to find harmony through the neutering of the passion "of the blood," through suspension of the carnal act. A couple whose fecundity, while loving, leads to real death. A couple forming the substrate for both the conceptualization and realization of the family and of the state which still hold sway today.

But, in this couple, whereas the brother is still able to see himself in his sister as if she were a living mirror, she finds in him no image of herself that would allow her to leave the family and have a right to the "for-itself" of the spirit "of daylight." It is understood that she accedes to generality through her husband and her child but only at the price of her singularity. She would have to give up her sensibility, the singularity of her desire, in order to enter into the immediately universal of her family duty. Woman would be wife and mother without desire. Pure obligation dissociates her from her affect.

This duty, abstract and empty of all feeling, is supposedly at the root of woman's identity, once the sister is dead and the chorus of women has been buried under the town so that the order of the city-state may be founded.

An ethical imperative would seem to require a practical and theoretical revision of the role historically allotted to woman. Whereas this role was still interpreted by Freud as anatomic destiny, we need to understand that it has been determined by the necessities of a traditional sociocultural organization—one admittedly in the process of evolving today.

Philosophy, thought, and discourse do not evolve swiftly enough in response to "popular" movements. One of the places in our time where we can locate a people is the "world of women." Nonetheless, if there is to be neither repression of this "people" nor ethical error on its part, an access to sexual difference becomes essential, and society must abandon the murderous hierarchy as well as the division of labor which bars woman from accomplishing the task reserved for her by Hegel: the task of going from the deepest depths to the highest heavens. In other words, of being faithful to a process of the divine which passes through her, whose course she must needs sustain, without regressing or yielding up her singular desire or falling prisoner to some fetish or idol of the question of "God." Could it be that one of the qualities of this divine process is to leave woman open, her threshold free, with no closure, no dogmatism? Could this be one of its ethical deeds, in sexual exchange as well?

This opportunity to question the ethical status of sexual difference is the result of an invitation to give the lecture series established in honor of Jan Tinbergen—a man who set himself the task, among others, of trying to solve certain socioeconomic problems of the third world. If I take this occasion to broach the problem of the sociocultural situation of women (sometimes referred to as the fourth world), at the request of women, and thanks to them, it will, I hope, be seen as a gesture of respect toward a vocation of generosity that is the motivation for this lectureship dedicated to theoretical research and social practice.

So let me return to the character of Antigone, though I shall not identify with it. Antigone, the antiwoman, is still a production of a culture that has been written by men alone. But this figure, who, according to Hegel, stands for ethics, has to be brought out of the night, out of the shadow, out of the rock, out of the total paralysis experienced by a social order that condemns itself even as it condemns her. Creon, who has forbidden burial for Polynices, who has suggested that Antigone keep quiet from now on about her relations with the gods, Creon who has ordered Antigone to be closed up in a hole in the rock, leaving just a little food so that he cannot be guilty of her death—this Creon has condemned society to a split in the order of reason that leaves nature without gods, without grace. Leaves the family with no future other than work for the state, procreation without joy, love without ethics.

Creon, the king, will, in the end, endure a fate as cruel as Antigone's. But he will be master of that destiny.

Antigone is silenced in her action. Locked up—paralyzed, on the edge of the city. Because she is neither master nor slave. And this upsets the order of the dialectic.

She is not a master, that much is clear.

She is not a slave. Especially because she does nothing by halves. Except for her suicide, perhaps? Suicide, the only act left to her. Given that society passes—as Hegel would say—onto the side of darkness when it is a question of the right of the female to act.

But who would dare condemn Antigone?

Not those who denied her air, love, the gods, and even the preparation of food.

Antigone has nothing to lose. She makes no attempt on another's life.

Hence the fear she arouses in Creon, who, for his part, has much at risk. I am no longer a man, he says; she is the man if I let her live. These words reveal the nature or the very essence of his crime. For him, the king, the only values are masculine, virile ones. Creon takes a risk when he wounds the other, the female, in the worship of her gods, in her right to love, to conscience, to speech. This wound will come back to haunt him as that abyss, that chasm, that night inscribed in the very heart of the dialectic, of reason, of society. Chasm or night that demands attention, like a "calvary" or a "chalice," writes Hegel.

If society today is afraid of certain men or certain women, we might ask ourselves what "crime" against them that fear might connote. And wonder if it is impossible to "imprison" or silence more than half of the world's population, for example.

This is all the more true when sensitivity becomes specularization, speculation, discourses that enter a loop of mutual interaction or lose their substance by depriving themselves of what once fed them, or fed them anew. Man is forced to search far and wide, within his memory, for the source of meaning. But by moving back into the past one risks losing the future. Discourse is a tight fabric that turns back upon the subject and wraps around and imprisons him in return. It is as if Agamemnon no longer needed Clytemnestra to catch him in her toils: discourse is net enough for him.

In the end, every "war" machine turns against the one who made it. At least according to Hegel? At least according to a certain logic of conscience? Unless we can pass into another?

Unless, at every opportunity, we ourselves take the negative upon ourselves. Which would amount to allowing the other his/her liberty, and sex. Which would assume that we accept losing ourselves by giving ourselves. Which would leave the decision about time to us. By giving us control over the debts we lay *on the future*.

Do we still have the time to face those debts?

Ethically, we have to give ourselves the time. Without forgetting to plan. Giving ourselves time is to plan on abjuring our deadly polemics so that we have time for living, and living together.

This ethical question can be approached from different perspectives, if I give myself, give us, time to think it through. Given that *science* is one of the last figures, if not the last figure, used to represent absolute knowledge, it is—ethically—essential that we ask science to reconsider the nonneutrality of the supposedly universal subject that constitutes its scientific theory and practice.

In actual fact, the self-proclaimed universal is the equivalent of an idiolect of men, a masculine imaginary, a sexed world. With no neuter. This will come as a surprise only to an out-and-out defender of idealism. It has always been men who spoke and, above all, wrote: in science, philosophy, religion, politics.

But, nothing is said about scientific intuition (except by a few rare scientists, notably physicists). Intuition would apparently arise ex nihilo, aseptic as by right. And yet a few modalities or qualities of that intuition can be sorted out. It is always a matter of:

—Positing *a* world in front of the self, constituting a world *in front of the self*.

—Imposing *a model* on the universe so as to take possession of it, an abstract, invisible, intangible model that is *thrown over* the universe like an encasing garment. Which amounts to clothing the universe in one's own identity. One's own blindness, perhaps?

—Claiming that, as a subject, one is rigorously alien to the model, i. e. , to prove that the model is purely and simply *objective*.

—Demonstrating that the model is "insensible" when in fact it has virtually been prescribed at least by the privilege accorded to the *visual* (i. e. , by the absence, the distancing, of a subject that is yet surreptitiously there).

—A move out of the world of the senses made possible by the *mediation of the instrument*, the intervention of a technique that separates the subject from the object under investigation. A process of moving away and delegating power to something that intervenes between the universe observed and the observing subject.

　　—Constructing an *ideal* or *idea-generated* model, independent of the physical and mental makeup of its producer. With games of induction, as well as deduction, passing through an ideal elaboration.

　　—Proving the *universality* of the model, at least within a given time. And its absolute power (independent of its producer), its constitution of a unique and total world.

　　—Buttressing that *universality* by protocols of experiments which at least two (identical?) subjects must agree on.

　　—Proving that the discovery is *efficient, productive, profitable, exploitable* (or is it rather *exploitative* of a natural world increasingly drained of life?). Which is assumed to mean *progress.*

These characteristics reveal an "isomorphism with man's sexual imaginary." Which has to be kept strictly under wraps. "Our subjective experiences or our personal opinions can never be used to justify any statement," claims the epistemologist of science.

But it is apparent in many ways that the subject in science is not neuter or neutral. Particularly in the way certain things are not discovered at a given period as well as in the research goals that science sets, or fails to set, for itself. Thus, in a more or less random list that refuses to respect the hierarchy of the sciences:

　　—*The physical sciences* constitute research targets in regard to a nature which they measure in an ever more formal, abstract, and modeled fashion. Their techniques, based on more and more sophisticated axiom-building, concern a matter which certainly still exists but cannot be perceived by the subject operating the experiment. At least in most sectors of these sciences. And "nature," the stake of the physical sciences, risks being exploited and torn apart at the hands of the physicist, even without his knowing. Given that the Newtonian dividing line has led scientific inquiry into a "universe" in which perception by the senses has almost no validity and which may even entail annulling precisely the thing that is at stake in the object of physics: the matter (whatever the predicates of matter may be) of the universe and of the bodies constituting it.

Within this very theory, in fact, there are deep divisions: theory of quanta/theory of fields, solid mechanics/fluid dynamics, for example. But the fact that the matter under study is inaccessible to the senses often involves the paradoxal privilege accorded to "solidity" in the discoveries, and science has been slow, or has even given up, trying to analyze the in-finite of force fields. Could this be interpreted as a refusal to take into account the dynamics of the subject researching himself?

—*The mathematical sciences*, in set theory, take an interest in closed and open spaces, in the infinitely large and infinitely small. They are less concerned with the question of the half-open, of fluid sets, of anything that analyzes the problem of edges, of the passage between things, of the fluctuations taking place from one threshold to the other of defined sets. (Even if topology raises such issues, does it not place far more emphasis on that which closes up than on that which remains without possible circularity?)

—*The biological sciences* have been very slow to take on certain problems. The constitution of the placental tissue, the permeability of membranes, for example. Are these not questions directly correlated to the female and the maternal sexual imaginary?

—*The logical sciences* are more concerned with bivalent theories than with trivalent or polyvalent ones. Is that because the latter still appear marginal? Because they upset the discursive economy?

—*The linguistic sciences* have concerned themselves with models for utterances, with synchronic structures of speech, with language models "known intuitively to any normally constituted subject." They have not faced, and at times even refuse to face, the question of the sexuation of discourse. They accept, perforce, that certain items of vocabulary may be added to the established lexicon, that new stylistic figures may potentially become acceptable, but they refuse to consider that syntax and the syntactic-semantic operation might be sexually determined, might not be neuter, universal, unchanging.

—*Economics* and perhaps even the social sciences have preferred to emphasize the phenomenon of scarcity and the question of survival rather than that of abundance and life.

—*Psychoanalytic science* is based on the two first principles of thermodynamics that underlie Freud's model of the libido. However, these two principles seem more isomorphic to male sexuality than to female. Given that female sexuality is less subject to alternations of tension-discharge, to conservation of required energy, to maintaining states of equilibrium, to functioning as a closed circuit that opens up through saturation, to the reversibility of time, etc.

If a scientific model is needed, female sexuality would perhaps fit better with what Prigogine calls "dissipatory" structures, which function through exchanges with the exterior world, which proceed in steps from one energy level to another, and which are not organized to search for equilibrium but rather to cross thresholds, a procedure that corresponds to going beyond disorder or entropy without discharge.

As we face these claims, these questions, this issue arises: *either* to do science *or* to become "militant." Or is it rather: to continue to do science *and* to divide oneself into several functions, several persons or characters? Should the "truth" of science and that of life remain separate, at least for the majority of researchers? What science or what life is at issue here, then? Particularly since life in our era is largely dominated by science and its techniques.

What is the origin of this split imposed and suffered by scientists? Is it a model of the subject that has not been analyzed? A "subjective" revolution that has not taken place? Given that the disintegration of the subject is programmed by the *episteme* and the power structures it has set up. Must we assume that the Copernican revolution has occurred but that the epistemological subject has yet to act on it and move beyond it? The discourse of the subject has been altered but finds itself even more disturbed by this revolution than the language of the world which preceded it. Given that the scientist, now, wants to be *in front of* the world: naming the world, making its laws, its axioms. Manipulating nature, exploiting it, but forgetting that he too is in nature. That he is still *physical*, and not only when faced with phenomena whose *physical* nature he tends to ignore. As he progresses according to an objective method designed to shelter him from any instability, any "mood," any feelings and affective fluctuations, from any intuition that has not been programmed in the name of science, from any influence of his desire, particularly his *sexual* desires, over his discoveries. Perhaps by installing himself within a system, within something that can be assimilated to what is already dead? Fearing, sterilizing the losses of equilibrium even though these are necessary to achieve a new horizon of discovery.

One of the ways most likely to occasion an interrogation of the scientific horizon is to question discourse about the subject of science, and the psychic and sexuate involvement of that subject in scientific discoveries and their formulation.

Such questions clamor to be answered, or at least raised, from somewhere outside, from a place in which the subject has not or has scarcely begun to be spoken. An outside placed on the other slope of sexual difference, the one which, while useful for reproducing the infrastructure of social order, has been condemned to imprisonment and silence within and by society. It remains true that the feminine, in and through her language, can, today, raise questions of untold richness. Still she must be allowed to speak; she must be heeded.

This may lead to the avoidance of two ethical mistakes, if I may return again to Hegel:

—Subordinating women to destiny without allowing them any access to mind, or consciousness of self and for self. Offering them only death and violence as their part.

—Closing man away in a consciousness of self and for self that leaves no space for the gods and whose discourse, even today and for that same reason, goes in search of its meaning.

In other words, in this division between the two sides of sexual difference, one part of the world would be searching for a way to find and speak its meaning, its side of signification, while the other would be questioning whether meaning is still to be found in language, values, and life.

This desperately important question of our time is linked to an injustice, an ethical mistake, a debt still owing to "natural law" and to its gods.

If this question is apparent in the dereliction of the feminine, it is also raised on the male side, in quest for its meaning. Humanity and humanism have proved that their ethos is difficult to apply outside certain limits of tolerance. Given that the world is not undifferentiated, not neuter, particularly insofar as the sexes are concerned.

The meaning that can be found on the male side is perhaps that of a debt contracted toward the one who gave and still gives man life, in language as well.

Language, however formal it may be, feeds on blood, on flesh, on material elements. Who and what has nourished language? How is this debt to be repaid? Must we produce more and more formal mechanisms and techniques which redound on man, like the inverted outcome of that mother who gave him a living body? And whom he fears in direct ratio to the unpaid debt that lies between them.

To remember that we must go on living and creating worlds is our task. But it can be accomplished only through the combined efforts of the two halves of the world: the masculine and the feminine.

And I shall end with an example of something that can constitute or entail an unpaid debt to the maternal, the natural, the matrical, the nourishing.

As we move farther away from our condition as living beings, we tend to forget the most indispensable element in life: *air*. The air we breathe, in which we live, speak, appear; the air in which everything "enters into presence" and can come into being.

This air that we never think of has been borrowed from a birth, a growth, a *phusis* and a *phuein* that the philosopher forgets.

To forget being is to forget the air, this first fluid given us gratis and free of interest in the mother's blood, given us again when we are born, like a natural profusion that raises a cry of pain: the pain of a being who comes into the world and is abandoned, forced henceforth to live without the immediate assistance of another body. Unmitigated mourning for the intrauterine nest, elemental homesickness that man will seek to assuage through his work as builder of worlds, and notably of the dwelling which seems to form the essence of his maleness: language.

In all his creations, all his works, man always seems to neglect thinking of himself as flesh, as one who has received his body as that primary home (that *Gestell*, as Heidegger would say, when, in "Logos," the seminar on Heraclitus, he recognizes that what metaphysics has not begun to address is the issue of the body) which determines the possibility of his coming into the world and the potential opening of a horizon of thought, of poetry, of celebration, that also includes the god or gods.

The fundamental dereliction in our time may be interpreted as our failure to remember or prize the element that is indispensable to life in all its manifestations: from the lowliest plant and animal forms to the highest. Science and technology are reminding men of their careless neglect by forcing them to consider the most frightening question possible, the question of a radical polemic: the destruction of the universe and of the human race through the splitting of the atom and its exploitation to achieve goals that are beyond our capacities as mortals.

"Only a god can save us now," said Heidegger, who was also remembering the words of Hölderlin, the poet with whom his thought was indissolubly linked. Hölderlin says that the god comes to us on a certain *wind* that blows from the icy cold of the North to the place where every sun rises: the East. The god arrives on the arms of a wind that sweeps aside everything that blocks the light, everything that separates fire and air and covers all with imperceptible ice and shadow. The god would refer back to a time before our space-time was formed into a closed world by an economy of natural elements forced to bow to man's affect and will. Demiurge that could have closed up the universe into a circle, or an egg, according to Empedocles.

Man's technical prowess today allows him to blow up the world just as, at the dawn of our culture, he was able to establish a finite horizon to it.

Is a god what we need, then? A god who can upset the limits of the possible, melt the ancient glaciers, a god who can make a future for us. A god carried on the breath of the *cosmos*, the song of the poets, the respiration of lovers.

We still have to await the god, remain ready and open to prepare a way for his coming. And, with him, for ourselves, to prepare, not an implacable decline, but a new birth, a new era in history.

Beyond the circularity of discourse, of the nothing that is in and of being. When the copula no longer veils the abyssal burial of the other in a gift of language which is neuter only in that it forgets the difference from which it draws its strength and energy. With a neuter, abstract *there is* giving way to or making space for a "we are" or "we become," "we live here" together.

This creation would be our opportunity, from the humblest detail of everyday life to the "grandest," by means of the opening of a *sensible transcendental* that comes into being through us, of which *we would be* the mediators and bridges. Not only in mourning for the dead God of Nietzsche, not waiting passively for the god to come, but by conjuring him up among us, within us, as resurrection and transfiguration of blood, of flesh, through a language and an ethics that is ours.

19. 伊利格瑞：《性别差异伦理学》

(Luce Irigaray，"An Ethics of Sexual Difference，" 1929)

作者小识

伊利格瑞(Luce Irigaray，1931—)，法国女性主义者、哲学家、心理语言学家、精神分析学家和文化理论家。她的女性主义理论有鲜明的后现代主义特色。伊利格瑞的思想脉络可分为三个阶段，第一阶段是对西方传统二元论的批判，第二阶段是建构女性主体间性，第三阶段是对男女性别差异的探究。她致力于各种场合的语言实证研究，探求男女说话方式的差异。伊利格瑞作品的关键特征是对于性别差异的关注，"语言和各再现系统无法翻译女人的欲望"。她志在寻找一个女性语言能自由发声之处。伊利格瑞的许多著作是关于西方著名先哲(包括柏拉图、黑格尔、尼采、海德格尔等)之间的虚拟对话的。她还曾借鉴马克思的资本和商品理论，认为女性的交换价值是由社会决定的，而她的使用价值来自她的自然特性。因此，一个女人的自我价值被分为使用价值和交换价值，她只因交换价值而被需要。这个价值系统创造了三种类型的女性：母亲，只有使用价值；处女，只有交换价值；妓女，既有使用价值又有交换价值。伊利格瑞的主要著作有：批判弗洛伊德"女人性"论断、挑战西方哲学家们尤其是拉康将"女人"对应于"空洞"这一男权话语视角的《他者女性窥镜》(*Speculum of the Other Woman*，1985)，试图从女性主体出发、打破对女性性欲的浅表化解读、展现女性欲望中的异质性的《此性非一》(*This Sex Which Is Not One*，1985)。

背景略说

巴黎公社的女英雄"红色贞女"路易丝·米歇尔(Louise Michel)是法国的女性主义先驱。生活在 20 世纪中期的伊利格瑞处于法国"知识典范的转移"时期，关注种族、阶级对立冲突的"人文主义"受到探究个人和社会之间的互动关系的"结构主义"的挑战。从"存在主义教母"——《第二性》的作者西蒙娜·德·波伏娃到"结构主义"的克丽丝缇娃亦是一种"现代性"转移。在这样一个转型时期，伊利格瑞的女性主义理论是对整个西方形而上学传统和文化组织的重构，她从哲学与精神分析学的角度展开对于女性的思考，具有后现代性。

二元对立是西方传统知识结构中根深蒂固的一种思维方式，这种固化思维导致人们习惯于对事物以好坏、高低进行二元区分。后现代女性主义从根本上反对二元对立，反思思维中"理性与非理性"等固化概念，并提出创新性的整合的思维模式，其中包括挖掘女性价值模式、提倡多元化模式等。伊利格瑞作为后现代女性主义者对于差异性十分关注，包括种族差异、民族差异、阶级差异、性别差异等，其中伊利格瑞最为关注的是性别差异。伊利格瑞认为性别差异是一种天然差异，在文化与社会领域都有所体现。按照伊利格瑞所处时代的主流观点，只要支持性别差异属于自然差异这一观点，都会被归于政治上的保守主义。从目的性来说，伊里格瑞关于性别差异的论述目的在于推动女性境遇的变革，而变革不仅要提升女性的社会价值，改善女性的生活状况，更要提升女性的自然价值，最后上升到改善人类与自然界的关系。

后期伊利格瑞对于性别差异的论述似乎越来越着力于凸显女性某些天生的品质。她认为男性和女性天生具有不同的自然条件，这意味着他们适宜进行不同的活动。这似乎很接近传统的对于男女之别的观点，即女性的自然条件使她们容易受到抚养子女等家庭领域的影响。

许多女性主义者试图批判伊利格瑞后期学说中的本质主义立场，即相信任何事物都存在着一个深藏着的唯一的本质，相信本质和现象的区分提供了人类观察万事万物的基本概念图式。然而，目前学者们对于伊利格瑞的性别差异理论是否属于本质主义理论还存在很多争议。认为伊利格瑞的作品属于本质主义的学者，比较集中地认为伊利格瑞对性别差异的关注只是异性恋行为的排演。但正如海伦·菲尔丁（Helen Fielding）所述，令女性主义者非常不安的伊利格瑞关于男性气质和女性气质的论述，并不能说明伊利格瑞的异质性倾向。她的批评者因所处的文化传承环境而产生了理解偏差，认为自然是不变的有机体或是可以被规定的、操控的、改写的事物。这些批评者对本质主义的理解是建立在二元思维基础之上的，他们将文化层面的层级概念加到了自然之上。

基本内容

本片段选自伊利格瑞文集第三部分《性别差异伦理学》，是她纪念简·丁伯根（Jan Tinbergen）系列讲座中的一篇演讲稿。文章伊始，伊利格瑞便提出每个时期对应着一定的思维方式，即使今天对于激情与伦理有关的问题也是需要仔细考虑的。斯宾诺莎、黑格尔等先哲曾提出遵循自然的一对对和谐夫妇构成了家庭和国家。伊利格瑞质疑这一论断的概念化与实现性基础，认为女人在这一伦理体系中是没有欲望的妻子和母亲，为了履行她的家庭义务，不得不放弃她的感性和欲望的独特性。

接下来，伊利格瑞以希腊神话中俄狄浦斯之女安提戈涅（Antigone）与国王克瑞翁（Creon）的冲突为例，引用剧中对白——"我不再是一个男人。如果我让她活着，她就是男人。"（"I am no longer a man, he says; she is the man if I let her live."）——说明现在的所谓伦理体系只涵盖男性个人，是一种男性化的想象世界，是虚假的、自封的。

最后，伊利格瑞总结道：我们必须继续努力生存，改造世界是我们的任务，但只有通过世界两个方面（男性和女性）的统一努力才能实现。

值得一提的是，为说明男人和女人本质上的不同性格对于他们在自然界中所处地位的影响，伊利格瑞着重在两个层面上定义"自然"这一概念。首先，对于她来说，某种东西的"本性"是指它的特征或本质。从这个意义上讲，男人和女人具有不同的本性。其次，对于伊利格瑞来说，"自然"指的是人们可感的物质世界或整个生存环境。这个物质世界包括人类，因为他们具有天性（并且根据这些天性行事），但是在另一层面上，这个物质世界将人类排除在外，因为人是独特的智慧生物，从事着改造自我和改造物质世界的活动。

总体来看，伊利格瑞试图重新以女性系谱评估女性的身份，以及传统意义上女性的自然性体现，但是伊利格瑞重新评估这些只是文化上的构思和象征，而且她的评估是以预设女性特性劣于男性特性为前提的。

拓展讨论

在男性话语体系占主导地位的社会中，男性总在有意或无意间试图拓展其话语的掌控范围，如将自己的姓氏给予其子女、妻子以及其他一切所有物，甚至将自己的性别给予上帝，给予宇宙法则，给予社会秩序。为了对抗"父亲之名"，伊利格瑞倡导建立一种女性话语体系，因为"当男性抓住了神谕和真理的时候，男性就从尘世和肉体根源中分离出来。这一变化也意味着法律、司法和修辞学的改变。当父神的这种逻各斯秩序被建立以后，就开始责难女性的话语权，并且使它处于消音（inaudible）状态"。伊利格瑞创造独立于男性话语体系之外的女性话语体系，意在创造属于女性的专属象征，从而解除女性话语的"消音状态"。

为了重构女性话语体系，伊利格瑞重新审视"男人和神、男人和男人、男人和世界、男人和女人的关系"。受结构主义和解构主义思潮的影响，伊利格瑞反对二元对立的思维方式，客观分析以往女性主义理论的不足，解构传统性别定式。她发现在"自然"意义上，男性在社会中理所当然地占据主体地位，建立了父权制社会。在这样一个社会中，女性依附男性建立婚姻关系，男性依照男性话语体系定义、阐释女人与世界。由此，女性逐渐丧失主体性，变成相对于男性的"他者"。伊利格瑞试图从"同一性"及男性的想象角度探索女性是如何被排除在现行话语体系之外的。她提出在性别差异基础上建构男、女两个主体，使人类只有性别差异而没有等级之分。在此情况下，男、女作为两个独立的主体，应当有对于性别差异的自知，并且既承认自己的世界，也承认他人的世界。两者可以用属于自身的语言和话语来表达自身感受，双方互相了解、尊重，形成和谐的社会关系。

伊利格瑞想要建构既尊重他者又认同主体的两性文化。在使用"他者"这个概念时，伊利格瑞首先承认"他者"列居从属地位，但更多的是强调"他者"所具有的包容性。她认为"他者"作为异质性的存在，并不是客体，也不是认知对象："他者可以是一种存在方式、思想方式和讲述方式，它使得开放、多重性和差异成为可能。"列维纳斯的"他者"理论是伊利格瑞构建男、女两个主体之间关系的重要思想来源。列维纳斯认为，没有任何全体真正包含实在，总是存在独立于全体的他者。列维纳斯所指的"他者"是不可化简的，在全体之外具有独立的地位，是不可以被纳入同一之中的。伊利格瑞则认为："他者是谁或者什么，我不知道，不过这个未知的他者是和我性别上有差异的东西。这种在未知事物面前惊奇、惊讶和吃惊的感觉应该被送回它合适的地方——性别差异的领域。"伊利格瑞指出，对女性的剥削来自性别差异，它的消除也只能从性别差异开始。伊利格瑞试图在性别差异基础上重建社会文化、女性主体。她希望把性别差异提升到身体现实之上的主体性层次——而这样的主体性是建立在对"女性"他者的认同和尊重基础之上的。

伊利格瑞在对性别差异进行阐释和探索的基础上，提出追求两性和谐的构想，认为只有让"性别差异真正成为自立自主的两个主体之间的差异，建立于此基础上的两性关系才是富有成效和创造性的"。伊利格瑞揭示出社会性别的人为性和可变性，认为关于社会性别的传统划分不过是男权中心文化的一种想象。从消除差异到差异基础上的平等，在对男性一元论进行解构的同时，伊利格瑞进行着对女性主体的建构。伊利格瑞呼吁构建女性话语体系，建立一种既要尊重他者又要认同主体的两性话语体系，以此保证社会关系中人与人之间的平等交流，创造更自由的发展空间。

延伸阅读

1. Gayatri Chakravorty Spivak，"Feminism and Critical Theory," in *The Spivak Reader*, ed. Donna Landry and Gerald MacLean，New York & London，Routledge，1996.

2. Luce Irigaray，"Woman Is a Woman as a Result of a Certain Lack of Characteristics," in *Speculum of the Other Woman*, trans. Gillian C. Gill，Ithaca，Cornell University Press，1985.

3. Luce Irigaray，"The Looking Glass from the Other Side," in *This Sex Which Is Not One*, trans. Catherine Porter& Carolyn Burke，Ithaca，Cornell University Press，1985.

4. Virginia Woolf，*A Room of One's Own*. New York，Harcourt Brace and Company，1929.

5. Luce Irigaray，*The Forgetting of Air in Martin Heidegger*, trans. Mary Beth Mader，Austin，University of Texas Press，1999.

6. Luce Irigaray，*Sexes and Genealogies*, trans. Gillian C. Gill，New York，Columbia University Press，1993.

20. Towards a Poetics of Culture[①](1986)

By Stephen J. Greenblatt

I feel in a somewhat false position, which is not a particularly promising way to begin, and I might as well explain why.[②] My own work has always been done with a sense of just having to go about and do it, without establishing first exactly what my theoretical position is. A few years ago I was asked by *Genre* to edit a selection of Renaissance essays, and I said OK. I collected a bunch of essays and then, out of a kind of desperation to get the introduction done, I wrote that the essays represented something I called a "new historicism." I've never been very good at making up advertising phrases of this kind; for reasons that I would be quite interested in exploring at some point, the name stuck much more than other names I'd very carefully tried to invent over the years. In fact I have heard—in the last year or so—quite a lot of talk about the "new historicism" (which for some reason in Australia is called Neo-historicism); there are articles about it, attacks on it, references to it in dissertations: the whole thing makes me quite giddy with amazement. In any case, as part of this peculiar phenomenon I have been asked to say something of a theoretical kind about the work I'm doing. So I shall try if not to define the new historicism, at least to situate it as a practice—a practice rather than a doctrine, since as far as I can tell (and I should be the one to know) it's no doctrine at all.

One of the peculiar characteristics of the "new historicism" in literary studies is precisely how unresolved and in some ways disingenuous it has been—I have been—about the relation to literary theory. On the one hand it

---

① This chapter was first published in *Learning to Curse: Essays in Early Modern Culture* (Stephen Greenblatt, 1990, pp. 146-160).

② This is the text of a lecture given at the University of Western Australia on September 4, 1986. A slightly different version appeared in Murray Krieger, ed., *The Aims of Representation: Subject/Text/History* (New York: Columbia University Press, 1987), pp. 257-273.

seems to me that an openness to the theoretical ferment of the last few years is precisely what distinguishes the new historicism from the positivist historical scholarship of the early twentieth century. Certainly, the presence of Michel Foucault on the Berkeley campus for extended visits during the last five or six years of his life, and more generally the influence in America of European (and especially French) anthropological and social theorists, has helped to shape my own literary critical practice. On the other hand the historicist critics have on the whole been unwilling to enrol themselves in one or the other of the dominant theoretical camps.

I want to speculate on why this should be so by trying to situate myself in relation to Marxism on the one hand, and poststructuralism on the other. In the 1970s I used to teach courses with names like "Marxist Aesthetics" on the Berkeley campus. This came to an inglorious end when I was giving such a course—it must have been the mid-1970s—and I remember a student getting very angry with me. Now it's true that I tended to like those Marxist figures who were troubled in relation to Marxism—Walter Benjamin, the early rather than the later Lukács, and so forth—and I remember someone finally got up and screamed out in class "You're either a Bolshevik or a Menshevik—make up your fucking mind," and then slammed the door. It was a little unsettling, but I thought about it afterwards and realized that I wasn't sure whether I was a Menshevik, but I certainly wasn't a Bolshevik. After that I started to teach courses with names like "Cultural Poetics. " It's true that I'm still more uneasy with a politics and a literary perspective that is untouched by Marxist thought, but that doesn't lead me to endorse propositions or embrace a particular philosophy, politics or rhetoric, *faute de mieux*.

Thus the crucial identifying gestures made by the most distinguished American Marxist aesthetic theorist, Fredric Jameson, seem to me highly problematic. Let us take, for example, the following eloquent passage from *The Political Unconscious*:

> the convenient working distinction between cultural texts that are so-cial and political and those that are not becomes something worse than an

error: namely, a symptom and a reinforcement of the reification and privatization of contemporary life. Such a distinction reconfirms that structural, experiential, and conceptual gap between the public and the private, between the social and the psychological, or the political and the poetic, between history or society and the 'individual,' which—the tendential law of social life under capitalism—maims our existence as individual subjects and paralyzes our thinking about time and change just as surely as it alienates us from our speech itself. [①]

A working distinction between cultural texts that are social and political and those that are not—that is, an aesthetic domain that is in some way marked off from the discursive institutions that are operative elsewhere in a culture—becomes for Jameson a malignant symptom of "privatization." Why should the "private" immediately enter into this distinction at all? Does the term refer to private property, that is, to the ownership of the means of production and the regulation of the mode of consumption? If so, what is the historical relation between this mode of economic organization and a working distinction between the political and the poetic? It would seem that in print, let alone in the electronic media, private ownership has led not to "privatization" but to the drastic communalization of all discourse, the constitution of an ever larger mass audience, the organization of a commercial sphere unimagined and certainly unattained by the comparatively modest attempts in pre-capitalist societies to organize public discourse. Moreover, is it not possible to have a communal sphere of art that is distinct from other communal spheres? Is this communal differentiation, sanctioned by the laws of property, not the dominant practice in capitalist society, manifestly in the film and television industries, but also, since the invention of movable type, in the production of poems and novels as well? Would we really find it less alienating to have no distinction at all between the political and the poetic—the situation, let us say, during China's Cultural Revolution? Or, for

---

① Fredric Jameson, *The Political Unconscious: Narrative as a Socially Symbolic Act* (Ithaca: Cornell University Press, 1981), p. 20.

that matter, do we find it notably liberating to have our own country governed by a film actor who is either cunningly or pathologically indifferent to the traditional differentiation between fantasy and reality?

For *The Political Unconscious* any demarcation of the aesthetic must be aligned with the private which is in turn aligned with the psychological, the poetic, and the individual, as distinct from the public, the social, and the political. All of these interlocking distinctions, none of which seems to me philosophically or even historically bound up with the original "working distinction," are then laid at the door of capitalism with its power to "maim" and "paralyze" us as "individual subjects." Though we may find a differentiation between cultural discourses that are artistic and cultural discourses that are social or political well before the European seventeenth century, and in cultures that seem far removed from the capitalist mode of production, Jameson insists that somehow the perpetrator and agent of the alleged maiming is capitalism. A shadowy opposition is assumed between the "individual" (bad) and the "individual subject" (good); indeed the maiming of the latter creates the former.

The whole passage has the resonance of an allegory of the fall of man: once we were whole, agile, integrated; we were individual subjects but not individuals, we had no psychology distinct from the shared life of the society; politics and poetry were one. Then capitalism arose and shattered this luminous, benign totality. The myth echoes throughout Jameson's book, though by the close it has been eschatologically reoriented so that the totality lies not in a past revealed to have always already fallen but in the classless future. A philosophical claim then appeals to an absent empirical event. And literature is invoked at once as the dark token of fallenness and the shimmering emblem of the absent transfiguration.

But, of course, poststructuralism has raised serious questions about such a vision, challenging both its underlying oppositions and the primal organic unity that it posits as either paradisal origin or utopian, eschatological end. ① This

---

① See Mark Poster, "Foucault, Poststructuralism, and the Mode of Information," in *The Aims of Representation*.

challenge has already greatly modified, though by no means simply displaced, Marxist discourse. I could exemplify this complex interaction between Marxism and poststructuralism by discussing Jameson's own most recent work in which he finds himself, from the perspective of postmodernism, deploring the loss of those "working distinctions" that at least enabled the left to identify its enemies and articulate a radical program. ① But to avoid confusions, I want to focus instead on the work of Jean-François Lyotard. Here, as in *The Political Unconscious*, the distinction between discursive fields is once again at stake: for Lyotard the existence of proper names makes possible.

> the co-existence of those worlds that Kant calls fields, territories, and domains—those worlds which of course present the same object, but which also make that object the stakes of heterogenous (or incommensurable) expectations in universes of phrases, none of which can be transformed into any other. ②

---

① Jameson himself does not directly account for the sudden reversal in his thinking; he suggests rather that it is not his thinking that has changed but capitalism itself. Following Ernest Mandel, he suggests that we have moved into late capitalism, and in this state cultural production and consumption operate by wholly different rules. In the cultural logic of postmodernism, the working distinctions Jameson earlier found paralyzing and malignant have in fact vanished, giving way to an organization of discourse and perception that is at once dreadful and visionary. Dreadful because the new postmodern condition has obliterated all the place markers—inside and outside, culture and society, orthodoxy and subversion—that made it possible to map the world and hence mount a critique of its power structures. Visionary because this new multi-national world, a world with intensities rather than emotions, elaborated surfaces rather than hidden depths, random, unreadable signs rather than signifiers, intimates a utopian release from the traditional nightmare of traditional history. The doubleness of the postmodern is perfectly figured for Jameson by contemporary architecture, most perfectly by the Bonaventura Hotel in Los Angeles.

The rapidity of the shift between modern and postmodern charted in Jameson's shift from *The Political Unconscious* (1981) to "Postmodernism, or The Cultural Logic of Late Capitalism," *New Left Review*, 146 (July-August 1984), 53-93, is, to say the least, startling.

② J.-F. Lyotard, "Judiciousness in Dispute or, Kant after Marx," in *The Aims of Representation*, p. 37.

Lyotard's model for these differentiated discourses is the existence of proper names. But now it is the role of capitalism not to demarcate discursive domains but, quite the opposite, to make such domains untenable. "Capital is that which wants a single language and a single network, and it never stops trying to present them" (p. 55). Lyotard's principal exhibit of this attempt by capital to institute a single language—what Bakhtin would call monologism—is Faurisson's denial of the Holocaust, and behind this denial, the Nazis' attempt to obliterate the existence of millions of Jews and other undesirables, an attempt Lyotard characterizes as the will "to strike from history and from the map entire worlds of names."

The immediate problem with this account is that the Nazis did not seem particularly interested in exterminating names along with the persons who possessed those names; on the contrary, they kept, in so far as was compatible with a compaign of mass murder, remarkably full records, and they looked forward to a time in which they could share their accomplishment with a grateful world by establishing a museum dedicated to the culture of the wretches they had destroyed. The Faurisson affair is at bottom not an epistemological dilemma, as Lyotard claims, but an attempt to wish away evidence that is both substantial and verifiable. The issue is not an Epicurean paradox—"if death is there, you are not there; if you are there, death is not there; hence it is impossible for you to prove that death is there"—but a historical problem: what is the evidence of mass murder? How reliable is this evidence? Are there convincing grounds for denying or doubting the documented events? And if there are not such grounds, how may we interpret the motives of those who seek to cast doubt upon the historical record?

There is a further problem in Lyotard's use of the Faurisson affair as an instance of capitalist hostility to names: the conflation of Fascist apologetics and capitalism would seem to be itself an instance of monologism, since it suppresses all the aspects of capitalism that are wedded to the generation and inscription of individual identities and to the demarcation of boundaries separating those identities. We may argue, of course, that the capitalist insistence upon individuality is fraudulent, but it is difficult, I think, to keep the principle of endlessly proliferated, irreducible individuality separate from the market place version against which it is set. For it is capitalism, as Marx suggested, that mounts the West's most powerful and sustained assault upon collective, communal values and identities. And it is in the market place and in the state apparatus linked to the circulation and accumulation of capital that names themselves are forged. Proper names, as distinct from common names, seem less the victims than the products of property—they are bound up not only with the property one has in oneself, that is, with the theory of possessive individualism, but quite literally with the property one possesses, for proper names are insisted upon in the early modern period precisely in order to register them in the official documents that enable the state to calculate and tax personal property. [1]

The difference between Jameson's capitalism, the perpetrator of separate discursive domains, the agent of privacy, psychology, and the individual, and Lyotard's capitalism, the enemy of such domains and the destroyer of privacy, psychology, and the individual, may in part be traced to a difference between the Marxist and poststructuralist projects. Jameson, seeking to expose the fallaciousness of a separate artistic sphere and to celebrate the materialist integration of all discourses, finds capitalism at the root of the false differentiation; Lyotard, seeking to celebrate the differentiation of all discourses and to expose the fallaciousness of monological unity, finds capitalism at the root of the false integration. History functions in both cases as a convenient anecdotal ornament upon a theoretical structure, and capitalism appears not as a complex social and economic development in the West but as a malign philosophical principle. [2]

I propose that the general question addressed by Jameson and Lyotard—

---

[1]   See, for example, William E. Tate, *The Parish Chest: A Study in the Records of Parochial Administration in England* (Cambridge: Cambridge University Press, 1946).

[2]   Alternatively, of course, we can argue, as Jameson in effect does, that there are two capitalisms. The older, industrial capitalism was the agent of distinctions; the new, late capitalism is the effacer of distinctions. The detection of one tendency or the other in the phase of capitalism where it does not theoretically belong can be explained by invoking the distinction between residual and emergent. I find this scholastic saving of the theory infinitely depressing.

what is the historical relation between art and society or between one institutionally demarcated discursive practice and another? —does not lend itself to a single, theoretically satisfactory answer of the kind that Jameson and Lyotard are trying to provide. Or rather theoretical satisfaction here seems to depend upon a utopian vision that collapses the contradictions of history into a moral imperative. The problem is not simply the incompatibility of two theories— Marxist and poststructuralist—with one another, but the inability of either of the theories to come to terms with the apparently contradictory historical effects of capitalism. In principle, of course, both Marxism and poststructuralism seize upon contradictions: for the former they are signs of repressed class conflicts, for the latter they disclose hidden cracks in the spurious certainties of logocentrism. But in practice Jameson treats capitalism as the agent of repressive differentiation, while Lyotard treats it as the agent of monological totalization. And this effacement of contradiction is not the consequence of an accidental lapse but rather the logical outcome of theory's search for the obstacle that blocks the realization of its eschatological vision.

If capitalism is invoked not as a unitary demonic principle, but as a complex historical movement in a world without paradisal origins or chiliastic expectations, then an inquiry into the relation between art and society in capitalist cultures must address both the formation of the working distinction upon which Jameson remarks and the totalizing impulse upon which Lyotard remarks. For capitalism has characteristically generated neither regimes in which all discourses seem coordinated, nor regimes in which they seem radically isolated or discontinuous, but regimes in which the drive towards differentiation and the drive towards monological organization operate simultaneously, or at least oscillate so rapidly as to create the impression of simultaneity.

In a brilliant paper that received unusual attention, elicited a response from a White House speech-writer, and most recently generated a segment on CBS's "Sixty Minutes," the political scientist and historian Michael Rogin recently observed the number of times President Reagan has, at critical moments in his career, quoted lines from his own or other popular films. The President is a man, Rogin remarks, "whose most spontaneous moments—('Where do we find such men?' about the American D-Day dead; 'I am paying for this microphone, Mr. Green,' during the 1980 New Hampshire primary debate)—are not only preserved and projected on film, but also turn out to be lines from old movies."① To a remarkable extent, Ronald Reagan, who made his final Hollywood film, *Hellcats of the Navy*, in 1957, continues to live within the movies; he has been shaped by them, draws much of his cold war rhetoric from them, and cannot or will not distinguish between them and an external reality. Indeed his political career has depended upon an ability to project himself and his mass audience into a realm in which there is no distinction between simulation and reality.

The response from Anthony Dolan, a White House speech-writer who was asked to comment on Rogin's paper, was highly revealing. "What he's really saying," Dolan suggested, "is that all of us are deeply affected by a uniquely American art form: the movies."② Rogin had in fact argued that the presidential character "was produced from the convergence of two sets of substitutions which generated Cold War countersubversion in the 1940s and underlie its 1980s revival—the political replacement of Nazism by Communism, from which the national security state was born; and the psychological shift from an embodied self to its simulacrum on film." Both the political and the psychological substitution were intimately bound up with Ronald Reagan's career in the movies. Dolan in response rewrites Rogin's thesis into a celebration of the power of "a uniquely American art form" to shape "all of us." Movies, Dolan told the *New York Times* reporter, "heighten reality rather than lessen it."

Such a statement appears to welcome the collapse of the working distinction between the aesthetic and the real; the aesthetic is not an alternative realm but a way of intensifying the single realm we all inhabit. But then the spokesman went on to assert that the President "usually credits the films whose lines

---

① Michael Rogin, " 'Ronald Reagan': *The Movie" and other Episodes in Political Demonology* (Berkeley: University of California Press, 1987).

② Quoted by reporter Michael Tolchin in the *New York Times* account of Rogin's paper, headlined. "How Reagan Always Gets the Best Lines," *New York Times*, September 9, 1985, p. 10.

he uses. " That is, at the moment of appropriation, the President acknowledges that he is borrowing from the aesthetic and hence acknowledges the existence of a working distinction. In so doing he respects and even calls attention to the difference between his own presidential discourse and the fictions in which he himself at one time took part; they are differences upon which his own transition from actor to politician in part depends, and they are the signs of the legal and economic system that he represents. For the capitalist aesthetic demands acknowledgments—hence the various marks of property rights that are flashed on the screen or inscribed in a text—and the political arena insists that it is not a fiction. That without acknowledgment the President delivers speeches written by Anthony Dolan or others does not appear to concern anyone; this has long been the standard operating procedure of American politicians. But it would concern people if the President recited speeches that were lifted without acknowledgment from old movies. He would then seem not to know the difference between fantasy and reality. And that might be alarming.

The White House, of course, was not responding to a theoretical problem, but to the implication that somehow the President did not fully recognize that he was quoting, or alternatively that he did realize it and chose to repress the fact in order to make a more powerful impression. In one version he is a kind of sleepwalker, in the other a plagiarist. To avoid these implications the White House spokesman needed in effect to invoke a difference that he had himself a moment before undermined.

The spokesman's remarks were hasty and *ad hoc*, but it did not take reflection to reproduce the complex dialectic of differentiation and identity that those remarks articulate. That dialectic is powerful precisely because it is by now virtually thoughtless; it takes a substantial intellectual effort to *separate* the boundaries of art from the subversion of those boundaries, an effort such as that exemplified in the work of Jameson or Lyotard. But the effect of such an effort is to remove itself from the very phenomenon it had proposed to analyze, namely, the relation between art and surrounding discourses in capitalist culture. For the effortless invocation of two apparently contradictory accounts of art is characteristic of American capitalism in the late twentieth century and an outcome of long-term tendencies in the relationship of art and capital: in the same moment a working distinction between the aesthetic and the real is established and abrogated.

We could argue, following Jameson, that the establishment of the distinction is the principal effect, with a view towards alienating us from our own imaginations by isolating fantasies in a private, apolitical realm. Or we could argue, following Lyotard, that the abrogation of the distinction is the principal effect, with a view towards effacing or evading differences by establishing a single, monolithic ideological structure. But if we are asked to choose between these alternatives, we will be drawn away from an analysis of the relation between capitalism and aesthetic production. For from the sixteenth century, when the effects for art of joint-stock company organization first began to be felt, to the present, capitalism has produced a powerful and effective oscillation between the establishment of distinct discursive domains and the collapse of those domains into one another. It is this restless oscillation rather than the securing of a particular fixed position that constitutes the distinct power of capitalism. The individual elements—a range of discontinuous discourses on the one hand, the monological unification of all discourses on the other—may be found fully articulated in other economic and social systems; only capitalism has managed to generate a dizzying, seemingly inexhaustible circulation between the two.

My use of the term *circulation* here is influenced by the work of Derrida, but sensitivity to the practical strategies of negotiation and exchange depends less upon poststructuralist theory than upon the circulatory rhythms of American politics. And the crucial point is that it is not politics alone but the whole structure of production and consumption—the systematic organization of ordinary life and consciousness—that generates the pattern of boundary making and breaking, the oscillation between demarcated objects and monological totality, that I have sketched. If we restrict our focus to the zone of political institutions, we can easily fall into the illusion that everything depends upon the unique talents—if that is the word—of Ronald Reagan, that he alone has managed to generate the enormously effective shuttling between massive, universalizing fantasies and centerlessness that characterizes his administration. This illusion leads in turn to what John Carlos Rowe has called the humanist trivialization of power, a trivialization that finds its local political expression in the belief that the fantasmatics of current American politics are the product of a single man and will pass with him. On the contrary, Ronald Reagan is manifestly the product of a larger and more durable American structure—not only a structure of power, ideological extremism and militarism, but of pleasure, recreation, and interest, a structure that shapes the spaces we construct for ourselves, the way we present "the news," the fantasies we daily consume on television or in the movies, the entertainments that we characteristically make and take.

I am suggesting then that the oscillation between totalization and difference, uniformity and the diversity of names, unitary truth and a proliferation of distinct entities—in short between Lyotard's capitalism and Jameson's—is built into the poetics of everyday behavior in America. ① Let us consider, for example, not the President's Hollywood career but a far more innocent California pastime, a trip to Yosemite National Park. One of the most popular walks at Yosemite is the Nevada Falls Trail. So popular, indeed, is this walk that the Park Service has had to pave the first miles of the trail in order to keep them from being dug into trenches by the heavy traffic. At a certain point the asphalt stops, and you encounter a sign that tells you that you are entering the wilderness. You have passed then from the National Forests that surround the park—forests that serve principally as state-subsidized nurseries for large timber companies and hence are not visibly distinguishable from the tracts of privately owned forest with which they are contiguous—to the park itself, marked by the payment of admission to the uniformed ranger at the entrance kiosk, and finally to a third and privileged zone of publicly demarcated Nature. This zone, called the wilderness, is marked by the abrupt termination of the asphalt and by a sign that lists the rules of behavior that you must now observe: no dogs, no litte-

---

① I borrow the phrase "the poetics of everyday behavior" from Iurii M. Lotman. See his essay in *The Semiotics of Russian Cultural History*, ed. A. D. Nakhimovsky and A. S. Nakhimovsky (Ithaca: Cornell University Press, 1985).

ring, no fires, no camping without a permit, and so forth. The wilderness then is signaled by an intensification of the rules, an intensification that serves as the condition of an escape from the asphalt.

You can continue on this trail then until you reach a steep cliff onto which the guardians of the wilderness have thoughtfully bolted a cast-iron stairway. The stairway leads to a bridge that spans a rushing torrent, and from the middle of the bridge you are rewarded with a splendid view of Nevada Falls. On the railing that keeps you from falling to your death as you enjoy your vision of the wilderness there are signs—information about the dimensions of the falls, warnings against attempting to climb the treacherous, mist-slickened rocks, trail markers for those who wish to walk further—and an anodyzed aluminum plaque on which are inscribed inspirational, vaguely Wordsworthian sentiments by the California environmentist John Muir. The passage, as best I can recall, assures you that in years to come you will treasure the image you have before you. And next to these words, also etched into the aluminum, is precisely an image: a photograph of Nevada Falls taken from the very spot on which you stand.

The pleasure of this moment—beyond the pleasure of the mountain air and the waterfall and the great boulders and the deep forests of Lodgepole and Jeffrey pine—arises from the unusually candid glimpse of the process of circulation that shapes the whole experience of the park. The wilderness is at once secured and obliterated by the official gestures that establish its boundaries; the natural is set over against the artificial through means that render such an opposition meaningless. The eye passes from the "natural" image of the waterfall to the aluminum image, as if to secure a difference (for why else bother to go to the park at all? Why not simply look at a book of pictures?), even as that difference is effaced. The effacement is by no means complete—on the contrary, parks like Yosemite are one of the ways in which the distinction between nature and artifice is constituted in our society—and yet the Park Service's plaque on the Nevada Falls bridge conveniently calls attention to the interpenetration of nature and artifice that makes the distinction possible.

What is missing from this exemplary fable of capitalist aesthetics is the question of property relations, since the National Parks exist precisely to suspend or marginalize that question through the ideology of protected public space. Everyone owns the parks. That ideology is somewhat bruised by the actual development of a park like Yosemite, with its expensive hotel, a restaurant that has a dress code, fancy gift shops and the like, but it is not entirely emptied out: even the administration of the right-wing Secretary of the Interior James Watt stopped short of permitting a private golf course to be constructed on park grounds, and there was public outrage when a television production company that had contracted to film a series in Yosemite decided to paint the rocks to make them look more realistic. What we need is an example that combines recreation or entertainment, aesthetics, the public sphere, and private property. The example most compelling to a literary critic like myself is not a political career or a national park but a novel.

In 1976, a convict named Gary Gilmore was released from a federal penitentiary and moved to Provo, Utah. Several months later, he robbed and killed two men, was arrested for the crimes, and convicted of murder. The case became famous when Gilmore demanded that he be executed—a punishment that had not been inflicted in America for some years, due to legal protections— and, over the strenuous objections of the American Civil Liberties Union and the National Association for the Advancement of Colored People, had his way. The legal maneuvers and the eventual firing-squad execution became national media events. Well before the denouement the proceedings had come to the attention of Norman Mailer and his publisher Warner Books which is, as it announces on its title pages, "a Warner Communications Company." Mailer's research assistant, Jere Herzenberg, and a hack writer and interviewer, Lawrence Schiller, conducted extensive interviews and acquired documents, records of court proceedings, and personal papers such as the intimate letters between Gilmore and his girlfriend. Some of these materials were in the public domain but many of them were not; they were purchased, and the details of the purchases themselves become part of the materials that were reworked by Mailer into *The Executioner's Song*, [1] a "true life novel" as it is called, that brilliantly

---

[1] N. Mailer, *The Executioner's Song* (New York: Warner Books, 1979).

combines documentary realism with Mailer's characteristic romance themes. The novel was a critical and popular success—a success signaled not only by the sheaves of admiring reviews but by the Universal Product Code printed on its paperback cover. It was subsequently made into an NBC-TV mini-series where on successive evenings it helped to sell cars, soap powder, and deodorant.

Mailer's book had further, and less predictable, ramifications. While he was working on *The Executioner's Song*, there was an article on Mailer in *People* magazine. The article caught the attention of a convict named Jack H. Abbott who wrote to offer him first-hand instruction on the conditions of prison life. An exchange of letters began, and Mailer grew increasingly impressed not only with their detailed information but with what he calls their "literary measure." The letters were cut and arranged by a Random House editor, Erroll McDonald, and appeared as a book called *In the Belly of the Beast*. This book too was widely acclaimed and contributed, with Mailer's help, to win a parole for its author.

"As I am writing these words," Mailer wrote in the Introduction to Abbott's book, "it looks like Abbott will be released on parole this summer. It is certainly the time for him to get out."[①]"I have never come into bodily contact with another human being in almost twenty years," wrote Abbott in his book, "except in combat; in acts of struggle, of violence" (p. 63). Shortly after his release, Abbott, now a celebrity, approached a waiter in an all-night restaurant and asked to use the men's room. The waiter—Richard Adan, an aspiring actor and playwright—told Abbott that the restaurant had no men's room and asked him to step outside. When Adan followed him on to the sidewalk, Abbott, apparently thinking that he was being challenged, stabbed Adan in the heart with a kitchen knife. Abbott was arrested and convicted once again of murder. The events have themselves been made into a play, also called *In the Belly of the Beast*, that recently opened to very favorable reviews.

Literary criticism has a familiar set of terms for the relationship between a

---

① Introduction to Jack Henry Abbott, *In the Belly of the Beast: Letters from Prison* (New York: Random House, 1981), p. xviii.

work of art and the historical events to which it refers: we speak of allusion, symbolization, allegorization, representation, and above all mimesis. Each of these terms has a rich history and is virtually indispensable, and yet they all seem curiously inadequate to the cultural phenomenon which Mailer's book and Abbott's and the television series and the play constitute. And their inadequacy extends to aspects not only of contemporary culture but of the culture of the past. We need to develop terms to describe the ways in which material—here official documents, private papers, newspaper clippings, and so forth—is transferred from one discursive sphere to another and becomes aesthetic proper-ty. It would, I think, be a mistake to regard this process as uni-directional—from social discourse to aesthetic discourse—not only because the aesthetic dis-course in this case is so entirely bound up with capitalist venture but because the social discourse is already charged with aesthetic energies. Not only was Gilmore explicitly and powerfully moved by the film version of *One Flew Over the Cuckoo's Nest*, but his entire pattern of behavior seems to have been shaped by the characteristic representations of American popular fiction, including Mailer's own.

Michael Baxandall has argued recently that "art and society are analytical concepts from two different kinds of categorization of human experience. ...un-homologous systematic constructions put upon interpenetrating subject-mat-ters." In consequence, he suggests, any attempt to relate the two must first "modify one of the terms till it matches the other, but keeping note of what modification has been necessary since this is a necessary part of one's infbrma-tion."[1] It is imperative that we acknowledge the modification and find a way to measure its degree, for it is only in such measurements that we can hope to chart the relationship between art and society. Such an admonition is impor-tant—methodological self-consciousness is one of the distinguishing marks of the new historicism in cultural studies as opposed to a historicism based upon faith in the transparency of signs and interpretive procedures—but it must be

---

① Michael Baxandall, "Art, Society, and the Bouger Principle," *Representations*, 12 (1985), 40-41.

supplemented by an understanding that the work of art is not itself a pure flame that lies at the source of our speculations. Rather the work of art is itself the product of a set of manipulations, some of them our own (most striking in the case of works that were not originally conceived as "art" at all but rather as something else—votive objects, propaganda, prayer, and so on), many others undertaken in the construction of the original work. That is, the work of art is the product of a negotiation between a creator or class of creators, equipped with a complex, communally shared repertoire of conventions, and the institutions and practices of society. In order to achieve the negotiation, artists need to create a currency that is valid for a meaningful, mutually profitable exchange. It is important to emphasize that the process involves not simply appropriation but exchange, since the existence of art always implies a return, a return normally measured in pleasure and interest. I should add that the society's dominant currencies, money, and prestige, are invariably involved, but I am here using the term "currency" metaphorically to designate the systematic adjustments, symbolizations and lines of credit necessary to enable an exchange to take place. The terms "currency" and "negotiation" are the signs of our manipulation and adjustment of the relative systems.

Much recent theoretical work must, I think, be understood in the context of a search for a new set of terms to understand the cultural phenomenon that I have tried to describe. Hence, for example, Wolfgang Iser writes of the creation of the aesthetic dimension through the "dynamic oscillation" between two discourses; the East German Marxist Robert Weimann argues that

> the process of making certain things one's own becomes inseparable from making other things (and persons) alien, so that the act of appropriation must be seen always already to involve not only self-projection and assimilation but alienation through reification and expropriation.

Anthony Giddens proposes that we substitute a concept of textual distanciation for that of the autonomy of the text, so that we can fruitfully grasp the "recursive character" of social life and of language. ① Each of these formulations—and, of course, there are significant differences among them—pulls away from a stable, mimetic theory of art and attempts to construct in its stead an interpretive model that will more adequately account for the unsettling circulation of materials and discourses that is, I have argued, the heart of modern aesthetic practice. It is in response to this practice that contemporary theory must situate itself: not outside interpretation, but in the hidden places of negotiation and exchange.

---

① All in *The Aims of Representation*.

20. 格林布拉特：《通向一种文化诗学》
(Stephen J. Greenblatt, "Towards a Poetics of Culture," 1986)

作者小识

　　格林布拉特（Stephen J. Greenblatt, 1943—　）美国学者，文学批评家，新历史主义和文化诗学的领军人物。他出生于美国的马萨诸塞州，博士毕业后任教于加州大学伯克利分校，后任教于哈佛大学，被授予"跨学科人文教授"和"新历史主义之父"的称号。

　　格林布拉特的学术生涯起步于 20 世纪六七十年代，其间出版了他的学士论文《三个现代讽刺作家：沃、奥威尔和赫胥黎》（*Three Modern Satirists：Waugh，Orwell，and Huxley*）以及博士论文《瓦尔特·雷莱爵士：文艺复兴人物和他的角色》（*Sir Walter Ralegh：The Renaissance Man and His Roles*）。这两部作品尚未使用新历史主义的批评方式，依然有新批评影响的痕迹，但已经开始思考文学和非文学的边界问题。20 世纪 80 年代，格林布拉特关注文艺复兴和莎士比亚的研究，提出了新历史主义和文化诗学的批评观念。《莎士比亚的商讨》（*Shakespearean Negotiations*）可被视为新历史主义和文化诗学批评的典范。20 世纪 90 年代，格林布拉特继续深耕新历史主义和文化诗学，出版了文集《学会诅咒：早期现代文化中的散文》（*Learning to Curse：Essays in Early Modern Culture*）和《不可思议的领地：新世界的奇迹》（*Marvelous Possessions：The Wonder of the New World*）。前者收录了 1975—1990 年的论文，后者收录了 1988 年以来的讲座。21 世纪以来，格林布拉特开始从学术界走入大众视野。2004 年出版的《俗世威尔：莎士比亚新传》（*Will in the World：How Shakespeare Became Shakespeare*）是一部面对大众的传记作品，畅销一时。2011 年出版的小说《大转向：世界如何步入现代》（*The Swerve：How the World Became Modern*）获得了美国国家图书奖和普利策奖。

背景略说

　　20 世纪初美国的文学批评以实证主义为主导。第二次世界大战后，英美新批评和形式主义逐渐代替实证主义在文学批评界站稳脚跟。20 世纪 60 年代，美国女性解放运动和民权运动爆发，总统肯尼迪遇刺，越南战争爆发。社会动荡逐渐波及学校内部，学术转向后结构主义、解构主义，学者们开始寻求对原有学术范式和观念的突破和瓦解。

格林布拉特成长在学术思想转变的时代，受到了形式主义和新批评的影响，接触了后结构主义和结构主义思想。20 世纪 70 年代，他在学校讲授马克思主义。此外，人类学的观念让他重新思考历史和文化的关系。格林布拉特将诸多的理论资源"拼贴"起来，解读文艺复兴和莎士比亚。1980 年发表的《文艺复兴时期自我造型：从莫尔到莎士比亚》（*Renaissance Self-Fashioning：From More to Shakespeare*）可被视为新历史主义的奠基之作。1982 年他在《文类》专刊中首次使用"新历史主义"的概念。

新历史主义多被视为文化诗学观念之下的一种具体的实践术语。文化诗学是将文学置入文化的观念中进行阐释，使得文学摆脱形式主义和新批评对文学的限制，利用故事、逸闻等"非文学"的文化因素来补充和丰富文学文本，以此得出新的观念。新历史主义强调对原有历史主义的否定。原有历史主义认为历史是可知的、明确的，文学只能生存在历史事件和人物的阴影之下，是它们简单的反映或表达。新历史主义认为历史是主观的，是历史与文化相结合的产物，要在文化、政治、经济等诸多要素中解读历史，对历史文本进行文学化的解读。

可见文化诗学和新历史主义打破了学科的确定性，解放了困于形式主义和新批评中的文学。文本是文化的产物，同时也形成文化。跨学科多领域的研究为文学、历史文化研究开拓了广阔的空间。由于文化诗学自身的跨学科性和多理论资源的交汇性，格林布拉特将其称为一种实践，而不是一种教义，表现出突破和开阔的研究思维和态度。

基本内容

选文《通向一种文化诗学》是格林布拉特 1986 年 9 月 4 日在西澳大学所做的一次演讲。通过这次演讲，格林布拉特旨在回应当时学界对他的"新历史主义"的质疑。他自陈在讲授马克思主义理论与"文化诗学"课程时遇到的理论困境，不知应当如何选择自己的研究方向。于是，他把后结构主义和马克思主义作为自身理论的坐标，将两种观念结合起来，在摇摆和振荡中陈述自己理论的位置。

马克思主义理论的代表人物詹姆逊认为：资本主义渗透在艺术领域当中，表面展现出公共性，实质上艺术受制于政治、经济的运作。因此，资本主义对艺术产生的异化作用只能通过区分政治领域和审美领域来研究。而后结构主义的代表人物利奥塔认为，资本主义通过单一的独白的意识结构，利用通用的概念抹杀或回避差异，是从共性的角度入手分析资本主义对人个性的忽视。可见，对于资本主义如何影响艺术领域，前者强调区分政治与美学从而揭露艺术中的欺骗性，而后者则从共性和独白中发现虚伪性。两者都试图阐释艺术与社会的关系，却互不相容。格林布拉特认为，阐释资本主义社会的运作方式不是非此即彼的状态。资本主义是复杂多层次的社会，两种模式很多时候是共同发生的。

为了论证资本主义运作的复杂性，格林布拉特列举了三个例子来论证。第一个是里根总统在电影中与政治中的形象的结合；第二个是在美国加利福尼亚州国家公园开发过程中，人工与自然因素在景观中所产生的作用；第三个是诺曼·米勒根据吉尔莫真实案件改编的小说《刽子手之歌》（*Executioner's Song*）。这三个例证都是艺术因素与社会因素的结合。电影中的里根总统与政治中的总统会相互影响，公众会将电影中的形象迁移到政治中，而政治中的里根也会喊出电影里的台词，两者相互补充；公园中的瀑布是人为的，也是自然的；《刽子手之歌》中的故事有真实内容，也有虚构内容。这三个例证说明，单独利用后结构主义或马克思主义来解读文化事件存在着局限性。格林布拉特强调要通过文化诗学来结合两种理论，在"流通"的过程中树立新的研究范式。

格林布拉特认为，传统观念中的隐喻、象征、语言、再现以及模仿都是必要的，但是如果用它们来解释电视报道、剧本等文化现象，就会显得不合适，因此就需要用文化诗学的观念，将文化领域中的文本与艺术结合起来，经过"流通"和"谈判"来重新确立审美、社会、文化之间的关系，走向文化诗学的研究方法。

拓展讨论

1980 年芝加哥大学出版社出版了格林布拉特所著的《文艺复兴时期自我造型：从莫尔到莎士比亚》。该书聚焦于 16 世纪的六位英国作家是如何"自我造型"的。格林布拉特将文学作品置入当时的文化背景中，利用文化诗学的方法，从作品人物的塑造、作家自我身份的认定、社会外部对人的影响以及他人自我意识之间的关系等角度来探索"自我"是如何建立起来的。文学内部"自我"的建立与外部社会"自我"的认知联系起来，在多层次互相关照中，重构"自我"。

格林布拉特认为"自我造型"是"权威"（authority）与"异质"（alien）相遇，即身份自我建立处在自我保留和自我消亡的斗争当中。权威和异质经过磨合与斗争，最终一同融入"自我"当中。这里以《文艺复兴时期自我造型：从莫尔到莎士比亚》最后一章为例，简单描述格林布拉特是如何通过《奥赛罗》（*Othello*）中的伊阿古（Iago）等人物来审视莎士比亚的"自我造型"的。格林布拉特认为《奥赛罗》中的人物具有即兴演绎的特质，他们面对不同的情境演绎出不同的状态，充满了流动性和不定性。伊阿古作为阴谋者，为了阴谋的成立不断即兴演绎，重塑他人的形象，转化自己的形象。格林布拉特认为，现实中的莎士比亚与戏剧中的人物一样也具有即兴演绎的性质。面对自身生存的社会，莎士比亚表面上遵守当时的政权、社会制度，而实际上通过即兴演绎进行反抗和改写，表现出自己的不屑。

格林布拉特由文学作品入手，分析戏剧中人物的特质。由于文学作品是当时整体文化的产物，是社会诸多因素的集合，因此格林布拉特将戏剧人物的特质迁移到作家身上，解读莎士比亚"自我"中所包含的"即兴演绎"的特质。这种特质正是呼应了权威与异质对立与融合的矛盾状态，自我的重塑没有那么容易。

延伸阅读

1. 张京媛：《新历史主义与文学批评》，北京，北京大学出版社，1993。该书是对新历史主义批评家作品的翻译与编选。通过此书可以更深入地了解新历史主义其他代表人物的思想与批评方法。

2. 格林布拉特：《莎士比亚的自由》，唐建清译，北京，社会科学文献出版社，2020。该书对莎士比亚和文艺复兴做出了细致的分析，通过难以察觉的细节来解读莎士比亚，认为莎士比亚拥抱又颠覆了时代常规。

21. *Heinrich von Ofterdingen* as Data Feed (1986)
By Friedrich A. Kittler

> And we know that messages are not simply reported;
> they also affect what people do and do not do.
> —Karl Knies, *Der Telegraph als Verkehrsmittel* (1857)

The story of *Heinrich von Ofterdingen* is simple. A youth of twenty years journeys with his mother through Germany. At the destination, he falls in love with a girl, but death steals her from him. On the final pages, an old man comforts the young man. Nothing more dramatic than this occurs, and the most momentous event is left out: on paper, the girl's death appears only in the hero's dream.

This plot is so meager that interpreters have overlooked it time and again. They only grow interested when the novel passes over to making theoretical statements. In this light, it becomes possible to read the plot as the illustration of theoretical discourse——to embed it in a history of the mind [*Geistesge-schichte*] transcending events. "Philosophy of history," "poetics," "conceptions of nature" or "representation of the Middle Ages in Romanticism" are the conventional rubrics under which the course of narration appears——and then disappears. It is as if the events recounted were merely a pretext for formulating theories. As if in other words, speech amounted to nothing more than what it says.

To be sure, Hardenberg's novel consists of innumerable conversations, possibly more so than any other work. The text says so itself: "idle conscience, in a smooth world that offers no resistance, turns into a gripping exchange—a

Fable that tells of all things [*zur alleserzählenden Fabel*]"(332). ① On the one hand, *Heinrich von Ofterdingen* presents a minimal quantity of actions and obstacles (leaving aside the book's one catastrophe, which is elided). On the other hand, it offers a maximal quantity of words that are exchanged. Because it features neither a lady stealing by night into the hero's chamber, nor a rival giving cause for a duel or suicide, Fable (ultimately, a character in the work) can ascend to a position of uncontested power and—as occurs in the inset fairy tale [*Märchen*] narrated by Klingsohr——allegorize the flow of information itself. ② Everything must be said, because there is nothing to say.

The innocence of speech even has a home in the text. Chapter five, in the first part of the novel, begins at a village inn. A simple observation is offered: "a large number of people, some of them travelers, others simply guests for a drink, sat in the room and conversed about anything and everything" (239). This place, then, is an earthly paradise—and one that stands far closer than poetic dreams of Atlantis or philosophical speculations about the Golden Age. Accordingly, it lies far below interpreters' threshold of perception. "People" (239) simply talk. Their names and what they say are not provided, much less recorded. This, everyone knows, is how it goes every day.

In a foreword which itself has vanished, Foucault described this everydayness:

The great *oeuvre* of the history of the world is indelibly accompanied by

---

① Quotations follow Novalis, *Schriften. Die Werke Friedrich von Hardenbergs*, ed. Paul Kluckhohn und Richard Samuel (Darmstadt: Wissenschaftliche Buchge-sellschaft, 1960-1968). Simple page numbers refer to the second edition of the first volume; Roman numerals and page numbers refer to the other volumes.

② On Klingsohr's tale, see Friedrich Kittler, "Die Irrwege des Eros und die 'absolute Familie.' Psychoanalytischer und diskursanalytischer Kommentar zu Klingsohrs Märchen in Novalis' 'Heinrich von Ofterdingen.'" *Psychoanalytische und psychopathologische Literaturinterpretation*, ed. Bernd Urban and Winfried Kudszus (Darmstadt: Wissenschaftliche Buchgesellschaft, 1981), 421-470. Whereas the latter study discusses what is necessarily unconscious in the text—its psychohistorical preconditions—the one at hand treats its surface: word processing [*Textverarbeitung*] as such.

the absence of an *oeuvre*, which renews itself at every instant, but which runs unaltered in its inevitable void the length of history; and from before history, as it is already there in the primitive decision, and after it again, as it will triumph in the last word uttered by history. The plenitude of history is only possible in the space, both empty and peopled at the same time, of all the words without language that appear to anyone who lends an ear, as a dull sound from beneath history, the obstinate murmur of a language talking *to itself*——without any speaking subject and without an interlocutor, wrapped up in itself, with a lump in its throat, collapsing before it ever reaches any formulation and returning without a fuss to the silence that it never shook off. The charred root of meaning. [①]

These words apply to literature every bit as much as they do to history. The work they perform is also measured and hemmed in by a murmur that cancels them out. No flow of information can occur without white noise, because channels of communication emit it themselves——as the chance distribution of interference. Whether they are drunken or not, the tavern murmurs constitute the unerasable background from which Hardenberg's novel extracts its characters' profiles and their words in the first place. Indeed, it is for this very reason that there are characters and words of a literary nature at all.

Right after the anonymous murmuring—which, in contrast to the systematic return of all other information [*Romaninformationen*], never receives further mention——the text passes over to a listener named Ofterdingen and to a narrator who, like all characters in novels (who occur verbally), not only has any number of things to say, but possesses knowledge as well. "The old man's discourse pleased Heinrich uncommonly, and he was inclined to hear yet more from him" (243). Interpreters overlook statements of this kind, too, because they possess no theoretical content and merely report the flow of information. Yet Hardenberg's novel absolutely abounds in them. Because this

---

① Michel Foucault, *History of Madness*, trans. Jonathan Murphy (London: Routledge, 2006), xxxi-xxxii.

white noise provides the zero value of literature, the transmission of knowledge (for example, when the Miner speaks) marks a discursive event and should be analyzed as such. The fact that speaking does not amount only to what it says constitutes its reality or history. For instead of simply reflecting so-called reality or history, every stream of information switches between dispositives of power. The fact that a budding poet like Ofterdingen listens "uncommonly" gladly to old miners provides information about the information networks of 1800.

That is to say, there can be no fiction—and certainly no Romanticism—if one uses labels that seek to measure the zero grades of discursive effectiveness [*Schwundstufen von Wirksamkeit*]. As the data feed that it is, *Heinrich von Ofterdingen*, the most Romantic of all the novels that Romanticism produced, displays the absoluteness [*Unhintergehbarkeit*] of an event. Its seeming poverty of plot [*Handlung*] simply offers space and a site for other, more forceful action [*Handeln*]: *the* action of speech itself. Fable, who tells of everything [*die alleserzählende Fabel*], is not a fairy tale or a myth. Without German poetry [*Dichtung*] of the kind that the Age of Goethe both produced and inaugurated in the first place, the *Bildungsstaat* of the revolutionary nineteenth century would not have existed.

To be sure, information networks must be reconstructed as such in order to demonstrate as much. Neither the unity of authorial intention nor the unity of the artistic work proves decisive for discourse analysis. If, according to Claude Shannon's theorem, information networks fundamentally connect a source, a transmitter, a channel, a receiver, and a destination,[1] then messages consisting of words (discourses, that is) must be recorded [*angeschrieben*] as a network that always—and as a matter of necessity—incorporates numerous other books, documents, archives, libraries, and institutions.

The task, then, involves reading along the lines that Novalis drew in his first, fragmentary novel. Here, an anonymous master instructs the *Novices of Sais* how to search for "crystals or flowers" which he, in turn, arranges in se-

---

[1] Cf. Claude E. Shannon and Warren Weaver, *The Mathematical Theory of Communication* (Urbana: University of Illinois Press, 1964), 33-35.

ries and columns—which he archives, that is. One morning, a pupil appears before him. Previously, the youth had "always looked sad." Now, however, he intones a "lofty, joyous song"—that is, he has grown up to be a poet. The novice has come to give his teacher "an unprepossessing little stone of a strange shape.""The teacher took it in hand and kissed it for a long time; then, he looked upon us with wetted eyes and placed this stone on an empty space between other stones, precisely where the rows touched each other, like rays" (81). It is impossible to state more clearly that poetry does not consist of radiant substance [*in strahlender Substantialität*] or of aesthetic appearance [*Schein*], but rather is defined by its place value [*Stellenwert*]. ① Even before they appear, all the stones, that is, units of information, count as part of a network plan or graph connecting them with each other. *Heinrich von Ofterdingen*—with a degree of precision that lies far ahead of conventional social histories of German literature——treats this same matter.

1.

At the beginning of the network plan—how could it be otherwise? —lies white noise. With its unheard-of opening words, the novel indicates the background against which it can become a novel in the first place. "His parents were already lying asleep, the clock on the wall struck its uniform beat, the wind rushed at the knocking windows; the room was intermittently lighted by the glow of the moon" (195). A twenty-year-old "youth," lying "restlessly upon his bed" in the same chamber, hears nothing of his parents' intercourse—verbal or otherwise. The information that reaches him consists solely of inhuman and stochastically distributed acoustic and optical data, which the text registers, but the hero does not. This is precisely how literature begins. To get started, it touches (on) other streams of information that—as rattling, ticking, whispering, and blinking—escape verbalization [*Sprachlichkeit*], because only

---

① On the development of the notion of place value in Schleiermacher's hermeneutics, cf. Manfred Frank, "Einleitung," F. D. E. Schleiermacher, *Hermeneutik und Kritik* (Frankfurt a. M. : Suhrkamp, 1977), 34-37.

gramophones can record actual acoustics and only films can record actual optics.

Around 1800, no medium besides words existed for serial data—that is, data in the succession of time. This is why the sleepless youth is predestined to become a poet, both in the opening scene and in general. Ofterdingen takes in all the sounds and faces that no word could possibly store as such; he does so in order, through the act of selection that he performs, to become estranged from his own presence [*aus seiner Gegenwart herauszufallen*]. Inasmuch as the Age of Goethe could only process serial data in and as language—which, Ofterdingen affirms, "man [*der Mensch*] commands" (287)—then he has no other choice. "The youth lay restlessly upon his bed, and thought of the Stranger and his tales" (195).

Therefore, it is a foreign person—about whom Ofterdingen "thinks" and, as the following makes clear, to whom he directs quiet conversations with himself—who makes him forget, first his parents, and second the white noise that surrounds him. From the outset, the novel determines that words, or more precisely, "tales" [*Erzählungen*], provide the source constituting its entire information network. The Stranger—their broadcaster—takes care of the initial selection. This also connects Ofterdingen, the aspiring poet, to the circuit of transmission called "literature." Both chance sounds and mere familial conversations fade away. A narrative takes their place, which individualizes its speaker as much as it does its auditor. According to Ofterdingen, no one has "ever" seen "a person similar" to the Stranger. Moreover—and even though everyone "has heard the same thing [*das Nämliche*]"—no one has ever "been gripped by his discourse [*Reden*]" as much as Ofterdingen himself (195). Therefore, the Stranger and his listener—the transmitter and the receiver—are separated by a marked proximity, which (as is the case everywhere in the novel) involves the object of discourse(s). This object both is and is not a word; it is like the Symbol, which Goethe defined as "the thing, without being it, yet being it after all [*die Sache, ohne die Sache zu sein, und doch die Sache*]."[1] Its name is "the

---

① Johann Wolfgang Goethe, "Über Philostrats Gemählde," *Werke*, *Weimarer Ausgabe* (Weimar: Böhlau, 1887-1919), XLIX/1, 142.

Blue Flower" (195).

Of all the words or things in the novel, this flower stands apart, for it functions both as a name and as an intuition [*Anschauung*]—as signifier and signified in one. ① Although the Blue Flower is only "given" in the Stranger's narratives, that is, it does not occur in sensory presence, it rouses a "passion" or "yearning" to "behold" it. At the same time, as a word that is transmitted [*weitergegebenes Wort*], it can also quiet this same passion: "Often, I am so delightfully well, and only when the Flower is not fully present [*wenn ich die Blume nicht recht gegenwärtig habe*] does a deep, heartfelt urging [*Treiben*] befall me" (195). Here, all at once, language proves capable of transporting an optical—that is, a sensory—flow of data.

In the quiet repetition of narratives that have already been heard, their referent really does become "present" [*gegenwärtig*]. Only when this wonder does not occur does Ofterdingen experience, in addition to the "deep, heartfelt urging," a fear that he "might be mad" (195). Here one may gauge just how hallucinatory the flower's appearance is—the extent to which, where this particular signifier is concerned, language trespasses its own borders. Ofterdingen's state, the ambiguity of deepest interiority and madness in one, describes the altogether poetic capacity of the soul [*das schlechthin poetische Seelenvermögen*] that Novalis—and all the aesthetics of the Age of Goethe②—called "imagination" [*Einbildungskraft*].

A fragment from 1798 offers the following definition:

Imagination is the wondrous sense that can replace all our other senses—and which stands so beautifully subject to our will [*der so sehr schön in*

---

① On the "symbol of intuition," cf. Horst Turk, "Goethes Wahlverwandtschaften: 'der doppelte Ehebruch der Phantasie,'" *Urszenen. Literaturwissenschaft als Diskursanalyse und Diskurskritik*, ed. Friedrich A. Kittler and Horst Turk (Frankfurt a. M.: Suhrkamp, 1977), 204-207.

② For documentation and media-technical conclusions, cf. Friedrich Kittler, *Discourse Networks*, 1800/1900, trans. Michael Metteer with Chris Cullens (Stanford: Stanford University Press, 1992), 113-119.

unsrer Willkür steht]. Even if the outer senses seem to be governed by mechanical laws—the imagination is obviously not tied to the presence and touch of external stimuli. (II, 650)

In this precise sense the merchants tell Ofterdingen about poetry [*Dichtung*], affirming that "this art is a truly wondrous matter. " The crafts of "painters and musicians [*Tonkünstler*]" pursue only the "artificial imitation of nature" for "eye" and "ear. " In contrast,

> of the art of poetry [*Dichtkunst*], there is nothing to be encountered externally. It also creates nothing with tools or hands; the eye and the ear perceive nothing of it: simply hearing the words is not the particular effect [*die eigentliche Wirkung*] of this secret art. Everything is internal, and just as those artists fill the outer senses with pleasant sensations, thus does the poet fill the inner shrine of the soul [*Heiligthum des Gemüths*] with new, wonderful and pleasing thoughts. He knows how to rouse those secret powers in us at will, and he gives, through words, an unknown, majestic world to be heard. As if from deep caverns, there emerged ancient and future times, countless human beings, wondrous regions, and the strangest occurrences within us—which tear us from the present with which we are familiar. (209ff.)

Lying on his lonesome bed, Ofterdingen—who can "dream and think [*dichten und denken*] of nothing" but the Blue Flower (195)—obeys this definition of poetry to the letter. Imagination replaces all his senses. That is, it provides, instead of signifiers that are heard, what the signifiers signify. Because of the simple fact that "merely hearing the words" does not constitute "the actual effect" of the "secret art" of poetry, the Stranger's tales do not exist as something present to the senses. Memory [*Erinnerung*] and memory alone—to employ Hegel's terminology—"has preserved them. " For this same reason, the words, to quote *Phenomenology of Spirit* once more, transform into a "picture gallery. "① In his "dreaming and thinking," Ofterdingen performs the elementary act that defined poetry in the Age of Goethe—and philosophy, too. Here lies the foundation of their historical alliance.

The matter has simply escaped readers' attention: the people of "thinkers and poets" is a people of readers. What novels and systems of philosophical aesthetics formulate as wonders or enigmas can be explained in very simple—that is, technical—terms. "If one reads properly," Novalis wrote elsewhere, "then there unfolds within us [*in unserm Innern*] a real, visible world following the words" (III, 377). Accordingly, the wondrous sense that can substitute for all our senses is called "literacy. " The unknown, majestic Word that poets make us hear through words opens a *fantastique de bibliothèque*—which, as Foucault has observed, represents the fundamental literary invention of the nineteenth century. ② For the first time in the history of a culture of writing [*Schriftkultur*], letters no longer needed to be laboriously deciphered, or even read in a muted voice. Silent and automated reading③ transported them immediately onto the "ground of subjective interiority" [*Boden der Innerlichkeit im Subjecte*],④ which as a matter of course consisted of hallucinated signifieds. That is why the novel—once again, in keeping with all the aesthetic systems of the day—need not acknowledge that poetry had long existed in book form, too. As the presence of the Stranger makes plain, it finds expression as a disembodied [*unsinnliche*] and absent voice that only appears in recollection [*nur noch erinnerte Stimme*].

To be sure, schools also teach silent reading today. However, no student still believes that for this reason he or she is hallucinating the meaning of what stands printed. Now wonders of this kind occur when one watches films and

---

① G. W. F. Hegel, *Phänomenologie des Geistes* (Hamburg: Meiner, 1980), 433.

② Cf. Michel Foucault, "La bibliothèque fantastique," *Travail de Flaubert*, ed. Raymond Debray-Genette et al. (Paris: Seuil, 1983), 103-122.

③ On literacy programs and "automatic" reading, cf. Joachim Gessinger, "Schriftspracherwerb im 18. Jahrhundert. Kulturelle Verelendung und politische Herrschaft," *Osnabrücker Beiträge zur Sprachtheorie* 11 (1979): 39.

④ G. W. F. Hegel, *System der Philosophie* (= *Encyclopädie*), ed. Hermann Glockner (Stuttgart: Frommann-Holzboog, 1927-1940), 351.

video clips. Ever since writing lost its monopoly on serial data processing, it has appeared for what it is: meaningless marks in black and white on paper.

Precisely this fact was inadmissible in the Age of Goethe. To recruit new initiates, the alphabet learned to make a new promise. As Ofterdingen puts it shortly before falling asleep:

> I heard tell, once, of olden times, how the animals and trees and rocks spoke with mankind. It seems to me as if, at any moment, they would begin again, and as if I could see in them what they want to tell me. There must yet be many words I do not know: if I did know more, I would understand everything much better. (195)

In the phantasm of an originary language or writing [*Ursprache oder Urschrift*],[1] then—even though this vision is guaranteed only by discourse(s)—signifiers and signified coincide in such a way that the latter themselves speak. This is reason enough for one, as the hearer or reader of natural language, to learn "many more words" oneself. Anyone who wished to become a poet around 1800 had to desire his own literacy first. And because all desire is erotic, the originary language had to beckon with a reward that promised the Impossible[2]: a recording of the relationship between the sexes.

No letter, no word, and no book says what women are. That is the reason why Ofterdingen drifts off. The riddle posed by his parents lying there and sleeping—which remains unanswered—is "solved" in a dream. The inaugural

---

[1] Cf. Alain Montandon, "Écriture et folie chez E. T. A. Hoffmann," *Romantisme* 24 (1979): 12.

[2] Cf. Jacques Lacan, *On Feminine Sexuality, the Limits of Love and Knowledge (Encore)*, trans. Bruce Fink (New York: Norton, 1999), 35:

Everything that is written stems from the fact that it will forever be impossible to write, as such, the sexual relationship. It is on that basis that there is a certain effect of discourse, which is called writing. One could, at a pinch, write $x\,R\,y$, and say x is man, y is woman, and R is the sexual relationship. Why not? The only problem is that it's stupid, because what is based on the signifier function (*la fonction de signifiant*) of "man" and "woman" are mere signifiers.

dream in the novel does not simply conduct all the tales told by the Stranger out of the words that they are into a real and visible world; it does not simply turn off—because, after all, "the slightest sound is not to be heard" (196)—the unrecordable sources of incidental noise. Rather, at its radiant ending, the dream, inasmuch as it embodies imagination, presents the very meaning [*gibt die Bedeutung selber zu sehen*] around which all the Stranger's words and all his auditor's dreaming and thinking have been circling:

> He saw nothing but the Blue Flower, and he gazed upon it for a long while with ineffable tenderness. Finally, he sought to approach it, when, all of a sudden, it began to move and change: the leaves became more luminous and nestled on the growing stalk; the Flower inclined toward him, and the petals unfolded a blue collar in which a delicate face was floating. (197)

In 1916, Hugo Münsterberg—who invented both the word for, and the practice of, "psychotechnics" [*Psychotechnik*]—published the first scientific theory of the feature film. His study sought to demonstrate that narrative cinema is able to simulate, implement, and thereby render superfluous all the unconscious processes of the mind. The logical consequence was that the medium of literature—should it represent something more than, and be something different from, printer's ink—had been surpassed.

> No theater could ever try to match such wonders, but for the camera they are not difficult. […] Rich artistic effects have been secured, and while on the stage every fairy play is clumsy and hardly able to create an illusion, in the film we really see the man transformed into a beast and the flower into a girl. [1]

---

[1] Hugo Münsterberg, *The Photoplay: A Psychological Study*, reprinted as *The Film: A Psychological Study. The Silent Photoplay in* 1916, ed. Richard Griffith (New York: Dover, 1970), 15.

The same fairy-tale wonders that have been simple matters of technology ever since Georges Méliès engineered his cinematic special effects were screened as literature and psychology around 1800. In the imagination of a dreamer enamored of words, the Blue Flower turns into a woman. The sleeper's hallucinatory vision receives an answer, and his "sight" [*Sehen*] sees a "face/sight" [*Gesicht*]. ① Such was media technology around 1800. "If one reads properly, then there unfolds, within us, a real, visible world following the words." In this *fantastique de bibliothèque*, words are not only capable of referring to women; they can *mean* them, too. Here speechless beings like a flower really speak with human beings—after all, the plant has become a girl. Ofterdingen will not be able to do otherwise than love the incarnate meaning of the signifier "flower" his whole life long. As soon as he encounters an empirically extant vision of a girl [*Mädchengesicht*](277), his own transformation—into a poet—is complete.

The transformation of words into flowers,② and of flowers into words, sustains all poetry in the Age of Goethe. Hardenberg's novel attests as much in the tale of Atlantis, which the merchants tell the budding poet Ofterdingen. The tale features a king who, "from youth onward, had read the works of the poets with rapturous delight," "devoted himself, with great zeal and at great expense, to collecting them from all languages, and always esteemed intercourse with singers above all else" (214). The poor monarch seems to lose his only daughter to death—a girl who "had grown up surrounded by hymns [*unter Gesängen*]" and whose "entire soul had become a tender song." When, at court,

> she harkened to the competing songs of the inspired [*begeisterte*] singers with deep attention [*mit tiefem Lauschen*], one took her for the visible

---

① On this relationship between seeing and being seen, cf. Jacques Lacan, *Le séminaire*, *livre XI: Les quatre concepts fondamentaux de la psychanalyse* (Paris: Seuil, 1973), 88ff.

② Cf. Anke Bennholdt-Thomsen, *Stern und Blume. Untersuchungen zur Sprachauffassung Hölderlins* (Bonn: Bouvier, 1967).

soul of the majestic art which had invoked those magical incantations, and ceased to marvel at the delights and melodies of the poets. (214)

It is no wonder, then, that her loss also robs a lover of letters like her father of the object of his desire. Without a woman to sign for it—as the "visible soul" of all songs and magical incantations—the medium of literature falls back into disconsolate literalness. Accordingly, the King "thinks" [*gedenkt*] to himself:

> what good does all this majesty, my high birth, do me now? Now I am more miserable than other men. Nothing can replace my daughter. Without her, the hymns are nothing but empty words and illusion [*Blendwerk*]. She was the magic that gave them life and joy, power and form. (223)

So that words would not be what they are—empty, that is—the poetry of the Age of Goethe underlaid them with a transcendental signified that transformed literacy into Desire itself. The transcendental signified could not be "replaced" by anything because—inasmuch as it involves the birth of a woman "out of the imagination"—"it can *replace* all the senses" (to say nothing of signifiers, which are defined by replaceability in the first place).

The idol of "Woman" forms the condition of possibility for Classical-Romantic poetry to the same extent that actual women remain silent. In the empirical sphere, women have nothing to do other than "listen" to actual singers—that is, men—"with deep attention." That is, women are consumers, a function of poetic discourse that is just as necessary as it is derivative. In transcendental terms, on the other hand—and as the visible soul of all words, which would otherwise be empty—the idol of "Woman" provides poets with an originary language whose depth is silence [*Stummheit*]. ① That is why Mathilde, the Blue Flower incarnate, appears to her lover in a dream and "speaks a wondrous, secret word into his mouth, which penetrate[s] his whole being." On

---

① Cf. Friedrich Schlegel, "Über die Philosophie. An Dorothea," *Kritische Friedrich-Schlegel-Ausgabe*, ed. Ernst Behler (Paderborn: Schöningh, 1958-), VIII, 42.

waking, Ofterdingen "would have given his very life still to know that word" (279). By the same token, "every future word will represent the effort to repeat that word, which is present within, yet unfixed."[①] In the first and final instance, poetry in the Age of Goethe means translating elementary, feminine speech—which never occurs—into articulated language.

As much is affirmed by another father in the novel when he discourses on his daughter and future son-in-law. Klingsohr—possibly an allegory for Goethe—speaks about Mathilde, the allegory "of Love," and Ofterdingen, the allegory "of Poetry":

> Just consider Love. Nowhere is the necessity of Poetry for the continued existence of mankind as clear as it is here. Love is mute, only Poetry can speak for it. Or Love is itself nothing but the highest Poetry of Nature. (287)[②]

With such technical precision does the mature, Classical Goethe impart a business secret to his Romantic heir. Even if the real Mathilde exchanges word after word with her lover, she remains mute all the same. "Since" women's "mere speech is already song" (276) mustering "scarcely audible words" (270), their discourse does not find its way into writing. [③] In order to be able to store the pure interiority of the transcendental signified, "natural poetry" [*Naturpoesie*] must first become "poetry" as a "strict art" (282). And that is a man's business.

---

① Johannes Mahr, *Übergang zum Endlichen. Der Weg des Dichters in Novalis' "Heinrich von Ofterdingen"* (Munich: Fink, 1970), 172.

② A novel written in 1808, which continued and completed the fragmentary *Ofterdingen*, turned the matter into plain speech and pragmatic plot points: "The Princess often seemed to have forgotten that she was mute, for none of her words escaped her father" (Ferdinand August Otto Heinrich Graf von Loeben [= Isidorus Orientalis], *Guido* [Mannheim: Schwan und Götz, 1808], 13).

③ Cf., once more, the parallel in Schlegel, "Über die Philosophie," VIII, 42.

2.

Secondly—and in empirical terms—literature in the Age of Goethe meant combining all the discourses that occur in disseminated form into unified poetic works. Klingsohr promises Ofterdingen "to read" with him "the strangest writings [*die merkwürdigsten Schriften*]" and to acquaint the aspiring poet "with all estates, all trades, all circumstances, and all demands of human society" (282). Even as a strict art, then, poetry involves translation. Discourses from the most varied times, places, and domains must be sampled, rewritten, and brought into a single channel. Put in terms of information technology, poetry means demultiplexing. Or as Novalis writes, "in the end, all poetry is translation"(IV, 237). That is precisely what Ofterdingen learns on his journey—that is, in the interval between meeting the Stranger, who initiates him, and encountering the Classical figure [*dem Klassiker*], who affords institutional recognition to his poet-heir [*Nachwuchsdichter*].

Ofterdingen's journey takes place without adventures or reversals of fortune. Everything happens so that he may be nothing more than an ear. "Heinrich listened very attentively to the new tales" (230), "heard their story, which was interrupted by many tears" (236), "paid attention to the conversation" (263), and so on, time and again. This occurs for good reason, for besides Mathilde—who must, after all, allegorize "Love" itself—no character in the novel suffers from muteness. All can speak of their station. Merchants speak of economic matters, knights of war, miners of geology and paleontology, Arab women of the Orient, and historians of history or literary history (cf. 265). All forms of contemporary knowledge, then, are provided in representative breadth and—as scholarly works put it so well—"in consideration of new findings in the cultural sciences." Therefore, even before pure poetic audition begins, an initial selection of discourses has already been made. The various forms of knowledge concern everyday lives, practices, and aptitudes, and they yield encyclopedic comprehensiveness. Delimited fields of knowledge emerge from the great murmur of daily routines——as if Ofterdingen were sitting in a library. Consequently, he can record all these discourses without effort (cf. 250).

And indeed, Ofterdingen's journey of education through oral narratives repeats Hardenberg's journey of education through all the books of the epoch. The one voyage provides the allegory of the other, and its orality represents a *fantastique de bibliothèque* that—as in the case of the merchants—simply emerges from translating quoted texts about the poet Arion back into speech and omitting the proper names of the protagonist and author (211-213). [1] With that, the novel guarantees the success of contemporary programs for instilling literacy. Ofterdingen is able to hear—that is, effortlessly absorb—everything that Hardenberg has read. When knowledge reaches the poet, it has already been distilled into meanings, that is, signifieds.

"Those calm, unknown people, whose world is their soul [*Gemüth*], whose action is contemplation, whose life is the quiet cultivation of their inner forces" (266) cannot be culturalized in any other way:

> Great and varied occurrences would disturb them. A simple life is their lot, and only through tales and writings need they become familiar with the rich contents and the infinite phenomena of the world. Only rarely in the course of their lives may an event pull them, for a while, into its rushing confusion—to teach them, through a little experience, more precisely of the circumstances and characters of those involved. For that, their perceptive sensibility is already busy with ⋯ matters near at hand, which present a rejuvenated world, and they make no step without experiencing the most surprising discoveries in themselves about the nature and meanings of the same. They are the poets. (267)

It makes no difference whether written works are at issue, as in Hardenberg's case, or oral accounts, as for Ofterdingen. For poets, the so-called world funnels into a news feed. The latter, however, functions along technologically precise lines—that is, in an altogether unromantic way. Time and again, the novel indicates the sources, broadcasters, channels, and receivers of messages that reach the poet; nor does it forget what goes missing en route (cf. 210f.).

---

[1]   On the function of these two deletions, cf. Kittler, *Discourse Networks*, 121-122.

But above all, data feeds are a matter of economy—to receive pure signifieds or "meanings," it is unnecessary to convey "the innumerable phenomena of the world." Information, according to Shannon's theorem, is the reciprocal of redundancy.

Hardenberg's novel sets up and enacts a principle of complexity reduction in precisely this sense: "rejuvenated representation" [*verjüngte Darstellung*]. *All* factual forms of knowledge of the epoch that reach Ofterdingen's ears are, by definition, miniatures—that is, depictions of similitude—that preserve relations but not dimensions. This is already taken care of inasmuch as elements of the messages get lost as they make their way to the poet. Precise phrasings are eroded until only pure meaning remains. Moreover, the narrative inlays in *Ofterdingen* assure the same: a tale within a tale (for example, when the merchants quote the myth of Arion or when Klingsohr's tale repeats Ofterdingen's family romance①) must necessarily have a lesser size than its frame and depict "the broadest stories, drawn together into tiny, shining minutes [*Minuten*]" (325).

Third, and finally, all the psychic conditions that the Age of Goethe called "poetic" perform miniaturization. Dreaming, Ofterdingen's father sees "the earth only as a golden bowl with the most intricate engraving" (202). In Ofterdingen's own vision, the heavenly realm shrinks to a "distant, small, wondrous majesty," while the earth lies "before him," "like an old, dear dwelling place" (321f.). Finally, in "childhood,"

> we see the full richness of infinite life, the tremendous forces of later time, the majesty of the end of the world, and the golden future of all things still closely woven into each other [*noch innig in einander verschlungen*]—and yet delicately rejuvenated in the clearest and most distinct way. (329)

Poetic imagination and complexity reduction coincide then. For Goethe, "true

---

① Cf. Kittler, "Die Irrwege des Eros," 449-463.

poetry" provided a "bird's-eye-view" of the earth in general. ① For Johann Christian Reil, the great psychiatrist, the mind itself was defined by the fact that it

> processes all matter that is given to it in keeping with its organization, and seeks at all times to introduce unity into the manifold. It winds together, in self-consciousness, the immeasurable thread of time into a knot, reproduces extinct centuries, and combines the elements of space extending into the Infinite—mountain ranges, rivers, forests, and the stars scattered in the firmament—into the miniature painting of imagination [*einer Vorstellung*]. ②

Of course, such abbreviations of space and time as occur throughout *Ofterdingen* are not materially performed by "the mind. " The mind is neither a film nor any other technological medium. The sole medium it has at its disposal is called language. According to Ofterdingen, however, language is "really a tiny world of signs and sounds" (287)—that is, the space of all possible miniatures that constitute poetry. For this reason, the rejuvenated depictions omitting the redundancy of the Real represent metaphors of reading itself. Just as the young Hardenberg read the sciences of his day only to be able to excerpt from book after book, the news feed reaching Ofterdingen's ear consists wholly and exclusively of prefabricated excerpts.

The greatest innovation in communications technology that occurred in the Age of Goethe was to combine storage and deletion. Hardenberg's philosophical preceptor, Johann Gottlieb Fichte, said so time and again. Only so long as the "art of printing" still stood in its infancy could the "sciences" (i. e. , universities) consider it their task to "set down the whole of book-learning once a-

---

① Johann Wolfgang Goethe, *Aus meinem Leben. Dichtung und Wahrheit*, *Sämtliche Werke. Jubiläums-Ausgabe*, ed. Eduard von der Hellen (Stuttgart: Cotta, 1904-1905), XXIV, 161.

② Johann Christian Reil, *Rhapsodieen über die Anwendung der psychischen Curmethode auf Geisteszerrüttungen* (Halle: Curtsche Buchhandlung, 1803), 55.

gain. " In the days when the early modern Republic of Letters was first institu-ted, storage simply involved repetition, either through written commentaries or oral lectures. However, ever since, first, the universal "spread of the book trade" and, second, the rise of literacy (a matter Fichte forgets)—since, that is, "there has existed no branch of learning about which there is not an excess of books"①—ROM (read-only memory) has become obsolete. "What the au-thor has said, we cannot tell our reader once more; for the former has already said it, and our reader can learn it from him in all respects [*in alle Wege*]."② Storage technology, therefore, must be refitted for RAM (random-access memory), which not only provides data in ROM format, but can also erase it and replace it with new information.

Accordingly, Fichte calls for an entirely new discourse of interpretation:

> We must uncover what the author himself is, inside—which is perhaps hidden to his own eyes, and through which all that is said becomes what it becomes to him. We must draw the spirit [*Geist*] out of the letter. ③

But if interpretations delete letters—that is, reduce them to "mind" or "spirit"—then they are identical to the miniature paintings that Reil extolled and Novalis implemented. As scientific as they may seem, inasmuch as they are discourses, they turn into works, art, and, more specifically, poetry.

> After all, one does not study to prepare for exams one's whole life long— to reproduce, verbally, what has been learned. Instead, one studies in order to apply knowledge to circumstances in life as they arise—and thereby to transform it into *works*; it is not just a matter of repetition, but

---

① Johann Gottlieb Fichte, "Deducirter Plan einer zu Berlin zu errichtenden höheren Lehranstalt," *Sämmtliche Werke*, ed. Immanuel Hermann Fichte (Berlin: Veit, 1845-1846), VIII, 98.

② Johann Gottlieb Fichte, *Die Grundzüge des gegenwärtigen Zeitalters*, *Sämmtliche Werke*, VII, 109.

③ Ibid.

of making something else out of and with, it: and so, here too, the final purpose is in no way knowledge, but rather the art of using knowledge. ①

No one followed Fichte more loyally than Novalis, and no one is truer to him than the hero of his novel. To be sure, literature—as a matter of definition and at all times—is a data stream.

All the same, in the Europe of old, there had been times when encyclopedic breadth and the literal reproduction of data made literature great and worthy of praise in the first place. Baroque novels—for example, Lohenstein's *Arminius*—restated the whole of book learning. ② That is, they operated without the deletions that prove constitutive for *Ofterdingen* and, for this reason, are depicted internally. Thus, Klingsohr's tale tells of a scribe, who clearly stands for the erstwhile Republic of Letters; this figure, however, must submit all his encyclopedically exact records to the censorship of a woman whose very name stands for the new philosophy. "Sophia's" magic dish "with limpid water" has the power to "erase" most of what the Scribe has written (294). Only very different pages—which "little Fable" (i. e. , Poetry) inscribes with the "quill of the Scribe"—pass the censor's office "fully shining and unscathed [*völlig glänzend und unversehrt*]" (295f.). After all, if one follows Fichte, these pages already are *works*, that is, reductions of complexity requiring no further reduction.

In an ingenious study, Heinrich Bosse has shown that the magical vessel in *Ofterdingen* and the wholly analogous magical water in E. T. A. Hoffmann's *Golden Pot* ③ are not mere symbols. Of course, the Age of Goethe had no writing materials that admitted thorough deletion. However, its schools invented a new surface of inscription that equipped even children with random-access

---

① Fichte, "Deducirter Plan," 100ff.

② Cf. , for example, the two encyclopedic reference works that Johann Christoph Männling compiled, around 1700, for Lohenstein's novel.

③ Cf. E. T. A. Hoffmann, "Der goldne Topf," *Fantasie- und Nachtstücke*, ed. Walter Müller-Seidel (Munich: Winkler, i960), 215.

memory: the slate [*Schiefertafel*]. Here, as everyone knows, chalk marks are made only to be corrected—that is, erased.

> The [old] writing exercises with pen and ink invariably formed—and endlessly, at that—the side-by-side arrangement of a tableau. Exercises with chalk and slate, on the other hand, opened the play of presence and absence—or, in less ludic terms, nothing other than the technology of spiritualization [*Technik der Vergeistigung*]. ① In writing and reading, they edged out mimicry both the refined Old-European art of *imitatio* as well as repetitive drills of spelling and copying. Instead, they encouraged students to do things themselves—a matter that was supposed to unfold in a framework of simulation that had already been shaped. ②

The new storage technology of the Age of Goethe, then, gave form to schools and poetry in equal measure. Ofterdingen's journey through Germany does not occur out of necessity. He could just as well have stayed in the classroom and taken in all the subjects of contemporary learning, spiritualizing them and transforming them into poetry. Hegel's dictum holds that pupils learn "the history of the world's development [*die Geschichte der Bildung der Welt*]" only "as if traced in silhouette." That, however, is precisely the point of complexity reduction, whether poetic or "pedagogical."③ Accordingly, between empirical and speculative approaches "for achieving knowledge of human history [*um zur Wissenschaft der menschlichen Geschichte zu gelangen*]." Ofterdingen chooses the second option: he considers each matter "in its living, manifold context"; on this basis, he can "easily compare it with all the others, like figures on a board" (208).

Through miniaturization, then, varying forms of knowledge—on the model

---

① Heinrich Bosse, "'Die Schüler müßen selbst schreiben lernen' oder Die Einrichtung der Schiefertafel,": *Schreiben—Schreiben lernen, Rolf Sanner zum 65. Geburtstag*, ed. Dietrich Boueke and Norbert Hopster (Tübingen: Narr, 1985), 194.

② Ibid. , 195.

③ Hegel, *Phänomenologie des Geistes*, 25.

of *The Novices in Sais* or, alternately, that of curricula invented around 1800—form constellations that permit the mathematical combination of their elements. This is how Hardenberg proceeds in *Allgemeines Brouillon*, and it is how his poetic protagonist makes his way as well. ① Comparisons and tabulations transfer individual forms of knowledge into place values within a system called "philosophy" in *Allgemeines Brouillon* and "poetry" in *Ofterdingen*. It is also exactly how Klingsohr summarizes the stations of Ofterdingen's journey of education. "The narrative of your journey," he tells Heinrich,

> afforded me pleasant entertainment yesterday evening. Indeed, I remarked that the spirit of the poetic art is your friend and companion [*freundlicher Begleiter*]. Your fellow travelers have, unnoticed, become its voices. In proximity to the Poet, Poetry bursts forth everywhere. The land of poetry, the Romantic Orient, has greeted you with its sweet melancholy; War has addressed you in its wild majesty; and Nature and History have approached you in the form of a miner and a hermit. (283)

After the fact, individual voices heard in the course of events become pure instances of discourse, whose speech, while particular to a discipline, is already standardized, that is, poetical. Ofterdingen—as he has often done already (cf. 238) and the novel will continue to do as a whole—only needs to pass on what he hears as a coherent "tale" in order to produce real literature, which simply involves demultiplexing separate chains of transmission or channels of knowledge.

In so doing, Ofterdingen brings back what, according to the novel, represents the original condition of all discourses: primordial unity. "In the most ancient times, in the lands of the Greek empire today," poets are said "to have been prophets and priests, lawmakers and doctors, all at once" (211). All four

---

① Compare formulations concerning the inversely proportional relation between the "Astrologist" and the "Miner" (260) with the innumerable passages in the *Brouillon*, where two or more sciences are chalked up as analogical proportions.

branches of university study (assuming that prophets were the precursors of philosophers) spoke from the same mouth then. And inasmuch as the mouth, in general, is "simply a mobile and answering ear" (211), Ofterdingen receives the task of renewing such unity by translating all discourses into the one true Poetry. According to the novel, however, this is obstructed by a historical circumstance: the monopoly of the church on knowledge. "It is bad enough," the merchants say, "that the sciences have come into the hands of an estate so distant from worldly life, and that princes are advised by such unsociable and truly inexperienced men." Therefore, they urge Ofterdingen "not to become a cleric" (207), but rather to take up the new profession—entirely unknown to monks or chaplains (208)—of Poet.

Hardenberg's novel, it could scarcely be said more clearly, does not take place in the Middle Ages where it is set, but in the present day of its discourse. The program concerns the creation of a historically new estate of civil servants that will prove more effective politically than their theological counterparts and unify the disciplines of all four fields of university study. This same reform of discourse took place in the Age of Goethe. "The separation of the order in schools [*Schulregiment*] from that of churches"[1]—which occurred in Prussia from 1794 on—replaced the same chaplains from whom Ofterdingen is obliged to receive his first instruction (204) with *Gymnasium* professors salaried by the state, and it replaced the Bible as the foundational text for alphabetization with poetic primers.[2] Only in this discursive space was the project undertaken by Schlegel and Novalis to found a new, poetic mythology—or Bible—not sacrilegious. In it alone can Ofterdingen transform "the world and history," by way of poetry, "into holy writ" (334) and declare that "the Bible and doctrine of Fable [*Bibel und Fabellehre*]" represent "Constellations of Heavenly Revolution [*SternBilder Eines Umlaufs*]"(333). Around 1800, the all-telling Fable

① Friedrich Paulsen, *Geschichte des gelehrten Unterrichts auf den deutschen Schulen und Universitäten vom Ausgange des Mittelalters bis zur Gegenwart. Mit besonderer Rücksicht auf den klassischen Unterricht*(Berlin, Leipzig: Veit, 1919-1921), II, 166.

② Cf. Ferdinand Bünger, *Entwicklungsgeschichte des Volksschullesebuches* (Leipzig: Dürr, 1898), esp. 231.

[*die alleserzählende Fabel*] replaced the Word made flesh, which was there in the Beginning.

"Fable," moreover, does not mean "fable." Instead, it means a discursive institution otherwise known as "German class" [*Deutschunterricht*]. Just as the novel translates and combines all forms of knowledge into poetry, so did the new field of instruction proceed. Teaching German, according to Friedrich Schleiermacher,

> is not just to be viewed as language learning; rather—because the mother tongue is the immediate organ of Understanding and the general organ of Fantasy—everything that can occur at schools for the free, formal cultivation of the Spirit flows into this instruction—all in preparation for Philosophy. ①

Imagination or "Fantasy" offers the altogether wondrous sense for replacing all senses, and German the wondrous discipline [*Fach*] for replacing all disciplines [*Fächer*]. Only when slates eliminated rhetorical imitation and German essays took the place of orality in schools could novels like *Ofterdingen* come into being. Every *Abitur* essay " documents " (once again, in Schleiermacher's words) the "education [*Bildung*] of Understanding and Fantasy"②—just as Ofterdingen's miniature depictions do for scientific discourses. The latter all represent poetically exalted allegories for a new method of testing that, around 1800, replaced rhetorical oral cultures with the written interpretive essay. To pass his *Abitur* as a poet, then, Ofterdingen must also find a German teacher. This is exactly what happens when Klingsohr "approaches, leading a lovely girl by the hand, to open stupid lips through the tones [*Laute*] of the mother tongue and the touch of a sweet, delicate mouth" (268). The

---

① Schleiermacher, "Gutachten vom 14. Dezember 1810," quoted in Paul Schwartz, "Die Gründung der Universität Berlin und der Anfang der Reform der höheren Schulen im Jahre 1810," *Mitteilungen der Gesellschaft für deutsche Erziehungs- und Schulgeschichte* 20 (1910): 173.

② Ibid. , 196.

mother tongue, as Klingsohr teaches his pupil in their shared readings (282), forms the immediate organ of the Understanding—and the kiss, as the school-boy dream of distant girls' lips, the general organ of Fantasy.

3.

Germany's higher school system—from the time it underwent fundamental reform in the Age of Goethe until 1908, when even Prussia finally admitted female students—was based on the exclusion of women. To be sure, girls could receive private tutoring, as Mathilde does from her father(282f.), and they could also attend schools for young ladies [*höhere Töchterschulen*], as Ottilie does in Goethe's *Elective Affinities*. However, since *Gymnasia* had the sole purpose of producing students (through the newly created *Abitur*), and universities bureaucrats (through the newly created *Staatsexamen*), women were left out of the system culminating in poets and thinkers, on the one hand, and civil servants, on the other (a development foreseen for the unwritten second half of Hardenberg's novel[①]). Because "Woman" meant "the Poetry of Nature," and because "the Poetry of Nature" was mute, her passing an *Abitur* or *Staatsexamen* was the very definition of the Impossible.

So that Ofterdingen may complete his course of education, then, Mathilde must return to the silence of blue flowers, which is where she came from in the first place. But this is also why Hardenberg's novel—even though it avoids all "great and manifold events [*große und vielfache Begebenheiten*]"—includes a "rushing whirl [*raschen Wirbel*]"(267) after all. Indeed, the words should be taken literally: Mathilde drowns in the waters of the Danube. Only when she dies are all the conditions of discourse fulfilled that lead Ofterdingen to the university and thereby make him a member of adult, male society [*Männergemeinschaft*]: "Terrible fear robbed him of consciousness. His heart [*das Herz*] was no longer beating. [...] His quiet mind [*Gemüth*] had disappeared"

---

① Cf. the keywords on the planned continuation: "Conversation with the Emperor on government, empire, etc." (340); "Conversation with the Emperor on government, etc. Mystical Emperor. Book *de Tribus Impostoribus*"(341).

(278). In other words, Ofterdingen has lost his love, his soul, and his proper name all at once. As "the Pilgrim"—which he is called from this point on (319)—he represents a purely discursive instance: "the Student."

As a purely discursive instance, Ofterdingen has to rediscover what constitutes his sole and essential medium: language. At the beginning of the second half of the novel, he wanders alone in desolate mountains. He hears, at first, only "a strong wind" whose "muffled, varied voices were lost as soon as they came" (319, cf. 349f.). For a second time, then, Ofterdingen encounters sources of noise that openly scorn words and books. This only occurs, however, so that the noise can be filtered away and, as fading background static, make "language and voice live again" within him (22). Both in the novel and in what is commonly called "life," such signal selection harkens to the name of love.

> Love is a logical inversion. Because—in the field of sexuality, sexualized bodies, and the sexes and sexual desire—many things occur without functioning, nothing happens in love. On the other hand, this means that there are no disturbances, either. The factors of "noise"—sexuality and its unfulfilled desire—are filtered out. [...] The totality and *pleroma* of love is maintained only through the paradox that want is wanting [*daß der Mangel mangelt*]—that is, sexuality. Here, poetry stands in as the language of love. [1]

Therefore, against the background of the wind and other noises that "dully drone," there appears a human and articulated "voice"—which the hallucinating "Pilgrim" recognizes as belonging to Mathilde (321). Just as soon, the voice secures an optical frame as well, and turns into the vision of that "distant, small, wondrous majesty" in which a miniaturized Mathilde appears as the

---

[1]   Jens Schreiber, *Das Symptom des Schreibens. Roman und absolutes Buch in der Frühromantik (Novalis/Schlegel)* (Frankfurt/M., Bern, New York: Peter Lang, 1983), 212.

Heavenly Mother (322). Through this fusion of Virgin and Mother, love and religion, and eroticism and maternity,① a woman [*Frau*] in the Real becomes the wife [*Frau*] of all men in the Imaginary. And because "it seemed as if she wanted to speak with him"—even "though nothing was to be heard" (322)—Ofterdingen finally learns what pure instances of discourse really are.

In the first poem that Ofterdingen succeeds at composing, the new author hails "Mathilde" as the "Mother and Beloved of God" (324). Because the signifier "Mathilde" no longer possesses reference (Mathilde is dead) or materiality (she is inaudible)—but at the same time and for this very reason means Meaning in general—it makes poetic [*poetisiert*] all past discourses (which parties like Ofterdingen have the task of uniting). This is also why "everything seems much more familiar and more prophetic than before" (322). Doubly absented or neutralized—first in the discourse of a father and then in the dream where she drowns—a real woman becomes the *Alma mater* of all forms of knowledge.

Accordingly, the place where Ofterdingen hallucinates the presence of absent parties is introduced as "a cloister, altogether wondrous, like an entrance to Paradise" (340). The site excludes real women as a matter of course. And if—as Hegel proudly put it—"our schools and universities are our churches,"② then its name is certain as well. Around 1800, the monopoly on knowledge formerly held by monasteries and churches shifted to the new, state-run educational system. Thus, it is no wonder that—in the shadow of Mathilde, who has been transfigured into an *Alma mater*—there appears a wise old man, whose conversations with Ofterdingen may serve as an ending even in a novel that remained a fragment. Sylvester—of whom it is not said for nothing that he, "as a father, sits alone, eternally tearful, at the [mother's] grave" (327)—represents Ofterdingen's philosophy teacher at university (just as Klingsohr taught him German in high school). Sylvester's expertise encompasses medicine (325), history (326), theology (332), the natural sciences (334),

---

① Cf. Gerhard Schulz, *Novalis* (Reinbek: Rowohlt, 1969), 141ff.

② Hegel, quoted in Karl Löwith, *Von Hegel zu Nietzsche. Der revolutionäre Bruch im Denken des* 19. *Jahrhunderts* (Stuttgart: Kohlhammer, 1950), 34.

and above all, philosophy (330-333). All disciplines—with the exception of jurisprudence—are represented when Sylvester initiates Ofterdingen into university learning. With that, both Poetry and the Poet achieve discursive legitimation.

Already in his exchange with Klingsohr, Ofterdingen had learned that poetry, despite the universality into which it can translate all discourses, has a limit:

> If there exists a proper sphere for the individual poet, within which he must remain ... there is also, for all human faculties, a certain limit to what can be represented ... Mature experience first teaches one to avoid such irregularity of objects and to leave the detection of the Simplest and the Highest to Wisdom of the World. (285ff.)

Also, and especially, the poet Klingsohr accords philosophy (and not theology, as Dante and the Middle Ages in general had done) a superiority that, when Sylvester appears, finally enters the novel itself. His doctrine—that "the cosmos [*das Weltall*] dissolves into infinite worlds which are always encompassed by greater worlds," and that "all senses, ultimately, are a single sense" (331)—formulates precisely the "Simplest and the Highest," which, according to Klingsohr, only philosophers (and not poets) can pronounce.

In passing from Klingsohr to Sylvester, from "expectation" [*Erwartung*] to "fulfillment" [*Erfüllung*]—as the two parts of the novel are called—Ofterdingen performs the final steps necessary for education in the Age of Goethe. Graduating from a preparatory school, where there were still women and the highest point was occupied by German poetry alone, he arrives at the peak of contemporary discourses. In the European university system of old, philosophy had simply provided a propaedeutic course of study for medicine, theology, and jurisprudence (the three discourses of absolute power). But around 1800, in the new *Bildungsstaat*, it achieved the rank and title of supreme knowledge. The careers of Fichte and Hegel attest as much.

Inasmuch as preparation for all university study passed to *Gymnasia*, the discipline of philosophy—previously the "preschool" of general knowledge for the three older fields of study—achieved an autonomous position at the beginning of the nineteenth century. In addition to the matter of cultivating scientific research, it was charged with the particular task of preparing [students] for the teaching profession. [1]

The formation of German teachers (in so-called reality) or poets (in so-called fiction) must occur by way of a discipline that surpasses even German. Not for nothing, in Schleiermacher's words, does "everything flow" into German lessons at the *Gymnasium*—everything, that is, "that can occur in schools for the free, formal education of the spirit, [which is] all preparation for philosophy." Klingsohr and Sylvester, Ofterdingen's two spiritual fathers, [2] are linked by this same information network. The one teaches the poetic, the other the philosophical, unity of all forms of learning.

Even though, as Sylvester tells the novel's protagonist, "Fable" is the "universal instrument [*Gesamtwerkzeug*]" of his "present world" (331), the wise old man considers Philosophy "the science of sciences" (III, 666). Here—at the highest level of reflection—resides his power. For all that, Sylvester is not unaware of the historical novelty of his position, nor does he leave room for others to doubt. He remarks "how far learning [*Wissenschaft*], which until now was called the Doctrine of Virtue or Ethics [*Tugend- oder Sittenlehre*]," has stood "from the pure form, of ethics as conceived by transcendental philosophy (332). In making this declaration, Sylvester is simply quoting Harden-berg, whose fragments and excerpts, in turn, quote "Fichte's moral doctrine [*Moral*]," which offers "the most correct views" (III, 685).

Hardenberg's novel is just that precise in securing its philosophical

---

① K. Fricke, "Die geschichtliche Entwicklung des Lehramts an den höheren Schulen," K. Fricke and K. Eulenburg, *Beiträge zur Oberlehrerfrage* (Leipzig: Teubner, 1903), 16.

② Cf. Schulz, *Novalis*, 139-141.

legitimation. A New Year that pronounces the words of Fichte [*ein Sylvester mit Fichte- Worten im Mund*] has nothing fictitious about it: the wise man's ascent to the highest instance of discourse in the text simply repeats the career path of philosophers in the disciplinary history of learning around 1800. Ever since a stranger told him about the Blue Flower, Ofterdingen has inhabited a realm of *Dichten und Denken*. Thus, when Ofterdingen and Sylvester meet at the end of the novel, the coupling of two discursive formations transforms into positive fact. The poetry that the Age of Goethe inaugurated cannot exist without the support of German Idealism.

From the inception, that is, starting with the works of Gustave Lanson and Georg Lukács, literary sociology has held a strangely vague conception of society. According to *The Theory of the Novel*, Hardenberg's work runs—indeed, it heightens—the "danger" of "lyrical, mood-dominated romanticizing of the structures of social reality," which "cannot, given the fact that reality at the present stage of development lacks pre-stabilized harmony, relate to the essential life of⋯ interiority. "[1] For all that, however, *Heinrich von Ofterdingen* does not set interiority in general against social formations that are (supposedly) hard at work dismantling the *deutsche Misere*. In actual fact, so-called interiority involves a student—that is, a man. By the same token, so-called social formations are actually the powers of discourse that institute the Social in the first place and steer it (for example, by way of readers' reactions to poetry). For this reason, Hardenberg's novel does not need to recruit readers—much less seduce them—with a world that is "beautiful and harmonious but closed within itself and unrelated to anything outside. "[2] Rather, the work simply needs to regulate its relationship with that instance of discursive power which, around 1800—and only then—took over literature. Of course, the reception of literature has always occurred via channels that determine in advance what

---

[1] Georg Lukács, *The Theory of the Novel: A Historico-Philosophical Essay on the Forms of Great Epic Literature*, trans. Anna Bostock (Cambridge: MIT Press, 1971), 140.

[2] Ibid.

qualifies as a text, an author, a work, a letter, and so on. But only in the Age of Goethe was this task performed by a philosophy that invented the new field of investigation that, ever since, has been called "literary interpretation."

Once Sylvester has taught him the philosophy of history, nature, and proper conduct [*des guten Handelns*], Ofterdingen can finally articulate what he has been doing unconsciously all along—ever since his dreaming and thinking came to revolve around a blue flower. Whereas at first he "didn't even have a clue" about "poets and singers" or "their peculiar [*sonderbar*] art" (208), he now brings forth a concept of poetry that (as Hegel would say) promptly submerges in the Concept itself. "O splendid Father," Ofterdingen apostrophizes the philosopher,

> with what joy does the light fill me that issues from your words. And so the true Spirit of Fable is a friendly disguise for the Spirit of Virtue, and the actual purpose of the Art of Poetry, which is subordinate to it, is the Activity of a most exalted and authentic Existence [*Regsamkeit des höchsten, eigenthümlichsten Daseyns*]. (332)

The logic of the signifieds—as determined by the discursive space around 1800—has been achieved. In a "friendly" way (i. e., one that moves the general public), Poetry, boiled down to its core spirit or concept, disguises Spirit [*Geist*] or the Concept itself; in other words, it disguises Philosophy (per the latter's self-definition). At the same time, because it explicitly stands "subordinate" to Philosophy, the "Art of Poetry" has both a mistress and an address into which its discourse—this unified articulation of all the information channels of the epoch—can truly flow [*münden*]. *Poetry* has achieved legitimation, as well as a storage unit into which Hardenberg's *Ofterdingen* merges just as completely as Goethe's *Faust* into Hegel's *Phenomenology*. [①] That is why, to this very day, interpreters of the novel, instead of analyzing the poetic-philosophical networking of discourses, have affirmed, time and again,

---

① Cf. Kittler, *Discourse Networks*, 154ff.

Ofterdingen's subordinate position—that is, subsumed the text under idealistic theorems.

Such is the power of authoritative discourses [*Herrendiskursen*]: whoever is able "freely" [*in "freyer Gewalt"*] to define what authority and a "master" possessed of "freedom" [*mit "freyer Gewalt"*] are makes what he says inescapable. Sylvester need not worry about leaving "the subordinate Art of Poetry"—this "disguise" of conscience—to the youthful Ofterdingen. As a philosopher, he has already claimed Conscience as such.

> Precisely this all-encompassing freedom, mastery, or dominion is the essence, the motor of conscience. In it is revealed the holy quality, the immediate creativity of personality; and every action of the master is, at the same time, the pronouncement of a lofty, simple, uncomplicated world— the Word of God. (331f.)

That is plain speech. Once again, Sylvester simply incarnates Fichte. A master of discourses says that God's dominion over discourse is over and done, now that Philosophy has assumed a position at the crown of all other disciplines. Formerly, perhaps, in the times of the "Bible," there existed "immediate exchange with Heaven"; maybe later, during the Middle Ages, "the Holy Ghost" spoke "to us" indirectly, "through the understanding of prudent and favorably-disposed men" (198). Around 1800, however, "the word of God" became identical with authorship. According to Sylvester, it appears as a "holy quality"—as the "immediate creativity of personality." According to Fichte, the "proof of the wrongfulness of reprinting books [*Unrechtmäßigkeit des Büchernachdrucks*]" can only be demonstrated when one recognizes that "everyone" has "his own course of thought [*Ideengang*]," "his own particular way of forming notions and connecting them with each other."

Around 1800 there arose for the first time a conception of copyright and authorship that understood books as the "exclusive property of [their] first master. "① Whoever—like Sylvester or Fichte—is magisterial enough to trump masters of this kind through reflection and provide reasons legitimating their own dominion truly speaks the Word of God.

A novel like *Heinrich von Ofterdingen*, which cycles through the discursive space of its epoch from beginning to end—from unrecordable noise up to the system of universal storage called "Philosophy"—and moreover does so for each and every word or author, does not depict "actions" [*Handlungen*]. Instead, it *acts*.

---

① Johann Gottlieb Fichte, "Beweis der Unrechtmässigkeit des Büchernachdrucks. Ein Räsonnement und eine Fabel," *Sämmtliche Werke*, VIII, 227. On the preparatory stages for such authorship—namely when Ofterdingen learns to identify as the protagonist of the poetic novels of education [*Dichterbildungsromane*] that he reads—cf. Kittler, *Discourse Networks*, 119ff.

21. 基特勒：《〈亨利希·奥夫特丁根〉作为数据传输记录》

(Friedrich A. Kittler, "*Heinrich von Ofterdingen* as Data Feed," 1986)

作者小识

基特勒（Friedrich A. Kittler，1943—2011），德国文学科学家和媒介理论家，被誉为"数字时代的德里达"，是媒介考古学德国学派的代表人物。他的研究以媒介技术文化为中心，广泛涉猎哲学、文学、历史、传播媒介与军事技术。以香农的信息论为科学基础，以海德格尔的"存在历史"为哲学方法，基特勒在后现代视野下分析文学语料，通过对 19 世纪以来的话语网络进行后结构主义分析，展开对媒介文化哲学的建构。他的媒介技术哲学极具原创性，不仅改变了技术研究的性质，而且引领着这一领域的学术方向。

基特勒是一位具有原创性且难以定位的理论家，其批判思维方式登峰造极，且被广泛地运用于文学、历史、哲学、交流甚至军事领域。他对于文学研究的贡献是将文学置于技术文化视野下，并专注于在复杂的历史脉络中对话语网络进行分析性重构。

基特勒的代表作包括《音乐与数学》（第一卷"希腊"，第一部"阿弗洛狄忒"）（*Musik und Mathematik* I: *Hellas* I: *Aphrodite*，2006）、《幽灵谈话录——不朽、讣告、记忆》（*Unsterbliche*: *Nachrufe*，*Erinnerungen*，*Geistergespräche*，2004）、《文化研究的历史》（*Eine Kulturgeschichte der Kulturwissenschaft*，2000）、《留声机　电影　打字机》（*Gramophone*，*Film*，*Typewriter*，1986）、《1800 年/1900 年的话语网络》（*Aufschreibesysteme 1800/1900*，1985）。

背景略说

基特勒不仅是媒介考古学德国学派的开创者之一，而且为审视文化技术世界提供了"存在论"的视角。总括其学术生涯，基特勒思想历经三变，呈现媒介文化研究历史之三种样态。20 世纪 80 年代，他分析文学话语网络（Aufschreibesysteme），开辟了技术与文学融合研究的新路，凸显女性，尤其是母亲形象在人文教化中的媒介地位（母亲即自然，自然即媒介，媒介即万物重返一体宇宙之归途)①；20 世纪 90 年代，他将硬件技术进化研究和软件编程开发研究结合起来，把话语分析导向技术基础结构和技术事件的描述，叙说 19 世纪 80 年代以后留声机、电影和打字机的相继诞生，将活字印刷术四个世纪的垄断地位的终结视为用数据记录人类记忆的技术新纪元②；21 世纪伊始，基特勒致力于"将心灵从人文科学之中驱逐出去"（Auftreibung des Geistes aus der Geistwissenschaften），以对技术的狂热之爱（media-phillia），甚至激进的技术先验论（the technological a prior），同英美技术文化研究中的"人类中心主义"分道扬镳。虽然其著述之中留下了福柯"人的消逝"之影响痕迹，"解构人"的法国后结构主义激进立场清晰可辨，但基特勒拒绝以二元论视野观照技术世纪，尤其否认其思想与"媒介考古学"的关联。此外，基特勒采用日耳曼农业工程中一个过时的词语"文化技术"（Kulturtechneken）来命名媒介研究工作，并像伊尼斯一样开启了朝着古典世界的转向。

　　基特勒浸润在法国后现代主义的理论氛围之下，其媒介文化批评凸显一个基本倾向：言说主体的权力去势（Entmachtung）导致了言语秩序的裂变。这项断言建立在三个假设之上。第一，语言之存在先于我们的存在，我们在语言的怀抱之中成长，语言是我们的主宰，所以人类并非语言的主人。从语言的自律性出发，基特勒断言：歌德的《浪游者的夜歌》和平克·弗洛伊德的《大脑损伤》（"Brain Damage"）都不是对现实的模仿，也不是情绪的表现，而是语言的自我表演。第二，媒介考古学表明，历史没有连续性可言，相反却受制于深刻的文化断裂。《1800 年/1900 年的话语网络》及其书写风格表明，历史相对于前面的"文人/学者共和国"是一场裂变，相对于后面的媒介技术的引导又是一段异质文化的表演。断裂阻碍了文化的连续性，却丰富了文化景观。这就印证了福柯的一个危言耸听的论断：从考古学层面上看，实证体系在 18 世纪末和 19 世纪初以一种规模宏大的方式实现了根本转型。第三，话语网络相对于存在结构具有优先性，甚至解构了以人为中心的存在结构。因此，基特勒的媒介文化批判彰显了反人文主义倾向。基于这一反人文主义前提，基特勒反对麦克卢汉的论断——"媒介是人的延伸"，反过来断言"人是媒介的延

　　① Friedrich A. Kittler, *Discourse Networks 1800/1900*, trans. Michael Metteer, with Chris Cullens, Stanford, CA: Stanford University Press, 1992.

　　② Friedrich A. Kittler, *Gramophone*, *Film*, *Typewriter*, trans. Geoffrey Winthrop-Young and Michael Wutz, Stanford, CA: Stanford University Press, 1999.

伸"，而人作为一个晚近的观念发明，则是一个年轻却濒临末日的"概念"。

于是，基特勒就必须将海德格尔的"存在历史"（The History of Being）与法国后现代话语融为一体，探索以媒介文化为主角的人类历史相位。海德格尔的"存在历史"，为人类理解存在、把握存在意蕴提供了一系列方式。基特勒以技术概念增补了存在的维度，赋予媒介以自律存在的意义，也就是以媒介技术为中心书写最新的存在历史。在媒介性之中反思媒介性，基特勒就势必将福柯的历史断裂观、拉康的镜像说运用于话语分析和媒介文化批判，致力于探索"技术世界之内在场的真理"。

基本内容

本章的选文集中研究诺瓦利斯的诗化教育小说《亨利希·奥夫特丁根》。基特勒运用香农的信息论，将这部诗兴流韵的小说读作"数据传输"，并借此深描"歌德时代"话语网络的特征及诗学诉求。

基特勒认为，诺瓦利斯的小说由无数的对话、复杂的文体、深邃的思辨、空灵的想象构成。它不像是一篇小说，而是多声部的音乐总谱。无待抒情主体，也无待描述对象，《亨利希·奥夫特丁根》的文本自我表演，自我言说：懒洋洋的良知，在一个毫无阻力的平滑世界，自由自主地变成了一场扣人心弦的交谈，这是一则无所不说的寓言。小说极少叙述情节，也没有描述主体的阻力，寓言却超越文类的限制升到了至高无上的地位。尤其是诗人克林索尔所讲述的大角星童话，这则小说之中的小说，将信息流寓言化了。一切都必须说，原因是完全没有什么可说。小说的有序之声，开始于白色噪声，有效信息源自无序紊乱。于是，基特勒断定，可以将福柯的知识考古学运用于对 1800 年德国文学话语网络生成的分析。福柯曾说：

> 世界历史的宏大巨著（Oeuvre）同一部缺席作品（oeuvre）之间的伴随性关联是不可磨灭的：缺席之作，时刻更新，但在其必然的虚空之中悄然掠过，对漫长的历史毫无影响；来自历史之前，它好像已经存在于源始的决断之中；源于历史之后，它好像再次在被历史改变的遗嘱之中大获全胜。唯有在空间之中，历史才臻于完满。这一空间既空无一物，又是人类的家园，由没有语言的全部语词构成。这些语词向每一个倾听它们的人敞开，显示为来自历史深处的沉闷音响，呈现为一种执拗的嗡嗡作响的语言。它们自言自语，没有言语的主体，也没有谈话的对手，内卷

于自身之内，如鱼鲠在喉，不吐不快，而又会在达到一种清晰的表述之前烟消云散，无怨无悔地归于永恒不可动摇的沉默。此乃焚烧至烬的意义之根。①

基特勒紧接着断言，这些论断运用于文学与运用于历史一样贴切。这些词语所造就的作品为这种嗡嗡作响的语言所测定和环绕。嘈杂音响让有意义的话语烟消云散。"没有白色噪声，就不会发生信息流，因为传播渠道主动删除了信息，因为它们只不过是随机的界面分布。"《亨利希·奥夫特丁根》第五章开篇对于乡村客栈嘈杂氛围的描写，便构成了诺瓦利斯诗性语言的意义之根。客栈里各色人等五方杂处，所谈内容无所不包，比对亚特兰蒂斯的诗意梦想和对黄金时代的哲学沉思更为接近现实人生。不管他们是否喝醉，乡村酒馆的客人们的嘈杂音响都构成了诺瓦利斯小说之不可磨灭的背景。正是从这些"来自历史深处的沉闷音响"中，作家塑造出栩栩如生的人物，编织出唯美的话语网络。"正是因为如此，才有最为符合文学本质的人物和词语。"

乡村酒馆里无名的喧嚣与骚动，完全对立于其他信息的系统递归，从来就不引人注意。在描写了这种混杂无序的音响之后，小说转向了一个名为"奥夫特丁根"的听众，以及一个叙述者。这个叙述者像小说中的其他人物一样，只存在于词语层面。他不仅有许多事情要说，而且还见多识广，无所不知。这个叙述者是个老人，他的话语令奥夫特丁根兴奋异常，渴望从他那里学得更多。但是，这些平淡无奇的陈述也容易被解释者忽略，因为它们并未包括任何理论内容，只不过是报道信息流而已。这种情形在《亨利希·奥夫特丁根》之中比比皆是。白色噪声提供了文学价值的零点，所以信息的传输是话语事件的标志，必须得到充分的分析。言语行为不只是臻于所说内容。这一事实构成了言语行为历史的现实性。信息流不只是简单地反映所谓现实或历史，而是在不同的权力装置（dispositives of powers）之间切换。"稚嫩的诗人，一如小说中的奥夫特丁根，兴奋异常地倾听老矿工的言谈；这就为 1800 年信息网络提供了典范的信息。"换言之，如果我们秉持这一标签去测定话语效用的零度相位（Schwundstufen von Wirksamkeit），那么，就没有小说，也没有浪漫主义。像事实存在的数据传输，《亨利希·奥夫特丁根》，这部浪漫主义小说

---

① Michel Foucault, *History of Madness*, ed. Jean Khalfa, trans. Jonathan Murphy and Jean Khalfa, London and New York, Routledge, 2006, pp. 31-32.

之中最为浪漫的小说，就被解释为浪漫的反面——"它展示了一种事件的绝对性（unhintergehbarkeit）"。显而易见，这部小说情节贫乏，却仅仅是为了给另一种更强大的情节腾出空间和场所——这就是言语本身的情节，或者言语本身的行动。在克林索尔所讲述的大角星童话中，那个无所不说的大写"寓言"就不是一则童话或一则神话。这个色彩绚丽但情调悲伤的童话表明，如果没有歌德时代所创造的德语诗歌，革命的 19 世纪人文共和国（教化国家，Bildungstaat）可能就不会存在。

因此，基特勒坚信，为了浪漫主义于"存在史"之中的意义，就必须重构 1800 年的话语网络。作者意图的整体，或者艺术作品的整体，对于话语分析均不具有决定性意义。基特勒话语分析的切入点，不是作家主体，不是读者接受，不是艺术作品，而是信息传输。也就是说，他将浪漫小说读作数据传输、编码解码，以及信息交换。按照香农的学说，信息网络从根本上将信源、传输者、信道、接受者和信宿联系在一起。所以，由语词或话语构成的信息必须被记录为网络。这一网络必然会永远吸纳其他的书籍、记录、档案、文献，以及制度要素。

基特勒将福柯的知识考古学、拉康的心理分析理论以及海德格尔的"存在历史"融于对 1800 年德语话语网络分析之中，完成了对网络计划的尼采式"价值全面重估"。

第一，1800 年左右，词语是传输时间进程之中数据流的唯一媒介。《亨利希·奥夫特丁根》之中词语传输最为显著的特色是"能指与所指"合一。恰如少年诗人梦境之中的"蓝花"，它超凡脱俗，不可方物，既是一个专名，又是一种直观，主宰着诗人/叙述者的梦境，象征着令人憔悴的浪漫渴望，以及对超验形式的激情。奥夫特丁根的心境，其最深的内在性与受激情驱动的迷狂合为一体，呈现出悖论与歧异。这种心境象征着灵魂的诗化潜能——诺瓦利斯以及歌德时代的全部美学称之为"诗性的想象"。幻象的诗学由此滥觞，其内在功能在于"将词语转换为图像的美术长廊"。于是，词语转型为花朵，花朵转换为词语，支撑起歌德时代的全部诗学。与此同时，浪漫时代的女性崇拜也构成了古典浪漫主义的可能性条件，因为现实之中的女性总是沉默无声。女性的偶像为诗人提供了源始的语言，沉默是词语的渊薮。而这就证明，玛蒂尔德作为蓝花的幻觉化身，出现在梦中情人面前，"将一种神奇诡秘的语言注入他的口中，渗透了他的整个存在"。

第二，歌德时代的文学蓄意要将一切以碎片形式呈现的话语融构为整体的诗学作品。克林索尔向奥夫特丁根允诺，要与他一起共读"天下至奇的文字"，让这位灵感蒸腾的诗人熟悉"一切产业、一切交易、一切环境，以及人类社会的一切要求"。这就意味着诗人不是创造者，而是信息搜集者。数据流经过旅行家、商人、旷工、隐士、诗人以及女人源源不断地输入他的想象官能之中，得以编码和建构，所得的作品也仿佛是一个百科全书式的数据库。即便是一门严格的艺术，诗歌也将翻译囊括其中，将数据系列转化为文学话语编程。这些来自不同时代、不同地域、不同领域的千差万别的话语必须变为标本，经过重写，而被转输到一个单一的频道。用信息技术的术语说，诗歌意味着"多路分解"（demultiplexing）。诺瓦利斯一言以蔽之："一切诗歌，终归是翻译转换。"在穿越德意志归向母亲家园的路途上，诗人学到的东西便是这么一种诗学教义。他先是邂逅陌生人，给他启蒙开悟，随后又遭遇作为古典人物的范本诗人，从制度上认同他便是诗人的后裔。

第三，歌德时代的所谓"诗学"，便是全部心灵条件的总和，而浪漫的心灵完成了世界的"微缩画"。在梦境之中，奥夫特丁根的父亲看到，"大地仅仅是一盏金碗，上面刻着最精致的图画"。在微型宇宙图景之中，诗性的想象和复杂的还原合而为一。一如歌德所说，"真正的诗歌"是对大地的鸟瞰。然而，心灵非物质，诗性的想象完成不了复杂的还原，浪漫诗人所控制的唯一媒介只有语言。语言毕竟是"符号和音响所构成的微型世界"。换言之，语言是构成诗歌的一切可能微型画之空间。正是因为如此，基特勒用拉康的话说，返老还童的图画删除了"实在界"的赘余信息，而再现了阅读自身的隐喻。而这就是歌德时代传播技术的最伟大创新：存储与删除并行不悖。书籍市场的扩大，素养教育的兴盛，以及学术分工的形成导致书籍的过剩，ROM（只读内存）就已经变得过时。存储技术必须改造以便适应 RAM（随机存取内存），它不仅为 ROM 格式提供了数据，而且可能删除数据，代之以新的信息。于是，诺瓦利斯与费希特一起呼吁："我们必须从字母之中救出精神。"精神化的技术由此发轫，不同的知识形式应运而生，歌德时代的新存储技术以同等力度赋予了学校教育与诗学创作以崭新形式。

第四，歌德时代的女性象征着"自然之诗"，而自然之诗沉默无言。在歌德时代以及 1800 年话语网络的封闭环路之内，现代男性从女性那里接受语言。可是，自然哑默，母亲无言，且被驱逐在文明体制之外，因此又必须由拥有庄严父权的男人来教授写作。女性话语或自然之声，通过男性的权威转化为诗歌。女性作为读者，从男性的作品之中学会说话，尔后便担负语言传播者的角色。随后，诸如黑格尔之类的哲学家阅读这些诗歌，通过逻辑来驯化神话，为新型教育和文学实践者提供形而上的正当性辩护。1800年话语网络建基于数据传输之流：话语网络从自然到书本，从书本到自然，往返穿梭，永无止境。基特勒更为明白地指出：

> 我将1800年前后的母亲、诗歌和治学的历史线性化了：母亲产生出大量的词汇，然后文学接过来，将它们变成作品，哲学又将作品理论化。我还将所有这一切形象化为一幅电路配置图，它解释了像"反馈"这样的技术隐喻何以突然出现。……母亲作为输入信息进入诗歌的频道，然后在另一头出来，为哲学的存储媒介搜集编码，而成为概念。于是，一本书一开始就被设计为一台机器。①

诺瓦利斯的《亨利希·奥夫特丁根》也是这样一台机器。自始至终，通过其时代空间周而复始地循环，这台机器将不可记录的白色噪声上升为"哲学"这种普遍存储系统，为了每一个词语或每一个作家，乐此不疲地进行这种转换。所以，这部作品从来就不注重描述"行动"。相反，它本身就是无休无止的行动、绵延不绝的"情节"。

拓展讨论

置身在数字技术时代，传承18世纪风靡德国和欧洲的希腊文化狂热之爱（Philhellenism），基特勒将古希腊世界当作一道屏幕，将现代世界的文化技术景观及其当代人的自恋想象投射其上，并赋予游牧存在、游吟诗人以一种存在论的意义。游吟诗人吟诵，我们在聆听中入迷和着魔。游吟诗人吟诵说，他们故事里的英雄在吟诵之中迷醉了所有的听众。不论男人还是女人，都应和着游吟诗人的吟诵而书写。基特勒的古典世界，是一个孤立绝缘的世界，一个拉康意义上的想象界。然而，作为一种时间性的存在物，人类永远被拒绝了认知时间的机遇。可是，时间、存在和文化技术，总是在互动与分裂的辩证之中。古希腊、早期现代以及现代—后现代，是这一互动与分裂的宏大叙事之三个阶段。在现代-后现代语境下，掠过早期现代和中世纪，而回望古

---

① F. Kittler and S. Banz, *Platz der Luftbrücke：Ein Gespräch*，Berlin：Oktagon，1996，p.45.

希腊，基特勒重构了一个免除了人之使命的文化技术世界。古代铭文，诗歌断章，塞壬之歌，游吟诗人之表演，希腊字母表所记录的话语乐谱，史诗中漫游的诸神、英雄、女人，如此等等，基特勒用这些碎片要素编织出古典世界的象征体系，将爱琴海玫瑰色曙光的文化魅力转化为大道多歧、永无休止、趣味全无的文明劳作，及其机械僵化的座架体系。这是一个直达衰落的悲剧性叙事，它强化了"希腊对德意志"甚至对整个欧洲的暴政。古典文化技术世界，一个没有所指的能指，却与海德格尔"存在历史"的划时代断裂、德里达"逻各斯中心主义"帝国的残像余韵相对照，从而形成一面感伤的镜像。

延伸阅读

1. 基特勒：《留声机　电影　打字机》，邢春丽译，上海，复旦大学出版社，2017。读书延续话语网络分析，对数字时代的文化特征进行了扣人心弦的描述。

2. 温斯洛普-扬：《基特勒论媒介》，张昱辰译，北京，中国传媒大学出版社，2019。该书追溯基特勒的法国、德国、古希腊思想谱系，剖析其技术迷恋，探寻文学、哲学融于媒介景观的可能性。

编者后记

　　这个选本的缘起，是研究生双语课程计划的设置与实施。中国语言文学学科硕士授权点比较文学与世界文学专业 2006 年落户北京第二外国语学院。为了凸显外语学院人才培养的优势和特色，研究生专业课程"西方文论"就理所当然地采用了中英文双语教学。限于见闻，中英文双语教学迄今尚无定论定法。作为授课教师，本书的主编认为，交替使用中文和英文讲课，这种理解勉强可算及格。选用英文原典，引领学生精读文献，自由切换语言发表观点和讨论，似乎更能彰显双语优势。说得哲学一点，即构筑两个"家园"，同时演练和提升两种语言水平。师生在两个"家园"里随意走动，尽情体会语言传递出来的文化神韵。这的确是一种很奢侈的享受，也是一种很艰难的游戏。

　　北京第二外国语学院研究生院启动"研究生教育质量提升计划"，下设"优质课程和精品教材"项目，为编撰本教材提供了一个契机。于是，编者斗胆进行了申请。感谢评审专家和研究生院人才培养处以及学科规划与建设办公室，是他们的信任，才使本项目得以顺利立项。2017 年秋天，首届文艺学三名研究生入学。主编立即将他们收编，组建团队，充分利用"西方文论"课内和课外活动，着手编撰这部教材。

　　主编总结编撰《比较文学经典导读》的经验，继续采用"英文原典，汉语导读"模式，尝试通过选文呈现从语言论形式主义批评到文化论跨学科批评转换转型的西方文论发展趋势。这个师生编撰团队效率很高，2018 年秋就选定了原典，撰写了八篇导读。他们遵循"作者小识""背景略说""基本内容""拓展讨论""延伸阅读"的设置，以简明的语言呈现艰深文本的要义，还尽可能与中国文论话语接轨讨论。后来由于种种原因，主编一直腾不出手来修改和统稿。

　　2020 年，重读选文，修改导读文字，加入新近反思，吸纳最新成果，对全书进行了彻底的修改。首先是更换原典，原则是让理论最大限度地体现在批评实践中；其次是修改导读文字，原则是让所选文本的亮点最大限度地凸显出来；然后是校对英文，这个工作量很大，因为软件转换出错率相当高；最后成稿。凡 21 篇，大体覆盖了形式主义、精神分析、结构主义、解构策略、后殖民文化、女性批评、文化诗学和媒介批评等重要论题，参编人员的分工如下：

　　胡继华（北京第二外国语学院教授）：设计全书架构，选定英文原典，设立导读文字规范，撰写第3、第7、第8、第9、第14、第15、第16、第18、第21篇的导读文字，并负责全书统稿。

　　杨旭（北京师范大学在读文艺学博士生）：撰写第1、第2、第4、第20篇的导读文字，并校对全书英文部分。

　　张泽恒（首都师范大学在读比较文学与世界文学博士生）：撰写第5、第10、第11、第12、第13篇的导读文字，并校对全书中文部分。

　　李静宜（外交部中国国际问题研究院研究员）：撰写第17、第19篇的导读文字，并承担了部分英文文章的格式转换工作。

　　研究生邵伊凡、王茜承担了部分文档合并、统一格式、排版的工作，这两位虽没有被列入参编人员名单，但必须在此表示感谢。

　　项目以北京第二外国语学院文学院（跨文化研究院）为单位申请获批，感谢王柯平教授、赵京华教授、杨平教授、刘燕教授、院成纯博士、黄薇薇博士的大力支持。在项目进展过程中，文学院（跨文化研究院）再次改名为"文化与传播学院"，感谢周连选书记、裴登峰教授、李洪波院长所做的大量协调工作。2017年至2020年，部分美学、文艺学和比较文学的研究生选修了"西方文论"课程。他们积极配合，认真学习，课上讨论奉献智慧，课后作业给予编者以启发，其部分观点被纳入导读文字中，在此深表感谢。文艺学教学科研团队中的兰善兴博士、王晓玉博士、李向利博士、单羽博士，在本书编撰过程中给予了各种各样的支持，在此亦表示谢意。研究生教学秘书杨玫芳老师、科研秘书郝京清老师，在教学与科研管理中对编者帮助甚多，关照有加，必须深表谢忱。

　　北京第二外国语学院研究生院学科规划与建设办公室、人才培养处对本书的编撰十分关注，职能部门的支持、组织、指导为本书顺利完成提供了根本保障。特别感谢郑承军教授、邹统钎教授、谢琼教授、佘伯川教授。

　　在出版了《比较文学经典导读》后若干年，北京师范大学出版社再次慷慨接纳本书。周粟先生、周劲含女士组织了高水平的编辑团队，为本书添加了华彩。为了这份书缘，编者必须真诚地表示感谢。

　　"巧言易标，拙辞难隐。"向支持和帮助我们的各位师友，谨表心曲，祈望各位平安、快乐、顺泰。

胡继华
辛丑盛夏于京西北郊中海枫涟山庄